A BOUNTY /of/ BLANDINGS

P. G. WODEHOUSE

W. W. Norton & Company
New York · London

For information about permission to reproduce selections from this book,
write to Permissions, W. W. Norton & Company, Inc.,
500 Fifth Avenue, New York, NY 10110

For information about special discounts for bulk purchases, please contact
W. W. Norton Special Sales at specialsales@wwnorton.com or 800-233-4830

Manufactured in the United States of America
Book design by Judith Abbate
Production manager: Louise Mattarelliano

Library of Congress Cataloging-in-Publication Data

Wodehouse, P. G. (Pelham Grenville), 1881–1975.
A bounty of Blandings / P.G. Wodehouse.—1st ed.
p. cm.
ISBN 978-0-393-34127-0 (pbk.)
1. Blandings Castle (England : Imaginary place)—Fiction. 2. Aristocracy
(Social class)—England—Fiction. 3. Shropshire (England)—Fiction.
4. Humorous stories, English. I. Title.
PR6045.O53A6 2011
823'.912—dc22

2011020687

W. W. Norton & Company, Inc.
500 Fifth Avenue, New York, N.Y. 10110
www.wwnorton.com

W. W. Norton & Company Ltd.
15 Carlisle Street, London W1D 3BS

3 4 5 6 7 8 9 0

A BOUNTY

of

BLANDINGS

Contents

Contents

BLANDINGS CASTLE

Contents

Contents

1

THE CUSTODY OF THE PUMPKIN

THE morning sunshine descended like an amber shower-bath on Blandings Castle, lighting up with a heartening glow its ivied walls, its rolling parks, its gardens, outhouses, and messuages, and such of its inhabitants as chanced at the moment to be taking the air. It fell on green lawns and wide terraces, on noble trees and bright flower-beds. It fell on the baggy trousers-seat of Angus McAllister, head-gardener to the ninth Earl of Emsworth, as he bent with dour Scottish determination to pluck a slug from its reverie beneath the leaf of a lettuce. It fell on the white flannels of the Hon. Freddie Threepwood, Lord Emsworth's second son, hurrying across the water-meadows. It also fell on Lord Emsworth himself and on Beach, his faithful butler. They were standing on the turret above the west wing, the former with his eye to a powerful telescope, the latter holding the hat which he had been sent to fetch.

'Beach,' said Lord Emsworth.

'M'lord?'

'I've been swindled. This dashed thing doesn't work.'

'Your lordship cannot see clearly?'

'I can't see at all, dash it. It's all black.'

The butler was an observant man.

'Perhaps if I were to remove the cap at the extremity of the instrument, m'lord, more satisfactory results might be obtained.'

'Eh? Cap? Is there a cap? So there is. Take it off, Beach.'

'Very good, m'lord.'

'Ah!' There was satisfaction in Lord Emsworth's voice. He twiddled and adjusted, and the satisfaction deepened. 'Yes, that's better. That's capital. Beach, I can see a cow.'

'Indeed, m'lord?'

'Down in the water-meadows. Remarkable. Might be two yards away. All right, Beach. Shan't want you any longer.'

'Your hat, m'lord?'

'Put it on my head.'

'Very good, m'lord.'

The butler, this kindly act performed, withdrew. Lord Emsworth continued gazing at the cow.

The ninth Earl of Emsworth was a fluffy-minded and amiable old gentleman with a fondness for new toys. Although the main interest of his life was his garden, he was always ready to try a side line, and the latest of these side lines was this telescope of his. Ordered from London in a burst of enthusiasm consequent upon the reading of an article on astronomy in a monthly magazine, it had been placed in position on the previous evening. What was now in progress was its trial trip.

Presently, the cow's audience-appeal began to wane. It was a fine cow, as cows go, but, like so many cows, it lacked sustained dramatic interest. Surfeited after awhile by the spectacle of it chewing the cud and staring glassily at nothing, Lord Emsworth decided to swivel the apparatus round in the hope of picking up something a trifle more sensational. And he was just about to do so, when into the range of his vision there came the Hon. Freddie. White and shining, he tripped along over the turf like a Theocritan shepherd hastening to keep an appointment with a nymph, and a sudden frown marred the serenity of Lord Emsworth's brow. He generally frowned when he saw Freddie, for with the passage of the years that youth had become more and more of a problem to an anxious father.

Unlike the male codfish, which, suddenly finding itself the parent of three million five hundred thousand little codfish, cheerfully resolves to love them all, the British aristocracy is apt to look with a somewhat jaundiced eye on its younger sons. And Freddie Threepwood was one of those younger sons who rather invite the jaundiced eye. It seemed to the head of the family that there was no way of coping with the boy. If he was allowed to live in London, he piled up debts and got into mischief; and when you jerked him back into the purer surroundings of Blandings Castle, he just mooned about the place, moping broodingly. Hamlet's society at Elsinore must have had much the same effect on his stepfather as did that of Freddie Threepwood at Blandings on Lord Emsworth. And it is probable that what induced the latter to keep a telescopic eye on him at this moment was the fact that his demeanour was so mysteriously jaunty, his bearing so intriguingly free from its customary crushed misery. Some inner voice whispered to Lord Emsworth that this smiling, prancing youth was up to no good and would bear watching.

The inner voice was absolutely correct. Within thirty seconds its case had been proved up to the hilt. Scarcely had his lordship had time to wish, as he invariably wished on seeing his offspring, that Freddie had been something entirely different in manners, morals, and appearance, and had been the son of somebody else living a considerable distance away, when out of a small spinney near the end of the meadow there bounded a girl. And Freddie, after a cautious glance over his shoulder, immediately proceeded to fold this female in a warm embrace.

Lord Emsworth had seen enough. He tottered away from the telescope, a shattered man. One of his favourite dreams was of some nice, eligible girl, belonging to a good family, and possessing a bit of money of her own, coming along some day and taking Freddie off his hands; but that inner voice, more confident now than ever, told him that this was not she. Freddie would not sneak off in this furtive fashion to meet eligible girls, nor could he imagine any eligible girl, in her right senses, rushing into Freddie's arms in that enthusiastic way. No, there was only one explanation. In the cloistral seclusion of Blandings, far from the Metropolis with all its conveniences for that sort of thing, Freddie had managed to get himself entangled. Seething with anguish and fury, Lord Emsworth hurried down the stairs and out on to the terrace. Here he prowled like an elderly leopard waiting for feeding-time, until in due season there was a flicker of white among the trees that flanked the drive and a cheerful whistling announced the culprit's approach.

It was with a sour and hostile eye that Lord Emsworth watched his son draw near. He adjusted his pince-nez, and with their assistance was able to perceive that a fatuous smile of self-satisfaction illumined the young man's face, giving him the appearance of a beaming sheep. In the young man's buttonhole there shone a nosegay of simple meadow flowers, which, as he walked, he patted from time to time with a loving hand.

'Frederick!' bellowed his lordship.

The villain of the piece halted abruptly. Sunk in a roseate trance, he had not observed his father. But such was the sunniness of his mood that even this encounter could not damp him. He gambolled happily up.

'Hullo, guv'nor!' he carolled. He searched in his mind for a pleasant topic of conversation—always a matter of some little difficulty on these occasions. 'Lovely day, what?'

His lordship was not to be diverted into a discussion of the weather. He drew a step nearer, looking like the man who smothered the young princes in the Tower.

'Frederick,' he demanded, 'who was that girl?'

The Hon. Freddie started convulsively. He appeared to be swallowing with difficulty something large and jagged.

'Girl?' he quavered. 'Girl? Girl, guv'nor?'

'That girl I saw you kissing ten minutes ago down in the water-meadows.'

'Oh!' said the Hon. Freddie. He paused. 'Oh, ah!' He paused again. 'Oh, ah, yes! I've been meaning to tell you about that, guv'nor.'

'You have, have you?'

'All perfectly correct, you know. Oh, yes, indeed! All most absolutely correct-o! Nothing fishy, I mean to say, or anything like that. She's my *fiancée*.'

A sharp howl escaped Lord Emsworth, as if one of the bees humming in the lavender-beds had taken time off to sting him in the neck.

'Who is she?' he boomed. 'Who is this woman?'

'Her name's Donaldson.'

'Who is she?'

'Aggie Donaldson. Aggie's short for Niagara. Her people spent their honeymoon at the Falls, she tells me. She's American and all that. Rummy names they give kids in America,' proceeded Freddie, with hollow chattiness. 'I mean to say! Niagara! I ask you!'

'Who is she?'

'She's most awfully bright, you know. Full of beans. You'll love her.'

'Who is she?'

'And can play the saxophone.'

'Who,' demanded Lord Emsworth for the sixth time, 'is she? And where did you meet her?'

Freddie coughed. The information, he perceived, could no longer be withheld, and he was keenly alive to the fact that it scarcely fell into the class of tidings of great joy.

'Well, as a matter of fact, guv'nor, she's a sort of cousin of Angus McAllister's. She's come over to England for a visit, don't you know, and is staying with the old boy. That's how I happened to run across her.'

Lord Emsworth's eyes bulged and he gargled faintly. He had had many unpleasant visions of his son's future, but they had never included one of him walking down the aisle with a sort of cousin of his head-gardener.

'Oh!' he said. 'Oh, indeed?'

'That's the strength of it, guv'nor.'

Lord Emsworth threw his arms up, as if calling on Heaven to witness a good man's persecution, and shot off along the terrace at a rapid trot. Having ranged the grounds for some minutes, he ran his quarry to earth at the entrance to the yew alley.

The head-gardener turned at the sound of his footsteps. He was a sturdy man of medium height, with eyebrows that would have fitted a bigger forehead. These, added to a red and wiry beard, gave him a formidable and uncompromising expression. Honesty Angus McAllister's face had in full measure, and also intelligence; but it was a bit short on sweetness and light.

'McAllister,' said his lordship, plunging without preamble into the matter of his discourse. 'That girl. You must send her away.'

A look of bewilderment clouded such of Mr McAllister's features as were not concealed behind his beard and eyebrows.

'Gurrul?'

'That girl who is staying with you. She must go!'

'Gae where?'

Lord Emsworth was not in the mood to be finicky about details.

'Anywhere,' he said. 'I won't have her here a day longer.'

'Why?' inquired Mr McAllister, who liked to thresh these things out.

'Never mind why. You must send her away immediately.'

Mr McAllister mentioned an insuperable objection.

'She's payin' me twa poon' a week,' he said simply.

Lord Emsworth did not grind his teeth, for he was not given to that form of displaying emotion; but he leaped some ten inches into the air and dropped his pince-nez. And, though normally a fair-minded and reasonable man, well aware that modern earls must think twice before pulling the feudal stuff on their *employés*, he took on the forthright truculence of a large landowner of the early Norman period ticking off a serf.

'Listen, McAllister! Listen to me! Either you send that girl away to-day or you can go yourself. I mean it!'

A curious expression came into Angus McAllister's face—always excepting the occupied territories. It was the look of a man who has not forgotten Bannockburn, a man conscious of belonging to the country of William Wallace and Robert the Bruce. He made Scotch noises at the back of his throat.

'Y'r lorrudsheep will accept ma notis,' he said, with formal dignity.

'I'll pay you a month's wages in lieu of notice and you will leave this afternoon,' retorted Lord Emsworth with spirit.

'Mphm!' said Mr McAllister.

Lord Emsworth left the battle-field with a feeling of pure exhilaration, still in the grip of the animal fury of conflict. No twinge of remorse did he feel at the thought that Angus McAllister had served him faithfully for ten years. Nor did it cross his mind that he might miss McAllister.

But that night, as he sat smoking his after-dinner cigarette, Reason, so violently expelled, came stealing timidly back to her throne, and a cold hand seemed suddenly placed upon his heart.

With Angus McAllister gone, how would the pumpkin fare?

• • •

The importance of this pumpkin in the Earl of Emsworth's life requires, perhaps, a word of explanation. Every ancient family in England has some little gap in its scroll of honour, and that of Lord Emsworth was no exception. For generations back his ancestors had been doing notable deeds; they had sent out from Blandings Castle statesmen and warriors, governors and leaders of the people: but they had not—in the opinion of the present holder of the title—achieved a full hand. However splendid the family record might appear at first sight, the fact remained that no Earl of Emsworth had ever won a first prize for pumpkins at the Shrewsbury Show. For roses, yes. For tulips true. For spring onions, granted. But not for pumpkins; and Lord Emsworth felt it deeply.

For many a summer past he had been striving indefatigably to remove this blot on the family escutcheon, only to see his hopes go tumbling down. But this year at last victory had seemed in sight, for there had been vouchsafed to Blandings a competitor of such amazing parts that his lordship, who had watched it grow practically from a pip, could not envisage failure. Surely, he told himself as he gazed on its golden roundness, even Sir Gregory Parsloe-Parsloe, of Matchingham Hall, winner for three successive years, would never be able to produce anything to challenge this superb vegetable.

And it was this supreme pumpkin whose welfare he feared he had jeopardized by dismissing Angus McAllister. For Angus was its official trainer. He understood the pumpkin. Indeed, in his reserved Scottish way, he even seemed to love it. With Angus gone, what would the harvest be?

Such were the meditations of Lord Emsworth as he reviewed the position of affairs. And though, as the days went by, he tried to tell himself that Angus McAllister was not the only man in the world who understood pumpkins, and that he had every confidence, the most complete and unswerving confidence, in Robert Barker, recently Angus's second-in-command, now promoted to the post of head-gardener and custodian of the Blandings Hope, he knew that this was but shallow bravado. When you are a pumpkin-owner with a big winner in your stable, you judge men by hard standards, and every day it became plainer that Robert Barker was only a makeshift. Within a week Lord Emsworth was pining for Angus McAllister.

It might be purely imagination, but to his excited fancy the pumpkin seemed to be pining for Angus too. It appeared to be drooping and losing weight. Lord Emsworth could not rid himself of the horrible idea that it was shrinking. And on the tenth night after McAllister's departure he dreamed a strange dream. He had gone with King George to show his Gracious Majesty the pumpkin, promising him the treat of a lifetime; and, when they arrived, there in the corner of the frame was a shrivelled thing the size of a pea. He woke, sweating, with his sovereign's disappointed screams ringing in his ears; and Pride gave its last quiver and collapsed. To reinstate Angus would be a surrender, but it must be done.

'Beach,' he said that morning at breakfast, 'do you happen to—er—to have McAllister's address?'

'Yes, your lordship,' replied the butler. 'He is in London, residing at number eleven Buxton Crescent.'

'Buxton Crescent? Never heard of it.'

'It is, I fancy, your lordship, a boarding-house or some such establishment off the Cromwell Road. McAllister was accustomed to make it his head-quarters whenever he visited the Metropolis on account of its handiness for Kensington Gardens. He liked,' said Beach with respectful reproach, for Angus had been a friend of his for nine years, 'to be near the flowers, your lordship.'

Two telegrams, passing through it in the course of the next twelve hours, caused some gossip at the post office of the little town of Market Blandings.

The first ran:

McAllister,
      11, Buxton Crescent,
            Cromwell Road,
                 London.
Return immediately.—Emsworth.

The second!

Lord Emsworth,
            Blandings Castle,
                        Shropshire.
I will not.—McAllister.

Lord Emsworth had one of those minds capable of accommodating but one thought at a time—if that; and the possibility that Angus McAllister might decline to return had not occurred to him. It was difficult to adjust himself to this new problem, but he managed it at last. Before nightfall he had made up his mind. Robert Barker, that broken reed, could remain in charge for another day or so, and meanwhile he would go up to London and engage a real head-gardener, the finest head-gardener that money could buy.

It was the opinion of Dr Johnson that there is in London all that life can afford. A man, he held, who is tired of London is tired of life itself. Lord Emsworth, had he been aware of this statement, would have contested it warmly. He hated London. He loathed its crowds, its smells, its noises; its omnibuses, its taxis, and its hard pavements. And, in addition to all its other defects, the miserable town did not seem able to produce a single decent head-gardener. He went from agency to agency, interviewing candidates, and not one of them came within a mile of meeting his requirements. He disliked their faces, he distrusted their references. It was a harsh thing to say of any man, but he was dashed if the best of them was even as good as Robert Barker.

It was, therefore, in a black and soured mood that his lordship, having lunched frugally at the Senior Conservative Club on the third day of his visit, stood on the steps in the sunshine, wondering how on earth he was to get through the afternoon. He had spent the morning rejecting head-gardeners, and the next batch was not due until the morrow. And what—besides rejecting head-gardeners—was there for a man of reasonable tastes to do with his time in this hopeless town?

And then there came into his mind a remark which Beach the butler had made at the breakfast-table about flowers in Kensington Gardens. He could go to Kensington Gardens and look at the flowers.

He was about to hail a taxicab from the rank down the street when there suddenly emerged from the Hotel Magnificent over the way a young man. This young man proceeded to cross the road, and, as he drew near, it seemed to Lord Emsworth that there was about his appearance something oddly familiar. He stared for a long instant before he could believe his eyes, then with a wordless cry bounded down the steps just as the other started to mount them.

'Oh, hullo, guv'nor!' ejaculated the Hon. Freddie, plainly startled.

'What—what are you doing here?' demanded Lord Emsworth.

He spoke with heat, and justly so. London, as the result of several spirited escapades which still rankled in the mind of a father who had had to foot the bills, was forbidden ground to Freddie.

The young man was plainly not at his ease. He had the air of one who is being pushed towards dangerous machinery in which he is loath to become entangled. He shuffled his feet for a moment, then raised his left shoe and rubbed the back of his right calf with it.

'The fact is, guv'nor—'

'You know you are forbidden to come to London.'

'Absolutely, guv'nor, but the fact is—'

'And why anybody but an imbecile should want to come to London when he could be at Blandings—'

'I know, guv'nor, but the fact is—' Here Freddie, having replaced his wandering foot on the pavement, raised the other, and rubbed the back of his left calf. 'I wanted to see you,' he said. 'Yes. Particularly wanted to see you.'

This was not strictly accurate. The last thing in the world which the Hon. Freddie wanted was to see his parent. He had come to the Senior Conservative Club to leave a carefully written note. Having delivered which, it had been his intention to bolt like a rabbit. This unforeseen meeting had upset his plans.

'To see me?' said Lord Emsworth. 'Why?'

'Got—er—something to tell you. Bit of news.'

'I trust it is of sufficient importance to justify your coming to London against my express wishes.'

'Oh, yes. Oh, yes, yes-yes. Oh, rather. It's dashed important. Yes—not to put too fine a point upon it—most dashed important. I say, guv'nor, are you in fairly good form to stand a bit of a shock?'

A ghastly thought rushed into Lord Emsworth's mind. Freddie's mysterious arrival—his strange manner—his odd hesitation and uneasiness—could it mean—? He clutched the young man's arm feverishly.

'Frederick! Speak! Tell me! Have the cats got at it?'

It was a fixed idea of Lord Emsworth, which no argument would have induced him to abandon, that cats had the power to work some dreadful mischief on his pumpkin and were continually lying in wait for the opportunity of doing so; and his behaviour on the occasion when one of the fast sporting set from the stables, wandering into the kitchen garden and finding him gazing at the Blandings Hope, had rubbed itself sociably against his leg, lingered long in that animal's memory.

Freddie stared.

'Cats? Why? Where? Which? What cats?'

'Frederick! Is anything wrong with the pumpkin?'

In a crass and materialistic world there must inevitably be a scattered few here and there in whom pumpkins touch no chord. The Hon. Freddie Threepwood was one of these. He was accustomed to speak in mockery of all pumpkins, and had even gone so far as to allude to the Hope of Blandings as 'Percy.' His father's anxiety, therefore, merely caused him to giggle.

'Not that I know of,' he said.

'Then what do you mean?' thundered Lord Emsworth, stung by the giggle. 'What do you mean, sir, by coming here and alarming me—scaring me out of my wits, by Gad!—with your nonsense about giving me shocks?'

The Hon. Freddie looked carefully at his fermenting parent. His fingers, sliding into his pocket, closed on the note which nestled there. He drew it forth.

'Look here, guv'nor,' he said nervously. 'I think the best thing would be for you to read this. Meant to leave it for you with the hall-porter. It's—well, you just cast your eye over it. Good-bye, guv'nor. Got to see a man.'

And, thrusting the note into his father's hand, the Hon. Freddie turned and was gone. Lord Emsworth, perplexed and annoyed, watched him skim up the road and leap into a cab. He seethed impotently. Practically any behaviour on the part of his son Frederick had the power to irritate him, but it was when he was vague and mysterious and incoherent that the young man irritated him most.

He looked at the letter in his hand, turned it over, felt it. Then—for it had suddenly occurred to him that if he wished to ascertain its contents he had better read it—he tore open the envelope.

The note was brief, but full of good reading matter.

> Dear Guv'nor,
>
> Awfully sorry and all that, but couldn't hold out any longer. I've popped up to London in the two-seater and Aggie and I were spliced this morning. There looked like being a bit of a hitch at one time, but Aggie's guv'nor, who has come over from America, managed to wangle it all right by getting a special licence or something of that order. A most capable Johnny. He's coming to see you. He wants to have a good long talk with you about the whole binge. Lush him up hospitably and all that, would you mind, because he's a really sound egg, and you'll like him.
>
> Well, cheerio!
>
> Your affectionate son,
>
> Freddie.
>
> P.S.—You won't mind if I freeze on to the two-seater for the nonce, what? It may come in useful for the honeymoon.

The Senior Conservative Club is a solid and massive building, but, as Lord Emsworth raised his eyes dumbly from the perusal of this letter, it seemed to him that it was performing a kind of whirling dance. The whole of the immediate neighbourhood, indeed, appeared to be shimmying in the middle of a thick mist. He was profoundly stirred. It is not too much to say that he was shaken to the core of his being. No father enjoys being flouted and defied by his own son; nor is it reasonable to expect a man to take a cheery view of life who is faced with the prospect of supporting for the remainder of his years a younger son, a younger son's wife, and possibly younger grandchildren.

For an appreciable space of time he stood in the middle of the pavement, rooted to the spot. Passers-by bumped into him or grumblingly made *détours* to avoid a collision. Dogs sniffed at his ankles. Seedy-looking individuals tried to arrest his attention in order to speak of their financial affairs. Lord Emsworth heeded none of them. He remained where he was, gaping like a fish, until suddenly his faculties seemed to return to him.

An imperative need for flowers and green trees swept upon Lord Emsworth. The noise of the traffic and the heat of the sun on the stone pavement were afflicting him like a nightmare. He signaled energetically to a passing cab.

'Kensington Gardens,' he said, and sank back on the cushioned seat.

Something dimly resembling peace crept into his lordship's soul as he paid off his cab and entered the cool shade of the gardens. Even from the road he had caught a glimpse of stimulating reds and yellows; and as he ambled up the asphalt path and plunged round the corner the flowerbeds burst upon his sight in all their consoling glory.

'Ah!' breathed Lord Emsworth, rapturously, and came to a halt before a glowing carpet of tulips. A man of official aspect, wearing a peaked cap and a uniform, stopped as he heard the exclamation and looked at him with approval and even affection.

'Nice weather we're 'avin',' he observed.

Lord Emsworth did not reply. He had not heard. There is that about a well-set-out bed of flowers which acts on men who love their gardens like a drug, and he was in a sort of trance. Already he had completely forgotten where he was, and seemed to himself to be back in his paradise of Blandings. He drew a step nearer to the flower-bed, pointing like a setter.

The official-looking man's approval deepened. This man with the peaked cap was the park-keeper, who held the rights of the high, the low, and the middle justice over that section of the gardens. He, too, loved these flower-beds, and he seemed to see in Lord Emsworth a kindred soul. The general public was too apt to pass by, engrossed in its own affairs, and this often wounded the park-keeper. In Lord Emsworth he thought that he recognized one of the right sort.

'Nice—' he began.

He broke off with a sharp cry. If he had not seen it with his own eyes, he would not have believed it. But, alas, there was no possibility of a mistake. With a ghastly shock he realized that he had been deceived in this attractive stranger. Decently, if untidily, dressed; clean; respectable to the outward eye; the stranger was in reality a dangerous criminal, the blackest type of evil-doer on the park-keeper's index. He was a Kensington Gardens flower-picker.

For, even as he uttered the word 'Nice,' the man had stepped lightly over the low railing, had shambled across the strip of turf, and before you could say 'weather' was busy on his dark work. In the brief instant in which the park-keeper's vocal chords refused to obey him, he was two tulips ahead of the game and reaching out to scoop in a third.

'Hi!!!' roared the park-keeper, suddenly finding speech. ' 'I there!!!'

Lord Emsworth turned with a start.

'Bless my soul!' he murmured reproachfully.

He was in full possession of his senses now, such as they were, and understood the enormity of his conduct. He shuffled back on to the asphalt, contrite.

'My dear fellow—' he began remorsefully.

The park-keeper began to speak rapidly and at length. From time to time Lord Emsworth moved his lips and made deprecating gestures, but he could not stem the flood. Louder and more rhetorical grew the park-keeper and denser and more interested the rapidly assembling crowd of spectators. And then through the stream of words another voice spoke.

'Wot's all this?'

The force had materialized in the shape of a large, solid constable.

The park-keeper seemed to understand that he had been superseded.

He still spoke, but no longer like a father rebuking an erring son. His attitude now was more that of an elder brother appealing for justice against a delinquent junior. In a moving passage he stated his case.

"E Says,' observed the constable judicially, speaking slowly and in capitals, as if addressing an untutored foreigner, "E Says You Was Pickin' The Flowers.'

'I saw 'im. I was standin' as close as I am to you.'

"E Saw You,' interpreted the constable. "E Was Standing At Your Side.'

Lord Emsworth was feeling weak and bewildered. Without a thought of annoying or doing harm to anybody, he seemed to have unchained the fearful passions of a French Revolution; and there came over him a sense of how unjust it was that this sort of thing should be happening to him, of all people—a man already staggering beneath the troubles of a Job.

'I'll 'ave to ask you for your name and address,' said the constable, more briskly. A stubby pencil popped for an instant into his stern mouth and hovered, well and truly moistened, over the virgin page of his notebook—that dreadful notebook before which taxi-drivers shrink and hardened bus-conductors quail.

'I—I—why, my dear fellow—I mean, officer—I am the Earl of Emsworth.'

Much has been written of the psychology of crowds, designed to show how extraordinary and inexplicable it is, but most of such writing is exaggeration. A crowd generally behaves in a perfectly natural and intelligible fashion. When, for instance, it sees a man in a badly-fitting tweed suit and a hat he ought to be ashamed of getting put through it for pinching flowers in the Park, and the man says he is an earl, it laughs. This crowd laughed.

'Ho?' The constable did not stoop to join in the merriment of the rabble, but his lip twitched sardonically. 'Have you a card, your lordship?'

Nobody intimate with Lord Emsworth would have asked such a foolish question. His card-case was the thing he always lost second when visiting London—immediately after losing his umbrella.

'I—er—I'm afraid—'

'R!' said the constable. And the crowd uttered another happy, hyena-like laugh, so intensely galling that his lordship raised his bowed head and found enough spirit to cast an indignant glance. And, as he did so, the hunted look faded from his eyes.

'McAllister!' he cried.

Two new arrivals had just joined the throng, and, being of rugged and nobbly physique, had already shoved themselves through to the ringside seats. One was a tall, handsome, smooth-faced gentleman of authoritative appearance, who, if he had not worn rimless glasses, would have looked like a Roman emperor. The other was a shorter, sturdier man with a bristly red beard.

'McAllister!' moaned his lordship piteously. 'McAllister, my dear fellow, do please tell this man who I am.'

After what had passed between himself and his late employer, a lesser man than Angus McAllister might have seen in Lord Emsworth's predicament merely a judgment. A man of little magnanimity would have felt that here was where he got a bit of his own back.

Not so this splendid Glaswegian.

'Aye,' he said. 'Yon's Lorrud Emsworruth.'

'Who are you?' inquired the constable searchingly.

'I used to be head-gardener at the cassel.'

'Exactly,' bleated Lord Emsworth. 'Precisely. My head-gardener.'

The constable was shaken. Lord Emsworth might not look like an earl, but there was no getting away from the fact that Angus McAllister was supremely head-gardeneresque. A staunch admirer of the aristocracy, the constable perceived that zeal had caused him to make a bit of a bloomer.

In this crisis, however, he comported himself with masterly tact. He scowled blackly upon the interested throng.

'Pass along there, please. Pass along,' he commanded austerely. 'Ought to know better than block up a public thoroughfare like this. Pass along!'

He moved off, shepherding the crowd before him. The Roman emperor with the rimless glasses advanced upon Lord Emsworth, extending a large hand.

'Pleased to meet you at last,' he said. 'My name is Donaldson, Lord Emsworth.'

For a moment the name conveyed nothing to his lordship. Then its significance hit him, and he drew himself up with hauteur.

'You'll excuse us, Angus,' said Mr Donaldson. 'High time you and I had a little chat, Lord Emsworth.'

Lord Emsworth was about to speak, when he caught the other's eye. It was a strong, keen, level grey eye, with a curious forcefulness about it that made him feel strangely inferior. There is every reason to suppose that Mr Donaldson had subscribed for years to those personality courses advertised in the magazines which guarantee to impart to the pupil who takes ten correspondence lessons the ability to look the boss in the eye and make him wilt. Mr Donaldson looked Lord Emsworth in the eye, and Lord Emsworth wilted.

'How do you do?' he said weakly.

'Now listen, Lord Emsworth,' proceeded Mr Donaldson. 'No sense in having hard feelings between members of a family. I take it you've heard by this that your boy and my girl have gone ahead and fixed it up? Personally, I'm delighted. That boy is a fine young fellow.'

Lord Emsworth blinked.

'You are speaking of my son Frederick?' he said incredulously.

'Of your son Frederick. Now, at the moment, no doubt, you are feeling a trifle sore. I don't blame you. You have every right to be sorer than a gumboil. But you must remember—young blood, eh? It will, I am convinced, be a lasting grief to that splendid young man—'

'You are still speaking of my son Frederick?'

'Of Frederick, yes. It will, I say, be a lasting grief to him if he feels he has incurred your resentment. You must forgive him, Lord Emsworth. He must have your support.'

'I suppose he'll have to have it, dash it!' said his lordship unhappily. 'Can't let the boy starve.'

'Mr Donaldson's hand swept round in a wide, grand gesture.

'Don't you worry about that. I'll look after that end of it. I am not a rich man—'

'Ah!' said Lord Emsworth rather bleakly. There had been something about the largeness of the other's manner which had led him to entertain hopes.

'I doubt,' continued Mr Donaldson frankly, for he was a man who believed in frankness in these matters, 'if, all told, I have as much as ten million dollars in the world.'

Lord Emsworth swayed like a sapling in the breeze.

'Ten million? Ten million? Did you say you had ten million dollars?'

'Between nine and ten, I suppose. Not more. You must remember,' said Mr Donaldson, with a touch of apology, 'that conditions have changed very much in America of late. We have been through a tough time, a mighty tough time. Many of my friends have been harder hit than I have. But things are coming back. Yes, sir, they're coming right back. I am a firm believer in President Roosevelt and the New Deal. Under the New Deal, the American dog is beginning to eat more biscuits. That, I should have mentioned, is my line. I am Donaldson's Dog-Biscuits.'

'Donaldson's Dog-Biscuits? Indeed? Really! Fancy that!'

'You have heard of Donaldson's Dog-Biscuits?' asked their proprietor eagerly.

'Never,' said Lord Emsworth cordially.

'Oh! Well, that's who I am. And, as I say, the business is beginning to pick up nicely after the slump. All over the country our salesmen are reporting that the American dog is once more becoming biscuit-conscious. And so I am in a position, with your approval, to offer Frederick a steady and possibly a lucrative job. I propose, always with your consent, of course, to send him over to Long Island City to start learning the business. I have no doubt that he will in time prove a most valuable asset to the firm.'

Lord Emsworth could conceive of no way in which Freddie could be of value to a dog-biscuit firm, except possibly as a taster; but he refrained from damping the other's enthusiasm by saying so. In any case, the thought of the young man actually earning his living, and doing so three thousand miles from Blandings Castle, would probably have held him dumb.

'He seems full of keenness. But, in my opinion, to be able to give of his best and push the Donaldson biscuit as it should be pushed, he must feel that he has your moral support, Lord Emsworth—his father's moral support.'

'Yes, yes, yes!' said Lord Emsworth heartily. A feeling of positive ado-
ration for Mr Donaldson was thrilling him. The getting rid of Freddie,
which he himself had been unable to achieve in twenty-six years, this
godlike dog-biscuit manufacturer had accomplished in less than a week.
What a man! felt Lord Emsworth. 'Oh, yes, yes, yes!' he said. 'Yes, indeed.
Most decidedly.'

'They sail on Wednesday.'

'Capital!'

'Early in the morning.'

'Splendid!'

'I may give them a friendly message from you? A forgiving, fatherly
message?'

'Certainly, certainly, certainly. Inform Frederick that he has my best
wishes.'

'I will.'

'Mention that I shall watch his future progress with considerable
interest.'

'Exactly.'

'Say that I hope he will work hard and make a name for himself.'

'Just so.'

'And,' concluded Lord Emsworth, speaking with a paternal earnest-
ness well in keeping with this solemn moment, 'tell him—er—not to
hurry home.'

He pressed Mr Donaldson's hand with feelings too deep for further speech. Then he galloped swiftly to where Angus McAllister stood
brooding over the tulip bed.

'McAllister!'

The head-gardener's beard waggled grimly. He looked at his late
employer with cold eyes. It is never difficult to distinguish between a
Scotsman with a grievance and a ray of sunshine, and Lord Emsworth,
gazing upon the dour man, was able to see at a glance into which cat-
egory Angus McAllister fell. His tongue seemed to cleave to his palate,
but he forced himself to speak.

'McAllister . . . I wish . . . I wonder . . .'

'Weel?'

'I wonder . . . I wish . . . What I want to say,' faltered Lord Emsworth humbly, 'is, have you accepted another situation yet?'

'I am conseederin' twa.'

'Come back to me!' pleaded his lordship, his voice breaking 'Robert Barker is worse than useless. Come back to me!'

Angus McAllister gazed woodenly at the tulips.

'A' weel—' he said at length.

'You will?' cried Lord Emsworth joyfully. 'Splendid! Capital! Excellent!'

'A' didna say I wud.'

'I thought you said "I will,"' said his lordship, dashed.

'I didna say "A' weel"; I said "A' weel,"' said Mr McAllister stiffly. 'Meanin' mebbe I might, mebbe not.'

Lord Emsworth laid a trembling hand upon his shoulder.

'McAllister, I will raise your salary.'

The beard twitched.

'Dash it, I'll double it!'

The eyebrows flickered.

'McAllister . . . Angus . . .' said Lord Emsworth in a low voice. 'Come back! The pumpkin needs you.'

In an age of rush and hurry like that of to-day, an age in which there are innumerable calls on the time of everyone, it is possible that here and there throughout the ranks of those who have read this chronicle there may be one or two who for various reasons found themselves unable to attend the last Agricultural Show at Shrewsbury. For these a few words must be added.

Sir Gregory Parsloe-Parsloe, of Matchingham Hall, was there, of course, but it would not have escaped the notice of a close observer that his mien lacked something of the haughty arrogance which had characterized it in other years. From time to time, as he paced the tent devoted to the exhibition of vegetables, he might have been seen to bite his lip, and his eye had something of that brooding look which Napoleon's must have worn at Waterloo.

But there was the right stuff in Sir Gregory. He was a gentleman and a sportsman. In the Parsloe tradition there was nothing small or mean. Half-way down the tent he stopped, and with a quick, manly gesture thrust out his hand.

'Congratulate you, Emsworth,' he said huskily.

Lord Emsworth looked up with a start. He had been deep in his thoughts.

'Eh? Oh, thanks. Thanks, my dear fellow, thanks, thanks. Thank you very much.' He hesitated. 'Er—can't both win, eh?'

Sir Gregory puzzled it out and saw that he was right.

'No,' he said. 'No. See what you mean. Can't both win. No getting round that.'

He nodded and walked on, with who knows what vultures gnawing at his broad bosom. And Lord Emsworth—with Angus McAllister, who had been a silent, beard-waggling witness of the scene, at his side—turned once more to stare reverently at that which lay on the strawy bottom of one of the largest packing-cases ever seen in Shrewsbury town.

A card had been attached to the exterior of the packing-case. It bore the simple legend:

PUMPKINS. FIRST PRIZE

2

LORD EMSWORTH ACTS
FOR THE BEST

THE housekeeper's room at Blandings Castle, G.H.Q. of the domestic staff that ministered to the needs of the Earl of Emsworth, was in normal circumstances a pleasant and cheerful apartment. It caught the afternoon sun; and the paper which covered its walls had been conceived in a jovial spirit by someone who held that the human eye, resting on ninety-seven simultaneous pink birds perched upon ninety-seven blue rose-bushes, could not but be agreeably stimulated and refreshed. Yet, with the entry of Beach, the butler, it was as though there had crept into its atmosphere a chill dreariness; and Mrs Twemlow, the housekeeper, laying down her knitting, gazed at him in alarm.

'Whatever is the matter, Mr Beach?'

The butler stared moodily out of the window. His face was drawn and he breathed heavily, as a man will who is suffering from a combination of strong emotion and adenoids. A ray of sunshine, which had been advancing jauntily along the carpet, caught sight of his face and slunk out, abashed.

'I have come to a decision, Mrs Twemlow.'

'What about?'

'Ever since his lordship started to grow it I have seen the writing on the wall plainer and plainer, and now I have made up my mind. The moment his lordship returns from London, I tender my resignation. Eighteen years have I served in his lordship's household, commencing as under-footman and rising to my present position, but now the end has come.'

'You don't mean you're going just because his lordship has grown a beard?'

'It is the only way, Mrs Twemlow. That beard is weakening his lordship's position throughout the entire country-side. Are you aware that at the recent Sunday school treat I heard cries of "Beaver!"?'

'No!'

'Yes! And this spirit of mockery and disrespect will spread. And, what is more, that beard is alienating the best elements in the County. I saw Sir Gregory Parsloe-Parsloe look very sharp at it when he dined with us last Friday.'

'It is not a handsome beard,' admitted the housekeeper.

'It is not. And his lordship must be informed. As long as I remain in his lordship's service, it is impossible for me to speak. So I shall tender my resignation. Once that is done, my lips will no longer be sealed. Is that buttered toast under that dish, Mrs Twemlow?'

'Yes, Mr Beach. Take a slice. It will cheer you up.'

'Cheer me up!' said the butler, with a hollow laugh that sounded like a knell.

It was fortunate that Lord Emsworth, seated at the time of this conversation in the smoking-room of the Senior Conservative Club in London, had no suspicion of the supreme calamity that was about to fall upon him; for there was already much upon his mind.

In the last few days, indeed, everything seemed to have gone wrong. Angus McAllister, his head-gardener, had reported an alarming invasion of greenfly among the roses. A favourite and respected cow, strongly fancied for the Milk-Giving Jerseys event at the forthcoming Cattle Show, had contracted a mysterious ailment which was baffling the skill of the local vet. And on top of all this a telegram had arrived from his lordship's younger son, the Hon. Frederick Threepwood, announcing that he was back in England and desirous of seeing his father immediately.

This, felt Lord Emsworth, as he stared bleakly before him at the little groups of happy Senior Conservatives, was the most unkindest cut of all. What on earth was Freddie doing in England? Eight months before he had married the only daughter of Donaldson's Dog-Biscuits, of Long Island City, in the United States of America; and in Long Island City he ought now to have been, sedulously promoting the dog-biscuit industry's best interests. Instead of which, here he was in London—and, according to his telegram, in trouble.

Lord Emsworth passed a hand over his chin, to assist thought, and was vaguely annoyed by some obstacle that intruded itself in the path of his fingers. Concentrating his faculties, such as they were, on this obstacle, he discovered it to be his beard. It irritated him. Hitherto, in moments of stress, he had always derived comfort from the feel of a clean-shaven chin. He felt now as if he were rubbing his hand over sea-weed; and most unjustly—for it was certainly not that young man's fault that he had decided to grow a beard—he became aware of an added sense of grievance against the Hon. Freddie.

It was at this moment that he perceived his child approaching him across the smoking-room floor.

'Hullo, guv'nor!' said Freddie.

'Well, Frederick?' said Lord Emsworth.

There followed a silence. Freddie was remembering that he had not met his father since the day when he had slipped into the latter's hand a note announcing his marriage to a girl whom Lord Emsworth had never seen—except once, through a telescope, when he, Freddie, was kissing her in the grounds of Blandings Castle. Lord Emsworth, on his side, was brooding on that phrase 'in trouble,' which had formed so significant a part of his son's telegram. For fifteen years he had been reluctantly help-ing Freddie out of trouble; and now, when it had seemed that he was off his hands for ever, the thing had started all over again.

'Do sit down,' he said testily.

Freddie had been standing on one leg, and his constrained attitude annoyed Lord Emsworth.

'Right-ho,' said Freddie, taking a chair. 'I say, guv'nor, since when the foliage?'

'What?'

'The beard. I hardly recognized you.'

Another spasm of irritation shot through his lordship.

'Never mind my beard!'

'I don't if you don't,' said Freddie agreeably. 'It was dashed good of you, guv'nor, to come bounding up to town so promptly.'

'I came because your telegram said that you were in trouble.'

'British,' said Freddie approvingly. 'Very British.'

'Though what trouble you can be in I cannot imagine. It is surely not money again?'

'Oh, no. Not money. If that had been all, I would have applied to the good old pop-in-law. Old Donaldson's an ace. He thinks the world of me.'

'Indeed? I met Mr Donaldson only once, but he struck me as a man of sound judgment.'

'That's what I say. He thinks I'm a wonder. If it were simply a question of needing a bit of the ready, I could touch him like a shot. But it isn't money that's the trouble. It's Aggie. My wife, you know.'

'Well?'

'She's left me.'

'Left you!'

'Absolutely flat. Buzzed off, and the note pinned to the pin-cushion. She's now at the Savoy and won't let me come near her; and I'm at a service-flat in King Street, eating my jolly old heart out, if you know what I mean.'

Lord Emsworth uttered a deep sigh. He gazed drearily at his son, marvelling that it should be in the power of any young man, even a specialist like Freddie, so consistently to make a mess of his affairs. By what amounted to a miracle this offspring of his had contrived to lure a millionaire's daughter into marrying him; and now, it seemed, he had let her get away. Years before, when a boy, and romantic as most boys are, his lordship had sometimes regretted that the Emsworths, though an ancient clan, did not possess a Family Curse. How little he had suspected that he was shortly about to become the father of it.

'The fault,' he said tonelessly, 'was, I suppose, yours?'

'In a way, yes. But—'

'What precisely occurred?'

'Well, it was like this, guv'nor. You know how keen I've always been on the movies. Going to every picture I could manage, and so forth. Well, one night, as I was lying awake, I suddenly got the idea for a scenario of my own. And dashed good it was, too. It was about a poor man who had an accident, and the coves at the hospital said that an operation was the only thing that could save his life. But they wouldn't operate without five hundred dollars down in advance, and he hadn't got five hundred dollars. So his wife got hold of a millionaire.'

'What,' inquired Lord Emsworth, 'is all this drivel?'

'Drivel, guv'nor?' said Freddie, wounded. 'I'm only telling you my scenario.'

'I have no wish to hear it. What I am anxious to learn from you—in as few words as possible—is the reason for the breach between your wife and yourself.'

'Well, I'm telling you. It all started with the scenario. When I'd written it, I naturally wanted to sell it to somebody; and just about then Pauline Petite came East and took a house at Great Neck, and a pal of mine introduced me to her.'

'Who is Pauline Petite?'

'Good Heavens, guv'nor!' Freddie stared, amazed. 'You don't mean to sit there and tell me you've never heard of Pauline Petite! The movie star. Didn't you see "Passion's Slaves"?'

'I did not.'

'Nor "Silken Fetters"?'

'Never.'

'Nor "Purple Passion"? Nor "Bonds of Gold"? Nor "Seduction"? Great Scott, guv'nor, you haven't lived!'

'What about this woman?'

'Well, a pal introduced me to her, you see, and I started to pave the way to getting her interested in this scenario of mine. Because, if she liked it, of course it meant everything. Well, this involved seeing a good deal of her, you understand, and one night Jane Yorke happened to come on us having a bite together at an inn.'

'Good God!'

'Oh, it was all perfectly respectable, guv'nor. All strictly on the up-and-up. Purely a business relationship. But the trouble was I had kept the thing from Aggie because I wanted to surprise her. I wanted to be able to come to her with the scenario accepted and tell her I wasn't such a fool as I looked.'

'Any woman capable of believing that—'

'And most unfortunately I had said that I had to go to Chicago that night on business. So, what with one thing and another—Well, as I said just now, she's at the Savoy and I'm—'

'Who is Jane Yorke?'

A scowl marred Freddie's smooth features.

'A pill, guv'nor. One of the worst. A Jebusite and Amalekite. If it hadn't been for her, I believe I could have fixed the thing. But she got hold of Aggie and whisked her away and poisoned her mind. This woman, guv'nor, has got a brother in the background, and she wanted Aggie to marry the brother. And my belief is that she is trying to induce Aggie to pop over to Paris and get a divorce, so as to give the blighted brother another look in, dash him! So now, guv'nor, is the time for action. Now is the moment to rally round as never before. I rely on you.'

'Me? What on earth do you expect me to do?'

'Why, go to her and plead with her. They do it in the movies. I've seen thousands of pictures where the white-haired old father—'

'Stuff and nonsense!' said Lord Emsworth, stung to the quick—for, like so many well-preserved men of ripe years, he was under the impression that he was merely slightly brindled. 'You have made your bed, and you must stew in it.'

'Eh?'

'I mean, you must stew in your own juice. You have brought this trouble on yourself by your own idiotic behaviour, and you must bear the consequences.'

'You mean you won't go and plead?'

'No.'

'You mean yes?'

'I mean no.'

'Not plead?' said Freddie, desiring to get this thing clear.

'I refuse to allow myself to be drawn into the matter.'

'You won't even give her a ring on the telephone?'

'I will not.'

'Oh, come, guv'nor. Be a sport. Her suite's Number Sixty-seven. You can get her in a second and state my case, all for the cost of twopence. Have a pop at it.'

'No.'

Freddie rose with set face.

'Very well,' he said tensely. 'Then I may as well tell you, guv'nor, that my life is as good as over. The future holds nothing for me. I am a spent egg. If Aggie goes to Paris and gets that divorce, I shall retire to some quiet spot and there pass the few remaining years of my existence, a blighted wreck. Good-bye, guv'nor.'

'Good-bye.'

'Honk-honk!' said Freddie moodily.

As a general rule, Lord Emsworth was an early and a sound sleeper, one of the few qualities which he shared with Napoleon Bonaparte being the ability to slumber the moment his head touched the pillow. But that night, weighed down with his troubles, he sought unconsciousness in vain. And somewhere in the small hours of the morning he sat up in bed, quaking. A sudden grisly thought had occurred to him.

Freddie had stated that, in the event of his wife obtaining a divorce, he proposed to retire for the rest of his life to some quiet spot. Suppose by 'quiet spot' he meant Blandings Castle! The possibility shook Lord Emsworth like an ague. Freddie had visited Blandings for extended periods before, and it was his lordship's considered opinion that the boy was a worse menace to the happy life of rural England than botts, greenfly, or foot-and-mouth disease. The prospect of having him at Blandings indefinitely affected Lord Emsworth like a blow on the base of the skull.

An entirely new line of thought was now opened. Had he in the recent interview, he asked himself, been as kind as he should have been? Had he not been a little harsh? Had he been just a shade lacking in sympathy? Had he played quite the part a father ought to have played?

The answers to the questions, in the order stated, were as follows: No. Yes. Yes. And No.

Waking after a belated sleep and sipping his early tea, Lord Emsworth found himself full of a new resolve. He had changed his mind. It was his intention now to go to this daughter-in-law of his and plead with her as no father-in-law had ever pleaded yet.

A man who has had a disturbed night is not at his best on the following morning. Until after luncheon Lord Emsworth felt much too heavy-headed to do himself justice as a pleader. But a visit to the flowers at Kensington Gardens, followed by a capital chop and half a bottle of claret at the Regent Grill, put him into excellent shape. The heaviness had vanished, and he felt alert and quick-witted.

So much so that, on arriving at the Savoy Hotel, he behaved with a cunning of which he had never hitherto suspected himself capable. On the very verge of giving his name to the desk-clerk, he paused. It might well be, he reflected, that this daughter-in-law of his, including the entire Emsworth family in her feud, would, did she hear that he was waiting below, nip the whole programme in the bud by refusing to see him. Better, he decided, not to risk it. Moving away from the desk, he headed for the lift, and presently found himself outside the door of Suite Sixty-seven.

He tapped on the door. There was no answer. He tapped again, and, once more receiving no reply, felt a little nonplussed. He was not a very far-seeing man, and the possibility that his daughter-in-law might not be at home had not occurred to him. He was about to go away when, peering at the door, he perceived that it was ajar. He pushed it open; and, ambling in, found himself in a cosy sitting-room, crowded, as feminine sitting-rooms are apt to be, with flowers of every description.

Flowers were always a magnet to Lord Emsworth, and for some happy minutes he pottered from vase to vase, sniffing.

It was after he had sniffed for perhaps the twentieth time that the impression came to him that the room contained a curious echo. It was almost as though, each time he sniffed, some other person sniffed too. And yet the place was apparently empty. To submit the acoustics to a final test, his lordship sniffed once more. But this time the sound that followed was of a more sinister character. It sounded to Lord Emsworth exactly like a snarl.

It was a snarl. Chancing to glance floorwards, he became immediately aware, in close juxtaposition to his ankles, of what appeared at first sight to be a lady's muff. But, this being one of his bright afternoons, he realized in the next instant that it was no muff, but a toy dog of the kind which women are only too prone to leave lying about their sitting-rooms.

'God bless my soul!' exclaimed Lord Emsworth, piously commending his safety to Heaven, as so many of his rugged ancestors had done in rather similar circumstances on the battlefields of the Middle Ages.

He backed uneasily. The dog followed him. It appeared to have no legs, but to move by faith alone.

'Go away, sir!' said Lord Emsworth.

He hated small dogs. They nipped you. Take your eye off them, and they had you by the ankle before you knew where you were. Discovering that his manœuvres had brought him to a door, he decided to take cover. He opened the door and slipped through. Blood will tell. An Emsworth had taken cover at Agincourt.

He was now in a bedroom, and, judging by the look of things, likely to remain there for some time. The woolly dog, foiled by superior intelligence, was now making no attempt to conceal its chagrin. It had cast off all pretence of armed neutrality and was yapping with a hideous intensity and shrillness. And ever and anon it scratched with baffled fury at the lower panels.

'Go away, sir!' thundered his lordship.

'Who's there?'

Lord Emsworth leaped like a jumping bean. So convinced had he been of the emptiness of this suite of rooms that the voice, speaking where no voice should have been, crashed into his nerve centres like a shell.

'Who is there?'

The mystery, which had begun to assume an aspect of the supernatural, was solved. On the other side of the room was a door, and it was from behind this that the voice had spoken. It occurred to Lord Emsworth that it was merely part of the general malignity of Fate that he should have selected for a formal father-in-lawful call the moment when his daughter-in-law was taking a bath.

He approached the door, and spoke soothingly.

'Pray do not be alarmed, my dear.'

'Who are you? What are you doing in my room?'

'There is no cause for alarm—'

He broke off abruptly, for his words had suddenly been proved fundamentally untrue. There was very vital cause for alarm. The door of the bedroom had opened, and the muff-like dog, shrilling hate, was scuttling in its peculiar legless manner straight for his ankles.

Peril brings out unsuspected qualities in every man. Lord Emsworth was not a professional acrobat, but the leap he gave in this crisis would have justified his being mistaken for one. He floated through the air like a homing bird. From where he had been standing the bed was a considerable distance away but he reached it with inches to spare, and stood there, quivering. Below him, the woolly dog raged like the ocean at the base of a cliff.

It was at this point that his lordship became aware of a young woman standing in the doorway through which he had just passed.

About this young woman there were many points which would have found little favour in the eyes of a critic of feminine charm. She was too short, too square, and too solid. She had a much too determined chin. And her hair was of an unpleasing gingery hue. But the thing Lord Emsworth liked least about her was the pistol she was pointing at his head.

A plaintive voice filtered through the bathroom door.

'Who's there?'

'It's a man,' said the girl behind the gun.

'I know it's a man. He spoke to me. Who is he?'

'I don't know. A nasty-looking fellow. I saw him hanging about the passage outside your door, and I got my gun and came along. Come on out.'

'I can't. I'm all wet.'

It is not easy for a man who is standing on a bed with his hands up to achieve dignity, but Lord Emsworth did the best he could.

'My dear madam!'

'What are you doing here?'

'I found the door ajar—'

'And walked in to see if there were any jewel-cases ajar, too. I think,' added the young woman, raising her voice so as to make herself audible to the unseen bather, 'it's Dopey Smith.'

'Who?'

'Dopey Smith. The fellow the cops said tried for your jewels in New York. He must have followed you over here.'

'I am not Dopey Smith, madam,' cried his lordship. 'I am the Earl of Emsworth.'

'You are?'

'Yes, I am.'

'Yes, you are!'

'I came to see my daughter-in-law.'

'Well, here she is.'

The bathroom door opened, and there emerged a charming figure draped in a kimono. Even in that tense moment Lord Emsworth was conscious of a bewildered astonishment that such a girl could ever have stooped to mate with his son Frederick.

'Who did you say he was?' she asked, recommending herself still more strongly to his lordship's esteem by scooping up the woolly dog and holding it securely in her arms.

'He says he's the Earl of Emsworth.'

'I *am* the Earl of Emsworth.'

The girl in the kimono looked keenly at him as he descended from the bed.

'You know, Jane,' she said, a note of uncertainty in her voice, 'it might be. He looks very like Freddie.'

The appalling slur on his personal appearance held Lord Emsworth dumb. Like other men, he had had black moments when his looks had not altogether satisfied him, but he had never supposed that he had a face like Freddie's.

The girl with the pistol uttered a stupefying whoop.

'Jiminy Christmas!' she cried. 'Don't you see?'

'See what?'

'Why, it *is* Freddie. Disguised. Trying to get at you this way. It's just the sort of movie stunt he would think clever. Take them off, Ralph Vandeleur—I know you!'

She reached out a clutching hand, seized his lordship's beard in a vice-like grip, and tugged with all the force of a modern girl, trained from infancy at hockey, tennis and Swedish exercises.

It had not occurred to Lord Emsworth a moment before that anything could possibly tend to make his situation more uncomfortable than it already was. He saw now that he had been mistaken in this view. Agony beyond his liveliest dreams flamed through his shrinking frame.

The girl regarded him with a somewhat baffled look.

'H'm!' she said disappointedly. 'It seems to be real. Unless,' she continued, on a more optimistic note, 'he's fixed it on with specially strong fish-glue or something. I'd better try again.'

'No, don't,' said his lordship's daughter-in-law. 'It isn't Freddie. I would have recognized him at once.'

'Then he's a crook after all. Kindly step into that cupboard, George, while I phone for the constabulary.'

Lord Emsworth danced a few steps.

'I will not step into cupboards. I insist on being heard. I don't know who this woman is—'

'My name's Jane Yorke, if you're curious.'

'Ah! The woman who poisons my son's wife's mind against him! I know all about you.' He turned to the girl in the kimono. 'Yesterday my son Frederick implored me by telegram to come to London. I saw him at my club. Stop that dog barking!'

'Why shouldn't he bark?' said Miss Yorke. 'He's in his own home.'

'He told me,' proceeded Lord Emsworth, raising his voice, 'that there had been a little misunderstanding between you—'

'Little misunderstanding is good,' said Miss Yorke.

'He dined with that woman for a purpose.'

'And directly I saw them,' said Miss Yorke, 'I knew what the purpose was.'

The Hon. Mrs Threepwood looked at her friend, wavering.

'I believe it's true,' she said, 'and he really is Lord Emsworth. He seems to know all that happened. How could he know if Freddie hadn't told him?'

'If this fellow is a crook from the other side, of course he would know. The thing was in *Broadway Whispers* and *Town Gossip*, wasn't it?'

'All the same—'

The telephone bell rang sharply.

'I assure you—' began Lord Emsworth.

'Right!' said the unpleasant Miss Yorke, at the receiver. 'Send him right up.' She regarded his lordship with a brightly triumphant eye. 'You're out of luck, my friend,' she said. 'Lord Emsworth has just arrived, and he's on his way up now.'

There are certain situations in which the human brain may be excused for reeling. Lord Emsworth's did not so much reel as perform a kind of dance, as if it were in danger of coming unstuck. Always a dreamy and absent-minded man, unequal to the rough hurly-burly of life, he had passed this afternoon through an ordeal which might well have unsettled the most practical. And this extraordinary announcement, coming on top of all he had been through, was too much for him. He tottered into the sitting-room and sank into a chair. It seemed to him that he was living in a nightmare.

And certainly in the figure that entered a few moments later there was nothing whatever to correct this impression. It might have stepped straight into anybody's nightmare and felt perfectly at home right from the start.

The figure was that of a tall, thin man with white hair and a long and flowing beard of the same venerable hue. Strange as it seemed that a person of such appearance should not have been shot on sight early in his career, he had obviously reached an extremely advanced age. He was either a man of about a hundred and fifty who was rather young for his years or a man of about a hundred and ten who had been aged by trouble.

'My dear child!' piped the figure in a weak, quavering voice.

'Freddie!' cried the girl in the kimono.

'Oh, dash it!' said the figure.

There was a pause, broken by a sort of gasping moan from Lord Emsworth. More and more every minute his lordship was feeling the strain.

'Good God, guv'nor!' said the figure, sighting him.

His wife pointed at Lord Emsworth.

'Freddie, is that your father?'

'Oh, yes. Rather. Of course. Absolutely. But he said he wasn't coming.'

'I changed my mind,' said Lord Emsworth in a low, stricken voice.

'I told you so, Jane,' said the girl. 'I thought he was Lord Emsworth all the time. Surely you can see the likeness now?'

A kind of wail escaped his lordship.

'Do I look like that?' he said brokenly. He gazed at his son once more and shut his eyes.

'Well,' said Miss Yorke, in her detestable managing way, turning her forceful personality on the newcomer, 'now that you are here, Freddie Threepwood, looking like Father Christmas, what's the idea? Aggie told you never to come near her again.'

A young man of his natural limpness of character might well have retired in disorder before this attack, but Love had apparently made Frederick Threepwood a man of steel. Removing his beard and eyebrows, he directed a withering glance at Miss Yorke.

'I don't want to talk to you,' he said. 'You're a serpent in the bosom. I mean a snake in the grass.'

'Oh, am I?'

'Yes, you are. You poisoned Aggie's mind against me. If it hadn't been for you, I could have got her alone and told her my story as man to man.'

'Well, let's hear it now. You've had plenty of time to rehearse it.'

Freddie turned to his wife with a sweeping gesture.

'I—' He paused. 'I say, Aggie, old thing, you look perfectly topping in that kimono.'

'Stick to the point,' said Miss Yorke.

'That is the point,' said Mrs Freddie, not without a certain softness. 'But if you think I look perfectly topping, why do you go running around with movie-actresses with carroty hair?'

'Red-gold,' suggested Freddie deferentially.

'Carroty!'

'Carroty it is. You're absolutely right. I never liked it all along.'

'Then why were you dining with it?'

'Yes, why?' inquired Miss Yorke.

'I wish you wouldn't butt in,' said Freddie petulantly. 'I'm not talking to you.'

'You might just as well, for all the good it's going to do you.'

'Be quiet, Jane. Well, Freddie?'

'Aggie,' said the Hon. Freddie, 'it was this way.'

'Never believe a man who starts a story like that,' said Miss Yorke.

'Do please be quiet, Jane. Yes, Freddie?'

'I was trying to sell that carroty female a scenario, and I was keeping it from you because I wanted it to be a surprise.'

'Freddie darling! Was that really it?'

'You don't mean to say—' began Miss Yorke incredulously.

'Absolutely it. And, in order to keep in with the woman—whom, I may as well tell you, I disliked rather heartily from the start—I had to lush her up a trifle from time to time.'

'Of course.'

'You have to with these people.'

'Naturally.'

'Makes all the difference in the world if you push a bit of food into them preparatory to talking business.'

'All the difference in the world.'

Miss Yorke, who seemed temporarily to have lost her breath, recovered it.

'You don't mean to tell me,' she cried, turning in a kind of wild despair to the injured wife, 'that you really believe this apple sauce?'

'Of course she does,' said Freddie. 'Don't you, precious?'

'Of course I do, sweetie-pie.'

'And, what's more,' said Freddie, pulling from his breast-pocket a buff-coloured slip of paper with the air of one who draws from his sleeve that extra ace which makes all the difference in a keenly-contested game, 'I can prove it. Here's a cable that came this morning from the Super-Ultra-Art Film Company, offering me a thousand solid dollars for the scenario. So another time, you, will you kindly refrain from judging your—er—fellows by the beastly light of your own—ah—foul imagination?'

'Yes,' said his wife, 'I must say, Jane, that you have made as much mischief as anyone ever did. I wish in future you would stop interfering in other people's concerns.'

'Spoken,' said Freddie, 'with vim and not a little terse good sense. And I may add—'

'If you ask me,' said Miss Yorke, 'I think it's a fake.'

'What's a fake?'

'That cable.'

'What do you mean, a fake?' cried Freddie indignantly. 'Read it for yourself.'

'It's quite easy to get cables cabled you by cabling a friend in New York to cable them.'

'I don't get that,' said Freddie, puzzled.

'I do,' said his wife; and there shone in her eyes the light that shines only in the eyes of wives who, having swallowed their husband's story, resent destructive criticism from outsiders. 'And I never want to see you again, Jane Yorke.'

'Same here,' agreed Freddie. 'In Turkey they'd shove a girl like that in a sack and drop her in the Bosphorus.'

'I might as well go,' said Miss Yorke.

'And don't come back,' said Freddie. 'The door is behind you.'

The species of trance which had held Lord Emsworth in its grip during the preceding conversational exchanges was wearing off. And now, perceiving that Miss Yorke was apparently as unpopular with the rest of the company as with himself, he came gradually to life again. His recovery was hastened by the slamming of the door and the spectacle of his son Frederick clasping in his arms a wife who, his lordship had never forgotten, was the daughter of probably the only millionaire in existence who had that delightful willingness to take Freddie off his hands which was, in Lord Emsworth's eyes, the noblest quality a millionaire could possess.

He sat up and blinked feebly. Though much better, he was still weak.

'What was your scenario about, sweetness?' asked Mrs Freddie.

'I'll tell you, angel-face. Or should we stir up the guv'nor? He seems a bit under the weather.'

'Better leave him to rest for awhile. That woman Jane Yorke upset him.'

'She would upset anybody. If there's one person I bar, it's the blister who comes between man and wife. Not right, I mean, coming between man and wife. My scenario's about a man and wife. This fellow, you understand, is a poor cove—no money, if you see what I mean—and he has an accident, and the hospital blokes say they won't operate unless he can chip in with five hundred dollars down in advance. But where to get it? You see the situation?'

'Oh, yes.'

'Strong, what?'

'Awfully strong.'

'Well, it's nothing to how strong it gets later on. The cove's wife gets hold of a millionaire bloke and vamps him and lures him to the flat and gets him to promise he'll cough up the cash. Meanwhile, cut-backs of the doctor at the hospital on the 'phone. And she laughing merrily so as not to let the millionaire bloke guess that her heart is aching. I forgot to tell you the cove had to be operated on immediately or he would hand in his dinner-pail. Dramatic, eh?'

'Frightfully.'

'Well, then the millionaire bloke demands his price. I thought of calling it "A Woman's Price."'

'Splendid.'

'And now comes the blow-out. They go into the bedroom and— Oh, hullo, guv'nor! Feeling better?'

Lord Emsworth had risen. He was tottering a little as he approached them, but his mind was at rest.

'Much better, thank you.'

'You know my wife, what?'

'Oh, Lord Emsworth,' said Mrs Freddie, 'I'm so dreadfully sorry. I wouldn't have had anything like this happen for the world. But—'

Lord Emsworth patted her hand paternally. Once more he was overcome with astonishment that his son Frederick should have been able to win the heart of a girl so beautiful, so sympathetic, so extraordinarily rich.

'The fault was entirely mine, my dear child. But—' He paused. Something was plainly troubling him. 'Tell me, when Frederick was wearing that beard—when Frederick was—was—when he was wearing that beard, did he really look like me?'

'Oh, yes. Very like.'

'Thank you, my dear. That was all I wanted to know. I will leave you now. You will wish to be alone. You must come down to Blandings, my dear child, at the very earliest opportunity.'

He walked thoughtfully from the room.

'Does this hotel,' he inquired of the man who took him down in the lift, 'contain a barber's shop?'

'Yes, sir.'

'I wonder if you would direct me to it?' said his lordship.

Lord Emsworth sat in his library at Blandings Castle, drinking that last restful whisky and soda of the day. Through the open window came the scent of flowers and the little noises of the summer night.

He should have been completely at rest, for much had happened since his return to sweeten life for him. Angus McAllister had reported that the green-fly were yielding to treatment with whale-oil solution; and the stricken cow had taken a sudden turn for the better, and at last advices was sitting up and taking nourishment with something of the old appetite. Moreover, as he stroked his shaven chin, his lordship felt a better, lighter man, as if some burden had fallen from him.

And yet, as he sat there, a frown was on his forehead.

He rang the bell.

'M'lord?'

Lord Emsworth looked at his faithful butler with appreciation. Deuce of a long time Beach had been at the Castle, and would, no doubt, be there for many a year to come. A good fellow. Lord Emsworth had liked the way the man's eyes had lighted up on his return, as if the sight of his employer had removed a great weight from his mind.

'Oh, Beach,' said his lordship, 'kindly put in a trunk-call to London on the telephone.'

'Very good, m'lord.'

'Get through to Suite Number Sixty-seven at the Savoy Hotel, and speak to Mr Frederick.'

'Yes, your lordship.'

'Say that I particularly wish to know how that scenario of his ended.'

'Scenario, your lordship?'

'Scenario.'

'Very good, m'lord.'

Lord Emsworth returned to his reverie. Time passed. The butler returned.

'I have spoken to Mr Frederick, your lordship.'

'Yes?'

'He instructed me to give your lordship his best wishes, and to tell you that, when the millionaire and Mr Cove's wife entered the bedroom, there was a black jaguar tied to the foot of the bed.'

'A jaguar?'

'A jaguar, your lordship. Mrs Cove stated that it was there to protect her honour, whereupon the millionaire, touched by this, gave her the money, and they sang the Theme Song as a duet. Mr Cove made a satisfactory recovery after his operation, your lordship.'

'Ah!' said Lord Emsworth, expelling a deep breath. 'Thank you, Beach, that is all.'

3

PIG - HOO - O - O - O - EY!

THANKS to the publicity given to the matter by *The Bridgnorth, Shifnal, and Albrighton Argus* (with which is incorporated *The Wheat-Growers' Intelligencer and Stock Breeders' Gazetteer*), the whole world to-day knows that the silver medal in the Fat Pigs class at the eighty-seventh annual Shropshire Agricultural Show was won by the Earl of Emsworth's black Berkshire sow, Empress of Blandings.

Very few people, however, are aware how near that splendid animal came to missing the coveted honour.

Now it can be told.

This brief chapter of Secret History may be said to have begun on the night of the eighteenth of July, when George Cyril Wellbeloved (twenty-nine), pig-man in the employ of Lord Emsworth, was arrested by Police-Constable Evans of Market Blandings for being drunk and disorderly in the tap-room of the Goat and Feathers. On July the nineteenth, after first offering to apologize, then explaining that it had been his birthday, and finally attempting to prove an alibi, George Cyril was very properly jugged for fourteen days without the option of a fine.

On July the twentieth, Empress of Blandings, always hitherto a hearty and even a boisterous feeder, for the first time on record declined all nourishment. And on the morning of July the twenty-first, the veterinary surgeon called in to diagnose and deal with this strange asceticism, was compelled to confess to Lord Emsworth that the thing was beyond his professional skill.

Let us just see, before proceeding, that we have got these dates correct:

July 18.—Birthday Orgy of Cyril Wellbeloved.

July 19.—Incarceration of Ditto.

July 20.—Pig Lays off the Vitamins.

July 21.—Veterinary Surgeon Baffled.

Right.

The effect of the veterinary surgeon's announcement on Lord Emsworth was overwhelming. As a rule, the wear and tear of our complex modern life left this vague and amiable peer unscathed. So long as he had sunshine, regular meals, and complete freedom from the society of his younger son Frederick, he was placidly happy. But there were chinks in his armour, and one of these had been pierced this morning. Dazed by the news he had received, he stood at the window of the great library of Blandings Castle, looking out with unseeing eyes.

As he stood there, the door opened. Lord Emsworth turned; and having blinked once or twice, as was his habit when confronted suddenly with anything, recognized in the handsome and imperious-looking woman who had entered his sister, Lady Constance Keeble. Her demeanour, like his own, betrayed the deepest agitation.

'Clarence,' she cried, 'an awful thing has happened!'

Lord Emsworth nodded dully.

'I know. He's just told me.'

'What! Has he been here?'

'Only this moment left.'

'Why did you let him go? You must have known I would want to see him.'

'What good would that have done?'

'I could at least have assured him of my sympathy,' said Lady Constance stiffly.

'Yes, I suppose you could,' said Lord Emsworth, having considered the point. 'Not that he deserves any sympathy. The man's an ass.'

'Nothing of the kind. A most intelligent young man, as young men go.'

'Young? Would you call him young? Fifty, I should have said, if a day.'

'Are you out of your senses? Heacham fifty?'

'Not Heacham. Smithers.'

As frequently happened to her when in conversation with her brother, Lady Constance experienced a swimming sensation in the head.

'Will you kindly tell me, Clarence, in a few simple words, what you imagine we are talking about?'

'I'm talking about Smithers. Empress of Blandings is refusing her food, and Smithers says he can't do anything about it. And he calls himself a vet!'

'Then you haven't heard? Clarence, a dreadful thing has happened. Angela has broken off her engagement to Heacham.'

'And the Agricultural Show on Wednesday week!'

'What on earth has that got to do with it?' demanded Lady Constance, feeling a recurrence of the swimming sensation.

'What has it got to do with it?' said Lord Emsworth warmly. 'My champion sow, with less than ten days to prepare herself for a most searching examination in competition with all the finest pigs in the county, starts refusing her food—'

'Will you stop maundering on about your insufferable pig and give your attention to something that really matters? I tell you that Angela—your niece Angela—has broken off her engagement to Lord Heacham and expresses her intention of marrying that hopeless ne'er-do-well, James Belford.'

'The son of old Belford, the parson?'

'Yes.'

'She can't. He's in America.'

'He is not in America. He is in London.'

'No,' said Lord Emsworth, shaking his head sagely. 'You're wrong. I remember meeting his father two years ago out on the road by Meeker's twenty-acre field, and he distinctly told me the boy was sailing for America next day. He must be there by this time.'

'Can't you understand? He's come back.'

'Oh? Come back? I see. Come *back?*'

'You know there was once a silly sentimental sort of affair between him and Angela; but a year after he left she became engaged to Heacham and I thought the whole thing was over and done with. And now it seems that she met this young man Belford when she was in London last week, and it has started all over again. She tells me she has written to Heacham and broken the engagement.'

There was a silence. Brother and sister remained for a space plunged in thought. Lord Emsworth was the first to speak.

'We've tried acorns,' he said. 'We've tried skim milk. And we've tried potato-peel. But, no, she won't touch them.'

Conscious of two eyes raising blisters on his sensitive skin, he came to himself with a start.

'Absurd! Ridiculous! Preposterous!' he said, hurriedly. 'Breaking the engagement? Pooh! Tush! What nonsense! I'll have a word with that young man. If he thinks he can go about the place playing fast and loose with my niece and jilting her without so much as a—'

'Clarence!'

Lord Emsworth blinked. Something appeared to be wrong, but he could not imagine what. It seemed to him that in his last speech he had struck just the right note—strong, forceful, dignified.

'Eh?'

'It is Angela who has broken the engagement.'

'Oh, Angela?'

'She is infatuated with this man Belford. And the point is, what are we to do about it?'

Lord Emsworth reflected.

'Take a strong line,' he said firmly. 'Stand no nonsense. Don't send 'em a wedding-present.'

There is no doubt that, given time, Lady Constance would have found and uttered some adequately corrosive comment on this imbecile suggestion; but even as she was swelling preparatory to giving tongue, the door opened and a girl came in.

She was a pretty girl, with fair hair and blue eyes which in their softer moments probably reminded all sorts of people of twin lagoons slumbering beneath a southern sky. This, however, was not one of those moments. To Lord Emsworth, as they met his, they looked like something out of an oxy-acetylene blowpipe; and, as far as he was capable of being disturbed by anything that was not his younger son Frederick, he was disturbed. Angela, it seemed to him, was upset about something; and he was sorry. He liked Angela.

To ease a tense situation, he said:

'Angela, my dear, do you know anything about pigs?'

The girl laughed. One of those sharp, bitter laughs which are so unpleasant just after breakfast.

'Yes, I do. You're one.'

'Me?'

'Yes, you. Aunt Constance says that, if I marry Jimmy, you won't let me have my money.'

'Money? Money?' Lord Emsworth was mildly puzzled. 'What money? You never lent me any money.'

Lady Constance's feelings found vent in a sound like an overheated radiator.

'I believe this absent-mindedness of yours is nothing but a ridiculous pose, Clarence. You know perfectly well that when poor Jane died she left you Angela's trustee.'

'And I can't touch my money without your consent till I'm twenty-five.'

'Well, how old are you?'

'Twenty-one.'

'Then what are you worrying about?' asked Lord Emsworth, surprised. 'No need to worry about it for another four years. God bless my soul, the money is quite safe. It is in excellent securities.'

Angela stamped her foot. An unladylike action, no doubt, but how much better than kicking an uncle with it, as her lower nature prompted.

'I have told Angela,' explained Lady Constance, 'that, while we naturally cannot force her to marry Lord Heacham, we can at least keep her money from being squandered by this wastrel on whom she proposes to throw herself away.'

'He isn't a wastrel. He's got quite enough money to marry me on, but he wants some capital to buy a partnership in a—'

'He is a wastrel. Wasn't he sent abroad because—'

'That was two years ago. And since then—'

'My dear Angela, you may argue until—'

'I'm not arguing. I'm simply saying that I'm going to marry Jimmy, if we both have to starve in the gutter.'

'What gutter?' asked his lordship, wrenching his errant mind away from thoughts of acorns.

'Any gutter.'

'Now, please listen to me, Angela.'

It seemed to Lord Emsworth that there was a frightful amount of conversation going on. He had the sensation of having become a mere bit of flotsam upon a tossing sea of female voices. Both his sister and his niece appeared to have much to say, and they were saying it simultaneously and fortissimo. He looked wistfully at the door.

It was smoothly done. A twist of the handle, and he was where beyond those voices there was peace. Galloping gaily down the stairs, he charged out into the sunshine.

His gaiety was not long-lived. Free at last to concentrate itself on the really serious issues of life, his mind grew sombre and grim. Once more there descended upon him the cloud which had been oppressing his soul before all this Heacham-Angela-Belford business began. Each step that took him nearer to the sty where the ailing Empress resided seemed a heavier step than the last. He reached the sty; and, draping himself over the rails, peered moodily at the vast expanse of pig within.

For, even though she had been doing a bit of dieting of late, Empress of Blandings was far from being an ill-nourished animal. She resembled a captive balloon with ears and a tail, and was as nearly circular as a pig can be without bursting. Nevertheless, Lord Emsworth, as he regarded her, mourned and would not be comforted. A few more square meals under her belt, and no pig in all Shropshire could have held its head up in the Empress's presence. And now, just for lack of those few meals, the supreme animal would probably be relegated to the mean obscurity of an 'Honourably Mentioned.' It was bitter, bitter.

He became aware that somebody was speaking to him; and, turning, perceived a solemn young man in riding breeches.

'I say,' said the young man.

Lord Emsworth, though he would have preferred solitude, was relieved to find that the intruder was at least one of his own sex. Women are apt to stray off into side-issues, but men are practical and can be relied on to stick to the fundamentals. Besides, young Heacham probably kept pigs himself and might have a useful hint or two up his sleeve.

'I say, I've just ridden over to see if there was anything I could do about this fearful business.'

'Uncommonly kind and thoughtful of you, my dear fellow,' said Lord Emsworth, touched. 'I fear things look very black.'

'It's an absolute mystery to me.'

'To me, too.'

'I mean to say, she was all right last week.'

'She was all right as late as the day before yesterday.'

'Seemed quite cheery and chirpy and all that.'

'Entirely so.'

'And then this happens—out of a blue sky, as you might say.'

'Exactly. It is insoluble. We have done everything possible to tempt her appetite.'

'Her appetite? Is Angela ill?'

'Angela? No, I fancy not. She seemed perfectly well a few minutes ago.'

'You've seen her this morning, then? Did she say anything about this fearful business?'

'No. She was speaking about some money.'

'It's all so dashed unexpected.'

'Like a bolt from the blue,' agreed Lord Emsworth. 'Such a thing has never happened before. I fear the worst. According to the Wolff-Lehmann feeding standards, a pig, if in health, should consume daily nourishment amounting to fifty-seven thousand eight hundred calories, these to consist of proteids four pounds five ounces, carbohydrates twenty-five pounds—'

'What has that got to do with Angela?'

'Angela?'

'I came to find out why Angela has broken off our engagement.'

Lord Emsworth marshalled his thoughts. He had a misty idea that he had heard something mentioned about that. It came back to him.

'Ah, yes, of course. She has broken off the engagement, hasn't she? I believe it is because she is in love with someone else. Yes, now that I recollect, that was distinctly stated. The whole thing comes back to me quite clearly. Angela has decided to marry someone else. I knew there was some satisfactory explanation. Tell me, my dear fellow, what are your views on linseed meal.'

'What do you mean, linseed meal?'

'Why, linseed meal,' said Lord Emsworth, not being able to find a better definition. 'As a food for pigs.'

'Oh, curse all pigs!'

'What!' There was a sort of astounded horror in Lord Emsworth's voice. He had never been particularly fond of young Heacham, for he was not a man who took much to his juniors, but he had not supposed him capable of anarchistic sentiments like this. 'What did you say?'

'I said, "Curse all pigs!" You keep talking about pigs. I'm not interested in pigs. I don't want to discuss pigs. Blast and damn every pig in existence!'

Lord Emsworth watched him, as he strode away, with an emotion that was partly indignation and partly relief—indignation that a landowner and a fellow son of Shropshire could have brought himself to utter such words, and relief that one capable of such utterance was not going to marry into his family. He had always in his woollen-headed way been very fond of his niece Angela, and it was nice to think that the child had such solid good sense and so much cool discernment. Many girls of her age would have been carried away by the glamour of young Heacham's position and wealth; but she, divining with an intuition beyond her years that he was unsound on the subject of pigs, had drawn back while there was still time and refused to marry him.

A pleasant glow suffused Lord Emsworth's bosom, to be frozen out a few moments later as he perceived his sister Constance bearing down upon him. Lady Constance was a beautiful woman, but there were times when the charm of her face was marred by a rather curious expression; and from nursery days onward his lordship had learned that this expression meant trouble. She was wearing it now.

'Clarence,' she said, 'I have had enough of this nonsense of Angela and young Belford. The thing cannot be allowed to go drifting on. You must catch the two o'clock train to London.'

'What! Why?'

'You must see this man Belford and tell him that, if Angela insists on marrying him, she will not have a penny for four years. I shall be greatly surprised if that piece of information does not put an end to the whole business.'

Lord Emsworth scratched meditatively at the Empress's tank-like back. A mutinous expression was on his mild face.

'Don't see why she shouldn't marry the fellow,' he mumbled.

'Marry James Belford?'

'I don't see why not. Seems fond of him and all that.'

'You never have had a grain of sense in your head, Clarence. Angela is going to marry Heacham.'

'Can't stand that man. All wrong about pigs.'

'Clarence, I don't wish to have any more discussion and argument. You will go to London on the two o'clock train. You will see Mr Belford. And you will tell him about Angela's money. Is that quite clear?'

'Oh, all right,' said his lordship moodily. 'All right, all right, all right.'

The emotions of the Earl of Emsworth, as he sat next day facing his luncheon-guest, James Bartholomew Belford, across a table in the main dining-room of the Senior Conservative Club, were not of the liveliest and most agreeable. It was bad enough to be in London at all on such a day of golden sunshine. To be charged, while there, with the task of blighting the romance of two young people for whom he entertained a warm regard was unpleasant to a degree.

For, now that he had given the matter thought, Lord Emsworth recalled that he had always liked this boy Belford. A pleasant lad, with, he remembered now, a healthy fondness for that rural existence which so appealed to himself. By no means the sort of fellow who, in the very presence and hearing of Empress of Blandings, would have spoken disparagingly and with oaths of pigs as a class. It occurred to Lord Emsworth, as it has occurred to so many people, that the distribution of money in this world is all wrong. Why should a man like pig-despising Heacham have a rent roll that ran into the tens of thousands, while this very deserving youngster had nothing?

These thoughts not only saddened Lord Emsworth—they embarrassed him. He hated unpleasantness, and it was suddenly borne in upon him that, after he had broken the news that Angela's bit of capital was locked up and not likely to get loose, conversation with his young friend during the remainder of lunch would tend to be somewhat difficult.

He made up his mind to postpone the revelation. During the meal, he decided, he would chat pleasantly of this and that; and then, later, while bidding his guest good-bye, he would spring the thing on him suddenly and dive back into the recesses of the club.

Considerably cheered at having solved a delicate problem with such adroitness, he started to prattle.

'The gardens at Blandings,' he said, 'are looking particularly attractive this summer. My head-gardener, Angus McAllister, is a man with whom I do not always find myself seeing eye to eye, notably in the matter of hollyhocks, on which I consider his views subversive to a degree; but there is no denying that he understands roses. The rose garden—'

'How well I remember that rose garden,' said James Belford, sighing slightly and helping himself to brussels sprouts. 'It was there that Angela and I used to meet on summer mornings.'

Lord Emsworth blinked. This was not an encouraging start, but the Emsworths were a fighting clan. He had another try.

'I have seldom seen such a blaze of colour as was to be witnessed there during the month of June. Both McAllister and I adopted a very strong policy with the slugs and plant lice, with the result that the place was a mass of flourishing Damasks and Ayrshires and—'

'Properly to appreciate roses,' said James Belford, 'You want to see them as a setting for a girl like Angela. With her fair hair gleaming against the green leaves she makes a rose garden seem a veritable Paradise.'

'No doubt,' said Lord Emsworth. 'No doubt. I am glad you liked my rose garden. At Blandings, of course, we have the natural advantage of loamy soil, rich in plant food and humus; but, as I often say to McAllister, and on this point we have never had the slightest disagreement, loamy soil by itself is not enough. You must have manure. If every autumn a liberal mulch of stable manure is spread upon the beds and the coarser parts removed in the spring before the annual forking—'

'Angela tells me,' said James Belford, 'that you have forbidden our marriage.'

Lord Emsworth choked dismally over his chicken. Directness of this kind, he told himself with a pang of self-pity, was the sort of thing young Englishmen picked up in America. Diplomatic circumlocution flourished only in a more leisurely civilization, and in those energetic and forceful surroundings you learned to Talk Quick and Do It Now, and all sorts of uncomfortable things.

'Er—well, yes, now you mention it, I believe some informal decision of that nature was arrived at. You see, my dear fellow, my sister Constance feels rather strongly—'

'I understand. I suppose she thinks I'm a sort of prodigal.'

'No, no, my dear fellow. She never said that. Wastrel was the term she employed.'

'Well, perhaps I did start out in business on those lines. But you can take it from me that when you find yourself employed on a farm in Nebraska belonging to an applejack-nourished patriarch with strong views on work and a good vocabulary, you soon develop a certain liveliness.'

'Are you employed on a farm?'

'I was employed on a farm.'

'Pigs?' said Lord Emsworth in a low, eager voice.

'Among other things.'

Lord Emsworth gulped. His fingers clutched at the table-cloth.

'Then perhaps, my dear fellow, you can give me some advice. For the last two days my prize sow, Empress of Blandings, has declined all nourishment. And the Agricultural Show is on Wednesday week. I am distracted with anxiety.'

James Belford frowned thoughtfully.

'What does your pig-man say about it?'

'My pig-man was sent to prison two days ago. Two days!' For the first time the significance of the coincidence struck him. 'You don't think that can have anything to do with the animal's loss of appetite?'

'Certainly. I imagine she is missing him and pining away because he isn't there.'

Lord Emsworth was surprised. He had only a distant acquaintance with George Cyril Wellbeloved, but from what he had seen of him he had not credited him with this fatal allure.

'She probably misses his afternoon call.'

Again his lordship found himself perplexed. He had had no notion that pigs were such sticklers for the formalities of social life.

'His call?'

'He must have had some special call that he used when he wanted her to come to dinner. One of the first things you learn on a farm is hog-calling. Pigs are temperamental. Omit to call them, and they'll starve rather than put on the nose-bag. Call them right, and they will follow you to the ends of the earth with their mouths watering.'

'God bless my soul! Fancy that.'

'A fact, I assure you. These calls vary in different parts of America. In Wisconsin, for example, the words "Poig, Poig, Poig" bring home—in both the literal and the figurative sense—the bacon. In Illinois, I believe they call "Burp, Burp, Burp," while in Iowa the phrase "Kus, Kus, Kus" is preferred. Proceeding to Minnesota, we find "Peega, Peega, Peega" or, alternatively, "Oink, Oink, Oink," whereas in Milwaukee, so largely inhabited by those of German descent, you will hear the good old Teuton "Komm Schweine, Komm Schweine." Oh, yes, there are all sorts of pig-calls, from the Massachusetts "Phew, Phew, Phew" to the "Loo-ey, Loo-ey, Loo-ey" of Ohio, not counting various local devices such as beating on tin cans with axes or rattling pebbles in a suit-case. I knew a man out in Nebraska who used to call his pigs by tapping on the edge of the trough with his wooden leg.'

'Did he, indeed?'

'But a most unfortunate thing happened. One evening, hearing a woodpecker at the top of a tree, they started shinning up it; and when the man came out he found them all lying there in a circle with their necks broken.'

'This is no time for joking,' said Lord Emsworth, pained.

'I'm not joking. Solid fact. Ask anybody out there.'

Lord Emsworth placed a hand to his throbbing forehead.

'But if there is this wide variety, we have no means of knowing which call Wellbeloved . . .'

'Ah,' said James Belford, 'but wait. I haven't told you all. There is a master-word.'

'A what?'

'Most people don't know it, but I had it straight from the lips of Fred Patzel, the hog-calling champion of the Western States. What a man! I've known him to bring pork chops leaping from their plates. He informed me that, no matter whether an animal has been trained to answer to the Illinois "Burp" or the Minnesota "Oink," it will always give immediate service in response to this magic combination of syllables. It is to the pig world what the Masonic grip is to the human. "Oink" in Illinois or "Burp" in Minnesota, and the animal merely raises its eyebrows' and stares coldly. But go to either state and call "Pig-hoo-oo-ey!" . . .'

The expression on Lord Emsworth's face was that of a drowning man who sees a lifeline.

'Is that the master-word of which you spoke?'

'That's it.'

'Pig—?'

'—hoo-oo-ey.'

'Pig-hoo-o-ey?'

'You haven't got it quite right. The first syllable should be short and staccato, the second long and rising into a falsetto, high but true.'

'Pig-hoo-o-o-ey.'

'Pig-hoo-o-o-ey.'

'Pig-hoo-o-o-ey!' yodelled Lord Emsworth, flinging his head back and giving tongue in a high, penetrating tenor which caused ninety-three Senior Conservatives, lunching in the vicinity, to congeal into living statues of alarm and disapproval.

'More body to the "hoo," ' advised James Belford.

'Pig-hoo-o-o-o-ey!'

The Senior Conservative Club is one of the few places in London where lunchers are not accustomed to getting music with their meals. White-whiskered financiers gazed bleakly at bald-headed politicians, as if asking silently what was to be done about this. Bald-headed politicians stared back at white-whiskered financiers, replying in the language of the eye that they did not know. The general sentiment prevailing was a vague determination to write to the Committee about it.

'Pig-hoo-o-o-o-ey!' carolled Lord Emsworth. And, as he did so, his eye fell on the clock over the mantelpiece. Its hands pointed to twenty minutes to two.

He started convulsively. The best train in the day for Market Blandings was the one which left Paddington station at two sharp. After that there was nothing till the five-five.

He was not a man who often thought; but, when he did, to think was with him to act. A moment later he was scudding over the carpet, making for the door that led to the broad staircase.

Throughout the room which he had left, the decision to write in strong terms to the Committee was now universal; but from the mind, such as it was, of Lord Emsworth the past, with the single exception of the word 'Pig-hoo-o-o-o-ey!' had been completely blotted.

Whispering the magic syllables, he sped to the cloak-room and retrieved his hat. Murmuring them over and over again, he sprang into a cab. He was still repeating them as the train moved out of the station; and he would doubtless have gone on repeating them all the way to Market Blandings, had he not, as was his invariable practice when travelling by rail, fallen asleep after the first ten minutes of the journey.

The stopping of the train at Swindon Junction woke him with a start. He sat up, wondering, after his usual fashion on these occasions, who and where he was. Memory returned to him, but a memory that was, alas, incomplete. He remembered his name. He remembered that he was on his way home from a visit to London. But what it was that you said to a pig when inviting it to drop in for a bite of dinner he had completely forgotten.

It was the opinion of Lady Constance Keeble, expressed verbally during dinner in the brief intervals when they were alone, and by means of silent telepathy when Beach, the butler, was adding his dignified presence to the proceedings, that her brother Clarence, in his expedition to London to put matters plainly to James Belford, had made an outstanding idiot of himself.

There had been no need whatever to invite the man Belford to lunch; but, having invited him to lunch, to leave him sitting, without having clearly stated that Angela would have no money for four years, was the act of a congenital imbecile. Lady Constance had been aware ever since their childhood days that her brother had about as much sense as a—

Here Beach entered, superintending the bringing-in of the savoury, and she had been obliged to suspend her remarks.

This sort of conversation is never agreeable to a sensitive man, and his lordship had removed himself from the danger zone as soon as he could manage it. He was now seated in the library, sipping port and straining a brain which Nature had never intended for hard exercise in an effort to bring back that word of magic of which his unfortunate habit of sleeping in trains had robbed him.

'Pig—'

He could remember as far as that; but of what avail was a single syllable? Besides, weak as his memory was, he could recall that the whole gist or nub of the thing lay in the syllable that followed. The 'pig' was a mere preliminary.

Lord Emsworth finished his port and got up. He felt restless, stifled. The summer night seemed to call to him like some silver-voiced swineherd calling to his pig. Possibly, he thought, a breath of fresh air might stimulate his brain-cells. He wandered downstairs; and, having dug a shocking old slouch hat out of the cupboard where he hid it to keep his sister Constance from impounding and burning it, he strode heavily out into the garden.

He was pottering aimlessly to and fro in the parts adjacent to the rear of the castle when there appeared in his path a slender female form. He recognized it without pleasure. Any unbiased judge would have said that his niece Angela, standing there in the soft, pale light, looked like some dainty spirit of the Moon. Lord Emsworth was not an unbiased judge. To him Angela merely looked like Trouble. The march of civilization has given the modern girl a vocabulary and an ability to use it which her grandmother never had. Lord Emsworth would not have minded meeting Angela's grandmother a bit.

'Is that you, my dear?' he said nervously.

'Yes.'

'I didn't see you at dinner.'

'I didn't want any dinner. The food would have choked me. I can't eat.'

'It's precisely the same with my pig,' said his lordship. 'Young Belford tells me—'

Into Angela's queenly disdain there flashed a sudden animation.

'Have you seen Jimmy? What did he say?'

'That's just what I can't remember. It began with the word "Pig"—'

'But after he had finished talking about you, I mean. Didn't he say anything about coming down here?'

'Not that I remember.'

'I expect you weren't listening. You've got a very annoying habit, Uncle Clarence,' said Angela maternally, 'of switching your mind off and just going blah when people are talking to you. It gets you very much disliked on all sides. Didn't Jimmy say anything about me?'

'I fancy so. Yes, I am nearly sure he did.'

'Well, what?'

'I cannot remember.'

There was a sharp clicking noise in the darkness. It was caused by Angela's upper front teeth meeting her lower front teeth; and was followed by a sort of wordless exclamation. It seemed only too plain that the love and respect which a niece should have for an uncle were in the present instance at a very low ebb.

'I wish you wouldn't do that,' said Lord Emsworth plaintively.

'Do what?'

'Make clicking noises at me.'

'I will make clicking noises at you. You know perfectly well, Uncle Clarence, that you are behaving like a bohunkus.'

'A what?'

'A bonhunkus,' explained his niece coldly, 'is a very inferior sort of worm. Not the kind of worm that you see on lawns, which you can respect, but a really degraded species.'

'I wish you would go in, my dear,' said Lord Emsworth. 'The night air may give you a chill.'

'I won't go in. I came out here to look at the moon and think of Jimmy. What are you doing out here, if it comes to that?'

'I came here to think. I am greatly exercised about my pig, Empress of Blandings. For two days she has refused her food, and young Belford says she will not eat until she hears the proper call or cry. He very kindly taught it to me, but unfortunately I have forgotten it.'

'I wonder you had the nerve to ask Jimmy to teach you pig-calls, considering the way you're treating him.'

'But—'

'Like a leper, or something. And all I can say is that, if you remember this call of his, and it makes the Empress eat, you ought to be ashamed of yourself if you still refuse to let me marry him.'

'My dear,' said Lord Emsworth earnestly, 'if through young Belford's instrumentality Empress of Blandings is induced to take nourishment once more, there is nothing I will refuse him—nothing.'

'Honour bright?'

'I give you my solemn word.'

'You won't let Aunt Constance bully you out of it?'

Lord Emsworth drew himself up.

'Certainly not,' he said proudly. 'I am always ready to listen to your Aunt Constance's views, but there are certain matters where I claim the right to act according to my own judgment.' He paused and stood musing. 'It began with the word "Pig—"'

From somewhere near at hand music made itself heard. The servants' hall, its day's labours ended, was refreshing itself with the housekeeper's gramophone. To Lord Emsworth the strains were merely an additional annoyance. He was not fond of music. It reminded him of his younger son Frederick, a flat but persevering songster both in and out of the bath.

'Yes, I can distinctly recall as much as that. Pig— Pig—'

'WHO—'

Lord Emsworth leaped in the air. It was as if an electric shock had been applied to his person.

'WHO stole my heart away?' howled the gramophone. 'WHO—?'

The peace of the summer night was shattered by a triumphant shout.

'Pig-HOO-o-o-o-ey!'

A window opened. A large, bald head appeared. A dignified voice spoke.

'Who is there? Who is making that noise?'

'Beach!' cried Lord Emsworth. 'Come out here at once.'

'Very good, your lordship.'

And presently the beautiful night was made still more lovely by the added attraction of the butler's presence.

'Beach, listen to this.'

'Very good, your lordship.'

'Pig-hoo-o-o-o-ey!'

'Very good, your lordship.'

'Now you do it.'

'I, your lordship?'

'Yes. It's a way you call pigs.'

'I do not call pigs, your lordship,' said the butler coldly.

'What do you want Beach to do it for?' asked Angela.

'Two heads are better than one. If we both learn it, it will not matter should I forget it again.'

'By Jove, yes! Come on, Beach. Push it over the thorax,' urged the girl eagerly. 'You don't know it, but this is a matter of life and death. At-a-boy, Beach! Inflate the lungs and go to it.'

It had been the butler's intention, prefacing his remarks with the statement that he had been in service at the castle for eighteen years, to explain frigidly to Lord Emsworth that it was not his place to stand in the moonlight practising pig-calls. If, he would have gone on to add, his lordship saw the matter from a different angle, then it was his, Beach's, painful duty to tender his resignation, to become effective one month from that day.

But the intervention of Angela made this impossible to a man of chivalry and heart. A paternal fondness for the girl, dating from the days when he had stooped to enacting—and very convincingly, too, for his was a figure that lent itself to the impersonation—the rôle of a hippopotamus for her childish amusement, checked the words he would have uttered. She was looking at him with bright eyes, and even the rendering of pig-noises seemed a small sacrifice to make for her sake.

'Very good, your lordship,' he said in a low voice, his face pale and set in the moonlight. 'I shall endeavour to give satisfaction. I would merely advance the suggestion, your lordship, that we move a few steps farther away from the vicinity of the servants' hall. If I were to be overheard by any of the lower domestics, it would weaken my position as a disciplinary force.'

'What chumps we are!' cried Angela, inspired. 'The place to do it is outside the Empress's sty. Then, if it works, we'll see it working.'

Lord Emsworth found this a little abstruse, but after a moment he got it.

'Angela,' he said, 'you are a very intelligent girl. Where you get your brains from, I don't know. Not from my side of the family.'

The bijou residence of the Empress of Blandings looked very snug and attractive in the moonlight. But beneath even the beautiful things of life there is always an underlying sadness. This was supplied in the present instance by a long, low trough, only too plainly full to the brim of succulent mash and acorns. The fast, obviously, was still in progress.

The sty stood some considerable distance from the castle walls, so that there had been ample opportunity for Lord Emsworth to rehearse his little company during the journey. By the time they had ranged themselves against the rails, his two assistants were letter-perfect.

'Now,' said his lordship.

There floated out upon the summer night a strange composite sound that sent the birds roosting in the trees above shooting off their perches like rockets. Angela's clear soprano rang out like the voice of the village blacksmith's daughter. Lord Emsworth contributed a reedy tenor. And the bass notes of Beach probably did more to startle the birds than any other one item in the programme.

They paused and listened. Inside the Empress's boudoir there sounded the movement of a heavy body. There was an inquiring grunt. The next moment the sacking that covered the doorway was pushed aside, and the noble animal emerged.

'Now!' said Lord Emsworth again.

Once more that musical cry shattered the silence of the night. But it brought no responsive movement from Empress of Blandings. She stood there motionless, her nose elevated, her ears hanging down, her eyes everywhere but on the trough where, by rights, she should now have been digging in and getting hers. A chill disappointment crept over Lord Emsworth, to be succeeded by a gust of petulant anger.

'I might have known it,' he said bitterly. 'That young scoundrel was deceiving me. He was playing a joke on me.'

'He wasn't,' cried Angela indignantly. 'Was he, Beach?'

'Not knowing the circumstances, miss, I cannot venture an opinion.'

'Well, why has it no effect, then?' demanded Lord Emsworth.

'You can't expect it to work right away. We've got her stirred up, haven't we? She's thinking it over, isn't she? Once more will do the trick. Ready, Beach?'

'Quite ready, miss.'

'Then when I say three. And this time, Uncle Clarence, do please for goodness' sake not yowl like you did before. It was enough to put any pig off. Let it come out quite easily and gracefully. Now, then. One, two—three!'

The echoes died away. And as they did so a voice spoke.

'Community singing?'

'Jimmy!' cried Angela, whisking round.

'Hullo, Angela. Hullo, Lord Emsworth. Hullo, Beach.'

'Good evening, sir. Happy to see you once more.'

'Thanks. I'm spending a few days at the Vicarage with my father. I got down here by the five-five.'

Lord Emsworth cut peevishly in upon these civilities.

'Young man,' he said, 'what do you mean by telling me that my pig would respond to that cry? It does nothing of the kind.'

'You can't have done it right.'

'I did it precisely as you instructed me. I have had, moreover, the assistance of Beach here and my niece Angela—'

'Let's hear a sample.'

Lord Emsworth cleared his throat.

'Pig-hoo-o-o-o-ey!'

James Belford shook his head.

'Nothing like it,' he said. 'You want to begin the "Hoo" in a low minor of two quarter notes in four-four time. From this build gradually to a higher note, until at last the voice is soaring in full crescendo, reaching F sharp on the natural scale and dwelling for two retarded half-notes, then breaking into a shower of accidental grace-notes.'

'God bless my soul!' said Lord Emsworth, appalled. 'I shall never be able to do it.'

'Jimmy will do it for you,' said Angela. 'Now that he's engaged to me, he'll be one of the family and always popping about here. He can do it every day till the show is over.'

James Belford nodded.

'I think that would be the wisest plan. It is doubtful if an amateur could ever produce real results. You need a voice that has been trained on the open prairie and that has gathered richness and strength from competing with tornadoes. You need a manly, sunburned, wind-scorched voice with a suggestion in it of the crackling of corn husks and the whisper of evening breezes in the fodder. Like this!'

Resting his hands on the rail before him, James Belford swelled before their eyes like a young balloon. The muscles on his cheekbones stood out, his forehead became corrugated, his ears seemed to shimmer. Then, at the very height of the tension, he let it go like, as the poet beautifully puts it, the sound of a great Amen.

'Pig-HOOOOO-OOO-OOO-O-O-ey!'

They looked at him, awed. Slowly, fading off across hill and dale, the vast bellow died away. And suddenly, as it died, another, softer sound succeeded it. A sort of gulpy, gurgly, plobby, squishy, wofflesome sound, like a thousand eager men drinking soup in a foreign restaurant. And, as he heard it, Lord Emsworth uttered a cry of rapture.

The Empress was feeding.

4

COMPANY FOR GERTRUDE

THE Hon. Freddie Threepwood, married to the charming daughter of Donaldson's Dog-Biscuits of Long Island City, N.Y., and sent home by his father-in-law to stimulate the sale of the firm's products in England, naturally thought right away of his aunt Georgiana. There, he reasoned, was a woman who positively ate dog-biscuits. She had owned, when he was last in the country, a matter of four Pekes, two Poms, a Yorkshire terrier, five Sealyhams, a Borzoi and an Airedale: and if that didn't constitute a promising market for Donaldson's Dog-Joy ('Get your dog thinking the Donaldson way'), he would like to know what did. The Alcester connection ought, he considered, to be good for at least ten of the half-crown cellophane-sealed packets a week.

A day or so after his arrival, accordingly, he hastened round to Upper Brook Street to make a sales-talk: and it was as he was coming rather pensively out of the house at the conclusion of the interview that he ran into Beefy Bingham, who had been up at Oxford with him. Several years had passed since the other, then a third year Blood and Trial Eights man, had bicycled along tow-paths saying rude things through a megaphone about Freddie's stomach, but he recognized him instantly. And this in spite of the fact that the passage of time appeared to have turned old

Beefers into a clergyman. For the colossal frame of this Bingham was now clad in sober black, and he was wearing one of those collars which are kept in position without studs, purely by the exercise of will-power.

'Beefers!' cried Freddie, his slight gloom vanishing in the pleasure of this happy reunion.

The Rev. Rupert Bingham, though he returned his greeting with cordiality, was far from exuberant. He seemed subdued, gloomy, as if he had discovered schism among his flock. His voice, when he spoke, was the voice of a man with a secret sorrow.

'Oh, hullo, Freddie. I haven't seen you for years. Keeping pretty fit?'

'As a fiddle, Beefers, old man, as a fiddle. And you?'

'Oh, I'm all right,' said the Rev. Rupert, still with that same strange gloom. 'What were you doing in that house?'

'Trying to sell dog-biscuits.'

'Do you sell dog-biscuits?'

'I do when people have sense enough to see that Donaldson's Dog-Joy stands alone. But could I make my fatheaded aunt see that? No, Beefers, not though I talked for an hour and sprayed her with printed matter like a—'

'Your aunt? I didn't know Lady Alcester was your aunt.'

'Didn't you, Beefers? I thought it was all over London.'

'Did she tell you about me?'

'What about you? Great Scott! Are you the impoverished bloke who wants to marry Gertrude?'

'Yes.'

'Well, I'm dashed.'

'I love her, Freddie,' said the Rev. Rupert Bingham. 'I love her as no man . . .'

'Rather. Quite. Absolutely. I know. All the usual stuff. And she loves you, what?'

'Yes. And now they've gone and sent her off to Blandings, to be out of my way.'

'Low. Very low. But why are you impoverished? What about tithes? I always understood you birds made a pot out of tithes.'

'There aren't any tithes where I am.'

'No tithes?'

'None.'

'H'm. Not so hot. Well, what are you going to do about it, Beefers?'

'I thought of calling on your aunt and trying to reason with her.'

Freddie took his old friend's arm sympathetically and drew him away.

'No earthly good, old man. If a woman won't buy Donaldson's Dog-Joy, it means she has some sort of mental kink and it's no use trying to reason with her. We must think of some other procedure. So Gertrude is at Blandings, is she? She would be. The family seem to look on the place as a sort of Bastille. Whenever the young of the species make a floater like falling in love with the wrong man, they are always shot off to Blandings to recover. The guv'nor has often complained about it bitterly. Now, let me think.'

They passed into Park Street. Some workmen were busy tearing up the paving with pneumatic drills, but the whirring of Freddie's brain made the sound almost inaudible.

'I've got it,' he said at length, his features relaxing from the terrific strain. 'And it's a dashed lucky thing for you, my lad, that I went last night to see that super-film, "Young Hearts Adrift," featuring Rosalie Norton and Otto Byng. Beefers, old man, you're legging it straight down to Blandings this very afternoon.'

'What!'

'By the first train after lunch. I've got the whole thing planned out. In this super-film, "Young Hearts Adrift," a poor but deserving young man was in love with the daughter of rich and haughty parents, and they took her away to the country so that she could forget, and a few days later a mysterious stranger turned up at the place and ingratiated himself with the parents and said he wanted to marry their daughter, and they gave their consent, and the wedding took place, and then he tore off his whiskers and it was Jim!'

'Yes, but . . .'

'Don't argue. The thing's settled. My aunt needs a sharp lesson. You would think a woman would be only too glad to put business in the way of her nearest and dearest, especially when shown samples and offered a fortnight's free trial. But no! She insists on sticking to Peterson's Pup-

Food, a wholly inferior product—lacking, I happen to know, in many of the essential vitamins—and from now on, old boy, I am heart and soul in your cause.'

'Whiskers?' said the Rev. Rupert doubtfully.

'You won't have to wear any whiskers. My guv'nor's never seen you. Or has he?'

'No, I've not met Lord Emsworth.'

'Very well, then.'

'But what good will it do me, ingratiating myself, as you call it, with your father? He's only Gertrude's uncle.'

'What good? My dear chap, are you aware that the guv'nor owns the country-side for miles around? He has all sorts of livings up his sleeve— livings simply dripping with tithes—and can distribute them to whoever he likes. I know, because at one time there was an idea of making me a parson. But I would have none of it.'

The Rev. Rupert's face cleared.

'Freddie, there's something in this.'

'You bet there's something in it.'

'But how can I ingratiate myself with your father?'

'Perfectly easy. Cluster round him. Hang on his every word. Interest yourself in his pursuits. Do him little services. Help him out of chairs. . . . Why, great Scott, I'd undertake to ingratiate myself with Stalin if I gave my mind to it. Pop off and pack the old toothbrush, and I'll go and get the guv'nor on the 'phone.'

At about the time when this pregnant conversation was taking place in London, W.1, far away in distant Shropshire Clarence, ninth Earl of Emsworth, sat brooding in the library of Blandings Castle. Fate, usually indulgent to this dreamy peer, had suddenly turned nasty and smitten him a grievous blow beneath the belt.

They say Great Britain is still a first-class power, doing well and winning respect from the nations: and, if so, it is, of course, extremely gratifying. But what of the future? That was what Lord Emsworth was asking himself. Could this happy state of things last? He thought not. Without wishing to be pessimistic, he was dashed if he saw how a country containing men like Sir Gregory Parsloe-Parsloe of Matchingham Hall could hope to survive.

Strong? No doubt. Bitter? Granted. But not, we think, too strong, not—in the circumstances—unduly bitter. Consider the facts.

When, shortly after the triumph of Lord Emsworth's preeminent sow, Empress of Blandings, in the Fat Pigs Class at the eighty-seventh annual Shropshire Agricultural Show, George Cyril Wellbeloved, his lordship's pig-man, had expressed a desire to hand in his portfolio and seek employment elsewhere, the amiable peer, though naturally grieved, felt no sense of outrage. He put the thing down to the old roving spirit of the Wellbeloveds. George Cyril, he assumed, wearying of Shropshire, wished to try a change of air in some southern or eastern country. A nuisance, undoubtedly, for the man, when sober, was beyond question a force in the piggery. He had charm and personality. Pigs liked him. Still, if he wanted to resign office, there was nothing to be done about it.

But when, not a week later, word was brought to Lord Emsworth that, so far from having migrated to Sussex or Norfolk or Kent or somewhere, the fellow was actually just round the corner in the neighbouring village of Much Matchingham, serving under the banner of Sir Gregory Parsloe-Parsloe of Matchingham Hall, the scales fell from his eyes. He realized that black treachery had been at work. George Cyril Wellbeloved had sold himself for gold, and Sir Gregory Parsloe-Parsloe, hitherto looked upon as a high-minded friend and fellow Justice of the Peace, stood revealed as that lowest of created things, a lurer-away of other people's pig-men.

And there was nothing one could do about it.

Monstrous!

But true.

So deeply was Lord Emsworth occupied with the consideration of this appalling state of affairs that it was only when the knock upon the door was repeated that it reached his consciousness.

'Come in,' he said hollowly.

He hoped it was not his niece Gertrude. A gloomy young woman. He could hardly stand Gertrude's society just now.

It was not Gertrude. It was Beach, the butler.

'Mr Frederick wishes to speak to your lordship on the telephone.'

An additional layer of greyness fell over Lord Emsworth's spirit as he toddled down the great staircase to the telephone closet in the hall. It was his experience that almost any communication from Freddie indicated trouble.

But there was nothing in his son's voice as it floated over the wire to suggest that all was not well.

'Hullo, guv'nor.'

'Well, Frederick?'

'How's everything at Blandings?'

Lord Emsworth was not the man to exhibit the vultures gnawing at his heart to a babbler like the Hon. Freddie. He replied, though it hurt him to do so, that everything at Blandings was excellent.

'Good-oh!' said Freddie. 'Is the old doss-house very full up at the moment?'

'If,' replied his lordship, 'you are alluding to Blandings Castle, there is nobody at present staying here except myself and your cousin Gertrude. Why?' he added in quick alarm. 'Were you thinking of coming down?'

'Good God, no!' cried his son with equal horror. 'I mean to say, I'd love it, of course, but just now I'm too busy with Dog-Joy.'

'Who is Popjoy?'

'Popjoy? Popjoy? Oh, ah, yes. He's a pal of mine and, as you've plenty of room, I want you to put him up for a bit. Nice chap. You'll like him. Right-ho, then, I'll ship him off on the three-fifteen.'

Lord Emsworth's face had assumed an expression which made it fortunate for his son that television was not yet in operation on the telephone systems of England: and he had just recovered enough breath for the delivery of a blistering refusal to have any friend of Freddie's within fifty miles of the place when the other spoke again.

'He'll be company for Gertrude.'

And at these words a remarkable change came over Lord Emsworth. His face untwisted itself. The basilisk glare died out of his eyes.

'God bless my soul! That's true!' he exclaimed. 'That's certainly true.

So he will. The three-fifteen, did you say? I will send the car to Market Blandings to meet it.'

Company for Gertrude? A pleasing thought. A fragrant, refreshing, stimulating thought. Somebody to take Gertrude off his hands occasionally was what he had been praying for ever since his sister Georgiana had dumped her down on him.

One of the chief drawbacks to entertaining in your home a girl who has been crossed in love is that she is extremely apt to go about the place doing good. All that life holds for her now is the opportunity of being kind to others, and she intends to be kind if it chokes them. For two weeks Lord Emsworth's beautiful young niece had been moving to and fro through the castle with a drawn face, doing good right and left: and his lordship, being handiest, had had to bear the brunt of it. It was with the first real smile he had smiled that day that he came out of the telephone-cupboard and found the object of his thoughts entering the hall in front of him.

'Well, well, well, my dear,' he said cheerily. 'And what have you been doing?'

There was no answering smile on his niece's face. Indeed, looking at her, you could see that this was a girl who had forgotten how to smile. She suggested something symbolic out of Maeterlinck.

'I have been tidying your study, Uncle Clarence,' she replied listlessly. 'It was in a dreadful mess.'

Lord Emsworth winced as a man of set habits will who has been remiss enough to let a Little Mother get at his study while his back is turned, but he continued bravely on the cheerful note.

'I have been talking to Frederick on the telephone.'

'Yes?' Gertrude sighed, and a bleak wind seemed to blow through the hall. 'Your tie's crooked, Uncle Clarence.'

'I like it crooked,' said his lordship, backing. 'I have a piece of news for you. A friend of Frederick's is coming down here tonight for a visit. His name, I understand, is Popjoy. So you will have some young society at last.'

'I don't want young society.'

'Oh, come, my dear.'

She looked at him thoughtfully with large, sombre eyes. Another sigh escaped her.

'It must be wonderful to be as old as you are, Uncle Clarence.'

'Eh?' said his lordship, starting.

'To feel that there is such a short, short step to the quiet tomb, to the ineffable peace of the grave. To me, life seems to stretch out endlessly, like a long, dusty desert. Twenty-three! That's all I am. Only twenty-three. And all our family live to sixty.'

'What do you mean, sixty?' demanded his lordship, with the warmth of a man who would be that next birthday. 'My poor father was seventy-seven when he was killed in the hunting-field. My uncle Robert lived till nearly ninety. My cousin Claude was eighty-four when he broke his neck trying to jump a five-barred gate. My mother's brother, Alistair . . .'

'Don't!' said the girl with a little shudder. 'Don't! It makes it all seem so awful and hopeless.'

Yes, that was Gertrude: and in Lord Emsworth's opinion she needed company.

The reactions of Lord Emsworth to the young man Popjoy, when he encountered him for the first time in the drawing-room shortly before dinner, were in the beginning wholly favourable. His son's friend was an extraordinarily large and powerful person with a frank, open, ingenuous face about the colour of the inside of a salmon, and he seemed a little nervous. That, however, was in his favour. It was, his lordship felt, a pleasant surprise to find in one of the younger generation so novel an emotion as diffidence.

He condoned, therefore, the other's trick of laughing hysterically even when the subject under discussion was the not irresistibly ludi- crous one of green-fly in the rose-garden. He excused him for appearing to find something outstandingly comic in the statement that the glass was going up. And when, springing to his feet at the entrance of Ger- trude, the young man performed some complicated steps in conjunction with a table covered with china and photograph-frames, he joined in the mirth which the feat provoked not only from the visitor but actually from Gertrude herself.

Yes, amazing though it might seem, his niece Gertrude, on seeing this young Popjoy, had suddenly burst into a peal of happy laughter. The gloom of the last two weeks appeared to be gone. She laughed. The young man laughed. They proceeded down to dinner in a perfect gale of merriment, rather like a chorus of revellers exiting after a concerted number in an old-fashioned comic opera.

And at dinner the young man had spilt his soup, broken a wine-glass, and almost taken another spectacular toss when leaping up at the end of the meal to open the door. At which Gertrude had laughed, and the young man had laughed, and his lordship had laughed—though not, perhaps, quite so heartily as the young folks, for that wine-glass had been one of a set which he valued.

However, weighing profit and loss as he sipped his port, Lord Emsworth considered that the ledger worked out on the right side. True, he had taken into his home what appeared to be a half-witted acrobat: but then any friend of his son Frederick was bound to be weak in the head, and, after all, the great thing was that Gertrude seemed to appreciate the newcomer's society. He looked forward contentedly to a succession of sunshine days of peace, perfect peace with loved ones far away; days when he would be able to work in his garden without the fear, which had been haunting him for the last two weeks, of finding his niece drooping wanly at his side and asking him if he was wise to stand about in the hot sun. She had company now that would occupy her elsewhere.

His lordship's opinion of his guest's mental deficiencies was strengthened late that night when, hearing footsteps on the terrace, he poked his head out and found him standing beneath his window, blowing kisses at it.

At the sight of his host he appeared somewhat confused.

'Lovely evening,' he said, with his usual hyenaesque laugh. 'I—er—thought . . . or, rather . . . that is to say . . . Ha, ha, ha!'

'Is anything the matter?'

'No, no! No! No, thanks, no! No! No, no! I—er—ho, ho, ho!—just came out for a stroll, ha, ha!'

Lord Emsworth returned to his bed a little thoughtfully. Perhaps some premonition of what was to come afflicted his subconscious mind, for, as he slipped between the sheets, he shivered. But gradually, as he dozed off, his equanimity became restored.

Looking at the thing in the right spirit, it might have been worse. After all, he felt, the mists of sleep beginning to exert their usual beneficent influence, he might have been entertaining at Blandings Castle one of his nephews, or one of his sisters, or even—though this was morbid— his younger son Frederick.

In matters where shades of feeling are involved, it is not always easy for the historian to be as definite as he could wish. He wants to keep the record straight, and yet he cannot take any one particular moment of time, pin it down for the scrutiny of Posterity and say 'This was the moment when Lord Emsworth for the first time found himself wishing that his guest would tumble out of an upper window and break his neck.' To his lordship it seemed that this had been from the beginning his constant day-dream, but such was not the case. When, on the second morning of the other's visit, the luncheon-gong had found them chatting in the library and the young man, bounding up, had extended a hand like a ham and, placing it beneath his host's arm, gently helped him to rise, Lord Emsworth had been quite pleased by the courteous attention.

But when the fellow did the same thing day after day, night after night, every time he caught him sitting; when he offered him an arm to help him across floors; when he assisted him up stairs, along corridors, down paths, out of rooms and into raincoats; when he snatched objects from his hands to carry them himself; when he came galloping out of the house on dewy evenings laden down with rugs, mufflers, hats and, on one occasion, positively a blasted respirator . . . why, then Lord Emsworth's proud spirit rebelled. He was a tough old gentleman and, like most tough old gentlemen, did not enjoy having his juniors look on him as something pathetically helpless that crawled the earth waiting for the end.

It had been bad enough when Gertrude was being the Little Mother. This was infinitely worse. Apparently having conceived for him one of those unreasoning, overwhelming devotions, this young Popjoy stuck closer than a brother; and for the first time Lord Emsworth began to appreciate what must have been the feelings of that Mary who aroused a similar attachment in the bosom of her lamb. It was as if he had been an Oldest Inhabitant fallen into the midst of a troop of Boy Scouts, all doing Good Deeds simultaneously, and he resented it with an indescribable bitterness. One can best illustrate his frame of mind by saying that, during the last phase, if he had been called upon to choose between his guest and Sir Gregory Parsloe-Parsloe as a companion for a summer ramble through the woods, he would have chosen Sir Gregory.

And then, on top of all this, there occurred the episode of the step-ladder.

The Hon. Freddie Threepwood, who had decided to run down and see how matters were developing, learned the details of this rather unfortunate occurrence from his cousin Gertrude. She met him at Market Blandings Station, and he could see there was something on her mind. She had not become positively Maeterlinckian again, but there was sorrow in her beautiful eyes: and Freddie, rightly holding that with a brainy egg like himself directing her destinies they should have contained only joy and sunshine, was disturbed by this.

'Don't tell me the binge has sprung a leak,' he said anxiously.

Gertrude sighed.

'Well, yes and no.'

'What do you mean, yes and no? Properly worked, the thing can't fail. This points to negligence somewhere. Has old Beefers been ingratiating himself?'

'Yes.'

'Hanging on the guv'nor's every word? Interesting himself in his pursuits? Doing him little services? And been at it two weeks? Good heavens! By now the guv'nor should be looking on him as a prize pig. Why isn't he?'

'I didn't say he wasn't. Till this afternoon I rather think he was. At any rate, Rupert says he often found Uncle Clarence staring at him in a sort of lingering, rather yearning way. But when that thing happened this afternoon, I'm afraid he wasn't very pleased.'

'What thing?'

'That step-ladder business. It was like this. Rupert and I sort of went for a walk after lunch, and by the time I had persuaded him that he ought to go and find Uncle Clarence and ingratiate himself with him, Uncle Clarence had disappeared. So Rupert hunted about for a long time and at last heard a snipping noise and found him miles away standing on a step-ladder, sort of pruning some kind of tree with a pair of shears. So Rupert said, "Oh, there you are!" And Uncle Clarence said, Yes, there he was, and Rupert said, "Ought you to tire yourself? Won't you let me do that for you?"'

'The right note,' said Freddie approvingly. 'Assiduity. Zeal. Well?'

'Well, Uncle Clarence said, "No, thank you!"—Rupert thinks it was "Thank you"—and Rupert stood there for a bit, sort of talking, and then he suddenly remembered and told Uncle Clarence that you had just 'phoned that you were coming down this evening, and I think Uncle Clarence must have got a touch of cramp or something, because he gave a kind of sudden sharp groan, Rupert says, and sort of quivered all over. This made the steps wobble, of course, so Rupert dashed forward to steady them, and he doesn't know how it happened, but they suddenly seemed to sort of shut up like a pair of scissors, and the next thing he knew Uncle Clarence was sitting on the grass, not seeming to like it much, Rupert says. He had ricked his ankle a bit and shaken himself up a bit, and altogether, Rupert says, he wasn't fearfully sunny. Rupert says he thinks he may have lost ground a little.'

Freddie pondered with knit brows. He was feeling something of the chagrin of a general who, after sweating himself to a shadow planning a great campaign, finds his troops unequal to carrying it out.

'It's such a pity it should have happened. One of the vicars near here has just been told by the doctor that he's got to go off to the south of France, and the living is in Uncle Clarence's gift. If only Rupert could have had that, we could have got married. However, he's bought Uncle Clarence some lotion.'

Freddie started. A more cheerful expression came into his sternly careworn face.

'Lotion?'

'For his ankle.'

'He couldn't have done better,' said Freddie warmly. 'Apart from showing the contrite heart, he has given the guv'nor medicine, and medicine to the guv'nor is what catnip is to the cat. Above all things he dearly loves a little bit of amateur doctoring. As a rule he tries it on somebody else— two years ago he gave one of the housemaids some patent ointment for chilblains and she went screaming about the house—but, no doubt, now that the emergency has occurred, he will be equally agreeable to treating himself. Old Beefers has made the right move.'

In predicting that Lord Emsworth would appreciate the gift of lotion, Freddie had spoken with an unerring knowledge of his father's character. The master of Blandings was one of those fluffy-minded old gentlemen who are happiest when experimenting with strange drugs. In a less censorious age he would have been a Borgia. It was not until he had retired to bed that he discovered the paper-wrapped bottle on the table by his side. Then he remembered that the pest Popjoy had mumbled something at dinner about buying him something or other for his injured ankle. He tore off the paper and examined the contents of the bottle with a lively satisfaction. The liquid was a dingy grey and sloshed pleasantly when you shook it. The name on the label—Blake's Balsam—was new to him, and that in itself was a recommendation.

His ankle had long since ceased to pain him, and to some men this might have seemed an argument against smearing it with balsam; but not to Lord Emsworth. He decanted a liberal dose into the palm of his hand. He sniffed it. It had a strong, robust, bracing sort of smell. He spent the next five minutes thoughtfully rubbing it in. Then he put the light out and went to sleep.

It is a truism to say that in the world as it is at present constituted few things have more far-reaching consequences than the accident of birth.

Lord Emsworth had probably suspected this. He was now to receive direct proof. If he had been born a horse instead of the heir to an earldom, that lotion would have been just right for him. It was for horses, though the Rev. Rupert Bingham had omitted to note the fact, that Blake had planned his balsam; and anyone enjoying even a superficial acquaintance with horses and earls knows that an important difference between them is that the latter have the more sensitive skins. Waking at a quarter to two from dreams of being burned at the stake by Red Indians, Lord Emsworth found himself suffering acute pain in the right leg.

He was a little surprised. He had not supposed that that fall from the ladder had injured him so badly. However, being a good amateur doctor, he bore up bravely and took immediate steps to cope with the trouble. Having shaken the bottle till it foamed at the mouth, he rubbed in some more lotion. It occurred to him that the previous application might have been too sketchy, so this time he did it thoroughly. He rubbed and kneaded for some twenty minutes. Then he tried to go to sleep.

Nature has made some men quicker thinkers than others. Lord Emsworth's was one of those leisurely brains. It was not till nearly four o'clock that the truth came home to him. When it did, he was just on the point of applying a fifth coating of the balsam to his leg. He stopped abruptly, replaced the cork, and, jumping out of bed, hobbled to the cold-water tap and put as much of himself under it as he could manage.

The relief was perceptible, but transitory. At five he was out again, and once more at half-past. At a quarter to six, succeeding in falling asleep, he enjoyed a slumber, somewhat disturbed by the intermittent biting of sharks, which lasted till a few minutes past eight. Then he woke as if an alarm clock had rung, and realized that further sleep was out of the question.

He rose from his bed and peered out of the window. It was a beautiful morning. There had been rain in the night and a world that looked as if it had just come back from the cleaner's sparkled under a beaming sun. Cedars cast long shadows over the smooth green lawns. Rooks cawed soothingly: thrushes bubbled in their liquid and musical way: and the air was full of a summer humming. Among those present of the insect world, Lord Emsworth noticed several prominent gnats.

Beyond the terrace, glittering through the trees, gleamed the waters of the lake. They seemed to call to him like a bugle. Although he had neglected the practice of late, there was nothing Lord Emsworth enjoyed more than a before-breakfast dip: and to-day anything in the nature of water had a particularly powerful appeal for him. The pain in his ankle had subsided by now to a dull throbbing, and it seemed to him that a swim might remove it altogether. Putting on a dressing-gown and slippers, he took his bathing-suit from its drawer and went downstairs.

The beauties of a really fine English summer day are so numerous that it is excusable in a man if he fails immediately to notice them all. Only when the sharp agony of the first plunge had passed and he was floating out in mid-water did Lord Emsworth realize that in some extraordinary way he had overlooked what was beyond dispute the best thing that this perfect morning had to offer him. Gazing from his bedroom window, he had observed the sun, the shadows, the birds, the trees, and the insects, but he had omitted to appreciate the fact that nowhere in this magic world that stretched before him was there a trace of his young guest, Popjoy. For the first time in two weeks he appeared to be utterly alone and free from him.

Floating on his back and gazing up into the turquoise sky, Lord Emsworth thrilled at the thought. He kicked sportively in a spasm of pure happiness. But this, he felt, was not enough. It failed to express his full happiness. To the ecstasy of this golden moment only music—that mystic language of the soul—could really do justice. The next instant there had cut quiveringly into the summer stillness that hung over the gardens of Blandings Castle a sudden sharp wail that seemed to tell of a human being in mortal distress. It was the voice of Lord Emsworth, raised in song.

It was a gruesome sound, calculated to startle the stoutest: and two bees, buzzing among the lavender, stopped as one bee and looked at each other with raised eyebrows. Nor were they alone affected. Snails withdrew into their shells: a squirrel doing calisthenics on the cedar nearly fell off its branch: and—moving a step up in the animal kingdom—the

Rev. Rupert Bingham, standing behind the rhododendron bushes and wondering how long it would be before the girl he loved came to keep her tryst, started violently, dropped his cigarette and, tearing off his coat, rushed to the water's edge.

Out in the middle of the lake, Lord Emsworth's transports continued undiminished. His dancing feet kicked up a flurry of foam. His short-sighted, but sparkling, eyes stared into the blue. His voice rose to a puls-ing scream.

'Love me,' sang Lord Emsworth, 'and the wo-o-o-o-rld is—ah—mi-yun!'

'It's all right,' said a voice in his ear. 'Keep cool. Keep quite cool.'

The effect of a voice speaking suddenly, as it were out of the void, is always, even in these days of wireless, disconcerting to a man. Had he been on dry land Lord Emsworth would have jumped. Being in ten feet of water, he went under as if a hand had pushed him. He experienced a momentary feeling of suffocation, and then a hand gripped him painfully by the fleshy part of the arm and he was on the surface again, spluttering.

'Keep quite cool,' murmured the voice. 'There's no danger.'

And now he recognized whose voice it was.

There is a point beyond which the human brain loses its kinship with the Infinite and becomes a mere seething mass of deleterious passions. Malays, when pushed past this point, take down the old *kris* from its hook and go out and start carving up the neighbours. Women have hys-terics. Earls, if Lord Emsworth may be taken as a sample, haul back their right fists and swing them as violently as their age and physique will permit. For two long weeks Lord Emsworth had been enduring this pes-tilential young man with outward nonchalance, but the strain had told. Suppressed emotions are always the most dangerous. Little by little, day by day, he had been slowly turning into a human volcano, and this final outrage blew the lid off him.

He raged with a sense of intolerable injury. Was it not enough that this porous plaster of a young man should adhere to him on shore? Must he even pursue him out into the waste of waters and come fooling about and pawing at him when he was enjoying the best swim he had had that summer? In all their long and honourable history no member of his ancient family had ever so far forgotten the sacred obligations of hospitality as to plug a guest in the eye. But then they had never had guests like this. With a sharp, passionate snort, Lord Emsworth extracted his right hand from the foam, clenched it, drew it back and let it go.

He could have made no more imprudent move. If there was one thing the Rev. Rupert Bingham, who in his time had swum for Oxford, knew, it was what to do when drowning men struggled. Something that might have been a very hard and knobbly leg of mutton smote Lord Emsworth violently behind the ear: the sun was turned off at the main: the stars came out, many of them of a singular brightness: there was a sound of rushing waters: and he knew no more.

W hen Lord Emsworth came to himself, he was lying in bed. And, as it seemed a very good place to be, he remained there. His head ached abominably, but he scarcely noticed this, so occupied was he with the thoughts which surged inside it. He mused on the young man Popjoy: he meditated on Sir Gregory Parsloe-Parsloe: and wondered from time to time which he disliked the more. It was a problem almost too nice for human solution. Here, on the one hand, you had a man who pestered you for two weeks and wound up by nearly murdering you as you bathed, but who did not steal pig-men: there, on the other, one who stole pig-men but stopped short of actual assault on the person. Who could hope to hold the scales between such a pair?

He had just remembered the lotion and was wondering if this might not be considered the deciding factor in this contest for the position of the world's premier blot, when the door opened and the Hon. Freddie Threepwood insinuated himself into the room.

'Hullo, guv'nor.'

'Well, Frederick?'

'How are you feeling?'

'Extremely ill.'

'Might have been worse, you know.'

'Bah!'

'Watery grave and all that.'

'Tchah!' said Lord Emsworth.

There was a pause. Freddie, wandering about the room, picked up and fidgeted with a chair, a vase, a hair-brush, a comb, and a box of matches: then, retracing his steps, fidgeted with them all over again in the reverse order. Finally, he came to the foot of his father's bed and dropped over it like, it seemed to that sufferer's prejudiced eye, some hideous animal gaping over a fence.

'I say, guv'nor.'

'Well, Frederick?'

'Narrow squeak, that, you know.'

'Pah!'

'Do you wish to thank your brave preserver?'

Lord Emsworth plucked at the coverlet.

'If that young man comes near me,' he said, 'I will not be answerable for the consequences.'

'Eh?' Freddie stared. 'Don't you like him?'

'Like him! I think he is the most appalling young man I ever met.'

It is customary when making statements of this kind to except present company, but so deeply did Lord Emsworth feel on the subject that he omitted to do so. Freddie, having announced that he was dashed, removed himself from the bed-rail and, wandering once more about the room, fidgeted with a toothbrush, a soap-dish, a shoe, a volume on spring bulbs, and a collar-stud.

'I say, guv'nor.'

'Well, Frederick?'

'That's all very well, you know, guv'nor,' said the Hon. Freddie, returning to his post and seeming to draw moral support from the feel of the bed-rail, 'but after what's happened it looks to me as if you were jolly well bound to lend your countenance to the union, if you know what I mean.'

'Union? What are you talking about? What union?'

'Gertrude and old Beefers?'

'Who the devil is old Beefers?'

'Oh, I forgot to tell you about that. This bird Popjoy's name isn't Popjoy. It's Bingham. Old Beefy Bingham. You know, the fellow Aunt Georgie doesn't want to marry Gertrude.'

'Eh?'

'Throw your mind back. They pushed her off to Blandings to keep her out of his way. And I had the idea of sending him down here *incog* to ingratiate himself with you. The scheme being that, when you had learned to love him, you would slip him a vacant vicarage, thus enabling them to get married. Beefers is a parson, you know.'

Lord Emsworth did not speak. It was not so much the shock of this revelation that kept him dumb as the astounding discovery that any man could really want to marry Gertrude, and any girl this Popjoy. Like many a thinker before him, he was feeling that there is really no limit to the eccentricity of human tastes. The thing made his head swim.

But when it had ceased swimming he perceived that this was but one aspect of the affair. Before him stood the man who had inflicted Popjoy on him, and with something of King Lear in his demeanour Lord Emsworth rose slowly from the pillows. Words trembled on his lips, but he rejected them as not strong enough and sought in his mind for others.

'You know, guv'nor,' proceeded Freddie, 'there's nothing to prevent you doing the square thing and linking two young hearts in the bonds of the Love God, if you want to. I mean to say, old Braithwaite at Much Matchingham has been ordered to the south of France by his doctor, so there's a living going that you've got to slip to somebody.'

Lord Emsworth sank back on the pillows.

'Much Matchingham!'

'Oh, dash it, you must know Much Matchingham, guv'nor. It's just round the corner. Where old Parsloe lives.'

'Much Matchingham!'

Lord Emsworth was blinking, as if his eyes had seen a dazzling light. How wrong, he felt, how wickedly mistaken and lacking in faith he had been when he had said to himself in his folly that Providence offers no method of retaliation to the just whose pig-men have been persuaded by Humanity's dregs to leave their employment and seek advanced wages elsewhere. Conscience could not bring remorse to Sir Gregory Parsloe-Parsloe, and the law, in its present imperfect state, was powerless to punish. But there was still a way. With this young man Popjoy— or Bingham—or whatever his name was, permanently established not a hundred yards from his park gates, would Sir Gregory Parsloe-Parsloe ever draw another really care-free breath? From his brief, but sufficient, acquaintance with the young man Bingham—Popjoy—Lord Emsworth thought not.

The punishment was severe, but who could say that Sir Gregory had not earned it?

'A most admirable idea,' said Lord Emsworth cordially. 'Certainly I will give your friend the living of Much Matchingham.'

'You will?'

'Most decidedly.'

'At-a-boy, guv'nor!' said Freddie. 'Came the Dawn!'

5

THE GO-GETTER

ON the usually unruffled brow of the Hon. Freddie Threepwood, as he paced the gardens of Blandings Castle, there was the slight but well-marked frown of one whose mind is not at rest. It was high summer and the gardens were at their loveliest, but he appeared to find no solace in their splendour. Calceolarias, which would have drawn senile yips of ecstasy from his father, Lord Emsworth, left him cold. He eyed the lobelias with an unseeing stare, as if he were cutting an undesirable acquaintance in the paddock at Ascot.

What was troubling this young man was the continued sales-resistance of his Aunt Georgiana. Ever since his marriage to the only daughter of Donaldson's Dog-Biscuits, of Long Island City, N.Y., Freddie Threepwood had thrown himself heart and soul into the promotion of the firm's wares. And, sent home to England to look about for likely prospects, he had seen in Georgiana, Lady Alcester, as has been already related, a customer who approximated to the ideal. The owner of four Pekingese, two Poms, a Yorkshire terrier, five Sealyhams, a Borzoi and an Airedale, she was a woman who stood for something in dog-loving circles. To secure her patronage would be a big thing for him. It would stamp him as a live wire and a go-getter. It would please his father-in-law hugely. And the proprietor of Donaldson's Dog-Joy was a man who, when even slightly pleased, had a habit of spraying five thousand dollar cheques like a geyser.

And so far, despite all his eloquence, callously oblivious of the ties of kinship and the sacred obligations they involve, Lady Alcester had refused to sign on the dotted line, preferring to poison her menagerie with some degraded garbage called, if he recollected rightly, Peterson's Pup-Food.

A bitter snort escaped Freddie. It was still echoing through the gardens, when he found that he was no longer alone. He had been joined by his cousin Gertrude.

'What-ho!' said Freddie amiably. He was fond of Gertrude, and did not hold it against her that she had a mother who was incapable of spotting a good dog-biscuit when she saw one. Between him and Gertrude there had long existed a firm alliance. It was to him that Gertrude had turned for assistance when the family were trying to stop her getting engaged to good old Beefy Bingham: and he had supplied assistance in such good measure that the engagement was now an accepted fact and running along nicely.

'Freddie,' said Gertrude, 'may I borrow your car?'

'Certainly. Most decidedly. Going over to see old Beefers?'

'No,' said Gertrude, and a closer observer than her cousin might have noted in her manner a touch of awkwardness. 'Mr. Watkins wants me to drive him to Shrewsbury.'

'Oh? Well, carry on, as far as I'm concerned. You haven't seen your mother anywhere, have you?'

'I think she's sitting on the lawn.'

'Ah? Is she? Right-ho. Thanks.'

Freddie moved off in the direction indicated, and presently came in sight of his relative, seated as described. The Airedale was lying at her feet. One of the Pekes occupied her lap. And she was gazing into the middle distance in a preoccupied manner, as if she, like her nephew, had a weight on her mind.

Nor would one who drew this inference from her demeanour have been mistaken. Lady Alcester was feeling disturbed.

A woman who stands in *loco parentis* to fourteen dogs must of necessity have her cares, but it was not the dumb friends that were worrying Lady Alcester now. What was troubling her was the disquieting behaviour of her daughter Gertrude.

Engaged to the Rev. Rupert Bingham, Gertrude seemed to her of late to have become infatuated with Orlo Watkins, the Crooning Tenor, one of those gifted young men whom Lady Constance Keeble, the chatelaine of Blandings, was so fond of inviting down for lengthy visits in the summer-time.

On the subject of the Rev. Rupert Bingham, Lady Alcester's views had recently undergone a complete change. In the beginning, the prospect of having him for a son-in-law had saddened and distressed her. Then, suddenly discovering that he was the nephew and heir of as opulent a shipping magnate as ever broke bread at the Adelphi Hotel, Liverpool, she had soared from the depths to the heights. She was now strongly pro-Bingham. She smiled upon him freely. Upon his appointment to the vacant Vicarage of Much Matchingham, the village nearest to Market Blandings, she had brought Gertrude to the Castle so that the young people should see one another frequently.

And, instead of seeing her betrothed frequently, Gertrude seemed to prefer to moon about with this Orlo Watkins, this Crooning Tenor. For days they had been inseparable.

Now, everybody knows what Crooning Tenors are. Dangerous devils. They sit at the piano and gaze into a girl's eyes and sing in a voice that sounds like gas escaping from a pipe about Love and the Moonlight and You: and, before you know where you are, the girl has scrapped the deserving young clergyman with prospects to whom she is affianced and is off and away with a man whose only means of livelihood consist of intermittent engagements with the British Broadcasting Corporation.

If a mother is not entitled to shudder at a prospect like that, it would be interesting to know what she is entitled to shudder at.

Lady Alcester, then, proceeded to shudder: and was still shuddering when the drowsy summer peace was broken by a hideous uproar. The Peke and the Airedale had given tongue simultaneously, and, glancing up, Lady Alcester perceived her nephew Frederick approaching.

And what made her shudder again was the fact that in Freddie's eye she noted with concern the familiar go-getter gleam, the old dog-biscuit glitter.

However, as it had sometimes been her experience, when cornered by her nephew, that she could stem the flood by talking promptly on other subjects, she made a gallant effort to do so now.

'Have you seen Gertrude, Freddie?' she asked.

'Yes. She borrowed my car to go to Shrewsbury.'

'Alone?'

'No. Accompanied by Watkins. The Yowler.'

A further spasm shook Lady Alcester.

'Freddie,' she said, 'I'm terribly worried.'

'Worried?'

'About Gertrude.'

Freddie dismissed Gertrude with a gesture.

'No need to worry about her,' he said. 'What you want to worry about is these dogs of yours. Notice how they barked at me? Nerves. They're a mass of nerves. And why? Improper feeding. As long as you mistakenly insist on giving them Peterson's Pup-Food—lacking, as it is, in many of the essential vitamins—so long will they continue to fly off the handle every time they see a human being on the horizon. Now, pursuant on what we were talking about this morning, Aunt Georgiana, there is a little demonstration I would like . . .'

'Can't you give her a hint, Freddie?'

'Who?'

'Gertrude.'

'Yes, I suppose I could give her a hint. What about?'

'She is seeing far too much of this man Watkins.'

'Well, so am I, for the matter of that. So is everybody who sees him more than once.'

'She seems quite to have forgotten that she is engaged to Rupert Bingham.'

'Rupert Bingham, did you say?' said Freddie with sudden animation. 'I'll tell you something about Rupert Bingham. He has a dog named Bottles who has been fed from early youth on Donaldson's Dog-Joy, and I wish you could see him. Thanks to the bone-forming properties of Donaldson's Dog-Joy, he glows with health. A fine, upstanding dog, with eyes sparkling with the joy of living and both feet on the ground. A credit to his master.'

'Never mind about Rupert's dog!'

'You've got to mind about Rupert's dog. You can't afford to ignore him. He is a dog to be reckoned with. A dog that counts. And all through Donaldson's Dog-Joy.'

'I don't want to talk about Donaldson's Dog-Joy.'

'I do. I want to give you a demonstration. You may not know it, Aunt Georgiana, but over in America the way we advertise this product, so rich in bone-forming vitamins, is as follows: We instruct our demonstrator to stand out in plain view before the many-headed and, when the audience is of sufficient size, to take a biscuit and break off a piece and chew it. By this means we prove that Donaldson's Dog-Joy is so superbly wholesome as actually to be fit for human consumption. Our demonstrator not only eats the biscuit—he enjoys it. He rolls it round his tongue. He chews it and mixes it with his saliva . . . .'

'Freddie, please!'

'With his saliva,' repeated Freddie firmly, 'And so does the dog. He masticates the biscuit. He enjoys it. He becomes a bigger and better dog. I will now eat a Donaldson's Dog-Biscuit.'

And before his aunt's nauseated gaze he proceeded to attempt this gruesome feat.

It was an impressive demonstration, but it failed in one particular. To have rendered it perfect, he should not have choked. Want of experience caused the disaster. Long years of training go to the making of the seasoned demonstrators of Donaldson's Dog-Joy. They start in a small way with carpet-tacks and work up through the flat-irons and patent breakfast cereals till they are ready for the big effort. Freddie was a novice. Endeavouring to roll the morsel round his tongue, he allowed it to escape into his windpipe.

The sensation of having swallowed a mixture of bricks and sawdust was succeeded by a long and painful coughing fit. And when at length the sufferer's eyes cleared, no human form met their gaze. There was the

Castle. There was the lawn. There were the gardens. But Lady Alcester had disappeared.

However, it is a well-established fact that good men, like Donaldson's Dog-Biscuits, are hard to keep down. Some fifty minutes later, as the Rev. Rupert Bingham sat in his study at Matchingham Vicarage, the parlourmaid announced a visitor. The Hon. Freddie Threepwood limped in, looking shop-soiled.

'What-ho, Beefers,' he said. 'I just came to ask if I could borrow Bottles.'

He bent to where the animal lay on the hearth-rug and prodded it civilly in the lower ribs. Bottles waved a long tail in brief acknowledgment. He was a fine dog, though of uncertain breed. His mother had been a popular local belle with a good deal of sex-appeal, and the question of his paternity was one that would have set a Genealogical College pursing its lips perplexedly.

'Oh, hullo, Freddie,' said the Rev. Rupert.

The young Pastor of Souls spoke in an absent voice. He was frowning. It is a singular fact—and one that just goes to show what sort of a world this is—that of the four foreheads introduced so far to the reader of this chronicle, three have been corrugated with care. And, if girls had consciences, Gertrude's would have been corrugated, too—giving us a full hand.

'Take a chair,' said the Rev. Rupert.

'I'll take a sofa,' said Freddie, doing so. 'Feeling a bit used up. I had to hoof it all the way over.'

'What's happened to your car?'

'Gertrude took it to drive Watkins to Shrewsbury.'

The Rev. Rupert sat for a while in thought. His face, which was large and red, had a drawn look. Even the massive body which had so nearly won him a Rowing Blue at Oxford gave the illusion of having shrunk. So marked was his distress that even Freddie noticed it.

'Something up, Beefers?' he inquired.

For answer the Rev. Rupert Bingham extended a ham-like hand which held a letter. It was written in a sprawling, girlish handwriting.

'Read that.'

'From Gertrude?'

'Yes. It came this morning. Well?'

Freddie completed his perusal and handed the document back. He was concerned.

'I think it's the bird,' he said.

'So do I.'

'It's long,' said Freddie, ' and it's rambling. It is full of stuff about "Are we sure?" and "Do we know our own minds?" and "Wouldn't it be better, perhaps?" But I think it is the bird.'

'I can't understand it.'

Freddie sat up.

'I can,' he said. 'Now I see what Aunt Georgiana was drooling about. Her fears were well founded. The snake Watkins has stolen Gertrude from you.'

'You think Gertrude's in love with Watkins?'

'I do. And I'll tell you why. He's a yowler, and girls always fall for yowlers. They have a glamour.'

'I've never noticed Watkins's glamour. He has always struck me as a bit of a weed.'

'Weed he may be, Beefers, but, none the less, he knows how to do his stuff. I don't know why it should be, but there is a certain type of tenor voice which acts on girls like catnip on a cat.'

The Rev. Rupert breathed heavily.

'I see,' he said.

'The whole trouble is, Beefers,' proceeded Freddie, 'that Watkins is romantic and you're not. Your best friend couldn't call you romantic. Solid worth, yes. Romance, no.'

'So it doesn't seem as if there was much to be done about it?'

Freddie reflected.

'Couldn't you manage to show yourself in a romantic light?'

'How?'

'Well—stop a runaway horse.'

'Where's the horse?'

' 'Myes,' said Freddie. 'That's by way of being the difficulty, isn't it? The horse—where is it?'

There was silence for some moments.

'Well, be that as it may,' said Freddie. 'Can I borrow Bottles?'

'What for?'

'Purposes of demonstration. I wish to exhibit him to my Aunt Georgiana, so that she may see for herself to what heights of robustness a dog can rise when fed sedulously on Donaldson's Dog-Joy. I'm having a lot of trouble with that woman, Beefers. I try all the artifices which win to success in salesmanship, and they don't. But I have a feeling that if she could see Bottles and poke him in the ribs and note the firm, muscular flesh, she might drop. At any rate, it's worth trying. I'll take him along, may I?'

'All right.'

'Thanks. And, in regard to your little trouble, I'll be giving it my best attention. You're looking in after dinner to-night?'

'I suppose so,' said the Rev. Rupert moodily.

The information that her impressionable daughter had gone off to roam the country-side in a two-seater car with the perilous Watkins had come as a grievous blow to Lady Alcester. As she sat on the terrace, an hour after Freddie had begun the weary homeward trek from Matchingham Vicarage, her heart was sorely laden.

The Airedale had wandered away upon some private ends, but the Peke lay slumbering in her lap. She envied it its calm detachment. To her the future looked black and the air seemed heavy with doom.

Only one thing mitigated her depression. Her nephew Frederick had disappeared. Other prominent local pests were present, such as flies and gnats, but not Frederick. The grounds of Blandings Castle appeared to be quite free from him.

And then even this poor consolation was taken from the stricken woman. Limping a little, as if his shoes hurt him, the Hon. Freddie came round the corner of the shrubbery, headed in her direction. He was accompanied by something having the outward aspect of a dog.

'What-ho, Aunt Georgiana!'

'Well, Freddie?' sighed Lady Alcester resignedly.

The Peke, opening one eye, surveyed the young man for a moment, seemed to be debating within itself the advisability of barking, came apparently to the conclusion that it was too hot, and went to sleep again.

'This is Bottles,' said Freddie.

'Who?'

'Bottles. The animal I touched on some little time back. Note the well-muscled frame.'

'I never saw such a mongrel in my life.'

'Kind hearts are more than coronets,' said Freddie. 'The point at issue is not this dog's pedigree, which, I concede, is not all Burke and Debrett, but his physique. Reared exclusively on a diet of Donaldson's Dog-Joy, he goes his way with his chin up, frank and fearless. I should like you, if you don't mind, to come along to the stables and watch him among the rats. It will give you some idea.'

He would have spoken further, but at this point something occurred, as had happened during his previous sales talk, to mar the effect of Freddie's oratory.

The dog Bottles, during this conversation, had been roaming to and fro in the inquisitive manner customary with dogs who find themselves in strange territory. He had sniffed at trees. He had rolled on the turf. Now, returning to the centre of things, he observed for the first time that on the lap of the woman seated in the chair there lay a peculiar something.

What it was Bottles did not know. It appeared to be alive. A keen desire came upon him to solve this mystery. To keep the records straight, he advanced to the chair, thrust an inquiring nose against the object, and inhaled sharply.

The next moment, to his intense surprise, the thing had gone off like a bomb, had sprung to the ground, and was moving rapidly towards him.

Bottles did not hesitate. A rough-and-tumble with one of his peers he enjoyed. He, as it were, rolled it round his tongue and mixed it with his saliva. But this was different. He had never met a Pekingese before, and no one would have been more surprised than himself if he had been informed that this curious, fluffy thing was a dog. Himself, he regarded it as an Act of God, and, thoroughly unnerved, he raced three times round the lawn and tried to climb a tree. Failing in this endeavour, he fitted his ample tail if possible more firmly into its groove and vanished from the scene.

The astonishment of the Hon. Freddie Threepwood was only equalled by his chagrin. Lady Alcester had begun now to express her opinion of the incident, and her sneers, her jeers, her unveiled innuendoes were hard to bear. If, she said, the patrons of Donaldson's Dog-Joy allowed themselves to be chased off the map in this fashion by Pekingese, she was glad she had never been weak enough to be persuaded to try it.

'It's lucky,' said Lady Alcester in her hard, scoffing way, 'that Susan wasn't a rat. I suppose a rat would have given that mongrel of yours heart failure.'

'Bottles,' said Freddie stiffly, 'is particularly sound on rats. I think, in common fairness, you ought to step to the stables and give him a chance of showing himself in a true light.'

'I have seen quite enough, thank you.'

'You won't come to the stables and watch him dealing with rats?'

'I will not.'

'In that case,' said Freddie sombrely, 'there is nothing more to be said. I suppose I may as well take him back to the Vicarage.'

'What Vicarage?'

'Matchingham Vicarage.'

'Was that Rupert's dog?'

'Of course it was.'

'Then have you seen Rupert?'

'Of course I have.'

'Did you warn him? About Mr Watkins?'

'It was too late to warn him. He had had a letter from Gertrude, giving him the raspberry.'

'What!'

'Well, she said Was he sure and Did they know their own minds, but you can take it from me that it was tantamount to the raspberry. Returning, however, to the topic of Bottles, Aunt Georgiana, I think you ought to take into consideration the fact that, in his recent encounter with the above Peke, he was undergoing a totally new experience and naturally did not appear at his best. I repeat once more that you should see him among the rats.'

'Oh, Freddie?'

'Hullo?'

'How can you babble about this wretched dog when Gertrude's whole future is at stake? It is simply vital that somehow she be cured of this dreadful infatuation . . .'

'Well, I'll have a word with her if you like, but, if you ask me, I think the evil has spread too far. Watkins has yowled himself into her very soul. However, I'll do my best. Excuse me, Aunt Georgiana.'

From a neighbouring bush the honest face of Bottles was protruding. He seemed to be seeking assurance that the All Clear had been blown.

It was at the hour of the ante-dinner cocktail that Freddie found his first opportunity of having the promised word with Gertrude. Your true salesman and go-getter is never beaten, and a sudden and brilliant idea for accomplishing the conversion of his Aunt Georgiana had come to him as he brushed his hair. He descended to the drawing-room with a certain jauntiness, and was reminded by the sight of Gertrude of his mission. The girl was seated at the piano, playing dreamy chords.

'I say,' said Freddie, 'a word with you, young Gertrude. What is all this bilge I hear about you and Beefers?'

The girl flushed.

'Have you seen Rupert?'

'I was closeted with him this afternoon. He told me all.'

'Oh?'

'He's feeling pretty low.'

'Oh?'

'Yes,' said Freddie, 'pretty low the poor old chap is feeling, and I don't blame him, with the girl he's engaged to rushing about the place getting infatuated with tenors. I never heard of such a thing, dash it! What do you see in this Watkins? Wherein lies his attraction? Certainly not in his ties. They're awful. And the same applies to his entire outfit. He looks as if he had bought his clothes off the peg at a second-hand gents' costumiers. And, as if that were not enough, he wears short, but distinct, side-whiskers. You aren't going to tell me that you're seriously considering chucking a sterling egg like old Beefers in favour of a whiskered warbler?'

There was a pause. Gertrude played more dreamy chords.

'I'm not going to discuss it,' she said. 'It's nothing to do with you.'

'Pardon me!' said Freddie. 'Excuse me! If you will throw your mind back to the time when Beefers was conducting his wooing, you may remember that I was the fellow who worked the whole thing. But for my resource and ingenuity you and the old bounder would never have got engaged. I regard myself, therefore, in the light of a guardian angel or something; and as such am entitled to probe the matter to its depths. Of course,' said Freddie, 'I know exactly how you're feeling. I see where you have made your fatal bloomer. This Watkins has cast his glamorous spell about you, and you're looking on Beefers as a piece of unromantic cheese. But mark this, girl . . .'

'I wish you wouldn't call me "girl."'

'Mark this, old prune,' amended Freddie. 'And mark it well. Beefers is tried, true and trusted. A man to be relied on. Whereas Watkins, if I have read those whiskers aright, is the sort of fellow who will jolly well let you down in a crisis. And then, when it's too late, you'll come moaning to me, weeping salt tears and saying, "Ah, why did I not know in time?" And I shall reply, "You unhappy little fathead . . . !"'

'Oh, go and sell your dog-biscuits, Freddie!'

Gertrude resumed her playing. Her mouth was set in an obstinate line. Freddie eyed her with disapproval.

'It's some taint in the blood,' he said. 'Inherited from female parent. Like your bally mother, you are constitutionally incapable of seeing reason. Pig-headed, both of you. Sell my dog-biscuits, you say? Ha! As if I hadn't boosted them to Aunt Georgiana till my lips cracked. And with what result? So far, none. But wait till to-night.'

'It is to-night.'

'I mean, wait till later on to-night. Watch my little experiment.'

'What little experiment?'

'Ah!'

'What do you mean, "Ah"?'

'Just "Ah!"' said Freddie.

The hour of the after-dinner coffee found Blandings Castle apparently an abode of peace. The superficial observer, peeping into the amber drawing-room through the French windows that led to the terrace, would have said that all was well with the inmates of this stately home of England. Lord Emsworth sat in a corner absorbed in a volume dealing with the treatment of pigs in sickness and in health. His sister, Lady Constance Keeble, was sewing. His other sister, Lady Alcester, was gazing at Gertrude. Gertrude was gazing at Orlo Watkins. And Orlo Watkins was gazing at the ceiling and singing in that crooning voice of his a song of Roses.

The Hon. Freddie Threepwood was not present. And that fact alone, if one may go by the views of his father, Lord Emsworth, should have been enough to make a success of any party.

And yet beneath this surface of cosy peace troubled currents were running. Lady Alcester, gazing at Gertrude, found herself a prey to gloom. She did not like the way Gertrude was gazing at Orlo Watkins. Gertrude, for her part, as the result of her recent conversation with the Hon. Freddie, was experiencing twinges of remorse and doubt. Lady Constance was still ruffled from the effect of Lady Alcester's sisterly frankness that evening on the subject of the imbecility of hostesses who deliberately let Crooning Tenors loose in castles. And Lord Emsworth was in that state of peevish exasperation which comes to dreamy old gentlemen who, wishing to read of Pigs, find their concentration impaired by voices singing of Roses.

Only Orlo Watkins was happy. And presently he, too, was to join the ranks of gloom. For just as he started to let himself go and handle this song as a song should be handled, there came from the other side of the door the sound of eager barking. A dog seemed to be without. And, apart from the fact that he disliked and feared all dogs, a tenor resents competition.

The next moment the door had opened, and the Hon. Freddie Threepwood appeared. He carried a small sack, and was accompanied by Bottles, the latter's manner noticeably lacking in repose.

On the face of the Hon. Freddie, as he advanced into the room, there was that set, grim expression which is always seen on the faces of those who are about to put their fortune to the test, to win or lose it all. The Old Guard at Waterloo looked much the same. For Freddie had decided to stake all on a single throw.

Many young men in his position, thwarted by an aunt who resolutely declined to amble across to the stables and watch a dog redeem himself among the rats, would have resigned themselves sullenly to defeat. But Freddie was made of finer stuff.

'Aunt Georgiana,' he said, holding up the sack, at which Bottles was making agitated leaps, 'you refused to come to the stables this afternoon to watch this Donaldson's Dog-Joy-fed animal in action, so you have left me no alternative but to play the fixture on your own ground.'

Lord Emsworth glanced up from his book.

'Frederick, stop gibbering. And take that dog out of here.'

Lady Constance glanced up from her sewing.

'Frederick, if you are coming in, come in and sit down. And take that dog out of here.'

Lady Alcester, glancing up from Gertrude, exhibited in even smaller degree the kindly cordiality which might have been expected from an aunt.

'Oh, do go away Freddie! You're a perfect nuisance. And take that dog out of here.'

The Hon. Freddie, with a noble look of disdain, ignored them all.

'I have here, Aunt Georgiana,' he said, 'a few simple rats. If you will kindly step out on to the terrace I shall be delighted to give a demonstration which should, I think, convince even your stubborn mind.'

The announcement was variously received by the various members of the company. Lady Alcester screamed. Lady Constance sprang for the bell. Lord Emsworth snorted. Orlo Watkins blanched and retired behind Gertrude. And Gertrude, watching him blench, seeing him retire, tightened her lips. A country-bred girl, she was on terms of easy familiarity with rats, and this evidence of alarm in one whom she had set on a pedestal disquieted her.

The door opened and Beach entered. He had come in pursuance of his regular duties to remove the coffee cups, but arriving, found other tasks assigned to him.

'Beach!' The voice was that of Lady Constance. 'Take away those rats.'

'Rats, m'lady?'

'Take that sack away from Mr Frederick!'

Beach understood. If he was surprised at the presence of the younger son of the house in the amber drawing-room with a sack of rats in his hand, he gave no indication of the fact. With a murmured apology, he secured the sack and started to withdraw. It was not, strictly, his place to carry rats, but a good butler is always ready to give and take. Only so can the amenities of a large country house be preserved.

'And don't drop the dashed things,' urged Lord Emsworth.

'Very good, m'lord.'

The Hon. Freddie had flung himself into a chair, and was sitting with his chin cupped in his hands, a bleak look on his face. To an ardent young go-getter these tyrannous actions in restraint of trade are hard to bear.

Lord Emsworth returned to his book.

Lady Constance returned to her sewing.

Lady Alcester returned to her thoughts.

At the piano Orlo Watkins was endeavouring to justify the motives which had led him a few moments before to retire prudently behind Gertrude.

'I hate rats,' he said. 'They jar upon me.'

'Oh?' said Gertrude.

'I'm not afraid of them, of course, but they give me the creeps.'

'Oh?' said Gertrude.

There was an odd look in her eyes. Of what was she thinking, this idealistic girl? Was it of the evening, a few short weeks before, when, suddenly encountering a beastly bat in the gloaming, she had found in the Rev. Rupert Bingham a sturdy and intrepid protector? Was she picturing the Rev. Rupert as she had seen him then—gallant, fearless, cleaving the air with long sweeps of his clerical hat, encouraging her the while with word and gesture?

Apparently so, for a moment later she spoke.

'How are you on bats?'

'Rats?'

'Bats.'

'Oh, bats?'

'Are you afraid of bats?'

'I don't like bats,' admitted Orlo Watkins.

Then dismissing the subject, he reseated himself at the piano and sang of June and the scent of unseen flowers.

Of all the little group in the amber drawing-room, only one member has now been left unaccounted for.

An animal of slow thought-processes, the dog Bottles had not at first observed what was happening to the sack. At the moment of its transference from the custody of Freddie to that of Beach, he had been engaged in sniffing at the leg of a chair. It was only as the door began to close that he became aware of the bereavement that threatened him. He bounded forward with a passionate cry, but it was too late. He found himself faced by unyielding wood. And when he started to scratch vehemently on this wood, a sharp pain assailed him. A book on the treatment of Pigs in sickness and in health, superbly aimed, had struck him in the small of the back. Then, for a space, he, like the Hon. Freddie Threepwood, his social sponsor, sat down and mourned.

'Take that beastly, blasted, infernal dog out of here,' cried Lord Emsworth.

Freddie rose listlessly.

'It's old Beefers' dog,' he said. 'Beefers will be here at any moment. We can hand the whole conduct of the affair over to him.'

Gertrude started.

'Is Rupert coming here to-night?'

'Said he would,' responded Freddie, and passed from the scene. He had had sufficient of his flesh and blood and was indisposed to linger. It was his intention to pop down to Market Blandings in his two-seater, soothe his wounded sensibilities, so far as they were capable of being soothed, with a visit to the local motion-picture house, look in at the Emsworth Arms for a spot of beer, and then home to bed, to forget.

Gertrude had fallen into a reverie. Her fair young face was overcast. A feeling of embarrassment had come upon her. When she had written that letter and posted it on the previous night, she had not foreseen that the Rev. Rupert would be calling so soon.

'I didn't know Rupert was coming to-night,' she said.

'Oh, yes,' said Lady Alcester brightly.

'Like a lingering tune, my whole life through, 'twill haunt me for EV-ah, that night in June with you-oo,' sang Orlo Watkins.

And Gertrude, looking at him, was aware for the first time of a curious sensation of not being completely in harmony with this young whiskered man. She wished he would stop singing. He prevented her thinking.

Bottles, meanwhile, had resumed his explorations. Dogs are philosophers. They soon forget. They do not waste time regretting the might-have-beens. Adjusting himself with composure to the changed conditions, Bottles moved to and fro in a spirit of affable inquiry. He looked at Lord Emsworth, considered the idea of seeing how he smelt, thought better of it, and advanced towards the French windows. Something was rustling in the bushes outside, and it seemed to him that this might as well be looked into before he went and breathed on Lady Constance's leg.

He had almost reached his objective, when Lady Alcester's Airedale, who had absented himself from the room some time before in order to do a bit of bone-burying, came bustling in, ready, his business completed, to resume the social whirl.

Seeing Bottles, he stopped abruptly.

Both then began a slow and cautious forward movement, of a crab-like kind. Arriving at close quarters, they stopped again. Their nostrils twitched a little. They rolled their eyes. And to the ears of those present there came, faintly at first, a low, throaty sound, like the far-off gargling of an octogenarian with bronchial trouble.

This rose to a sudden crescendo. And the next moment hostilities had begun.

In underrating Bottles's qualities and scoffing at him as a fighting force, Lady Alcester had made an error. Capable though he was of pusillanimity in the presence of female Pekingese, there was nothing of the weakling about this sterling animal. He had cleaned up every dog in Much Matchingham and was spoken of on all sides—from the Blue Boar in the High Street to the distant Cow and Caterpillar on the Shrewsbury Road—as an ornament to the Vicarage and a credit to his master's Cloth.

On the present occasion, moreover, he was strengthened by the fact that he felt he had right on his side. In spite of a certain coldness on the part of the Castle circle and a soreness about the ribs where the book on Pigs and their treatment had found its billet, there seems to be no doubt that Bottles had by this time become thoroughly convinced that this drawing-room was his official home. And, feeling that all these delightful people were relying on him to look after their interests and keep alien and subversive influences at a distance, he advanced with a bright willingness to the task of ejecting this intruder.

Nor was the Airedale disposed to hold back. He, too, was no stranger to the ring. In Hyde Park, where, when at his London residence, he took his daily airing, he had met all comers and acquitted himself well. Dogs from Mayfair, dogs from Bayswater, dogs from as far afield as the Brompton Road and West Kensington had had experience of the stuff of which he was made. Bottles reminded him a little of an animal from Pont Street, over whom he had once obtained a decision on the banks of the Serpentine; and he joined battle with an easy confidence,

The reactions of a country-house party to an after-dinner dog-fight in the drawing-room always vary considerably according to the individual natures of its members. Lady Alcester, whose long association with the species had made her a sort of honorary dog herself, remained tranquil. She surveyed the proceedings with unruffled equanimity through a tortoise-shell-rimmed lorgnette. Her chief emotion was one of surprise at the fact that Bottles was unquestionably getting the better of the exchanges. She liked his footwork. Impressed, she was obliged to admit that, if this was the sort of battler it turned out, there must be something in Donaldson's Dog-Joy after all.

The rest of the audience were unable to imitate her nonchalance. The two principals were giving that odd illusion, customary on these occasions, of being all over the place at the same time: and the demeanour of those in the ring-side seats was frankly alarmed. Lady Constance had backed against the wall, from which position she threw a futile cushion. Lord Emsworth, in his corner, was hunting feebly for ammunition and wishing that he had not dropped the pince-nez, without which he was no sort of use in a crisis.

And Gertrude? Gertrude was staring at Orlo Watkins, who, with a resource and presence of mind unusual in one so young, had just climbed on top of a high cabinet containing china.

His feet were on a level with her eyes, and she saw that they were feet of clay.

And it was at this moment, when a girl stood face to face with her soul, that the door opened.

'Mr Bingham,' announced Beach.

Men of the physique of the Rev. Rupert Bingham are not as a rule quick thinkers. From earliest youth, the Rev. Rupert had run to brawn rather than brain. But even the dullest-witted person could have told, on crossing that threshold, that there was a dog-fight going on. Beefy Bingham saw it in a flash, and he acted promptly.

There are numerous methods of stopping these painful affairs. Some advocate squirting water, others prefer to sprinkle pepper. Good results may be obtained, so one school of thought claims, by holding a lighted match under the nearest nose. Beefy Bingham was impatient of these subtleties.

To Beefy all this was old stuff. Ever since he had been given his Cure of Souls, half his time, it sometimes seemed to him, had been spent in hauling Bottles away from the throats of the dogs of his little flock. Experience had given him a technique. He placed one massive hand on the neck of the Airedale, the other on the neck of Bottles, and pulled. There was a rending sound, and they came apart.

'Rupert!' cried Gertrude.

Gazing at him, she was reminded of the heroes of old. And few could have denied that he made a strangely impressive figure, this large young man, standing there with bulging eyes and a gyrating dog in each hand. He looked like a statue of Right triumphing over Wrong. You couldn't place it exactly, because it was so long since you had read the book, but he reminded you of something out of 'Pilgrim's Progress.'

So, at least, thought Gertrude. To Gertrude it was as if the scales had fallen from her eyes and she had wakened from some fevered dream. Could it be she, she was asking herself, who had turned from this noble youth and strayed towards one who, though on the evidence he seemed to have a future before him as an Alpine climber, was otherwise so contemptible?

'Rupert!' said Gertrude.

Beefy Bingham had now completed his masterly campaign. He had thrown Bottles out of the window and shut it behind him. He had dropped the Airedale to the carpet, where it now sat, licking itself in a ruminative way. He had produced a handkerchief and was passing it over his vermilion brow.

'Oh, Rupert!' said Gertrude, and flung herself into his arms.

The Rev. Rupert said nothing. On such occasions your knowledgeable Vicar does not waste words.

Nor did Orlo Watkins speak. He had melted away. Perhaps, perched on his eyrie, he had seen in Gertrude's eyes the look which, when seen in the eyes of a girl by any interested party, automatically induces the latter to go to his room and start packing, in readiness for the telegram which he will receive on the morrow, summoning him back to London on urgent business. At any rate, he had melted.

It was late that night when the Hon. Freddie Threepwood returned to the home of his fathers. Moodily undressing, he was surprised to hear a knock on the door.

His Aunt Georgiana entered. On her face was the unmistakable look of a mother whose daughter has seen the light and will shortly be marrying a deserving young clergyman with a bachelor uncle high up in the shipping business.

'Freddie,' said Lady Alcester, 'you know that stuff you're always babbling about—I've forgotten its name . . .'

'Donaldson's Dog-Joy,' said Freddie. 'It may be obtained either in the small (or one-and-threepenny) packets or in the half-crown (or large) size. A guarantee goes with each purchase. Unique in its health-giving properties . . .'

'I'll take two tons to start with,' said Lady Alcester.

6

LORD EMSWORTH
AND THE GIRL FRIEND

THE day was so warm, so fair, so magically a thing of sunshine and blue skies and bird-song that anyone acquainted with Clarence, ninth Earl of Emsworth, and aware of his liking for fine weather, would have pictured him going about the place on this summer morning with a beaming smile and an uplifted heart. Instead of which, humped over the breakfast-table, he was directing at a blameless kippered herring a look of such intense bitterness that the fish seemed to sizzle beneath it. For it was August Bank Holiday, and Blandings Castle on August Bank Holiday became, in his lordship's opinion, a miniature Inferno.

This was the day when his park and grounds broke out into a noisome rash of swings, roundabouts, marquees, toy balloons and paper bags; when a tidal wave of the peasantry and its squealing young engulfed those haunts of immemorial peace. On August Bank Holiday he was not allowed to potter pleasantly about his gardens in an old coat: forces beyond his control shoved him into a stiff collar and a top hat and told him to go out and be genial. And in the cool of the quiet evenfall they put him on a platform and made him make a speech. To a man with a day like that in front of him fine weather was a mockery.

His sister, Lady Constance Keeble, looked brightly at him over the coffee-pot.

'What a lovely morning!' she said.

Lord Emsworth's gloom deepened. He chafed at being called upon—by this woman of all others—to behave as if everything was for the jolliest in the jolliest of all possible worlds. But for his sister Constance and her hawk-like vigilance, he might, he thought, have been able at least to dodge the top-hat.

'Have you got your speech ready?'

'Yes.'

'Well, mind you learn it by heart this time and don't stammer and dodder as you did last year.'

Lord Emsworth pushed plate and kipper away. He had lost his desire for food.

'And don't forget you have to go to the village this morning to judge the cottage gardens.'

'All right, all right, all right,' said his lordship testily. 'I've not forgotten.'

'I think I will come to the village with you. There are a number of those Fresh Air London children staying there now, and I must warn them to behave properly when they come to the Fête this afternoon. You know what London children are. McAllister says he found one of them in the gardens the other day, picking his flowers.'

At any other time the news of this outrage would, no doubt, have affected Lord Emsworth profoundly. But now, so intense was his self-pity, he did not even shudder. He drank coffee with the air of a man who regretted that it was not hemlock.

'By the way, McAllister was speaking to me again last night about that gravel path through the yew alley. He seems very keen on it.'

'Glug!' said Lord Emsworth—which, as any philologist will tell you, is the sound which peers of the realm make when stricken to the soul while drinking coffee.

Concerning Glasgow, that great commercial and manufacturing city in the county of Lanarkshire in Scotland, much has been written. So lyrically does the Encyclopædia Britannica deal with the place that it covers twenty-seven pages before it can tear itself away and go on to Glass, Glastonbury, Glatz and Glauber. The only aspect of it, however, which immediately concerns the present historian is the fact that the citizens it breeds are apt to be grim, dour, persevering, tenacious men; men with red whiskers who know what they want and mean to get it. Such a one was Angus McAllister, head-gardener at Blandings Castle.

For years Angus McAllister had set before himself as his earthly goal the construction of a gravel path through the Castle's famous yew alley. For years he had been bringing the project to the notice of his employer, though in anyone less whiskered the latter's unconcealed loathing would have caused embarrassment. And now, it seemed, he was at it again.

'Gravel path!' Lord Emsworth stiffened through the whole length of his stringy body. Nature, he had always maintained, intended a yew alley to be carpeted with a mossy growth. And, whatever Nature felt about it, he personally was dashed if he was going to have men with Clydeside accents and faces like dissipated potatoes coming along and mutilating that lovely expanse of green velvet. 'Gravel path, indeed! Why not asphalt? Why not a few hoardings with advertisements of liver pills and a filling-station? That's what the man would really like.'

Lord Emsworth felt bitter, and when he felt bitter he could be terribly sarcastic.

'Well, I think it is a very good idea,' said his sister. 'One could walk there in wet weather then. Damp moss is ruinous to shoes.'

Lord Emsworth rose. He could bear no more of this. He left the table, the room and the house and, reaching the yew alley some minutes later, was revolted to find it infested by Angus McAllister in person. The head-gardener was standing gazing at the moss like a high priest of some ancient religion about to stick the gaff into the human sacrifice.

'Morning, McAllister,' said Lord Emsworth coldly.

'Good morrrrning, your lorrudsheep.'

There was a pause. Angus McAllister, extending a foot that looked like a violin-case, pressed it on the moss. The meaning of the gesture was plain. It expressed contempt, dislike, a generally anti-moss spirit:

and Lord Emsworth, wincing, surveyed the man unpleasantly through his pince-nez. Though not often given to theological speculation, he was wondering why Providence, if obliged to make head-gardeners, had found it necessary to make them so Scotch. In the case of Angus McAllister, why, going a step farther, have made him a human being at all? All the ingredients of a first-class mule simply thrown away. He felt that he might have liked Angus McAllister if he had been a mule.

'I was speaking to her leddyship yesterday.'

'Oh?'

'About the gravel path I was speaking to her leddyship.'

'Oh?'

'Her leddyship likes the notion fine.'

'Indeed! Well . . .'

Lord Emsworth's face had turned a lively pink, and he was about to release the blistering words which were forming themselves in his mind when suddenly he caught the head-gardener's eye and paused. Angus McAllister was looking at him in a peculiar manner, and he knew what that look meant. Just one crack, his eye was saying—in Scotch, of course—just one crack out of you and I tender my resignation. And with a sickening shock it came home to Lord Emsworth how completely he was in this man's clutches.

He shuffled miserably. Yes, he was helpless. Except for that kink about gravel paths, Angus McAllister was a head-gardener in a thousand, and he needed him. He could not do without him. That, unfortunately, had been proved by experiment. Once before, at the time when they were grooming for the Agricultural Show that pumpkin which had subsequently romped home so gallant a winner, he had dared to flout Angus McAllister. And Angus had resigned, and he had been forced to plead— yes, plead—with him to come back. An employer cannot hope to do this sort of thing and still rule with an iron hand. Filled with the coward rage that dares to burn but does not dare to blaze, Lord Emsworth coughed a cough that was undisguisedly a bronchial white flag.

'I'll—er—I'll think it over, McAllister.'

'Mphm.'

'I have to go to the village now. I will see you later.'

'Mphm.'

'Meanwhile, I will—er—think it over.'

'Mphm.'

The task of judging the floral displays in the cottage gardens of the little village of Blandings Parva was one to which Lord Emsworth had looked forward with pleasurable anticipation. It was the sort of job he liked. But now, even though he had managed to give his sister Constance the slip and was free from her threatened society, he approached the task with a downcast spirit. It is always unpleasant for a proud man to realize that he is no longer captain of his soul; that he is to all intents and purposes ground beneath the number twelve heel of a Glaswegian head-gardener; and, brooding on this, he judged the cottage gardens with a distrait eye. It was only when he came to the last on his list that anything like animation crept into his demeanour.

This, he perceived, peering over its rickety fence, was not at all a bad little garden. It demanded closer inspection. He unlatched the gate and pottered in. And a dog, dozing behind a water-butt, opened one eye and looked at him. It was one of those hairy, nondescript dogs, and its gaze was cold, wary and suspicious, like that of a stockbroker who thinks someone is going to play the confidence trick on him.

Lord Emsworth did not observe the animal. He had pottered to a bed of wallflowers and now, stooping, he took a sniff at them.

As sniffs go, it was an innocent sniff, but the dog for some reason appeared to read into it criminality of a high order. All the indignant householder in him woke in a flash. The next moment the world had become full of hideous noises, and Lord Emsworth's preoccupation was swept away in a passionate desire to save his ankles from harm.

As these chronicles of Blandings Castle have already shown, he was not at his best with strange dogs. Beyond saying 'Go away, sir!' and leaping to and fro with an agility surprising in one of his years, he had accomplished little in the direction of a reasoned plan of defence when the cottage door opened and a girl came out.

'Hoy!' cried the girl.

And on the instant, at the mere sound of her voice, the mongrel, suspending hostilities, bounded at the new-comer and writhed on his back at her feet with all four legs in the air. The spectacle reminded Lord Emsworth irresistibly of his own behaviour when in the presence of Angus McAllister.

He blinked at his preserver. She was a small girl, of uncertain age— possibly twelve or thirteen, though a combination of London fogs and early cares had given her face a sort of wizened motherliness which in some odd way caused his lordship from the first to look on her as belonging to his own generation. She was the type of girl you see in back streets carrying a baby nearly as large as herself and still retaining sufficient energy to lead one little brother by the hand and shout recrimination at another in the distance. Her cheeks shone from recent soaping, and she was dressed in a velveteen frock which was obviously the pick of her wardrobe. Her hair, in defiance of the prevailing mode, she wore drawn tightly back into a short pigtail.

'Er—thank you,' said Lord Emsworth.

'Thank you, sir,' said the girl.

For what she was thanking him, his lordship was not able to gather. Later, as their acquaintance ripened, he was to discover that this strange gratitude was a habit with his new friend. She thanked everybody for everything. At the moment, the mannerism surprised him. He continued to blink at her through his pince-nez.

Lack of practice had rendered Lord Emsworth a little rusty in the art of making conversation to members of the other sex. He sought in his mind for topics.

'Fine day.'

'Yes, sir. Thank you, sir.'

'Are you'—Lord Emsworth furtively consulted his list—'are you the daughter of—ah—Ebenezer Sprockett?' he asked, thinking, as he had often thought before, what ghastly names some of his tenantry possessed.

'No, sir. I'm from London, sir.'

'Ah? London, eh? Pretty warm it must be there.' He paused. Then, remembering a formula of his youth: 'Er—been out much this Season?'

'No, sir.'

'Everybody out of town now, I suppose? What part of London?'

'Drury Line, sir.'

'What's your name? Eh, what?'

'Gladys, sir. Thank you, sir. This is Ern.'

A small boy had wandered out of the cottage, a rather hard-boiled specimen with freckles, bearing surprisingly in his hand a large and beautiful bunch of flowers. Lord Emsworth bowed courteously and with the addition of this third party to the *tête-à-tête* felt more at his ease.

'How do you do,' he said. 'What pretty flowers.'

With her brother's advent, Gladys, also, had lost diffidence and gained conversational aplomb.

'A treat, ain't they?' she agreed eagerly. 'I got 'em for 'im up at the big 'ahse. Coo! The old josser the plice belongs to didn't arf chase me. 'E found me picking 'em and 'e sharted somefin at me and come runnin' after me, but I copped 'im on the shin wiv a stone and 'e stopped to rub it and I come away.'

Lord Emsworth might have corrected her impression that Blandings Castle and its gardens belonged to Angus McAllister, but his mind was so filled with admiration and gratitude that he refrained from doing so. He looked at the girl almost reverently. Not content with controlling savage dogs with a mere word, this super-woman actually threw stones at Angus McAllister—a thing which he had never been able to nerve himself to do in an association which had lasted nine years—and, what was more, copped him on the shin with them. What nonsense, Lord Emsworth felt, the papers talked about the Modern Girl. If this was a specimen, the Modern Girl was the highest point the sex had yet reached.

'Ern,' said Gladys, changing the subject, 'is wearin' 'air-oil todiy.'

Lord Emsworth had already observed this and had, indeed, been moving to windward as she spoke.

'For the Feet,' explained Gladys.

'For the feet?' It seemed unusual.

'For the Feet in the pork this afternoon.'

'Oh, you are going to the Fête?'

'Yes, sir, thank you, sir.'

For the first time, Lord Emsworth found himself regarding that grisly social event with something approaching favour.

'We must look out for one another there,' he said cordially. 'You will remember me again? I shall be wearing'—he gulped—'a top hat.'

'Ern's going to wear a stror penamaw that's been give 'im.'

Lord Emsworth regarded the lucky young devil with frank envy. He rather fancied he knew that panama. It had been his constant companion for some six years and then had been torn from him by his sister Constance and handed over to the vicar's wife for her rummage-sale.

He sighed.

'Well, good-bye.'

'Good-bye, sir. Thank you, sir.'

Lord Emsworth walked pensively out of the garden and, turning into the little street, encountered Lady Constance.

'Oh, there you are, Clarence.'

'Yes,' said Lord Emsworth, for such was the case.

'Have you finished judging the gardens?'

'Yes.'

'I am just going into this end cottage here. The vicar tells me there is a little girl from London staying there. I want to warn her to behave this afternoon. I have spoken to the others.'

Lord Emsworth drew himself up. His pince-nez were slightly askew, but despite this his gaze was commanding and impressive.

'Well, mind what you say,' he said authoritatively. 'None of your district-visiting stuff, Constance.'

'What do you mean?'

'You know what I mean. I have the greatest respect for the young lady to whom you refer. She behaved on a certain recent occasion—on two recent occasions—with notable gallantry and resource, and I won't have her ballyragged. Understand that!'

The technical title of the orgy which broke out annually on the first Monday in August in the park of Blandings Castle was the Blandings Parva School Treat, and it seemed to Lord Emsworth, wanly watching the proceedings from under the shadow of his top hat, that if this was the sort of thing schools looked on as pleasure he and they were mentally poles apart. A function like the Blandings Parva School Treat blurred his conception of Man as Nature's Final Word.

The decent sheep and cattle to whom this park normally belonged had been hustled away into regions unknown, leaving the smooth expanse of turf to children whose vivacity scared Lord Emsworth and adults who appeared to him to have cast aside all dignity and every other noble quality which goes to make a one hundred per cent British citizen. Look at Mrs Rossiter over there, for instance, the wife of Jno. Rossiter, Provisions, Groceries and Home-Made Jams. On any other day of the year, when you met her, Mrs Rossiter was a nice, quiet, docile woman who gave at the knees respectfully as you passed. To-day, flushed in the face and with her bonnet on one side, she seemed to have gone completely native. She was wandering to and fro drinking lemonade out of a bottle and employing her mouth, when not so occupied, to make a devastating noise with what he believed was termed a squeaker.

The injustice of the thing stung Lord Emsworth. This park was his own private park. What right had people to come and blow squeakers in it? How would Mrs Rossiter like it if one afternoon he suddenly invaded her neat little garden in the High Street and rushed about over her lawn, blowing a squeaker?

And it was always on these occasions so infernally hot. July might have ended in a flurry of snow, but directly the first Monday in August arrived and he had to put on a stiff collar out came the sun, blazing with tropic fury.

Of course, admitted Lord Emsworth, for he was a fair-minded man, this cut both ways. The hotter the day, the more quickly his collar lost its starch and ceased to spike him like a javelin. This afternoon, for instance, it had resolved itself almost immediately into something which felt like a wet compress. Severe as were his sufferings, he was compelled to recognize that he was that much ahead of the game.

A masterful figure loomed at his side.

'Clarence!'

Lord Emsworth's mental and spiritual state was now such that not even the advent of his sister Constance could add noticeably to his discomfort.

'Clarence, you look a perfect sight.'

'I know I do. Who wouldn't in a rig-out like this? Why in the name of goodness you always insist . . .'

'Please don't be childish, Clarence. I cannot understand the fuss you make about dressing for once in your life like a reasonable English gentleman and not like a tramp.'

'It's this top hat. It's exciting the children.'

'What on earth do you mean, exciting the children?'

'Well, all I can tell you is that just now, as I was passing the place where they're playing football—Football! In weather like this!—a small boy called out something derogatory and threw a portion of a coco-nut at it.'

'If you will identify the child,' said Lady Constance warmly, 'I will have him severely punished.'

'How the dickens,' replied his lordship with equal warmth, 'can I identify the child? They all look alike to me. And if I did identify him, I would shake him by the hand. A boy who throws coco-nuts at top hats is fundamentally sound in his views. And stiff collars . . .'

'Stiff! That's what I came to speak to you about. Are you aware that your collar looks like a rag? Go in and change it at once.'

'But, my dear Constance . . .'

'At once, Clarence. I simply cannot understand a man having so little pride in his appearance. But all your life you have been like that. I remember when we were children . . .'

Lord Emsworth's past was not of such a purity that he was prepared to stand and listen to it being lectured on by a sister with a good memory.

'Oh, all right, all right, all right,' he said. 'I'll change it, I'll change it.'

'Well, hurry. They are just starting tea.'

Lord Emsworth quivered.

'Have I got to go into that tea-tent?'

'Of course you have. Don't be so ridiculous. I do wish you would realize your position. As master of Blandings Castle . . .'

A bitter, mirthless laugh from the poor peon thus ludicrously described drowned the rest of the sentence.

It always seemed to Lord Emsworth, in analysing these entertainments, that the August Bank Holiday Saturnalia at Blandings Castle reached a peak of repulsiveness when tea was served in the big marquee. Tea over, the agony abated, to become acute once more at the moment when he stepped to the edge of the platform and cleared his throat and tried to recollect what the deuce he had planned to say to the goggling audience beneath him. After that, it subsided again and passed until the following August.

Conditions during the tea hour, the marquee having stood all day under a blazing sun, were generally such that Shadrach, Meshach and Abednego, had they been there, could have learned something new about burning fiery furnaces. Lord Emsworth, delayed by the revision of his toilet, made his entry when the meal was half over and was pleased to find that his second collar almost instantaneously began to relax its iron grip. That, however, was the only gleam of happiness which was to be vouchsafed him. Once in the tent, it took his experienced eye but a moment to discern that the present feast was eclipsing in frightfulness all its predecessors.

Young Blandings Parva, in its normal form, tended rather to the stolidly bovine than the riotous. In all villages, of course, there must of necessity be an occasional tough egg—in the case of Blandings Parva the names of Willie Drake and Thomas (Rat-Face) Blenkiron spring to the mind—but it was seldom that the local infants offered anything beyond the power of a curate to control. What was giving the present gathering its striking resemblance to a reunion of *sans-culottes* at the height of the French Revolution was the admixture of the Fresh Air London visitors.

About the London child, reared among the tin cans and cabbage stalks of Drury Lane and Clare Market, there is a breezy insouciance which his country cousin lacks. Years of back-chat with annoyed parents and relatives have cured him of any tendency he may have had towards shyness, with the result that when he requires anything he grabs for it, and when he is amused by any slight peculiarity in the personal appearance of members of the governing classes he finds no difficulty in translating his thoughts into speech. Already, up and down the long tables, the curate's unfortunate squint was coming in for hearty comment, and the front teeth of one of the school-teachers ran it a close second for popularity. Lord Emsworth was not, as a rule, a man of swift inspirations, but it occurred to him at this juncture that it would be a prudent move to take off his top hat before his little guests observed it and appreciated its humorous possibilities.

The action was not, however, necessary. Even as he raised his hand a rock cake, singing through the air like a shell, took it off for him.

Lord Emsworth had had sufficient. Even Constance, unreasonable woman though she was, could hardly expect him to stay and beam genially under conditions like this. All civilized laws had obviously gone by the board and Anarchy reigned in the marquee. The curate was doing his best to form a provisional government consisting of himself and the two school-teachers, but there was only one man who could have coped adequately with the situation and that was King Herod, who—regrettably—was not among those present. Feeling like some aristocrat of the old *régime* sneaking away from the tumbril, Lord Emsworth edged to the exit and withdrew.

Outside the marquee the world was quieter, but only comparatively so. What Lord Emsworth craved was solitude, and in all the broad park there seemed to be but one spot where it was to be had. This was a red-tiled shed, standing beside a small pond, used at happier times as a lounge or retiring-room for cattle. Hurrying thither, his lordship had just begun to revel in the cool, cow-scented dimness of its interior when from one of the dark corners, causing him to start and bite his tongue, there came the sound of a subdued sniff.

He turned. This was persecution. With the whole park to mess about in, why should an infernal child invade this one sanctuary of his? He spoke with angry sharpness. He came of a line of warrior ancestors and his fighting blood was up.

'Who's that?'

'Me, sir. Thank you, sir.'

Only one person of Lord Emsworth's acquaintance was capable of expressing gratitude for having been barked at in such a tone. His wrath died away and remorse took its place. He felt like a man who in error has kicked a favourite dog.

'God bless my soul!' he exclaimed. 'What in the world are you doing in a cow-shed?'

'Please, sir, I was put.'

'Put? How do you mean, put? Why?'

'For pinching things, sir.'

'Eh? What? Pinching things? Most extraordinary. What did you—er—pinch?'

'Two buns, two jem-sengwiches, two apples and a slicer cake.'

The girl had come out of her corner and was standing correctly at attention. Force of habit had caused her to intone the list of the pur-loined articles in the singsong voice in which she was wont to recite the multiplication-table at school, but Lord Emsworth could see that she was deeply moved. Tear-stains glistened on her face, and no Emsworth had ever been able to watch unstirred a woman's tears. The ninth Earl was visibly affected.

'Blow your nose,' he said, hospitably extending his handkerchief.

'Yes, sir. Thank you, sir.'

'What did you say you had pinched? Two buns . . .'

'. . . Two jem-sengwiches, two apples and a slicer cake.'

'Did you eat them?'

'No, sir. They wasn't for me. They was for Ern.'

'Ern? Oh, ah, yes. Yes, to be sure. For Ern, eh?'

'Yes, sir.'

'But why the dooce couldn't Ern have—er—pinched them for him-self? Strong, able-bodied young feller, I mean.'

Lord Emsworth, a member of the old school, did not like this disposi-tion on the part of the modern young man to shirk the dirty work and let the woman pay.

'Ern wasn't allowed to come to the treat, sir.'

'What! Not allowed? Who said he mustn't?'

'The lidy, sir.'

'What lidy?'

'The one that come in just after you'd gorn this morning.'

A fierce snort escaped Lord Emsworth. Constance! What the devil did Constance mean by taking it upon herself to revise his list of guests without so much as a . . . Constance, eh? He snorted again. One of these days Constance would go too far.

'Monstrous!' he cried.

'Yes, sir.'

'High-handed tyranny, by Gad. Did she give any reason?'

'The lidy didn't like Ern biting 'er in the leg, sir.'

'Ern bit her in the leg?'

'Yes, sir. Pliying 'e was a dorg. And the lidy was cross and Ern wasn't allowed to come to the treat, and I told 'im I'd bring 'im back somefing nice.'

Lord Emsworth breathed heavily. He had not supposed that in these degenerate days a family like this existed. The sister copped Angus McAllister on the shin with stones, the brother bit Constance in the leg . . . It was like listening to some grand old saga of the exploits of heroes and demigods.

'I thought if I didn't 'ave nothing myself it would make it all right.'

'Nothing?' Lord Emsworth started. 'Do you mean to tell me you have not had tea?'

'No, sir. Thank you, sir. I thought if I didn't 'ave none, then it would be all right Ern 'aving what I would 'ave 'ad if I 'ad 'ave 'ad.'

His lordship's head, never strong, swam a little. Then it resumed its equilibrium. He caught her drift.

'God bless my soul!' said Lord Emsworth. 'I never heard anything so monstrous and appalling in my life. Come with me immediately.'

'The lidy said I was to stop 'ere, sir.'

Lord Emsworth gave vent to his loudest snort of the afternoon.

'Confound the lidy!'

'Yes, sir. Thank you, sir.'

Five minutes later Beach, the butler, enjoying a siesta in the housekeeper's room, was roused from his slumbers by the unexpected ringing of a bell. Answering its summons, he found his employer in the library, and with him a surprising young person in a velveteen frock, at the sight of whom his eyebrows quivered and, but for his iron self-restraint, would have risen.

'Beach!'

'Your lordship?'

'This young lady would like some tea.'

'Very good, your lordship.'

'Buns, you know. And apples, and jem—I mean jam-sandwiches, and cake, and that sort of thing.'

'Very good, your lordship.'

'And she has a brother, Beach.'

'Indeed, your lordship?'

'She will want to take some stuff away for him.' Lord Emsworth turned to his guest. 'Ernest would like a little chicken, perhaps?'

'Coo!'

'I beg your pardon?'

'Yes, sir. Thank you, sir.'

'And a slice or two of ham?'

'Yes, sir. Thank you, sir.'

'And—he has no gouty tendency?'

'No, sir. Thank you, sir.'

'Capital! Then a bottle of that new lot of port, Beach. It's some stuff they've sent me down to try,' explained his lordship. 'Nothing special, you understand,' he added apologetically, 'but quite drinkable. I should like your brother's opinion of it. See that all that is put together in a parcel, Beach, and leave it on the table in the hall. We will pick it up as we go out.'

A welcome coolness had crept into the evening air by the time Lord Emsworth and his guest came out of the great door of the castle. Gladys, holding her host's hand and clutching the parcel, sighed contentedly. She had done herself well at the tea-table. Life seemed to have nothing more to offer.

Lord Emsworth did not share this view. His spacious mood had not yet exhausted itself.

'Now, is there anything else you can think of that Ernest would like?' he asked. 'If so, do not hesitate to mention it. Beach, can you think of anything?'

The butler, hovering respectfully, was unable to do so.

'No, your lordship. I ventured to add—on my own responsibility, your lordship—some hard-boiled eggs and a pot of jam to the parcel.'

'Excellent! You are sure there is nothing else?'

A wistful look came into Glady's eyes.

'Could he 'ave some flarze?'

'Certainly,' said Lord Emsworth. 'Certainly, certainly, certainly. By all means. Just what I was about to suggest my—er—what *is* flarze?'

Beach, the linguist, interpreted.

'I think the young lady means flowers, your lordship.'

'Yes, sir. Thank you, sir. Flarze.'

'Oh?' said Lord Emsworth. 'Oh? Flarze?' he said slowly. 'Oh, ah, yes. Yes. I see. H'm!'

He removed his pince-nez, wiped them thoughtfully, replaced them, and gazed with wrinkling forehead at the gardens that stretched gaily out before him. Flarze! It would be idle to deny that those gardens contained flarze in full measure. They were bright with Achillea, Bignonia Radicans, Campanula, Digitalis, Euphorbia, Funkia, Gypsophila, Helianthus, Iris, Liatris, Monarda, Phlox Drummondi, Salvia, Thalictrum, Vinca and Yucca. But the devil of it was that Angus McAllister would have a fit if they were picked. Across the threshold of this Eden the ginger whiskers of Angus McAllister lay like a flaming sword.

As a general rule, the procedure for getting flowers out of Angus McAllister was as follows. You waited till he was in one of his rare moods of complaisance, then you led the conversation gently round to the subject of interior decoration, and then, choosing your moment, you asked if he could possibly spare a few to be put in vases. The last thing you thought of doing was to charge in and start helping yourself.

'I—er— . . .' said Lord Emsworth.

He stopped. In a sudden blinding flash of clear vision he had seen himself for what he was—the spineless, unspeakably unworthy descendant of ancestors who, though they may have had their faults, had certainly known how to handle employees. It was 'How now, varlet!' and 'Marry come up, thou malapert knave!' in the days of previous Earls of Emsworth. Of course, they had possessed certain advantages which he lacked. It undoubtedly helped a man in his dealings with the domestic staff to have, as they had had, the rights of the high, the middle and the low justice—which meant, broadly, that if you got annoyed with your head-gardener you could immediately divide him into four head-gardeners with a battle-axe and no questions asked—but even so, he realized that they were better men than he was and that, if he allowed craven fear of Angus McAllister to stand in the way of this delightful girl and her charming brother getting all the flowers they required, he was not worthy to be the last of their line.

Lord Emsworth wrestled with his tremors.

'Certainly, certainly, certainly,' he said, though not without a qualm. 'Take as many as you want.'

And so it came about that Angus McAllister, crouched in his potting-shed like some dangerous beast in its den, beheld a sight which first froze his blood and then sent it boiling through his veins. Flitting to and fro through his sacred gardens, picking his sacred flowers, was a small girl in a velveteen frock. And—which brought apoplexy a step closer—it was the same small girl who two days before had copped him on the shin with a stone. The stillness of the summer evening was shattered by a roar that sounded like boilers exploding, and Angus McAllister came out of the potting-shed at forty-five miles per hour.

Gladys did not linger. She was a London child, trained from infancy to bear herself gallantly in the presence of alarms and excursions, but this excursion had been so sudden that it momentarily broke her nerve. With a horrified yelp she scuttled to where Lord Emsworth stood and, hiding behind him, clutched the tails of his morning-coat.

'Oo-er!' said Gladys.

Lord Emsworth was not feeling so frightfully good himself. We have pictured him a few moments back drawing inspiration from the nobility of his ancestors and saying, in effect, 'That for McAllister!' but truth now compels us to admit that this hardy attitude was largely due to the fact that he believed the head-gardener to be a safe quarter of a mile away among the swings and roundabouts of the Fête. The spectacle of the man charging vengefully down on him with gleaming eyes and bristling whiskers made him feel like a nervous English infantryman at the Battle of Bannockburn. His knees shook and the soul within him quivered.

And then something happened, and the whole aspect of the situation changed.

It was, in itself, quite a trivial thing, but it had an astoundingly stimulating effect on Lord Emsworth's morale. What happened was that Gladys, seeking further protection, slipped at this moment a small, hot hand into his.

It was a mute vote of confidence, and Lord Emsworth intended to be worthy of it.

'He's coming,' whispered his lordship's Inferiority Complex agitatedly.

'What of it?' replied Lord Emsworth stoutly.

'Tick him off,' breathed his lordship's ancestors in his other ear.

'Leave it to me,' replied Lord Emsworth.

He drew himself up and adjusted his pince-nez. He felt filled with a cool masterfulness. If the man tendered his resignation, let him tender his damned resignation.

'Well, McAllister?' said Lord Emsworth coldly.

He removed his top hat and brushed it against his sleeve.

'What is the matter, McAllister?'

He replaced his top hat.

'You appear agitated, McAllister.'

He jerked his head militantly. The hat fell off. He let it lie. Freed from its loathsome weight he felt more masterful than ever. It had just needed that to bring him to the top of his form.

'This young lady,' said Lord Emsworth, 'has my full permission to pick all the flowers she wants, McAllister. If you do not see eye to eye with me in this matter, McAllister, say so and we will discuss what you are going to do about it, McAllister. These gardens, McAllister, belong to me, and if you do not—er—appreciate that fact you will, no doubt, be able to find another employer—ah—more in tune with your views. I value your services highly, McAllister, but I will not be dictated to in my own garden, McAllister. Er—dash it,' added his lordship, spoiling the whole effect.

A long moment followed in which Nature stood still, breathless. The Achillea stood still. So did the Bignonia Radicans. So did the Campanula, the Digitalis, the Euphorbia, the Funkia, the Gypsophila, the Helianthus, the Iris, the Liatris, the Monarda, the Phlox Drummondi, the Salvia, the Thalictrum, the Vinca and the Yucca. From far off in the direction of the park there sounded the happy howls of children who were probably breaking things, but even these seemed hushed. The evening breeze had died away.

Angus McAllister stood glowering. His attitude was that of one sorely perplexed. So might the early bird have looked if the worm ear-marked for its breakfast had suddenly turned and snapped at it. It had never occurred to him that his employer would voluntarily suggest that he sought another position, and now that he had suggested it Angus McAllister disliked the idea very much. Blandings Castle was in his bones. Elsewhere, he would feel an exile. He fingered his whiskers, but they gave him no comfort.

He made his decision. Better to cease to be a Napoleon than be a Napoleon in exile.

'Mphm,' said Angus McAllister.

'Oh, and by the way, McAllister,' said Lord Emsworth, 'that matter of the gravel path through the yew alley. I've been thinking it over, and I won't have it. Not on any account. Mutilate my beautiful moss with a beastly gravel path? Make an eyesore of the loveliest spot in one of the finest and oldest gardens in the United Kingdom? Certainly not. Most decidedly not. Try to remember, McAllister, as you work in the gardens of Blandings Castle, that you are not back in Glasgow, laying out recreation grounds. That is all, McAllister. Er—dash it—that is all.'

'Mphm,' said Angus McAllister.

He turned. He walked away. The potting-shed swallowed him up. Nature resumed its breathing. The breeze began to blow again. And all over the gardens birds who had stopped on their high note carried on according to plan.

Lord Emsworth took out his handkerchief and dabbed with it at his forehead. He was shaken, but a novel sense of being a man among men thrilled him. It might seem bravado, but he almost wished—yes, dash it, he almost wished—that his sister Constance would come along and start something while he felt like this.

He had his wish.

'Clarence!'

Yes, there she was, hurrying towards him up the garden path. She, like McAllister, seemed agitated. Something was on her mind.

'Clarence!'

'Don't keep saying "Clarence!" as if you were a dashed parrot,' said Lord Emsworth haughtily. 'What the dickens is the matter, Constance?'

'Matter? Do you know what the time is? Do you know that everybody is waiting down there for you to make your speech?'

Lord Emsworth met her eye sternly.

'I do not,' he said. 'And I don't care. I'm not going to make any dashed speech. If you want a speech, let the vicar make it. Or make it yourself. Speech! I never heard such dashed nonsense in my life.' He turned to Gladys. 'Now, my dear,' he said, 'if you will just give me time to get out of these infernal clothes and this ghastly collar and put on something human, we'll go down to the village and have a chat with Ern.'

SUMMER
LIGHTNING

PREFACE

A CERTAIN critic—for such men, I regret to say, do exist—made the nasty remark about my last novel that it contained 'all the old Wodehouse characters under different names'. He has probably by now been eaten by bears, like the children who made mock of the prophet Elisha: but if he still survives he will not be able to make a similar charge against *Summer Lightning*. With my superior intelligence, I have outgeneralled the man this time by putting in all the old Wodehouse characters under the same names. Pretty silly it will make him feel, I rather fancy.

This story is a sort of Old Home Week for my—if I may coin a phrase—puppets. Hugo Carmody and Ronnie Fish appeared in *Money for Nothing*. Pilbeam was in *Bill the Conqueror*. And the rest of them, Lord Emsworth, the Efficient Baxter, Butler Beach, and the others have all done their bit before in *Something Fresh* and *Leave it to Psmith*. Even Empress of Blandings, that pre-eminent pig, is coming up for the second time, having made her debut in a short story called 'Pig-hoo-oo-ey!', which, with other Blandings Castle stories too fascinating to mention, will eventually appear in volume form.

The fact is, I cannot tear myself away from Blandings Castle. The place exercises a sort of spell over me. I am always popping down to Shropshire and looking in there to hear the latest news, and there always seems to be something to interest me. It is in the hope that it will also interest My Public that I have jotted down the bit of gossip from the old spot which I have called *Summer Lightning*.

A word about the title. It is related of Thackeray that, hitting upon *Vanity Fair* after retiring to rest one night, he leaped out of bed and ran seven times round the room, shouting at the top of his voice. Oddly enough, I behaved in exactly the same way when I thought of *Summer Lightning*. I recognized it immediately as the ideal title for a novel. My exuberance has been a little diminished since by the discovery that I am not the only one who thinks highly of it. Already I have been informed that two novels with the same name have been published in England, and my agent in America cables to say that three have recently been placed on the market in the United States. As my story has appeared in serial form under its present label, it is too late to alter it now. I can only express the modest hope that this story will be considered worthy of inclusion in the list of the Hundred Best Books Called Summer Lightning.

P. G. WODEHOUSE

Contents

to

DENIS MACKAIL

author of 'Greenery Street,' 'The Flower Show,'

and other books which I wish I had written

TROUBLE BREWING AT BLANDINGS

· 1 ·

Blandings Castle slept in the sunshine. Dancing little ripples of heat-mist played across its smooth lawns and stone-flagged terraces. The air was full of the lulling drone of insects. It was that gracious hour of a summer afternoon, midway between luncheon and tea, when Nature seems to unbutton its waistcoat and put its feet up.

In the shade of a laurel bush outside the back premises of this stately home of England, Beach, butler to Clarence, ninth Earl of Emsworth, its proprietor, sat sipping the contents of a long glass and reading a weekly paper devoted to the doings of Society and the Stage. His attention had just been arrested by a photograph in an oval border on one of the inner pages: and for perhaps a minute he scrutinized this in a slow, thorough, pop-eyed way, absorbing its every detail. Then, with a fruity chuckle, he took a penknife from his pocket, cut out the photograph, and placed it in the recesses of his costume.

At this moment, the laurel bush, which had hitherto not spoken, said 'Psst!'

The butler started violently. A spasm ran through his ample frame.

'Beach!' said the bush.

Something was now peering out of it. This might have been a wood-nymph, but the butler rather thought not, and he was right. It was a tall young man with light hair. He recognized his employer's secretary, Mr Hugo Carmody, and rose with pained reproach. His heart was still jumping, and he had bitten his tongue.

'Startle you, Beach?'

'Extremely, sir.'

'I'm sorry. Excellent for the liver, though. Beach, do you want to earn a quid?'

The butler's austerity softened. The hard look died out of his eyes.

'Yes, sir.'

'Can you get hold of Miss Millicent alone?'

'Certainly, sir.'

'Then give her this note, and don't let anyone see you do it. Especially—and this is where I want you to follow me very closely, Beach—Lady Constance Keeble.'

'I will attend to the matter immediately, sir.'

He smiled a paternal smile. Hugo smiled back. A perfect understanding prevailed between these two. Beach understood that he ought not to be giving his employer's niece surreptitious notes: and Hugo understood that he ought not to be urging a good man to place such a weight upon his conscience.

'Perhaps you are not aware, sir,' said the butler, having trousered the wages of sin, 'that her ladyship went up to London on the three-thirty train?'

Hugo uttered an exclamation of chagrin.

'You mean that all this Red Indian stuff—creeping from bush to bush and not letting a single twig snap beneath my feet—has simply been a waste of time?' He emerged, dusting his clothes. 'I wish I'd known that before,' he said. 'I've severely injured a good suit, and it's a very moot question whether I haven't got some kind of a beetle down my back. However, nobody ever took a toss through being careful.'

'Very true, sir.'

Relieved by the information that the X-ray eye of the aunt of the girl he loved was operating elsewhere, Mr Carmody became conversational.

'Nice day, Beach.'

'Yes, sir.'

'You know, Beach, life's rummy. I mean to say, you never can tell what the future holds in store. Here I am at Blandings Castle, loving it. Sing of joy, sing of bliss, home was never like this. And yet, when the project of my coming here was first placed on the agenda, I don't mind telling you the heart was rather bowed down with weight of woe.'

'Indeed, sir?'

'Yes. Noticeably bowed down. If you knew the circumstances, you would understand why.'

Beach did know the circumstances. There were few facts concerning the dwellers in Blandings Castle of which he remained in ignorance for long. He was aware that young Mr Carmody had been, until a few weeks back, co-proprietor with Mr Ronald Fish, Lord Emsworth's nephew, of a night-club called the Hot Spot, situated just off Bond Street in the heart of London's pleasure-seeking area; that, despite this favoured position, it had proved a financial failure; that Mr Ronald had gone off with his mother, Lady Julia Fish, to recuperate at Biarritz; and that Hugo, on the insistence of Ronnie that unless some niche was found for his boyhood friend he would not stir a step towards Biarritz or any other blighted place, had come to Blandings as Lord Emsworth's private secretary.

'No doubt you were reluctant to leave London, sir?'

'Exactly. But now, Beach, believe me or believe me not, as far as I am concerned, anyone who likes can have London. Mark you, I'm not saying that just one brief night in the Piccadilly neighbourhood would come amiss. But to dwell in, give me Blandings Castle. What a spot, Beach!'

'Yes, sir.'

'A Garden of Eden, shall I call it?'

'Certainly, sir, if you wish.'

'And now that old Ronnie's coming here, joy, as you might say, will be unconfined.'

'Is Mr Ronald expected, sir?'

'Coming either to-morrow or the day after. I had a letter from him this morning. Which reminds me. He sends his regards to you, and asks me to tell you to put your shirt on Baby Bones for the Medbury Selling Plate.'

The butler pursed his lips dubiously.

'A long shot, sir. Not generally fancied.'

'Rank outsider. Leave it alone, is my verdict.'

'And yet Mr Ronald is usually very reliable. It is many years now since he first began to advise me in these matters, and I have done remarkably well by following him. Even as a lad at Eton he was always singularly fortunate in his information.'

'Well, suit yourself,' said Hugo, indifferently. 'What was that thing you were cutting out of the paper just now?'

'A photograph of Mr Galahad, sir. I keep an album in which I paste items of interest relating to the Family.'

'What that album needs is an eye-witness's description of Lady Constance Keeble falling out of a window and breaking her neck.'

A nice sense of the proprieties prevented Beach from endorsing this view verbally, but he sighed a little wistfully. He had frequently felt much the same about the chatelaine of Blandings.

'If you would care to see the clipping, sir? There is a reference to Mr Galahad's literary work.'

Most of the photographs in the weekly paper over which Beach had been relaxing were of peeresses trying to look like chorus-girls and chorus-girls trying to look like peeresses: but this one showed the perky features of a dapper little gentleman in the late fifties. Beneath it, in large letters, was the single word:

GALLY

Under this ran a caption in smaller print.

'The Hon. Galahad Threepwood, brother of the Earl of Emsworth. A little bird tells us that "Gally" is at Blandings Castle, Shropshire, the ancestral seat of the family, busily engaged in writing his Reminiscences. As every member of the Old Brigade will testify, they ought to be as warm as the weather, if not warmer.'

Hugo scanned the exhibit thoughtfully, and handed it back, to be placed in the archives.

'Yes,' he observed, 'I should say that about summed it up. That old bird must have been pretty hot stuff, I imagine, back in the days of Edward the Confessor.'

'Mr Galahad was somewhat wild as a young man,' agreed the butler with a sort of feudal pride in his voice. It was the opinion of the Servants' Hall that the Hon. Galahad shed lustre on Blandings Castle.

'Has it ever occurred to you, Beach, that that book of his is going to make no small stir when it comes out?'

'Frequently, sir.'

'Well, I'm saving up for my copy. By the way, I knew there was something I wanted to ask you. Can you give me any information on the subject of a bloke named Baxter?'

'Mr Baxter, sir? He used to be private secretary to his lordship.'

'Yes, so I gathered. Lady Constance was speaking to me about him this morning. She happened upon me as I was taking the air in riding kit and didn't seem overpleased. "You appear to enjoy a great deal of leisure, Mr Carmody," she said. "Mr Baxter," she continued, giving me the meaning eye, "never seemed to find time to go riding when he was Lord Emsworth's secretary. Mr Baxter was always so hard at work. But, then, Mr Baxter," she added, the old lamp becoming more meaning than ever, "loved his work. Mr Baxter took a real interest in his duties. Dear me! What a very conscientious man Mr Baxter was, to be sure!" Or words to that effect. I may be wrong, but I classed it as a dirty dig. And what I want to know is, if Baxter was such a world-beater, why did they ever let him go?'

The butler gazed about him cautiously.

'I fancy, sir, there was some Trouble.'

'Pinched the spoons, eh? Always the way with those zealous workers.'

'I never succeeded in learning the full details, sir, but there was something about some flower-pots.'

'He pinched the flower-pots?'

'Threw them at his lordship, I was given to understand.'

Hugo looked injured. He was a high-spirited young man who chafed at injustice.

'Well, I'm dashed if I see then,' he said, 'where this Baxter can claim to rank so jolly high above me as a secretary. I may be leisurely, I may forget to answer letters, I may occasionally on warm afternoons go in to some extent for the folding of the hands in sleep, but at least I don't throw flower-pots at people. Not so much as a pen-wiper have I ever bunged at Lord Emsworth. Well, I must be getting about my duties. That ride this morning and a slight slumber after lunch have set the schedule back a bit. You won't forget that note, will you?'

'No, sir.'

Hugo reflected.

'On second thoughts,' he said, 'perhaps you'd better hand it back to me. Safer not to have too much written matter circulating about the place. Just tell Miss Millicent that she will find me in the rose-garden at six sharp.'

'In the rose-garden . . ,'

'At six sharp.'

'Very good, sir. I will see that she receives the information.'

· II ·

For two hours after this absolutely nothing happened in the grounds of Blandings Castle. At the end of that period there sounded through the mellow, drowsy stillness a drowsy, mellow chiming. It was the clock over the stables striking five. Simultaneously, a small but noteworthy procession filed out of the house and made its way across the sun-bathed lawn to where the big cedar cast a grateful shade. It was headed by James, a footman, bearing a laden tray. Following him came Thomas, another footman, with a gate-leg table. The rear was brought up by Beach, who carried nothing, but merely lent a tone.

The instinct which warns all good Englishmen when tea is ready immediately began to perform its silent duty. Even as Thomas set the gate-leg table to earth there appeared, as if answering a cue, an elderly gentleman in stained tweeds and a hat he should have been ashamed of. Clarence, ninth Earl of Emsworth, in person. He was a long, lean, stringy man of about sixty, slightly speckled at the moment with mud, for he had spent most of the afternoon pottering round pig-styes. He surveyed the preparations for the meal with vague amiability through rimless pince-nez.

'Tea?'

'Yes, your lordship.'

'Oh?' said Lord Emsworth. 'Ah? Tea, eh? Tea? Yes. Tea. Quite so. To be sure, tea. Capital.'

One gathered from his remarks that he realized that the tea hour had arrived and was glad of it. He proceeded to impart his discovery to his niece, Millicent, who, lured by that same silent call, had just appeared at his side.

'Tea, Millicent.'

'Yes.'

'Er—tea,' said Lord Emsworth, driving home his point.

Millicent sat down, and busied herself with the pot. She was a tall, fair girl with soft blue eyes and a face like the Soul's Awakening. Her whole appearance radiated wholesome innocence. Not even an expert could have told that she had just received a whispered message from a bribed butler and was proposing at six sharp to go and meet a quite ineligible young man among the rose-bushes.

'Been down seeing the Empress, Uncle Clarence?'

'Eh? Oh, yes. Yes, my dear. I have been with her all the afternoon.'

Lord Emsworth's mild eyes beamed. They always did when that noble animal, Empress of Blandings, was mentioned. The ninth Earl was a man of few and simple ambitions. He had never desired to mould the destinies of the State, to frame its laws and make speeches in the House of Lords that would bring all the peers and bishops to their feet, whooping and waving their hats. All he yearned to do, by way of ensuring admittance to England's Hall of Fame, was to tend his prize sow, Empress of Blandings, so sedulously that for the second time in two consecutive years he would win the silver medal in the Fat Pigs class at the Shropshire Agricultural Show. And every day, it seemed to him, the glittering prize was coming more and more within his grasp.

Earlier in the summer there had been one breathless sickening moment of suspense, and disaster had seemed to loom. This was when his neighbour, Sir Gregory Parsloe-Parsloe, of Matchingham Hall, had basely lured away his pig-man, the superbly gifted George Cyril Wellbeloved, by the promise of higher wages. For a while Lord Emsworth had feared lest the Empress, mourning for her old friend and valet, might refuse food and fall from her high standard of obesity. But his apprehensions had proved groundless. The Empress had taken to Pirbright, George Cyril's successor, from the first, and was tucking away her meals with all the old abandon. The Right triumphs in this world far more often than we realize.

'What do you do to her?' asked Millicent, curiously. 'Read her bedtime stories?'

Lord Emsworth pursed his lips. He had a reverent mind, and disliked jesting on serious subjects.

'Whatever I do, my dear, it seems to effect its purpose. She is in wonderful shape.'

'I didn't know she had a shape. She hadn't when I last saw her.'

This time Lord Emsworth smiled indulgently. Gibes at the Empress's rotundity had no sting for him. He did not desire for her that school-girl slimness which is so fashionable nowadays.

'She has never fed more heartily,' he said. 'It is a treat to watch her.'

'I'm so glad. Mr Carmody,' said Millicent, stooping to tickle a spaniel which had wandered up to take pot-luck, 'told me he had never seen a finer animal in his life.'

'I like that young man,' said Lord Emsworth emphatically. 'He is sound on pigs. He has his head screwed on the right way.'

'Yes, he's an improvement on Baxter, isn't he?'

'Baxter!' His lordship choked over his cup.

'You didn't like Baxter much, did you, Uncle Clarence?'

'Hadn't a peaceful moment while he was in the place. Dreadful feller! Always fussing. Always wanting me to *do* things. Always coming round corners with his infernal spectacles gleaming and making me sign papers when I wanted to be out in the garden. Besides he was off his head. Thank goodness I've seen the last of Baxter.'

'But have you?'

'What do you mean?'

'If you ask me,' said Millicent, 'Aunt Constance hasn't given up the idea of getting him back.'

Lord Emsworth started with such violence that his pince-nez fell off. She had touched on his favourite nightmare. Sometimes he would wake trembling in the night, fancying that his late secretary had returned to the castle. And though on these occasions he always dropped off to sleep again with a happy smile of relief, he had never ceased to be haunted by the fear that his sister Constance, in her infernal managing way, was scheming to restore the fellow to office.

'Good God! Has she said anything to you?'

'No. But I have a feeling. I know she doesn't like Mr Carmody.'

Lord Emsworth exploded.

'Perfect nonsense! Utter, absolute, dashed nonsense. What on earth does she find to object to in young Carmody? Most capable, intelligent boy. Leaves me alone. Doesn't fuss me. I wish to heaven she would . . .'

He broke off, and stared blankly at a handsome woman of middle age who had come out of the house and was crossing the lawn.

'Why, here she is!' said Millicent, equally and just as disagreeably surprised. 'I thought you had gone up to London, Aunt Constance.'

Lady Constance Keeble had arrived at the table. Declining, with a distrait shake of the head, her niece's offer of the seat of honour by the tea-pot, she sank into a chair. She was a woman of still remarkable beauty, with features cast in a commanding mould and fine eyes. These eyes were at the moment dull and brooding.

'I missed my train,' she explained. 'However, I can do all I have to do in London to-morrow. I shall go up by the eleven-fifteen. In a way, it will be more convenient, for Ronald will be able to motor me back. I will look in at Norfolk Street and pick him up there before he starts.'

'What made you miss your train?'

'Yes,' said Lord Emsworth, complainingly. 'You started in good time.'

The brooding look in his sister's eyes deepened.

'I met Sir Gregory Parsloe.' Lord Emsworth stiffened at the name. 'He kept me talking. He is extremely worried.' Lord Emsworth looked pleased. 'He tells me he used to know Galahad very well a number of years ago, and he is very much alarmed about this book of his.'

'And I bet he isn't the only one,' murmured Millicent.

She was right. Once a man of the Hon. Galahad Threepwood's ante-

cedents starts taking pen in hand and being reminded of amusing incidents that happened to my dear old friend So-and-So, you never know
where he will stop; and all over England, among the more elderly of the
nobility and gentry, something like a panic had been raging ever since the
news of his literary activities had got about. From Sir Gregory Parsloe-
Parsloe, of Matchingham Hall, to grey-headed pillars of Society in distant Cumberland and Kent, whole droves of respectable men who in
their younger days had been rash enough to chum with the Hon. Galahad were recalling past follies committed in his company and speculat-
ing agitatedly as to how good the old pest's memory was.

For Galahad in his day had been a notable lad about town. A *beau sab-
reur* of Romano's. A Pink 'Un. A Pelican. A crony of Hughie Drummond
and Fatty Coleman; a brother-in-arms of the Shifter, the Pitcher, Peter
Blobbs and the rest of an interesting but not strait-laced circle. Bookmakers had called him by his pet name, barmaids had simpered beneath
his gallant chaff. He had heard the chimes at midnight. And when he
had looked in at the old Gardenia, commissionaires had fought for the
privilege of throwing him out. A man, in a word, who should never have
been taught to write and who, if unhappily gifted with that ability, should
have been restrained by Act of Parliament from writing Reminiscences.

So thought Lady Constance, his sister. So thought Sir Gregory
Parsloe-Parsloe, his neighbour. And so thought the pillars of society in
distant Cumberland and Kent. Widely as they differed on many points,
they were unanimous on this.

'He wanted me to try to find out if Galahad was putting anything
about him into it.'

'Better ask him now,' said Millicent. 'He's just come out of the house
and seems to be heading in this direction.'

Lady Constance turned sharply: and, following her niece's pointing
finger, winced. The mere sight of her deplorable brother was generally
enough to make her wince. When he began to talk and she had to listen,
the wince became a shudder. His conversation had the effect of making
her feel as if she had suddenly swallowed something acid.

'It always makes me laugh,' said Millicent, 'when I think what a frightfully bad shot Uncle Gally's godfathers and godmothers made when they
christened him.'

She regarded her approaching relative with that tolerant—indeed, admiring—affection which the young of her sex, even when they have Madonna-like faces, are only too prone to lavish on such of their seniors as have had interesting pasts.

'Doesn't he look marvellous?' she said. 'It really is an extraordinary thing that anyone who has had as good a time as he has can be so amazingly healthy. Everywhere you look, you see men leading model lives and pegging out in their prime, while good old Uncle Gally, who apparently never went to bed till he was fifty, is still breezing along as fit and rosy as ever.'

'All our family have had excellent constitutions,' said Lord Emsworth.

'And I'll bet Uncle Gally needed every ounce of his,' said Millicent.

The Author, ambling briskly across the lawn, had now joined the little group at the tea-table. As his photograph had indicated, he was a short, trim, dapper little man of the type one associates automatically in one's mind with checked suits, tight trousers, white bowler hats, pink carnations, and race-glasses bumping against the left hip. Though bare-headed at the moment and in his shirt-sleeves, and displaying on the tip of his nose the ink-spot of the literary life, he still seemed out of place away from a paddock or an American bar. His bright eyes, puckered at the corners, peered before him as though watching horses rounding into the straight. His neatly-shod foot had about it a suggestion of pawing in search of a brass rail. A jaunty little gentleman, and, as Millicent had said, quite astonishingly fit and rosy. A thoroughly misspent life had left the Hon. Galahad Threepwood, contrary to the most elementary justice, in what appeared to be perfect, even exuberantly perfect physical condition. How a man who ought to have had the liver of the century could look and behave as he did was a constant mystery to his associates. His eye was not dimmed nor his natural force abated. And when, skipping blithely across the turf, he tripped over the spaniel, so graceful was the agility with which he recovered his balance that he did not spill a drop of the whisky-and-soda in his hand. He continued to bear the glass aloft like some brave banner beneath which he had often fought and won. Instead of the blot on the proud family, he might have been a teetotal acrobat.

Having disentangled himself from the spaniel and soothed the animal's wounded feelings by permitting it to sniff the whisky-and-soda, the

Hon. Galahad produced a black-rimmed monocle, and, screwing it into his eye, surveyed the table with a frown of distaste.

'Tea?'

Millicent reached for a cup.

'Cream and sugar, Uncle Gally?'

He stopped her with a gesture of shocked loathing.

'You know I never drink tea. Too much respect for my inside. Don't tell me you are ruining your inside with that poison.'

'Sorry, Uncle Gally. I like it.'

'You be careful,' urged the Hon. Galahad, who was fond of his niece and did not like to see her falling into bad habits. 'You be very careful how you fool about with that stuff. Did I ever tell you about poor Buffy Struggles back in 'ninety-three? Some misguided person lured poor old Buffy into one of those temperance lectures illustrated with coloured slides, and he called on me next day ashen, poor old chap—ashen. "Gally," he said. "What would you say the procedure was when a fellow wants to buy tea? How would a fellow set about it?" "Tea?" I said. "What do you want tea for?" "To drink," said Buffy. "Pull yourself together, dear boy," I said. "You're talking wildly. You can't drink tea. Have a brandy-and-soda." "No more alcohol for me," said Buffy. "Look what it does to the common earthworm." "But you're not a common earthworm," I said, putting my finger on the flaw in his argument right away. "I dashed soon shall be if I go on drinking alcohol," said Buffy. Well, I begged him with tears in my eyes not to do anything rash, but I couldn't move him. He ordered in ten pounds of the muck and was dead inside the year.'

'Good heavens! Really?'

The Hon. Galahad nodded impressively.

'Dead as a door-nail. Got run over by a hansom cab, poor dear old chap, as he was crossing Piccadilly. You'll find the story in my book.'

'How's the book coming along?'

'Magnificently, my dear. Splendidly. I had no notion writing was so easy. The stuff just pours out. Clarence, I wanted to ask you about a date. What year was it there was that terrible row between young Gregory Parsloe and Lord Burper, when Parsloe stole the old chap's false teeth, and pawned them at a shop in the Edgware Road? '96? I should have said later than that—'97 or '98. Perhaps you're right, though. I'll pencil in '96 tentatively.'

Lady Constance uttered a sharp cry. The sunlight had now gone quite definitely out of her life. She felt, as she so often felt in her brother Galahad's society, as if foxes were gnawing her vitals. Not even the thought that she could now give Sir Gregory Parsloe-Parsloe the inside information for which he had asked was able to comfort her.

'Galahad! You are not proposing to print libellous stories like that about our nearest neighbour?'

'Certainly I am.' The Hon. Galahad snorted militantly. 'And, as for libel, let him bring an action if he wants to. I'll fight him to the House of Lords. It's the best documented story in my book. Well, if you insist it was '96, Clarence . . . I'll tell you what,' said the Hon. Galahad, inspired. 'I'll say "towards the end of the nineties". After all, the exact date isn't so important. It's the facts that matter.'

And, leaping lightly over the spaniel, he flitted away across the lawn.

Lady Constance sat rigid in her chair. Her fine eyes were now protruding slightly, and her face was drawn. This and not the Mona Lisa's, you would have said, looking at her, was the head on which all the sorrows of the world had fallen.

'Clarence!'

'My dear?'

'What are you going to do about this?'

'Do?'

'Can't you see that something must be done? Do you realize that if this awful book of Galahad's is published it will alienate half our friends? They will think we are to blame. They will say we ought to have stopped him somehow. Imagine Sir Gregory's feelings when he reads that appalling story!'

Lord Emsworth's amiable face darkened.

'I am not worrying about Parsloe's feelings. Besides, he did steal Burper's false teeth. I remember him showing them to me. He had them packed up in cotton-wool in a small cigar-box.'

The gesture known as wringing the hands is one that is seldom seen in real life, but Lady Constance Keeble at this point did something with hers which might by a liberal interpretation have been described as wringing.

'Oh, if Mr Baxter were only here!' she moaned.

Lord Emsworth started with such violence that his pince-nez fell off and he dropped a slice of seed-cake.

'What on earth do you want that awful feller here for?'

'He would find a way out of this dreadful business. He was always so efficient.'

'Baxter's off his head.'

Lady Constance uttered a sharp exclamation.

'Clarence, you really can be the most irritating person in the world. You get an idea and you cling to it in spite of whatever anybody says. Mr Baxter was the most wonderfully capable man I ever met.'

'Yes, capable of anything,' retorted Lord Emsworth with spirit. 'Threw flower-pots at me in the middle of the night. I woke up in the small hours and found flower-pots streaming in at my bedroom window and looked out and there was this feller Baxter standing on the terrace in lemon-coloured pyjamas, hurling the dashed things as if he thought he was a machine-gun, or something. I suppose he's in an asylum by this time.'

Lady Constance had turned a bright scarlet. Even in their nursery days she had never felt quite so hostile towards the head of the family as now.

'You know perfectly well that there was a quite simple explanation. My diamond necklace had been stolen, and Mr Baxter thought the thief had hidden it in one of the flower-pots. He went to look for it and got locked out and tried to attract attention by . . .'

'Well, I prefer to think the man was crazy, and that's the line that Galahad takes in his book.'

'His . . . ! Galahad is not putting that story in his book?'

'Of course he's putting it in his book. Do you think he's going to waste excellent material like that? And, as I say, the line Galahad takes—and he's a clear-thinking, level-headed man—is that Baxter was a raving, roaring lunatic. Well, I'm going to have another look at the Empress.'

He pottered off pigwards.

· III ·

For some moments after he had gone, there was silence at the tea-table.
Millicent lay back in her chair, Lady Constance sat stiffly upright in hers.
A little breeze that brought with it a scent of wall-flowers began whisper-
ing the first tidings that the cool of evening was on its way.

'Why are you so anxious to get Mr Baxter back, Aunt Constance?'
asked Millicent.

Lady Constance's rigidity had relaxed. She was looking her calm,
masterful self again. She had the air of a woman who has just solved a
difficult problem.

'I think his presence here essential,' she said.

'Uncle Clarence doesn't seem to agree with you.'

'Your Uncle Clarence has always been completely blind to his best
interests. He ought never to have dismissed the only secretary he has
ever had who was capable of looking after his affairs.'

'Isn't Mr Carmody any good?'

'No. He is not. And I shall never feel easy in my mind until Mr Baxter
is back in his old place.'

'What's wrong with Mr Carmody?'

'He is grossly inefficient. And,' said Lady Constance, unmasking her
batteries, 'I consider that he spends far too much of his time mooning around you, my dear. He appears to imagine that he is at Blandings
Castle simply to dance attendance on you.'

The charge struck Millicent as unjust. She thought of pointing out
that she and Hugo only met occasionally and then on the sly, but it
occurred to her that the plea might be injudicious. She bent over the
spaniel. A keen observer might have noted a defensiveness in her manner. She looked like a girl preparing to cope with an aunt.

'Do you find him an entertaining companion?'

Millicent yawned.

'Mr Carmody? No, not particularly.'

'A dull young man, I should have thought.'

'Deadly.'

'Vapid.'

'Vap to a degree.'

'And yet you went riding with him last Tuesday.'

'Anything's better than riding alone.'

'You play tennis with him, too.'

'Well, tennis is a game I defy you to play by yourself.'

Lady Constance's lips tightened.

'I wish Ronald had never persuaded your uncle to employ him. Clarence should have seen by the mere look of him that he was impossible.' She paused.

'It will be nice having Ronald here,' she said.

'Yes.'

'You must try to see something of him. If,' said Lady Constance, in the manner which her intimates found rather less pleasant than some of her other manners, 'Mr Carmody can spare you for a moment from time to time.'

She eyed her niece narrowly. But Millicent was a match for any number of narrow glances, and had been from her sixteenth birthday. She was also a girl who believed that the best form of defence is attack.

'Do you think I'm in love with Mr Carmody, Aunt Constance?'

Lady Constance was not a woman who relished the direct methods of the younger generation. She coloured.

'Such a thought never entered my head.'

'That's fine. I was afraid it had.'

'A sensible girl like you would naturally see the utter impossibility of marriage with a man in his position. He has no money and very little prospects. And, of course, your uncle holds your own money in trust for you and would never dream of releasing it if you wished to make an unsuitable marriage.

'So it does seem lucky I'm not in love with him, doesn't it?'

'Extremely fortunate.'

Lady Constance paused for a moment, then introduced a topic on which she had frequently touched before. Millicent had seen it coming by the look in her eyes.

'Why you won't marry Ronald, I can't think. It would be so suitable in every way. You have been fond of one another since you were children.'

'Oh, I like old Ronnie a lot.'

'It has been a great disappointment to your Aunt Julia.'

'She must cheer up. She'll get him off all right, if she sticks at it.'

Lady Constance bridled.

'It is not a question of . . . If you will forgive my saying so, my dear, I think you have allowed yourself to fall into a way of taking Ronald far too much for granted. I am afraid you have the impression that he will always be there, ready and waiting for you when you at last decide to make up your mind. I don't think you realize what a very attractive young man he is.'

'The longer I wait, the more fascinating it will give him time to become.'

At a moment less tense, Lady Constance would have taken time off to rebuke this flippancy; but she felt it would be unwise to depart from her main theme.

'He is just the sort of young man that girls are drawn to. In fact, I have been meaning to tell you. I had a letter from your Aunt Julia, saying that during their stay at Biarritz they met a most charming American girl, a Miss Schoonmaker, whose father, it seems, used to be a friend of your Uncle Galahad. She appeared to be quite taken with Ronald, and he with her. He travelled back to Paris with her and left her there.'

'How fickle men are!' sighed Millicent.

'She had some shopping to do,' said Lady Constance sharply. 'By this time she is probably in London. Julia invited her to stay at Blandings, and she accepted. She may be here any day now. And I do think, my dear,' proceeded Lady Constance earnestly, 'that, before she arrives, you ought to consider very carefully what your feelings towards Ronald really are.'

'You mean, if I don't watch my step, this Miss Doopenhacker may steal my Ronnie away from me?'

It was not quite how Lady Constance would have put it herself, but it conveyed her meaning.

'Exactly.'

Millicent laughed. It was plain that her flesh declined to creep at the prospect.

'Good luck to her,' she said. 'She can count on a fish-slice from me, and I'll be a bridesmaid, too, if wanted. Can't you understand, Aunt Constance, that I haven't the slightest desire to marry Ronnie. We're great pals, and all that, but he's not my style. Too short, for one thing.'

'Short?'

'I'm inches taller than he is. When we went up the aisle, I should look like someone taking her little brother for a walk.'

Lady Constance would undoubtedly have commented on this remark, but before she could do so the procession reappeared, playing an unexpected return date. Footman James bore a dish of fruit, Footman Thomas a salver with a cream-jug on it. Beach, as before, confined himself to a straight ornamental role.

'Oo!' said Millicent welcomingly. And the spaniel, who liked anything involving cream, gave a silent nod of approval.

'Well,' said Lady Constance, as the procession withdrew, giving up the lost cause, 'if you won't marry Ronald, I suppose you won't.'

'That's about it,' agreed Millicent, pouring cream.

'At any rate, I am relieved to hear that there is no nonsense going on between you and this Mr Carmody. That I could not have endured.'

'He's only moderately popular with you, isn't he?'

'I dislike him extremely.'

'I wonder why. I should have thought he was fairly all right, as young men go. Uncle Clarence likes him. So does Uncle Gally.'

Lady Constance had a high, arched nose, admirably adapted for sniffing. She used it now to the limits of its power.

'Mr Carmody,' she said, 'is just the sort of young man your Uncle Galahad would like. No doubt he reminds him of the horrible men he used to go about London with in his young days.'

'Mr Carmody isn't a bit like that.'

'Indeed?' Lady Constance sniffed again. 'Well, I dislike mentioning it to you, Millicent, for I am old-fashioned enough to think that young girls should be shielded from a knowledge of the world, but I happen to know that Mr Carmody is not at all a nice young man. I have it on the most excellent authority that he is entangled with some impossible chorus-girl.'

It is not easy to sit suddenly bolt-upright in a deep garden-chair, but Millicent managed the feat.

'What!'

'Lady Allardyce told me so.'

'And how does she know?'

'Her son Vernon told her. A girl of the name of Brown. Vernon Allardyce says that he used to see her repeatedly, lunching and dining and dancing with Mr Carmody.'

There was a long silence.

'Nice boy, Vernon,' said Millicent.

'He tells his mother everything.'

'That's what I meant. I think it's so sweet of him.' Millicent rose. 'Well, I'm going to take a short stroll.'

She wandered off towards the rose-garden.

· IV ·

A young man who has arranged to meet the girl he loves in the rose-garden at six sharp naturally goes there at five-twenty-five, so as not to be late. Hugo Carmody had done this, with the result that by three minutes to six he was feeling as if he had been marooned among roses since the beginning of the summer.

If anybody had told Hugo Carmody six months before that half-way through the following July he would be lurking in trysting-places like this, his whole being alert for the coming of a girl, he would have scoffed at the idea. He would have laughed lightly. Not that he had not been fond of girls. He had always liked girls. But they had been, as it were, the mere playthings, so to speak, of a financial giant's idle hour. Six months ago he had been the keen, iron-souled man of business, all his energies and thoughts devoted to the management of the Hot Spot.

But now he stood shuffling his feet and starting hopefully at every sound, while the leaden moments passed sluggishly on their way. Then his vigil was enlivened by a wasp, which stung him on the back of the hand. He was leaping to and fro, licking his wounds, when he perceived the girl of his dreams coming down the path.

'Ah!' cried Hugo.

He ceased to leap and, rushing forward, would have clasped her in a fond embrace. Many people advocate the old-fashioned blue-bag for wasp-stings, but Hugo preferred this treatment.

To his astonishment she drew back. And she was not a girl who usually drew back on these occasions.

'What's the matter?' he asked, pained. It seemed to him that a spanner had been bunged into a holy moment.

'Nothing.'

Hugo was concerned. He did not like the way she was looking at him. Her soft blue eyes appeared to have been turned into stone.

'I say,' he said, 'I've just been stung by a beastly great wasp.'

'Good!' said Millicent.

The way she was talking seemed to him worse than the way she was looking.

Hugo's concern increased.

'I say, what's up?'

The granite eye took on an added hardness.

'You want to know what's up?'

'Yes—what's up?'

'I'll tell you what's up.'

'Well, what's up?' asked Hugo.

He waited for enlightenment, but she had fallen into a chilling silence.

'You know,' said Hugo, breaking it, 'I'm getting pretty fed up with all this secrecy and general snakiness. Seeing you for an occasional odd five minutes a day and having to put on false whiskers and hide in bushes to manage that. I know the Keeble looks on me as a sort of cross between a leper and a nosegay of deadly nightshade, but I'm strong with the old boy. I talk pig to him. You might almost say I play on him as on a stringed instrument. So what's wrong with going to him and telling him in a frank and manly way that we love each other and are going to get married?'

The marble of Millicent's face was disturbed by one of those quick, sharp, short, bitter smiles that do nobody any good.

'Why should we lie to Uncle Clarence?'

'Eh?'

'I say, why should we tell him something that isn't true?'

'I don't get your drift.'

'I will continue snowing,' said Millicent coldly. 'I am not quite sure if I am ever going to speak to you again in this world or the next. Much will depend on how good you are as an explainer. I have it on the most excellent authority that you are entangled with a chorus-girl. How about it?'

Hugo reeled. But then St Anthony himself would have reeled if a charge like that had suddenly been hurled at him. The best of men require time to overhaul their conscience on such occasions. A moment and he was himself again.

'It's a lie!'

'Name of Brown.'

'Not a word of truth in it. I haven't set eyes on Sue Brown since I first met you.'

'No. You've been down here all the time.'

'And when I *was* setting eyes on her—why, dash it, my attitude from start to finish was one of blameless, innocent, one hundred per cent brotherliness. A wholesome friendship. Brotherly. Nothing more. I liked dancing and she liked dancing and our steps fitted. So occasionally we would go out together and tread the measure. That's all there was to it. Pure brotherliness. Nothing more. I looked on myself as a sort of brother.'

'Brother, eh?'

'Absolutely a brother. Don't,' urged Hugo earnestly, 'go running away, my dear old thing, with any sort of silly notion that Sue Brown was something in the nature of a vamp. She's one of the nicest girls you would ever want to meet.'

'Nice, is she?'

'A sweet girl. A girl in a million. A real good sort. A sound egg.'

'Pretty, I suppose?'

The native good sense of the Carmodys asserted itself at the eleventh hour.

'Not pretty,' said Hugo decidedly. 'Not pretty, no. Not at all pretty. Far from pretty. Totally lacking in sex-appeal, poor girl. But nice. A good sort. No nonsense about her. Sisterly.'

Millicent pondered.

'H'm,' she said.

Nature paused, listening. Birds checked their song, insects their droning. It was as if it had got about that this young man's fate hung in the balance and the returns would be in shortly.

'Well, all right,' she said at length. 'I suppose I'll have to believe you.'

"At's the way to talk!'

'But just you bear this in mind, my lad. Any funny business from now on . . .'

'As if . . .!'

'One more attack of that brotherly urge . . .'

'As though . . .!'

'All right, then.'

Hugo inhaled vigorously. He felt like a man who has just dodged a wounded tigress.

'Banzai!' he said. 'Sweethearts still!'

· V ·

Blandings Castle dozed in the twilight. Its various inmates were variously occupied. Clarence, ninth Earl of Emsworth, after many a longing lingering look behind, had dragged himself away from the Empress's boudoir and was reading his well-thumbed copy of *British Pigs*. The Hon. Galahad, having fixed up the Parsloe–Burper passage, was skimming through his day's output with an artist's complacent feeling that this was the stuff to give 'em. Butler Beach was pasting the Hon. Galahad's photograph into his album. Millicent, in her bedroom, was looking a little thoughtfully into her mirror. Hugo, in the billiard-room, was practising pensive cannons and thinking loving thoughts of his lady, coupled with an occasional reflection that a short, swift binge in London would be a great wheeze if he could wangle it.

And in her boudoir on the second floor, Lady Constance Keeble had taken pen in hand and was poising it over a sheet of notepaper.

'Dear Mr Baxter,' she wrote.

2

THE COURSE OF TRUE LOVE

• I •

The brilliant sunshine which so enhanced the attractions of life at Blandings Castle had brought less pleasure to those of England's workers whose duties compelled them to remain in London. In his offices on top of the Regal Theatre in Shaftesbury Avenue, Mr Mortimer Mason, the stout senior partner in the firm of Mason and Saxby, Theatrical Enterprises, Ltd, was of opinion that what the country really needed was one of those wedge-shaped depressions off the Coast of Iceland. Apart from making him feel like a gaffed salmon, Flaming July was ruining business. Only last night, to cut down expenses, he had had to dismiss some of the chorus from the show downstairs, and he hated dismissing chorus-girls. He was a kind-hearted man, and, having been in the profession himself in his time, knew what it meant to get one's notice in the middle of the summer.

There was a tap on the door. The human watchdog who guarded the outer offices entered.

'Well?' said Mortimer Mason wearily.

'Can you see Miss Brown, sir?'

'Which Miss Brown? Sue?'

'Yes, sir.'

'Of course.' In spite of the heat, Mr Mason brightened. 'Is she outside?'

'Yes, sir.'

'Then pour her in.'

Mortimer Mason had always felt a fatherly fondness for this girl, Sue Brown. He liked her for her own sake, for her unvarying cheerfulness and the honest way she worked. But what endeared her more particularly to him was the fact that she was Dolly Henderson's daughter. London was full of elderly gentlemen who became pleasantly maudlin when they thought of Dolly Henderson and the dear old days when the heart was young and they had had waists. He heaved himself from his chair: then fell back again, filled with a sense of intolerable injury.

'My God!' he cried. 'Don't look so cool.'

The rebuke was not undeserved. On an afternoon when the asphalt is bubbling in the roadways and theatrical managers melting where they sit, no girl has a right to resemble a dewy rose plucked from some old-world garden. And that, Mr Mason considered, was just what this girl was deliberately resembling. She was a tiny thing, mostly large eyes and a wide, happy smile. She had a dancer's figure and in every movement of her there was Youth.

'Sorry, Pa.' She laughed, and Mr Mason moaned faintly. Her laugh had reminded him, for his was a nature not without it's poetical side, of ice tinkling in a jug of beer. 'Try not looking at me.'

'Well, Sue, what's on your mind? Come to tell me you're going to be married?'

'Not at the moment, I'm afraid.'

'Hasn't that young man of yours got back from Biarritz yet?'

'He arrived this morning. I had a note during the *matinée*. I suppose he's outside now, waiting for me. Want to have a look at him?'

'Does it mean walking downstairs?' asked Mr Mason, guardedly.

'No. He'll be in his car. You can see him from the window.'

Mr Mason was equal to getting to the window. He peered down at the rakish sports-model two-seater in the little street below. Its occupant was lying on his spine, smoking a cigarette in a long holder and looking austerely at certain children of the neighbourhood whom he seemed to suspect of being about to scratch his paint.

'They're making fiancés very small this season,' said Mr Mason, concluding his inspection.

'He is small, isn't he? He's sensitive about it, poor darling. Still, I'm small, too, so that's all right.'

'Fond of him?'

'Frightfully.'

'Who is he, anyway? Yes, I know his name's Fish, and it doesn't mean a thing to me. Any money?'

'I believe he's got quite a lot, only his uncle keeps it all. Lord Emsworth. He's Ronnie's trustee, or something.'

'Emsworth? I knew his brother years ago.' Mr Mason chuckled reminiscently. 'Old Gally! What a lad! I've got a scheme I'd like to interest old Gally in. I wonder where he is now.'

'The *Prattler* this week said he was down at Blandings Castle. That's Lord Emsworth's place in Shropshire. Ronnie's going down there this evening.'

'Deserting you so soon?' Mortimer Mason shook his head. 'I don't like this.'

Sue laughed.

'Well, I don't,' said Mr Mason. 'You be careful. These lads will all bear watching.'

'Don't worry, Pa. He means to do right by our Nell.'

'Well, don't say I didn't warn you. So old Gally is at Blandings, is he? I must remember that. I'd like to get in touch with him. And now, what was it you wanted to see me about?'

Sue became grave.

'I've come to ask you a favour.'

'Go ahead. You know me.'

'It's about those girls you're getting rid of.'

Mr Mason's genial face took on a managerial look.

'Got to get rid of them.'

'I know. But one of them's Sally Field.'

'Meaning what?'

'Well, Sally's awfully hard up, Pa. And what I came to ask,' said Sue breathlessly, 'was, will you keep her on and let me go instead?'

Utter amazement caused Mortimer Mason momentarily to forget the heat. He sat up, gaping.

'Do what?'

'Let me go instead.'

'Let you go instead?'

'Yes.'

'You're crazy.'

'No, I'm not. Come on, Pa. Be a dear.'

'Is she a great friend of yours?'

'Not particularly. I'm sorry for her.'

'I won't do it.'

'You must. She's down to her last bean.'

'But I need you in the show.'

'What nonsense! As if I made the slightest difference.'

'You do. You've got—I don't know—' Mr Mason twiddled his fingers. 'Something. Your mother used to have it. Did you know I was the second juvenile in the first company she was ever in?'

'Yes, you told me. And haven't you got on! There's enough of you now to make two second juveniles. Well, you will do it, won't you?'

Mr Mason reflected.

'I suppose I'll have to, if you insist,' he said at length. 'If I don't, you'll just hand your notice in anyway. I know you. You're a sportsman, Sue. Your mother was just the same. But are you sure you'll manage all right? I shan't be casting the new show till the end of August, but I may be able to fix you up somewhere if I look round.'

'I don't see how you could look any rounder if you tried, you poor darling. Do you realize, Pa, that if you got up early every morning and did half an hour's Swedish exercises . . .'

'If you don't want to be murdered, stop!'

'It would do you all the good in the world, you know. Well, it's awfully sweet of you to bother about me, Pa, but you mustn't. You've got enough to worry you already. I shall be all right. Good-bye. You've been an angel about Sally. It'll save her life.'

'If she's that cross-eyed girl at the end of the second row who's always out of step, I'm not sure I want to save her life.'

'Well, you're going to do it, anyway. Good-bye.'

'Don't run away.'

'I must. Ronnie's waiting. He's going to take me to tea somewhere. Up the river, I hope. Think how nice it will be there, under the trees, with the water rippling . . .'

'The only thing that stops me hitting you with this ruler,' said Mr Mason, 'is the thought that I shall soon be getting out of this Turkish Bath myself. I've a show opening at Blackpool next week. Think how nice and cool it will be on the sands there, with the waves splashing . . .'

'. . . And you with your little spade and bucket, paddling! Oh, Pa, do send me a photograph. Well, I can't stand here all day, chatting over your vacation plans. My poor Ronnie must be getting slowly fried.'

· II ·

The process of getting slowly fried, especially when you are chafing for a sight of the girl you love after six weeks of exile from her society, is never an agreeable one. After enduring it for some time, the pink-faced young man with the long cigarette-holder had left his seat in the car and had gone for shade and comparative coolness to the shelter of the stage entrance, where he now stood reading the notices on the call-board. He read them moodily. The thought that, after having been away from Sue for all these weeks, he was now compelled to leave her again and go to Blandings Castle was weighing on Ronald Overbury Fish's mind sorely.

Mac, the guardian of the stage door, leaned out of his hutch. The *matinée* over, he had begun to experience that solemn joy which comes to camels approaching an oasis and stage-door men who will soon be at liberty to pop round the corner. He endeavoured to communicate his happiness to Ronnie.

'Won't be long now, Mr Fish.'

'Eh?'

'Won't be long now, sir.'

'Ah,' said Ronnie.

Mac was concerned at his companion's gloom. He liked smiling faces about him. Reflecting, he fancied he could diagnose its cause.

'I was sorry to hear about that, Mr Fish.'

'Eh?'

'I say I was sorry to hear about that, sir.'

'About what?'

'About the Hot Spot, sir. That night-club of yours. Busting up that way. Going West so prompt.'

Ronnie Fish winced. He presumed the man meant well, but there are certain subjects one does not want mentioned. When you have contrived with infinite pains to wheedle a portion of your capital out of a reluctant trustee and have gone and started a night-club with it and seen that night-club flash into the receiver's hands like some frail egg-shell engulfed by a whirl-pool, silence is best.

'Ah,' he said briefly, to indicate this.

Mac had many admirable qualities, but not tact. He was the sort of man who would have tried to cheer Napoleon up by talking about the Winter Sports at Moscow.

'When I heard that you and Mr Carmody was starting one of those places, I said to the fireman "I give it two months," I said. And it was six weeks, wasn't it, sir?'

'Seven.'

'Six or seven. Immaterial which. Point is I'm usually pretty right I said to the fireman "It takes brains to run a night-club," I said. "Brains and a certain what-shall-I-say." Won me half-a-dollar, that did.'

He searched in his mind for other topics to interest and amuse.

'Seen Mr Carmody lately, sir?'

'No. I've been in Biarritz. He's down in Shropshire. He's got a job as secretary to an uncle of mine.'

'And I shouldn't wonder,' said Mac cordially, 'if he wouldn't make a mess of *that*.'

He began to feel that the conversation was now going with a swing.

'Used to see a lot of Mr Carmody round here at one time.'

The advance guard of the company appeared, in the shape of a flock of musicians. They passed out of the stage door, first a couple of thirsty-looking flutes, then a group of violins, finally an oboe by himself with a scowl on his face. Oboes are always savage in captivity.

'Yes, sir. Came here a lot, Mr Carmody did. Asking for Miss Brown. Great friends those two was.'

'Oh?' said Ronnie thickly.

'Used to make me laugh to see them together.'

Ronnie appeared to swallow something large and jagged.

'Why?'

'Well, him so tall and her so small. But there,' said Mac philosophically, 'they say it's opposites that get on best. I know I weigh seventeen stone and my missus looks like a ninepenny rabbit, and yet we're as happy as can be.'

Ronnie's interest in the poundage of the stage-door keeper's domestic circle was slight.

'Ah,' he said.

Mac, having got on to the subject of Sue Brown, stayed there.

'You see the flowers arrived all right, sir.'

'Eh?'

'The flowers you sent Miss Brown, sir,' said Mac, indicating with a stubby thumb a bouquet on the shelf behind him. 'I haven't given her them yet. Thought she'd rather have them after the performance.'

It was a handsome bouquet, but Ronnie Fish stared at it with a sort of dumb horror. His pink face had grown pinker, and his eyes were glassy.

'Give me those flowers, Mac,' he said in a strangled voice.

'Right, sir. Here you are, sir. Now you look just like a bride-groom, sir,' said the stage-door keeper, chuckling the sort of chuckle that goes with seventeen stone and a fat head.

This thought had struck Ronnie, also. It was driven home a moment later by the displeasing behaviour of two of the chorus-girls who came flitting past. Both looked at him in a way painful to a sensitive young man, and one of them giggled. Ronnie turned to the door.

'When Miss Brown comes, tell her I'm waiting outside in my car.'

'Right, sir. You'll be in again, I suppose, sir?'

'No.' The sombre expression deepened on Ronnie's face. 'I've got to go down to Shropshire this evening.'

'Be away long?'

'Yes. Quite a time.'

'Sorry to hear that, sir. Well, good-bye, sir. Thank you, sir.'

Ronnie, clutching the bouquet, walked with leaden steps to the two-seater. There was a card attached to the flowers. He read it, frowned darkly, and threw the bouquet into the car.

Girls were passing now in shoals. They meant nothing to Ronnie Fish. He eyed them sourly, marvelling why the papers talked about 'beauty choruses'. And then, at last, there appeared one at the sight of whom his heart, parting from its moorings, began to behave like a jumping bean. It had reached his mouth when she ran up with both hands extended.

'Ronnie, you precious angel lambkin!'

'Sue!'

To a young man in love, however great the burden of sorrows beneath which he may be groaning, the spectacle of the only girl in the world, smiling up at him, seldom fails to bring a temporary balm. For the moment, Ronnie's gloom ceased to be. He forgot that he had recently lost several hundred pounds in a disastrous commercial venture. He forgot that he was going off that evening to live in exile. He even forgot that this girl had just been sent a handsome bouquet by a ghastly bargee named P. Frobisher Pilbeam, belonging to the Junior Constitutional Club. These thoughts would return, but for the time being the one that occupied his mind to the exclusion of all others was the thought that after six long weeks of separation he was once more looking upon Sue Brown.

'I'm so sorry I kept you waiting, precious. I had to see Mr Mason.'

Ronnie started.

'What about?'

A student of the motion-pictures, he knew what theatrical managers were.

'Just business.'

'Did he ask you to lunch, or anything?'

'No. He just fired me.'

'Fired you!'

'Yes, I've lost my job,' said Sue happily.

Ronnie quivered.

'I'll go and break his neck.'

'No, you won't. It isn't his fault. It's the weather. They have to cut down expenses when there's a heat-wave. It's all the fault of people like you for going abroad instead of staying in London and coming to the theatre.' She saw the flowers and uttered a delighted squeal. 'For me?'

A moment before, Ronnie had been all chivalrous concern—a knight prepared to battle to the death for his lady-love. He now froze.

'Apparently,' he said coldly.

'How do you mean, apparently?'

'I mean they are.'

'You pet!'

'Leap in.'

Ronnie's gloom was now dense and foglike once more. He gestured fiercely at the clustering children and trod on the self-starter. The car moved smoothly round the corner into Shaftesbury Avenue.

Opposite the Monico, there was a traffic-block, and he unloaded his soul.

'In re those blooms.'

'They're lovely.'

'Yes, but I didn't send them.'

'You brought them. Much nicer.'

'What I'm driving at,' said Ronnie heavily, 'is that they aren't from me at all. They're from a blighter named P. Frobisher Pilbeam.'

Sue's smile had faded. She knew her Ronald's jealousy so well. It was the one thing about him which she could have wished changed.

'Oh?' she said dismally.

The crust of calm detachment from all human emotion, built up by years of Eton and Cambridge, cracked abruptly, and there peeped forth a primitive Ronald Overbury Fish.

'Who is this Pilbeam?' he demanded. 'Pretty much the Boy Friend, I take it, what?'

'I've never even met him!'

'But he sends you flowers.'

'I know he does,' wailed Sue, mourning for a golden afternoon now probably spoiled beyond repair. 'He keeps sending me his beastly flowers and writing me his beastly letters . . .'

Ronnie gritted his teeth.

'And I tell you I've never set eyes on him in my life.'

'You don't know who he is?'

'One of the girls told me that he used to edit that paper *Society Spice*. I don't know what he does now.'

'When he isn't sending you flowers, you mean?'

'I can't help him sending me flowers.'

'I don't suppose you want to.'

Sue's eyes flickered. Realizing, however, that her Ronnie in certain moods resembled a child of six, she made a pathetic attempt to lighten the atmosphere.

'It's not my fault if I get persecuted with loathsome addresses is it? I suppose, when you go to the movies, you blame Lilian Gish for being pursued by the heavy.'

Ronnie was not to be diverted.

'Sometimes I ask myself,' he said darkly, 'if you really care a hang for me.'

'Oh, Ronnie!'

'Yes, I do—repeatedly. I look at you and I look at myself and that's what I ask myself. What on earth is there about me to make a girl like you fond of a fellow? I'm a failure. Can't even run a night-club. No brains. No looks.'

'You've got a lovely complexion.'

'Too pink. Much too pink. And I'm so damned short.'

'You're not a bit too short.'

'I am. My Uncle Gally once told me I looked like the protoplasm of a minor jockey.'

'He ought to have been ashamed of himself.'

'Why the dickens,' said Ronnie, laying bare his secret dreams, 'I couldn't have been born a decent height, like Hugo . . .' He paused. His hand shook on the steering-wheel. 'That reminds me. That fellow Mac

at the stage door was saying that you and Hugo used to be as thick as
thieves. Always together, he said.'

Sue sighed. Things were being difficult to-day.

'That was before I met you,' she explained patiently. 'I used to like
dancing with him. He's a beautiful dancer. You surely don't suppose for a
minute that I could ever be in love with Hugo?'

'I don't see why not.'

'Hugo!' Sue laughed. There was something about Hugo Carmody that
always made her want to laugh.

'Well, I don't see why not. He's better looking than I am. Taller. Not
so pink. Plays the saxophone.'

'Will you stop being silly about Hugo.'

'Well, I fear that bird. He's my best pal and I know his work. He's
practically handsome. And lissom, to boot.' A hideous thought smote
Ronnie like a blow. 'Did he ever . . .' He choked. Did he ever hold your
hand?'

'Which hand?'

'Either hand.'

'How can you suggest such a thing!' cried Sue, shocked.

'Well, will you swear there's nothing between him and you?'

'Of course there isn't.'

'And nothing between this fellow Pilbeam and you?'

'Of course not.'

'Ah!' said Ronnie. 'Then I can go ahead, as planned.'

His was a mercurial temperament, and it had lifted him in an instant
from the depths to the heights. The cloud had passed from his face, the
look of Byronic despair from his eyes. He beamed.

'Do you know why I'm going down to Blandings to-night?' he asked.

'No. I only wish you weren't.'

'Well, I'll tell you. I've got to get round my uncle.'

'Do what?'

'Make myself solid with my Uncle Clarence. If you've ever had anything to do with trustees you'll know that the one thing they bar like
poison is parting with money. And I've simply got to have another chunk
of my capital, and a good big one, too. Without money, how on earth can

I marry you? Let me get hold of funds, and we'll dash off to the registrar's the moment you say the word. So now you understand why I've got to get to Blandings at the earliest possible moment and stay there till further notice.'

'Yes. I see. And you're a darling. Tell me about Blandings, Ronnie.'

'How do you mean?'

'Well, what sort of a place is it? I want to imagine you there while you're away.'

Ronnie pondered. He was not at his best as a word painter.

'Oh, you know the kind of thing. Parks and gardens and terraces and immemorial elms and all that. All the usual stuff.'

'Any girls there?'

'My cousin Millicent. She's my Uncle Lancelot's daughter. He's dead. The family want Millicent and me to get married.'

'To each other, you mean? What a perfectly horrible idea!'

'Oh, it's all right. We're both against the scheme.'

'Well, that's some comfort. What other girls will there be at Blandings?'

'Only one that I know of. My mother met a female called Schoonmaker at Biarritz. American. Pots of money, I believe. One of those beastly tall girls. Looked like something left over from Dana Gibson. I couldn't stand her myself, but my mother was all for her, and I didn't at all like the way she seemed to be trying to shove her off on to me. You know—"Why don't you ring up Myra Schoonmaker, Ronnie? I'm sure she would like to go to the Casino to-night. And then you could dance afterwards." Sinister, it seemed to me.'

'And she's going to Blandings? H'm!'

'There's nothing to h'm about.'

'I'm not so sure. Oh, well, I suppose your family are quite right. I suppose you ought really to marry some nice girl in your own set.'

Ronnie uttered a wordless cry, and in his emotion allowed the mudguard of the two-seater to glide so closely past an Austin Seven that Sue gave a frightened squeak and the Austin Seven went on its way thinking black thoughts.

'Do be careful, Ronnie, you old chump!'

'Well, what do you want to go saying things like that for? I got enough of that from the family, without having *you* start.'

'Poor old Ronnie! I'm sorry. Still, you must admit that they'd be quite within their rights, objecting to me. I'm not so hot, you know. Only a chorus-girl. Just one of the Ensemble!'

Ronnie said something between his teeth that sounded like 'Juk!' What he meant was, Be her station never so humble, a pure, sweet girl is a fitting mate for the highest in the land.

'And my mother was a music-hall singer.'

'A what!'

'A music-hall singer. What they used to call a Serio. You know—pink tights and rather risky songs.'

This time Ronnie did not say 'Juk!' He merely swallowed painfully. The information had come as a shock to him. Somehow or other, he had never thought of Sue as having encumbrances in the shape of relatives; and he could not hide from himself the fact that a pink-tighted Serio might stir the Family up quite a little. He pictured something with per-oxide hair who would call his Uncle Clarence 'dearie'.

'English, do you mean? On the Halls here in London?'

'Yes. Her stage name was Dolly Henderson.'

'Never heard of her.'

'I dare say not. But she was the rage of London twenty years ago.'

'I always thought you were American,' said Ronnie, aggrieved. 'I dis-tinctly recollect Hugo, when he introduced us, telling me that you had just come over from New York.'

'So I had. Father took me to America soon after mother died.'

'Oh, your mother is—er—no longer with us?'

'No.'

'Too bad,' said Ronnie, brightening.

'My father's name was Cotterleigh. He was in the Irish Guards.'

'What!'

Ronnie's ecstatic cry seriously inconvenienced a traffic policeman in the exercise of his duties.

'But this is fine! This is the goods! It doesn't matter to me, of course, one way or the other. I'd love you just the same if your father had sold jellied eels. But think what an enormous difference this will make to my blasted family!'

'I doubt it.'

'But it will. We must get him over at once and spring him on them. Or is he in London?'

Sue's brown eyes clouded.

'He's dead.'

'Eh? Oh? Sorry!' said Ronnie.

He was dashed for a moment.

'Well, at least let me tell the family about him,' he urged, recovering. 'Let me dangle him before their eyes a bit.'

'If you like. But they'll still object to me because I'm in the chorus.'

Ronnie scowled. He thought of his mother, he thought of his Aunt Constance, and reason told him that her words were true.

'Dash all this rot people talk about chorus-girls!' he said. "They seem to think that just because a girl works in the chorus she must be a sort of animated champagne vat. . . .'

'Ugh!'

'Spending her life dancing on supper-tables with tight stockbrokers. . . .'

'And not a bad way of passing an evening,' said Sue meditatively. 'I must try it some time.'

'. . . with the result that when it's a question of her marrying anybody, the fellow's people look down their noses and kick like mules. It's happened in our family before. My Uncle Gally was in love with some girl on the stage back in the dark ages, and they formed a wedge and bust the thing up and shipped him off to South Africa or somewhere to forget her. And look at him! Drew three sober breaths in the year nineteen-hundred and then decided that was enough. I expect I shall be the same. If I don't take to drink, cooped up at Blandings a hundred miles away from you, I shall be vastly surprised. It's all a lot of silly nonsense. I haven't any patience with it. I've a jolly good mind to go to Uncle Clarence to-night and simply tell him that I'm in love with you and intend to marry you and that if the family don't like it they can lump it.'

'I wouldn't.'

Ronnie simmered down.

'Perhaps you're right.'

'I'm sure I am. If he hears about me, he certainly won't give you your money. Whereas, if he doesn't, he may. What sort of a man is he?'

'Uncle Clarence? Oh, a mild, dreamy old boy. Mad about gardening and all that. At the moment, I hear, he's wrapped up in his pig.'

'That sounds cosy.'

'I'd feel a lot easier in my mind, I can tell you, going down there to tackle him, if I were a pig. I'd expect a much warmer welcome.'

'You were rather a pig just now, weren't you?'

Ronnie quivered. Remorse gnawed the throbbing heart beneath his beautifully cut waistcoat.

'I'm sorry. I'm frightfully sorry. The fact is, I'm so crazy about you, I get jealous of everybody you meet. Do you know, Sue, if you ever let me down, I'd . . . I don't know what I'd do. Er—Sue!'

'Hullo?'

'Swear something.'

'What?'

'Swear that, while I'm at Blandings, you won't go out with a soul. Not even to dance.'

'Not even to dance?'

'No.'

'All right.'

'Especially this man Pilbeam.'

'I thought you were going to say Hugo.'

'I'm not worrying about Hugo. He's safe at Blandings.'

'Hugo at Blandings?'

'Yes. He's secretarying for my Uncle Clarence. I made my mother get him the job when the Hot Spot conked.'

'So you'll have him *and* Millicent *and* Miss Schoonmaker there to keep you company! How nice for you.'

'Millicent!'

'It's all very well to say "Millicent!" like that. If you ask me, I think she's a menace. She sounds coy and droopy. I can see her taking you for walks by moonlight under those immemorial elms and looking up at you with big, dreamy eyes . . .'

'Looking down at me, you mean. She's about a foot taller than I am. And, anyway, if you imagine there's a girl on earth who could extract so much as a kindly glance from me when I've got you to think about, you're very much mistaken. I give you my honest word . . .'

He became lyrical. Sue, leaning back, listened contentedly. The cloud had been a threatening cloud, blackening the skies for a while, but it had passed. The afternoon was being golden, after all.

· III ·

'By the way,' said Ronnie, the flood of eloquence subsiding. 'A thought occurs. Have you any notion where we're headed for?'

'Heaven.'

'I mean at the moment.'

'I supposed you were taking me to tea somewhere.'

'But where? We've got right out of the tea zone. What with one thing and another, I've just been driving at random—to and fro, as it were—and we seem to have worked round to somewhere in the Swiss Cottage neighbourhood. We'd better switch back and set a course for the Carlton or some place. How do you feel about the Carlton?'

'All right.'

'Or the Ritz?'

'Whichever you like.'

'Or—gosh!'

'What's the matter?'

'Sue! I've got an idea.'

'Beginner's luck.'

'Why not go to Norfolk Street?'

'To your home?'

'Yes. There's nobody there. And our butler is a staunch bird. He'll get us tea and say nothing.'

'I'd like to meet a staunch butler.'

'Then shall we?'

'I'd love it. You can show me all your little treasures and belongings and the photographs of you as a small boy.'

Ronnie shook his head. It irked him to discourage her pretty enthusiasm, but a man cannot afford to take risks.

'Not those. No love could stand up against the sight of me in a sailor suit at the age of ten. I don't mind,' he said, making a concession, 'letting you see the one of me and Hugo, taken just before the Public Schools Rackets Competition, my last year at school. We were the Eton pair.'

'Did you win?'

'No. At a critical moment in the semi-final that ass Hugo foozled a shot a one-armed cripple ought to have taken with his eyes shut. It dished us.'

'Awful!' said Sue. 'Well, if I ever had any impulse to love Hugo, that's killed it.' She looked about her. 'I don't know this aristocratic neighbourhood at all. How far is it to Norfolk Street?'

'Next turning.'

'You're sure there's nobody in the house? None of the dear old Family?'

'Not a soul.'

He was right. Lady Constance Keeble was not actually in the house. At the moment when he spoke she had just closed the front door behind her. After waiting half an hour in the hope of her nephew's return, she had left a note for him on the hall table, and was going to Claridge's to get a cup of tea.

It was not until he had drawn up immediately opposite the house that Ronnie perceived what stood upon the steps. Having done so, he blenched visibly.

'Oh, my sainted aunt!' he said.

And seldom can the familiar phrase have been used with more appropriateness.

The sainted aunt was inspecting the two-seater and its contents with a frozen stare. Her eyebrows were two marks of interrogation. As she had told Millicent, she was old-fashioned, and when she saw her flesh and blood snuggled up to girls of attractive appearance in two-seaters, she suspected the worst.

'Good afternoon, Ronald.'

'Er—hullo, Aunt Constance.'

'Will you introduce me?'

There is no doubt that peril sharpens the intellect. His masters at school and his tutors at the University, having had to do with Ronald Overbury Fish almost entirely at times when his soul was at rest, had classed him among the less keen-witted of their charges. Had they seen him now in this crisis they would have pointed at him with pride. And, being the sportsmen and gentlemen that they were, they would have hastened to acknowledge that they had grossly underestimated his ingenuity and initiative.

For, after turning a rather pretty geranium tint and running a finger round the inside of his collar for an instant, as if he found it too tight, Ronnie Fish spoke the only two words in the language which could have averted disaster.

'Miss Schoonmaker,' he said, huskily.

Sue at his side gave a little gasp. These were unsuspected depths.

'Miss Schoonmaker!'

Lady Constance's resemblance to Apollyon straddling right across the way had vanished abruptly. Remorse came upon her that she should have wronged her blameless nephew with unfounded suspicions.

'Miss Schoonmaker, my aunt, Lady Constance Keeble,' said Ronnie, going from strength to strength, and speaking now quite easily and articulately.

Sue was not the girl to sit dumbly by and fail a partner in his hour of need. She smiled brightly.

'How do you do, Lady Constance?' she said. She smiled again, if possible even more brightly than before. 'I feel I know you already. Lady Julia told me so much about you at Biarritz.'

A momentary qualm lest, in the endeavour to achieve an easy cordiality, she had made her manner a shade too patronizing, melted in the sunshine of the older woman's smile. Lady Constance had become charming, almost effusive. She had always hoped that Ronald and Millicent would make a match of it: but, failing that, this rich Miss Schoonmaker was certainly the next best thing. And driving chummily about

London together like this must surely, she thought, mean something, even in these days when chummy driving is so prevalent between the sexes. At any rate, she hoped so.

'So here you are in London!'

'Yes.'

'You did not stay long in Paris.'

'No.'

'When can you come down to Blandings?'

'Oh, very soon, I hope.'

'I am going there this evening. I only ran up for the day. I want you to drive me back, Ronald.'

Ronnie nodded silently. The crisis passed, a weakness had come upon him. He preferred not to speak, if speech could be avoided.

'Do try to come soon. The gardens are looking delightful. My brother will be so glad to see you. I was just on my way to Claridge's for a cup of tea. Won't you come too?'

'I'd love to,' said Sue, 'but I really must be getting on. Ronnie was taking me shopping.'

'I thought you stayed in Paris to do your shopping.'

'Not all of it.'

'Well, I shall hope to see you soon.'

'Oh, yes.'

'At Blandings.'

'Thank you so much. Ronnie, I think we ought to be getting along.'

'Yes.' Ronnie's mind was blurred, but he was clear on that point. 'Yes, getting along. Pushing off.'

'Well, I'm so delighted to have seen you. My sister told me so much about you in her letters. After you have put your luggage on the car, Ronald, will you come and pick me up at Claridge's?'

'Right ho.'

'I would like to make an early start, if possible.'

'Right ho.'

'Well, good-bye for the present, then.'

'Right ho.'

'Good-bye, Lady Constance.'

'Good-bye.'

The two-seater moved off, and Ronnie, taking his right hand from the wheel as it turned the corner, groped for a handkerchief, found it, and passed it over his throbbing brow.

'So that was Aunt Constance!' said Sue.

Ronnie breathed deeply.

'Nice meeting one of whom I have heard so much.'

Ronnie replaced his hand on the wheel and twiddled it feebly to avoid a dog. Reaction had made him limp.

Sue was gazing at him almost reverently.

'What genius, Ronnie! What ready wit! What presence of mind! If I hadn't heard it with my own ears, I wouldn't have believed it. Why didn't you ever tell me you were one of those swift thinkers?'

'I didn't know it myself.'

'Of course, I'm afraid it has complicated things a little.'

'Eh?' Ronnie started. This aspect of the matter had not struck him. 'How do you mean?'

'When I was a child, they taught me a poem . . .'

Ronnie raised a suffering face to hers.

'Don't let's talk about your childhood now, old thing,' he pleaded. 'Feeling rather shaken. Any other time . . .'

'It's all right. I'm not wandering from the subject. I can only remember two lines of the poem. They were, "Oh, what a tangled web we weave when first we practise to deceive." You do see the web is a bit tangled, don't you, Ronnie, darling?'

'Eh? Why? Everything looks pretty smooth to me. Aunt Constance swallowed you without a yip.'

'And when the real Miss Schoonmaker arrives at Blandings with her jewels and her twenty-four trunks?' said Sue gently.

The two-seater swerved madly across Grosvenor Street.

'Gosh!' said Ronnie.

Sue's eyes were sparkling.

'There's only one thing to do,' she said. 'Now you're in, you'll have to go in deeper. You'll have to put her off.'

'How?'

'Send her a wire saying she mustn't come to Blandings, because scarlet fever or something has broken out.'

'I couldn't!'

'You must. Sign it in Lady Constance's name.'

'But suppose . . .'

'Well, suppose they do find out? You won't be in any worse hole than you will be if she comes sailing up to the front door, all ready to stay a couple of weeks. And she will unless you wire.'

'That's true.'

'What it means,' said Sue, 'is that instead of having plenty of time to get that money out of Lord Emsworth you'll have to work quick.' She touched his arm. 'Here's a post-office,' she said. 'Go and send that wire before you weaken.'

Ronnie stopped the car.

'You will have to do the most rapid bit of trustee-touching in the history of the world, I should think,' said Sue reflectively. 'Do you think you can manage it?'

'I'll have a jolly good prod.'

'Remember what it means.'

'I'll do that all right. The only trouble is that in the matter of biting Uncle Clarence's ear I've nothing to rely on but my natural charm. And as far as I've been able to make out,' said Ronnie, 'he hasn't noticed yet that I have any.'

He strode into the post-office, thinking deeply.

3

SENSATIONAL THEFT OF A PIG

· I ·

It was the opinion of the poet Calverley, expressed in his immortal 'Ode to Tobacco', that there is no heaviness of the soul which will not vanish beneath the influence of a quiet smoke. Ronnie Fish would have disputed this theory. It was the third morning of his sojourn at Blandings Castle; and, taking with him a tennis-ball which he proposed to bounce before him in order to assist thought, he had wandered out into the grounds, smoking hard. And tobacco, though Turkish and costly, was not lightening his despondency at all. It seemed to Ronnie that the present was bleak and the future grey. Roaming through the sun-flooded park, he bounced his tennis-ball and groaned in spirit.

On the credit side of the ledger one single item could be inscribed. Hugo was at the castle. He had the consolation, therefore, of knowing that that tall and lissom young man was not in London, exercising his fatal fascination on Sue. But, when you had said this, you had said everything. After all, even eliminating Hugo, there still remained in the metropolis a vast population of adult males, all either acquainted with

Sue or trying to make her acquaintance. The poison-sac Pilbeam, for instance. By now it might well be that that bacillus had succeeded in obtaining an introduction to her. A devastating thought.

And even supposing he hadn't, even supposing that Sue, as she had promised, was virtuously handing the mitten to all the young thugs who surged around her with invitations to lunch and supper; where did that get a chap? What, in other words, of the future?

In coming to Blandings Castle, Ronnie was only too well aware, he had embarked on an expedition, the success or failure of which would determine whether his life through the years was to be roses, roses all the way or a dreary desert. And so far, in his efforts to win the favour and esteem of his Uncle Clarence, he seemed to have made no progress whatsoever. On the occasions when he had found himself in Lord Emsworth's society, the latter had looked at him sometimes as if he did not know he was there, more often as if he wished he wasn't. It was only too plain that the collapse of the Hot Spot had left his stock in bad shape. There had been a general sagging of the market. Fish Preferred, taking the most sanguine estimate, could scarcely be quoted at more than about thirty to thirty-five.

Plunged in thought, and trying without any success to conjure up a picture of a benevolent uncle patting him on the head with one hand while writing cheques with the other, he had wandered some distance from the house and was passing a small spinney, when he observed in a little dell to his left a peculiar object.

It was a large yellow caravan. And what, he asked himself, was a caravan doing in the grounds of Blandings Castle?

To aid him in grappling with the problem, he flung the tennis-ball at it. Upon which, the door opened and a spectacled head appeared.

'Hullo!' said the head.

'Hullo!' said Ronnie.

'Hullo!'

'Hullo!'

The thing threatened to become a hunting-chorus. At this moment, however, the sun went behind a cloud and Ronnie was enabled to recognize the head's proprietor. Until now, the light, shining on the other's glasses, had dazzled him.

'Baxter!' he exclaimed.

The last person he would have expected to meet in the park of Blandings. He had heard all about that row a couple of years ago. He knew that, if his own stock with Lord Emsworth was low, that of the Efficient Baxter was down in the cellar, with no takers. Yet here the fellow was, shoving his head out of caravans as if nothing had ever happened.

'Ah, Fish!'

Rupert Baxter descended the steps, a swarthy-complexioned young man with a supercilious expression which had always been displeasing to Ronnie.

'What are you doing here?' asked Ronnie.

'I happened to be taking a caravan holiday in the neighbourhood. And, finding myself at Market Blandings last night, I thought I would pay a visit to the place where I had spent so many happy days.'

'I see.'

'Perhaps you could tell me where I could find Lady Constance?'

'I haven't seen her since breakfast. She's probably about somewhere?'

'I will go and inquire. If you meet her, perhaps you would not mind mentioning that I am here.'

The Efficient Baxter strode off, purposeful as ever; and Ronnie, having speculated for a moment as to how his Uncle Clarence would comport himself if he came suddenly round a corner and ran into this bit of the dead past, and having registered an idle hope that, when this happened, he might be present with a camera, inserted another cigarette in its holder and passed on his way.

· II ·

Five minutes later, Lord Emsworth, leaning pensively out of the library window and sniffing the morning air, received an unpleasant shock. He could have sworn he had seen his late secretary, Rupert Baxter, cross the gravel and go in at the front door.

'Bless my soul!' said Lord Emsworth.

The only explanation that occurred to him was that Baxter, having met with some fatal accident, had come back to haunt the place. To suppose the fellow could be here in person was absurd. When you shoot a secretary out for throwing flower-pots at you in the small hours, he does not return to pay social calls. A frown furrowed his lordship's brow. The spectre of one of his ancestors he could have put up with, but the idea of a Blandings Castle haunted by Baxter he did not relish at all. He decided to visit his sister Constance in her boudoir and see what she had to say about it.

'Constance, my dear.'

Lady Constance looked up from the letter she was writing. She clicked her tongue, for it annoyed her to be interrupted at her correspondence.

'Well, Clarence?'

'I say, Constance, a most extraordinary thing happened just now. I was looking out of the library window and—you remember Baxter?'

'Of course I remember Mr Baxter.'

'Well, his ghost has just walked across the gravel.'

'What *are* you talking about, Clarence?'

'I'm telling you. I was looking out of the library window and I suddenly saw—'

'Mr Baxter,' announced Beach, flinging open the door.

'Mr Baxter!'

'Good morning, Lady Constance.'

Rupert Baxter advanced with joyous camaraderie glinting from both lenses. Then he perceived his former employer and his exuberance diminished. 'Er—good morning, Lord Emsworth,' he said, flashing his spectacles austerely upon him.

There was a pause. Lord Emsworth adjusted his pince-nez and regarded the visitor dumbly. Of the relief which was presumably flooding his soul at the discovery that Rupert Baxter was still on this side of the veil, he gave no outward sign.

Baxter was the first to break an uncomfortable silence.

'I happened to be taking a caravan holiday in this neighbourhood, Lady Constance, and finding myself near Market Blandings last night, I thought I would . . .'

'Why, of course! We should never have forgiven you if you had not come to see us. Should we, Clarence?'

'Eh?'

'I said, should we?'

'Should we what?' said Lord Emsworth, who was still adjusting his mind.

Lady Constance's lips tightened, and a moment passed during which it seemed always a fifty-fifty chance that a handsome silver ink-pot would fly through the air in the direction of her brother's head. But she was a strong woman. She fought down the impulse.

'Did you say you were travelling in a caravan, Mr Baxter?'

'In a caravan. I left it in the park.'

'Well, of course you must come and stay with us. The castle,' she continued, raising her voice a little, to compete with a sort of wordless bubbling which had begun to proceed from her brother's lips, 'is almost empty just now. We shall not be having our first big house-party till the middle of next month. You must make quite a long visit. I will send some-body over to fetch your things.'

'It is exceedingly kind of you.'

'It will be delightful having you here again. Won't it, Clarence?'

'Eh?'

'I said won't it?'

'Won't it what?'

Lady Constance's hand trembled above the ink-pot like a hovering butterfly. She withdrew it.

'Will it not be delightful,' she said, catching her brother's eye and holding it like a female Ancient Mariner, 'having Mr Baxter back at the castle again?'

'I'm going down to see my pig,' said Lord Emsworth.

A silence followed his departure, such as would have fallen had a cof-fin just been carried out. Then Lady Constance shook off gloom.

'Oh, Mr Baxter, I'm so glad you were able to come. And how clever of you to come in a caravan. It prevented your arrival seeming pre-arranged.'

'I thought of that.'

'You think of everything.'

Rupert Baxter stepped to the door, opened it, satisfied himself that no listeners lurked in the passage, and returned to his seat.

'Are you in any trouble, Lady Constance? Your letter seemed so very urgent.'

'I am in dreadful trouble, Mr Baxter.'

If Rupert Baxter had been a different type of man and Lady Constance Keeble a different type of woman he would probably at this point have patted her hand. As it was, he merely hitched his chair an inch closer to hers.

'If there is anything I can do?'

'There is nobody except you who can do anything. But I hardly like to ask you.'

'Ask me whatever you please. And if it is in my power . . .'

'Oh, it is.'

Rupert Baxter gave his chair another hitch.

'Tell me.'

Lady Constance hesitated.

'It seems such an impossible thing to ask of anyone.'

'Please!'

'Well . . . you know my brother?'

Baxter seemed puzzled. Then an explanation of the peculiar question presented itself.

'Oh you mean Mr . . . ?'

'Yes, yes, yes. Of course I wasn't referring to Lord Emsworth. My brother Galahad.'

'I have never met him. Oddly enough, though he visited the castle twice during the period when I was Lord Emsworth's secretary, I was away both times on my holiday. Is he here now?'

'Yes. Finishing his Reminiscences.'

'I saw in some paper that he was writing the history of his life.'

'And if you know what a life his has been you will understand why I am distracted.'

'Certainly I have heard stories,' said Baxter guardedly.

Lady Constance performed that movement with her hands which came so close to wringing.

'The book is full from beginning to end of libellous anecdotes, Mr Baxter. About all our best friends. If it is published we shall not have a friend left. Galahad seems to have known everybody in England when they were young and foolish, and to remember everything particularly foolish and disgraceful that they did. So . . .'

'So you want me to get hold of the manuscript and destroy it?'

Lady Constance stared, stunned by this penetration. She told herself that she might have known that she would not have to make long explanations to Rupert Baxter. His mind was like a searchlight, darting hither and thither, lighting up whatever it touched.

'Yes,' she gasped. She hurried on. 'It does seem, I know, an extraordinary thing to . . .'

'Not at all.'

'. . . but Lord Emsworth refuses to do anything.'

'I see.'

'You know how he is in the face of any emergency.'

'Yes, I do, indeed.'

'So supine. So helpless. So vague and altogether incompetent.'

'Precisely.'

'Mr Baxter, you are my only hope.'

Baxter removed his spectacles, polished them, and put them back again.

'I shall be delighted, Lady Constance, to do anything to help you that lies in my power. And to obtain possession of this manuscript should be an easy task. But is there only one copy of it in existence?'

'Yes, yes, yes. I am sure of that. Galahad told me that he was waiting till it was finished before sending it to the typist.'

'Then you need have no further anxiety.'

It was a moment when Lady Constance Keeble would have given much for eloquence. She sought for words that should adequately express her feelings, but could find none.

'Oh, Mr Baxter!' she said.

· III ·

Ronnie Fish's aimlessly wandering feet had taken him westward. It was not long, accordingly, before there came to his nostrils a familiar and penetrating odour, and he found that he was within a short distance of the detached residence employed by Empress of Blandings as a combined bedroom and restaurant. A few steps, and he was enabled to observe that celebrated animal in person. With her head tucked well down and her tail wiggling with pure *joie de vivre*, the Empress was hoisting in a spot of lunch.

Everybody likes to see somebody eating. Ronnie leaned over the rail, absorbed. He poised the tennis-ball and with an absent-minded flick of the wrist bounced it on the silver medallist's back. Finding the pleasant, ponging sound which resulted soothing to harassed nerves, he did it again. The Empress made excellent bouncing. She was not one of your razor-backs. She presented a wide and resistant surface. For some minutes, therefore, the pair carried on according to plan—she eating, he bouncing, until presently Ronnie was thrilled to discover that this outdoor sport of his was assisting thought. Gradually—mistily at first, then assuming shape, a plan of action was beginning to emerge from the murk of his mind.

How would this be, for instance?

If there was one thing calculated to appeal to his Uncle Clarence, to induce in his Uncle Clarence a really melting mood, it was the announcement that somebody desired to return to the Land. He loved to hear of people returning to the Land. How, then, would this be? Go to the old boy, state that one had seen the light and was in complete agreement with him that England's future depended on checking the Drift to the Towns, and then ask for a good fat slice of capital with which to start a farm.

The project of starting a farm was one which was bound to . . . Half a minute. Another idea on the way. Yes, here it came, and it was a pippin. Not merely just an ordinary farm, but a pig-farm! Wouldn't Uncle Clarence leap in the air and shower gold on anybody who wanted to live in the country and breed pigs? You bet your Sunday cuffs he would. And, once the money was safely deposited to the account of Ronald Overbury Fish in Cox's Bank, then ho! For the registrar's hand in hand with Sue.

There was a musical *plonk* as Ronnie bounced the ball for the last time on the Empress's complacent back. Then, no longer with dragging steps but treading on air, he wandered away to sketch out the last details of the scheme before going indoors and springing it.

· IV ·

Too often it happens that, when you get these brain-waves, you take another look at them after a short interval and suddenly detect some fatal flaw. No such disappointment came to mar the happiness of Ronnie Fish.

'I say, Uncle Clarence,' he said, prancing into the library, some half-hour later.

Lord Emsworth was deep in the current issue of a weekly paper of porcine interest. It seemed to Ronnie, as he looked up, that his eye was not any too chummy. This, however, did not disturb him. That eye, he was confident, would melt anon. If, at the moment, Lord Emsworth could hardly have sat for his portrait in the role of a benevolent uncle, there would, Ronnie felt, be a swift change of demeanour in the very near future.

'I say, Uncle Clarence, you know that capital of mine.'

'That what?'

'My capital. My money. The money you're trustee of. And a jolly good trustee,' said Ronnie handsomely. 'Well, I've been thinking things over and I want you, if you will, to disgorge a segment of it for a sort of venture I've got in mind.'

He had not expected the eye to melt yet, and it did not. Seen through the glass of his uncle's pince-nez, it looked like an oyster in an aquarium.

'You wish to start another night-club?'

Lord Emsworth's voice was cold, and Ronnie hastened to disabuse him of the idea.

'No, no. Nothing like that. Night-clubs are a mug's game. I ought never to have touched them. As a matter of fact, Uncle Clarence, London as a whole seems to me a bit of a washout these days. I'm all for the country. What I feel is that the drift to the towns should be checked. What England wants is more blokes going back to the land. That's the way it looks to me.'

Ronnie Fish began to experience the first definite twinges of uneasiness. This was the point at which he had been confident that the melting process would set in. Yet, watching the eye, he was dismayed to find it as oysterlike as ever. He felt like an actor who has been counting on a round of applause and goes off after his big speech without a hand. The idea occurred to him that his uncle might possibly have grown a little hard of hearing.

'To the Land,' he repeated, raising his voice. 'More blokes going back to the Land. So I want a dollop of capital to start a farm.'

He braced himself for the supreme revelation.

'I want to breed pigs,' he said reverently.

Something was wrong. There was no blinking the fact any longer. So far from leaping in the air and showering gold, his uncle merely stared at him in an increasingly unpleasant manner. Lord Emsworth had removed his pince-nez and was wiping them; and Ronnie thought that his eye looked rather less agreeable in the nude than it had done through glass.

'Pigs!' he cried, fighting against a growing alarm.

'Pigs?'

'Pigs.'

'You wish to breed pigs?'

'That's right,' bellowed Ronnie. 'Pigs!' And from somewhere in his system he contrived to dig up and fasten on his face an ingratiating smile.

Lord Emsworth replaced his pince-nez.

'And I suppose,' he said throatily, quivering from his bald head to his roomy shoes, 'that when you've got 'em you'll spend the whole day bouncing tennis-balls on their backs?'

Ronnie gulped. The shock had been severe. The ingratiating smile lingered on his lips, as if fastened there with pins, but his eyes were round and horrified.

'Eh?' he said feebly.

Lord Emsworth rose. So long as he insisted on wearing an old shoot-ing jacket with holes in the elbows and letting his tie slip down and show the head of a brass stud, he could never hope to be completely satisfactory as a figure of outraged majesty; but he achieved as imposing an effect as his upholstery would permit. He drew himself up to his full height, which was considerable, and from this eminence glared balefully down on his nephew.

'I saw you! I was on my way to the piggery and I saw you there bounc-ing your infernal tennis-balls on my pig's back. Tennis-balls!' Fire seemed to stream from the pince-nez. 'Are you aware that Empress of Blandings is an excessively nervous, highly-strung animal, only too ready on the slightest provocation to refuse her meals? You might have undone the work of months with your idiotic tennis-ball.'

'I'm sorry. . . .'

'What's the good of being sorry?'

'I never thought. . . .'

'You never do. That's what's the trouble with you. Pig-farm! said Lord Emsworth vehemently, his voice soaring into the upper register. 'You couldn't manage a pig-farm. You aren't fit to manage a pig-farm. You aren't worthy to manage a pig-farm. If I had to select somebody out of the whole world to manage a pig-farm, I would choose you last.'

Ronnie Fish groped his way to the table and supported himself on it. He had a sensation of dizziness. On one point he was reasonably clear, viz. that his Uncle Clarence did not consider him ideally fitted to manage a pig-farm, but apart from that his mind was in a whirl. He felt as if he had stepped on something and it had gone off with a bang.

'Here! What *is* all this?'

It was the Hon. Galahad who had spoken, and he had spoken pee-vishly. Working in the small library with the door ajar, he had found the babble of voices interfering with literary composition and, justifiably annoyed, had come to investigate.

'Can't you do your reciting some time when I'm not working, Clar-ence?' he said. 'What's all the trouble about?'

Lord Emsworth was still full of his grievance.

'He bounced tennis-balls on my pig!'

The Hon. Galahad was not impressed. He did not register horror.

'Do you mean to tell me,' he said sternly, 'that all this fuss, ruining my morning's work, was simply about that blasted pig of yours?'

'I refuse to allow you to call the Empress a blasted pig! Good heavens!' cried Lord Emsworth passionately. 'Can none of my family appreciate the fact that she is the most remarkable animal in Great Britain? No pig in the whole annals of the Shropshire Agricultural Show has ever won the silver medal two years in succession. And that, if only people will leave her alone and refrain from incessantly pelting her with tennis-balls, is what the Empress is quite certain to do. It is an unheard of feat.'

The Hon. Galahad frowned. He shook his head reprovingly. It was all very well, he felt, a stable being optimistic about its nominee, but he was a man who could face facts. In a long and chequered life he had seen so many good things unstuck. Besides, he had his superstitions, and one of them was that counting your chickens in advance brought bad luck.

'Don't you be too cocksure, my boy,' he said gravely. I looked in at the Emsworth Arms the other day for a glass of beer, and there was a fellow in there offering three to one on an animal called Pride of Matchingham. Offering it freely. Tall, red-haired fellow with a squint. Slightly bottled.'

Lord Emsworth forgot Ronnie, forgot tennis-balls, forgot, in the shock of this announcement, everything except that deeper wrong which so long had been poisoning his peace.

'Pride of Matchingham belongs to Sir Gregory Parsloe,' he said, 'and I have no doubt that the man offering such ridiculous odds was his pig-man, Wellbeloved. As you know, the fellow used to be in my employment, but Parsloe lured him away from me by the promise of higher wages.' Lord Emsworth's expression had now become positively ferocious. The thought of George Cyril Wellbeloved, that perjured pig-man, always made the iron enter into his soul. 'It was a most abominable and unneighbourly thing to do.'

The Hon. Galahad whistled.

'So that's it, is it? Parsloe's pig-man going about offering three to one—against the form-book, I take it?'

'Most decidedly. Pride of Matchingham was awarded second prize last year, but it is a quite inferior animal to the Empress.'

'Then you look after that pig of yours, Clarence.' The Hon. Galahad spoke earnestly. 'I see what this means. Parsloe's up to his old games, and intends to queer the Empress somehow.'

'Queer her?'

'Nobble her. Or, if he can't do that, steal her.'

'You don't mean that.'

'I do mean it. The man's as slippery as a greased eel. He would nobble his grandmother if it suited his book. Let me tell you I've known young Parsloe for thirty years and I solemnly state that if his grandmother was entered in a competition for fat pigs and his commitments made it desirable for him to get her out of the way, he would dope her bran-mash and acorns without a moment's hesitation.'

'God bless my soul!' said Lord Emsworth, deeply impressed.

'Let me tell you a little story about young Parsloe. One or two of us used to meet at the Black Footman in Gossiter Street in the old days—they've pulled it down now—and match our dogs against rats in the room behind the bar. Well, I put my Towser, an admirable beast, up against young Parsloe's Banjo on one occasion for a hundred pounds a side. And when the night came and he was shown the rats, I'm dashed if he didn't just give a long yawn and roll over and go to sleep. I whistled him . . . called him . . . Towser, Towser . . . No good . . . Fast asleep. And my firm belief has always been that young Parsloe took him aside just before the contest was to start and gave him about six pounds of steak and onions. Couldn't prove anything, of course, but I sniffed the dog's breath and it was like opening the kitchen door of a Soho chophouse on a summer night. That's the sort of man young Parsloe is.'

'Galahad!'

'Fact. You'll find the story in my book.'

Lord Emsworth was tottering to the door.

'God bless my soul! I never realized . . . I must see Pirbright at once. I didn't suspect . . . It never occurred . . .'

The door closed behind him. The Hon. Galahad, preparing to return to his labours, was arrested by the voice of his nephew Ronald.

'Uncle Gally!'

The young man's pink face had flamed to a bright crimson. His eyes gleamed strangely.

'Well?'

'You don't really think Sir Gregory will try to steal the Empress?'

'I certainly do. Known him for thirty years, I tell you.'

'But how could he?'

'Go to her sty at night, of course, and take her away.'

'And hide her somewhere?'

'Yes.'

'But an animal that size. Rather like looking in at the Zoo and pocketing one of the elephants, what?'

'Don't talk like an idiot. She's got a ring through her nose, hasn't she?'

'You mean, Sir Gregory could catch hold of the ring and she would breeze along quite calmly?'

'Certainly. Puffy Benger and I stole old Wivenhoe's pig the night of the Bachelors' Ball at Hammer's Easton in the year '95. We put it in Plug Basham's bedroom. There was no difficulty about the thing whatsoever. A little child could have led it.'

He withdrew into the small library, and Ronnie slid limply into the chair which Lord Emsworth had risen from so majestically. He felt the need of sitting. The inspiration which had just come to him had had a stunning effect. The brilliance of it most frightened him. That idea about starting a pig-farm had shown that this was one of his bright mornings, but he had never foreseen that he would be as bright as this.

'Golly!' said Ronnie.

Could he . . . ?

Well, why not?

Suppose . . . ?

No, the thing was impossible.

Was it? Why? Why was it impossible? Suppose he had a stab at it. Suppose, following his Uncle Galahad's expert hints, he were to creep out to-night, abstract the Empress from her home, hide her somewhere for a day or two and then spectacularly restore her to her bereaved owner? What would be the result? Would Uncle Clarence sob on his neck, or

would he not? Would he feel that no reward was too good for his benefactor or wouldn't he? Most decidedly he would. Fish Preferred would
soar immediately. That little matter of the advance of capital would solve
itself. Money would stream automatically from the Emsworth coffers.

But could it be done? Ronnie forced himself to examine the scheme
dispassionately, with a mind alert for snags.

He could detect none. A suitable hiding place occurred to him immediately—that disused gamekeeper's cottage in the West Wood. Nobody
ever went there. It would be as good as a Safe Deposit.

Risk of Detection? Why should there be any risk of detection? Who
would think of connecting Ronald Fish with the affair?

Feeding the animal . . . ?

Ronnie's face clouded. Yes, here at last was the snag. This did present difficulties. He was vague as to what pigs ate, but he knew that they
needed a lot of whatever it was. It would be no use restoring to Lord
Emsworth a skeleton Empress. The cuisine must be maintained at its
existing level, or the thing might just as well be left undone.

For the first time he began to doubt the quality of his recent inspiration. Scanning the desk with knitted brows, he took from the book-rest
the volume entitled *Pigs, and How to Make Them Pay.* A glance at page
61, and his misgivings were confirmed.

"Myes,' said Ronnie, having skimmed through all the stuff about bar-
ley meal and maize meal and linseed meal and potatoes and separated
milk or buttermilk. This, he now saw clearly, was no one man job. It
called not only for a dashing principal but a zealous assistant.

And what assistant?

Hugo?

No. In many respects the ideal accomplice for an undertaking of this
nature, Hugo Carmody had certain defects which automatically disqual-
ified him. To enrol Hugo as his lieutenant would mean revealing to him
the motives that lay at the back of the venture. And if Hugo knew that
he, Ronnie, was endeavouring to collect funds in order to get married,
the thing would be all over Shropshire in a couple of days. Short of putting it on the front page of the *Daily Mail* or having it broadcast over the
wireless, the surest way of obtaining publicity for anything you wanted

kept dark was to confide it to Hugo Carmody. A splendid chap, but the real, genuine human colander. No, not Hugo.

Then who? . . .

Ah!

Ronnie Fish sprang from his chair, threw his head back and uttered a yodel of joy so loud and penetrating that the door of the small library flew open as if he had touched a spring.

A tousled literary man emerged.

'Stop that damned noise! How the devil can I write with a row like that going on?'

'Sorry, Uncle. I was just thinking of something.'

'Well, think of something else. How do you spell "intoxicated"?'

'One "x".'

'Thanks,' said the Hon. Galahad, and vanished again.

· V ·

In his pantry, in shirt-sleeved ease, Beach, the butler, sat taking the well-earned rest of a man whose silver is all done and who has no further duties to perform till lunch-time. A bullfinch sang gaily in a cage on the window-sill, but it did not disturb him, for he was absorbed in the Racing Intelligence page of the *Morning Post*.

Suddenly he rose, palpitating. A sharp rap had sounded on the door, and he was a man who reacted nervously to sudden noises. There entered his employer's nephew, Mr Ronald Fish.

'Hullo, Beach.'

'Sir?'

'Busy?'

'No, sir.'

'Just thought I'd look in.'

'Yes, sir.?'

'For a chat.'

'Very good, sir.'

Although the butler spoke with his usual smooth courtesy, he was far from feeling easy in his mind. He did not like Ronnie's looks. It seemed to him that his young visitor was feverish. The limbs twitched, the eyes gleamed, the blood-pressure appeared heightened, and there was a super-normal pinkness in the epidermis of the cheek.

'Long time since we had a real, cosy talk, Beach.'

'Yes, sir.'

'When I was a kid, I was in and out of this pantry of yours all day long.'

'Yes, sir.'

A mood of extreme sentimentality now appeared to grip the young man. He sighed like a centenarian recalling far off, happy things.

'Those were the days, Beach.'

'Yes, sir.'

'No problems then. No worries. And even if I had worries, I could always bring them to you, couldn't I?'

'Yes, sir.'

'Remember the time I hid in here when my Uncle Gally was after me with a whangee for putting tin-tacks on his chair?'

'Yes, sir.'

'It was a close call, but you saved me. You were staunch and true. A man in a million. I've always thought that if there were more people like you in the world, it would be a better place.'

'I do my best to give you satisfaction, sir.'

'And how you succeed! I shall never forget your kindness in those dear old days, Beach.'

'Extremely good of you to say so, sir.'

'Later, as the years went by, I did my best to repay you, by sharing with you such snips as came my way. Remember the time I gave you Black-bird for the Manchester November Handicap?'

'Yes, sir.'

'You collected a packet.'

'It did prove a remarkably sound investment, sir.'

'Yes. And so it went on. I look back through the years, and I seem to see you and me standing side by side, each helping each, each doing the square thing by the other. You certainly always did the square thing by me.'

'I trust I shall always continue to do so, sir.'

'I know you will, Beach. It isn't in you to do otherwise. And that,' said Ronnie, beaming on him lovingly, 'is why I feel so sure that, when I have stolen my uncle's pig, you will be there helping to feed it till I give it back.'

The butler's was not a face that registered nimbly. It took some time for a look of utter astonishment to cover its full acreage. Such a look had spread to perhaps two-thirds of its surface when Ronnie went on.

'You see, Beach, strictly between ourselves, I have made up my mind to sneak the Empress away and keep her hidden in that gamekeeper's cottage in the West Wood and then, when Uncle Clarence is sending out SOS's and offering large rewards, I shall find it there and return it, thus winning his undying gratitude and putting him in the right frame of mind to yield up a bit of my money that I want to dig out of him. You get the idea?'

The butler blinked. He was plainly endeavouring to conquer a suspicion that his mind was darkening. Ronnie nodded kindly at him as he fought for speech.

'It's the scheme of a lifetime, you were going to say? You're quite right. It is. But it's one of those schemes that call for a sympathetic fellow-worker. You see, pigs like the Empress, Beach, require large quantities of food at frequent intervals. I can't possibly handle the entire commissariat department myself. That's where you're going to help me, like the splendid fellow you are and always have been.'

The butler had now begun to gargle slightly. He cast a look of agonized entreaty at the bullfinch, but the bird had no comfort to offer. It continued to chirp reflectively to itself, like a man trying to remember a tune in his bath.

'An enormous quantity of food they need,' proceeded Ronnie. 'You'd be surprised. Here it is in this book I took from my uncle's desk. At least six pounds of meal a day, not to mention milk or buttermilk and bran made sloppy with swill.'

Speech at last returned to the butler. It took the form at first of a faint sound like the cry of a frightened infant. Then words came.

'But, Mr Ronald . . . !'

Ronnie stared at him incredulously. He seemed to be wrestling with an unbelievable suspicion.

'Don't tell me you're thinking of throwing me down, Beach? You? My friend since I was so high?' He laughed. He could see now how ridiculous the idea was. 'Of course you aren't! You couldn't. Apart from wanting to do me a good turn, you've gathered by this time with that quick intelligence of yours, that there's money in the thing. Ten quid down, Beach, the moment you give the nod. And nobody knows better than yourself that ten quid, invested on Baby Bones for the Medbury Selling Plate at the current odds, means considerably more than a hundred in your sock on settling-day.'

'But, sir . . . It's impossible . . . I couldn't dream . . . if ever it was found out . . . Really, I don't think you ought to ask me, Mr Ronald . . .'

'Beach!'

'Yes, but, really, sir . . .'

Ronnie fixed him with a compelling eye.

'Think well, Beach. Who gave you Creole Queen for the Lincolnshire?'

'But Mr Ronald . . .'

'Who gave you Mazzawattee for the Jubilee Stakes, Beach? What a beauty!'

A tense silence fell upon the pantry. Even the bullfinch was hushed.

'And it may interest you to know,' said Ronnie, 'that just before I left London I heard of something really hot for the Goodwood Cup.'

A low gasp escaped Beach. All butlers are sportsmen, and Beach had been a butler for eighteen years. Mere gratitude for past favours might not have been enough in itself to turn the scale, but this was different. On the subject of form for the Goodwood Cup he had been quite unable to reach a satisfying decision. It had baffled him. For days he had been groping in the darkness.

'Jujube, sir?' he whispered.

'Not Jujube.'

'Ginger George?'

'Not Ginger George. It's no use your trying to guess, for you'll never do it. Only two touts and the stable-cat know this one. But you shall know it, Beach, the minute I give that pig back and claim my reward. And that pig needs to be fed. Beach, how about it?'

For a long minute the butler stared before him, silent. Then, as if he felt that some simple, symbolic act of the sort was what this moment demanded, he went to the bullfinch's cage and put a green-baize cloth over it.

'Tell me just what it is you wish me to do, Mr Ronald,' he said.

· VI ·

The dawn of another day crept upon Blandings Castle. Hour by hour the light grew stronger till, piercing the curtains of Ronnie's bedroom, it woke him from a disturbed slumber. He turned sleepily on the pillow. He was dimly conscious of having had the most extraordinary dream, all about stealing pigs. In this dream . . .

He sat up with a jerk. Like cold water dashed in his face had come the realization that it had been no dream.

'Gosh!' said Ronnie, blinking.

Few things have such a tonic effect on a young man accustomed to be a little heavy on waking in the morning as the discovery that he has stolen a prize pig overnight. Usually, at this hour, Ronnie was more or less of an inanimate mass till kindly hands brought him his early cup of tea: but to-day he thrilled all down his pyjama-clad form with a novel alertness. Not since he had left school had he 'sprung out of bed', but he did so now. Bed, generally so attractive to him, had lost its fascination. He wanted to be up and about.

He had bathed, shaved, and was slipping into his trousers when his toilet was interrupted by the arrival of his old friend Hugo Carmody. On Hugo's face there was an expression which it was impossible to misread. It indicated as plainly as a label that he had come bearing news, and Ronnie, guessing the nature of this news, braced himself to be suitably startled.

'Ronnie!'

'Well?'

'Heard what's happened?'

'What?'

'You know that pig of your uncle's?'

'What about it?'

'It's gone.'

'Gone?'

'Gone!' said Hugo, rolling the word round his tongue. 'I met the old boy half a minute ago, and he told me. It seems he went down to the pig-bin for a before-breakfast look at the animal, and it wasn't there.'

'Wasn't there?'

'Wasn't there.'

'How do you mean, wasn't there?'

'Well, it wasn't. Wasn't there at all. It had gone.'

'Gone?'

'Gone! Its room was empty and its bed had not been slept in.'

'Well, I'm dashed!' said Ronnie.

He was feeling pleased with himself. He felt he had played his part well. Just the right incredulous amazement, changing just soon enough into stunned belief.

'You don't seem very surprised,' said Hugo.

Ronnie was stung. The charge was monstrous.

'Yes, I do,' he cried. 'I seem frightfully surprised. I *am* surprised. Why shouldn't I be surprised?'

'All right. Just as you say. Spring about a bit more, though, another time when I bring you these sensational items. Well, I'll tell you one thing,' said Hugo with satisfaction. 'Out of evil, cometh good. It's an ill wind that has no turning. For me, this startling occurrence has been a life-saver. I've got thirty-six hours leave out of it. The old boy is sending me up to London to get a detective.'

'A what?'

'A detective.'

'A detective!'

Ronnie was conscious of a marked spasm of uneasiness. He had not bargained for detectives.

'From a place called the Argus Enquiry Agency.'

Ronnie's uneasiness increased. This thing was not going to be so simple after all. He had never actually met a detective, but he had read a lot about them. They nosed about and found clues. For all he knew, he might have left a hundred clues.

'Naturally I shall have to stay the night in town. And, much as I like this place,' said Hugo, 'there's no denying that a night in town won't hurt. I've got fidgety feet, and a spot of dancing will do me all the good in the world. Bring back the roses to my cheeks.'

'Whose idea was it, getting down this blighted detective?' demanded Ronnie. He knew he was not being nonchalant, but he was disturbed.

'Mine.'

'Yours, eh?'

'All mine. I suggested it.'

'You did, did you?' said Ronnie.

He directed at his companion a swift glance of a kind that no one should have directed at an old friend.

'Oh?' he said morosely. 'Well, buzz off. I want to dress.'

· VII ·

A morning spent in solitary wrestling with a guilty conscience had left Ronnie Fish thoroughly unstrung. By the time the clock over the stable struck the hour of one, his mental condition had begun to resemble that of the late Eugene Aram. He paced the lower terrace with bent head, starting occasionally at the sudden chirp of a bird, and longed for Sue. Five minutes of Sue, he felt, would make him a new man.

It was perfectly foul, mused Ronnie, this being separated from the girl he loved. There was something about Sue . . . he couldn't describe it, but something that always seemed to act on a fellow's whole system like a powerful pick-me-up. She was the human equivalent of those pink drinks you went and got—or, rather, which you used to go and get before a good woman's love had made you give up all that sort of thing—at that chemist's at the top of the Haymarket after a wild night on the moors. It must have been with a girl like Sue in mind, he felt, that the poet had written those lines 'When something something something brow, a ministering angel thou!'

At this point in his meditations, a voice from immediately behind him spoke his name.

'I say, Ronnie.'

It was only his cousin Millicent. He became calmer. For an instant, so deep always is a criminal's need for a confidant, he had a sort of idea of sharing his hideous secret with this girl, between whom and himself there had long existed a pleasant friendship. Then he abandoned the notion. His secret was not one that could be lightly shared. Momentary relief of mind was not worth purchasing at the cost of endless anxiety.

'Ronnie, have you seen Mr Carmody anywhere?'

'Hugo? He went up to London on the ten-thirty.'

'Went up to London? What for?'

'He's gone to a place called the Argus Enquiry Agency to get a detective.'

'What, to investigate this business of the Empress?'

'Yes.'

Millicent laughed. The idea tickled her.

'I'd like to be there to see old man Argus's face when he finds that all he's wanted for is to track down missing pigs. I should think he would beat Hugo over the head with a blood-stain.'

Her laughter trailed away. There had come into her face the look of one suddenly visited by a displeasing thought.

'Ronnie!'

'Hullo?'

'Do you know what?'

'What?'

'This looks fishy to me.'

'How do you mean?'

'Well, I don't know how it strikes you, but this Argus Enquiry Agency is presumably on the phone. Why didn't Uncle Clarence just ring them up and ask them to send down a man?'

'Probably didn't think of it.'

'Whose idea was it, anyway, getting down a man?'

'Hugo's.'

'He suggested that he should run up to town?'

'Yes.'

'I thought as much,' said Millicent darkly.

'What do you mean?'

Millicent's eyes narrowed. She kicked moodily at a passing worm.

'I don't like it,' she said. 'It's fishy. Too much zeal. It looks very much to me as if our Mr Carmody had a special reason for wanting to get up to London for the night. And I think I know what the reason was. Did you ever hear of a girl named Sue Brown?'

The start which Ronnie gave eclipsed in magnitude all the other starts he had given that morning. And they had been many and severe.

'It isn't true?'

'What isn't true?'

'That there's anything whatever between Hugo and Sue Brown.'

'Oh? Well, I had it from an authoritative source.'

It was not the worm's lucky morning. It had now reached Ronnie, and he kicked at it, too. The worm had the illusion that it had begun to rain shoes.

'I've got to go in and make a phone call,' said Millicent, abruptly.

Ronnie scarcely noticed her departure. He had supposed himself to have been doing some pretty tense thinking all the morning, but, compared with its activity now, his brain hitherto had been stagnant.

It couldn't be true, he told himself. Sue had said definitely that it wasn't, and she couldn't have been lying to him. Girls like Sue didn't lie. And yet . . .

The sound of the luncheon gong floated over the garden.

Well, one thing was certain. It was simply impossible to remain here at Blandings Castle, getting his mind poisoned with doubts and speculations which for the life of him he could not keep out of it. If he took the two-seater and drove off in it the moment this infernal meal was over, he could be in London before eight. He could call at Sue's flat; receive her assurance once more that Hugo Carmody, tall and lissom though he might be, expert on the saxophone though he admittedly was, meant nothing to her; take her out to dinner and, while dining, ease his mind of that which weighed upon it. Then, fortified with comfort and advice, he could pop into the car and be back at the castle by lunch-time on the following day.

It wasn't, of course, that he didn't trust her implicitly. Nevertheless . . . Ronnie went in to lunch.

4

NOTICEABLE BEHAVIOUR OF
RONALD FISH

• I •

If you go up Beeston Street in the south-western postal division of London and follow the pavement on the right-hand side, you come to a blind alley called Hayling Court. If you enter the first building on the left of this blind alley and mount a flight of stairs, you find yourself facing a door, on the ground-glass of which is the legend:

ARGUS

ENQUIRY

AGENCY

LTD

and below it, to one side, the smaller legend

P. FROBISHER PILBEAM, MGR

And if, at about the hour when Ronnie Fish had stepped into his two-seater in the garage of Blandings Castle, you had opened this door and gone in and succeeded in convincing the gentlemanly office-boy that yours was a *bona fide* visit, having nothing to do with the sale of life insurance, proprietary medicines or handsomely bound sets of Dumas, you would have been admitted to the august presence of the Mgr himself. P. Frobisher Pilbeam was seated at his desk, reading a telegram which had arrived during his absence at lunch.

This is peculiarly an age of young men starting out in business for themselves; of rare, unfettered spirits chafing at the bonds of employment and refusing to spend their lives working forty-eight weeks in the year for a salary. Quite early in his career Pilbeam had seen where the big money lay, and decided to go after it.

As editor of that celebrated weekly scandal-sheet, *Society Spice*, Percy Pilbeam had had exceptional opportunities of discovering in good time the true bent of his genius: with the result that, after three years of nosing out people's discreditable secrets on behalf of the Mammoth Publishing Company, his employers, he had come to the conclusion that a man of his gifts would be doing far better for himself nosing out such secrets on his own behalf. Considerably to the indignation of Lord Tilbury, the Mammoth's guiding spirit, he had borrowed some capital, handed in his portfolio, and was now in an extremely agreeable financial position.

The telegram over which he sat brooding with wrinkled forehead was just the sort of telegram an Enquiry agent ought to have been delighted to receive, being thoroughly cryptic and consequently a pleasing challenge to his astuteness as a detective, but Percy Pilbeam, in his ten minutes' acquaintance with it, had come to dislike it heartily. He preferred his telegrams easier.

It ran as follows:

Be sure send best man investigate big robbery.

It was unsigned.

What made the thing particularly annoying was that it was so tantalizing. A big robbery probably meant jewels, with a correspondingly big fee attached to their recovery. But you cannot scour England at random, asking people if they have had a big robbery in their neighbourhood.

Reluctantly, he gave the problem up; and, producing a pocket mirror, began with the aid of a pen nib to curl his small and revolting moustache. His thoughts had drifted now to Sue. They were not altogether sunny thoughts, for the difficulty of making Sue's acquaintance was beginning to irk Percy Pilbeam. He had written her notes. He had sent her flowers. And nothing had happened. She ignored the notes, and what she did with the flowers he did not know. She certainly never thanked him for them.

Brooding upon these matters, he was interrupted by the opening of the door. The gentlemanly office-boy entered. Pilbeam looked up, annoyed.

'How many times have I told you not to come in here without knocking?' he asked sternly.

The office-boy reflected.

'Seven,' he replied.

'What would you have done if I had been in conference with an important client?'

'Gone out again,' said the office-boy. Working in a Private Enquiry Agency, you drop into the knack of solving problems.

'Well, go out now.'

'Very good, sir. I merely wished to say that, while you were absent at lunch, a gentleman called.'

'Eh? Who was he?'

The office-boy, who liked atmosphere, and hoped some day to be promoted to the company of Mr Murphy and Mr Jones, the two active assistants who had their lair on the ground floor, thought for a moment of saying that, beyond the obvious facts that the caller was a Freemason, left-handed, a vegetarian and a traveller in the East, he had made no deductions from his appearance. He perceived, however, that his employer was not in the vein for that sort of thing.

'A Mr Carmody, sir. Mr Hugo Carmody.'

'Ah!' Pilbeam displayed interest. 'Did he say he would call again?'

'He mentioned the possibility, sir.'

'Well, if he does, inform Mr Murphy and tell him to be ready when I ring.'

The office-boy retired, and Pilbeam returned to his thoughts of Sue.

He was quite certain now that he did not like her attitude. Her attitude wounded him. Another thing he deplored was the reluctance of stage-door keepers to reveal the private addresses of the personnel of the company. Really, there seemed to be no way of getting to know the girl at all.

Eight respectful knocks sounded on the door. The office-boy, though occasionally forgetful, was conscientious. He had restored the average.

'Well?'

'Mr Carmody to see you, sir.'

Pilbeam once more relegated Sue to the hinterland of his mind. Business was business.

'Show him in.'

'This way, sir,' said the office-boy with a graceful courtliness which, even taking into account the fact that he suffered adenoids, had an old-world flavour, and Hugo sauntered across the threshold.

Hugo felt, and was looking, quietly happy. He seemed to bring the sunshine with him. Nobody could have been more wholeheartedly attached than he to Blandings Castle and the society of his Millicent, but he was finding London, revisited, singularly attractive.

'And this, if I mistake not, Watson, is our client now,' said Hugo genially.

Such was his feeling of universal benevolence that he embraced with his good-will even the repellent-looking young man who had risen from the desk. Percy Pilbeam's eyes were too small and too close together and he marcelled his hair in a manner distressing to right-thinking people, but to-day he had to be lumped in with the rest of the species as a man and a brother, so Hugo bestowed a dazzling smile upon him. He still thought Pilbeam should not have been wearing pimples with a red tie. One or the other if he liked. But not both. Nevertheless he smiled upon him.

'Fine day,' he said.

'Quite,' said Pilbeam.

'Very jolly, the smell of the asphalt and carbonic gas.'

'Quite.'

'Some people might call London a shade on the stuffy side on an afternoon like this. But not Hugo Carmody.'

'No?'

'No. H. Carmody finds it just what the doctor ordered.' He sat down. 'Well, sleuth,' he said, 'to business. I called before lunch, but you were out.'

'Yes.'

'But here I am again. And I suppose you want to know what I've come about?'

'When you're ready to get round to it,' said Pilbeam patiently.

Hugo stretched his long legs comfortably.

'Well, I know you detective blokes always want a fellow to begin at the beginning and omit no detail, for there is no saying how important some seemingly trivial fact may be. Omitting birth and early education then, I am at the moment private secretary to Lord Emsworth, at Blandings Castle, in Shropshire. And,' said Hugo, 'I maintain, a jolly good secretary. Others may think differently, but that is my view.'

'Blandings Castle?'

A thought had struck the proprietor of the Argus Enquiry Agency. He fumbled in his desk and produced the mysterious telegram. Yes, as he had fancied, it had been handed in at a place called Market Blandings.

'Do you know anything about this?' he asked, pushing it across the desk.

Hugo glanced at the document.

'The old boy must have sent that after I left,' he said. 'The absence of signature is, no doubt, due to mental stress. Lord Emsworth is greatly perturbed. A-twitter. Shaken to the core, you might say.'

'About this robbery?'

'Exactly. It has got right in amongst him.'

Pilbeam reached for pen and paper. There was a stern, set, bloodhound sort of look in his eyes.

'Kindly give me the details.'

Hugo pondered a moment.

'It was a dark and stormy night . . . No, I'm a liar. The moon was riding serenely in the sky . . .'

'This big robbery? Tell me about it.'

Hugo raised his eyebrows.

'Big?'

'The telegram says "big".'

'These telegraph-operators will try to make sense. You can't stop them editing. The word should be "pig". Lord Emsworth's pig has been stolen!'

'Pig!' cried Percy Pilbeam.

Hugo looked at him a little anxiously.

'You know what a pig is, surely? If not, I'm afraid there is a good deal of tedious spade work ahead of us.'

The roseate dreams which the proprietor of the Argus had had of missing jewels broke like bubbles. He was deeply affronted. A man of few ideals, the one deep love of his life was for this Enquiry Agency which he had created and nursed to prosperity through all the dangers and vicissitudes which beset Enquiry Agencies in their infancy. And the thought of being expected to apply its complex machinery to a search for lost pigs cut him, as Millicent had predicted, to the quick.

'Does Lord Emsworth seriously suppose that I have time to waste looking for stolen pigs?' he demanded shrilly. 'I never heard such non-sense in my life.'

'Almost the exact words which all the other Hawkshaws used. Finding you not at home,' explained Hugo, 'I spent the morning going round to other Agencies. I think I visited six in all, and every one of them took the attitude you do.'

'I am not surprised.'

'Nevertheless, it seemed to me that they, like you, lacked vision. This pig, you see, is a prize pig. Don't picture to yourself something with a kink in its tail sporting idly in the mud. Imagine, rather, a favourite daughter kidnapped from her ancestral home. This is heavy stuff, I assure you. Restore the animal in time for the Agricultural Show, and you may ask of Lord Emsworth what you will, even unto half his kingdom.'

Percy Pilbeam rose. He had heard enough.

'I will not trouble Lord Emsworth. The Argus Enquiry Agency . . .'

'. . . does not detect pigs? I feared as much. Well, well, so be it. And now,' said Hugo, affably, 'may I take advantage of the beautiful friendship which has sprung up between us to use your telephone?'

Without waiting for permission—for which, indeed, he would have had to wait some time—he drew the instrument to him and gave a number. He then began to chat again.

'You seem a knowledgeable sort of bloke,' he said. 'Perhaps you can tell me where the village swains go these days when they want to dance upon the green? I have been absent for some little time from the centre of the vortex, and I have become as a child in these matters. What is the best that London has to offer to a young man with his blood up and the vine leaves more or less in his hair?'

Pilbeam was a man of business. He had no wish to converse with this client who had disappointed him and wounded his finest feelings, but it so happened that he had recently bought shares in a rising restaurant.

'Mario's,' he replied promptly. 'It's the only place.'

Hugo sighed. Once he had dreamed that the answer to a question like that would have been 'The Hot Spot'. But where was the Hot Spot now? Gone like the flowers that wither in the first frost. The lion and the lizard kept the courts where Jamshyd gloried and—after hours, unfortunately, which had started all the trouble—drank deep. Ah well, life was pretty complex.

A voice from the other end of the wire broke in on his reverie. He recognized it as that of the porter of the block of flats where Sue had her tiny abode.

'Hullo? Bashford? Mr Carmody speaking. Will you make a long arm and haul Miss Brown to the instrument. Eh? Miss Sue Brown, of course. No other Browns are any use to me whatsoever. Right ho, I'll wait.'

The astute detective never permits himself to exhibit emotion. Pilbeam turned his start of surprise into a grave, distrait nod, as if he were thinking out deep problems. He took up his pen and drew three crosses and a squiggle on the blotting-paper. He was glad that no gentlemanly instinct had urged him to leave his visitor alone to do his telephoning.

'Mario's, eh?' said Hugo. 'What's the band like?'

'It's Leopold's.'

'Good enough for me,' said Hugo with enthusiasm. He hummed a bar or two, and slid his feet dreamily about the carpet. 'I'm shockingly out of practice, dash it. Well, that's that. Touching this other matter, you're sure you won't come to Blandings?'

'Quite.'

'Nice place. Gravel soil, spreading views, well laid-out pleasure grounds, Company's own water . . . I would strongly advise you to bring your magnifying-glass and spend the summer. However, if you really feel . . . Sue! Hullo-ullo-ullo! This is Hugo. Yes, just up in town for the night on a mission of extraordinary secrecy and delicacy which I am not empowered to reveal. Speaking from the Argus Enquiry Agency, by courtesy of proprietor. I was wondering if you would care to come out and help me restore my lost youth, starting at about eight-thirty. Eh?'

A silence had fallen at the other end of the wire. What was happening was that in the hall of the block of flats Sue's conscience was fighting a grim battle against heavy odds. Ranged in opposition to it were her loneliness, her love of dancing and her desire once more to see Hugo, who, though he was not a man one could take seriously, always cheered her up and made her laugh. And she had been needing a laugh for days.

Hugo thought he had been cut off.

'Hullo-ullo-ullo-ullo-ullo-ullo!' he barked peevishly.

'Don't yodel like that,' said Sue. 'You've nearly made me deaf.'

'Sorry, dear heart. I thought the machine had conked. Well, how do you react? Is it a bet?'

'I do want to see you again,' said Sue, hesitatingly.

'You shall. In person. Clean shirt, white waistcoat, the Carmody studs, and everything.'

'Well . . . !'

A psychically gifted bystander, standing in the hall of the block of flats, would have heard at this moment a faint moan. It was Sue's conscience collapsing beneath an unexpected flank attack. She had just remembered that if she went to dine with Hugo she would learn all the latest news about Ronnie. It put the whole thing in an entirely different light. Surely Ronnie himself could have no objection to the proposed feast if he knew that all she was going for was to talk about him? She might dance a little, of course, but purely by the way. Her real motive in accepting the invitation, she now realized quite clearly, was to hear all about Ronnie.

'All right,' she said. 'Where?'

'Mario's. They tell me it's the posh spot these days.'

'Mario's?'

'Yes. M for mange, A for asthma, R for rheumatism . . . oh, you've got it? All right, then. At eight-thirty.'

Hugo put the receiver back. Once more he allowed his dazzling smile to play upon the Argus's proprietor.

'Much obliged for use of instrument,' he said. 'Thank you.'

'Thank *you*,' said Pilbeam.

'Well, I'll be pushing along. Ring us up if you change your mind. Market Blandings 32X. If you don't take on the job no one will. I suppose there are other sleuths in London besides the bevy I've interviewed to-day, but I'm not going to see them. I consider that I have done my bit and am through.' He looked about him. 'Make a good thing out of this business?' he asked, for he was curious on these points and was never restrained by delicacy from seeking information.

'Quite.'

'What does the work consist of? I've often wondered. Measuring foot-prints and putting the tips of your fingers together, and all that, I suppose?'

'We are frequently asked to follow people and report on their movements.'

Hugo laughed amusedly.

'Well, don't go following me and reporting on my movements. Much trouble might ensue. Bung-oh.'

'Good-bye,' said Percy Pilbeam.

He pressed a bell on the desk, and moved to the door to show his visitor out.

· II ·

Leopold's justly famous band, its cheeks puffed out and its eyeballs roll-ing, was playing a popular melody with lots of stomp in it, and for the first time since she had accepted Hugo's invitation to the dance, Sue, glid-ing round the floor, was conscious of a spiritual calm. Her conscience, quieted by the moaning of the saxophones, seemed to have retired from business. It realized, no doubt, the futility of trying to pretend that there was anything wrong in a girl enjoying this delightful exercise.

How absurd, she felt, Ronnie's objections were. It was, considered Sue, becoming analytical, as if she were to make a tremendous fuss because he played tennis and golf with girls. Dancing was just a game like those two pastimes, and it so happened that you had to have a man with you or you couldn't play it. To get all jealous and throaty just because one went out dancing was simply ridiculous.

On the other hand, placid though her conscience now was, she had to admit that it was a relief to feel that he would never know of this little outing.

Men were such children when they were in love. Sue found herself sighing over the opposite sex's eccentricities. If they were only sensible, how simple life would be. It amazed her that Ronnie could ever have any possible doubt, however she might spend her leisure hours, that her heart belonged to him alone. She marvelled that he should suppose for a moment that even if she danced all night and every night with every other man in the world it would make any difference to her feelings towards him.

All the same, holding the peculiar views he did, he must undoubtedly be humoured.

'You won't breathe a word to Ronnie about our coming here, will you, Hugo?' she said, repeating an injunction which had been her opening speech on arriving at the restaurant.

'Not a syllable.'

'I can trust you?'

'Implicitly. Telegraphic address, Discretion, Market Blandings.'

'Ronnie's funny, you see.'

'One long scream.'

'I mean, he wouldn't understand.'

'No. Great surprise it was to me,' said Hugo, doing complicated things with his feet, 'to hear that you and the old hound had decided to team up. You could have knocked me down with a feather. Odd he never confided in his boyhood friend.'

'Well, it wouldn't do for it to get about.'

'Are you suggesting that Hugo Carmody is a babbler?'

'You do like gossiping. You know you do.'

'I know nothing of the sort,' said Hugo with dignity. 'If I were asked to give my opinion, I should say that I was essentially a strong, silent man.'

He made a complete circle of the floor in that capacity. His taciturnity surprised Sue.

'What's the matter?' she asked.

'Dudgeon,' said Hugo.

'What?'

'I'm sulking. That remark of yours rankles. That totally unfounded accusation that I cannot keep a secret. It may interest you to know that I, too, am secretly engaged and have never so much as mentioned it to a soul.'

'Hugo!'

'Yes. Betrothed. And so at long last came a day when Love wound his silken fetters about Hugo Carmody.'

'Who's the unfortunate girl?'

'There is no unfortunate girl. The lucky girl . . . Was that your foot?'

'Yes.'

'Sorry. I haven't got the hang of these new steps yet. The lucky girl, I was saying, is Miss Millicent Threepwood.'

As if stunned by the momentousness of the announcement, the band stopped playing; and, chancing to be immediately opposite their table, the man who never revealed secrets led his partner to her chair. She was gazing at him ecstatically.

'You don't mean that?'

'I do mean that. What did you think I meant?'

'I never heard anything so wonderful in my life!'

'Good news?'

'I'm simply delighted.'

'I'm pleased, too,' said Hugo.

'I've been trying not to admit it to myself, but I was very scared about Millicent. Ronnie told me the family wanted him and her to marry, and you never know what may happen when families throw their weight about. And now it's all right!'

'Quite all right.'

The music had started again, but Sue remained in her seat.

'Not?' said Hugo, astonished.

'Not just yet. I want to talk. You don't realize what this means to me. Besides, your dancing's gone off, Hugo. You're not the man you were.'

'I need practice.' He lit a cigarette and tapped a philosophical vein of thought, eyeing the gyrating couples meditatively. 'It's the way they're always introducing new steps that bothers the man who has been living out in the woods. I have become a rusty rustic.'

'I didn't mean you were bad. Only you used to be such a marvel. Dancing with you was like floating on a pink cloud above an ocean of bliss.'

'A very accurate description, I should imagine,' agreed Hugo. 'But don't blame me. Blame these Amalgamated Professors of the Dance, or whatever they call themselves—the birds who get together every couple of weeks or so to decide how they can make things more difficult. Amazing thing that they won't leave well alone.'

'You must have change.'

'I disagree with you,' said Hugo. 'No other walk in life is afflicted by a gang of thugs who are perpetually altering the rules of the game. When you learn to play golf, the professional doesn't tell you to bring the club up slowly and keep the head steady and roll the forearms and bend the left knee and raise the left heel and keep your eye on the ball and not sway back and a few more things, and then, after you've sweated yourself to the bone learning all that, suddenly add "Of course, you understand that this is merely intended to see you through till about three weeks from next Thursday. After that the Supreme Grand Council of Consolidated Divot-Shifters will scrap these methods and invent an entirely new set!"'

'Is this more dudgeon?'

'No. Not dudgeon.'

'It sounds like dudgeon. I believe your little feelings are hurt because I said your dancing wasn't as good as it used to be.'

'Not at all. We welcome criticism.'

'Well, get your mind off it and tell me all about you and Millicent and . . .'

'When I was about five,' resumed Hugo, removing his cigarette from the holder and inserting another, 'I attended my first dancing-school. I'm a bit shaky on some of the incidents of the days when I was trailing clouds of glory, but I do remember that dancing-school. At great trouble and expense I was taught to throw up a rubber ball with my left hand and catch it with my right, keeping the small of the back rigid and generally behaving in a graceful and attractive manner. It doesn't sound a likely sort of thing to learn at a dancing-school, but I swear to you that that's what the curriculum was. Now, the point I am making . . .'

'Did you fall in love with Millicent right away, or was it gradual?'

'The point I am making is this. I became very good at throwing and catching that rubber ball. I dislike boasting, but I stood out conspicuously among a pretty hot bunch. People would nudge each other and say "Who is he?" behind their hands. I don't suppose, when I was feeling right, I missed the rubber ball more than once in twenty goes. But what good does it do me now? Absolutely none. Long before I got a chance of exhibiting my accomplishment in public and having beautiful women fawn on me for my skill, the Society of Amalgamated Professors of the Dance decided that the Rubber-Ball Glide, or whatever it was called, was out of date.'

'Is she very pretty?'

'And what I say is that all this chopping and changing handicaps a chap. I am perfectly prepared at this moment to step out on that floor and heave a rubber ball about, but it simply isn't being done nowadays. People wouldn't understand what I was driving at. In other words, all the time and money and trouble that I spent on mastering the Rubber-Ball Shimmy is a dead loss. I tell you, if the Amalgamated Professors want to make people cynics, they're going the right way to work.'

'I wish you would tell me all about Millicent.'

'In a moment. Dancing, they taught me at school, dates back to the early Egyptians, who ascribed the invention to the god Thoth. The Phrygian Corybantes danced in honour of somebody whose name I've forgotten, and every time the festival of Rhea Silvia came round the ancient Roman hoofers were there with their hair in a braid. But what was good enough for the god Thoth isn't good enough for these blighted Amalgamated Professors! Oh no! And it's been the same all through the ages. I don't suppose there has been a moment in history when some poor, well-meaning devil, with ambition at one end of him and two left feet at the other, wasn't getting it in the neck.'

'And all this,' said Sue, 'because you trod on my foot for just one half-second.'

'Hugo Carmody dislikes to tread on women's feet, even for half a second. He has his pride. Ever hear of Father Mariana?'

'No.'

'Mariana, George. Born twelve hundred and something. Educated privately and at Leipzig University. Hobbies, fishing, illuminating vellum and mangling the wurzel. You must have heard of old Pop Mariana?'

'I haven't, and I don't want to. I want to hear about Millicent.'

'It was the opinion of Father Mariana that dancing was a deadly sin. He was particularly down, I may mention, on the saraband. He said the saraband did more harm than the Plague. I know just how he felt. I'll bet he had worked like a dog at twenty-five pazazas the complete course of twelve lessons, guaranteed to teach the fandango: and, just when his instructor had finally told him that he was fit to do it at the next Saturday Night Social, along came the Amalgamated Brothers with their new-fangled saraband, and where was Pop? Leaning against the wall with the other foot-and-mouth diseasers, trying to pretend dancing bored him. Did I hear you say you wanted a few facts about Millicent?'

'You did.'

'Sweetest girl on earth.'

'Really?'

'Absolutely. It's well known. All over Shropshire.'

'And she really loves you?'

'Between you and me,' said Hugo confidentially, 'I don't wonder you speak in that amazed tone. If you saw her, you'd be still more surprised. I am a man who thinks before he speaks. I weigh my words. And I tell you solemnly that that girl is too good for me.'

'But you're a sweet darling precious pet.'

'I know I'm a sweet darling precious pet. Nevertheless, I still maintain that she is too good for me. She is the nearest thing to an angel that ever came glimmering through the laurels in the quiet evenfall in the garden by the turrets of the old manorial hall.'

'Hugo! I'd no idea you were so poetical.'

'Enough to make a chap poetical, loving a girl like that.'

'And you really do love her?'

Hugo took a feverish gulp of champagne and rolled his eyeballs as if he had been a member of Leopold's justly famous band.

'Madly. Devotedly. And when I think how I have deceived her my soul sickens.'

'Have you deceived her?'

'Not yet. But I'm going to in about five minutes. I put in a phone call to Blandings just now, and when I get through I shall tell her I'm speaking from my hotel bedroom, where I am on the point of going to bed. You see,' said Hugo confidentially, 'Millicent, though practically perfect in every other respect, is one of those girls who might misunderstand this little night out of mine, did it but come to her ears. Speaking of which, you ought to see them. Like alabaster shells.'

'I know what you mean. Ronnie's like that.'

Hugo stared.

'Ronnie?'

'Yes.'

'You mean to sit there and tell me that Ronnie's ears are like alabaster shells?'

'No, I meant that he would be furious if he knew that I had come out dancing. And, oh, I do love dancing so,' sighed Sue.

'He must never know!'

'No. That's why I asked you just now not to tell him.'

'I won't. Secrecy and silence. Thank goodness there's nobody who could tell Millicent, even if they wanted to. Ah! This must be the bringer of glad tidings, come to say my call is through. All set?' he asked the pageboy who had threaded his way through the crowd to their table.

'Yes, sir.'

Hugo rose.

'Amuse yourself somehow till I return.'

'I shan't be dull,' said Sue.

She watched him disappear, then leaned back in her seat, watching the dancers. Her eyes were bright, and Hugo's news had brought a flush to her cheeks. Percy Pilbeam, who had been hovering in the background, hoping for such an opportunity ever since his arrival at the restaurant, thought he had never seen her looking prettier. He edged between the tables and took Hugo's vacated chair. There are men who, approaching a member of the other sex, wait for permission before sitting down, and men who sit down without permission. Pilbeam was one of the latter.

'Good evening,' he said.

She turned, and was aware of a nasty-looking little man at her elbow. He seemed to have materialized from nowhere.

'May I introduce myself, Miss Brown?' said this blot. 'My name is Pilbeam.'

At the same moment there appeared in the doorway and stood there raking the restaurant with burning eyes the flannel-suited figure of Ronald Overbury Fish.

· III ·

Ronnie Fish's estimate of the time necessary for reaching London from Blandings Castle in a sports-model two-seater had been thrown out of gear by two mishaps. Half-way down the drive the car had developed some mysterious engine-trouble, which had necessitated taking it back to the stables and having it overhauled by Lord Emsworth's chauffeur. It was not until nearly an hour later that he had been able to resume his journey, and a blowout near Oxford had delayed him still further. He arrived at Sue's flat just as Sue and Hugo were entering Mario's.

Ringing Sue's front-door bell produced no result. Ronnie regretted that in the stress of all the other matters that occupied his mind he had forgotten to send her a telegram. He was about to creep away and have a bite of dinner at the Drones Club—a prospect which pleased him not at all, for the Drones at dinner-time was always full of hearty eggs who talked much too loud for a worried man's nerves, and might even go so far as to throw bread at him, when, descending the stairs into the hall, he came upon Bashford, the porter.

Bashford, who knew Ronnie well, said "Ullo, Mr Fish,' and Ronnie said 'Hullo, Bashford,' and Bashford said the weather seemed to keep up, and Ronnie said 'Yes, that's right, it did,' and it was at this point that the porter uttered these memorable—and, as events proved, epoch-making words:

'If you're looking for Miss Brown, Mr Fish, I've an idea she's gone to a place called Mario's.'

He poured further details into Ronnie's throbbing ear. Mr Carmody had rung up on the phone, might have been ar-parse four, and he, Bashford, not listening but happening to hear, had thought he had caught something said about this place Mario's.

'Mario's?' said Ronnie. 'Thanks, Bashford. Mario's, eh? Right!'

The porter, for Eton and Cambridge train their sons well, found nothing in the way Mr Fish spoke to cause a thrill. Totally unaware that he had been conversing with Othello's younger brother, he went back to his den in the basement and sat down with a good appetite to steak and chips. And Ronnie, quivering from head to foot, started the car and drove off.

Jealousy, said Shakespeare, and he was about right, is the green-eyed monster which doth mock the meat he feeds on. By the time Ronald Overbury Fish pushed through the swinging-door that guards the revelry at Mario's from the gaze of the passer-by, he was, like the Othello he so much resembled, perplexed in the extreme. He felt hot all over, then cold all over, then hot again, and the waiter who stopped him on the threshold of the dining-room to inform him that evening-dress was indispensable on the dancing-floor, and that flannel suits must go up to the balcony, was running a risk which would have caused his insurance company to purse its lips and shake its head.

Fortunately for him, Ronnie did not hear. He was scanning the crowd before him in an effort to find Sue.

'Plenty of room in the balcony, sir,' urged the waiter, continuing to play with fire.

This time Ronnie did become dimly aware that somebody was

addressing him, and he was about to turn and give the man one look, when half-way down a grove of black coats and gaily-decorated frocks he suddenly saw what he was searching for. The next moment he was pushing a path through the throng, treading on the toes of brave men and causing fair women to murmur bitterly that this sort of thing ought to be prevented by the management.

Five yards from Sue's table, Ronnie Fish would have said that his cup was full and could not possibly be made any fuller. But when he had covered another two and pushed aside a fat man who was standing in the fairway, he realized his mistake. It was not Hugo who was Sue's companion, but a reptilian-looking squirt with narrow eyes and his hair done in ridges. And, as he saw him, something seemed to go off in Ronnie's brain like a released spring.

A waiter, pausing with a tray of glasses, pointed out to him that on the dancing-floor evening-dress was indispensable.

Gentleman in flannel suits, he added, could be accommodated in the balcony.

'Plenty of room in the balcony, sir,' said the waiter.

Ronnie reached the table. Pilbeam at the moment was saying that he had wanted for a long time to meet Sue. He hoped she had got his flowers all right.

It was perhaps a natural desire to look at anything but this odious and thrusting individual who had forced his society upon her, that caused Sue to raise her eyes.

Raising them, she met Ronnie's. And, as she saw him, her conscience, which she had supposed lulled for the night, sprang to life more vociferous than ever. It had but been crouching, the better to spring.

'Ronnie!'

She started up. Pilbeam also rose. The waiter with the glasses pressed the edge of his tray against Ronnie's elbow in a firm but respectful manner and told him that on the dancing-floor evening-dress was indispensable. Gentleman in flannel suits, however, would find ample accommodation in the balcony.

Ronnie did not speak. And it would have been better if Sue had not done so. For, at this crisis, some subconscious instinct, of the kind which is always waiting to undo us at critical moments, suggested to her dazed mind that when men who do not know each other are standing side by side in a restaurant one ought to introduce them.

'Mr Fish, Mr Pilbeam,' murmured Sue.

Only the ringing of the bell that heralds the first round a heavy-weight championship fight could have produced more instant and violent results. Through Ronnie's flannel-clad body a sort of galvanic shock seemed to pass. Pilbeam! He had come expecting Hugo, and Hugo would have been bad enough. But Pilbeam! The man she had said she didn't even know. The man she hadn't met. The man whose gifts of flowers she had professed to resent. In person! In the flesh! Hobnobbing with her in a restaurant! By Gad, he meant to say! By George! Good Gosh!

His fist clenched. Eton was forgotten, Cambridge not even a memory. He inhaled so sharply that a man at the next table who was eating a mousse of chicken stabbed himself in the chin with his fork. He turned on Pilbeam with a hungry look. And at this moment, the waiter, raising his voice a little, for he was beginning to think that Ronnie's hearing was slightly affected, mentioned as an interesting piece of information that the management of Mario's preferred to reserve the dancing-floor exclusively for clients in evening-dress. But there was a bright side. Gentlemen in flannel suits could be accommodated in the balcony.

It was the waiter who saved Percy Pilbeam. Just as a mosquito may divert for an instant a hunter who is about to spring at and bite in the neck a tiger of the jungle, so did this importunate waiter divert Ronnie Fish. What it was all about, he was too overwrought to ascertain, but he knew that the man was annoying him, pestering him, trying to chat with him when he had business elsewhere. With all the force of a generous nature, sorely tried, he plugged the waiter in the stomach with his elbow. There was a crash which even Leopold's band could not drown. The man who had stabbed himself with the fork had his meal still further spoiled by the fact that it suddenly began to rain glass. And, as regards the other occupants of the restaurant, the word 'Sensation' about sums the situation up.

Ronnie and the management of Mario's now formed two sharply contrasted schools of thought. To Ronnie the only thing that seemed to matter was this Pilbeam—this creeping, slinking, cuckoo-in-the-nest Pilbeam, the Lothario who had lowered all speed records in underhand villainy by breaking up his home before he had got one. He concentrated all his faculties to the task of getting round the table, to the other side of which the object of his dislike had prudently withdrawn, and showing him in no uncertain manner where he got off.

To the management, on the other hand, the vital issue was all this broken glassware. The waiter had risen from the floor, but the glasses were still there, and scarcely one of them was in a condition ever to be used again for the refreshment of Mario's customers. The head-waiter, swooping down on the fray like some god in the Iliad descending from a cloud, was endeavouring to place this point of view before Ronnie. Assisting him with word and gesture were two inferior waiters—Waiter A and Waiter B.

Ronnie was in no mood for abstract debate. He hit the headwaiter in the abdomen, Waiter A in the ribs, and was just about to dispose of Waiter B, when his activities were hampered by the sudden arrival of reinforcements. From all parts of the room other waiters had assembled—to name but a few, Waiters C, D, E, F, G, and H—and he found himself hard pressed. It seemed to him that he had dropped into a Waiter's Convention. As far as the eye could reach, the arena was crammed with waiters, and more coming. Pilbeam had disappeared altogether, and so busy was Ronnie now that he did not even miss him. He had reached that condition of mind which the old Vikings used to call Berserk and which among modern Malays is termed running amok.

Ronnie Fish in the course of his life had had many ambitions. As a child, he had yearned some day to become an engine-driver. At school, it had seemed to him that the most attractive career the world had to offer was that of the professional cricketer. Later, he had hoped to run a prosperous night-club. But now, in his twenty-sixth year, all these desires were cast aside and forgotten. The only thing in life that seemed really worth while was to massacre waiters; and to this task he addressed himself with all the energy and strength at his disposal.

Matters now began to move briskly. Waiter C, who rashly clutched the sleeve of Ronnie's coat, reeled back with a hand pressed to his right eye. Waiter D, a married man, contented himself with standing on the outskirts and talking Italian. But Waiter E, made of sterner stuff, hit Ronnie rather hard with a dish containing *omelette aux champignons*, and it was as the latter reeled beneath this buffet that there suddenly appeared in the forefront of the battle a figure wearing a gay uniform and almost completely concealed behind a vast moustache, waxed at the ends. It was the commissionaire from the street-door; and anybody who has ever been bounced from a restaurant knows that commissionaires are heavy metal.

This one, whose name was McTeague, and who had spent many lively years in the army before retiring to take up his present duties, had a grim face made of some hard kind of wood and the muscles of a village blacksmith. A man of action rather than words, he clove his way through the press in silence. Only when he reached the centre of the maelstrom did he speak. This was when Ronnie, leaping upon a chair the better to perform the operation, hit him on the nose. On receipt of this blow, he uttered the brief monosyllable 'Ho!' and then, without more delay, scooped Ronnie into an embrace of steel and bore him towards the door, through which was now moving a long, large, leisurely policeman.

· IV ·

It was some few minutes later that Hugo Carmody, emerging from the telephone-booth on the lower floor where the cocktail bar is, sauntered back into the dancing-room and was interested to find waiters massaging bruised limbs, other waiters replacing fallen tables, and Leopold's band playing in a sort of hushed undertone like a band that has seen strange things.

'Hullo!' said Hugo. 'Anything up?'

He eyed Sue inquiringly. She looked to him like a girl who has had some sort of a shock. Not, or his eyes deceived him, at all her old bright self.

'What's up?' he asked.

'Take me home, Hugo!'

Hugo stared.

'Home? Already? With the night yet young?'

'Oh, Hugo, take me home, quick.'

'Just as you say,' assented Hugo agreeably. He was now pretty certain that something was up. 'One second to settle the bill, then homeward ho. And on the way you shall tell me all about it. For I jolly well know,' said Hugo, who prided himself on his keenness of observation, 'that something is—or has been—up.'

5

A PHONE CALL FOR HUGO

THE Law of Great Britain is a remorseless machine, which, once set in motion, ignores first causes and takes into account only results. It will not accept shattered dreams as an excuse for shattering glassware; nor will you get far by pleading a broken heart in extenuation of your behaviour in breaking waiters. Haled on the morrow before the awful majesty of Justice at Bosher Street Police Court and charged with disorderly conduct in a public place—to wit, Mario's Restaurant, and resisting an officer—to wit, P.C. Murgatroyd, in the execution of his duties, Ronald Fish made no impassioned speeches. He did not raise clenched fists aloft and call upon heaven to witness that he was a good man wronged. Experience, dearly bought in the days of his residence at the University, had taught him that when the Law gripped you with its talons the only thing to do was to give a false name, say nothing and hope for the best.

Shortly before noon, accordingly, on the day following the painful scene just described, Edwin Jones, of 7 Nasturtium Villas, Cricklewood, poorer by the sum of five pounds, was being conveyed in a swift taxi-cab to his friend Hugo Carmody's hotel, there to piece together his broken life and try to make a new start.

On the part of the man Jones himself during the ride there was a disposition towards silence. He gazed before him bleakly and gnawed his lower lip. Hugo Carmody, on the other hand, was inclined to be rather jubilant. It seemed to Hugo that after a rocky start things had panned out pretty well.

'A nice, smooth job,' he said approvingly. 'I was scanning the beak's face closely during the summing up and I couldn't help fearing for a moment that it was going to be a case of fourteen days without the option. As it is, here you are, a free man, and no chance of your name being in the papers. A moral victory, I call it.'

Ronnie released his lower lip in order to bare his teeth in a bitter sneer.

'I wouldn't care if my name were in every paper in London.'

'Oh, come, old loofah! The honoured name of Fish?'

'What do I care about anything now?'

Hugo was concerned. This morbid strain, he felt, was unworthy of a Nasturtium Villas Jones.

'Aren't you rather tending to make a bit too much heavy weather over this?'

'Heavy weather!'

'I think you are. After all, when you come right down to it, what has happened? You find poor little Sue . . .'

'Don't call her "poor little Sue"!'

'You find the party of the second part,' amended Hugo, 'at a dance place. Well, why not? What, if you follow me, of it? Where's the harm in her going out to dance?'

'With a man she swore she didn't know!'

'Well, at the time when you asked her, probably she didn't know him. Things move quickly in a great city. I wish I had a quid for every girl I've been out dancing with, whom I hadn't known from Eve a couple of days before.'

'She promised me she wouldn't go out with a soul.'

'Ah, but with a merry twinkle in her eye, no doubt? I mean to say, you can't expect a girl nowadays to treat a promise like that seriously. I mean, dash it, be reasonable!'

'And with that little worm of all people!'

Hugo cleared his throat. He was conscious of a slight embarrassment. He had not wished to touch on this aspect of the affair, but Ronnie's last words gave a Carmody and a gentleman no choice.

'As a matter of fact, Ronnie, old man,' he said, 'you are wrong in supposing that she went to Mario's with the above Pilbeam. She went with me. Blameless Hugo, what. I mean, more like a brother than anything.'

Ronnie declined to be comforted.

'I don't believe you.'

'My dear chap!'

'I suppose you think you're damned clever, trying to smooth things over. She was at Mario's with Pilbeam.'

'I took her there.'

'You may have taken her. But she was dining with Pilbeam.'

'Nothing of the kind.'

'Do you think I can't believe my own eyes? It's no use your saying anything, Hugo, I'm through with her. She's let me down. Less than a week I've been away,' said Ronnie, his voice trembling, 'and she lets me down. Well, it serves me right for being such a fool as to think she ever cared a curse for me.'

He relapsed into silence. And Hugo, after turning over in his mind a few specimen remarks, decided not to make them. The cab drew up before the hotel, and Ronnie, getting out, uttered a wordless exclamation.

'No, let me,' said Hugo considerately. A bit rough on a man, he felt, after coughing up five quid to the hell-hounds of the Law, to be expected to pay the cab. He produced money and turned to the driver. It was some moments before he turned back again, for the driver, by the rules of the taxi-chauffeurs' Union, kept his petty cash tucked into his underclothing. When he did so, he was considerably astonished to find that Ronnie, while his back was turned, had, in some unaccountable manner, become Sue. The changeling was staring unhappily at him from the exact spot where he had left his old friend.

'Hullo!' he said.

'Ronnie's gone,' said Sue.

'Gone?'

'Yes. He walked off as quick as he could round the corner when he saw me. He . . .' Sue's voice broke. 'He didn't say a word.'

'How did you get here?' asked Hugo. There were other matters, of course, to be discussed later, but he felt he must get this point cleared up first.

'I thought you would bring him back to your hotel, and I thought that if I could see him I could . . . say something.'

Hugo was alarmed. He was now practically certain that this girl was going to cry, and if there was one thing he disliked it was being with crying girls in a public spot. He would not readily forget the time when a female named Yvonne Something had given way to a sudden twinge of neuralgia in his company not far from Piccadilly Circus, and an old lady had stopped and said that it was brutes like him who caused all the misery in the world.

'Come inside,' he urged quickly. 'Come and have a cocktail or a cup of tea or a bun or something. I say,' he said, as he led the way into the hotel lobby and found two seats in a distant corner. 'I'm frightfully sorry about all this. I can't help feeling it's my fault.'

'Oh, no.'

'If I hadn't asked you to dinner . . .'

'It isn't that that's the trouble. Ronnie might have been a little cross for a minute or two if he had found you and me together, but he would soon have got over it. It was finding me with that horrid little man Pilbeam. You see, I told him—and it was quite true—that I didn't know him.'

'Yes, so he was saying to me in the cab.'

'Did he—what did he say?'

'Well, he plainly resented the Pilbeam, I'm afraid. His manner, when touching on the Pilbeam, was austere. I tried to drive into his head that that was just an accidental meeting and that you had come to Mario's with me, but he would have none of it. I fear, old thing, there's nothing to be done but leave the whole binge to Time, the Great Healer.'

A page-boy was making a tour of the lobby. He seemed to be seeking a Mr Gregory.

'If only I could get hold of him and make him listen. I haven't been given a chance to explain.'

'You think you could explain, even if given a chance?'

'I could try. Surely he couldn't help seeing that I really loved him, if we had a real talk?'

'And the trouble is, you're here and he'll be back at Blandings in a few hours. Difficult,' said Hugo, shaking his head. 'Complex.'

'Mr Carmody,' chanted the page-boy, coming nearer. 'Mr Carmody.'

'Hi!' cried Hugo.

'Mr Carmody? Wanted on the telephone, sir.'

Hugo's face became devout and saint-like.

'Awfully sorry to leave you for an instant,' he said, 'but do you mind if I rush? It must be Millicent. She's the only person who knows I'm here.'

He sped away, and Sue, watching him, found herself choking with sudden tears. It seemed to emphasize her forlornness so, this untimely evidence of another love-story that had not gone awry. She seemed to be listening to that telephone-conversation, hearing Hugo's delighted yelps as the voice of the girl he loved floated to him over the wire.

She pulled herself together. Beastly of her to be jealous of Hugo just because he was happy. . . .

Sue sat up abruptly. She had had an idea.

It was a breath-taking idea, but simple. It called for courage, for audacity, for a reckless disregard of consequences, but nevertheless it was simple.

'Hugo,' she cried, as that lucky young man returned and dropped into the chair at her side. 'Hugo, listen!'

'I say,' said Hugo.

'I've suddenly thought . . .'

'I say,' said Hugo.

'Do listen!'

'I say,' said Hugo, 'that was Millicent on the phone.'

'Was it? How nice. Listen, Hugo . . .'

'Speaking from Blandings.'

'Yes. But . . .'

'And she has broken off the engagement!'

'What!'

'Broken off the bally engagement,' repeated Hugo. He signalled urgently to a passing waiter. 'Get me a brandy-and-soda, will you?' he said. His face was pale and set. 'A stiffish brandy-and-soda, please.'

'Brandy-and-soda, sir?'

'Yes,' said Hugo. 'Stiffish.'

$$\boxed{6}$$

SUE HAS AN IDEA

S UE stared at him, bewildered.
'Broken off the engagement?'
'Broken off the engagement.'

In moments of stress, the foolish question is always the one that comes uppermost in the mind.

'Are you sure?'

Hugo emitted a sound which resembled the bursting of a paper bag. He would have said himself, if asked, that he was laughing mirthlessly.

'Sure? Not much doubt about it.'

'But why?'

'She knows all.'

'All what?'

'Everything, you poor fish,' said Hugo, forgetting in a strong man's agony the polish of the Carmodys. 'She's found out that I took you to dinner last night.'

'What!'

'She has.'

'But how?'

The paper bag exploded again. A look of intense bitterness came into Hugo's face.

'If ever I meet that slimy, slinking, marcel-waved by-product Pilbeam again,' he said, 'let him commend his soul to God! If he has time,' he added.

He took the brandy-and-soda from the waiter, and eyed Sue dully.

'Anything on similar lines for you?'

'No, thanks.'

'Just as you like. It's not easy for a man in my position to realize,' said Hugo, drinking deeply, 'that refusing a brandy-and-soda is possible. I shouldn't have said, off-hand, that it could be done.'

Sue was a warm-hearted girl. In the tragedy of this announcement she had almost forgotten that she had troubles herself.

'Tell me all about it, Hugo.'

He put down the empty glass.

'I came up from Blandings yesterday,' he said, 'to interview the Argus Enquiry Agency on the subject of sending a man down to investigate the theft of Lord Emsworth's pig.'

Sue would have liked to hear more about this pig, but she knew that this was no time for questions.

'I went to the Argus and saw this wen Pilbeam, who runs it.'

Again Sue would have liked to speak. Once more she refrained. She felt as if she were at a sick-bed, hearing a dying man's last words. On such occasions one does not interrupt.

'Meanwhile,' proceeded Hugo tonelessly, 'Millicent, suspecting—and I am surprised at her having a mind like that. I always looked on her as a pure, white soul—suspecting that I might be up to something in London, got the Argus on the long-distance telephone and told them to follow my movements and report to her. And, apparently, just before she called me up, she had been talking to them on the wire and getting their statement. All this she revealed to me in short, burning sentences, and then she said that if I thought we were still engaged, I could have three more guesses. But, to save me trouble, she would tell me the answer—viz.: No wedding-bells for me. And to think,' said Hugo, picking up the glass and putting it down again, after inspection, with a hurt and disappointed look, 'that I actually rallied this growth Pilbeam on the subject of following people and reporting on their movements. Yes, I assure you. Rallied him blithely. Just as I was leaving his office, we kidded merrily back and forth. And then I went out into the world, happy and carefree, little knowing that my every step was dogged by a blasted bloodhound. Well, all I can say is that, if Ronnie wants this Pilbeam's gore, and I gather that he does, he will jolly well have to wait till I've helped myself.'

Sue, womanlike, blamed the woman.

'I don't think Millicent can be a very nice girl,' she said, primly.

'An angel,' said Hugo. 'Always was. Celebrated for it. I don't blame her.'

'I do.'

'I don't.'

'I do.'

'Well, have it your own way,' said Hugo handsomely. He beckoned to the waiter. 'Another of the same, please.'

'This settles it,' said Sue.

Her eyes were sparkling. Her chin a resolute tilt.

'Settles what?'

'While you were at the telephone, I had an idea.'

'I have had ideas in my time,' said Hugo. 'Many of them. At the moment, I have but one. To get within arm's length of the yam Pilbeam and twist his greasy neck till it comes apart in my hands. "What do you do here?" I said. "Measure footprints?" "We follow people and report on their movements," said he. "Ha, ha!" I laughed carelessly. "Ha, ha!" laughed he. General mirth and jollity. And all the while . . .'

'Hugo, will you listen?'

'And this is the bitter thought that now strikes me. What chance have I of scooping out the man's inside with my bare hands? I've got to go back to Blandings on the two-fifteen, or I lose my job. Leaving him unscathed in his bally lair, chuckling over my downfall and following some other poor devil's movements.'

'Hugo!'

The broken man passed a weary hand over his forehead.

'You spoke?'

'I've been speaking for the last ten minutes, only you won't listen.'

'Say on,' said Hugo, listlessly starting on the second restorative.

'Have you ever heard of a Miss Schoonmaker?'

'I seem to know the name. Who is she?'

'Me.'

Hugo lowered his glass, pained.

'Don't talk drip to a broken-hearted man,' he begged. 'What do you mean?'

'When Ronnie was driving me in his car, we met Lady Constance Keeble.'

'A blister,' said Hugo. 'Always was. Generally admitted all over Shropshire.'

'She thought I was this Miss Schoonmaker.'

'Why?'

'Because Ronnie said I was.'

Hugo sighed hopelessly.

'Complex. Complex. My God! How complex.'

'It was quite simple and natural. Ronnie had just been telling me about this girl—how he had met her at Biarritz and that she was coming to Blandings and so on, and when he saw Lady Constance looking at me with frightful suspicion it suddenly occurred to him to say that I was her.'

'That you were Lady Constance?'

'No, idiot. Miss Schoonmaker. And now I'm going to wire her—Lady Constance, not Miss Schoonmaker, in case you were going to ask—saying that I'm coming to Blandings right away.'

'Pretending to be this Miss Schoonmaker?'

'Yes.'

Hugo shook his head.

'Imposs.'

'Why?'

'Absolutely out of the q.'

'Why? Lady Constance is expecting me. Do be sensible.'

'I'm being sensible all right. But somebody is gibbering and, naming no names, it's you. Don't you realize that, just as you reach the front door, this Miss Schoonmaker will arrive in person, dishing the whole thing?'

'No, she won't.'

'Why won't she?'

'Because Ronnie sent her a telegram, in Lady Constance's name, saying that there's scarlet fever or something at Blandings and she wasn't to come.'

Hugo's air of the superior critic fell from him like a garment. He sat up in his chair. So moved was he that he spilled his brandy-and-soda and did not give it so much as a look of regret. He let it soak into the carpet, unheeded.

'Sue!'

'Once I'm at Blandings, I shall be able to see Ronnie and make him be sensible.'

'That's right.'

'And then you'll be able to tell Millicent that there couldn't have been much harm in my being out with you last night, because I'm engaged to Ronnie.'

'That's right, too.'

'Can you see any flaws?'

'Not a flaw.'

'I suppose, as a matter of fact, you'll give the whole thing away in the first five minutes by calling me Sue.'

Hugo waved an arm buoyantly.

'Don't give the possibility another thought,' he said. 'If I do, I'll cover it up adroitly by saying I meant, "Schoo". Short for Schoonmaker. And now go and send her another telegram. Keep on sending telegrams. Leave nothing to chance. Send a dozen and pitch it strong. Say that Blandings Castle is ravaged with disease. Not merely scarlet fever. Scarlet fever *and* mumps. Not to mention housemaid's knee, diabetes, measles, shingles, and the botts. We're on to a big thing, my Susan. Let us push it along.'

7

A JOB FOR PERCY PILBEAM

· I ·

Sunshine, calling to all right-thinking men to come out and revel in its heartening warmth, poured in at the windows of the great library of Blandings Castle. But to Clarence, ninth Earl of Emsworth, much as he liked sunshine as a rule, it brought no cheer. His face drawn, his pince-nez askew, his tie drooping away from its stud like a languorous lily, he sat staring sightlessly before him. He looked like something that had just been prepared for stuffing by a taxidermist.

A moralist, watching Lord Emsworth in his travail, would have reflected smugly that it cuts both ways, this business of being a peer of the realm with large private means and a good digestion. Unalloyed prosperity, he would have pointed out in his offensive way, tends to enervate; and in this world of ours, full of alarms and uncertainties, where almost anything is apt to drop suddenly on top of your head without warning at almost any moment, what one needs is to be tough and alert.

When some outstanding disaster happens to the ordinary man, it finds him prepared. Years of missing the eight-forty-five, taking the dog for a run on rainy nights, endeavouring to abate smoky chimneys, and coming down to breakfast and discovering that they have burned the bacon again, have given his soul a protective hardness, so that by the time his wife's relations arrive for a long visit he is ready for them.

Lord Emsworth had had none of this salutary training. Fate, hitherto, had seemed to spend its time thinking up ways of pampering him. He ate well, slept well, and had no money troubles. He grew the best roses in Shropshire. He had won a first prize for Pumpkins at that county's Agricultural Show, a thing no Earl of Emsworth had ever done before. And, just previous to the point at which this chronicle opens, his younger son, Frederick, had married the daughter of an American millionaire and had gone to live three thousand miles away from Blandings Castle, with lots of good, deep water in between him and it. He had come to look on himself as Fate's spoiled darling.

Can we wonder, then, that in the agony of this sudden, treacherous blow he felt stunned and looked eviscerated? Is it surprising that the sunshine made no appeal to him? May we not consider him justified, as he sat there, in swallowing a lump in his throat like an ostrich gulping down a brass door-knob?

The answer to these questions, in the order given, is No, No, and Yes.

The door of the library opened, revealing the natty person of his brother Galahad. Lord Emsworth straightened his pince-nez and looked at him apprehensively. Knowing how little reverence there was in the Hon. Galahad's composition, and how tepid was his interest in the honourable struggles for supremacy of Fat Pigs, he feared that the other was about to wound him in his bereavement with some jarring flippancy. Then his gaze softened and he was conscious of a soothing feeling of relief. There was no frivolity in his brother's face, only a gravity which became him well. The Hon. Galahad sat down, hitched up the knees of his trousers, cleared his throat, and spoke in a tone that could not have been more sympathetic or in better taste.

'Bad business, this, Clarence.'

'Appalling, my dear fellow.'

'What are you going to do about it?'

Lord Emsworth shrugged his shoulders hopelessly. He generally did when people asked him what he was going to do about things.

'I am at a loss,' he confessed. 'I do not know how to act. What young Carmody tells me has completely upset all my plans.'

'Carmody?'

'I sent him to the Argus Enquiry Agency in London to engage the services of a detective. It is a firm that Sir Gregory Parsloe once mentioned to me, in the days when we were on better terms. He said, in rather a meaning way, I thought, that if ever I had any trouble of any sort that needed expert and tactful handling, these were the people to go to. I gathered that they had assisted him in some matter the details of which he did not confide to me, and had given complete satisfaction.'

'Parsloe!' said the Hon. Galahad, and sniffed.

'So I sent young Carmody to London to approach them about finding the Empress. And now he tells me that his errand proved fruitless. They were firm in their refusal to trace missing pigs.'

'Just as well.'

'What do you mean?'

'Save you a lot of unnecessary expense. There's no need for you to waste money employing detectives.'

'I thought that possibly the trained mind . . .'

'I can tell you who's got the Empress. I've known it all along.'

'What!'

'Certainly.'

'Galahad!'

'It's as plain as the nose on your face.'

Lord Emsworth felt his nose.

'Is it?' he said doubtfully.

'I've just been talking to Constance . . .'

'Constance?' Lord Emsworth opened his mouth feebly. 'She hasn't got my pig?'

'I've just been talking to Constance,' repeated the Hon. Galahad, 'and she called me some very unpleasant names.'

'She does, sometimes. Even as a child, I remember . . .'

'Most unpleasant names. A senile mischief-maker, among others, and a meddling old penguin. And all because I told her that the man who had stolen Empress of Blandings was young Gregory Parsloe.'

'Parsloe!'

'Parsloe. Surely it's obvious? I should have thought it would have been clear to the meanest intelligence.'

From boyhood up, Lord Emsworth had possessed an intelligence about as mean as an intelligence can be without actually being placed under restraint. Nevertheless, he found his brother's theory incredible.

'Parsloe?'

'Don't keep saying "Parsloe".'

'But, my dear Galahad . . .'

'It stands to reason.'

'You don't really think so?'

'Of course I think so. Have you forgotten what I told you the other day?'

'Yes,' said Lord Emsworth. He always forgot what people told him the other day.

'About young Parsloe,' said the Hon. Galahad impatiently. 'About his nobbling my dog Towser.'

Lord Emsworth started. It all came back to him. A hard expression crept into the eyes behind the pince-nez, which emotion had just jerked crooked again.

'To be sure. Towser. Your dog. I remember.'

'He nobbled Towser, and he's nobbled the Empress. Dash it, Clarence, use your intelligence. Who else except young Parsloe had any interest in getting the Empress out of the way? And, if he hadn't known there was some dirty work being planned, would that pig-man of his, Brotherhood or whatever his name is, have been going about offering three to one on Pride of Matchingham? I told you at the time it was fishy.'

The evidence was damning, and yet Lord Emsworth found himself once more a prey to doubt. Of the blackness of Sir Gregory Parsloe-Parsloe's soul he had, of course, long been aware. But could the man actually be capable of the Crime of the Century? A fellow-landowner? A Justice of the Peace? A man who grew pumpkins? A Baronet?

'But Galahad . . . A man in Parsloe's position . . .'

'What do you mean a man in his position? Do you suppose a fellow changes his nature just because a cousin of his dies and he comes into a baronetcy? Haven't I told you a dozen times that I've known young Parsloe all his life? Known him intimately. He was always as hot as mustard and as wide as Leicester Square. Ask anybody who used to go around Town in those days. When they saw young Parsloe coming, strong men winced and hid their valuables. He hadn't a penny except what he could get by telling the tale, and he always did himself like a prince. When I knew him first, he was living down on the river at Shepperton. His old father, the Dean, had made an arrangement with the keeper of the pub there to give him breakfast and bed and nothing else. "If he wants dinner, he must earn it," the old boy said. And do you know how he used to earn it? He trained that mongrel of his, Banjo, to go and do tricks in front of parties that came to the place in steam-launches. And then he would stroll up and hope his dog was not annoying them and stand talking till they went in to dinner and then go in with them and pick up the wine-list, and before they knew what was happening he would be bursting with their champagne and cigars. That's the sort of fellow young Parsloe was.'

'But even so . . .'

'I remember him running up to me outside that pub one afternoon—the Jolly Miller it was called, his face shining with positive ecstasy. "Come in, quick!" he said. "There's a new bar-maid, and she hasn't found out yet I'm not allowed credit."'

'But, Galahad . . .'

'And if young Parsloe thinks I've forgotten a certain incident that occurred in the early summer of the year '95, he's very much mistaken. He met me in the Haymarket and took me into the Two Goslings for a drink—there's a hat-shop now where it used to be—and after we'd had it he pulls a sort of dashed little top affair out of his pocket, a thing with numbers written round it. Said he'd found it in the street and wondered who thought of these ingenious little toys and insisted on our spinning it for half-crowns. "You take the odd numbers, I'll take the even," says young Parsloe. And before I could fight my way out into the fresh air, I was ten pounds seven and sixpence in the hole. And I discovered next morning that they make those beastly things so that if you push the stem through and spin them the wrong way up you're bound to get an even number. And when I asked him the following afternoon to show me that top again, he said he'd lost it. That's the sort of fellow young Parsloe was. And you expect me to believe that inheriting a baronetcy and settling down in the country has made him so dashed pure and high-minded that he wouldn't stoop to nobbling a pig.'

Lord Emsworth uncoiled himself. Cumulative evidence had done its work. His eyes glittered, and he breathed stertorously.

'The scoundrel!'

'Tough nut, always was.'

'What shall I do?'

'Do? Why, go to him right away and tax him.'

'Tax him?'

'Yes. Look him squarely in the eye and tax him with his crime.'

'I will! Immediately.'

'I'll come with you.'

'Look him squarely in the eye!'

'And tax him!'

'And tax him.' Lord Emsworth had reached the hall and was peering agitatedly to right and left. 'Where the devil's my hat? I can't find my hat. Somebody's always hiding my hat. I will not have my hats hidden.'

'You don't need a hat to tax a man with stealing a pig,' said the Hon. Galahad, who was well versed in the manners and rules of good society.

· II ·

In his study at Matchingham Hall in the neighbouring village of Much Matchingham, Sir Gregory Parsloe-Parsloe sat gazing at the current number of a weekly paper. We have seen that weekly paper before. On that occasion it was in the plump hands of Beach. And, oddly enough, what had attracted Sir Gregory's attention was the very item which had interested the butler.

The Hon. Galahad Threepwood, brother of the Earl of Emsworth. A little bird tells us that "Gally" is at Blandings Castle, Shropshire, the ancestral seat of the family, busily engaged in writing his Reminis-

cences. As every member of the Old Brigade will testify, they ought to
be as warm as the weather, if not warmer!'

But whereas Beach, perusing this, had chuckled, Sir Gregory Parsloe-Parsloe shivered, like one who on a country ramble suddenly perceives a snake in his path.

Sir Gregory Parsloe-Parsloe, of Matchingham Hall, seventh baronet of his line, was one of those men who start their lives well, skid for a while, and then slide back on to the straight and narrow path and stay there. That is to say, he had been up to the age of twenty a blameless boy and from the age of thirty-one, when he had succeeded to the title, a practically blameless Bart. So much so that now, in his fifty-second year, he was on the eve of being accepted by the local Unionist Committee as their accredited candidate for the forthcoming by-election in the Bridgeford and Shifley Parliamentary Division of Shropshire.

But there had been a decade in his life, that dangerous decade of the twenties, when he had accumulated a past so substantial that a less able man would have been compelled to spread it over a far longer period. It was an epoch in his life to which he did not enjoy looking back, and years of irreproachable Barthood had enabled him, as far as he personally was concerned, to bury the past. And now, it seemed, this pestilential companion of his youth was about to dig it up again.

The years had turned Sir Gregory into a man of portly habit; and, as portly men do in moments of stress, he puffed. But, puff he never so shrewdly, he could not blow away that paragraph. It was still there, looking up at him, when the door opened and the butler announced Lord Emsworth and Mr Galahad Threepwood.

Sir Gregory's first emotion on seeing the taxing party file into the room was one of pardonable surprise. Aware of the hard feelings which George Cyril Wellbeloved's transference of his allegiance had aroused in the bosom of that gifted pig-man's former employer, he had not expected to receive a morning call from the Earl of Emsworth. As for the Hon. Galahad, he had ceased to be on cordial terms with him as long ago as the winter of the year nineteen hundred and six.

Then, following quickly on the heels of surprise, came indignation.

That the author of the Reminiscences should be writing scurrilous stories about him with one hand and strolling calmly into his private study with, so to speak, the other occasioned him the keenest resentment. He drew himself up and was in the very act of staring haughtily, when the Hon. Galahad broke the silence.

'Young Parsloe,' said the Hon. Galahad, speaking in a sharp, unpleasant voice, 'your sins have found you out!'

It had been the baronet's intention to inquire to what he was indebted for the pleasure of this visit, and to inquire it icily; but at this remarkable speech the words halted on his lips.

'Eh?' he said blankly.

The Hon. Galahad was regarding him through his monocle rather as a cook eyes a black-beetle on discovering it in the kitchen sink. It was a look which would have aroused pique in a slug, and once more the Squire of Matchingham's bewilderment gave way to wrath.

'What the devil do you mean?' he demanded.

'See his face?' asked the Hon. Galahad in a rasping aside.

'I'm looking at it now,' said Lord Emsworth.

'Guilt written upon it.'

'Plainly,' agreed Lord Emsworth.

The Hon. Galahad, who had folded his arms in a menacing manner, unfolded them and struck the desk a smart blow.

'Be very careful, Parsloe! Think before you speak. And, when you speak, speak the truth. I may say, by way of a start, that we know all.'

How low an estimate Sir Gregory Parsloe had formed of his visitors' collective sanity was revealed by the fact that it was actually to Lord Emsworth that he now turned as the more intelligent of the pair.

'Emsworth! Explain! What the deuce are you doing here? And what the devil is that old image talking about?'

Lord Emsworth had been watching his brother with growing admiration. The latter's spirited opening of the case for the prosecution had won his hearty approval.

'You know,' he said curtly.

'I should say he dashed well does know,' said the Hon. Galahad. 'Parsloe, produce that pig!'

Sir Gregory pushed his eyes back into their sockets a split second before they would have bulged out of his head beyond recovery. He did his best to think calm, soothing thoughts. He had just remembered that he was a man who had to be careful about his blood-pressure.

'Pig?'

'Pig.'

'Did you say pig?'

'Pig.'

'What pig?'

'He says "What pig?"'

'I heard him,' said Lord Emsworth.

Sir Gregory Parsloe again had trouble with his eyes.

'I don't know what you are talking about.'

The Hon. Galahad unfolded his arms again and smote the desk a blow that unshipped the cover of the ink-pot.

'Parsloe, you sheep-faced, shambling exile from hell,' he cried. 'Disgorge that pig immediately!'

'My Empress,' added Lord Emsworth.

'Precisely. Empress of Blandings. The pig you stole last night.'

Sir Gregory Parsloe-Parsloe rose slowly from his chair. The Hon. Galahad pointed an imperious finger at him, but he ignored the gesture. His blood-pressure was now hovering around the hundred-and-fifty mark.

'Do you mean to tell me that you seriously accuse . . .'

'Parsloe, sit down!'

Sir Gregory choked.

'I always knew, Emsworth, that you were as mad as a coot.'

'As a what?' whispered his lordship.

'Coot,' said the Hon. Galahad curtly. 'Sort of duck.' He turned to the defendant again. 'Vituperation will do you no good, young Parsloe. We *know* that you have stolen that pig.'

'I haven't stolen any damned pig. What would I want to steal a pig for?'

The Hon. Galahad snorted.

'What did you want to nobble my dog Towser for in the back room of the Black Footman in the spring of the year '97?' he said. 'To queer the favourite, that's why you did it. And that's what you're after now, trying to queer the favourite again. Oh, we can see through you all right, young Parsloe. We read you like a book.'

Sir Gregory had stopped worrying about his blood-pressure. No amount of calm, soothing thoughts could do it any good now.

'You're crazy! Both of you. Stark, staring mad.'

'Parsloe, will you or will you not cough up that pig?'

'I have not got your pig.'

'That is your last word, is it?'

'I haven't seen the creature.'

'Why a coot?' asked Lord Emsworth, who had been brooding for some time in silence.

'Very well,' said the Hon. Galahad. 'If that is the attitude you propose to adopt, there is no course before me but to take steps. And I'll tell you the steps I'm going to take, young Parsloe. I see now that I have been foolishly indulgent. I have allowed my kind heart to get the better of me. Often and often, when I've been sitting at my desk, I've remembered a good story that simply cried out to be put into my Reminiscences, and every time I've said to myself, "No," I've said. "That would wound young Parsloe. Good as it is, I can't use it. I must respect young Parsloe's feelings." Well, from now on there will be no more forbearance. Unless you restore that pig, I shall insert in my book every dashed thing I can remember about you—starting with our first meeting, when I came into Romano's and was introduced to you while you were walking round the supper-table with a soup tureen on your head and stick of celery in your hand, saying that you were a sentry outside Buckingham Palace. The world shall know you for what you are—the only man who was ever thrown out of the Café de l'Europe for trying to raise the price of a bottle of champagne by raffling his trousers at the main bar. And, what's more, I'll tell the full story of the prawns.'

A sharp cry escaped Sir Gregory. His face had turned a deep magenta. In these affluent days of his middle age, he always looked rather like a Regency buck who has done himself well for years among the flesh-pots. He now resembled a Regency buck who, in addition to being on the verge of apoplexy, has been stung in the leg by a hornet.

'I will,' said the Hon. Galahad firmly. 'The full, true and complete story of the prawns, omitting nothing.'

'What was the story of the prawns, my dear fellow?' asked Lord Emsworth, interested.

'Never mind. I know. And young Parsloe knows. And if Empress of Blandings is not back in her sty this afternoon, you will find it in my book.'

'But I keep telling you,' cried the suffering baronet, 'that I know nothing whatever about your pig.'

'Ha!'

'I've not seen the animal since last year's Agricultural Show.'

'Ho!'

'I didn't know it had disappeared till you told me.'

The Hon. Galahad stared fixedly at him through the black-rimmed monocle. Then, with a gesture of loathing, he turned to the door.

'Come, Clarence!' he said.

'Are we going?'

'Yes,' said the Hon. Galahad with quiet dignity. 'There is nothing more that we can do here. Let us get away from this house before it is struck by a thunderbolt.'

· III ·

The gentlemanly office-boy who sat in the outer room of the Argus Enquiry Agency read the card which the stout visitor had handed to him and gazed at the stout visitor with respect and admiration. A polished lad, he loved the aristocracy. He tapped on the door of the inner office.

'A gentleman to see me?' asked Percy Pilbeam.

'A *baronet* to see you, sir,' corrected the office-boy. 'Sir Gregory Parsloe-Parsloe, Matchingham Hall, Salop.'

'Show him in immediately,' said Pilbeam with enthusiasm.

He rose and pulled down the lapels of his coat. Things, he felt, were looking up. He remembered Sir Gregory Parsloe. One of his first cases. He had been able to recover for him some letters which had fallen into the wrong hands. He wondered, as he heard the footsteps outside, if his client had been indulging in correspondence again.

From the baronet's sandbagged expression, as he entered, such might well have been the case. It is the fate of Sir Gregory Parsloe-Parsloe to come into this chronicle puffing and looking purple. He puffed and looked purple now.

'I have called to see you, Mr Pilbeam,' he said, after the preliminary civilities had been exchanged and he had lowered his impressive bulk into a chair, 'because I am in a position of serious difficulty.'

'I am sorry to hear that, Sir Gregory.'

'And because I remember with what discretion and resource you once acted on my behalf.'

Pilbeam glanced at the door. It was closed. He was now convinced that his visitor's little trouble was the same as on the previous occasion, and he looked at the indefatigable man with frank astonishment.

Didn't these old bucks, he was asking himself, ever stop writing compromising letters? You would have thought they would have got writer's cramp.

'If there is any way in which I can assist you, Sir Gregory . . . Perhaps you will tell me the facts from the beginning?'

'The beginning?' Sir Gregory pondered. 'Well, let me put it this way. At one time, Mr Pilbeam, I was younger than I am to-day.'

'Quite.'

'Poorer.'

'No doubt.'

'And less respectable. And during that period of my life I unfortunately went about a good deal with a man named Threepwood.'

'Galahad Theepwood?'

'You know him?' said Sir Gregory, surprised.

Pilbeam chuckled reminiscently.

'I know his name. I wrote an article about him once, when I was editing a paper called *Society Spice*. Number One of the Thriftless Aristocrats series. The snappiest thing I ever did in my life. They tell me he called twice at the office with a horsewhip, wanting to see me.'

Sir Gregory exhibited concern.

'You have met him, then?'

'I have not. You are probably not familiar with the inner workings of a paper like Society Spice, Sir Gregory, but I may tell you that it is foreign to the editorial policy ever to meet visitors who call with horsewhips.'

'Would he have heard your name?'

'No. There was a very strict rule in the Spice office that the names of the editorial staff were not to be divulged.'

'Ah!' said Sir Gregory, relieved.

His relief gave place to indignation. There was an inconsistency about the Hon. Galahad's behaviour which revolted him.

'He cut up rough, did he, because you wrote things about him in your paper? And yet he doesn't seem to mind writing things himself about other people, damn him. That's quite another matter. A different thing altogether. Oh yes!'

'Does he write? I didn't know.'

'He's writing his Reminiscences at this very moment. He's down at Blandings Castle, finishing them now. And the book's going to be full of stories about me. That's why I've come to see you. Dashed, infernal, damaging stories, which'll ruin my reputation in the county. There's one about some prawns . . .'

Words failed Sir Gregory. He sat puffing. Pilbeam nodded gravely. He understood the position now. As to what his client expected him to do about it, however, he remained hazy.

'But if these stories you speak of are libelous . . .'

'What has that got to do with it? They're true.'

'The greater the truth, the greater the . . .'

'Oh, I know all about that,' interrupted Sir Gregory impatiently. 'And a lot of help it's going to be to me. A jury could give me the heaviest damages on record and it wouldn't do me a bit of good. What about my reputation in the county? What about knowing that every damned fool I met was laughing at me behind my back? What about the Unionist Committee? I may tell you, Mr Pilbeam, apart from any other consideration, that I am on the point of being accepted by our local Unionist Committee as their candidate at the next election. And if that old pest's book is published, they will drop me like a hot coal. Now do you understand?'

Pilbeam picked up a pen, and with it scratched his chin thoughtfully. He liked to take an optimistic view with regard to his clients' affairs, but he could not conceal from himself that Sir Gregory appeared to be out of luck.

'He is determined to publish this book?'

'It's the only object he's got in life, the miserable old fossil.'

'And he is resolved to include the stories?'

'He called on me this morning expressly to tell me so. And I caught the next train to London to put the matter in your hands.'

Pilbeam scratched his left cheekbone.

'H'm!' he said. 'Well, in the circumstances, I really don't see what is to be done except . . .'

'. . . get hold of the manuscript and destroy it, you were about to say? Exactly. That's precisely what I've come to ask you to do for me.'

Pilbeam opened his mouth, startled. He had not been about to say anything of the kind. What he had been intending to remark was that, the situation being as described, there appeared no course to pursue but to fold the hands, set the teeth, and await the inevitable disaster like a man and a Briton. He gazed blankly at this lawless Bart. Baronets are proverbially bad, but surely, felt Percy Pilbeam, there was no excuse for them to be as bad as all that.

'Steal the manuscript?'

'Only possible way.'

'But that's rather a tall order, isn't it Sir Gregory?'

'Not,' replied the baronet ingratiatingly, 'for a clever young fellow like you.'

The flattery left Pilbeam cold. His distant, unenthusiastic manner underwent no change. However clever a man is, he was thinking, he cannot very well abstract the manuscript of a book of Reminiscences from a house unless he is first able to enter that house.

'How could I get into the place?'

'I should have thought you would have found a dozen ways.'

'Not even one,' Pilbeam assured him.

'Look how you recovered those letters of mine.'

'That was easy.'

'You told them you had come to inspect the gas meter.'

'I could scarcely go to Blandings Castle and say I had come to inspect the gas meter and hope to be invited to make a long visit on the strength of it. You do not appear to realize, Sir Gregory, that the undertaking you suggest would not be a matter of a few minutes. I might have to remain in the house for quite a considerable time.'

Sir Gregory found his companion's attitude damping. He was a man who, since his accession to the baronetcy and its accompanying wealth, had grown accustomed to seeing people jump smartly to it when he issued instructions. He became peevish.

'Why couldn't you go there as a butler or something?'

Percy Pilbeam's only reply to this was a tolerant smile. He raised the pen and scratched his head with it.

'Scarcely feasible,' he said. And again that rather pitying smile flitted across his face.

The sight of it brought Sir Gregory to the boil. He felt an irresistible desire to say something to wipe it away. It reminded him of the smiles he had seen on the faces of bookmakers in his younger days when he had suggested backing horses with them on credit and in a spirit of mutual trust.

'Well, have it your own way,' he snapped. 'But it may interest you to know that to get that manuscript into my possession I am willing to pay a thousand pounds.'

It did, as he had foreseen, interest Pilbeam extremely. So much so that in his emotion he jerked the pen wildly, inflicting a nasty scalp wound.

'A thuth?' he stammered.

Sir Gregory, a prudent man in money matters, perceived that he had allowed his sense of the dramatic to carry him away.

'Well, five hundred,' he said, rather quickly. 'And five hundred pounds is a lot of money, Mr Pilbeam.'

The point was one which he had no need to stress. Percy Pilbeam had grasped it without assistance, and his face grew wan with thought. The day might come when the proprietor of the Argus Enquiry Agency would remain unmoved by the prospect of adding five hundred pounds to his bank balance, but it had not come yet.

'A cheque for five hundred the moment that old weasel's manuscript is in my hands,' said Sir Gregory, insinuatingly.

Nature had so arranged it that in no circumstances could Percy Pilbeam's face ever become really beautiful; but at this moment there stole into it an expression which did do something to relieve, to a certain extent, its normal unpleasantness. It was an expression of rapture, of joy, of almost beatific happiness—the look, in short, of a man who sees his way clear to laying his hands on five hundred pounds.

There is about the mention of any substantial sum of money something that seems to exercise a quickening effect on the human intelligence. A moment before, Pilbeam's mind had been an inert mass. Now, abruptly, it began to function like a dynamo.

Get into Blandings Castle? Why, of course he could get into Blandings Castle. And not sneak in, either, with a trouser-seat itching in apprehension of the kick that should send him out again, but bowl proudly up to the front door in his two-seater and hand his suit-case to the butler and be welcomed as the honoured guest. Until now he had forgotten, for he had deliberately set himself to forget, the outrageous suggestion of that young idiot whose name escaped him that he should come to Blandings and hunt about for lost pigs. It had wounded his self-respect so deeply at the time that he had driven it from his thoughts. When he found himself thinking about Hugo, he had immediately pulled himself together and started thinking about something else. Now it all came back to him. And Hugo's parting words, he recalled, had been that if ever he changed his mind the commission would still be open.

'I will take this case, Sir Gregory,' he said.

'Woof?'

'You may rely on my being at Blandings Castle by to-morrow evening at the latest. I have thought of a way of getting there.'

He rose from his desk, and paced the room with knitted brows. That agile brain had begun to work under its own steam. He paused once to look in a distrait manner out of the window; and when Sir Gregory cleared his throat to speak, jerked an impatient shoulder at him. He could not have baronets, even with hyphens in their names, interrupting him at a moment like this.

'Sir Gregory,' he said at length. 'The great thing in matters like this is to be prepared with a plan. I have a plan.'

'Woof!' said Sir Gregory.

This time he meant that he had thought all along that his companion would get one after pacing like that.

'When you arrive home, I want you to invite Mr Galahad Threepwood to dinner to-morrow night.'

The baronet shook like a jelly. Wrath and amazement fought within him. Ask the man to dinner? After what had occurred?

'As many others of the Blandings Castle party as you think fit, of course, but Mr Threepwood without fail. Once he is out of the house, my path will be clear.'

Wrath and amazement died away. The baronet had grasped the idea. The beauty and simplicity of the stratagem stirred his admiration. But was it not, he felt, a simpler matter to issue such an invitation than to get it accepted? A vivid picture rose before his eyes of the Hon. Galahad as he had last seen him.

Then there came to him the blessed, healing thought of Lady Constance Keeble. He would send the invitation to her and—yes, dash it!—he would tell her the full facts, put his cards on the table and trust to her sympathy and proper feeling to enlist her in the cause. He had been long aware that her attitude towards the Reminiscences resembled his own. He could rely on her to help him. He could also rely on her somehow—by what strange feminine modes of coercion he, being a bachelor, could only guess at—to deliver the Hon. Galahad Threepwood at Matchingham Hall in time for dinner. Women, he knew, had this strange power over their near relations.

'Splendid!' he said. 'Excellent! Capital. Woof! I'll see it's done.'

'Then you can leave the rest to me.'

'You think, if I can get him out of the house, you will be able to secure the manuscript?'

'Certainly.'

Sir Gregory rose and extended a trembling hand.

'Mr Pilbeam,' he said, with deep feeling, 'coming to see you was the wisest thing I ever did in my life.'

'Quite,' said Percy Pilbeam.

8

THE STORM CLOUDS HOVER
OVER BLANDINGS

HAVING re-read the half-dozen pages which he had written since luncheon, the Hon. Galahad Threepwood attached them with a brass paper-fastener to the main body of his monumental work and placed the manuscript in its drawer—lovingly, like a young mother putting her first-born to bed. The day's work was done. Rising from the desk, he yawned and stretched himself.

He was ink-stained but cheerful. Happiness, as solid thinkers have often pointed out, comes from giving pleasure to others; and the little anecdote which he had just committed to paper would, he knew, give great pleasure to a considerable number of his fellow-men. All over England they would be rolling out of their seats when they read it. True, their enjoyment might possibly not be shared to its fullest extent by Sir Gregory Parsloe-Parsloe, of Matchingham Hall, for what the Hon. Galahad had just written was the story of the prawns: but the first lesson an author has to learn is that he cannot please everybody.

He left the small library which he had commandeered as a private study and, descending the broad staircase, observed Beach in the hall below. The butler was standing mountainously beside the tea-table, staring in a

sort of trance at a plateful of anchovy sandwiches: and it struck the Hon.
Galahad, not for the first time in the last few days, that he appeared to
have something on his mind. A strained, haunted look he seemed to have,
as if he had done a murder and was afraid somebody was going to find the
body. A more practised physiognomist would have been able to interpret
that look. It was the one that butlers always wear when they have allowed
themselves to be persuaded against their better judgement into becoming
accessories before the fact in the theft of their employers' pigs.

'Beach,' he said, speaking over the banisters, for he had just remembered there was a question he wanted to ask the man about the somewhat eccentric Major-General Magnus in whose employment he had
once been.

'What's the matter with you?' he added with some irritation. For the
butler, jerked from his reverie, had jumped a couple of inches and shaken
all over in a manner that was most trying to watch. A butler, felt the Hon.
Galahad, is a butler, and a startled fawn is a startled fawn. He disliked
the blend of the two in a single body.

'I beg your pardon, sir?'

'Why on earth do you spring like that when anyone speaks to you?
I've noticed it before. He leaps,' he said complainingly to his niece Millicent, who now came down the stairs with slow, listless steps. 'When
addressed, he quivers like a harpooned whale.'

'Oh?' said Millicent dully. She had dropped into a chair and picked up
a book. She looked like something that might have occurred to Ibsen in
one of his less frivolous moments.

'I am extremely sorry, Mr Galahad.'

'No use being sorry. Thing is not to do it. If you are practising the
Shimmy for the Servants' Ball, be advised by an old friend and give it up.
You haven't the build.'

'I think I may have caught a chill, sir.'

'Take a stiff whisky toddy. Put you right in no time. What's the car
doing out there?'

'Her ladyship ordered it, sir. I understand that she and Mr Baxter are
going to Market Blandings to meet the train arriving at four-forty.'

'Somebody expected?'

'The American young lady, sir. Miss Schoonmaker.'

'Of course, yes. I remember. She arrives to-day, does she?'

'Yes, sir.'

The Hon. Galahad mused.

'Schoonmaker. I used to know old Johnny Schoonmaker well. A great fellow. Mixed the finest mint-juleps in America. Have you ever tasted a mint-julep, Beach?'

'Not to my recollection, sir.'

'Oh, you'd remember all right if you had. Insidious things. They creep up to you like a baby sister and slide their little hands into yours and the next thing you know the Judge is telling you to pay the clerk of the court fifty dollars. Seen Lord Emsworth anywhere?'

'His lordship is at the telephone, sir.'

'Don't do it, I tell you!' said the Hon. Galahad petulantly. For once again the butler had been affected by what appeared to be a kind of palsy.

'I beg your pardon, Mr Galahad. It was something I was suddenly reminded of. There was a gentleman just after luncheon who desired to communicate with you on the telephone. I understood him to say that he was speaking from Oxford, being on his way from London to Blackpool in his automobile. Knowing that you were occupied with your literary work, I refrained from disturbing you. And till I mentioned the word "telephone", the matter slipped my mind.'

'Who was he?'

'I did not get the gentleman's name, sir. The wire was faulty. But he desired me to inform you that his business had to do with a dramatic entertainment.'

'A play?'

'Yes, sir,' said Beach, plainly impressed by this happy way of putting it. 'I took the liberty of advising him that you might be able to see him later in the afternoon. He said that he would call after tea.'

The butler passed from the hall with heavy, haunted steps, and the Hon. Galahad turned to his niece.

'I know who it is,' he said. 'He wrote to me yesterday. It's a theatrical manager fellow I used to go about with years ago. Man named

Mason. He's got a play, adapted from the French, and he's had the idea of changing it into the period of the nineties and getting me to put my name to it.'

'Oh?'

'On the strength of my book coming out at the same time. Not a bad notion, either. Galahad Threepwood's a name that's going to have box-office value pretty soon. The house'll be sold out for weeks to all the old buffers who'll come flocking up to London to see if I've put anything about them into it.'

'Oh?' said Millicent.

The Hon. Galahad frowned. He sensed a lack of interest and sympathy.

'What's the matter with you?' he demanded.

'Nothing.'

'Then why are you looking like that?'

'Like what?'

'Pale and tragic, as if you'd just gone into Tattersall's and met a bookie you owed money to.'

'I am perfectly happy.'

The Hon. Galahad snorted.

'Yes, radiant. I've seen fogs that were cheerier. What's that book you're reading?'

'It belongs to Aunt Constance.' Millicent glanced wanly at the cover. 'It seems to be about Theosophy.'

'Theosophy! Fancy a young girl in the spring-time of life . . . What the devil has happened to everybody in this house? There's some excuse, perhaps, for Clarence. If you admit the possibility of a sane man getting so attached to a beastly pig, he has a right to be upset. But what's wrong with all the rest of you? Ronald! Goes about behaving like a bereaved tomato. Beach! Springs up and down when you speak to him. And that young fellow Carmody . . .'

'I am not interested in Mr Carmody.'

'This morning,' said the Hon. Galahad, aggrieved, 'I told that boy one of the most humorous limericks I ever heard in my life—about an Old Man Of—however, that is neither here nor there—and he just gaped at me with his jaw dropping, like a spavined horse looking over a fence. There are mysteries afoot in this house, and I don't like 'em. The atmosphere of Blandings Castle has changed all of a sudden from that of a normal, happy English home into something Edgar Allan Poe might have written on a rainy Sunday. It's getting on my nerves. Let's hope this girl of Johnny Schoonmaker's will cheer us up. If she's anything like her father, she ought to be a nice, lively girl. But I suppose, when she arrives, it'll turn out that she's in mourning for a great-aunt or brooding over the situation in Russia or something. I don't know what young people are coming to nowadays. Gloomy. Introspective. The old gay spirit seems to have died out altogether. In my young days a girl of your age would have been upstairs making an apple-pie bed for somebody instead of lolling on chairs reading books about Theosophy.'

Snorting once more, the Hon. Galahad disappeared into the smoking-room, and Millicent, tight-lipped, returned to her book. She had been reading for some minutes when she became aware of a long, limp, drooping figure at her side.

'Hullo,' said Hugo, for this ruin of a fine young man was he.

Millicent's ear twitched, but she did not reply.

'Reading?'

He had been standing on his left leg. With a sudden change of policy, he now shifted, and stood on his right.

'Interesting book?'

Millicent looked up.

'I beg your pardon?'

'Only said—is that an interesting book?'

'Very,' said Millicent.

Hugo decided that his right leg was not a success. He stood on his left again.

'What's it about?'

'Transmigration of Souls.'

'A thing I'm not very well up on.'

'One of the many, I should imagine,' said the haughty girl. 'Every day you seem to know less and less about more and more.' She rose, and made for the stairs. Her manner suggested that she was disappointed in the hall of Blandings Castle. She had supposed it a nice place for a girl to sit and study the best literature, and now, it appeared, it was overrun by the Underworld. 'If you're really anxious to know what Transmigration means, it's simply that some people believe that when you die your soul goes into something else.'

'Rum idea,' said Hugo, becoming more buoyant. He began to draw hope from her chattiness. She had not said as many consecutive words as this to him for quite a time. 'Into something else, eh? Odd notion. What do you suppose made them think of that?'

'Yours, for instance, would probably go into a pig. And then I would come along and look into your sty and I'd say, "Good gracious! Why, there's Hugo Carmody. He hasn't changed a bit!"'

The spirit of the Carmodys had been a good deal crushed by recent happenings, but at this it flickered into feeble life.

'I call that a beastly thing to say.'

'Do you?'

'Yes, I do.'

'I oughtn't to have said it?'

'No, you oughtn't.'

'Well, I wouldn't have, if I could have thought of anything worse.'

'And when you let a little thing like what happened the other night rot up a great love like ours, I—well, I call it a bit rotten. You know perfectly well that you're the only girl in the world I ever . . .'

'Shall I tell you something?'

'What?'

'You make me sick.'

Hugo breathed passionately through his nose.

'So all is over, is it?'

'You can jolly well bet all is over. And if you're interested in my future plans, I may mention I intend to marry the first man who comes along and asks me. And you can be a page at the wedding if you like. You couldn't look any sillier than you do now, even in a frilly shirt and satin knickerbockers.'

Hugo laughed raspingly.

'Is that so?'

'It is.'

'And once you said there wasn't another man like me in the world.'

'Well, I should hate to think there was,' said Millicent. And as the celebrated James–Thomas–Beach procession had entered with cakes and gate-leg tables and her last word seemed about as good a last word as a girl might reasonably consider herself entitled to, she passed proudly up the stairs.

James withdrew. Thomas withdrew. Beach remained gazing with a hypnotized eye at the cake.

'Beach!' said Hugo.

'Sir?'

'Curse all women!'

'Very good, sir,' said Beach.

He watched the young man disappear through the open front door, heard his footsteps crunch on the gravel, and gave himself up to meditation again. How gladly, he was thinking, if it had not been for upsetting Mr Ronald's plans, would he have breathed in his employer's ear as he filled his glass at dinner, 'The pig is in the gamekeeper's cottage in the west wood, your lordship. Thank you, your lordship.' But it was not to be. His face twisted, as if with sudden pain, and he was aware of the Hon. Galahad emerging from the smoking-room.

'Just remembered something I wanted to ask you, Beach. You were with old General Magnus, weren't you, some years ago, before you came here?'

'Yes, Mr Galahad.'

'Then perhaps you can tell me the exact facts about that trouble in 1912. I know the old chap chased young Mandeville three times round the lawn in his pyjamas, but did he merely try to stab him with the bread-knife or did he actually get home?'

'I could not say, sir. He did not honour me with his confidence.'

'Infernal nuisance,' said the Hon. Galahad. 'I like to get these things right.'

He eyed the butler discontentedly as he retired. More than ever was he convinced that the fellow had something on his mind. The very way he walked showed it. He was about to return to the smoking-room when his brother Clarence came into the hall. And there was in Lord Emsworth's bearing so strange a gaiety that he stood transfixed. It seemed to the Hon. Galahad years since he had seen anyone looking cheerful in Blandings Castle.

'Good God, Clarence! What's happened?'

'What, my dear fellow?'

'You're wreathed in smiles, dash it, and skipping like the high hills. Found that pig under the drawing-room sofa or something?'

Lord Emsworth beamed.

'I have had the most cheering piece of news, Galahad. That detective—the one I sent young Carmody to see—the Argus man, you know—he has come after all. He drove down in his car and is at this moment in Market Blandings, at the Emsworth Arms. I have been speaking to him on the telephone. He rang up to ask if I still required his services.'

'Well, you don't.'

'Certainly I do, Galahad. I consider his presence vital.'

'He can't tell you any more than you know already. There's only one man who can have stolen that pig, and that's young Parsloe.'

'Precisely. Yes. Quite true. But this man will be able to collect evidence and bring the thing home and—er—bring it home. He has the trained mind. I consider it most important that the case should be in the hands of a man with a trained mind. We should be seeing him very shortly. He is having what he describes as a bit of a snack at the Emsworth Arms. When he has finished, he will drive over. I am delighted. Ah, Constance, my dear.'

Lady Constance Keeble, attended by the Efficient Baxter, had appeared at the foot of the stairs. His lordship eyed her a little warily. The châtelaine of Blandings was apt sometimes to react unpleasantly to the information that visitors not invited by herself were expected at the castle.

'Constance, my dear, a friend of mine is arriving this evening, to spend a few days. I forgot to tell you.'

'Well, we have plenty of room for him,' replied Lady Constance, with surprising amiability. 'There is something I forgot to tell you, too. We are dining at Matchingham tonight.'

'Matchingham?' Lord Emsworth was puzzled. He could think of no one who lived in the village of Matchingham except Sir Gregory Parsloe-Parsloe. 'With whom?'

'Sir Gregory, of course. Who else do you suppose it could be?'

'What!'

'I had a note from him after luncheon. It is short notice, of course, but that doesn't matter in the country. He took it for granted that we would not be engaged.'

'Constance!' Lord Emsworth swelled slightly. 'Constance, I will not—dash it, I will not—dine with that man. And that's final.'

Lady Constance smiled a sort of lion-tamer's smile. She had foreseen a reaction of this kind. She had expected sales-resistance, and was prepared to cope with it. Not readily, she knew, would her brother become Parsloe-conscious.

'Please do not be absurd, Clarence. I thought you would say that. I have already accepted for you, Galahad, myself, and Millicent. You may as well understand at once that I do not intend to be on bad terms with our nearest neighbour, even if a hundred of your pig-men leave you and go to him. Your attitude in the matter has been perfectly childish from the very start. If Sir Gregory realizes that there has been a coolness, and has most sensibly decided to make the first move towards a reconciliation, we cannot possibly refuse the overture.'

'Indeed? And what about my friend? Arriving this evening.'

'He can look after himself for a few hours, I should imagine.'

'Abominable rudeness he'll think it.' This line of attack had occurred to Lord Emsworth quite suddenly. He found it good. Almost an inspiration, it seemed to him. 'I invite my friend Pilbeam here to pay us a visit, and the moment he arrives we meet him at the front door, dash it, and say, "Ah, here you are, Pilbeam! Well, amuse yourself, Pilbeam. We're off." And this Miss—er—this American girl. What will she think?'

'Did you say Pilbeam?' asked the Hon. Galahad.

'It is no use talking, Clarence. Dinner is at eight. And please see that your dress clothes are nicely pressed. Ring for Beach and tell him now. Last night you looked like a scarecrow.'

'Once and for all, I tell you . . .'

At this moment an unexpected ally took the arena on Lady Constance's side.

'Of course we must go, Clarence,' said the Hon. Galahad, and Lord Emsworth, spinning round to face this flank attack, was surprised to see a swift, meaning wink come and go on his brother's face. 'Nothing gained by having unpleasantness with your neighbours in the country. Always a mistake. Never pays.'

'Exactly,' said Lady Constance, a little dazed at finding this Saul among the prophets, but glad of the helping hand. 'In the country one is quite dependent on one's neighbours.'

'And young Parsloe—not such a bad chap, Clarence. Lots of good in Parsloe. We shall have a pleasant evening.'

'I am relieved to find that you, at any rate, have sense, Galahad,' said Lady Constance handsomely. 'I will leave you to try and drive some of it into Clarence's head. Come, Mr Baxter, we shall be late.'

The sound of the car's engine had died away before Lord Emsworth's feelings found relief in speech.

'But, Galahad, my dear fellow!'

The Hon. Galahad patted his shoulder reassuringly.

'It's all right, Clarence, my boy. I know what I'm doing. I have the situation well in hand.'

'Dine with Parsloe after what has occurred? After what occurred yesterday? It's impossible. Why on earth the man is inviting us, I can't understand.'

'I suppose he thinks that if he gives us a dinner I shall relent and omit the prawn story. Oh, I see Parsloe's motive all right. A clever move. Not that it'll work.'

'But what do you want to go for?'

The Hon. Galahad raked the hall with a conspiratorial monocle. It appeared to be empty. Nevertheless, he looked under a settee and, going to the front door, swiftly scanned the gravel.

'Shall I tell you something, Clarence?' he said, coming back. 'Something that'll interest you?'

'Certainly, my dear fellow. Certainly. Most decidedly.'

'Something that'll bring the sparkle to your eyes?'

'By all means. I should enjoy it.'

'You know what we're going to do? To-night? After dining with Parsloe and sending Constance back in the car?'

'No.'

The Hon. Galahad placed his lips to his brother's ear.

'We're going to steal his pig, my boy.'

'What!'

'It came to me in a flash while Constance was talking. Parsloe stole the Empress. Very well, we'll steal Pride of Matchingham. Then we'll be in a position to look young Parsloe squarely in the eye and say, "What about it?"'

Lord Emsworth swayed gently. His brain, never a strong one, had tottered perceptibly on its throne.

'Galahad!'

'Only thing to do. Reprisals. Recognized military manoeuvre.'

'But how? Galahad, how can it be done?'

'Easily. If young Parsloe stole the Empress, why should we have any difficulty in stealing his animal? You show me where he keeps it, my boy, and I'll do the rest. Puffy Benger and I stole old Wivenhoe's pig at Hammer's Easton in the year '95. We put it in Plug Basham's bedroom. And we'll put Parsloe's pig in a bedroom, too.'

'In a bedroom?'

'Well, a sort of bedroom. Where are we to hide the animal—that's what you've been asking yourself, isn't it? I'll tell you. We're going to put it in that caravan that your flower-pot-throwing friend Baxter arrived in. Nobody's going to think of looking there. Then we'll be in a position to talk terms to young Parsloe, and I think he will very soon see the game is up.'

Lord Emsworth was looking at his brother almost devoutly. He had always known that Galahad's intelligence was superior to his own, but he had never realized it could soar to quite such lofty heights as this. It was, he supposed, the result of the life his brother had lived. He himself, sheltered through the peaceful, uneventful years at Blandings Castle, had allowed his brain to become comparatively atrophied. But Galahad, battling through these same years with hostile skittle-sharps and the sort of man that used to be a member of the old Pelican Club, had kept his clear and vigorous.

'You really think it would be feasible?'

'Trust me. By the way, Clarence, this man Pilbeam of yours. Do you know if he was ever anything except a detective?'

'I have no idea, my dear fellow. I know nothing of him. I have merely spoken to him on the telephone. Why?'

'Oh, nothing. I'll ask him when he arrives. Where are you going?'

'Into the garden.'

'It's raining.'

'I have my macintosh. I really—I feel I really must walk about after what you have told me. I am in a state of considerable excitement.'

'Well, work it off before you see Constance again. It won't do to have her start suspecting there's something up. If there's anything you want to ask me about, you'll find me in the smoking-room.'

For some twenty minutes the hall of Blandings Castle remained empty. Then Beach appeared. At the same moment, from the gravel outside there came the purring of a high-powered car and the sound of voices. Beach posed himself in the doorway, looking, as he always did on these occasions, like the Spirit of Blandings welcoming the lucky guest.

9

ENTER SUE

'LEAVE the door open, Beach,' said Lady Constance.

'Very good, your ladyship.'

'I think the smell of the wet earth and the flowers is so refreshing, don't you?'

The butler did not. He was not one of your fresh-air men. Rightly conjecturing, however, that the question had been addressed not to him but to the girl in the beige suit who had accompanied the speaker up the steps, he forbore to reply. He cast an appraising bulging-eyed look at this girl and decided that she met with his approval. Smaller and slighter than the type of woman he usually admired, he found her, nevertheless, even by his own exacting standards of criticism, noticeably attractive. He liked her face and he liked the way she was dressed. Her frock was right, her shoes were right, her stockings were right, and her hat was right. As far as Beach was concerned, Sue had passed the Censor.

Her demeanour pleased him, too. From the flush on her face and the sparkle in her eyes, she seemed to be taking her first entry into Blandings Castle in quite the proper spirit of reverential excitement. To be at Blandings plainly meant something to her, was an event in her life: and Beach, who after many years of residence within its walls had come to look on the Castle as a piece of personal property, felt flattered and gratified.

'I don't think this shower will last long,' said Lady Constance.

'No,' said Sue, smiling brightly.

'And now you must be wanting some tea after your journey.'

'Yes,' said Sue, smiling brightly.

It seemed as if she had been smiling brightly for centuries. The moment she had alighted from the train and found her formidable hostess and this strangely sinister Mr Baxter waiting to meet her on the platform, she had begun to smile brightly and had been doing it ever since.

'Usually we have tea on the lawn. It is so nice there.'

'It must be.'

'When the rain is over, Mr Baxter, you must show Miss Schoonmaker the rose-garden.'

'I shall be delighted,' said the Efficient Baxter.

He flashed gleaming spectacles in her direction, and a momentary panic gripped Sue. She feared that already this man had probed her secret. In his glance, it seemed to her, there shone suspicion.

Such, however, was not the case. It was only the combination of large spectacles and heavy eyebrows that had created the illusion. Although Rupert Baxter was a man who generally suspected everybody on principle, it so happened that he had accepted Sue without question. The glance was an admiring, almost a loving glance. It would be too much to say that Baxter had already fallen a victim to Sue's charms, but the good looks which he saw and the wealth which he had been told about were undeniably beginning to fan the hidden fire.

'My brother is a great rose-grower.'

'Yes, isn't he? I mean, I think roses are so lovely.' The spectacles were beginning to sap Sue's morale. They seemed to be eating into her soul like some sort of corrosive acid. 'How nice and old everything is here,' she went on hurriedly. 'What is that funny-looking gargoyle thing over there?'

What she actually referred to was a Japanese mask which hung from the wall, and it was unfortunate that the Hon. Galahad should have chosen this moment to come out of the smoking-room. It made the question seem personal.

'My brother Galahad,' said Lady Constance. Her voice lost some of the kindly warmth of the hostess putting the guest at her ease and took on the cold disapproval which the author of the Reminiscences always induced in her. 'Galahad, this is Miss Schoonmaker.'

'Really?' The Hon. Galahad trotted briskly up. 'It is? Bless my soul! Well, well, well!'

'How do you do?' said Sue, smiling brightly.

'How are you, my dear? I know your father intimately.'

The bright smile faded. Sue had tried to plan this venture of hers carefully, looking ahead for all possible pitfalls, but that she would encounter people who knew Mr Schoonmaker intimately she had not foreseen.

'Haven't seen him lately, of course. Let me see . . . Must be twenty-five years since we met. Yes, quite twenty-five years.'

A warm and lasting friendship was destined to spring up between Sue and the Hon. Galahad Threepwood, but never in the whole course of it did she experience again quite the gush of whole-hearted affection which surged over her at these words.

'I wasn't born then,' she said.

The Hon. Galahad was babbling on happily.

'A great fellow, old Johnny. You'll find some stories about him in my book. I'm writing my Reminiscences, you know. Fine sportsman, old Johnny. Great grief to him, I remember, when he broke his leg and had to go into a nursing-home in the middle of the racing season. However, he made the best of it. Got the nurses interested in current form, and used to make a book with them in fruit and cigarettes and things. I recollect coming to see him one day and finding him quite worried. He was a most conscientious man, with a horror of not settling up when he lost, and apparently one of the girls had had a suet dumpling on the winner of the three o'clock race at fifteen to eight, and he couldn't figure out what he had got to pay her.'

Sue, laughing gratefully, was aware of a drooping presence at her side.

'My niece Millicent,' said Lady Constance. 'Millicent, my dear, this is Miss Schoonmaker.'

'How do you do?' said Sue, smiling brightly.

'How do you do?' said Millicent, like the silent tomb breaking its silence.

Sue regarded her with interest. So this was Hugo's Millicent. The sight of her caused Sue to wonder at the ardent nature of that young man's devotion. Millicent was pretty, but she would have thought that one of Hugo's exuberant disposition would have preferred something a little livelier.

She was startled to observe in the girl's eye a look of surprise. In a situation as delicate as hers was, Sue had no wish to occasion surprise to anyone.

'Ronnie's friend?' asked Millicent. 'The Miss Schoonmaker Ronnie met at Biarritz?'

'Yes,' said Sue faintly.

'But I had the impression that you were very tall. I'm sure Ronnie told me so.'

'I suppose almost anyone seems tall to that boy,' said the Hon. Galahad.

Sue breathed again. She had had a return of the unpleasant feeling of being boneless which had come upon her when the Hon. Galahad had spoken of knowing Mr Schoonmaker intimately. But, though she breathed, she was still shaken. Life at Blandings Castle was plainly going to be a series of shocks. She sat back with a sensation of dizziness. Baxter's spectacles seemed to her to be glittering more suspiciously than ever.

'Have you seen Ronald anywhere, Millicent?' asked Lady Constance.

'Not since lunch. I suppose he's out in the grounds somewhere.'

'I saw him half an hour ago,' said the Hon. Galahad. 'He came mooning along under my window while I was polishing up some stuff I wrote this afternoon. I called to him, but he just grunted and wandered off.'

'He will be surprised to find you here,' said Lady Constance, turning to Sue. 'Your telegram did not arrive till after lunch, so he does not know that you were planning to come to-day. Unless you told him, Galahad.'

'I didn't tell him. Never occurred to me that he knew Miss Schoonmaker. Forgot you'd met him at Biarritz. What was he like then? Reasonably cheerful?'

'Yes, I think so.'

'Didn't scowl and jump and gasp and quiver all over the place?'

'No.'

'Then something must have happened when he went up to London. It was after he came back that I remember noticing that he seemed upset about something. Ah, the rain's stopped.'

Lady Constance looked over her shoulder.

'The sky still looks very threatening,' she said, 'but you might be able to get out for a few minutes. Mr Baxter,' she explained, 'is going to show Miss Schoonmaker the rose-garden.'

'No, he isn't,' said the Hon. Galahad, who had been scrutinizing Sue through his monocle with growing appreciation. 'I am. Old Johnny Schoonmaker's little girl . . . why, there are a hundred things I want to discuss.'

The last thing Sue desired was to be left alone with the intimidating Baxter. She rose quickly.

'I should love to come,' she said.

The prospect of discussing the intimate affairs of the Schoonmaker family was not an agreeable one, but anything was better than the society of the spectacles.

'Perhaps,' said the Hon. Galahad, as he led her to the door, 'you'll be able to put me right about that business of old Johnny and the mysterious woman at the New Year's Eve party. As I got the story, Johnny suddenly found this female—a perfect stranger, mind you—with her arms round his neck, telling him in a confidential undertone that she had made up her mind to go straight back to Des Moines, Iowa, and stick a knife into Fred. What he had done to win her confidence and who Fred was and whether she ever did stick a knife into him, your father hadn't found out by the time I left for home.'

His voice died away, and a moment later the Efficient Baxter, starting as if a sudden thought had entered his powerful brain rose abruptly and made quickly for the stairs.

10

A SHOCK FOR SUE

· I ·

The rose-garden of Blandings Castle was a famous beauty-spot. Most people who visited it considered it deserving of a long and leisurely inspection. Enthusiastic horticulturists frequently went pottering and sniffing about it for hours on end. The tour through its fragrant groves personally conducted by the Hon. Galahad Threepwood lasted some six minutes.

'Well, that's what it is, you see,' he said, as they emerged, waving a hand vaguely. 'Roses and—er—roses, and all that sort of thing. You get the idea. And now, if you don't mind, I ought to be getting back. I want to keep in touch with the house. It slipped my mind, but I'm expecting a man to call to see me at any moment on some rather important business.'

Sue was quite willing to return. She liked her companion, but she had found his company embarrassing. The subject of the Schoonmaker family history showed a tendency to bulk too largely in his conversation for comfort. Fortunately, his practice of asking a question and answering it himself and then rambling off into some anecdote of the person or persons involved enabled her so far to avoid disaster: but there was no saying how long this happy state of things would last. She was glad of the opportunity of being alone.

Besides, Ronnie was somewhere out in these grounds. At any moment, if she went wandering through them, she might come upon him. And then, she told herself, all would be well. Surely he could not preserve his sullen hostility in the face of the fact that she had come all this way, pretending dangerously to be Miss Schoonmaker, of New York, simply in order to see him?

Her companion, she found, was still talking.

'He wants to see me about a play. This book of mine is going to make a stir, you see, and he thinks that if he can get me to put my name to the play . . .'

Sue's thoughts wandered again. She gathered that the caller he was expecting had to do with the theatrical industry, and wondered for a moment if it was anyone she had ever heard of. She was not sufficiently interested to make inquiries. She was too busy thinking of Ronnie.

'I shall be quite happy,' she said, as the voice beside her ceased. 'It's such a lovely place. I shall enjoy just wandering about by myself.'

The Hon. Galahad seemed shocked at the idea.

'Wouldn't dream of leaving you alone. Clarence will look after you, and I shall be back in a few minutes.'

The name seemed to Sue to strike a familiar chord. Then she remembered. Lord Emsworth. Ronnie's Uncle Clarence. The man who held Ronnie's destinies in the hollow of his hand.

'Hi! Clarence!' called the Hon. Galahad.

Sue perceived pottering towards them a long, stringy man of mild and benevolent aspect. She was conscious of something of a shock. In Ronnie's conversation, the Earl of Emsworth had always appeared in the light of a sort of latter-day ogre, a man at whom the stoutest nephew might well shudder. She saw nothing formidable in this new-comer.

'Is that Lord Emsworth?' she asked, surprised.

'Yes. Clarence, this is Miss Schoonmaker.'

His lordship had pottered up and was beaming amiably.

'Is it, indeed? Oh, ah, yes, to be sure. Delighted. How are you? How are you? Miss Who?'

'Schoonmaker. Daughter of my old friend Johnny Schoonmaker. You knew she was arriving. Considering that you were in the hall when Constance went to meet her . . .'

'Oh, yes.' The cloud was passing from what, for want of a better word, must be called Lord Emsworth's mind. 'Yes, yes, yes. Yes, to be sure.'

'I've got to leave you to look after her for a few minutes, Clarence.'

'Certainly, certainly.'

'Take her about and show her things. I wouldn't go too far from the house, if I were you. There's a storm coming up.'

'Exactly. Precisely. Yes, I will take her about and show her things. Are you fond of pigs?'

Sue had never considered this point before. Hers had been an urban life, and she could not remember ever having come into contact with a pig on what might be termed a social footing. But, remembering that this was the man whom Ronnie had described as being wrapped up in one of these animals, she smiled her bright smile.

'Oh, yes. Very.'

'Mine has been stolen.'

'I'm so sorry.'

Lord Emsworth was visibly pleased at this womanly sympathy.

'But I now have strong hopes that she may be recovered. The trained mind is everything. What I always say . . .'

What it was that Lord Emsworth always said was unfortunately destined to remain unrevealed. It would probably have been something good, but the world was not to hear it; for at this moment, completely breaking his train of thought, there came from above, from the direction of the window of the small library, an odd, scrabbling sound. Something shot through the air. And the next instant there appeared in the middle of a flower-bed containing lobelias something that was so manifestly not a lobelia that he stared at it in stunned amazement, speech wiped from his lips as with a sponge.

It was the Efficient Baxter. He was on all fours, and seemed to be groping about for his spectacles, which had fallen off and got hidden in the undergrowth.

· II ·

Properly considered, there is no such thing as an insoluble mystery. It may seem puzzling at first sight when ex-secretaries start falling as the gentle rain from heaven upon the lobelias beneath, but there is always a reason for it. That Baxter did not immediately give the reason was due to the fact that he had private and personal motives for not doing so.

We have called Rupert Baxter efficient, and efficient he was. The word, as we interpret it, implies not only a capacity for performing the ordinary tasks of life with a smooth firmness of touch but in addition a certain alertness of mind, a genius for opportunism, a gift for seeing clearly, thinking swiftly, and Doing It Now. With these qualities Rupert Baxter was pre-eminently equipped; and it had been with him the work of a moment to perceive, directly the Hon. Galahad had left the house with Sue, that here was his chance of popping upstairs, nipping in to the small library, and abstracting the manuscript of the Reminiscences. Having popped and nipped, as planned, he was in the very act of searching the desk when the sound of a footstep outside froze him from his spectacles to the soles of his feet. The next moment, fingers began to turn the door-handle.

You may freeze a Baxter's body, but you cannot numb his active brain. With one masterful, lightning-like flash of clear thinking he took in the situation and saw the only possible way out. To reach the door leading to the large library, he would have to circumnavigate the desk. The window, on the other hand, was at his elbow. So he jumped out of it.

All these things Baxter could have explained in a few words. Refraining from doing so, he rose to his feet and began to brush the mould from his knees.

'Baxter! What on earth?'

The ex-secretary found the gaze of his late employer trying to nerves which had been considerably shaken by his fall. The occasions on which he disliked Lord Emsworth most intensely were just these occasions when the other gaped at him open-mouthed like a surprised halibut.

'I overbalanced,' he said curtly.

'Overbalanced?'

'Slipped.'

'Slipped?'

'Yes. Slipped.'

'How? Where?'

It now occurred to Baxter that by a most fortunate chance the window of the small library was not the only one that looked out on to this arena into which he had precipitated himself. He might equally well have descended from the larger library which adjoined it.

'I was leaning out of the library window . . .'

'Why?'

'Inhaling the air . . .'

'What for?'

'And I lost my balance.'

'Lost your balance?'

'I slipped.'

'Slipped?'

Baxter had the feeling—it was one which he had often had in the old days when conversing with Lord Emsworth—that an exchange of remarks had begun which might go on for ever. A keen desire swept over him to be—and that right speedily—in some other place. He did not care where it was. So long as Lord Emsworth was not there, it would be Paradise enow.

'I think I will go indoors and wash my hands,' he said.

'And face,' suggested the Hon. Galahad.

'My face, also,' said Rupert Baxter coldly.

He started to move round the angle of the house, but long before he had got out of hearing Lord Emsworth's high and penetrating tenor was dealing with the situation. His lordship, as so often happened on these occasions, was under the impression that he spoke in a hushed whisper.

'Mad as a coot!' he said. And the words rang out through the still summer air like a public oration.

They cut Baxter to the quick. They were not the sort of words to which a man with an inch and a quarter of skin off his left shinbone ought ever to have been called upon to listen. With flushed ears and glowing spectacles, the Efficient Baxter passed on his way. Statistics relating to madness among coots are not to hand, but we may safely doubt whether even in the ranks of these notoriously unbalanced birds there could have been found at this moment one who was feeling half as mad as he did.

Lord Emsworth continued to gaze at the spot where his late secretary had passed from sight.

'Mad as a coot,' he repeated.

In his brother Galahad he found a ready supporter.

'Madder,' said the Hon. Galahad.

'Upon my word, I think he's actually worse than he was two years ago. Then, at least, he never fell out of windows.'

'Why on earth do you have the fellow here?'

Lord Emsworth sighed.

'It's Constance, my dear Galahad. You know what she is. She insisted on inviting him.'

'Well, if you take my advice, you'll hide the flower-pots. One of the things this fellow does when he gets these attacks,' explained the Hon. Galahad, taking Sue into the family confidence, 'is to go about hurling flower-pots at people.'

'Really?'

'I assure you. Looking for me, Beach?'

The careworn figure of the butler had appeared, walking as one pacing behind the coffin of an old friend.

'Yes, sir. The gentleman has arrived, Mr Galahad. I looked in the small library, thinking that you might possibly be there, but you were not.'

'No, I was out here.'

'Yes, sir.'

'That's why you couldn't find me. Show him up to the small library, Beach, and tell him I'll be with him in a moment.'

'Very good, sir.'

The Hon. Galahad's temporary delay in going to see his visitor was due to his desire to linger long enough to tell Sue, to whom he had taken a warm fancy and whom he wished to shield as far as it was in his power from the perils of life, what every girl ought to know about the Efficient Baxter.

'Never let yourself be alone with that fellow in a deserted spot, my dear,' he counselled. 'If he suggests a walk in the woods, call for help. Been off his head for years. Ask Clarence.'

Lord Emsworth nodded solemnly.

'And it looks to me,' went on the Hon. Galahad, 'as if his mania had now taken a suicidal turn. Overbalanced, indeed! How the deuce could he have overbalanced? Flung himself out bodily, that's what he did. I couldn't think who it was he reminded me of till this moment. He's the living image of a man I used to know in the nineties. The first intimation any of us had that this chap had anything wrong with him was when he turned up to supper at the house of a friend of mine—George Pallant. You remember George, Clarence?—with a couple of days' beard on him. And when Mrs George, who had known him all her life, asked why he hadn't shaved—"Shaved?" says this fellow, surprised. Packleby, his name was. One of the Leicestershire Packlebys. "Shaved, dear lady?" he says. "Well, considering that they even hide the butter-knife when I come down to breakfast for fear I'll try to cut my throat with it, is it reasonable to suppose they'd trust me with a razor?" Quite stuffy about it, he was, and it spoiled the party. Look after Miss Schoonmaker, Clarence. I shan't be long.'

Lord Emsworth had little experience in the art of providing diversion for young girls. Left thus to his native inspiration, he pondered a while. If the Empress had not been stolen, his task would, of course, have been simple. He could have given this Miss Schoonmaker a half-hour of sheer entertainment by taking her down to the piggeries to watch that superb animal feed. As it was, he was at something of a loss.

'Perhaps you would care to see the rose-garden?' he hazarded.

'I should love it,' said Sue.

'Are you fond of roses?'

'Tremendously.'

Lord Emsworth found himself warming to this girl. Her personality pleased him. He seemed dimly to recall something his sister Constance had said about her—something about wishing that her nephew Ronald would settle down with some nice girl with money like that Miss Schoonmaker whom Julia had met at Biarritz. Feeling so kindly towards her, it occurred to him that a word in season, opening her eyes to his nephew's true character, might prevent the girl making a mistake which she would regret for ever when it was too late.

'I think you know my nephew Ronald?' he said.

'Yes.'

Lord Emsworth paused to smell a rose. He gave Sue a brief biography of it before returning to the theme.

'That boy's an ass,' he said.

'Why?' said Sue sharply. She began to feel less amiable towards this stringy old man. A moment before, she had been thinking that it was rather charming, that funny, vague manner of his. Now she saw him clearly for what he was—a dodderer, and a Class A dodderer at that.

'Why?' His lordship considered the point. 'Well, heredity, probably, I should say. His father, old Miles Fish, was the biggest fool in the Brigade of Guards.' He looked at her impressively through slanting pince-nez, as if to call her attention to the fact that this was something of an achievement. 'The boy bounces tennis-balls on pigs,' he went on, getting down to the ghastly facts.

Sue was surprised. The words, if she had caught them correctly, seemed to present a side of Ronnie's character of which she had been unaware.

'Does what?'

'I saw him with my own eyes. He bounced a tennis-ball on Empress of Blandings. And not once but repeatedly.'

The motherly instinct which all girls feel towards the men they love urged Sue to say something in Ronnie's defence. But, apart from suggesting that the pig had probably started it, she could not think of anything. They left the rose-garden and began to walk back to the lawn, Lord Emsworth still exercised by the thought of his nephew's shortcomings. For one reason and another, Ronnie had always been a source of vague annoyance to him since boyhood. There had even been times when he had felt that he would almost have preferred the society of his younger son, Frederick.

'Aggravating boy,' he said. 'Most aggravating. Always up to something or other. Started a night-club the other day. Lost a lot of money over it. Just the sort of thing he would do. My brother Galahad started some kind of a club many years ago. It cost my old father nearly a thousand pounds, I recollect. There is something about Ronald that reminds me very much of Galahad at the same age.'

Although Sue had found much in the author of the Reminiscences to attract her, she was able to form a very fair estimate of the sort of young man he must have been in the middle twenties. This charge, accordingly, struck her as positively libellous.

'I don't agree with you, Lord Emsworth.'

'But you never knew my brother Galahad as a young man,' his lordship pointed out cleverly.

'What is the name of that hill over there?' asked Sue in a cold voice, changing the unpleasant subject.

'That hill? Oh, that one?' It was the only one in sight. 'It is called the Wrekin.'

'Oh?' said Sue.

'Yes,' said Lord Emsworth.

'Ah,' said Sue.

They had crossed the lawn and were on the broad terrace that looked out over the park. Sue leaned on the low stone wall that bordered it and gazed before her into the gathering dusk.

The castle had been built on a knoll of rising ground, and on this terrace one had the illusion of being perched up at a great height. From where she stood, Sue got a sweeping view of the park and of the dim, misty Vale of Blandings that dreamed beyond. In the park, rabbits were scuttling to and fro. In the shrubberies birds called sleepily. From somewhere out across the fields there came the faint tinkling of sheep-bells. The lake shone like old silver, and there was a river in the distance, dull grey between the dull green of the trees.

It was a lovely sight, age-old, orderly and English, but it was spoiled by the sky. The sky was overcast and looked bruised. It seemed to be made of dough, and one could fancy it pressing down on the world like a heavy blanket. And it was muttering to itself. A single heavy drop of rain splashed on the stone beside Sue, and there was a low growl far away as if some powerful and unfriendly beast had spied her.

She shivered. She had been gripped by a sudden depression, a strange foreboding that chilled the spirit. That muttering seemed to say that there was no happiness anywhere and never could be any. The air was growing close and clammy. Another drop of rain fell, squashily like a toad, and spread itself over her hand.

Lord Emsworth was finding his companion unresponsive. His stream of prattle slackened and died away. He began to wonder how he was to escape from a girl who, though undeniably pleasing to the eye, was proving singularly difficult to talk to. Raking the horizon in search of aid, he perceived Beach approaching, a silver salver in his hand. The salver had a card on it, and an envelope.

'For me, Beach?'

'The card, your lordship. The gentleman is in the hall.'

Lord Emsworth breathed a sigh of relief.

'You will excuse me, my dear? It is most important that I should see this fellow immediately. My brother Galahad will be back very shortly, I have no doubt. He will entertain you. You don't mind?'

He bustled away, glad to go, and Sue became conscious of the salver, thrust deferentially towards her.

'For you, miss.'

'For me?'

'Yes, miss,' moaned Beach, like a winter wind wailing through dead trees.

He inclined his head sombrely, and was gone. Sue tore open the envelope. For one breath-taking instant she had thought it might be from Ronnie. But the writing was not Ronnie's familiar scrawl. It was bold, clear, decisive writing, the writing of an efficient man.

She looked at the last page.

'Yours sincerely,

'R. J. BAXTER'

Sue's heart was beating faster as she turned back to the beginning. When a girl in the position in which she had placed herself has been stared at through steel-rimmed spectacles in the way this R. J. Baxter had stared at her through his spectacles, her initial reaction to mysterious notes from the man behind the lenses cannot but be a panic fear that all has been discovered.

The opening sentence dispelled her alarm. Purely personal motives, it appeared, had caused Rupert Baxter to write these few lines. The mere fact that the letter began with the words,

'Dear Miss Schoonmaker,'

was enough in itself to bring comfort.

'At the risk of annoying you by the intrusion of my private affairs (wrote the Efficient Baxter), I feel that I must give you an explanation of the incident which occurred in the garden in your presence this afternoon. From the observation—in the grossest taste—which Lord Emsworth let fall in my hearing, I fear you may have placed a wrong construction on what took place. (I allude to the expression "Mad as a coot", which I distinctly heard Lord Emsworth utter as I moved away.)

'The facts were precisely as I stated. I was leaning out of the library window, and, chancing to lean too far, I lost my balance and fell. That I might have received serious injuries and was entitled to expect sympathy, I overlook. But the words "Mad as a coot" I resent extremely.

'Had this incident not occurred, I would not have dreamed of saying anything to prejudice you against your host. As it is, I feel that in justice to myself I must tell you that Lord Emsworth is a man to whose utterances no attention should be paid. He is to all intents and purposes half-witted. Life in the country, with its lack of intellectual stimulus, has caused his natural feebleness of mind to reach a stage which borders closely on insanity. His relatives look on him as virtually an imbecile and have, in my opinion, every cause to do so.

'In these circumstances, I think I may rely on you to attach no importance to his remarks this afternoon.

'Yours sincerely,

'R. J. BAXTER

'P. S. *You will, of course, treat this as entirely confidential.*

'P. P. S. *If you are fond of chess and would care for a game after dinner, I am a good player.*

'P. P. S. S. *Or Bezique.'*

Sue thought it a good letter, neat and well-expressed. Why it had been written, she could not imagine. It had not occurred to her that love—or, at any rate, a human desire to marry a wealthy heiress—had begun to burgeon in R. J. Baxter's bosom. With no particular emotions, other than the feeling that if he was counting on playing Bezique with her after dinner he was due for a disappointment, she put the letter in her pocket, and looked out over the park again.

The object of all good literature is to purge the soul of its petty troubles. This, she was pleased to discover, Baxter's letter had succeeded in doing. Recalling its polished phrases, she found herself smiling appreciatively.

That muttering sky did not look so menacing now. Everything, she told herself, was going to be all right. After all, she did not ask much from Fate—just an uninterrupted five minutes with Ronnie. And if Fate so far had denied her this very moderate demand . . .

'All alone?'

Sue turned, her heart beating quickly. The voice, speaking close behind her, had had something of the effect of a douche of iced water down her back. For, restorative though Baxter's letter had been, it had not left her in quite the frame of mind to enjoy anything so sudden and jumpy as an unexpected voice.

It was the Hon. Galahad, back from his interview with the gentleman, and the sight of him did nothing to calm her agitation. He was eyeing her, she thought, with a strange and sinister intentness. And though his manner, as he planted himself beside her and began to talk, seemed all that was cordial and friendly, she could not rid herself of a feeling of uneasiness. That look still lingered in her mind's eye. With the air all heavy and woolly and the sky growling pessimistic prophecies, it had been a look to alarm the bravest girl.

Chattering amiably, the Hon. Galahad spoke of this and that; of scenery and the weather; of birds and rabbits; of friends of his who had served terms in prison and of other friends who, one would have said on the evidence, had been lucky to escape. Then his monocle was up again, and that look was back on his face.

The air was more breathless than ever.

'You know,' said the Hon. Galahad, 'it's been a great treat to me, meeting you, my dear. I haven't seen any of your people for a number of years, but your father and I correspond pretty regularly. He tells me all the news. Did you leave your family well?'

'Quite well.'

'How was your Aunt Edna?'

'Fine,' said Sue feebly.

'Ah,' said the Hon. Galahad. 'Then your father must have been mistaken when he told me she was dead. But perhaps you thought I meant your Aunt Edith?'

'Yes,' said Sue gratefully.

'She's all right, I hope?'

'Oh, yes.'

'What a lovely woman!'

'Yes.'

'You mean she still is?'

'Oh, yes.'

'Remarkable! She must be well over seventy by now. No doubt you mean beautiful considering she is over seventy?'

'Yes.'

'Pretty active?'

'Oh, yes.'

'When did you see her last?'

'Oh—just before I sailed.'

'And you say she's active? Curious! I heard two years ago that she was paralysed. I suppose you mean active for a paralytic.'

The little puckers at the corners of his eyes deepened into wrinkles. The monocle gleamed like the eye of a dragon. He smiled genially.

'Confide in me, Miss Brown,' he said. 'What's the game?'

11

MORE SHOCKS FOR SUE

· I ·

Sue did not answer. When the solid world melts abruptly beneath the feet, one feels disinclined for speech. Avoiding the monocle, she stood looking with wide, blank eyes at a thrush which hopped fussily about the lawn. Behind her, the sky gave a low chuckle, as if this was what it had been waiting for.

'Up there,' proceeded the Hon. Galahad, pointing to the small library, 'is the room where I work. And sometimes, when I'm not working, I look out of the window. I was looking out a short while back when you were down here talking to my brother Clarence. There was a fellow with me. He looked out, too.' His voice sounded blurred and far-away. 'A theatrical manager fellow whom I used to know very well in the old days. A man named Mason.'

The thrush had flown away. Sue continued to gaze at the spot where it had been. Across the years, for the mind works oddly in times of stress, there had come to her a vivid recollection of herself at the age of ten, taken by her mother to the Isle of Man on her first steamer trip and just beginning to feel the motion of the vessel. There had been a moment then, just before the supreme catastrophe, when she had felt exactly as she was feeling now.

'We saw you, and he said "Why, there's Sue!"—I said "Sue? Sue Who?" "Sue Brown," said this fellow Mason. He said you were one of the girls at his theatre. He didn't seem particularly surprised to see you here. He said he took it that everything had been fixed up all right and he was glad, because you were one of the best. He wanted to come and have a chat with you, but I headed him off. I thought you might prefer to talk over this little matter of your being Miss Sue Brown alone with me. Which brings me back to my original question. What, Miss Brown, is the game?'

Sue felt dizzy, helpless, hopeless.

'I can't explain,' she said.

The Hon. Galahad tut-tutted protestingly.

'You don't mean to say you propose to leave the thing as just another of those historic mysteries? Don't you want me ever to get a good night's sleep again?'

'Oh, it's so long.'

'We have the evening before us. Take it bit by bit, a little at a time. To begin with, what did Mason mean by saying that everything was all right?'

'I had told him about Ronnie.'

'Ronnie? My nephew Ronald?'

'Yes. And, seeing me here, he naturally took it for granted that Lord Emsworth and the rest of you had consented to the engagement and invited me to the castle.'

'Engagement?'

'I used to be engaged to Ronnie.'

'What! That young Fish?'

'Yes.'

'Good God!' said the Hon. Galahad.

Suddenly Sue began to feel conscious of a slackening of the tension. Mysteriously, the conversation was seeming less difficult. In spite of the fact that Reason scoffed at the absurdity of such an idea, she felt just as if she were talking to a potential friend and ally. The thought had come to her at the moment when, looking up, she caught sight of her companion's face. It is an unpleasant thing to say of any man, but there is no denying that the Hon. Galahad's face, when he was listening to the confessions of those who had behaved as they ought not to have behaved, very frequently lacked the austerity and disapproval which one likes to see in faces on such occasions.

'But however did Pa Mason come to be here?' asked Sue.

'He came to discuss some business in connexion with . . . Never mind about that,' said the Hon. Galahad, calling the meeting to order. 'Kindly refrain from wandering from the point. I'm beginning to see daylight. You are engaged to Ronald, you say?'

'I was.'

'But you broke it off?'

'He broke it off.'

'He did?'

'Yes. That's why I came here. You see, Ronnie was here and I was in London and you can't put things properly in letters, so I thought that if I could get down to Blandings I could see him and explain and put everything right . . . and I'd met Lady Constance in London one day when I was with Ronnie and he had introduced me as Miss Schoonmaker, so that part of it was all right . . . so . . . Well, so I came.'

If this chronicle has proved anything, it has proved by now that the moral outlook of the Hon. Galahad Threepwood was fundamentally unsound. A man to shake the head at. A man to view with concern. So felt his sister, Lady Constance Keeble, and she was undoubtedly right. If final evidence were needed, his next words supplied it.

'I never heard,' said the Hon. Galahad, beaming like one listening to a tale of virtue triumphant, 'anything so dashed sporting in my life.'

Sue's heart leaped. She had felt all along that Reason, in denying the possibility that this man could ever approve of what she had done, had been mistaken. These pessimists always are.

'You mean,' she cried, 'you won't give me away?'

'Me?' said the Hon. Galahad, aghast at the idea. 'Of course I won't. What do you take me for?'

'I think you're an angel.'

The Hon. Galahad seemed pleased at the compliment, but it was plain that there was something that worried him. He frowned a little.

'What I can't make out,' he said, 'is why you want to marry my nephew Ronald.'

'I love him, bless his heart.'

'No, seriously!' protested the Hon. Galahad. 'Do you know that he once put tin-tacks on my chair?'

'And he bounces tennis-balls on pigs. All the same, I love him.'

'You can't!'

'I do.'

'How can you possibly love a fellow like that?'

'That's just what he always used to say,' said Sue softly. 'And I think that's why I love him.'

The Hon. Galahad sighed. Fifty years' experience had taught him that it was no use arguing with women on this particular point, but he had conceived a warm affection for this girl, and it shocked him to think of her madly throwing herself away.

'Don't you go doing anything in a hurry, my dear. Think it over carefully. I've seen enough of you to know that you're a very exceptional girl.'

'I don't believe you like Ronnie.'

'I don't dislike him. He's improved since he was a boy. I'll admit that. But he isn't worthy of you.'

'Why not?'

'Well, he isn't.'

She laughed.

'It's funny that you of all people should say that. Lord Emsworth was telling me just now that Ronnie is exactly like what you used to be at his age.'

'What!'

'That's what he said.'

The Hon. Galahad stared incredulously.

'That boy like me?' He spoke with indignation, for his pride had been sorely touched. 'Ronald like me? Why, I was twice the man he is. How many policemen do you think it used to take to shift me from the Alhambra to Vine Street when I was in my prime? Two! Sometimes three. And one walking behind carrying my hat. Clarence ought to be more careful what he says, dash it. It's just this kind of loose talk that makes trouble. The fact of the matter is, he's gone and got his brain so addled with pigs he doesn't know what he is saying half the time.'

He pulled himself together with a strong effort. He became calmer.

'What did you and that young poop quarrel about?' he asked.

'He is not a poop!'

'He is. It's astonishing to me that any one individual can be such a poop. You'd have thought it would have required a large syndicate. How long have you known him?'

'About nine months.'

'Well, I've known him all his life. And I say he's a poop. If he wasn't, he wouldn't have quarrelled with you. However, we won't split straws. What did you quarrel about?'

'He found me dancing.'

'What's wrong with that?'

'I had promised I wouldn't.'

'And is that all the trouble?'

'It's quite enough for me.'

The Hon. Galahad made light of the tragedy.

'I don't see what you're worrying about. If you can't smooth a little thing like that over, you're not the girl I take you for.'

'I thought I might be able to.'

'Of course you'll be able to. Girls were always doing that sort of thing to me in my young days, and I never held out for five minutes, once the crying started. Go and sob on the boy's waist-coat. How are you as a sobber?'

'Not very good, I'm afraid.'

'Well, there are all sorts of other tricks you can try. Every girl knows a dozen. Falling on your knees, fainting, laughing hysterically, going rigid all over . . . scores of them.'

'I think it will be all right if I can just talk to him. The difficulty is to get an opportunity.'

The Hon. Galahad waved a hand spaciously.

'Make an opportunity! Why, I knew a girl years ago—she's a grandmother now—who had a quarrel with the fellow she was engaged to, and a week or so later she found herself staying at the same country-house with him—Heron's Hill it was. The Matchelows' place in Sussex—and she got him into her room one night and locked the door and said she was going to keep him there all night and ruin both their reputations unless he handed back the ring and agreed that the engagement was on again. And she'd have done it, too. Her name was Frederica Something. Red-haired girl.'

'I suppose you have to have red hair to do a thing like that. I was thinking of a quiet meeting in the rose-garden.'

The Hon. Galahad seemed to consider this tame, but he let it pass.

'Well, whatever you do, you'll have to be quick about it, my dear. Suppose old Johnny Schoonmaker's girl really turns up? She said she was going to.'

'Yes, but I made Ronnie send her a telegram, signed with Lady Constance's name, saying that there was scarlet fever at the castle and she wasn't to come.'

One dislikes the necessity of perpetually piling up the evidence against the Hon. Galahad Threepwood, to show ever more and more clearly how warped was his moral outlook. Nevertheless the fact must be stated that at these words he threw his head up and uttered a high, piercing laugh that sent the thrush, which had just returned to the lawn, starting back as if a bullet had hit it. It was a laugh which, when it had rung out in days of yore in London's more lively night-resorts, had caused commissionaires to leap like war-horses at the note of the bugle, to spit on their hands, feel their muscles and prepare for action.

'It's the finest thing I ever heard!' cried the Hon. Galahad. It restores my faith in the younger generation. And a girl like you seriously contemplates marrying a boy like . . . Oh, well!' he said resignedly, seeming to brace himself to make the best of a distasteful state of affairs, 'It's your business, I suppose. You know your own mind best. After all, the great thing is to get you into the family. A girl like you is what this family has been needing for years.'

He patted her kindly on the shoulder, and they started to walk towards the house. As they did so, two men came out of it.

One was Lord Emsworth. The other was Percy Pilbeam.

· II ·

There is about a place like Blandings Castle something which, if you are not in the habit of visiting country-houses planned on the grand scale, tends to sap the morale. At the moment when Sue caught sight of him, the proprietor of the Argus Enquiry Agency was not feeling his brightest and best.

Beach, ushering him through the front door, had started the trouble. He had merely let his eye rest upon Pilbeam, but it had been enough. The butler's eye, through years of insufficient exercise and too hearty feeding, had acquired in the process of time a sort of glaze which many people found trying when they saw it. In Pilbeam it created an inferiority complex of the severest kind.

He could not know that to this godlike man he was merely a blur. To Beach, tortured by the pangs of a guilty conscience, almost everything nowadays was merely a blur. Misinterpreting his gaze, Pilbeam had read into it a shocked contempt, a kind of wincing agony at the thought that things like himself should be creeping into Blandings Castle. He felt as if he had crawled out from under a flat stone.

And it was at this moment that somebody in the dimness of the hall had stepped forward and revealed himself as the young man, name unknown, who had showed such a lively disposition to murder him on the dancing-floor of Mario's restaurant. And from the violent start which he gave, it was plain that the young man's memory was as good as his own.

So far, things had not broken well for Percy Pilbeam. But now his luck turned. There had appeared in the nick of time an angel from heaven, effectively disguised in a shabby shooting-coat and an old hat. He had introduced himself as Lord Emsworth, and he had taken Pilbeam off with him into the garden. Looking back over his shoulder, Pilbeam saw that the young man was still standing there, staring after him—wistfully, it seemed to him; and he was glad, as he followed his host out into the fresh air, to be beyond the range of his eye. Between it and the eye of Beach, the butler, there seemed little to choose.

Relief, however, by the time he arrived on the terrace, had not completely restored his composure. That inferiority complex was still at work, and his surroundings intimidated him. At any moment, he felt, on a terrace like this, there might suddenly appear to confront him and complete his humiliation some brilliant shattering creature indigenous to this strange and disturbing world—a Duchess, perhaps—a haughty hunting woman it might be—the dashing daughter of a hundred Earls, possibly who would look at him as Beach had looked at him and raising beautifully pencilled eyebrows in aristocratic disdain, turn away with a murmured 'Most extraordinary!' He was prepared for almost anything.

One of the few things he was not prepared for was Sue. And at the sight of her he leaped three clear inches and nearly broke a collar stud.

'Gaw!' he said.

'I beg your pardon?' said Lord Emsworth. He had not caught his companion's remark and hoped he would repeat it. The lightest utterance of a detective with the trained mind is something not to be missed. 'What did you say, my dear fellow?'

He, too, perceived Sue; and with a prodigious effort of the memory, working by swift stages through Schofield, Maybury, Coolidge and Spooner, recalled her name.

'Mr Pilbeam, Miss Schoonmaker,' he said. 'Galahad, this is Mr Pilbeam. Of the Argus, you remember.'

'Pilbeam?'

'How do you do?'

'Pilbeam?'

'My brother,' said Lord Emsworth, exerting himself to complete the introduction. 'This is my brother Galahad.'

'Pilbeam?' said the Hon. Galahad, looking intently at the proprietor of the Argus. 'Were you ever connected with a paper called *Society Spice*, Mr Pilbeam?'

The gardens of Blandings Castle seemed to the detective to rock gently. There had, he knew, been a rigid rule in the office of that bright, but frequently offensive, paper that the editor's name was never to be revealed to callers: but it now appeared only too sickeningly evident that a leakage had occurred. Underlings, he realized too late, can be bribed.

He swallowed painfully. Force of habit had come within a hair's-breath of making him say 'Quite.'

'Never,' he gasped. 'Certainly not. No! Never.'

'A fellow of your name used to edit it. Uncommon name, too.'

'Relation, perhaps. Distant.'

'Well, I'm sorry you're not the man,' said the Hon. Galahad regretfully. 'I've been wanting to meet him. He wrote a very offensive thing about me once. Most offensive thing.'

Lord Emsworth, who had been according the conversation the rather meagre interest which he gave to all conversations that did not deal with pigs, created a diversion.

'I wonder,' he said, 'if you would like to see some photographs?'

It seemed to Pilbeam, in his disordered state, strange that anyone should suppose that he was in a frame of mind to enjoy the Family Album, but he uttered a strangled sound which his host took for acquiescence.

'Of the Empress, I mean, of course. They will give you some idea of what a magnificent animal she is. They will . . .' He sought for the *mot juste*. '. . . stimulate you. I'll go to the library and get them out.'

The Hon. Galahad was now his old, affable self again.

'You doing anything after dinner?' he asked Sue.

'There was some talk,' said Sue, 'of a game of Bezique with Mr Baxter.'

'Don't dream of it,' said the Hon. Galahad vehemently. 'The fellow would probably try to brain you with the mallet. I was thinking that if I hadn't got to go out to dinner I'd like to read you some of my book. I think you would appreciate it. I wouldn't read it to anybody except you. I somehow feel you've got the right sort of outlook. I let my sister Constance see a couple of pages once, and she was too depressing for words. An author can't work if people depress him. I'll tell you what I'll do. I'll give you the thing to read. Which is your room?'

'The Garden Room, I think it's called.'

'Oh yes. Well, I'll bring the manuscript to you before I leave.'

He sauntered off. There was a moment's pause. Then Sue turned to Pilbeam. Her chin was tilted. There was defiance in her eye.

'Well?' she said.

· III ·

Percy Pilbeam breathed a sigh of relief. At the first moment of their meeting, all that he had ever read about doubles had raced through his mind. This question clarified the situation. It put matters on a firm basis. His head ceased to swim. It was Sue Brown and no other who stood before him.

'What on earth are you doing here?' he asked.

'Never mind.'

'What's the game?'

'Never mind.'

'There's no need to be so dashed unfriendly.'

'Well, if you must know, I came here to see Ronnie and try to explain about that night at Mario's.'

There was a pause.

'What was that name the old boy called you?'

'Schoonmaker.'

'Why did he call you that?'

'Because that's who he thinks I am.'

'What on earth made you choose a name like that?'

'Oh, don't keep on asking questions.'

'I don't believe there is such a name. And when it comes to asking questions,' said Pilbeam warmly, 'what do you expect me to do? I never got such a shock in my life as when I met you just now. I thought I was seeing things. Do you mean to say you're here under a false name, pretending to be somebody else?'

'Yes.'

'Well, I'm hanged! And as friendly as you please with everybody.'

'Yes.'

'Everybody except me.'

'Why should I be friendly with you? You've done your best to ruin my life.'

'Eh?'

'Oh, never mind,' said Sue impatiently.

There was another pause.

'Chatty!' said Pilbeam, wounded again.

He fidgeted his fingers along the wall.

'That Galahad fellow seems to look on you as a daughter or something.'

'We are great friends.'

'So I see. And he's going to give you his book to read.'

'Yes.'

A keen, purposeful, Argus-Enquiry-Agent sort of look shot into Pilbeam's face.

'Well, this is where you and I get together,' he said.

'What do you mean?'

'I'll tell you what I mean. Do you want to make some money?'

'No,' said Sue.

'What! Of course you do. Everybody does. Now listen. Do you know why I'm here?'

'I've stopped wondering why you're anywhere. You just seem to pop up.'

She started to move away. A sudden, disturbing thought had come to her. At any moment Ronnie might appear on the terrace. If he found her here, closeted, so to speak, with the abominable Pilbeam, what would he think? What, rather, would he not think?

'Where are you going?'

'Into the house.'

'Come back,' said Pilbeam urgently.

'I'm going.'

'But I've got something important to say.'

'Well?'

She stopped.

'That's right,' said Pilbeam approvingly. 'Now listen. You'll admit that, if I liked, I could give you away and spoil whatever game it is that you're up to in this place?'

'Well?'

'But I'm not going to do it. If you'll be sensible.'

'Sensible?'

Pilbeam looked cautiously up and down the terrace.

'Now listen,' he said. 'I want your help. I'll tell you why I'm here. The old boy thinks I've come down to find his pig, but I haven't. I've come to get that book your friend Galahad is writing.'

'What!'

'I thought you'd be surprised. Yes, that's what I'm after. There's a man living near here who's scared stiff that there's going to be a lot of stories about him in that book, and he came to see me at my office yesterday and offered me . . .' He hesitated a moment. '. . . Offered me,' he went on, 'a hundred pounds if I'd get into the house somehow and snitch the manuscript. And you being friendly with the old buster has made everything simple.'

'You think so?'

'Easy,' he assured her. 'Especially now he's going to give you the thing to read. All you have to do is hand it over to me, and there's fifty quid for you. For doing practically nothing.'

Sue's eyes lit up. Pilbeam had expected that they would. He could not conceive of a girl whose eyes would not light up at such an offer.

'Oh?' said Sue.

'Fifty quid,' said Pilbeam. 'I'm going halves with you.'

'And if I don't do what you want I suppose you will tell them who I really am?'

'That's it,' said Pilbeam, pleased at her ready intelligence.

'Well, I'm not going to do anything of the kind.'

'What!'

'And if,' said Sue, 'you want to tell these people who I am, go ahead and tell them.'

'I will.'

'Do. But just bear in mind that the moment you do I shall tell Mr Threepwood that it was you who wrote that thing about him in *Society Spice*.'

Percy Pilbeam swayed like a sapling in the breeze. The blow had unmanned him. He found no words with which to reply.

'I will,' said Sue.

Pilbeam continued speechless. He was still trying to recover from this deadly thrust through an unexpected chink in his armour when the opportunity for speech passed. Millicent had appeared, and was walking along the terrace towards them. She wore her customary air of settled gloom. On reaching them, she paused.

'Hullo,' said Millicent, from the depths.

'Hullo,' said Sue.

The library window framed the head and shoulders of Lord Emsworth.

'Pilbeam, my dear fellow, will you come up to the library. I have found the photographs.'

Millicent eyed the detective's retreating back with a mournful curiosity.

'Who's he?'

'A man named Pilbeam.'

'Pill, I should say, is right. What makes him waddle like that?'

Sue was unable to supply a solution to this problem. Millicent came and stood beside her, and, leaning on the stone parapet, gazed disparagingly at the park. She gave the impression of disliking all parks, but this one particularly.

'Ever read Schopenhauer?' she asked, after a silence.

'No.'

'You should. Great stuff.'

She fell into a heavy silence again, her eyes peering into the gathering gloom. Somewhere in the twilight world a cow had begun to emit long, nerve-racking bellows. The sound seemed to sum up and underline the general sadness.

'Schopenhauer says that all the suffering in the world can't be mere chance. Must be meant. He says life's a mixture of suffering and boredom. You've got to have one or the other. His stuff's full of snappy cracks like that. You'd enjoy it. Well, I'm going for a walk. You coming?'

'I don't think I will, thanks.'

'Just as you like. Schopenhauer says suicide's absolutely O.K. He says Hindoos do it instead of going to church. They bung themselves into the Ganges and get eaten by crocodiles and call it a well-spent day.'

'What a lot you seem to know about Schopenhauer.'

'I've been reading him up lately. Found a copy in the library. Schopenhauer says we are like lambs in a field, disporting themselves under the eye of the butcher, who chooses first one and then another for his prey. Sure you won't come for a walk?'

'No thanks. I think I'll go in.'

'Just as you like,' said Millicent. 'Liberty Hall.'

She moved off a few steps, then returned.

'Sorry if I seem loopy,' she said. 'Something on my mind. Been giving it a spot of thought. The fact is, I've just got engaged to be married to my cousin Ronnie.'

The trees that stood out against the banking clouds seemed to swim before Sue's eyes. An unseen hand had clutched her by the throat and was crushing the life out of her.

'Ronnie!'

'Yes,' said Millicent, rather in the tone of voice which Schopenhauer would have used when announcing the discovery of a caterpillar in his salad. 'We fixed it up just now.'

She wandered away, and Sue clung to the terrace wall. That at least was solid in a world that rocked and crashed.

'I say!'

It was Hugo. She was looking at him through a mist, but there was never any mistaking Hugo Carmody.

'I say! Did she tell you?'

Sue nodded.

'She's engaged.'

Sue nodded.

'She's going to marry Ronnie.'

Sue nodded.

'Death, where is thy sting?' said Hugo, and vanished in the direction taken by Millicent.

12

ACTIVITIES OF BEACH THE BUTLER

· I ·

The firm and dignified note in which Rupert Baxter had expressed his considered opinion of the Earl of Emsworth had been written in the morning-room immediately upon the ex-secretary's return to the house and delivered into Beach's charge with hands still stained with garden-mould. Only when this urgent task had been performed did he start to go upstairs in quest of the wash and brush-up which he so greatly needed. He was mounting the stairs to his bedroom and had reached the first floor when a door opened and his progress was arrested by what in a lesser woman would have been a yelp. Proceeding, as it did, from the lips of Lady Constance Keeble, we must call it an exclamation of surprise.

'Mr Baxter!'

She was standing in the doorway of her boudoir, and she eyed his dishevelled form with such open-mouthed astonishment that for an instant the ex-secretary came near to including her with the head of the family in the impromptu Commination Service which was taking shape in his mind. He was in no mood for wide-eyed looks of wonder.

'May I come in?' he said curtly. He could explain all, but he did not wish to do so on the first floor landing of a house where almost anybody might be listening with flapping ears.

'But, Mr Baxter!' said Lady Constance.

He paused for a moment to grit his teeth, then closed the door.

'What *have* you been doing, Mr Baxter?'

'Jumping out of window.'

'Jumping out of *win*-dow?'

He gave a brief synopsis of the events which had led up to his spirited act. Lady Constance drew in her breath with a remorseful hiss.

'Oh, dear!' she said. 'How foolish of me. I should have told you.'

'I beg your pardon?'

Even though she was in the safe retirement of her boudoir Lady Constance Keeble looked cautiously over her shoulder. In the stirring and complicated state into which life had got itself at Blandings Castle, practically everybody in the place except Lord Emsworth, had fallen into the habit nowadays of looking cautiously over his or her shoulder before he or she spoke.

'Sir Gregory Parsloe said in his note,' she explained, 'that this man Pilbeam who is coming here this evening is acting for him.'

'Acting for him?'

'Yes. Apparently Sir Gregory went to see him yesterday and has promised him a large sum of money if he will obtain possession of my brother Galahad's manuscript. That is why he has invited us to dinner to-night, to get Galahad out of the house. So there was no need for you to have troubled.'

There was a silence.

'So there was no need,' repeated the Efficient Baxter slowly, wiping from his eye the remains of a fragment of mould which had been causing him some inconvenience, 'for me to have troubled.'

'I am so sorry, Mr Baxter.'

'Pray do not mention it, Lady Constance.'

His eye, now that the mould was out of it, was able to work again with its customary keenness. His spectacles, as he surveyed the remorseful woman before him, had a cold, steely look.

'I see,' he said. 'Well, it might perhaps have spared me some little inconvenience had you informed me of this earlier, Lady Constance. I have bruised my left shin somewhat severely and, as you see, made myself rather dirty.'

'I am so sorry.'

'Furthermore, I gathered from the remark he let fall that the impression my actions have made upon Lord Emsworth is that I am insane.'

'Oh, dear.'

'He even specified the precise degree of insanity. As mad as a coot, were his words.'

He softened a little. He reminded himself that this woman before him, who was so nearly doing what is described as wringing her hands, had always been his friend, had always wished him well, had never slackened her efforts to restore him to the secretarial duties which he had once enjoyed.

'Well, it cannot be helped,' he said. 'The thing now is to think of some way of recovering the lost ground.'

'You mean, if you could find the Empress?'

'Exactly.'

'Oh, Mr Baxter, if you only could!'

'I can.'

Lady Constance stared at his dark, purposeful, efficient face in dumb admiration. To another man who had spoken those words she would have replied 'How?' or even 'How on earth?' But, as they had proceeded from Rupert Baxter, she merely waited silently for enlightenment.

'Have you given this matter any consideration, Lady Constance?'

'Yes.'

'To what conclusions have you come?'

Lady Constance felt dull and foolish. She felt like Doctor Watson— almost like a Scotland Yard Bungler.

'I don't think I have come to any,' she said, avoiding the spectacles guiltily. 'Of course,' she added, 'I think it is absurd to suppose that Sir Gregory . . .'

Baxter waved aside the notion. It was not even worth a 'Tchah!'

'In any matter of this kind,' he said, 'the first thing to do is to seek motive. Who is there in Blandings Castle who could have had a motive for stealing Lord Emsworth's pig?'

Lady Constance would have given a year's income to have been able to make some reasonably intelligent reply, but all she could do was look and listen. Baxter was not annoyed. He would not have had it otherwise. He preferred his audiences dumb and expectant.

'Carmody.'

'Mr Carmody?'

'Precisely. He is Lord Emsworth's secretary, and a most inefficient secretary, a secretary who stands hourly in danger of losing his position. He sees me arrive at the castle, a man who formerly held the post he holds. He is alarmed. He suspects. He searches wildly about in his mind for means of consolidating himself in Lord Emsworth's regard. Then he has an idea, the sort of wild, motion-picture-bred idea which would come to a man of his stamp. He thinks to himself that if he removes the pig and conceals it somewhere and then pretends to have found it and restores it to its owner, Lord Emsworth's gratitude will be so intense that all danger of his dismissal will be at an end.'

He removed his spectacles and wiped them. Lady Constance uttered a low cry. In anybody else it would have been a squeak. Baxter replaced his spectacles.

'I have no doubt the pig is somewhere in the grounds at this moment,' he said.

'But, Mr Baxter . . . !'

The ex-secretary raised a compelling hand.

'But he would not have undertaken a thing like this single-handed. A secretary's time is not his own, and it would be necessary to feed the pig at regular intervals. He would require an accomplice. And I think I know who that accomplice is. Beach!'

This time not even the chronicler's desire to place Lady Constance's utterances in the best and most attractive light can hide the truth. She bleated.

'Be-ee-ee-ee-ach!'

The spectacles raked her keenly.

'Have you observed Beach closely of late?'

She shook her head. She was not a woman who observed butlers closely.

'He has something on his mind. He is nervous. Guilty. Conscience-stricken. He jumps when you speak to him.'

'Does he?'

'Jumps,' repeated the Efficient Baxter. 'Just now I gave him a—I happened to address him, and he sprang in the air.' He paused. 'I have half a mind to go and question him.'

'Oh, Mr Baxter! Would that be wise?'

Rupert Baxter's intention of interrogating the butler had been merely a nebulous one, a sort of idle dream, but these words crystallized it into a resolve. He was not going to have people asking him if things would be wise.

'A few searching questions should force him to reveal the truth.'

'But he'll give notice!'

This interview had been dotted with occasions on which Baxter might reasonably have said 'Tchah!' but, as we have seen, until this moment he had refrained. He now said it.

'Tchah!' said the Efficient Baxter. 'There are plenty of other butlers.'

And with this undeniable truth he stalked from the room. The wash and brush-up were still as necessary as they had been ten minutes before, but he was too intent on the chase to think about washes and brushes-up. He hurried down the stairs. He crossed the hall. He passed through the green-baize door that led to the quarters of the Blandings Castle staff. And he was making his way along the dim passage to the pantry where at this hour Beach might be supposed to be, when its door opened abruptly and a vast form emerged.

It was the butler. And from the fact that he was wearing a bowler hat it was plain that he was seeking the great outdoors.

Baxter stopped in mid-stride and remained on one-leg, watching. Then, as his quarry disappeared in the direction of the back entrance he followed quickly.

Out in the open it was almost as dark as it had been in the passage. That grey, threatening sky had turned black by now. It was a swollen mass of inky clouds, heavy with the thunder, lightning and rain which so often come in the course of an English summer to remind the island race that they are hardy Nordics and must not be allowed to get their fibre all sapped by eternal sunshine like the less favoured dwellers in more southerly climes. It bayed at Baxter like a bloodhound.

But it took more than dirty weather to quell the Efficient Baxter when duty called. Like the character in Tennyson's poem who followed the gleam, he followed the butler. There was but one point about Beach which even remotely resembled a gleam, but it happened to be the only one which at this moment really mattered. He was easy to follow.

The shrubbery swallowed the butler. A few seconds later, it had swallowed the Efficient Baxter.

· II ·

There are those who maintain—and make a nice income by doing so in the evening papers—that in these degenerate days the old, hardy spirit of the Briton has died out. They represent themselves as seeking vainly for evidence of the survival of those qualities of toughness and endurance which once made Englishmen what they were. To such, the spectacle of Rupert Baxter braving the elements could not have failed to bring cheer and consolation. They would have been further stimulated by the conduct of Hugo Carmody.

It had not escaped Hugo's notice, as he left Sue on the terrace and started out in the wake of Millicent, that the weather was hotting up for a storm. He saw the clouds. He heard the fast-approaching thunder. For neither did he give a hoot. Let it rain, was Hugo's verdict. Let it jolly well rain as much as it dashed well wanted to. As if encouraged, the sky sent down a fat, wet drop which insinuated itself just between his neck and collar.

He hardly noticed it. The information confided to him by his friend Ronald Fish had numbed his senses so thoroughly that water down the back of the neck was merely an incident. He was feeling as he had not felt since the evening some years ago when, boxing for his University in the light-weight division, he had incautiously placed the point of his jaw in the exact spot at the moment occupied by his opponent's right fist. When you have done this or—equally—when you have just been told that the girl you love is definitely betrothed to another, you begin to understand how Anarchists must feel when the bomb goes off too soon.

In all the black days through which he had been living recently, Hugo had never really lost hope. It had been dim sometimes, but it had always been there. It was his opinion that he knew women, just as it was Sue's idea that she knew men. Like Sue, he had placed his trust in the thought that true love conquers all obstacles; that coldness melts; that sundered hearts may at long last be brought together again by a little judicious pleading and reasoning. Even the fact that Millicent stared at him, when they met, with large, scornful eyes that went through him like stilettos, unpleasant though it was, had not caused him to despair. He had looked forward to the moment when he should contrive to get her alone and do a bit of snappy talking along the right lines.

But this was final. This was the end. This put the tin hat on it. She was engaged to Ronnie. Soon she would be married to Ronnie. Like a gadfly the hideous thought sent Hugo Carmody reeling on through the gloom.

It was so dark now that he could scarcely see before him. And, looking about him, he discovered that the reason for this was that he had made his way into a wood of sorts. The West Wood, he deduced dully, taking into consideration the fact that there was no other in this particular part of the estate. Well, he might just as well be in the West Wood as anywhere. He trudged on.

The ground beneath his feet was spongy, and equipped with low-lying brambles which pricked through his thin flannels and would have caused him discomfort if he had been in the frame of mind to notice brambles. There were trees against which he bumped, and logs over which he tripped. And ahead of him, in a small clearing, there was a dilapidated-looking cottage. He noticed this because it seemed the sort of place where a man, now that a warm, gusty wind had sprung up, might shelter and light a cigarette. The need for tobacco had become imperative.

He was surprised to find that it was raining, and had apparently, from the state of his clothes, been raining for quite some time. It was also thundering. The storm had broken, and the boom of it seemed to be all round him. A flash of lightning reminded him that he was in just the kind of place, among all these trees, where blokes get struck. At dinner-time they are missed, and later on search-parties come out with lanterns. Somebody stumbles over something soft, and the rays of the lantern fall on a charred and blackened form. Here, quickly, we have found him! Where? Over here. Is *that* Hugo Carmody? Well, well! Pick him up, boys, and bring him along. He was a good chap once. Moody, though, of late. Some trouble about a girl, wasn't it? She will be sorry when she hears of this. Drove him to it, you might almost say. Steady with that stretcher. Now, when I say 'To me.' Right!

There was something about this picture which quite cheered Hugo up. Ajax defied the lightning. Hugo Carmody rather encouraged it than otherwise. He looked approvingly at a more than usually vivid flash that seemed to dart among the tree-tops like a snake. All the same, he was forced to reflect, he was getting dashed wet. No sense, when you came right down to it, in getting dashed wet. After all, a man could be struck by lightning just as well in that cottage sort of place over there. Ho! for the cottage, felt Hugo, and headed for it at a gallop.

He had just reached the door, when it was flung open. There was a noise rather like that made by a rising pheasant, and the next moment something white had flung itself into his arms and was weeping emotionally on his chest.

'Hugo! Hugo, darling!'

Reason told Hugo it could scarcely be Millicent who was clinging to him like this and speaking to him like this. And yet Millicent it most certainly appeared to be. She continued to speak, still in the same friendly, even chatty strain.

'Hugo! Save me!'

'Right ho!'

'I wur-wur-went in thur-thur-there to shush-shush-shelter from the rain and it's all pitch dark.'

Hugo squeezed her fondly and with the sort of relief that comes to men who find themselves squeezing where they had not thought to squeeze. No need for that snappy bit of talking now. No need for arguments and explanations, for pleadings and entreaties. No need for anything but a good biceps.

He was bewildered. But mixed with his bewilderment had come a certain feeling of complacency. There was no denying that it was enjoyable, this exhibition of tremulous weakness in one who, if she had had the shadow of a fault, had always been inclined to matter-of-factness and the display of that rather hard, bright self-sufficiency which is so characteristic of the modern girl. If this melting mood was due to the fact that Millicent, while in the cottage, had seen a ghost, Hugo wanted to meet that ghost and shake its hand. Every man likes to be in a position to say 'There, there, little woman!' to the girl of his heart, particularly if for the last few days she has been treating him like a more than ordinarily unpleasant worm, and Hugo Carmody felt that he was in that position now.

'There, there!' he said, not quite feeling up to risking the 'little woman'. 'It's all right.'

'But it tut-tut-tut . . .'

'It what?' said Hugo puzzled.

'It tut-tut-tut-tisn't. There's a man in there!'

'A man?'

'Yes. I didn't know there was anyone there, and it was pitch dark and I heard something move and I said "Who's that?" and then he suddenly spoke to me in German.'

'In German?'

'Yes.'

Hugo released her gently. His face was determined.

'I'm going in to have a look.'

'Hugo! Stop! You'll be killed.'

She stood there, rigid. The rain lashed about her, but she did not heed it. The lightning gleamed. She paid it no attention. For the minute that lasts an hour she waited, straining her ears for sounds of the death-struggle. Then a dim form appeared.

'I say, Millicent.'

'Hugo! Are you all right?'

'Yes. I'm all right. I say, Millicent, do you know what?'

'No, what?'

A chuckle came to her through the darkness.

'It's the pig.'

'It's what?'

'The pig.'

'Who's a pig?'

'This is. Your friend in here. It's Empress of Blandings, as large as life. Come and have a look.'

· III ·

Millicent had a look. She came to the door of the cottage and peered in. Yes, just as he had said, there was the Empress. In the feeble light of the match which Hugo was holding, the noble animal's attractive face was peering up at her—questioningly, as if wondering if she might be the bearer of the evening snack which would be so exceedingly welcome. The picture was one which would have set Lord Emsworth screaming with joy. Millicent merely gaped.

'How on earth did she get here?'

'That's what I'm going to find out,' said Hugo. 'One always knew she must be cached somewhere, of course. What is this place, anyway?'

'It used to be a gamekeeper's cottage, I believe.'

'Well, there seems to be a room up above,' said Hugo, striking another match. 'I'm going to go up there and wait. It's quite likely that somebody will be along to feed the animal, and I'm going to see who it is.'

'Yes, that's what we'll do. How clever of you!'

'Not you. You get back home.'

'I won't.'

There was a pause. A strong man would, no doubt, have asserted himself. But Hugo, though feeling better than he had done for days, was not feeling quite so strong as all that.

'Just as you like.' He shut the door. 'Well, come on. We'd better be making a move. The fellow may be here at any moment.'

They climbed the crazy stairs and lowered themselves cautiously to a floor which smelled of mice and mildew. Below, all was in darkness, but there were holes through which it would be possible to look when the time should come for looking. Millicent could feel one near her face.

'You don't think this floor will give way?' she asked rather nervously.

'I shouldn't think so. Why?'

'Well, I don't want to break my neck.'

'You don't, don't you? Well, I would jolly well like to break mine,' said Hugo, speaking tensely in the darkness. It had just occurred to him that now would be a good time for a heart-to-heart talk. 'If you suppose I'm keen on going on living with you and Ronnie doing the Wedding Glide all over the place, you're dashed well mistaken. I take it you're aware that you've broken my bally heart, what?'

'Oh, Hugo!' said Millicent.

Silence fell. Below, the Empress rustled. Aloft, something scuttered.

'Oo!' cried Millicent. 'Was that a rat?'

'I hope so.'

'What!'

'Rats gnaw you,' explained Hugo. 'They cluster round and chew you to the bone and put an end to your misery.'

There was silence again. Then Millicent spoke in a small voice.

'You're being beastly,' she said.

Remorse poured over Hugo in a flood.

'I'm frightfully sorry. Yes, I know I am, dash it. But, look here, you know . . . I mean, all this getting engaged to Ronnie. A bit thick, what? You don't expect me to give three hearty cheers, do you? Wouldn't want me to break into a few carefree dance-steps?'

'I can't believe it's really happened.'

'Well, how did it happen?'

'It sort of happened all of a sudden. I was feeling miserable and very angry with you and . . . and all that. And I met Ronnie and he took me for a stroll and we went down by the lake and started throwing little bits of stick at the swans, and suddenly Ronnie sort of grunted and said "I say!" and I said "Hullo?" and he said "Will you marry me?" and I said "All right," and he said "I ought to warn you, I despise all women," and I said "And I loathe all men" and he said "Right ho, I think we shall be very happy."'

'I see.'

'I only did it to score off you.'

'You succeeded.'

A trace of spirit crept into Millicent's voice.

'You never really loved me,' she said. 'You know jolly well you didn't.'

'Is that so?'

'Well, what did you want to go sneaking off to London for, then, and stuffing that beastly girl of yours with food?'

'She isn't my girl. And she isn't beastly.'

'She is.'

'Well, you seem to get on with her all right. I saw you chatting on the terrace together as cosily as dammit.'

'What!'

'Miss Schoonmaker.'

'I don't know what you're talking about. What's Miss Schoonmaker got to do with it?'

'Miss Schoonmaker isn't Miss Schoonmaker. She's Sue Brown.'

For a moment it seemed to Millicent that the crack in her companion's heart had spread to his head. Futile though the action was, she stared in the direction from which his voice had proceeded. Then, suddenly, his words took on a meaning. She gasped.

'She's followed you down here!'

'She hasn't followed me down here. She's followed Ronnie down here. Can't you get it into your nut,' said Hugo with justifiable exasperation, 'that you've been making floaters and bloomers and getting everything mixed up all along? Sue Brown has never cared a curse for me, and I've never thought anything about her, except that she's a jolly girl and nice to dance with. That's absolutely and positively the only reason I went out with her. I hadn't had a dance for six weeks and my feet had begun to itch so that I couldn't sleep at night. So I went to London and took her out and Ronnie found her talking to that pestilence Pilbeam and thought he had taken her out and she had told him she didn't even know the man, which was quite true, but Ronnie cut up rough and said he was through with her and came down here and she wanted to get a word with him, so she came down here, pretending to be Miss Schoonmaker, and the moment she gets here she finds Ronnie is engaged to you. A nice surprise for the poor girl!'

Millicent's head had begun to swim long before the conclusion of this recital.

'But what is Pilbeam doing down here?'

'Pilbeam?'

'He was on the terrace talking to her.'

A low snarl came through the darkness.

'Pilbeam here? Ah! So he came, after all, did he? He's the fellow Lord Emsworth sent me to, about the Empress. He runs the Argus Enquiry Agency. It was Pilbeam's minions that dogged my steps that night, at your request. So he's here, is he? Well, let him enjoy himself while he can. Let him sniff the country air while the sniffing is good. A bitter reckoning awaits that bloke.'

From the disorder of Millicent's mind another point emerged insistently demanding explanation.

'You said she wasn't pretty!'

'Who?'

'Sue Brown.'

'Nor she is.'

'You don't call her pretty? She's fascinating.'

'Not to me,' said Hugo doggedly. 'There's only one girl in the world that I call pretty, and she's going to marry Ronnie.' He paused. 'If you haven't realized by this time that I love you, and always shall love you, and have never loved anybody else, and never shall love anybody else, you're a fathead. If you brought me Sue Brown or any other girl in the world on a plate with water-cress round her, I wouldn't so much as touch her hand.'

Another rat—unless it was an exceptionally large mouse—had begun to make its presence felt in the darkness. It seemed to be enjoying an early dinner off a piece of wood. Millicent did not even notice it. She had reached out, and her hand had touched Hugo's arm. Her fingers closed on it desperately.

'Oh, Hugo!' she said.

The arm became animated. It clutched her, drew her along the mouse-and-mildew-scented floor. And time stood still.

Hugo was the first to break the silence.

'And to think that not so long ago I was wishing that a flash of lightning would strike me amidships!' he said.

The aroma of mouse and mildew had passed away. Violets seemed to be spreading their fragrance through the cottage. Violets and roses. The rat, a noisy feeder, had changed into an orchestra of harps, dulcimers and sackbuts that played soft music.

And then, jarring upon these sweet strains, there came the sound of the cottage door opening. And a moment later light shone through the holes in the floor.

Millicent gave Hugo's arm a warning pinch. They looked down. On the floor below stood a lantern, and beside it a man of massive build who, from the golloping noises that floated upwards, appeared to be giving the Empress those calories and proteins which a pig of her dimensions requires so often and in such large quantities.

This Good Samaritan had been stooping. Now he straightened himself and looked about him with an apprehensive eye. He raised the lantern, and its light fell upon his face.

And, as she saw that face, Millicent, forgetting prudence, uttered in a high, startled voice a single word.

'Beach!' cried Millicent.

Down below, the butler stood congealed. It seemed to him that the Voice of Conscience had spoken.

· IV ·

Conscience, besides having a musical voice, appeared also to be equipped with feet. Beach could hear them clattering down the stairs, and the volume of noise was so great that it seemed as if Conscience must be a centipede. But he did not stir. It would have required at that moment a derrick to move him, and there was no derrick in the game-keeper's cottage in the West Wood. He was still standing like a statue when Hugo and Millicent arrived. Only when the identity of the new-comers impressed itself on his numbed senses did his limbs begin to twitch and show some signs of relaxing. For he looked on Hugo as a friend. Hugo, he felt, was one of the few people in his world who, finding him in his present questionable position, might be expected to take the broad and sympathetic view.

He nerved himself to speak.

'Good evening, sir. Good evening, miss.'

'What's all this?' said Hugo.

Years ago, in his hot and reckless youth, Beach had once heard that question from the lips of a policeman. It had disconcerted him then. It disconcerted him now.

'Well, sir,' he replied.

Millicent was staring at the Empress, who, after one courteous look of inquiry at the intruders, had given a brief grunt of welcome and returned to the agenda.

'*You* stole her, Beach? *You!*'

The butler quivered. He had known this girl since her long hair and rompers days. She had sported in his pantry. He had cut elephants out of paper for her and taught her tricks with bits of string. The shocked note in her voice seared him like vitriol. To her, he felt, niece to the Earl of Emsworth and trained by his lordship from infancy in the best traditions of pig-worship, the theft of the Empress must seem the vilest of crimes. He burned to re-establish himself in her eyes.

There comes in the life of every conspirator a moment when loyalty to his accomplices wavers before the urge to make things right for himself. We can advance no more impressive proof of the nobility of the butler's soul than that he did not obey this impulse. Millicent's accusing eyes were piercing him, but he remained true to his trust. Mr Ronald had sworn him to secrecy: and even to square himself he could not betray him.

And, as if by way of a direct reward from Providence for this sterling conduct, inspiration descended upon Beach.

'Yes, miss,' he replied.

'Oh, Beach!'

'Yes, miss. It was I who stole the animal. I did it for your sake, miss.'

Hugo eyed him sternly.

'Beach,' he said. 'This is pure apple-sauce.'

'Sir?'

'Apple-sauce, I repeat. Why endeavour to swing the lead, Beach? What do you mean, you stole the pig for her sake?'

'Yes,' said Millicent. 'Why for my sake?'

The butler was calm now. He had constructed his story, and he was going to stick to it.

'In order to remove the obstacles in your path, miss.'

'Obstacles?'

'Owing to the fact that you and Mr Carmody have frequently entrusted me with your—may I say surreptitious correspondence, I have long been cognizant of your sentiments towards one another, miss. I am aware that it is your desire to contract a union with Mr Carmody, and I knew that there would be objections raised on the part of certain members of the family.'

'So far,' said Hugo critically, 'this sounds to me like drivel of the purest water. But go on.'

'Thank you, sir. And then it occurred to me that, were his lordship's pig to disappear, his lordship would, on recovering the animal, be extremely grateful to whoever restored it. It was my intention to apprise you of the animal's whereabouts, and suggest that you should inform his lordship that you had discovered it. In his gratitude, I fancied, his lordship would consent to the union.'

There could never be complete silence in any spot where Empress of Blandings was partaking of food; but something as near silence as was possible followed this speech. In the rays of the lantern Hugo's eyes met Millicent's. In hers, as in his, there was a look of stunned awe. They had heard of faithful old servitors. They had read about faithful old servitors. They had seen faithful old servitors on the stage. But never had they dreamed that faithful old servitors could be as faithful as this.

'Oh, Beach!' said Millicent.

She had used the words before. But how different this 'Oh, Beach!' was from that other, earlier 'Oh, Beach!' On that occasion, the exclamation had been vibrant with reproach, pain, disillusionment. Now, it contained gratitude, admiration, an affection almost too deep for speech.

And the same may be said of Hugo's 'Gosh!'

'Beach,' cried Millicent, 'you're an angel!'

'Thank you, miss.'

'A topper!' agreed Hugo.

'Thank you, sir.'

'However did you get such a corking idea?'

'It came to me, miss.'

'I'll tell you what it is, Beach,' said Hugo earnestly. 'When you hand in your dinner-pail in due course of time—and may the moment be long distant!—you've got to leave your brain to the nation. You've simply got to. Have it pickled and put in the British Museum, because it's the outstanding brain of the century. I never heard of anything so brilliant in my puff. Of course the old boy will be all over us.'

'He'll do anything for us,' said Millicent.

'This is not merely a scheme. It is more. It is an egg. Pray silence for your chairman. I want to think.'

Outside, the storm had passed. Birds were singing. Far away, the thunder still rumbled. It might have been the sound of Hugo's thoughts, leaping and jostling one another.

'I've worked it all out,' said Hugo at length. 'Some people might say, Rush to the old boy now and tell him we've found his pig. I say, No. In my opinion we ought to hold this pig for a rising market. The longer we wait, the more grateful he will be. Give him another forty-eight hours, I suggest, and he will have reached the stage where he will deny us nothing.'

'But . . .'

'No! Act precipitately and we are undone. Don't forget that it is not merely a question of getting your uncle's consent to our union. We've got to break it to him that you aren't going to marry Ronnie. And the family have always been pretty keen on your marrying Ronnie. To my mind, another forty-eight hours at the very least is essential.'

'Perhaps you're right.'

'I know I'm right.'

'Then we'll simply leave the Empress here?'

'No,' said Hugo decidedly. 'This place doesn't strike me as safe. If we found her here, anybody might. We require a new safe-deposit, and I know the very one. It's . . .'

Beach came out of the silence. His manner betrayed agitation.

'If it is all the same to you, sir, I would much prefer not to hear it.'

'Eh?'

'It would be a great relief to me, sir, to be able to expunge the entire matter from my mind. I have been under a considerable mental strain of late, sir, and I really don't think I could bear any more of it. Besides, supposing I were questioned, sir. It may be my imagination, but I have rather fancied from the way he has looked at me occasionally that Mr Baxter harbours suspicions.'

'Baxter always harbours suspicions about something,' said Millicent.

'Yes, miss. But in this case they are well-grounded, and if it is all the same to you and Mr Carmody, I would greatly prefer that he was not in a position to go on harbouring them.'

'All right, Beach,' said Hugo. 'After what you have done for us, your lightest wish is law. You can be out of this, if you want to. Though I was going to suggest that, if you cared to go on feeding the animal . . .'

'No, sir . . . really . . . if you please . . .'

'Right ho, then. Come along, Millicent. We must be shifting.'

'Are you going to take her away now?'

'This very moment. I pass this handkerchief through the handy ring which you observe in the nose and . . . Ho! Allezoop! Good-bye, Beach. It is a far, far better thing that I do than I have ever done—I think.'

'Good-bye, Beach,' said Millicent. 'I can't tell you how grateful we are.'

'I am glad to have given satisfaction, miss. I wish you every success and happiness, sir.'

Left alone, the butler drew in his breath till he swelled like a balloon, then poured it out again in a long, sighing puff. He picked up the lantern and left the cottage. His walk was the walk of a butler from whose shoulders a great weight has rolled.

· V ·

It is a fact not generally known, for a nice sense of the dignity of his position restrained him from exercising it, that Beach possessed a rather attractive singing-voice. It was a mellow baritone, in timbre not unlike that which might have proceeded from a cask of very old, dry sherry, had it had vocal cords; and we cannot advance a more striking proof of the lightness of heart which had now come upon him than by mentioning that, as he walked home through the wood, he broke his rigid rule and definitely warbled.

> 'There's a light in thy bow-er'

sang Beach,

> 'A light in thy BOW-er . . .'

He felt more like a gay young second footman than a butler of years' standing. He listened to the birds with an uplifted heart. Upon the rabbits that sported about his path he bestowed a series of indulgent smiles. The shadow that had darkened his life had passed away. His conscience was at rest.

So completely was this so that when, on reaching the house, he was informed by Footman James that Lord Emsworth had been inquiring for him and desired his immediate presence in the library, he did not even tremble. A brief hour ago, and what menace this announcement would have seemed to him to hold. But now it left him calm. It was with some little difficulty that, as he mounted the stairs, he kept himself from resuming his song.

'Er—Beach.'

'Your lordship?'

The butler now became aware that his employer was not alone. Dripping in an unpleasant manner on the carpet, for he seemed somehow to have got himself extremely wet, stood the Efficient Baxter. Beach regarded him with a placid eye. What was Baxter to him or he to Baxter now?

'Your lordship?' he said again, for Lord Emsworth appeared to be experiencing some difficulty in continuing the conversation.

'Eh? What? What? Oh, yes.'

The ninth Earl braced himself with a visible effort.

'Er—Beach.'

'Your lordship?'

'I—er—I sent for you, Beach . . .'

'Yes, your lordship?'

At this moment Lord Emsworth's eye fell on a volume on the desk dealing with Diseases in Pigs. He seemed to draw strength from it.

'Beach,' he said, in quite a crisp, masterful voice, 'I sent for you because Mr Baxter has made a remarkable charge against you. Most extraordinary.'

'I should be glad to be acquainted with the gravamen of the accusation, your lordship.'

'The what?' asked Lord Emsworth, starting.

'If your lordship would be kind enough to inform me of the substance of Mr Baxter's charge?'

'Oh, the substance? Yes. You mean the substance? Precisely. Quite so. The substance. Yes, to be sure. Quite so. Quite so. Yes, Exactly. No doubt.'

It was plain to the butler that his employer had begun to dodder. Left to himself this human cuckoo-clock would go maundering on like this indefinitely. Respectfully, but with the necessary firmness, he called him to order.

'What is it that Mr Baxter says, your lordship?'

'Eh? Oh, tell him, Baxter. Yes, tell him, dash it.'

The Efficient Baxter moved a step closer and began to drip on another part of the carpet. His spectacles gleamed determinedly. Here was no stammering, embarrassed Peer of the Realm, but a man who knew his own mind and could speak it.

'I followed you to the gamekeeper's cottage in the West Wood just now, Beach.'

'Sir?'

'You heard what I said.'

'Undoubtedly, sir. But I fancied I must be mistaken. I have not been to the spot you mention, sir.'

'I saw you with my own eyes.'

'I can only repeat my asseveration, sir,' said the butler with a saintly meekness.

Lord Emsworth, who had taken another look at *Diseases in Pigs*, became brisk again.

'He says he peeped through the window, dash it.'

Beach raised a respectful eyebrow. It was as if he had said that it was not his place to comment on the pastimes of the Castle's guests, however childish. If Mr Baxter wished to go out into the woods in the rain and play solitary games of Peep-Bo, that, said the eyebrow, that was a matter that concerned Mr Baxter alone.

'And you were in there, he says, feeding the Empress.'

'Your lordship?'

'And you were in there . . . Dash it, you heard.'

'I beg your pardon, your lordship, but I really fail to comprehend.'

'Well, if you want it in a nutshell, Mr Baxter says it was you who stole my pig.'

There were few things in the world that the butler considered worth raising both eyebrows at. This was one of the few. He stood for a moment, exhibiting them to Lord Emsworth; then turned to Baxter, so that he could see them, too. This done, he lowered them and permitted about three-eighths of a smile to play for a moment about his lips.

'Might I speak frankly, your lordship?'

'Dash it, man, we want you to speak frankly. That's the whole idea. That's why I sent for you. We want a full confession and the name of your accomplice and all that sort of thing.'

'I hesitate only because what I should like to say may possibly give offence to Mr Baxter, your lordship, which would be the last thing I should desire.'

The prospect of offending the Efficient Baxter, which caused such concern to Beach, appeared to disturb his lordship not at all.

'Get on. Say what you like.'

'Well, then, your lordship, I think it possible that Mr Baxter, if he will pardon my saying so, may have been suffering from a hallucination.'

'Tchah!' said the Efficient Baxter.

'You mean he's potty?' said Lord Emsworth, struck with the idea. In the excitement of his late secretary's information, he had overlooked this simple explanation. Now there came surging back to him all the evidence that went to support such a theory. Those flower-pots . . . That leap from the library window. He looked at Baxter keenly. There *was* a sort of wild gleam in his eyes. The old coot glitter.

'Really, Lord Emsworth!'

'Oh, I'm not saying you are, my dear fellow. Only . . .'

'It is quite obvious to me,' said Baxter stiffly, 'that this man is lying. Wait!' he continued, raising a hand. 'Are you prepared to come with his lordship and me to the cottage now, at this very moment, and let his lordship see for himself?'

'No, sir.'

'Ha!'

'I should first,' said Beach, 'wish to go downstairs and get my hat.'

'Quite right,' agreed Lord Emsworth cordially. 'Very sensible. Might catch a nasty cold in the head. Certainly get your hat, Beach, and meet us at the front door.'

'Very good, your lordship.'

A bystander, observing the little party that was gathered some five minutes later on the gravel outside the great door of Blandings Castle, would have noticed about it a touch of chill, a certain restraint. None of its three members seemed really in the mood for a ramble through the woods. Beach, though courtly, was not cordial. The face under his bowler hat was the face of a good man misjudged. Baxter was eyeing the sullen sky as though he suspected it of something. As for Lord Emsworth, he had just become conscious that he was about to accompany through dark and deserted ways one who, though on this afternoon's evidence the trend of his tastes seemed to be towards suicide, might quite possibly become homicidal.

'One moment,' said Lord Emsworth.

He scuttled into the house again, and came out looking happier. He was carrying a stout walking-stick with an ivory knob on it.

13

COCKTAILS BEFORE DINNER

· I ·

Blandings Castle basked in the afterglow of a golden summer evening. Only a memory now was the storm which, two hours since, had raged with such violence through its parks, pleasure grounds and messuages. It had passed, leaving behind it peace and bird-song and a sunset of pink and green and orange and opal and amethyst. The air was cool and sweet, and the earth sent up a healing fragrance. Little stars were peeping down from a rain-washed sky.

To Ronnie Fish, slumped in an armchair in his bedroom on the second floor, the improved weather conditions brought no spiritual uplift. He could see the sunset, but it left him cold. He could hear the thrushes calling in the shrubberies, but did not think much of them. It is, in short, in no sunny mood that we reintroduce Ronald Overbury Fish to the reader of this chronicle.

The meditations of a man who has recently proposed to and been accepted by a girl, some inches taller than himself, for whom he entertains no warmer sentiment than a casual feeling that, take her for all in all, she isn't a bad sort of egg, must of necessity tend towards the sombre: and the surroundings in which Ronnie had spent the latter part of the afternoon had not been of a kind to encourage optimism. At the moment when the skies suddenly burst asunder and the world became a shower-bath, he had been walking along the path that skirted the wall of the kitchen-garden: and the only shelter that offered itself was a gloomy cave or dug-out that led to the heating apparatus of the hothouses. Into this he had dived like a homing rabbit, and here, sitting on a heap of bricks, he had remained for the space of fifty minutes with no company but one small green frog and his thoughts.

The place was a sort of Sargasso Sea into which had drifted all the flotsam and jetsam of the kitchen-garden which it adjoined. There was a wheelbarrow, lacking its wheel and lying drunkenly on its side. There were broken pots in great profusion. There was a heap of withered flowers, a punctured watering-can, a rake with large gaps in its front teeth, some potatoes unfit for human consumption and half a dead blackbird. The whole effect was extraordinarily like Hell, and Ronnie's spirits, not high at the start, had sunk lower and lower.

Sobered by rain, wheelbarrows, watering-cans, rakes, potatoes, and dead blackbirds, not to mention the steady, supercilious eye of a frog which resembled that of a Bishop at the Athenaeum inspecting a shy new member, Ronnie had begun definitely to repent of the impulse which had led him to ask Millicent to be his wife. And now, in the cosier environment of his bedroom, he was regretting it more than ever.

Like most people who have made a defiant and dramatic gesture and then have leisure to reflect, he was oppressed by a feeling that he had gone considerably farther than was prudent. Samson, as he heard the pillars of the temple begin to crack, must have felt the same. Gestures are all very well while the intoxication lasts. The trouble is that it lasts such a very little while.

In asking Millicent to marry him, he had gone, he now definitely realized, too far. He had overdone it. It was not that he had any objection to Millicent as a wife. He had none whatever—provided she were somebody else's wife. What was so unpleasant was the prospect of being married to her himself.

He groaned in spirit, and became aware that he was no longer alone.

The door had opened, and his friend Hugo Carmody was in the room. He noted with a dull surprise that Hugo was in the conventional costume of the English gentleman about to dine. He had not supposed the hour so late.

'Hullo,' said Hugo. 'Not dressed? The gong's gone.'

It now became clear to Ronnie that he simply was not equal to facing his infernal family at the dinner-table. He supposed that Millicent had spread the news of their engagement by this time, and that meant discussion, wearisome congratulations, embraces from his Aunt Constance, chaff of the vintage of 1895 from his Uncle Galahad—in short, fuss and gabble. And he was in no mood for fuss and gabble. Pot-luck with a tableful of Trappist monks he might just have endured, but not a hearty feed with the family.

'I don't want any dinner.'

'No dinner?'

'No.'

'Ill or something?'

'No.'

'But you don't want any dinner? I see. Rummy! However, your affair, of course. It begins to look as if I should have to don the nose-bag alone. Beach tells me that Baxter also will be absent from the trough. He's upset about something, it seems, and has asked for a snort and sandwiches in the smoking-room. And as for the pustule Pilbeam,' said Hugo grimly, 'I propose to interview him at the earliest possible date. And after that he won't want any dinner, either.'

'Where are the rest of them?'

'Didn't you know?' said Hugo, surprised. 'They're dining over at old Parsloe's. Your aunt, Lord Emsworth, old Galahad, and Millicent.' He coughed. A moment of some slight embarrassment impended. 'I say, Ronnie, old man, while on the subject of Millicent.'

'Well?'

'You know that engagement of yours?'

'What about it?'

'It's off.'

'Off?'

'Right off. A wash-out. She's changed her mind.'

'What!'

'Yes. She's going to marry me. I may tell you we have been engaged for weeks—one of those secret betrothals—but we had a row. Row now over. Complete reconciliation. So she asked me to break it to you gently that in the circs. she proposes to return you to store.'

A thrill of ecstasy shot through Ronnie. He felt as men on the scaffold feel when the messenger bounds in with the reprieve.

'Well, that's the first bit of good news I've had for a long time,' he said.

'You mean you didn't want to marry Millicent?'

'Of course I didn't.'

'Not so much of the "of course", laddie,' said Hugo, offended.

'She's an awfully nice girl . . .'

'An angel. Shropshire's leading seraph.'

'. . . but I'm not in love with her any more than she's in love with me.'

'In that case,' said Hugo, with justifiable censure, 'why propose to her? A goofy proceeding, it seems to me.' He clicked his tongue. 'Of course! I see what happened. You grabbed Millicent to score off Sue, and she grabbed you to score off me. And now, I suppose, you've fixed it up with Sue again. Very sound. Couldn't have made a wiser move. She's obviously the girl for you.'

Ronnie winced. The words had touched a nerve. He had been trying not to think of Sue, but without success. Her picture insisted on rising before him. Not being able to exclude her from his thoughts, he had tried to think of her bitterly.

'I haven't,' he cried.

Extraordinary how difficult it was, even now, to think bitterly of Sue. Sue was Sue. That was the fundamental fact that hampered him. Try as he might to concentrate it on the tragedy of Mario's restaurant, his mind insisted on slipping back to earlier scenes of sunshine and happiness.

'You haven't?' said Hugo, damped.

That Ronnie could possibly be in ignorance of Sue's arrival at the castle never occurred to him. Long ere this, he took it for granted, they must have met. And he assumed, from the equanimity with which his friend had received the news of the loss of Millicent, that Sue and he must have had just such another heart-to-heart talk as had taken place in the room above the gamekeeper's cottage. The dour sullenness of Ronnie's face made his kindly heart sink.

'You mean you haven't fixed things up?'

'No.'

Ronnie writhed. Sue in his car. Sue up the river. Sue in his arms to the music of sweet saxophones. Sue laughing. Sue smiling. Sue in the springtime, with the little breezes ruffling her hair . . .

He forced his mind away from these weakening visions. Sue at Mario's . . . That was better . . . Sue letting him down. . . . Sue hobnobbing with the blister Pilbeam . . . That was much better.

'I think you're being very hard on that poor little girl, Ronnie.'

'Don't call her a poor little girl.'

'I will call her a poor little girl,' said Hugo firmly. 'To me, she is a poor little girl, and I don't care who knows it. I don't mind telling you that my heart bleeds for her. Bleeds profusely. And I must say I should have thought . . .'

'I don't want to talk about her.'

'. . . after her doing what she has done . . .'

'I don't want to talk about her, I tell you.'

Hugo sighed. He gave it up. The situation was what they called an *impasse*. Too bad. His best friend and a dear little girl like that parted for ever. Two jolly good eggs sundered for all eternity. Oh, well, that was Life.

'If you want to talk about anything,' said Ronnie, 'you had much better talk about this engagement of yours.'

'Only too glad, old man. Was afraid it might bore you, or would have touched more freely on subject.'

'I suppose you realize the Family will squash it flat?'

'Oh, no, they won't.'

'You think my Aunt Constance is going to leap about and bang the cymbals?'

'The Keeble, I admit,' said Hugo, with a faint shiver, 'may make her presence felt to some extent. But I rely on the ninth Earl's support and patronage. Before long, I shall be causing the ninth to look on me as a son.'

'How?'

For a moment Hugo almost yielded to the temptation to confide in this friend of his youth. Then he realized the unwisdom of such a course. By an odd coincidence, he was thinking exactly the same of Ronnie as Ronnie at an earlier stage of this history had thought of him. Ronnie, he considered, though a splendid chap, was not fitted to be a repository of secrets. A babbler. A sieve. The sort of fellow who would spread a secret hither and thither all over the place before nightfall.

'Never mind,' he said. 'I have my methods.'

'What are they?'

'Just methods,' said Hugo, 'and jolly good ones. Well, I'll be pushing off. I'm late. Sure you won't come down to dinner? Then I'll be going. It is imperative that I get hold of Pilbeam with all possible speed. Don't want the sun to go down on my wrath. All has ended happily in spite of him, but that's no reason why he shouldn't be massacred. I look on myself as a man with a public duty.'

For some minutes after the door had closed, Ronnie remained humped up in the chair. Then, in spite of everything, there began to creep upon him a desire for food, too strong to be resisted. Perfect health and a tealess afternoon in the open had given him a compelling appetite. He still shrank from the thought of the dining-room. Fond as he was of Hugo, he simply could not stand his conversation tonight. A chop at the Emsworth Arms would meet the case. He could get down there in five minutes in his two-seater.

He rose. His mind, as he moved to the door, was not entirely occupied with thoughts of food. Hugo's parting words had turned it in the direction of Pilbeam again.

What had brought Pilbeam to the castle, he did not know. But, now that he was here, let him look out for himself! A couple of minutes alone with P. Frobisher Pilbeam was just the medicine his bruised soul required. Apparently, from what he had said, Hugo also entertained some grievance against the man. It could be nothing compared with his own.

Pilbeam! The cause of all his troubles. Pilbeam! The snake in the grass. Pilbeam . . . ! Yes . . . ! His heart might be broken, his life a wreck, but he could still enjoy the faint consolation of dealing faithfully with Pilbeam.

He went out into the corridor. And, as he did so, Percy Pilbeam came out of the room opposite.

· II ·

Pilbeam had dressed for dinner with considerable care. Owing to the fact that Lord Emsworth, in his woollen-headed way, had completely forgotten to inform him of the exodus to Matchingham Hall, he was expecting to meet a gay and glittering company at the meal, and had prepared himself accordingly. Looking at the result in the mirror, he had felt a glow of contentment. This glow was still warming him as he passed into the corridor. As his eyes fell on Ronnie, it faded abruptly.

In the days of his editorship of *Society Spice*, that frank and fearless journal, P. Frobisher Pilbeam had once or twice had personal encounters with people having no cause to wish him well. They had not appealed to him. He was a man who found no pleasure in physical violence. And that physical violence threatened now was only too sickeningly plain. It was foreshadowed in the very manner in which this small but sturdy young man confronting him had begun to creep forward. Pilbeam, who was an F.R.Z.S., had seen leopards at the Zoo creep just like that.

Years of conducting a weekly scandal-sheet, followed by a long period of activity as a private enquiry agent, undoubtedly train a man well for the exhibition of presence-of-mind in sudden emergencies. One finds it difficult in the present instance to over-praise Percy Pilbeam's ready resource. Had a great military strategist been present, he would have nodded approval. With the grim menace of Ronnie Fish coming closer and closer, Percy Pilbeam did exactly what Napoleon, Hannibal, or the great Duke of Marlborough would have done. Reaching behind him for the handle and twisting it sharply, he slipped through the door of his bedroom, banged it, and was gone. Many an eel has disappeared into the mud with less smoothness and celerity.

If the leopard which he resembled had seen its prey vanish into the undergrowth just before dinner-time, it would probably have expressed its feelings in exactly the same kind of short, rasping cry as proceeded from Ronnie Fish, witnessing this masterly withdrawal. For an instant he was completely taken aback. Then he plunged for the door and plunged into the room.

He stood, baffled. Pilbeam had vanished. To Ronnie's astonished eyes the apartment appeared entirely free from detectives in any shape or form whatsoever. There was the bed. There were the chairs. There were the carpet, the dressing-table, and the book-shelf. But of private enquiry agents there was a complete shortage.

How long this miracle would have continued to afflict him one cannot say. His mind was still dealing dazedly with it, when there came to his ears a sharp click, as of a key being turned in the lock. It seemed to proceed from a hanging-cupboard at the other side of the room.

Old Miles Fish, Ronnie's father, might, as Lord Emsworth had asserted, have been the biggest fool in the Brigade of Guards, but his son could reason and deduce. Springing forward, he tugged at the handle of the cupboard door. The door stood fast.

At the same moment there filtered through it the sound of muffled breathing.

Ronnie was already looking grim. He now looked grimmer. He placed his lips to the panel.

'Come out of that!'

The breathing stopped.

'All right,' said Ronnie, with a hideous calm. 'Right jolly ho! I can wait.'

For some moments there was silence. Then from the beyond a voice spoke in reply.

'Be reasonable!' said the voice.

'Reasonable?' said Ronnie thickly. 'Reasonable, eh?' He choked. 'Come out! I only want to pull your head off,' he added, with a note of appeal.

The voice became conciliatory.

'I know what you're upset about,' it said.

'You do, eh?'

'Yes, I quite understand. But I can explain everything.'

'What?'

'I say I can explain everything.'

'You can, can you?'

'Quite,' said the voice.

Up till now Ronnie had been pulling. It now occurred to him that pushing might possibly produce more satisfactory results. So he pushed. Nothing, however, happened. Blandings Castle was a house which rather prided itself on its solidity. Its walls were walls and its doors doors. No jimcrack work here. The cupboard creaked, but did not yield.

'I say!'

'Well?'

'I wish you'd listen. I tell you I can explain everything. About that night at Mario's, I mean. I know exactly how it is. You think Miss Brown is fond of me. I give you my solemn word she can't stand the sight of me. She told me so herself.'

A pleasing thought came to Ronnie.

'You can't stay in there all night,' he said.

'I don't want to stay in here all night.'

'Well, come on out, then.'

The voice became plaintive.

'I tell you she had never set eyes on me before that night at Mario's. She was dining with that fellow Carmody, and he went out and I came over and introduced myself. No harm in that, was there?'

Ronnie wondered if kicking would do any good. A tender feeling for his toes, coupled with the reflection that his Uncle Clarence might have something to say if he started breaking up cupboard doors, caused him to abandon the scheme. He stood, breathing tensely.

'Just a friendly word, that's all I came over to say. Why shouldn't a fellow introduce himself to a girl and say a friendly word?'

'I wish I'd got there earlier.'

'I'd have been glad to see you,' said Pilbeam courteously.

'Would you?'

'Quite.'

'I shall be glad to see *you*,' said Ronnie, 'when I can get this damned door open.'

Pilbeam began to fear asphyxiation. The air inside the cupboard was growing closer. Peril lent him the inspiration which it so often does.

'Look here,' he said, 'are you Ronnie?'

Ronnie turned pinker.

'I don't want any of your dashed cheek.'

'No, but listen. Is your name Ronnie?'

Silence without.

'Because, if it is,' said Pilbeam, 'you're the fellow she's come here to see.'

More silence.

'She told me so. In the garden this evening. She came here calling herself Miss Shoemaker or some such name, just to see you. That ought to show you that I'm not the man she's keen on.'

The silence was broken by a sharp exclamation.

'What's that?'

Pilbeam repeated his remark. A growing hopefulness lent an almost finicky clearness to his diction.

'Come out!' cried Ronnie.

'That's all very well, but . . .'

'Come out, I want to talk to you.'

'You are talking to me.'

'I don't want to bellow this through a door. Come on out. I swear I won't touch you.'

It was not so much Pilbeam's faith in the knightly word of the Fishes that caused him to obey the request as a feeling that, if he stayed cooped up in this cupboard much longer, he would get a rush of blood to the head. Already he was beginning to feel as if he were breathing a solution of dust and mothballs. He emerged. His hair was rumpled, and he regarded his companion warily. He had the air of a man who has taken his life in his hands. But the word of the Fishes held good. As far as Ronnie was concerned, the war appeared to be over.

'What did you say? She's here?'

'Quite.'

'What do you mean, quite?'

'Certainly. Quite. She got here just before I did. Haven't you seen her?'

'No.'

'Well, she's here. She's in the room they call the Garden Room. I heard her tell that old bird Galahad so. If you go there now,' said Pilbeam insinuatingly, 'you could have a quiet word with her before she goes down to dinner.'

'And she said she had come here to see me?'

'Yes. To explain about that night at Mario's. And what I say,' proceeded Pilbeam warmly, 'is, if a girl didn't love a fellow, would she come to a place like this, calling herself Miss Shoolbred or something, simply to see him? I ask you!' said Pilbeam.

Ronnie did not answer. His feelings held him speechless. He was too deep in a morass of remorse to be able to articulate. Indeed, he was in a frame of mind so abased that he almost asked Pilbeam to kick him. The thought of how he had wronged his blameless Sue was almost too bitter to be borne. It bit like a serpent and stung like an adder.

From the surge and riot of his reflections one thought now emerged clearly, shining like a beacon on a dark night. The Garden Room!

Turning without a word, he shot out of the door as quickly as Percy Pilbeam a short while ago had shot in. And Percy Pilbeam, with a deep sigh, went to the dressing-table, took up the brush, and started to restore his hair to a state fit for the eyes of the nobility and gentry. This done, he smoothed his moustache and went downstairs to the drawing-room.

· III ·

The drawing-room was empty. And, to Pilbeam's surprise, it continued to be empty for quite a considerable time. He felt puzzled. He had expected to meet a reproachful host with an eye on the clock and a haughty hostess clicking her tongue. As the minutes crept by and his solitude remained unbroken, he began to grow restless.

He wandered about the room staring at the pictures, straightening his tie and examining the photographs on the little tables. The last of these was one of Lord Emsworth, taken apparently at about the age of thirty, in long whiskers and the uniform of the Shropshire Yeomanry. He was gazing at this with the fascinated horror which it induced in everyone who saw it suddenly for the first time, when the door at last opened; and with a sinking sensation of apprehension Pilbeam beheld the majestic form of Beach.

For an instant he stood eyeing the butler with that natural alarm which comes to all of us when in the presence of a man who a few short hours earlier has given us one look and made us feel like a condemned food product. Then his tension relaxed.

It has been well said that for every evil in this world Nature supplies an antidote. If butlers come, can cocktails be far behind? Beach was carrying a tray with glasses and a massive shaker on it; and Pilbeam, seeing these, found himself regarding their formidable bearer almost with equanimity.

'A cocktail, sir?'

'Thanks.'

He accepted a brimming glass. The darkness of its contents suggested a welcome strength. He drank. And instantaneously all through his system beacon-fires seemed to burst into being.

He drained the glass. His whole outlook on life was now magically different. Quite suddenly he had begun to feel equal to a dozen butlers, however glazed their eyes might be.

And it might have been an illusion caused by gin and vermouth, but this butler seemed to have changed considerably for the better since their last meeting. His eye, though still glassy, had lost the old basilisk quality. There appeared now, in fact, to be something so positively light-hearted about Beach's whole demeanour that the proprietor of the Argus Enquiry Agency was emboldened to plunge into conversation.

'Nice evening.'

'Yes, sir.'

'Nice after the storm.'

'Yes, sir.'

'Came down a bit, didn't it?'

'The rain was undoubtedly extremely heavy, sir. Another cocktail?'

'Thanks.'

The re-lighting of the beacons had the effect of removing from Pil-beam the last trace of diffidence and shyness. He saw now that he had been entirely mistaken in this butler. Encountering him in the hall at the moment of his arrival, he had supposed him supercilious and hostile. He now perceived that he was a butler and a brother. More like Old King Cole, that jolly old soul, indeed, than anybody Pilbeam had met for months.

'I got caught in it,' he said affably.

'Indeed, sir?'

'Yes. Lord Emsworth had been showing me some photographs of that pig of his . . . By the way, in strict confidence . . . what's your name?'

'Beach, sir.'

'In strict confidence, Beach, I know something about that pig.'

'Indeed, sir?'

'Yes. Well, after I had seen the photographs, I went for a walk in the park and the rain came on and I got pretty wet. In fact, I don't mind tell-ing you I had to get under cover and take my trousers off to dry.'

He laughed merrily.

'Another cocktail, sir?'

'Making three in all?'

'Yes, sir.'

'Perhaps you're right,' said Pilbeam.

For some moments he sat, pensive and distrait, listening to the strains of a brass band which seemed to have started playing somewhere in the vicinity. Then his idly floating thoughts drifted back to the mystery which had been vexing him before this delightful butler's entry.

'I say, Beach, I've been waiting here hours and hours. Where's this dinner I heard you beating gongs about?'

'Dinner is ready, sir, but I put it back some little while, as gentlemen aren't punctual in the summer time.'

Pilbeam considered this statement. It sounded to him as if it would make rather a good song-title. Gentlemen aren't punctual in the summertime, in the summertime (I said, In the summertime), So take me back to that old Kentucky shack . . . He tried to fit it to the music which the brass band was playing, but it did not go very well and he gave it up.

'Where is everybody?' he asked.

'His lordship and her ladyship and Mr Galahad and Miss Threepwood are dining at Matchingham Hall.'

'What! With old Pop Parsloe?'

'With Sir Gregory Parsloe-Parsloe, yes, sir.'

Pilbeam chuckled.

'Well, well, well! Quick worker, old Parsloe. Don't you think so, Beach? I mean, you advise him to do a thing, to act in a certain way, to adopt a certain course of action, and he does it right away. You agree with me, Beach?'

'I fear my limited acquaintance with Sir Gregory scarcely entitles me to offer an opinion, sir.'

'Talking of old Parsloe, Beach . . . you did say your name was Beach?'

'Yes, sir.'

'With a capital B?'

'Yes, sir.'

'Well, talking of old Parsloe, Beach, I could tell you something about him. Something he's up to.'

'Indeed, sir?'

'But I'm not going to. Respect client's confidence. Lips sealed. Professional secret.'

'Yes, sir?'

'As you rightly say, yes. Any more of that stuff in the shaker, Beach?'

'A little, sir, if you consider it judicious.'

'That's just what I do consider it. Start pouring.'

The detective sipped luxuriously, fuller and fuller every moment of an uplifting sense of well-being. If the friendship which had sprung up between himself and the butler was possibly a little one-sided, on the one side on which it did exist it was warm, even fervent. It seemed to Pilbeam that for the first time since he had arrived at Blandings Castle he had found a real chum, a kindred soul in whom he might confide. And he was filled with an overwhelming desire to confide in somebody.

'As a matter of fact, Beach,' he said, 'I could tell you all sorts of things about all sorts of people. Practically everybody in this house I could tell you something about. What's the name of that chap with the light hair, for instance? The old boy's secretary?'

'Mr Carmody, sir.'

'Carmody! That's the name. I've been trying to remember it. Well, I could tell you something about Carmody.'

'Indeed, sir?'

'Yes. Something about Carmody that would interest you very much. I saw Carmody this afternoon when Carmody didn't see me.'

'Indeed, sir?'

'Yes. Where is Carmody?'

'I imagine he will be down shortly, sir. Mr Ronald also.'

'Ronald!' Pilbeam drew in his breath sharply. 'There's a tough baby, Beach. That Ronnie. Do you know what he wanted to do just now? Murder me!'

In Beach's opinion, for he did not look on Percy Pilbeam as a very necessary member of society, this would have been a commendable act, and he regretted that its consummation had been prevented. He was also feeling that the conscientious butler he had always prided himself on being would long ere this have withdrawn and left this man to talk to himself. But even the best of butlers have human emotions, and the magic of Pilbeam's small-talk held Beach like a spell. It reminded him of the Gossip page of *Society Spice*, a paper to which he was a regular subscriber. He was piqued and curious. So far, it was true, his companion had merely hinted, but something seemed to tell him that, if he lingered on, a really sensational news-item would shortly emerge.

He had never been more right in his life. Pilbeam by this time had finished the fourth cocktail, and the urge to confide had become overpowering. He looked at Beach, and it nearly made him cry to think that he was holding anything back from such a splendid fellow.

'And do you know why he wanted to murder me, Beach?'

It scarcely seemed to the butler that the action required anything in the nature of a reasoned explanation, but he murmured the necessary response.

'I could not say, sir.'

'Of course you couldn't. How could you? You don't know. That's why I'm telling you. Well, listen. He's in love with a girl in the chorus at the Regal, a girl named Sue Brown, and he thought I had been taking her out to dinner. That's why he wanted to murder me, Beach.'

'Indeed, sir?'

The butler spoke calmly, but he was deeply stirred. He had always flattered himself that the inmates of Blandings Castle kept few secrets from him, but this was something new.

'Yes. That's why. I had the dickens of a job holding him off, I can tell you. Do you know what saved me, Beach?'

'No, sir.'

'Presence of mind. I put it to him—to Ronnie—I put it to Ronnie as a reasonable man that, if this girl loved me, would she have come to this place, pretending to be Miss Shoemaker, simply so as to see him?'

'Sir!'

'Yes, that's who Miss Shoemaker is, Beach. She's a chorus-girl called Sue Brown, and she's come here to see Ronnie.'

Beach stood transfixed. His eyes swelled bulbously from their sockets. He was incapable of even an 'Indeed, sir?'

He was still endeavouring to assimilate this extraordinary revelation when Hugo Carmody entered the room.

'Ah!' said Hugo, his eye falling on Pilbeam. He stiffened. He stood looking at the detective like Schopenhauer's butcher at the selected lamb.

'Leave us, Beach,' he said, in a grave, deep voice.

The butler came out of his trance.

'Sir?'

'Pop off.'

'Very good, sir.'

The door closed.

'I've been looking for you, viper,' said Hugo.

'Have you Carmody?' said Percy Pilbeam effervescently. 'I've been looking for you, too. Got something I want to talk to you about. Each looking for each. Or am I thinking of a couple of other fellows? Come right in, Carmody, and sit down. Good old Carmody! Jolly old Carmody! Splendid old Carmody! Well, well, well, well, well!'

If the lamb mentioned above had suddenly accosted the above-mentioned butcher in a similar strain of hearty camaraderie, it could have hardly disconcerted him more than Pilbeam with these cheery words disconcerted Hugo. His stern, set gaze became a gaping stare.

Then he pulled himself together. What did words matter? He had no time to bother about words. Action was what he was after. Action!

'I don't know if you're aware of it, worm,' he said, 'but you came jolly near to blighting my life.'

'Doing what, Carmody?'

'Blighting my life.'

'List to me while I tell you of the Spaniard who blighted my life,' sang Percy Pilbeam, letting it go like a lark in the springtime. He had never felt happier or in more congenial society. 'How did I blight your life, Carmody?'

'You didn't.'

'You said I did.'

'I said you tried to.'

'Make up your mind, Carmody.'

'Don't keep calling me Carmody.'

'But, Carmody,' protested Pilbeam, 'it's your name, isn't it? Certainly it is. Then why try to hush it up, Carmody? Be frank and open. I don't mind people knowing my name. I glory in it. It's Pilbeam—Pilbeam—Pilbeam—that's what it is—Pilbeam!'

'In about thirty seconds,' said Hugo, 'it will be Mud.'

It struck Percy Pilbeam for the first time that in his companion's manner there was a certain peevishness.

'Something the matter?' he asked, concerned.

'I'll tell you what's the matter.'

'Do, Carmody, do,' said Pilbeam. 'Do, do, do. Confide in me. I like your face.'

He settled himself in a deep armchair, and putting the tips of his fingers together after a little preliminary difficulty in making them meet, leaned back, all readiness to listen to whatever trouble it was that was disturbing this new friend of his.

'Some days ago, insect . . .'

Pilbeam opened his eyes.

'Speak up, Carmody,' he said. 'Don't mumble.'

Hugo's fingers twitched. He regarded his companion with a burning eye, and wondered why he was wasting time talking instead of at once proceeding to the main business of the day and knocking the fellow's head off at the roots. What saved Pilbeam was the reclining position he had assumed. If you are a Carmody and a sportsman, you cannot attack even a viper, if it persists in lying back on its spine and keeping its eyes shut.

'Some days ago,' he began again, 'I called at your office. And after we had talked of this and that, I left. I discovered later that immediately upon my departure you had set your foul spies on my trail and had instructed them to take notes of my movements and report on them. The result being that I came jolly close to having my bally life ruined. And, if you want to know what I'm going to do, I'm going to haul you out of that chair and turn you round and kick you hard and go on kicking you till I kick you out of the house. And if you dare to shove your beastly little nose back inside the place, I'll disembowel you.'

Pilbeam unclosed his eyes.

'Nothing,' he said, 'could be fairer than that. Nevertheless, that's no reason why you should go about stealing pigs.'

Hugo had often read stories in which people reeled and would have fallen, had they not clutched at whatever it was that they clutched at. He had never expected to undergo that experience himself. But it is undoubtedly the fact that, if he had not at this moment gripped the back of a chair, he would have been hard put to it to remain perpendicular.

'Pig-pincher!' said Pilbeam austerely, and closed his eyes again.

Hugo, having established his equilibrium by means of the chair, had now moved away. He was making a strong effort to recover his morale. He picked up the photograph of Lord Emsworth in his Yeomanry uniform and looked at it absently; then, as if it had just dawned upon him, put it down with a shudder, like a man who finds that he had been handling a snake.

'What do you mean?' he said thickly.

Pilbeam's eyes opened.

'What do I mean? What do you think I mean? I mean you're a pig-pincher. That's what I mean. You go to and fro, sneaking pigs and hiding them in caravans.'

Hugo took up Lord Emsworth's photograph again, saw what he was doing, and dropped it quickly. Pilbeam had closed his eyes once more, and, looking at him, Hugo could not repress a reluctant thrill of awe. He had often read about the superhuman intuition of detectives, but he had never before been privileged to observe it in operation. Then an idea occurred to him.

'Did you see me?'

'What say, Carmody?'

'Did you see me?'

'Yes, I see you, Carmody,' said Pilbeam playfully. 'Peep-bo!'

'Did you see me put that pig in the caravan?'

Pilbeam nodded eleven times in rapid succession.

'Certainly I saw you, Carmody. Why shouldn't I see you, considering I'd been caught in the rain and taken shelter in the caravan and was in there with my trousers off, trying to dry them because I'm subject to lumbago?'

'I didn't see you.'

'No, Carmody, you did not. And I'll tell you why, Carmody. Because I heard a girl's voice outside saying "Be quick, or somebody will come along!" and I hid. You don't suppose I would let a sweet girl see me in knee-length mesh-knit underwear, do you? Not done, Carmody,' said Pilbeam, severely. 'Not cricket.'

Hugo was experiencing the bitterness which comes to all criminals who discover, too late, that they have undone themselves by trying to be clever. It had seemed at the time such a good idea to remove the Empress from the gamekeeper's cottage in the West Wood and place her in Baxter's caravan, where nobody would think of looking. How could he have anticipated that the caravan would be bulging with blighted detectives?

At this tense moment, the door opened and Beach appeared.

'I beg your pardon, sir, but do you propose to wait any longer for Mr Ronald?'

'Eh?'

'Certainly not,' said Pilbeam. 'Who the devil's Mr Ronald, I should like to know? I didn't come to this place to do a fast-cure. I want my dinner, and I want it now. And if Mr Ronald doesn't like it, he can do the other thing.' He strode in a dominating manner to the door. 'Come along, Carmody. Din-dins.'

Hugo had sunk into a chair.

'I don't want any dinner,' he said, dully.

'You don't want any dinner?'

'No.'

'No dinner?'

'No.'

Pilbeam shrugged his shoulders impatiently.

'The man's an ass,' he said.

He headed for the stairs. His manner seemed to indicate that he washed his hands of Hugo.

Beach lingered.

'Shall I bring you some sandwiches, sir?'

'No thanks. What's that?'

A loud crash had sounded. The butler went to the door and looked out.

'It is Mr Pilbeam, sir. He appears to have fallen downstairs.'

For an instant a look of hope crept into Hugo's careworn face.

'Has he broken his neck?'

'Apparently not, sir.'

'Ah,' said Hugo regretfully.

14

SWIFT THINKING BY THE EFFICIENT BAXTER

· I ·

The Efficient Baxter had retired to the smoking-room shortly before half-past seven. He desired silence and solitude, and in this cosy haven he got both. For a few minutes nothing broke the stillness but the slow ticking of a clock on the mantelpiece. Then from the direction of the hall there came a new sound, faint at first but swelling and swelling to a frenzied blare, seeming to throb through the air with a note of passionate appeal like a woman wailing for her demon lover. It was that tocsin of the soul, that muezzin of the country-house, the dressing-for-dinner gong.

Baxter did not stir. The summons left him unmoved. He had heard it, of course. Butler Beach was a man who swung a pretty gong-stick. He had that quick forearm flick and wristy follow-through which stamp the master. If you were anywhere within a quarter of a mile or so, you could not help hearing him. But the sound had no appeal for Baxter. He did not propose to go in to dinner. He wanted to be alone with his thoughts.

They were not the sort of thoughts with which most men would have wished to be left alone, being both dark and bitter. That expedition to the gamekeeper's cottage in the West Wood had not proved a pleasure-trip for Rupert Baxter. Reviewing it in his mind, he burned with baffled rage.

And yet everybody had been very nice to him—very nice and tactful. True, at the moment of the discovery that the cottage contained no pig and appeared to have been pigless from its foundation, there had been perhaps just the slightest suspicion of constraint. Lord Emsworth had grasped his ivory-knobbed stick a little more tightly, and had edged behind Beach in a rather noticeable way, his manner saying more plainly than was agreeable, 'If he springs, be ready!' And there had come into the butler's face a look, hard to bear, which was a blend of censure and pity. But after that both of them had been charming.

Lord Emsworth had talked soothingly about light and shade effects. He had said—and Beach agreed with him—that in the darkness of a thunderstorm anybody might have been deceived into supposing that he had seen a butler feeding a pig in the gamekeeper's cottage. It was probably, said Lord Emsworth—and Beach thought so, too—a bit of wood sticking out of the wall or something. He went on to tell a longish story of how he himself, when a boy, had fancied he had seen a cat with flaming eyes. He had concluded by advising Baxter—and Beach said the suggestion was a good one—to hurry home and have a nice cup of hot tea and go to bed.

His attitude, in short, could not have been pleasanter or more considerate. Yet Baxter, as he sat in the smoking-room, burned, as stated, with baffled rage.

The door-handle turned. Beach stood on the threshold.

'If you have changed your mind, sir, about taking dinner, the meal is quite ready.'

He spoke as friend to friend. There was nothing in his manner to suggest that the man he addressed had ever accused him of stealing pigs. As far as Beach was concerned, all was forgotten and forgiven.

But the milk of human kindness, of which the butler was so full, had not yet been delivered on Baxter's doorstep. The hostility in his eye, as he fixed it on his visitor, was so marked that a lesser man than Beach might have been disconcerted.

'I don't want any dinner.'

'Very good, sir.'

'Bring me that whisky-and-soda quick.'

'Yes, sir.'

The door closed as softly as it had opened, but not before a pang like a red-hot needle had pierced the ex-secretary's bosom. It was caused by the fact that he had distinctly heard the butler, as he withdrew, utter a pitying sigh.

It was the sort of sigh which a kind-hearted man would have given on peeping into a padded cell in which some old friend was confined, and Baxter resented it with all the force of an imperious nature. He had not ceased to wonder what, if anything, could be done about it when the refreshments arrived, carried by James the footman. James placed them gently on the table, shot a swift glance of respectful commiseration at the patient, and passed away.

The sigh had cut Baxter like a knife. The look stabbed him like a dagger. For a moment he thought of calling the man back and asking him what the devil he meant by staring at him like that, but wiser counsels prevailed. He contented himself with draining a glass of whisky-and-soda and swallowing two sandwiches.

This done, he felt a little—not much, but a little—better. Before, he would gladly have murdered Beach and James and danced on their graves. Now, he would have been satisfied with straight murder.

However, he was alone at last. That was some slight consolation. Beach had come and gone. Footman James had come and gone. Everybody else must by now be either at Matchingham Hall or assembled in the dining-room. On the solitude which he so greatly desired there could be no further intrusion. He resumed his meditations.

For a time these dealt exclusively with the recent past, and were, in consequence, of a morbid character. Then, as the grateful glow of the whisky began to make itself felt, a softer mood came to Rupert Baxter. His mind turned to thoughts of Sue.

Men as efficient as Rupert Baxter do not fall in love in the generally accepted sense of the term. Their attitude towards the tender passion is more restrained than that of the ordinary feckless young man who loses his heart at first sight with a whoop and a shiver. Baxter approved of Sue. We cannot say more. But this approval, added to the fact that he had been informed by Lady Constance that the girl was the only daughter of a man who possessed sixty million dollars, had been enough to cause him to ear-mark her in his mind as the future Mrs Baxter. In that capacity he had docketed her and filed her away at the first moment of their meeting.

Naturally, therefore, the remarks which Lord Emsworth had let fall in her hearing had caused him grave concern. It hampers a man in his wooing if the girl he has selected for his bride starts with the idea that he is as mad as a coot. He congratulated himself on the promptitude with which he had handled the situation. That letter which he had written her could not fail to put him right in her eyes.

Rupert Baxter was a man in whose lexicon there was no such word as failure. An heiress like this Miss Schoonmaker would not, he was aware, lack for suitors: but he did not fear them. If only she were making a reasonably long stay at the castle, he felt that he could rely on his force of character to win the day. In fact, it seemed to him that he could almost hear the wedding bells ringing already. Then, coming out of his dreams, he realized that it was the telephone.

He reached for the instrument with a frown, annoyed at the interruption, and spoke with an irritated sharpness.

'Hullo?'

A ghostly voice replied. The storm seemed to have affected the wires.

'Speak up!' barked Baxter.

He banged the telephone violently on the table. The treatment, as is so often the case, proved effective.

'Blandings Castle?' said the voice, no longer ghostly.

'Yes.'

'Post Office, Market Blandings, speaking. Telegram for Lady Constance Keeble.'

'I will take it.'

The voice became faint again. Baxter went through the movements as before.

'Lady Constance Keeble, Blandings Castle, Market Blandings, Shropshire, England,' said the voice, recovering strength, as if it had shaken off a wasting sickness. 'Handed in at Paris.'

'Where?'

'Paris, France.'

'Oh? Well?'

The voice gathered volume.

'"Terribly sorry hear news . . ."'

'What?'

'"News."'

'Yes?'

'"Terribly sorry hear news stop Quite understand stop So disappointed shall be unable come to you later as going back America at end of month stop Do hope we shall be able arrange something when I return next year stop Regards stop!"'

'Yes?'

'Signed "Myra Schoonmaker".'

'Signed—*what?*'

'Myra Schoonmaker.'

Baxter's mouth had fallen open. The forehead above the spectacles was wrinkled, the eyes behind them staring blankly and with a growing horror.

'Shall I repeat?'

'What?'

'Do you wish the message repeated?'

'No,' said Baxter in a choking voice.

He hung up the receiver. There seemed to be something crawling down his back. His brain was numbed.

Myra Schoonmaker! Telegraphing from Paris!

Then who was this girl who was at the castle calling herself by that preposterous name? An imposter, an adventuress. She must be.

And if he made a move to expose her she would revenge herself by showing Lord Emsworth that letter of his.

In his agitation of the moment he had risen to his feet. He now sat down heavily.

That letter . . . !

He must recover it. He must recover it at once. As long as it remained in the girl's possession, it was a pistol pointed at his head. Once let Lord Emsworth become acquainted with those very frank criticisms of himself which it contained, and not even his ally, Lady Constance, would be able to restore him to his lost secretaryship. The ninth Earl was a mild man, accustomed to bowing to his sister's decrees, but there were limits beyond which he could not be pushed.

And Baxter yearned to be back at Blandings Castle in the position he had once enjoyed. Blandings was his spiritual home. He had held other secretaryships—he held one now, at a salary far higher than that which Lord Emsworth had paid him—but never had he succeeded in recapturing that fascinating sense of power, of importance, of being the man who directed the destinies of one of the largest houses in England.

At all costs he must recover that letter. And the present moment, he perceived, was ideal for the venture. The girl must have the thing in her room somewhere, and for the next hour at least she would be in the dining-room. He would have ample opportunity for a search.

He did not delay. Thirty seconds later he was mounting the stairs, his face set, his spectacles gleaming grimly. A minute later, he reached his destination. No good angel, aware of what the future held, stood on the threshold to bar his entry. The door was ajar. He pushed it open and went in.

· II ·

Blandings Castle, like most places of its size and importance, contained bedrooms so magnificent that they were never used. With their four-poster beds and their superb but rather oppressive tapestries, they had remained untenanted since the time when Queen Elizabeth I, dodging from country-house to country-house in that restless, snipe-like way of hers, had last slept in them. Of the guest-rooms still in commission, the most luxurious was that which had been given to Sue.

At the moment when Baxter stole cautiously in, it was looking its best in the gentle evening light. But Baxter was not in sight-seeing mood. He ignored the carved bedstead, the cosy armchairs, the pictures, the decorations, and the soft carpet into which his feet sank. The beauty of the sky through the french windows that gave on to the balcony drew but a single brief glance from him. Without delay, he made for the writing-desk which stood against the wall near the bed. It seemed to him a good point of departure for his search.

There were several pigeon-holes in the desk. They contained single sheets of notepaper, double sheets of notepaper, postcards, envelopes, telegraph-forms, and even a little pad on which the room's occupant was presumably expected to jot down any stray thoughts and reflections on Life which might occur to him or her before turning in for the night. But not one of them contained the fatal letter.

He straightened himself and looked about the room. The drawer of the dressing-table now suggested itself as a possibility. He left the desk and made his way towards it.

The primary requisite of dressing-tables being a good supply of light, they are usually placed in a position to get as much of it as possible. This one was no exception. It stood so near to the open windows that the breeze was ruffling the tassels on its lamp-shades: and Baxter, arriving in front of it, was enabled for the first time to see the balcony in its entirety.

And, as he saw it, his heart seemed to side-slip. Leaning upon the parapet and looking out over the sea of gravel that swept up to the front door from the rhododendron-fringed drive, stood a girl. And not even the fact that her back was turned could prevent Baxter identifying her.

For an instant he remained frozen. Even the greatest men congeal beneath the chill breath of the totally unexpected. He had assumed as a matter of course that Sue was down in the dining-room, and it took him several seconds to adjust his mind to the unpleasing fact that she was up on her balcony. When he recovered his presence of mind sufficiently to draw noiselessly away from the line of vision, his first emotion was one of irritation. This chopping and changing, this eleventh hour alteration of plans, these sudden decisions to remain upstairs when they ought to be downstairs, were what made women as a sex so unsatisfactory.

To irritation succeeded a sense of defeat. There was nothing for it, he realized, but to give up his quest and go. He started to tip-toe silently to the door, agreeably conscious now of the softness and thickness of the Axminster pile that made it possible to move unheard, and had just reached it, when from the other side there came to his ears a sound of chinking and clattering—the sound, in fact, which is made by plates and dishes when they are carried on a tray to a guest who, after a long railway journey, has asked her hostess if she may take dinner in her room.

Practice makes perfect. This was the second time in the last three hours that Baxter had found himself trapped in a room in which it was vitally urgent that he should not be discovered: and he was getting the technique of the thing. On the previous occasion, in the small library, he had taken to himself wings like a bird and sailed out of the window. In the present crisis, such a course, he perceived immediately, was not feasible. The way of an eagle would profit him nothing. Soaring over the balcony, he would be observed by Sue and would, in addition, unquestionably break his neck. What was needed here was the way of a diving-duck.

And so, as the door-handle turned, Rupert Baxter, even in this black hour efficient, dropped on all-fours and slid under the bed as smoothly as if he had been practising for weeks.

· III ·

Owing to the restricted nature of his position and the limited range of vision which he enjoys, virtually the only way in which a man who is hiding under a bed can entertain himself is by listening to what is going on outside. He may hear something of interest, or he may hear only the draught sighing along the floor: but, for better or for worse, that is all he is able to do.

The first sound that came to Rupert Baxter was that made by the placing of the tray on the table. Then, after a pause, a pair of squeaking shoes passed over the carpet and squeaked out of hearing. Baxter recognized them as those of Footman Thomas, a confirmed squeaker.

After this, somebody puffed, causing him to deduce the presence of Beach.

'Your dinner is quite ready, miss.'

'Oh, thank you.'

The girl had apparently come in from the balcony. A chair scraped to the table. A savoury scent floated to Baxter's nostrils, causing him acute discomfort. He had just begun to realize how extremely hungry he was and how rash he had been, firstly to attempt to dine off a couple of sandwiches, and secondly to undertake a mission like his present one without a square meal inside him.

'That is chicken, miss. *En casserole.*'

Baxter had deduced as much, and was trying not to let his mind dwell on it. He uttered a silent groan. In addition to the agony of having to smell food, he was beginning to be conscious of a growing cramp in his left leg. He turned on one side and did his best to emulate the easy nonchalance of those Indian fakirs who, doubtless from the best motives, spend the formative years of their lives lying on iron spikes.

'It looks very good.'

'I trust you will enjoy it, miss. Is there anything further that I can do for you?'

'No, thank you. Oh, yes. Would you mind fetching that manuscript from the balcony. I was reading it out there, and I left it on the chair. It's Mr Threepwood's book.'

'Indeed, miss? An exceedingly interesting compilation, I should imagine?'

'Yes, very.'

'I wonder if it would be taking a liberty, miss, to ask you to inform me later, at your leisure, if I make any appearance in its pages.'

'You?'

'Yes, miss. From what Mr Galahad has let fall from time to time, I fancy it was his intention to give me printed credit as his authority for certain of the stories which appear in the book.'

'Do you want to be in it?'

'Most decidedly, miss. I should consider it an honour. And it would please my mother.'

'Have you a mother?'

'Yes, miss. She lives at Eastbourne.'

The butler moved majestically on to the balcony, and Sue's mind had turned to speculation about his mother and whether she looked anything like him, when there was a sound of hurrying feet without, the door flew open, and Beach's mother passed from her mind like the unsubstantial fabric of a dream. With a little choking cry she rose to her feet. Ronnie was standing before her.

15

OVER THE TELEPHONE

A ND meanwhile, if we may borrow an expression from a sister art, what
of Hugo Carmody?

It is a defect unfortunately inseparable from any such document as
this faithful record of events in and about Blandings Castle that the
chronicler, in order to give a square deal to each of the individuals whose
fortunes he has undertaken to narrate, is compelled to flit abruptly from
one to the other in the manner popularized by the chamois of the Alps
leaping from crag to crag. The activities of the Efficient Baxter seeming
to him to demand immediate attention, he was reluctantly compelled
some little while back to leave Hugo in the very act of reeling beneath a
crushing blow. The moment has now come to return to him.

The first effect on a young man of sensibility and gentle upbringing
of the discovery that an unfriendly detective has seen him placing stolen
pigs in caravans is to induce a stunned condition of mind, a sort of mental coma. The face lengthens. The limbs grow rigid. The tie slips side-
ways and the cuffs recede into the coat-sleeves. The subject becomes
temporarily, in short, a total loss.

It is perhaps as well, therefore, that we did not waste valuable time watching Hugo in the process of digesting Percy Pilbeam's sensational announcement, for it would have been like looking at a statue. If the reader will endeavour to picture Rodin's Thinker in a dinner-jacket and trousers with braid down the sides, he will have got the general idea. At the instant when Hugo Carmody makes his reappearance, life has just begun to return to the stiffened frame.

And with life came the dawning of intelligence. This ghastly snag which had popped up in his path was too big, reflected Hugo, for any man to tackle. It called for a woman's keener wit. His first act on emerging from the depths, therefore, was to leave the drawing-room and totter downstairs to the telephone. He got the number of Matchingham Hall and, establishing communication with Sir Gregory Parsloe-Parsloe's butler, urged him to summon Miss Millicent Threepwood from the dinner-table. The butler said in rather a reproving way that Miss Threepwood was at the moment busy drinking soup. Hugo, with the first flash of spirit he had shown for a quarter of an hour, replied that he didn't care if she was bathing in it. Fetch her, said Hugo, and almost added the words 'You scurvy knave.' He then clung weakly to the receiver, waiting, and in a short while a sweet, but agitated, voice floated to him across the wire.

'Hugo?'

'Millicent?'

'Is that you?'

'Yes. Is that you?'

'Yes.'

Anything in the nature of misunderstanding was cleared away. It was both of them.

'What's up?'

'Everything's up.'

'How do you mean?'

'I'll tell you,' said Hugo, and did so. It was not a difficult story to tell. Its plot was so clear that a few whispered words sufficed.

'You don't mean that?' said Millicent, the tale concluded.

'I do mean that.'

'Oh, golly!' said Millicent.

Silence followed. Hugo waited palpitatingly. The outlook seemed to him black. He wondered if he had placed too much reliance in woman's wit. That 'Golly!' had not been hopeful.

'Hugo!'

'Hullo?'

'This is a bit thick.'

'Yes,' agreed Hugo. The thickness had not escaped him.

'Well, there's only one thing to do.'

A faint thrill passed through Hugo Carmody. One would be enough. Woman's wit was going to bring home the bacon after all.

'Listen!'

'Well?'

'The only thing to do is for me to go back to the dining-room and tell Uncle Clarence you've found the Empress.'

'Eh?'

'Found her, fathead.'

'How do you mean?'

'Found her in the caravan.'

'But weren't you listening to what I was saying?' There were tears in Hugo's voice. 'Pilbeam saw us putting her there.'

'I know.'

'Well, what's our move when he says so?'

'Stout denial.'

'Eh?'

'We stoutly deny it,' said Millicent.

The thrill passed through Hugo again, stronger than before. It might work. Yes, properly handled, it would work. He poured broken words of love and praise into the receiver.

'That's right,' he cried. 'I see daylight. I will go to Pilbeam and tell him privily that if he opens his mouth I'll strangle him.'

'Well, hold on. I'll go and tell Uncle Clarence. I expect he'll be out in a moment to have a word with you.'

'Half a minute! Millicent!'

'Well?'

'When am I supposed to have found this ghastly pig?'

'Ten minutes ago, when you were taking a stroll before dinner. You happened to pass the caravan and you heard an odd noise inside, and you looked to see what it was, and there was the Empress and you raced back to the house to telephone.'

'But, Millicent! Half a minute!'

'Well?'

'The old boy will think Baxter stole her.'

'So he will! Isn't that splendid! Well, hold on.'

Hugo resumed his vigil. It was some moments later that a noise like the clucking of fowls broke out at the Matchingham Hall end of the wire. He deduced correctly that this was caused by the ninth Earl of Emsworth endeavouring to clothe his thoughts in speech.

'Kuk-kuk-kuk . . .'

'Yes, Lord Emsworth?'

'Kuk-Carmody!'

'Yes, Lord Emsworth?'

'Is this true?'

'Yes, Lord Emsworth.'

'You've found the Empress?'

'Yes, Lord Emsworth.'

'In that feller Baxter's caravan?'

'Yes, Lord Emsworth.'

'Well, I'll be damned!'

'Yes, Lord Emsworth.'

So far Hugo Carmody had found his share of the dialogue delightfully easy. On these lines he would have been prepared to continue it all night. But there was something else besides, 'Yes, Lord Emsworth' that he must now endeavour to say. There is a tide in the affairs of men which, taken at the flood, leads on to fortune: and that tide, he knew, would never rise higher than at the present moment. He swallowed twice to unlimber his vocal cords.

'Lord Emsworth,' he said, and, though his heart was beating fast, his voice was steady, 'there is something I would like to take this opportunity of saying. It will come as a surprise to you, but I hope not as an unpleasant surprise. I love your niece Millicent, and she loves me,

Lord Emsworth. We have loved each other for many weeks and it is my hope that you will give your consent to our marriage. I am not a rich man, Lord Emsworth. In fact, strictly speaking, except for my salary I haven't a bean in the world. But my Uncle Lester owns Rudge Hall, in Worcestershire—I dare say you have heard of the place? You turn to the left off the main road to Birmingham and go about a couple of miles . . . well, anyway, it's a biggish sort of place in Worcestershire and my Uncle Lester owns it and the property is entailed and I'm next in succession . . . I won't pretend that my Uncle Lester shows any indications of passing in his checks, he was extremely fit last time I saw him, but, after all, he's getting on and all flesh is as grass and, as I say, I'm next man in, so I shall eventually succeed to quite a fairish bit of the stuff and a house and park and rent-roll and all that, so what I mean is, it isn't as if I wasn't in a position to support Millicent later on, and if you realized, Lord Emsworth, how we love one another I'm sure you would see that it wouldn't be playing the game to put any obstacles in the way of our happiness, so what I'm driving at, if you follow me, is, may we charge ahead?'

There was dead silence at the other end of the wire. It seemed as if the revelation of a good man's love had struck Lord Emsworth dumb. It was only some moments later, after he had said 'Hullo!' six times and 'I say, are you there?' twice that it was borne in upon Hugo that he had wasted two hundred and eighty words of the finest eloquence on empty space.

His natural chagrin at this discovery was sensibly diminished by the sudden sound of Millicent's voice in his ear.

'Hullo!'

'Hullo!'

'Hullo!'

'Hullo!'

'Hugo!'

'Hullo!'

'I say, Hugo!' She spoke with the joyous excitement of a girl who has just emerged from the centre of a family dog-fight. 'I say, Hugo, things are hotting up here properly. I sprung it on Uncle Clarence just now that I want to marry you!'

'So did I. Only he wasn't there.'

'I said "Uncle Clarence, aren't you grateful to Mr Carmody for find-ing the Empress?" and he said "Yes, yes, yes, yes, yes, to be sure. Capital boy! Capital boy! Always liked him." And I said "I suppose you wouldn't by any chance let me marry him?" and he said "Eh, what? Marry him?" "Yes," I said. "Marry him." And he said "Certainly, certainly, certainly, certainly, by all means." And then Aunt Constance had a fit, and Uncle Gally said she was a kill-joy and ought to be ashamed of herself for throw-ing the gaff into love's young dream, and Uncle Clarence kept on saying "Certainly, certainly, certainly." I don't know what old Parsloe thinks of it all. He's sitting in his chair, looking at the ceiling and drinking hock. The butler left at the end of round one. I'm going back to see how it's all coming out. Hold the line.'

A man for whom Happiness and Misery are swaying in the scales three miles away, and whose only medium of learning the result of the contest is a telephone wire, is not likely to ring off impatiently. Hugo sat tense and breathless, like one listening in on the radio to a championship fight in which he has a financial interest. It was only when a cheery voice spoke at his elbow that he realized that his solitude had been invaded, and by Percy Pilbeam at that.

Percy Pilbeam was looking rosy and replete. He swayed slightly and his smile was rather wider and more pebble-beached than a total abstainer's would have been.

'Hullo, Carmody,' said Percy Pilbeam. 'What ho, Carmody. So here you are, Carmody.'

It came to Hugo that he had something to say to this man.

'Here, you!' he cried.

'Yes, Carmody?'

'Do you want to be battered to a pulp?'

'No, Carmody.'

'Then listen. You didn't see me put that pig in the caravan. Understand?'

'But I did, Carmody.'

'You didn't—not if you want to go on living.'

Percy Pilbeam appeared to be in a mood not only of keen intelligence but of the utmost reasonableness and amiability.

'Say no more, Carmody,' he said agreeably. 'I take your point. You want me not to tell anybody I saw you put that caravan in the pig. Quite, Carmody, quite.'

'Well, bear it in mind.'

'I will, Carmody. Oh yes, Carmody, I will. I'm going for a stroll outside, Carmody. Care to join me?'

'Go to hell!'

'Quite,' said Percy Pilbeam.

He tacked unsteadily to the door, aimed himself at it and passed through. And a moment later Millicent's voice spoke.

'Hugo?'

'Hullo?'

'Oh, Hugo, darling, the battle's over. We've won. Uncle Clarence has said "Certainly" sixty-five times, and he's just told Aunt Constance that if she thinks she can bully him she's very much mistaken. It's a walkover. They're all coming back right away in the car. Uncle Clarence is an angel.'

'So are you.'

'Me?'

'Yes, you.'

'Not such an angel as you are.'

'Much more of an angel than I am,' said Hugo, in the voice of one trained to the appraising and classifying of angels.

'Well, anyway, you precious old thing, I'm going to give them the slip and walk home along the road. Get out Ronnie's two-seater and come and pick me up and we'll go for a drive together, miles and miles through the country. It's the most perfect evening.'

'You bet it is!' said Hugo fervently. 'What I call something like an evening. Give me two minutes to get the car out and five to make the trip and I'll be with you.'

''At-a-boy!' said Millicent.

''At-a-baby!' said Hugo.

16

LOVERS' MEETING

S UE stood staring, wide-eyed. This was the moment which she had tried to picture to herself a hundred times. And always her imagination had proved unequal to the task. Sometimes she had seen Ronnie in her mind's eye cold, aloof, hostile; sometimes gasping and tottering, dumb with amazement; sometimes pointing a finger at her like a character in a melodrama and denouncing her as an impostor. The one thing for which she had not been prepared was what happened now.

Eton and Cambridge train their sons well. Once they have grasped the fundamental fact of life that all exhibitions of emotion are bad form, bombshells cannot disturb their poise and earthquakes are lucky if they get so much as an 'Eh, what?' from them. But Cambridge has its limitations, and so has Eton. And remorse had goaded Ronnie Fish to a point where their iron discipline had ceased to operate. He was stirred to his depths, and his scarlet face, his rumpled hair, his starting eyes and his twitching fingers all proclaimed the fact.

'Ronnie!' cried Sue.

It was all she had time to say. The thought of what she had done for his sake; the thought that for love of him she had come to Blandings Castle under false colours—an impostor—faced at every turn by the risk of detection—liable at any moment to be ignominiously exposed and looked at through a lorgnette by his Aunt Constance; the thought of the shameful way he had treated her . . . all these thoughts were racking Ronald Fish with a searing anguish. They had brought the hot blood of the Fishes to the boil, and now, face to face with her, he did not hesitate.

He sprang forward, clasped her in his arms, hugged her to him. To Baxter's revolted ears, though he tried not to listen, there came in a husky cataract the sound of a Fish's self-reproaches. Ronnie was saying what he thought of himself, and his opinion appeared not to be high. He said he was a beast, a brute, a swine, a cad, a hound, and a worm. If he had been speaking of Percy Pilbeam, he could scarcely have been less complimentary.

Even up to this point, Baxter had not liked the dialogue. It now became perfectly nauseating. Sue said it had all been her fault. Ronnie said, No, his. No, hers, said Sue. No, his, said Ronnie. No, hers, said Sue. No, altogether his, said Ronnie. It must have been his, he pointed out, because, as he had observed before, he was a hound and a worm. He now went further. He revealed himself as a blister, a tick, and a perishing outsider.

'You're not!'

'I am!'

'You're not!'

'I am!'

'Of course you're not!'

'I certainly am!'

'Well, I love you anyway.'

'You can't.'

'I do.'

'You can't.'

'I do.'

Baxter writhed in silent anguish.

'How long?' said Baxter to his immortal soul. 'How long?'

The question was answered with a startling promptitude. From the neighbourhood of the french windows there sounded a discreet cough. The debaters sprang apart, two minds with but a single thought.

'Your manuscript, miss,' said Beach sedately.

Sue looked at him. Ronnie looked at him. Sue until this moment had forgotten his existence. Ronnie had supposed him downstairs, busy about his butlerine duties. Neither seemed very glad to see him.

Ronnie was the first to speak.

'Oh—hullo, Beach!'

There being no answer to this except 'Hullo, sir!' which is a thing that butlers do not say, Beach contented himself with a benignant smile. It had the unfortunate effect of making Ronnie think that the man was laughing at him, and the Fishes were men at whom butlers may not lightly laugh. He was about to utter a heated speech, indicating this, when the injudiciousness of such a course presented itself to his mind. Beach must be placated. He forced his voice to a note of geniality.

'So there you are, Beach?'

'Yes, sir.'

'I suppose all this must seem tolerably rummy to you?'

'No, sir.'

'No?'

'I had already been informed, Mr Ronald, of the nature of your feelings towards this lady.'

'What!'

'Yes, sir.'

'Who told you?'

'Mr Pilbeam, sir.'

Ronnie uttered a gasp. Then he became calmer. He had suddenly remembered that this man was his ally, his accomplice, linked to him not only by a friendship dating back to his boyhood but by the even stronger bond of mutual crime. Between them there need be no reserves. Delicate though the situation was, he now felt equal to it.

'Beach,' he said. 'How much do you know?'

'All, sir.'

'All?'

'Yes, sir.'

'Such as—?'

Beach coughed.

'I am aware that this lady is a Miss Sue Brown. And, according to my informant, she is employed in the chorus of the Regal Theatre.'

'Quite the Encyclopaedia, aren't you?'

'Yes, sir.'

'I want to marry Miss Brown, Beach.'

'I can readily appreciate such a desire on your part, Mr Ronald,' said the butler with a paternal smile.

Sue caught at the smile.

'Ronnie! He's all right. I believe he's a friend.'

'Of course he's a friend! Old Beach. One of my earliest and stoutest pals.'

'I mean, he isn't going to give us away.'

'Me, miss?' said Beach, shocked. 'Certainly not.'

'Splendid fellow, Beach!'

'Thank you, sir.'

'Beach,' said Ronnie, 'the time has come to act. No more delay. I've got to make myself solid with Uncle Clarence at once. Directly he gets back to-night, I shall go to him and tell him that Empress of Blandings is in the gamekeeper's cottage in the West Wood, and then, while he's still weak, I shall spring on him the announcement of my engagement.'

'Unfortunately, Mr Ronald, the animal is no longer in the cottage.'

'You've moved it?'

'Not I, sir. Mr Carmody. By a most regrettable chance Mr Carmody found me feeding it this afternoon. He took it away and deposited it in some place of which I am not cognizant, sir.'

'But, good heavens, he'll dish the whole scheme. Where is he?'

'You wish me to find him, sir?'

'Of course I wish you to find him. Go at once and ask him where that pig is. Tell him it's vital.'

'Very good, sir.'

Sue had listened with bewilderment to this talk of pigs.

'I don't understand, Ronnie.'

Ronnie was pacing the room in agitation. Once he came so close to where Baxter lay in his snug harbour that the ex-secretary had a flashing glimpse of a sock with a lavender clock. It was the first object of beauty that he had seen for a long time, and he should have appreciated it more than he did.

'I can't explain now,' said Ronnie. 'It's too long. But I can tell you this. If we don't get that pig back, we're in the soup.'

'Ronnie!'

Ronnie had ceased to pace the room. He was standing in a listening attitude.

'What's that?'

He sprang quickly to the balcony, looked over the parapet and came softly back.

'Sue!'

'What!'

'It's that blighter Pilbeam,' said Ronnie in a guarded undertone. 'He's climbing up the waterspout!'

17

SPIRITED CONDUCT OF LORD EMSWORTH

FROM the moment when it left the door of Matchingham Hall and started on its journey back to Blandings Castle, a silence as of the tomb had reigned in the Antelope car which was bringing Lord Emsworth, his sister Lady Constance Keeble, and his brother, the Hon. Galahad Threepwood, home from their interrupted dinner-party. Not so much as a syllable proceeded from one of them.

In the light of what Millicent, an eyewitness at the Front, had told Hugo over the telephone of the family battle which had been raging at Sir Gregory Parsloe's table, this will appear strange. If ever three people with plenty to say to one another were assembled together in a small space, these three, one would have thought, were those three. Lady Constance alone might have been expected to provide enough conversation to keep the historian busy for hours.

The explanation, like all explanations, is simple. It is supplied by that one word Antelope.

Owing to the fact that some trifling internal ailment had removed from the active list the Hispano-Suiza in which Blandings Castle usually went out to dinner, Voules, the chauffeur, had to fall back upon this secondary and inferior car; and anybody who has ever owned an Antelope is aware that there is no glass partition inside it shutting off the driver from the cash customers. He is right there in their midst, ready and eager to hear everything that is said and to hand it on in due course to the Servant's Hall.

In these circumstances, though the choice seemed one between speech and spontaneous combustion, the little company kept their thoughts to themselves. They suffered, but they did it. It would be difficult to find a better illustration of all that is implied in the fine old phrase *Noblesse oblige*. At Lady Constance we point with particular pride. She was a woman, and silence weighed hardest on her.

There were times during the drive when even the sight of Voules' large, red ears, all pricked up to learn the reason for this sudden and sensational return, was scarcely sufficient to restrain Lady Constance Keeble from telling her brother Clarence just what she thought of him. From boyhood up, he had not once come near to being her ideal man; but never had he sunk so low in her estimation as at the moment when she heard him giving his consent to the union of her niece Millicent with a young man who, besides being penniless, had always afflicted her with a nervous complaint for which she could find no name, but which is known to Scientists as the heeby-jeebies.

Nor had he re-established himself in any way by his outspoken remarks on the subject of the Efficient Baxter. He had said things about Baxter which no admirer of that energetic man could forgive. The adjectives mad, crazy, insane, gibbering—and, worse, potty—had played in and out of his conversation like flashes of lightning. And from the look in his eye she gathered that he was still saying them all over again to himself.

Her surmise was correct. To Lord Emsworth the events of this day had come as a stunning revelation. On the strength of that flower-pot incident two years ago, he had always looked on Baxter as mentally unbalanced; but, being a fair-minded man, he had recognized the possibility that a quiet, regular life and freedom from worries might, in the interval which had elapsed since his late secretary's departure from the castle, have effected a cure. Certainly the man had appeared quite normal on the day of his arrival. And now into the space of a few hours he had crammed enough variegated lunacy to equip all the March Hares in England and leave some over for the Mad Hatters.

The ninth Earl of Emsworth was not a man who was easily disturbed. His was a calm which, as a rule, only his younger son Frederick could shatter. But it was not proof against the sort of thing that had being going on to-day. No matter how placid you may be, if you find yourself in close juxtaposition with a man who, when he is not hurling himself out of windows, is stealing pigs and trying to make you believe they were stolen by your butler, you begin to think a bit. Lord Emsworth was thoroughly upset. As the car bowled up the drive, he was saying to himself that nothing could surprise him now.

And yet something did. As the car turned the corner by the rhododendrons and wheeled into the broad strip of gravel that faced the front door, he beheld a sight which brought the first sound he had uttered since the journey began bursting from his lips.

'Good God!'

The words were spoken in a high, penetrating tenor, and they made Lady Constance jump as if they had been pins running into her. This unexpected breaking of the great silence was agony to her taut nerves.

'What *is* the matter?'

'Matter? Look! Look at that fellow!'

Voules took it upon himself to explain. Never having met Lady Constance socially, as it were, he ought perhaps not to have spoken. He considered, however, that the importance of the occasion justified the solecism.

'A man is climbing the waterspout, m'lady.'

'What! Where? I don't see him.'

'He has just got into the balcony outside one of the bedrooms,' said the Hon. Galahad.

Lord Emsworth went straight to the heart of the matter.

'It's that fellow Baxter!' he exclaimed.

The summer day, for all the artificial aid lent by daylight saving, was now definitely over, and gathering night had spread its mantle of dusk over the world. The visibility, therefore, was not good: and the figure which had just vanished over the parapet of the balcony of the Garden

Room had been unrecognizable except to the eye of intuition. This, however, was precisely the sort of eye that Lord Emsworth possessed.

He reasoned closely. There were, he knew, on the premises of Blandings Castle other male adults besides Rupert Baxter: but none of these would climb up waterspouts and disappear over balconies. To Baxter, on the other hand, such a pursuit would seem the normal, ordinary way of passing an evening. It would be his idea of wholesome relaxation. Soon, no doubt, he would come out on the balcony again and throw himself to the ground. That was the sort of fellow Baxter was—a man of strange pleasures.

And so, going as we say, straight to the heart of the matter, Lord Emsworth, jerking the pince-nez off his face in his emotion, exclaimed:

'It's that fellow Baxter!'

Not since a certain day in their mutual nursery many years ago had Lady Constance gone to the length of actually hauling off and smiting her elder brother on the head with the flat of an outraged hand: but she came very near to doing it now. Perhaps it was the presence of Voules that caused her to confine herself to words.

'Clarence, you're an idiot!'

Even Voules could not prevent her saying that. After all, she was revealing no secrets. The chauffeur had been in service at the castle quite long enough to have formed the same impression for himself.

Lord Emsworth did not argue the point. The car had drawn up now outside the front door. The front door was open, as always of a summer evening, and the ninth Earl, accompanied by his brother Galahad, hurried up the steps and entered the hall. And, as they did so, there came to their ears the sound of running feet. The next moment, the flying figure of Percy Pilbeam came into view, taking the stairs four at a time.

'God bless my soul!' said Lord Emsworth.

If Pilbeam heard the words or saw the speaker, he gave no sign of having done so. He was plainly in a hurry. He shot through the hall and, more like a startled gazelle than a private enquiry agent, vanished down the steps. His shirt-front was dark with dirt-stains, his collar had burst from its stud, and it seemed to Lord Emsworth, in the brief moment during which he was able to focus him, that he had a black eye. The next instant, there descended the stairs and flitted past with equal speed the form of Ronnie Fish.

Lord Emsworth got an entirely wrong conception of the affair. He had no means of knowing what had taken place in the Garden Room when Pilbeam, inspired by alcohol and flushed with the thought that now was the time to get into that apartment and possess himself of the manuscript of the Hon. Galahad's reminiscences, had climbed the waterspout to put the plan into operation. He knew nothing of the detective's sharp dismay at finding himself unexpectedly confronted with the menacing form of Ronnie Fish. He was ignorant of the lively and promising mix-up which had been concluded by Pilbeam's tempestuous dash for life. All he saw was two men fleeing madly for the open spaces, and he placed the obvious interpretation upon this phenomenon.

Baxter, he assumed, had run amok and had done it with such uncompromising thoroughness that strong men ran panic-stricken before him.

Mild though the ninth Earl was by nature, a lover of rural peace and the quiet life, he had, like all Britain's aristocracy, the right stuff in him. It so chanced that during the years when he had held his commission in the Shropshire Yeomanry the motherland had not called to him to save her. But, had that call been made, Clarence, ninth Earl of Emsworth, would have answered it with as prompt a 'Bless my Soul! Of course. Certainly!' as any of his Crusader ancestors. And in his sixtieth year the ancient fire still lingered. The Hon. Galahad, who had turned to watch the procession through the front door with a surprised monocle, turned back and found that he was alone. Lord Emsworth had disappeared. He now beheld him coming back again. On his amiable face was a look of determination. In his hand was a gun.

'Eh? What?' said the Hon. Galahad, blinking.

The head of the family did not reply. He was moving towards the stairs. In just that same silent purposeful way had an Emsworth advanced on the foe at Agincourt.

A sound as of disturbed hens made the Hon. Galahad turn again.

'Galahad! What is all this? What is happening?'

The Hon. Galahad placed his sister in possession of the facts as known to himself.

'Clarence has just gone upstairs with a gun.'

'With a gun!'

'Yes. Looked like mine, too. I hope he takes care of it.'

He perceived that Lady Constance had also been seized with the urge to climb. She was making excellent time up the broad staircase. So nimbly did she move that she was on the second landing before he came up with her.

And, as they stood there, a voice made itself heard from a room down the corridor.

'Baxter! Come out! Come out, Baxter, my dear fellow, immediately.'

In the race for the room from which the words had appeared to proceed, Lady Constance, getting off to a good start, beat her brother by a matter of two lengths. She was thus the first to see a sight unusual even at Blandings Castle, though strange things had happened there from time to time.

Her young guest, Miss Schoonmaker, was standing by the window, looking excited and alarmed. Her brother Clarence, pointing a gun expertly from the hip, was staring fixedly at the bed. And from under the bed, a little like a tortoise protruding from its shell, there was coming into view the spectacled head of the Efficient Baxter.

18

PAINFUL SCENE IN A BEDROOM

A MAN who has been lying under a bed for a matter of some thirty minutes and, while there, has been compelled to listen to the sort of dialogue which accompanies a lovers' reconciliation seldom appears at his best or feels his brightest. There was fluff in Baxter's hair, dust on his clothes, and on Baxter's face a scowl of concentrated hatred of all humanity. Lord Emsworth, prepared for something pretty wild-looking, found his expectations exceeded. He tightened his grasp on the gun, and to ensure a more accurate aim raised the butt of it to his shoulder, closing one eye and allowing the other to gleam along the barrel.

'I have you covered, my dear fellow,' he said mildly.

Rupert Baxter had not yet begun to stick straws in his hair, but he seemed on the verge of that final piece of self-expression.

'Don't point that damned thing at me!'

'I shall point it at you,' replied Lord Emsworth with spirit. He was not a man to be dictated to in his own house. 'And at the slightest sign of violence . . .'

'Clarence!' It was Lady Constance who spoke. 'Put that gun down.'

'Certainly not.'

'Clarence!'

'Oh, all right.'

'And now, Mr Baxter,' said Lady Constance, proceeding to dominate the scene in her masterly way, 'I am sure you can explain.'

Her agitation had passed. It was not in this strong woman to remain agitated long. She had been badly shaken, but her faith in her idol still held good. Remarkable as his behaviour might appear, she was sure that he could account for it in a perfectly satisfactory manner.

Baxter did not speak. His silence gave Lord Emsworth the opportunity of advancing his own views.

'Explain?' He spoke petulantly, for he resented the way in which his sister had thrust him from the centre of the stage. 'What on earth is there to explain? The thing's obvious.'

'Can't say I've quite got to the bottom of it,' murmured the Hon. Galahad. 'Fellow under bed. Why? Why under bed? Why here at all?'

Lord Emsworth hesitated. He was a kind-hearted man, and he felt that what he had to say would be better said in Baxter's absence. However, there seemed no way out of it, so he proceeded.

'My dear Galahad, think!'

'Eh?'

'That flower-pot affair. You remember?'

'Oh!' Understanding shone in the Hon. Galahad's monocle. 'You mean . . .?'

'Exactly.'

'Yes, yes. Of course. Subject to these attacks, you mean?'

'Precisely.'

This was not the first time Lady Constance Keeble had had the opportunity of hearing a theory ventilated by her brothers which she found detestable. She flushed brightly.

'Clarence!'

'My dear?'

'Kindly stop talking in that offensive way.'

'God bless my soul!' Lord Emsworth was stung. 'I like that. What have I said that is offensive?'

'You know perfectly well.'

'If you mean that I was reminding Galahad in the most delicate way that poor Baxter here is not quite . . .'

'Clarence!'

'All very well to say "Clarence!" like that. You know yourself he isn't right in the head. Didn't he throw flower-pots at me? Didn't he leap out of the window this very afternoon? Didn't he try to make me think that Beach . . .'

Baxter interrupted. There were certain matters on which he considered silence best, but this was one on which he could speak freely.

'Lord Emsworth!'

'Eh?'

'It has now come to my knowledge that Beach was not the prime mover in the theft of your pig. But I have ascertained that he was an accessory.'

'A what?'

'He helped,' said Baxter, grinding his teeth a little. 'The man who committed the actual theft was your nephew Ronald.'

Lord Emsworth turned to his sister with a triumphant gesture, like one who has been vindicated.

'There! Now perhaps you'll say he's not potty? It won't do, Baxter, my dear fellow,' he went on, waggling a reproachful gun at his late employee. 'You really mustn't excite yourself by making up these stories.'

'Bad for the blood-pressure,' agreed the Hon. Galahad.

'The Empress was found this evening in your caravan,' said Lord Emsworth.

'What!'

'In your caravan. Where you put her when you stole her. And, bless my soul,' said Lord Emsworth, with a start, 'I must be going and seeing that she is put back in her sty. I must find Pirbright. I must . . .'

'In my caravan?' Baxter passed a feverish hand across his dust-stained forehead. Illumination came to him. 'Then that's what that fellow Carmody did with the animal!'

Lord Emsworth had had enough of this. Empress of Blandings was waiting for him. Counting the minutes to that holy reunion, he chafed at having to stand here listening to these wild ravings.

'First Beach, then Ronald, then Carmody! You'll be saying I stole her next, or Galahad here, or my sister Constance. Baxter, my dear fellow, we aren't blaming you. Please don't think that. We quite see how it is. You will overwork yourself, and, of course, nature demands the penalty. I wish you would go quietly to your room, my dear fellow, and lie down. All this must be very bad for you.'

Lady Constance intervened. Her eye was aflame, and she spoke like Cleopatra telling an Ethiopian slave where he got off.

'Clarence, will you kindly use whatever slight intelligence you may possess? The theft of your pig is one of the most trivial and unimportant things that ever happened in this world, and I consider the fuss that has been made about it quite revolting. But whoever stole the wretched animal . . .'

Lord Emsworth blenched. He started as if wondering if he had heard aright.

'. . . and wherever it has been found, it was certainly not Mr Baxter who stole it. It is, as Mr Baxter says, much more likely to have been a young man like Mr Carmody. There is a certain type of young man, I believe, to which Mr Carmody belongs, which considers practical joking amusing. Do ask yourself, Clarence, and try to answer the question as reasonably as is possible for a man of your mental calibre: What earthly motive would Mr Baxter have for coming to Blandings Castle and stealing pigs?'

It may have been the feel of the gun in his hand which awoke in Lord Emsworth old memories of dashing days with the Shropshire Yeomanry and lent him some of the hot spirit of his vanished youth. The fact remains that he did not wilt beneath his sister's dominating eye. He met it boldly, and boldly answered back.

'And ask yourself, Constance,' he said, 'what earthly motive Mr Baxter has for anything he does.'

'Yes,' said the Hon. Galahad loyally. 'What motive had our friend Baxter for coming to Blandings Castle and scaring girls stiff by hiding under beds?'

Lady Constance gulped. They had found the weak spot in her defences. She turned to the man who she still hoped could deal efficiently with this attack.

'Mr Baxter!' she said, as if she were calling on him for an after-dinner speech.

But Rupert Baxter had had no dinner. And it was perhaps this that turned the scale. Quite suddenly there descended on him a frenzied desire to be out of this, cost what it might. An hour before, half an hour before, even five minutes before, his tongue had been tied by a still lingering hope that he might yet find his way back to Blandings Castle in the capacity of private secretary to the Earl of Emsworth. Now, he felt that he would not accept that post, were it offered to him on bended knee.

A sudden overpowering hatred of Blandings Castle and all it contained gripped the Efficient Baxter. He marvelled that he had ever wanted to come back. He held at the present moment the well-paid and responsible position of secretary and adviser to J. Horace Jevons, the American millionaire, a man who not only treated him with an obsequiousness and respect which were balm to his soul, but also gave him such sound advice on the investment of money that already he had trebled his savings. And it was this golden-hearted Chicagoan whom he had been thinking of deserting, purely to satisfy some obscure sentiment which urged him to return to a house which, he now saw, he loathed as few houses have been loathed since human beings left off living in caves.

His eyes flashed through their lenses. His mouth tightened.

'I will explain!'

'I knew you would have an explanation,' cried Lady Constance.

'I have. A very simple one.'

'And short, I hope?' asked Lord Emsworth, restlessly. He was aching to have done with all this talk and discussion and to be with his pig once more. To think of the Empress languishing in a beastly caravan was agony to him.

'Quite short,' said Rupert Baxter.

The only person in the room who so far had remained entirely outside this rather painful scene was Sue. She had looked on from her place by the window, an innocent bystander. She now found herself drawn abruptly into the maelstrom of the debate. Baxter's spectacles were raking her from head to foot, and he had pointed at her with an accusing forefinger.

'I came to this room,' he said, 'to try to recover a letter which I had written to this lady who calls herself Miss Schoonmaker.'

'Of course she calls herself Miss Schoonmaker,' said Lord Emsworth, reluctantly dragging his thoughts from the Empress. 'It's her name, my dear fellow. That,' he explained gently, 'is why she calls herself Miss Schoonmaker. God bless my soul!' he said, unable to restrain a sudden spurt of irritability. 'If a girl's name is Schoonmaker, naturally she calls herself Miss Schoonmaker.'

'Yes, if it is. But hers is not. It is Brown.'

'Listen, my dear fellow,' said Lord Emsworth soothingly. 'You are only exciting yourself by going on like this. Probably doing yourself a great deal of harm. Now, what I suggest is, that you go to your room and put a cool compress on your forehead and lie down and take a good rest. I will send Beach up to you with some nice bread-and-milk.'

'Rum and milk,' amended the Hon. Galahad. 'It's the only thing. I knew a fellow in the year '97 who was subject to these spells—you probably remember him, Clarence. Bellamy. Barmy Bellamy we used to call him—and whenever . . .'

'Her name is Brown!' repeated Baxter, his voice soaring in a hysterical crescendo. 'Sue Brown. She is a chorus-girl at the Regal Theatre in London. And she is apparently engaged to be married to your nephew Ronald.'

Lady Constance uttered a cry. Lord Emsworth expressed his feelings with a couple of tuts. The Hon. Galahad alone was silent. He caught Sue's eye, and there was concern in his gaze.

'I overheard Beach saying so in this very room. He said he had had the information from Mr Pilbeam. I imagine it to be accurate. But in any case, I can tell you this much. Whoever she is, she is an impostor who has come here under a false name. While I was in the smoking-room some time back a telegram came through on the telephone from Market Blandings. It was signed Myra Schoonmaker, and it had been handed in in Paris this afternoon. That is all I have to say,' concluded Baxter. 'I will now leave you, and I sincerely hope I shall never set eyes on any of you again. Good evening!'

His spectacles glinting coldly, he strode from the room and in the doorway collided with Ronnie, who was entering.

'Can't you look where you're going?' he asked.

'Eh?' said Ronnie.

'Clumsy idiot!' said the Efficient Baxter, and was gone.

In the room he had left, Lady Constance Keeble had become a stony figure of menace. She was not at ordinary times a particularly tall woman, but she seemed now to tower like something vast and awful: and Sue quailed before her.

'Ronnie!' cried Sue weakly.

It was the cry of the female in distress, calling to her mate. Just so in prehistoric days must Sue's cavewoman ancestress have cried to the man behind the club when suddenly cornered by the sabre-toothed tiger which Lady Constance Keeble so closely resembled.

'Ronnie!'

'What's all this?' asked the last of the Fishes.

He was breathing rather quickly, for the going had been fast. Pilbeam, once out in the open, had shown astonishing form at the short sprint. He had shaken off Ronnie's challenge twenty yards down the drive, and plunged into a convenient shrubbery, and Ronnie, giving up the pursuit, had come back to Sue's room to report. It occasioned him some surprise to find that in his absence it had become the scene of some sort of public meeting.

'What's all this?' he said, addressing that meeting.

Lady Constance wheeled round upon him.

'Ronald, who is this girl?'

'Eh?' Ronnie was conscious of a certain uneasiness, but he did his best. He did not like his aunt's looks, but then he never had. Something was evidently up, but it might be that airy nonchalance would save the day. 'You know her, don't you? Miss Schoonmaker? Met her with me in London.'

'Is her name Brown? And is she a chorus-girl?'

'Why, yes,' admitted Ronnie. It was a bombshell, but Eton and Cambridge stood it well. 'Why, yes,' he said, 'as a matter of fact, that's right.'

Words seemed to fail Lady Constance. Judging from the expression on her face this was just as well.

'I'd been meaning to tell you about that,' said Ronnie. 'We're engaged.'

Lady Constance recovered herself sufficiently to find one word.

'Clarence!'

'Eh?' said Lord Emsworth. His thoughts had been wandering.

'You heard?'

'Heard what?'

Beyond the stage of turbulent emotion, Lady Constance had become suddenly calm and icy.

'If you have not been sufficiently interested to listen,' she said, 'I may inform you that Ronald has just announced his intention of marrying a chorus-girl.'

'Oh, ah?' said Lord Emsworth. Would a man of Baxter's outstandingly unbalanced intellect, he was wondering, have remembered to feed the Empress regularly? The thought was like a spear quivering in his heart. He edged in agitation towards the door, and had reached it when he perceived that his sister had not yet finished talking to him.

'So that is all the comment you have to make, is it?'

'Eh? What about?'

'The point I have been endeavouring to make you understand,' went on Lady Constance, with laborious politeness, 'is that your nephew Ronald has announced his intention of marrying into the Regal Theatre chorus.'

'Who?'

'Ronald. This is Ronald. He is anxious to marry Miss Brown, a chorus-girl. This is Miss Brown.'

'How do you do?' said Lord Emsworth. He might be vague, but he had the manners of the old school.

Ronnie interposed. The time had come to play the ace of trumps.

'She isn't an ordinary chorus-girl.'

'From the fact of her coming to Blandings Castle under a false name,' said Lady Constance, 'I imagine not. It shows unusual enterprise.'

'What I mean,' continued Ronnie, 'is, I know what a bally snob you are, Aunt Constance—no offence, but you know what I mean—keen on birth and family and all that sort of rot . . . well, what I'm driving at is that Sue's father was in the Guards.'

'A private? Or a corporal?'

'Captain. A fellow named . . .'

'Cotterleigh,' said Sue in a small voice.

'Cotterleigh,' said Ronnie.

'Cotterleigh!'

It was the Hon. Galahad who had spoken. He was staring at Sue open-mouthed.

'Cotterleigh? Not Jack Cotterleigh?'

'I don't know whether it was Jack Cotterleigh,' said Ronnie. 'The point I'm making is that it was Cotterleigh and that he was in the Irish Guards.'

The Hon. Galahad was still staring at Sue.

'My dear,' he cried, and there was an odd sharpness in his voice, 'was your mother Dolly Henderson, who used to be a Serio at the old Oxford and the Tivoli?'

Not for the first time Ronald Fish was conscious of a feeling that his Uncle Galahad ought to be in some kind of a home. He would drag in Dolly Henderson! He would stress the Dolly Henderson note at just this point in the proceedings! He would spoil the whole thing by calling attention to the Dolly Henderson aspect of the matter, just when it was vital to stick to the Cotterleigh, the whole Cotterleigh, and nothing but the Cotterleigh. Ronnie sighed wearily. Padded cells, he felt, had been invented specially for the Uncle Galahads of this world, and the Uncle Galahads, he considered, ought never to be permitted to roam about outside them.

'Yes,' said Sue. 'She was.'

The Hon. Galahad was advancing on her with outstretched hands. He looked like some father in melodrama welcoming the prodigal daughter.

'Well, I'm dashed!' he said. He repeated three times that he was in this condition. He seized Sue's limp paws and squeezed them fondly. 'I've been trying to think all this while who it was that you reminded me of, my dear girl. Do you know that in the years '96, '97, and '98, I was madly in love with your mother myself? Do you know that if my infernal family hadn't shipped me off to South Africa I would certainly have married her? Fact, I assure you. But they got behind me and shoved me on to the boat, and when I came back I found that young Cotterleigh had cut me out. Well!'

It was a scene which some people would have considered touching. Lady Constance Keeble was not one of them.

'Never mind about that now, Galahad,' she said. 'The point is . . .'

'The point is,' retorted the Hon. Galahad warmly, 'that that young Fish there wants to marry Dolly Henderson's daughter, and I'm for it. And I hope, Clarence, that you'll have some sense for once in your life and back them up like a sportsman.'

'Eh?' said the ninth Earl. His thoughts had once more been wandering. Even assuming that Baxter had fed the Empress, would he have given her the right sort of food and enough of it?

'You see for yourself what a splendid girl she is.'

'Who?'

'This girl.'

'Charming,' agreed Lord Emsworth courteously, and returned to his meditations.

'Clarence!' cried Lady Constance, jerking him out of them.

'Eh?'

'You are not to consent to this marriage.'

'Who says so?'

'I say so. And think what Julia will say.'

She could not have advanced a more impressive argument. In this chronicle the Lady Julia Fish, relict of the late Major-General Sir Miles Fish, C.B.O. of the Brigade of Guards, has made no appearance. We, therefore, know nothing of her compelling eye, her dominant chin, her determined mouth, and her voice, which, at certain times—as, for example, when rebuking a brother—could raise blisters on a sensitive skin. Lord Emsworth was aware of all these things. He had had experience of them from boyhood. His idea of happiness was to be where Lady Julia Fish was not. And the thought of her coming down to Blandings Castle and tackling him in his library about this business froze him to the mar-

row. It had been his amiable intention until this moment to do whatever
the majority of those present wanted him to do. But now he hesitated.

'You think Julia wouldn't like it?'

'Of course Julia would not like it.'

'Julia's an ass,' said the Hon. Galahad.

Lord Emsworth considered this statement, and was inclined to agree
with it. But it did not alter the main point.

'You think she would make herself unpleasant about it?'

'I do.'

'In that case . . .' Lord Emsworth paused. Then a strange soft light
came into his eyes. 'Well, see you all later,' he said. 'I'm going down to
look at my pig.'

His departure was so abrupt that it took Lady Constance momentarily by surprise, and he was out of the room and well down the corridor
before she could recover herself sufficiently to act. Then she, too, hurried out. They could hear her voice diminishing down the stairs. It was
calling 'Clarence!'

The Hon. Galahad turned to Sue. His manner was brisk, yet soothing.

'A shame to inflict these fine old English family rows on a visitor,' he
said, patting her shoulder as one who, if things had broken right and
there had not been a regular service of boats to South Africa in the nineties, might have been her father. 'What you need, my dear, is a little rest
and quiet. Come along, Ronald, we'll leave you. The place to continue
this discussion is somewhere outside this room. Cheer up, my dear.
Everything may come out all right yet.'

Sue shook her head.

'It's no good,' she said hopelessly.

'Don't you be too sure,' said the Hon. Galahad.

'I'll jolly well tell you one thing,' said Ronnie. 'I'm going to marry you,
whatever happens. And that's that. Good heavens! I can work, can't I?'

'What at?' asked the Hon. Galahad.

'What at?' Why—er—why, at anything.'

'The market value of any member of this family,' said the Hon.
Galahad, who harboured no illusions about his nearest and dearest, 'is

about threepence-ha-penny per annum. No! What we've got to do is get round old Clarence somehow, and that means talk and argument, which had better take place elsewhere. Come along, my boy. You never know your luck. I've seen stickier things than this come out right in my time.'

19

GALLY TAKES MATTERS IN HAND

S UE stood on the balcony, looking out into the night. Velvet darkness shrouded the world, and from the heart of it came the murmur of rustling trees and the clean, sweet smell of earth and flowers. A little breeze had sprung up, stirring the ivy at her side. Somewhere in it a bird was chirping drowsily, and in the distance sounded the tinkle of running water.

She sighed. It was a night made for happiness. And she was quite sure now that happiness was not for her.

A footstep sounded behind her, and she turned eagerly.

'Ronnie?'

It was the voice of the Hon. Galahad Threepwood that answered.

'Only me, I'm afraid, my dear. May I come on to your balcony? God bless my soul, as Clarence would say, what a wonderful night!'

'Yes,' said Sue doubtfully.

'You don't think so.'

'Oh, yes.'

'I bet you don't. I know I didn't, that night when my old father put his foot down and told me I was leaving for South Africa on the next boat.

Just such a night as this it was, I remember.' He rested his arms on the parapet. 'I never saw your mother after she was married,' he said.

'No?'

'No. She left the stage and. . . . Oh, well, I was rather busy at the time—lot of heavy drinking to do, and so forth—and somehow we never met. The next thing I heard—two or three years ago—was that she was dead. You're very like her, my dear. Can't think why I didn't spot the resemblance right away.'

He became silent. Sue did not speak. She slid her hand under his arm. It was all that there seemed to do. A corncrake began to call monotonously in the darkness.

'That means rain,' said the Hon. Galahad. 'Or not. I forget which. Did you ever hear your mother sing that song . . . ? No, you wouldn't. Before your time. About young Ronald,' he said, abruptly.

'What about him?'

'Fond of him?'

'Yes.'

'I mean really fond?'

'Yes.'

'How fond?'

Sue leaned out over the parapet. At the foot of the wall beneath her Percy Pilbeam, who had been peering out of a bush, popped his head back again. For the detective, possibly remembering with his subconscious mind stories heard in childhood of Bruce and the spider, had refused to admit defeat and had returned by devious ways to the scene of his disaster. Five hundred pounds is a lot of money, and Percy Pilbeam was not going to be deterred from attempting to earn it by the fact that at his last essay he had only just succeeded in escaping with his life. The influence of his potations had worn off to some extent, and he was his calm, keen self again. It was his intention to lurk in these bushes till the small hours, if need be, and then to attack the waterspout again and so the Garden Room where the manuscript of the Hon. Galahad's Reminiscences lay. You cannot be a good detective if you are easily discouraged.

'I can't put it into words,' said Sue.

'Try.'

'No. Everything you say straight out about the way you feel about anybody always sounds silly. Besides, to you Ronnie isn't the sort of man you could understand anyone raving about. You look on him just as something quite ordinary.'

'If that,' said the Hon. Galahad critically.

'Yes, if that. Whereas to me he's something . . . rather special. In fact, if you really want to know how I feel about Ronnie, he's the whole world to me. There! I told you it would sound silly. It's like something out of a song, isn't it? I've worked in the chorus of that sort of song a hundred times. Two steps left, two steps right, kick, smile, both hands on heart— because he's all the wo-orld to me-ee! You can laugh if you like.'

There was a momentary pause.

'I'm not laughing,' said the Hon. Galahad. 'My dear, I only wanted to find out if you really cared for that young Fish . . .'

'I wish you wouldn't call him "that young Fish".'

'I'm sorry, my dear. It seems to describe him so neatly. Well, I just wanted to be quite sure you really were fond of him, because . . .'

'Well?'

'Well, because I've just fixed it all up.'

She clutched at the parapet.

'What!'

'Oh, yes,' said the Hon. Galahad. 'It's all settled. I don't say that you can actually count on an aunt-in-law's embrace from my sister Constance—in fact, if I were you, I wouldn't risk it. She might bite you—but, apart from that, everything's all right. The wedding bells will ring out. Your young man's in the garden somewhere. You had better go and find him and tell him the news. He'll be interested.'

'But . . . but . . .'

Sue was clutching his arm. A wild impulse was upon her to shout and sob. She had no doubts now as to the beauty of the night.

'But . . . how? Why? What has happened?'

'Well . . . You'll admit I might have married your mother?'

'Yes.'

'Which makes me a sort of honorary father to you.'

'Yes'

'In which capacity, my dear, your interests are mine. More than mine, in fact. So what I did was to make your happiness the *Price of the Papers*. Ever see that play? No, before your time. It ran at the Adelphi before you were born. There was a scene where . . .'

'What do you mean?'

The Hon. Galahad hesitated a moment.

'Well, the fact of the matter is, my dear, knowing how strongly my sister Constance has always felt on the subject of those Reminiscences of mine, I went to her and put it to her squarely. "Clarence," I said to her, "is not the sort of man to make any objection to anyone marrying anybody, so long as he isn't expected to attend the wedding. You're the real obstacle," I said. "You and Julia. And if you come round, you can talk Julia over in five minutes. You know she relies on your judgement." And then I said that, if she gave up acting like a barbed-wire entanglement in the path of true love, I would undertake not to publish the Reminiscences.'

Sue clung to his arm. She could find no words.

Percy Pilbeam, who, for the night was very still, had heard all, could have found many. Nothing but the delicate nature of his present situation kept him from uttering them, and that only just. To Percy Pilbeam it was as if he had seen five hundred pounds flutter from his grasp like a vanishing blue bird. He raged dumbly. In all London and the Home Counties there were few men who liked five hundred pounds better than P. Frobisher Pilbeam.

'Oh!' said Sue. Nothing more. Her feelings were too deep. She hugged his arm. 'Oh!' she said, and again 'Oh!'

She found herself crying, and was not ashamed.

'Now, come!' said the Hon. Galahad protestingly. 'Nothing so very extraordinary in that, was there? Nothing so exceedingly remarkable in one pal helping another?'

'I don't know what to say.'

'Then don't say it,' said the Hon. Galahad, much relieved. 'Why, bless you, I don't care whether the damned things are published or not. At least. . . . No, certainly I don't. . . . Only cause a lot of unpleasantness. Besides, I'll leave the dashed book to the Nation and have it published in a hundred years and become the Pepys of the future, what? Best thing that could have happened. Homage of Posterity and all that.'

'Oh!' said Sue.

The Hon. Galahad chuckled.

'It is a shame, though, that the world will have to wait a hundred years before it hears the story of young Gregory Parsloe and the prawns. Did you get to that when you were reading the thing this evening?'

'I'm afraid I didn't read very much,' said Sue. 'I was thinking of Ronnie rather a lot.'

'Oh? Well, I can tell you. You needn't wait a hundred years. It was at Ascot, the year Martingale won the Gold Cup . . .'

Down below, Percy Pilbeam rose from his bush. He did not care now if he were seen. He was still a guest in this hole of a castle, and if a guest cannot pop in and out of bushes if he likes, where does British hospitality come in? It was his intention to shake the dust of Blandings off his feet, to pass the night at the Emsworth Arms, and on the morrow to return to London, where he was appreciated.

'Well, my dear, it was like this. Young Parsloe . . .'

Percy Pilbeam did not linger. The story of the prawns meant nothing to him. He turned away, and the summer night swallowed him. Somewhere in the darkness an owl hooted. It seemed to Pilbeam that there was derision in the sound. He frowned. His teeth came together with a click.

If he could have found it, he would have had a word with that owl.

HEAVY
WEATHER

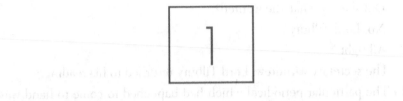

1

SUNSHINE pierced the haze that enveloped London. It came down Fleet Street, turned to the right, stopped at the premises of the Mammoth Publishing Company, and, entering through an upper window, beamed pleasantly upon Lord Tilbury, founder and proprietor of that vast factory of popular literature, as he sat reading the batch of weekly papers which his secretary had placed on the desk for his inspection. Among the secrets of this great man's success was the fact that he kept a personal eye on all the firm's products.

Considering what a pleasant rarity sunshine in London is, one might have expected the man behind the Mammoth to beam back. Instead, he merely pressed the buzzer. His secretary appeared. He pointed silently. The secretary drew the shade, and the sunshine, having called without an appointment, was excluded.

'I beg your pardon, Lord Tilbury . . .'

'Well?'

'A Lady Julia Fish has just rung up on the telephone.'

'Well?'

'She says she would like to see you this morning.'

Lord Tilbury frowned. He remembered Lady Julia Fish as an agreeable hotel acquaintance during his recent holiday at Biarritz. But this was Tilbury House, and at Tilbury House he did not desire the company of hotel acquaintances, however agreeable.

'Did she say what she wanted?'

'No, Lord Tilbury.'

'All right.'

The secretary withdrew. Lord Tilbury returned to his reading.

The particular periodical which had happened to come to hand was the current number of that admirable children's paper, *Tiny Tots*, and for some moments he scanned its pages with an attempt at his usual conscientious thoroughness. But it was plain that his heart was not in his work. The Adventures of Pinky, Winky, and Pop in Slumberland made little impression upon him. He passed on to a thoughtful article by Laura J. Smedley on what a wee girlie can do to help mother, but it was evident that for once Laura J. had failed to grip. Presently with a grunt he threw the paper down and for the third time since it had arrived by the morning post picked up a letter which lay on the desk. He already knew it by heart, so there was no real necessity for him to read it again, but the human tendency to twist the knife in the wound is universal.

It was a brief letter. Its writer's eighteenth-century ancestors, who believed in filling their twelve sheets when they took pen in hand, would have winced at the sight of it. But for all its brevity it had ruined Lord Tilbury's day.

It ran as follows:

> *Blandings Castle,*
> *Shropshire.*
>
> Dear Sir,
>
> *Enclosed find cheque for the advance you paid me on those Reminiscences of mine.*
>
> *I have been thinking it over, and have decided not to publish them, after all.*
>
> *Yours truly,*
> *G. Threepwood.*

'Cor!' said Lord Tilbury, an ejaculation to which he was much addicted in times of mental stress.

He rose from his chair and began to pace the room. Always Napoleonic of aspect, being short and square and stumpy and about twenty-five pounds overweight, he looked now like a Napoleon taking his morning walk at St Helena.

And yet, oddly enough, there were men in England who would have whooped with joy at the sight of that letter. Some of them might even have gone to the length of lighting bonfires and roasting oxen whole for the tenantry about it. Those few words over that signature would have spread happiness in every county from Cumberland to Cornwall. So true is it that in this world everything depends on the point of view.

When, some months before, the news had got about that the Hon. Galahad Threepwood, brother of the Earl of Emsworth and as sprightly an old gentleman as was ever thrown out of a Victorian music-hall, was engaged in writing the recollections of his colourful career as a man about town in the nineties, the shock to the many now highly respectable members of the governing classes who in their hot youth had shared it was severe. All over the country decorous Dukes and steady Viscounts, who had once sown wild oats in the society of the young Galahad, sat quivering in their slippers at the thought of what long-cupboarded skeletons those Reminiscences might disclose.

They knew their Gally, and their imagination allowed them to picture with a crystal clearness the sort of book he would be likely to produce. It would, they felt in their ageing bones, be essentially one of those of which the critics say 'A veritable storehouse of diverting anecdote.' To not a few—Lord Emsworth's nearest neighbour, Sir Gregory Parsloe-Parsloe of Matchingham Hall, was one of them—it was as if the Recording Angel had suddenly decided to rush into print.

Lord Tilbury, however, had looked on the thing from a different angle. He knew—no man better—what big money there was in this type of literature. The circulation of his nasty little paper, *Society Spice*, proved that. Even though Percy Pilbeam, its nasty little editor, had handed in his portfolio and gone off to start a Private Inquiry Agency, it was still a gold-mine. He had known Gally Threepwood in the old days—not intimately, but quite well enough to cause him now to hasten to acquire all rights to the story of his life, sight unseen. It seemed to him that the book could not fail to be the *succès de scandale* of the year.

Acute, therefore, as had been the consternation of the Dukes and Viscounts on learning that the dead past was about to be disinterred, it paled in comparison with that of Lord Tilbury on suddenly receiving this intimation that it was not. There is a tender spot in all great men. Achilles had his heel. With Lord Tilbury it was his pocket. He hated to see money get away from him, and out of this book of Gally Threepwood's he had been looking forward to making a small fortune.

Little wonder, then, that he mourned and was unable to concentrate on *Tiny Tots*. He was still mourning when his secretary entered bearing a slip of paper.

Name—Lady Julia Fish.   *Business*—Personal.

Lord Tilbury snorted irritably. At a time like this!

'Tell her I'm . . .'

And then there flashed into his mind a sudden recollection of something he had heard somebody say about this Lady Julia Fish. The words 'Blandings Castle' seemed to be connected with it. He turned to the desk and took up *Debrett's Peerage*, searching among the E's for Emsworth, Earl of'.

Yes, there it was. Lady Julia Fish had been born Lady Julia Threepwood. She was a sister of the perjured Galahad.

That altered things. Here, he perceived, was an admirable opportunity of working off some of his stored-up venom. His knowledge of life told him that the woman would not be calling unless she wanted to get something out of him. To inform her in person that she was most certainly not going to get it would be balm to his lacerated feelings.

'Ask her to come up,' he said.

• • •

Lady Julia Fish was a handsome middle-aged woman of the large blonde type, of a personality both breezy and commanding. She came into the room a few moments later like a galleon under sail, her resolute chin and her china-blue eyes proclaiming a supreme confidence in her ability to get anything she wanted out of anyone. And Lord Tilbury, having bowed stiffly, stood regarding her with a pop-eyed hostility. Even setting aside her loathsome family connexions, there was a patronizing good humour about her manner which he resented. And certainly, if Lady Julia Fish's manner had a fault, it was that it resembled a little too closely that of the great lady of a village amusedly trying to make friends with the backward child of one of her tenants.

'Well, well, well,' she said, not actually patting Lord Tilbury on the head but conveying the impression that she might see fit to do so at any moment, 'you're looking very bonny. Biarritz did you good.'

Lord Tilbury, with the geniality of a trapped wolf, admitted to being in robust health.

'So this is where you get out all those jolly little papers of yours, is it? I must say I'm impressed. Quite awe-inspiring, all that ritual on the threshold. Admirals in the Swiss Navy making you fill up forms with your name and business, and small boys in buttons eyeing you as if anything you said might be used in evidence against you.'

'What *is* your business?' asked Lord Tilbury.

'The practical note!' said Lady Julia, with indulgent approval. 'How stimulating that is. Time is money, and all that. Quite. Well, cutting the preamble, I want a job for Ronnie.'

Lord Tilbury looked like a trapped wolf who had thought as much.

'Ronnie?' he said coldly.

'My son. Didn't you meet him at Biarritz? He was there. Small and pink.'

Lord Tilbury drew in breath for the delivery of the nasty blow.

'I regret . . .'

'I know what you're going to say. You're very crowded here. Fearful congestion, and so on. Well, Ronnie won't take up much room. And I shouldn't think he could do any actual harm to a solidly established concern like this. Surely you could let him mess about at *something?* Why, Sir Gregory Parsloe, our neighbour down in Shropshire, told me that you were employing his nephew, Monty. And while I would be the last woman to claim Ronnie is a mental giant, at least he's brighter than young Monty Bodkin.'

A quiver ran through Lord Tilbury's stocky form. This woman had unbared his secret shame. A man who prided himself on never letting himself be worked for jobs, he had had a few weeks before a brief moment of madness when, under the softening influence of a particularly good public dinner, he had yielded to the request of the banqueter on his left that he should find a place at Tilbury House for his nephew.

He had regretted the lapse next morning. He had regretted it more on seeing the nephew. And he had not ceased to regret it now.

'That,' he said tensely, 'has nothing to do with the case.'

'I don't see why. Swallowing camels and straining at gnats is what I should call it.'

'Nothing,' repeated Lord Tilbury, 'to do with the case.'

He was beginning to feel that this interview was not working out as he had anticipated. He had meant to be strong, brusque, decisive—the man of iron. And here this woman had got him arguing and explaining—almost in a position of defending himself. Like so many people who came into contact with her, he began to feel that there was something disagreeably hypnotic about Lady Julia Fish.

'But what do you want your son to work here *for?*' he asked, realizing as he spoke that a man of iron ought to have scorned to put such a question.

Lady Julia considered.

'Oh, a pittance. Whatever the dole is you give your slaves.'

Lord Tilbury made himself clearer.

'I mean, why? Has he shown any aptitude for journalism?'

This seemed to amuse Lady Julia.

'My dear man,' she said, tickled by the quaint conceit, 'no member of my family has ever shown any aptitude for anything except eating and sleeping.'

'Then why do you want him to join my staff?'

'Well, primarily, to distract his mind.'

'What!'

'To distract his . . . well, yes, I suppose in a loose way you could call it a mind.'

'I don't understand you.'

'Well, it's like this. The poor half-wit is trying to marry a chorus-girl, and it seemed to me that if he were safe at Tilbury House, inking his nose and getting bustled about by editors and people, it might take his mind off the tender passion.'

Lord Tilbury drew a long, deep, rasping breath. The weakness had passed. He could be strong now. This outrageous insult to the business he loved had shattered the spell which those china-blue eyes and that confident manner had been weaving about him. He spoke curtly, placing his thumbs in the armholes of his waistcoat to lend emphasis to his remarks.

'I fear you have mistaken the functions of Tilbury House, Lady Julia.'

'I beg your pardon?'

'We publish newspapers, magazines, weekly journals. We are not a Home for the Lovelorn.'

There was a brief silence.

'I see,' said Lady Julia. She looked at him inquiringly. 'You sound very stuffy,' she went on. 'Not your old merry Biarritz self at all. Did your breakfast disagree with you this morning?'

'Cor!'

'Something's the matter. Why, at Biarritz you were known as Sunny Jim.'

Lord Tilbury was ill attuned to badinage.

'Yes,' he said. 'Something is the matter. If you really wish to know, I am scarcely in a frame of mind today to go out of my way to oblige members of your family. After what has occurred.'

'What has occurred?'

'Your brother Galahad . . .' Lord Tilbury choked. 'Look at this,' he said.

He extended the letter rather in the manner of one anxious to rid himself of a snake which has somehow come into his possession. Lady Julia scrutinized it with languid interest.

'It's monstrous. Abominable. He accepted the contract, and he ought to fulfil it. At the very least, in common decency, he might have given his reasons for behaving in this utterly treacherous and unethical way. But does he? Not at all. Explanations? None. Apologies? Regrets? Oh dear, no. He merely "decides not to publish". In all my thirty years of . . .'

Lady Julia was never a very good listener.

'Odd,' she said handing the letter back. 'My brother Galahad is a man who moves in a mysterious way his wonders to perform. A quite unaccountable mentality. I knew he was writing this book, of course, but I have no notion whatever why he has had this sudden change of heart. Perhaps some Duke who doesn't want to see himself in the "Peers I Have Been Thrown Out Of Public-Houses With" chapter has been threatening to take him for a ride.'

'Cor!'

'Or some Earl with a guilty conscience. Or a Baronet. "Society Scribe Bumped Off By Baronets"—that would make a good headline for one of your papers.'

'This is not a joking matter.'

'Well, at any rate, my dear man, it's no good savaging *me*. I'm not responsible for Galahad's eccentricities. I'm simply an innocent widow-woman trying to wangle a cushy job for her only son. Coming back to which, I rather gather from what you said just now that you do not intend to set Ronnie punching the clock?'

Lord Tilbury shook from stem to stern. His eyes gleamed balefully. Nature in the raw is seldom mild.

'I absolutely and positively refuse to employ your son at Tilbury House in any capacity whatsoever.'

'Well, that's a fair answer to a fair question, and seems to close the discussion.'

Lady Julia rose.

'Too bad about Gally's little effort,' she said silkily. 'You'll lose a lot of money, won't you? There's a mint of it in a really indiscreet book of Reminiscences. They tell me that Lady Wensleydale's *Sixty Years Near The Knuckle In Mayfair*, or whatever it was called, sold a hundred thousand copies. And, knowing Gally, I'll bet he would have started remembering where old Jane Wensleydale left off. *Good* morning, Lord Tilbury. So nice to have seen you again.'

The door closed. The proprietor of the Mammoth sat staring before him, his agony too keen to permit him even to say 'Cor!'

2

THE spasm passed. Presently life seemed to steal back to that rigid form. It would be too much to say that Lord Tilbury became himself, but at least he began to function once more. Though pain and anguish rack the brow, the world's work has to be done. Like a convalescent reaching for his barley-water, he stretched out a shaking hand and took up *Tiny Tots* again.

And here it would be agreeable to leave him—the good man restoring his *morale* with refreshing draughts at the fount of wholesome literature. But this happy ending was not to be. Once more it was to be proved that this was not Lord Tilbury's lucky morning. Scarcely had he begun to read, when his eyes suddenly protruded from their sockets, his stout body underwent a strong convulsion, and from his parted lips there proceeded a loud snort. It was as if a viper had sprung from between the pages and bitten him on the chin.

And this was odd, because *Tiny Tots* is a journal not as a rule provocative of violent expressions of feeling. Ably edited by that well-known writer of tales for the young, the Rev. Aubrey Sellick, it strives always to take the sane middle course. Its editorial page, in particular, is a model of non-partisan moderation. And yet, amazingly, it was this same editorial page which had just made Lord Tilbury's blood-pressure hit a new high.

It occurred to him that mental strain might have affected his eyesight. He blinked and took another look.

No, there it was, just as before.

UNCLE WOGGLY TO HIS CHICKS

Well, chickabiddies, how are you all? Minding what Nursie says and eating your spinach like good little men? That's right. I know the stuff tastes like a motorman's glove, but they say there's iron in it, and that's what puts hair on the chest.

Lord Tilbury, having taken time out to make a noise like a leaking siphon, resumed his reading.

Well, now let's get down to it. This week, my dear little souls, Uncle Woggly is going to put you on to a good thing. We all want to make a spot of easy money these hard times, don't we? Well, here's the low down, straight from the horse's mouth. All you have to do is to get hold of some mug and lure him into betting that a quart whisky bottle holds a quart of whisky.

Sounds rummy, what? I mean, that's what you would naturally think it would hold. So does the mug. But it isn't. It's really more, and I'll tell you why.

First you fill the bottle. This gives you your quart. Then you shove the cork in. And then—follow me closely here—you turn the bottle upside down and you'll find there's a sort of bulging-in part at the bottom. Well, slosh some whisky into that, and there you are. Because the bot. is now holding more than a quart and you scoop the stakes.

I have to acknowledge a sweet little letter from Frankie Kendon (Hendon) about his canary which goes tweet-tweet-tweet. Also one from Muriel Poot (Stow-in-the-Wold), who is going to lose her shirt if she ever bets anyone she knows how to spell 'tortoise'. . . .

Lord Tilbury had read enough. There was some good stuff further on about Willy Waters (Ponders End) and his cat Miggles, but he did not wait for it. He pressed the buzzer emotionally.

'Tots!' he cried, choking. 'Tiny Tots! Who is editing Tiny Tots now?'

'Mr Sellick is the regular editor, Lord Tilbury,' replied his secretary, who knew everything and wore horn-rimmed spectacles to prove it, 'but he is away on his vacation. In his absence, the assistant editor is in charge of the paper. Mr Bodkin.'

'Bodkin!'

So loud was Lord Tilbury's voice and so sharply did his eyes bulge that the secretary recoiled a step, as if something had hit her.

'That popinjay!' said Lord Tilbury, in a strange, low, grating voice. 'I might have guessed it. I might have foreseen something like this. Send Mr Bodkin here at once.'

It was a judgement, he felt. This was what came of going to public dinners and allowing yourself to depart from the principles of a lifetime. One false step, one moment of weakness when there were wheedling snakes of Baronets at your elbow, and what a harvest, what a reckoning!

He leaned back in his chair, tapping the desk with a paper knife. He had just broken this, when there was a knock at the door and his young subordinate entered.

'Good morning, good morning, good morning,' said the latter affably. 'Want to see me about something?'

Monty Bodkin was rather an attractive popinjay, as popinjays go. He was tall and slender and lissom, and many people considered him quite good-looking. But not Lord Tilbury. He had disapproved of his appearance from their first meeting, thinking him much too well dressed, much too carefully groomed, and much too much like what he actually was, a member in good standing of the Drones Club. The proprietor of the Mammoth Publishing Company could not have put into words his ideal of a young journalist, but it would have been something rather shaggy, preferably with spectacles, certainly not wearing spats. And while Montry Bodkin was not actually spatted at the moment, there did undoubtedly hover about him a sort of spat aura.

'Ha!' said Lord Tilbury, sighting him.

He stared bleakly. His demeanour now was that of a Napoleon who, suffering from toothache, sees his way to taking it out of one of his minor Marshals.

'Come in,' he growled.

'Shut the door,' he grunted.

'And don't grin like that,' he snarled. 'What the devil are you grinning for?'

The words were proof of the deeps of misunderstanding which yawned between the assistant editor of *Tiny Tots* and himself. Certainly something was splitting Monty Bodkin's face in a rather noticeable manner, but the latter could have taken his oath it was an ingratiating smile. He had intended it for an ingratiating smile, and unless something had gone extremely wrong with the works in the process of assembling it, that is what it should have come out as.

However, being a sweet-tempered popinjay and always anxious to oblige, he switched it off. He was feeling a little puzzled. The atmosphere seemed to him to lack chumminess, and he was at a loss to account for it.

'Nice day,' he observed tentatively.

'Never mind the day.'

'Right ho. Heard from Uncle Gregory lately?'

'Never mind your Uncle Gregory.'

'Right ho.'

'And don't say "Right ho."'

'Right ho,' said Monty dutifully.

'Read this.'

Monty took the proffered copy of *Tots*.

'You want me to read aloud to you?' he said, feeling that this was matier.

'You need not trouble. I have already seen the passage in question. Here, where I am pointing.'

'Oh, ah, yes. Uncle Woggly. Right ho.'

'Will you stop saying "Right ho"! . . . Well?'

'Eh?'

'You wrote that, I take it?'

'Oh, rather.'

'Cor!'

Monty was now definitely perplexed. He could conceal it from him-self no longer that there was ill-will in the air. Lord Tilbury's had never been an elfin personality, but he had always been a good deal more win-some than this.

A possible solution of his employer's emotion occurred to him.

'You aren't worrying about it not being accurate, are you? Because that's quite all right. I had it on the highest authority—from an old boy called Galahad Threepwood. Lord Emsworth's brother. You wouldn't have heard of him, of course, but he was a great lad about the metropo-lis at one time, and you can rely absolutely on anything he says about whisky bottles.'

He broke off, puzzled once more. He could not understand what had caused his companion to strike the desk in that violent manner.

'What the devil do you mean, you wretched imbecile,' demanded Lord Tilbury, speaking a little indistinctly, for he was sucking his fist, 'by putting stuff of this sort in *Tiny Tots?*'

'You don't like it?' said Monty, groping.

'How do you suppose the mothers who read that drivel to their chil-dren will feel?'

Monty was concerned. This opened up a new line of thought.

'Wrong tone, do you think?'

'Mugs . . . Betting . . . Whisky . . . You have probably lost us ten thou-sand subscribers.'

'I say, that never occurred to me. Yes, by Jove, I see what you mean now. Unfortunate slip, what? May quite easily cause alarm and despon-dency. Yes, yes, yes, to be sure. Oh, yes, indeed. Well, I can only say I'm sorry.'

'You can not only say you are sorry,' said Lord Tilbury, correcting this view, 'you can go to the cashier, draw a month's salary, get to blazes out of here, and never let me see your face in the building again.'

Monty's concern increased.

'But this sounds like the sack. Don't tell me that what you are hinting at is the sack?'

Speech failed Lord Tilbury. He jerked his thumb doorwards. And such was the magic of his personality that Monty found himself a moment later with his fingers on the handle. Its cold hardness seemed to wake him from a trance. He halted, making a sort of Custer's Last Stand.

'Reflect!' he said.

Lord Tilbury busied himself with his papers.

'Uncle Gregory won't like this,' said Monty reproachfully.

Lord Tilbury quivered for an instant as if somebody had struck a brad-awl into him, but preserved an aloof silence.

'Well, he won't, you know.' Monty had no wish to be severe, but he felt compelled to point this out. 'He takes all the trouble to get me a job, I mean to say, and now this happens. Oh, no, don't deceive yourself, Uncle Gregory will be vexed.'

'Get out,' said Lord Tilbury.

Monty fondled the door handle for a space, marshalling his thoughts. He had that to say which he rather fancied would melt the other's heart a goodish bit, but he was not quite sure how to begin.

'Haven't you gone?' said Lord Tilbury.

Monty reassured him.

'Not yet. The fact is, there's something I rather wanted to call to your attention. You don't know it, but for private and personal reasons I particularly want to hold this *Tiny Tots* job for a year. There are wheels within wheels. It's a sort of bet, as a matter of fact. Have you ever met a girl called Gertrude Butterwick? . . . However, it's a long story and I won't bother you with it now. But you can take it from me that there definitely are wheels within wheels and unless I continue in your employment, till somewhere around the middle of next June, my life will be a blank and all my hopes and dreams shattered. So how about it? Would you, on second thoughts, taking this into consideration, feel disposed to postpone the rash act till then? If you've any doubts as to my doing my bit, dismiss them. I would work like the dickens. First at the office, last to come away, and solid, selfless service all the time—no clock-watching, no folding of the hands in . . .'

'Get OUT!' said Lord Tilbury.

There was a silence.

'You will not reconsider?'

'No.'

'You are not to be moved?'

'No.'

Monty Bodkin drew himself up.

'Oh, right ho,' he said stiffly. 'Now we know where we are. Now we know where we stand. If that is the attitude you take, I suppose there is nothing to be done about it. Since you have no heart, no sympathy, no feeling, no bowels—of compassion, I mean—I have no alternative but to shove off. I have only two things to say to you, Lord Tilbury. One is that you have ruined a man's life. The other is Pip-pip.'

He passed from the room, erect and dignified, like some young aristocrat of the French Revolution stepping into the tumbril. Lord Tilbury's secretary removed her ear from the door just in time to avoid a nasty flesh-wound.

A month's salary in his pocket, chagrin in his heart, and in his soul that urgent desire for a quick one which comes to young men at times like this, Monty Bodkin stood hesitating in the doorway of Tilbury House. And Fate, watching him, found itself compelled to do a bit of swift thinking.

'Now, shall I,' mused Fate, 'send this sufferer to have his snort at the Bunch of Grapes round the corner? Or shall I put him in a taxi and shoot him off to the Drones Club, where he will meet his old friend, Hugo Carmody, with momentous results?'

It was no light decision to have to make. Much depended on it. It would affect the destinies of Ronald Fish and his betrothed, Sue Brown; of Clarence, ninth Earl of Emsworth, and his pig, Empress of Blandings; of Lord Tilbury, of the Mammoth Publishing Company; of Sir Gregory Parsloe-Parsloe, Bart, of Matchingham Hall; and of that unpleasant little man, Percy Pilbeam, late editor of *Society Spice* and now proprietor of the Argus Private Inquiry Agency.

'H'm!' said Fate.

'Oh, dash it!' said Fate. 'Let's make it the Drones.'

And so it came about that Monty, some twenty minutes later, was seated in the club smoking-room, side by side with young Mr Carmody, sipping a Lizard's Breath and relating the story of his shattered career.

'Turfed out!' he concluded, with a bitter laugh. 'Driven into the snow! Well, that's Life, I suppose.'

Hugo Carmody was not unsympathetic, but he had a fair mind and privately considered that Lord Tilbury had acted with great good sense. Obviously, felt Hugo, the whole secret of success, if you were running a business and had Monty Bodkin working for you, was to get rid of him at the earliest possible moment.

'Tough,' he said. 'Still, what do you want with a job? You're rolling in the stuff.'

Monty admitted that he was not unblessed with this world's goods, but said that that was not the point.

'Money's got nothing to do with it. It was holding down the job that mattered. There are wheels within wheels. I'll tell you all about it, shall I?'

'No thanks.'

'Just as you like. Another spot? Waiter, two more spots.'

'Anyway,' said Hugo, with a kindly desire to point out the bright side, 'if you hadn't got fired now, you'd have been bound to have got fired sooner or later, what? I mean to say, I don't see how you could ever have been much good to a concern like the Mammoth, unless they had used you as a paperweight. And I'll bet you were all wrong about that whisky bottle.'

Monty's spirit had been a good deal reduced by recent happenings, but he could not let this pass.

'I'll bet I wasn't,' he said warmly. 'I had the information straight from an authoritative source. Lord Emsworth's brother, old Gally Threepwood. My Uncle Gregory's place in Shropshire is only about a couple of miles from Blandings, and when I was a kid I used to be popping in and out all the time, and one day old Gally drew me aside . . .'

Hugo was interested.

'Your Uncle Gregory? Would that be Sir Gregory Parsloe?'

'Yes.'

'Well, well. I never knew you were Parsloe's nephew.'

'Why, have you met him?'

'Of course I've met him. I've been down at Blandings all the summer.'

'Not really? Oh, but, of course, I was forgetting. You and Ronnie Fish have always been pals, haven't you? You were staying with him?'

'No. I was secretarying for old Emsworth. A nice, soft job. I've chucked it now.'

'I thought a fellow called Baxter was his secretary.'

'My dear chap, you aren't abreast. Baxter left ages ago.'

Monty sighed, as a young man will who is made to realize that time is passing.

'Yes,' he agreed, 'I've lost touch with Blandings a bit. It must be three years since I was there. Somehow, ever since this business of going to the south of France in the summer started, I've never seemed to be able to get down. How are they all? Is old Emsworth much about the same?'

'What was he like when you used to infest the place?'

'Oh, a mild, dreamy, absent-minded sort of old bird. Talked about nothing but roses and pumpkins.'

'Then he is much about the same, except that now he talks about nothing but pigs.'

'Pigs, eh?'

'His Empress of Blandings won the silver medal in the Fat Pigs' Class at last year's Shropshire Agricultural Show, and is confidently expected to repeat this year. This gives the ninth Earl's conversation a porcine trend.'

'How's old Gally?'

'Still going strong.'

'And Beach?'

'Buttling away as hard as ever.'

'Well, well, well,' said Monty sentimentally. 'The old spot certainly doesn't seem to have changed much since . . . Good Lord!' he exclaimed abruptly, spilling the remains of his cocktail over his trousers and in his emotion not noticing it. He had been electrified by a sudden idea.

Although since his arrival at the Drones we have seen Monty Bodkin relaxed, at his ease, chatting of this and that, he had never forgotten that he had just lost a job and that, owing to there being wheels within wheels, it was imperative that he secure another. And a bright light had just flashed upon him.

Minds like Monty Bodkin's may not always work at express speed, but they are subject to the same subconscious processes as those of more brain-burdened men. Right from the moment when Hugo had mentioned that he had been acting as secretary to the Earl of Emsworth, he had had a sort of nebulous idea that there was a big and important message wrapped up in this information, if only he could locate it. His subconscious mind had been having a go at the problem ever since, and now it passed the solution up to headquarters.

He quivered with excitement.

'Just a second,' he said. 'Let's get this straight. You say you were old Emsworth's secretary.'

'Yes.'

'And you've been fired?'

'I have not been fired,' said Hugo Carmody with justifiable annoy-ance, 'I've resigned. If you really want to know, I'm engaged to Lord Emsworth's niece, and I'm taking her down to Worcestershire in about half an hour to meet the head of the clan.'

Monty was too preoccupied to offer felicitations.

'When did you leave?'

'Day before yesterday.'

'Anybody been engaged to take your place?'

'Not that I know of.'

'Hugo,' said Monty earnestly. 'I'm going to get that job. I'm going to phone straight off to my Uncle Gregory to snaffle it for me without delay.'

Hugo looked at him commiseratingly. It was painful to him to be in the position of having to throw spanners into an old friend's daydreams, but he felt the poor chap ought to be told the truth.

'I shouldn't count too much on Sir G. Parsloe getting you jobs with old Emsworth,' he said. 'As I remarked before, you aren't quite abreast of modern Blandings history. Relations between Blandings Castle and

Matchingham Hall are a bit strained just at the moment. Not long ago your uncle did the dirty on old Emsworth by luring his pig-man away from him.'

'Oh, a little thing like that . . .'

'Well, try this one. Lord Emsworth has a fixed idea that your uncle is plotting to nobble Empress of Blandings.'

'What! Why?'

'He's got it all worked out. Your uncle owns a pig called Pride of Matchingham, and with the Empress out of the way it would probably cop the silver medal at the Show. So when the Empress was stolen the other day . . .'

'Stolen! Who stole her?'

'Ronnie.'

Monty's head, never strong, was beginning to swim.

'What Ronnie? Do you mean Ronnie Fish?'

'That's right. It's a complicated story. Ronnie's engaged to a girl, and he can't marry her unless old Emsworth coughs up his money.'

'He's Ronnie's trustee?'

'Yes.'

'Trustees are tough eggs,' said Monty thoughtfully. 'I had one till I was twenty-five, and it used to take me weeks of patient spadework to extract so much as a tenner from the man.'

'So, in order to ingratiate himself with old Emsworth, Ronnie pinched his pig.'

Once more Monty became conscious of that swimming sensation. He could not follow this.

'But why—?'

'Quite simple. His idea was to kidnap the pig, hide it somewhere for a day or two, and then pretend to find it and so win the old boy's gratitude. After which, to have put the bite on him would have been an easy task. It was a very sound scheme indeed. Of course, it all went wrong. Any scheme of Ronnie's would.'

'What went wrong?'

'Well, various unforeseen events occurred, and in the end the animal was discovered in a caravan belonging to Baxter. I told you it was a little complicated,' said Hugo kindly, noting the strained expression on his friend's face.

Monty agreed, but on one point he found himself reasonably clear.

'Then old Emsworth must have known that my uncle didn't steal the pig? I mean, if it was found in Baxter's . . .'

'Not at all. He thinks Baxter was working for your uncle. I tell you once more, as I was saying at the beginning, that, taking it by and large, I don't think I'd rely too much on Sir Gregory's pull, if I were you.'

Monty chewed his lip thoughtfully.

'There's no harm in trying.'

'Oh, have a shot, by all means. I'm only saying it isn't one of those stone-cold certainties that old Emsworth will engage you as his secretary purely out of love for Sir G. Parsloe.' Hugo looked at the clock, and rose. 'I've got to be going,' he said, 'if I don't want to miss that train.'

Monty accompanied him to the front steps, and Hugo hailed a cab.

'It might work,' said Monty pensively.

'Oh, rather. Certainly.'

'They might have had a what-is-it—a reconciliation by this time.'

'I didn't see any signs of it when I left. And now I must really rush,' said Hugo, getting into the cab. 'Oh, by the way,' he added, leaning out of the window, 'there's just one thing. If you do go to Blandings, you'll find the second prettiest girl in England there. Keep well away, is my advice.'

'Eh?'

'Ronnie's fiancée. They're both at the Castle, and if you exhibit too much enthusiasm about her he is extremely apt to strangle you with his bare hands. Personally,' said Hugo, 'I regard jealousy as a mug's game, my view being that where there is thingummy there should be what-d'you-call-it. Perfect love, ditto trust. But Ronnie belongs more to the Othello or green-eyed monster school of thought. He was so jealous of a fellow called Pilbeam that he went so far on one occasion as to wreck a restaurant when he found him apparently dining with Sue in it. Oh, yes, a bird of strong feelings and keen sensibilities, old Ronnie.'

'How do you mean apparently dining?'

'She was really dining with me. Blameless Hugo. But Ronnie didn't know that. He discovered Sue in conversation with this Pilbeam—you'll find him at the Castle, too . . .'

'Sue?' said Monty.

'Her name's Sue. Sue Brown.'

'What!'

'Sue Brown.'

'Not Sue Brown? You don't mean a girl called Sue Brown who was in the chorus at the Regal?'

'That's the one. You seem to know her.'

'Know her? I should say I do know her. Certainly I know her. I haven't seen her for about a couple of years, but at one time. . . Dear old Sue! Good old Sue! One of the sweetest things on earth, old Sue. You don't often come across such a ripper. Why . . .'

Hugo shook his head deprecatingly.

'Precisely the spirit against which I am warning you. Just the very tone you would do well to avoid. I think we may say that it is an excellent thing that your chances of getting to Blandings Castle are so remote. I should hate to read in my morning paper that your swollen body had been found floating in the lake.'

For some moments after the cab had rolled away, Monty remained in deep thought on the steps. The news that Sue Brown, of all people, was at Blandings Castle had certainly made the prospect of securing employment there additionally attractive. It would be great seeing old Sue again.

As for all that pig business, he refused to allow himself to be discouraged. Probably much exaggerated. An excellent fellow, Hugo Carmody, one of the best, but always inclined to make a good story out of everything.

Full of optimism, Monty Bodkin went along the passage to the telephone-room.

'I want a trunk call,' he said. 'Matchingham 8-3.'

3

S OME twenty-four hours after Monty Bodkin had put in his long-distance call to Matchingham 8-3, an observant bird, winging its way over Blandings Castle and taking a bird's-eye view of its parks, gardens, and messuages, would have noticed a couple walking up and down the terrace which fronts the main entrance of that stately home of England. And narrowing its gaze and shading its eyes with a claw, for the morning sun was strong, it would have seen that one of the pair was a small, sturdy young man of pink complexion, the other an extremely pretty girl in a green linen dress with a Quaker collar. Ronald Overbury Fish was saying good-bye to his Sue preparatory to driving in to Market Blandings and taking the twelve-forty train east. He was going to Norfolk to be best man at the wedding of his cousin George.

He did not anticipate that the parting would be a long one, for he expected to return on the morrow. Nevertheless, he felt constrained to give Sue a few words of advice as to her deportment during his absence.

First and foremost, he urged, she must use every feminine wile to fascinate his Uncle Clarence.

'Right,' said Sue. She was a tiny girl, with an enchanting smile and big blue eyes. These last were now sparkling with ready intelligence. She followed his reasoning perfectly. Lord Emsworth, though he had prom-ised Ronnie his money, had not yet given it to him and might conceivably change his mind. Obviously, therefore, he must be fascinated. The task, moreover, would not be a distasteful one. In the brief time during which she had had the pleasure of his acquaintance, she had grown very fond of that mild and dreamy peer.

'Right,' she said.

'Keep surging round him like glue.'

'Right,' said Sue.

'In fact, I think you had better go and talk pig to him the moment I've left.'

'Right,' said Sue.

'And about Aunt Constance . . .' said Ronnie.

He paused, frowning. He always frowned when he thought of his aunt, Lady Constance Keeble.

When Ronald Fish, the Last of the Fishes, only son of Lady Julia Fish, and nephew to Clarence, ninth Earl of Emsworth, had announced that a marriage had been arranged and would shortly take place between himself and a unit of the Regal Theatre chorus, he had had what might be called a mixed Press. Some of the notices were good, others not.

Beach, the Castle butler, who had fostered for eighteen years a semi-paternal attitude towards Ronnie and had fallen in love with Sue at first sight, liked the idea. So did the Hon. Galahad Threepwood, who when a dashing young man about town in the nineties had wanted to marry Sue's mother. As for Lord Emsworth himself, he had said 'Oh, ah?' in an absent voice on hearing the news and had gone on thinking about pigs.

It was, as so often happens on these occasions, from the female side of the family that the jarring note had proceeded. Women are seldom without their class prejudices. Their views on the importance of Rank diverge from those of the poet Burns. We have seen how Lady Julia felt about the match. The disapproval of her sister Constance was equally pronounced. She grieved over this blot which was about to be splashed upon the escutcheon of a proud family, and let the world see that she grieved. She sighed a good deal, and when she was not sighing kept her lips tightly pressed together.

So now when Ronnie mentioned her name, he frowned.

'About Aunt Constance . . .'

He was going on to add that, should his Aunt Constance have the nerve during his absence to put on dog and do any of that haughty County stuff to his betrothed, the latter would be well advised to kick her in the face; when there emerged from the house a young man with marcelled hair, a shifty expression, and a small and repellent moustache. He stood for an instant on the threshold, hesitated, caught Ronnie's eye, smiled weakly, and disappeared again. Ronnie stood gazing tensely at the spot where he had been.

'Little blighter!' he growled, grinding his teeth gently. The sight of P. Frobisher Pilbeam always tended to wake the fiend that slept in Ronald Fish. 'Looking for you, I suppose!'

Sue started nervously.

'Oh, I shouldn't think so. We've hardly spoken for days.'

'He doesn't ever bother you now?'

'Oh, no.'

'What's he doing here, anyway? I thought he'd left.'

'I suppose Lord Emsworth asked him to stay on. What *does* he matter?'

'He used to send you flowers!'

'I know, but . . .'

'He trailed you to that restaurant that night.'

'I know. But surely you aren't worried about him any longer?'

'Me?' said Ronnie. 'No! Of course not.'

He spoke a little gruffly, for he was embarrassed. It is always embarrassing for a young man of sensibility to realize that he is making a priceless ass of himself. He knew perfectly well that there was nothing between Sue and this Pilbeam perisher and never had been anything. And yet the sight of him about the place could make him flush and scowl and get all throaty.

Of course, the whole trouble with him was that where Sue was concerned he suffered from an inferiority complex. He found it so difficult to believe that a girl like her could really care for a bird so short and pink as himself. He was always afraid that one of these days it would suddenly dawn upon her what a mistake she had made in supposing herself to be in love with him and would race off and fall in love with somebody else. Not Pilbeam, of course, but suppose somebody tall and lissom came along . . .

Sue was pressing her point. She wanted this thing settled and out of the way. The only cloud on her happiness was that tendency of her Ronald's towards jealousy, to which Hugo Carmody had alluded so feelingly in his conversation with Monty Bodkin. Jealousy when two people had come together and knew that they loved one another always seemed to her silly and incomprehensible. She had the frank, uncomplicated mind of a child.

'You promise you won't worry about him again?'

'Absolutely not.'

'Nor about anybody else?'

'Positively not. Couldn't possibly happen again.' He paused. 'The only thing is,' he said broodingly, 'I *am* so dashed short!'

'You're just the right height.'

'And pink.'

'My favourite colour. You're a precious little pink cherub, and I love you.'

'You really do?'

'Of course I do.'

'But suppose you changed your mind?'

'You are a chump, Ronnie.'

'I know I'm a chump, but I still say—Suppose you changed your mind?'

'It's much more likely that you'll change yours.'

'What!'

'Suppose when your mother arrives she talks you over?'

'What absolute rot!'

'I don't imagine she will approve of me.'

'Of course she'll approve of you.'

'Lady Constance doesn't.'

Ronnie uttered a spirited cry.

'Aunt Constance! I was trying to think who it was we were talking about when that Pilbeam blister came to a head. Listen. If Aunt Constance tries to come the old aristocrat over you while I'm away, punch her in the eye. Don't put up for a moment with any pursed-lip-and-lorgnette stuff.'

'And what do I do when your mother reaches for her lorgnette?'

'Oh, you won't have anything of that sort from Mother.'

'Hasn't she got a lorgnette?'

'Mother's all right.'

'Not like Lady Constance?'

'A bit, to look at. But quite different, really. Aunt Constance is straight Queen Elizabeth. Mother's a cheery soul.'

'She'll try to talk you over, all the same.'

'She won't.'

'She will. "Ronald, my dear boy, really! This absurd infatuation. Most extraordinary!" I can feel it in my bones.'

'Mother couldn't talk like that if you paid her. I keep telling you she's a genial egg.'

'She won't like me.'

'Of course she'll like you. Don't be . . . what the dickens is that word.'

Sue was biting her lip with her small, very white tooth. Her blue eyes had clouded.

'I wish you weren't going away, Ronnie.'

'It's only for tonight.'

'Have you really got to go?'

'Afraid so. Can't very well let poor old George down. He's relying on me. Besides, I want to watch his work at the altar rails. Pick up some hints on technique which'll come in useful when you and I . . .'

'If ever we do.'

'Do stop talking like that,' begged Ronnie.

'I'm sorry. But I do wish you hadn't got to go away. I'm scared. It's this place. It's so big and old. It makes me feel like a puppy that's got into a cathedral.'

Ronnie turned and gave his boyhood home an appraising glance.

'I suppose it is a fairly decent-sized old shack,' he admitted, having run his eye up to the battlements and back again. 'I never really gave the thing much thought before, but, now you mention it, I have seen smaller places. But there's nothing about it to scare anybody.'

'There is—if you were born and brought up in a villa in the suburbs. I feel that at any moment all the ghosts of your ancestors will come popping out, pointing at me and shouting "What business have *you* here, you little rat?"'

'They'd better not let me catch them at it,' said Ronnie warmly. 'Don't be so . . . what on earth is that word? I know it begins with an *m*. You mustn't feel like that. You've gone like a breeze here. Uncle Clarence likes you. Uncle Gally likes you. Everybody likes you—except Aunt Constance. And a fat lot we care what Aunt Constance thinks, what?'

'I keep worrying about your mother.'

'And I keep telling you . . .'

'I know. But I've got that funny feeling you get sometimes that things are going to happen. Trouble, trouble. A dark lady coming over the water.'

'Mother's fair.'

'It doesn't make it any better. I've got that presentiment.'

'Well, I don't see why you should. Everything's gone without a hitch so far.'

'That's just what I mean. I've been so frightfully happy, and I feel that all the beastly things that spoil happiness are just biding their time. Waiting. They can't do nothin' till Martin gets here!'

'Eh?'

'I was thinking of a thing one of the girls used to play on her gramophone in the dressing-room, the last show I was in. It was about a Negro who goes to a haunted house, and demon cats keep coming in, each bigger and more horrible than the last, and as each one comes in it says to the others, "Shall we start in on him now?" and they shake their heads and say, "Not yet. We can't do nothin' till Martin gets here." Well, I can't help feeling that Martin soon will be here.'

Ronnie had found the word for which he had been searching.

'Morbid. I knew it began with an *m*. Don't be so dashed morbid!'

Sue gave herself a little shake, like a dog coming out of a pond. She put her arm in Ronnie's and gave it a squeeze.

'I suppose it is morbid.'

'Of course it is.'

'Everything may be all right.'

'Everything's going to be fine. Mother will be crazy about you. She won't be able to help herself. Because of all the . . .'

On the verge of becoming lyrical, Ronnie broke off abruptly. The Castle car had just come round the corner from the stables with Voules, the chauffeur, at the helm.

'I didn't know it was as late as that,' said Ronnie discontentedly.

The car drew up beside them, and he eyed Voules with a touch of austerity. It was not that he disliked the chauffeur, a man whom he had known since his boyhood and one with whom he had many a time played village cricket. It was simply that there are moments when a fellow wishes to be free from observation, and one of these is when he is about to bid farewell to his affianced.

However, there was good stuff in Ronald Fish. Ignoring the chauffeur's eye, which betrayed a disposition to be roguish, he gathered his loved one to him and, his face now a pretty cerise, kissed her with all a Fish's passion. This done, he entered the car, leaned out of the window, waved, went on waving, and continued to wave till Sue was out of sight. Then, sitting down, he gazed straight before him, breathing a little heavily through the nostrils.

Sue, having lingered until the car had turned the corner of the drive and was hidden by a clump of rhododendrons, walked pensively back to the terrace.

The August sun was now blazing down in all its imperious majesty. Insects were chirping sleepily in the grass, and the hum of bees in the lavender borders united with the sun and the chirping to engender sloth. A little wistfully Sue looked past the shrubbery at the cedar-shaded lawn where the Hon. Galahad Threepwood, thoughtfully sipping a whisky and soda, lay back in a deep chair, cool and at his ease. There was another chair beside him, and she knew that he had placed it there for her.

But duty is duty, no matter how warm the sun and drowsy the drone of insects. Ronnie had asked her to go and talk pig to Lord Emsworth, and the task must be performed.

She descended the broad stone steps and, turning westward, made for the corner of the estate sacred to that noble Berkshire sow, Empress of Blandings.

• • •

The boudoir of the Empress was situated in a little meadow, dappled with buttercups and daisies, round two sides of which there flowed in a silver semicircle the stream which fed the lake. Lord Emsworth, as his custom was, had pottered off there directly after breakfast, and now, at half past twelve, he was still standing, in company with his pig-man Pirbright, draped bonelessly over the rail of the sty, his mild eyes beaming with the light of a holy devotion.

From time to time he sniffed sensuously. Elsewhere throughout this fair domain the air was fragrant with the myriad scents of high summer, but not where Lord Emsworth was doing his sniffing. Within a liberal radius of the Empress's headquarters other scents could not compete. This splendid animal diffused an aroma which was both distinctive and arresting. Attractive, too, if you liked that sort of thing, as Lord Emsworth did.

Between Empress of Blandings and these two human beings who ministered to her comfort there was a sharp contrast in physique. Lord Emsworth was tall and thin and scraggy, Pirbright tall and thin and scraggier. The Empress, on the other hand, could have passed in a dim light for a captive balloon, fully inflated and about to make its trial trip. The modern craze for slimming had found no votary in her. She liked her meals large and regular, and had never done a reducing exercise in her life. Watching her now as she tucked into a sort of hash of bran, acorns, potatoes, linseed, and swill, the ninth Earl of Emsworth felt his heart leap up in much the same way as that of the poet Wordsworth used to do when he beheld a rainbow in the sky.

'What a picture, Pirbright!' he said reverently.

'Ur, m'lord.'

'She's bound to win. Can't help herself.'

'Yur, m'lord.'

'Unless . . . We mustn't let her get stolen again, Pirbright.'

'Nur, m'lord.'

Lord Emsworth adjusted his pince-nez thoughtfully. The ecstatic pig-gleam had faded from his eyes. His face was darkened by a cloud of concern. He was thinking of that bad Baronet, Sir Gregory Parsloe.

The theft of the Empress and the subsequent discovery of her in his ex-secretary Baxter's caravan had at first mystified Lord Emsworth completely. Why Baxter, though a recognized eccentric, should have been going about Shropshire stealing pigs seemed to him a problem incapable of solution.

But calm reflection had brought the answer to the riddle. Obviously the fellow had been a minion in the pay of Sir Gregory, operating throughout under orders from the Big Shot. And what was disquieting him now was the conviction that the danger was not yet past. Baffled once, the Baronet, he felt, was crouching for another spring. With two weeks still to pass before the Agricultural Show, there was ample time for his subtle brain to conceive another hideous plot. At any moment, in short, the bounder was liable to come sneaking in, mask on face and poison-needle in hand, intent on nobbling the favourite.

His eyes roamed the paddock. It was a lonely spot, far from human habitation. A pig, assaulted here by Baronets, might well cry for help unheard.

'Do you think she's safe in this sty, Pirbright?' he asked anxiously. 'I feel we ought to move her to that new one by the kitchen garden. It's near your cottage.'

What reply the Vice-President in charge of Pigs would have made to this suggestion—whether it would have been an 'Ur', a 'Yur', or a 'Nur'—will never be known. For at this moment there appeared a figure at the sight of whom he touched his forelock and receded respectfully into the background.

Lord Emsworth, whose pince-nez had fallen off, put them on again and peered mildly, like a sheep looking over a fence.

'Ah, Connie, my dear.'

There had been times when the sudden advent of his sister, Lady Constance Keeble, at a moment when he was drooping his long body over the rail of the Empress's sanctum would have caused him agitation and discomfort. She had a way of appearing from nowhere and upbraid-

ing him for expending on pigs time which had better have been devoted
to correspondence connected with the business of the estate. But for the
last two days, since the departure of that young fellow Carmody, he had
had no secretary; and a man can't be expected to attend to his correspondence without a secretary. His conscience, accordingly, was clear, and he
spoke with none of that irritable defensiveness, as of some wild creature
at bay, which he sometimes displayed on these occasions.

'Ah, Connie, my dear, you are just in time to give me your advice. I
was saying to Pirbright . . .'

Lady Constance did not wait for the sentence to be completed. In her
dealings with the head of the family she was always inclined to infuse
into her manner a suggestion of a rather short-tempered nurse with a
rather fat-headed child.

'Never mind what you were saying to Pirbright. Do you know what
time it is?'

Lord Emsworth did not. He never did. Beyond a vague idea that when
it got too dark for him to see the Empress at a range of four feet it was
getting on for dinner-time, he took little account of the hours.

'It's nearly one, and we have people coming to lunch at half past.'

Lord Emsworth assimilated this.

'Lunch? Oh, ah, yes. Yes, of course. Lunch, to be sure. Yes, lunch. You
think I ought to come in and wash my hands?'

'And your face. It's covered with mud. And change those clothes. And
those shoes. And put on a clean collar. Really, Clarence, you're as much
trouble as a baby. Why you want to waste your time staring at beastly
pigs, I can't imagine.'

Lord Emsworth accompanied her across the paddock, but his face—
there was hardly any mud on it at all, really, just a couple of splashes
or so—was sullen and mutinous. This was not the first time his sister
had alluded in this offensive manner to one whom he regarded as the
supreme ornament of her sex and species. Beastly pigs, indeed! He pondered moodily on the curious inability of his immediate circle to appreciate the importance of the Empress in the scheme of things. Not one of
them seemed to have the sagacity to realize her true worth.

Well, yes, one, perhaps. That little girl what-was-her-name, who was going to marry his nephew Ronald, had always displayed a pleasing interest in the silver medallist.

'Nice girl,' he said, following this train of thought to its conclusion.

'What *are* you talking about, Clarence?' asked Lady Constance wearily. 'Who is a nice girl?'

'That little girl of Ronald's. I've forgotten her name. Smith, is it?'

'Brown,' said Lady Constance shortly.

'That's right, Brown. Nice girl.'

'You are entitled to your opinion, I suppose,' said Lady Constance.

They walked on in silence for some moments.

'While we are on the subject of Miss Brown,' said Lady Constance, speaking the name as she always did with her teeth rather tightly clenched and a stony look in her eyes, 'I forgot to tell you that I had a letter from Julia this morning.'

'*Did* you?' said Lord Emsworth, giving the matter some two-fifty-sevenths of his attention. 'Capital, capital. Who,' he asked politely, 'is Julia?'

Lady Constance was within easy reach of his head and could quite comfortably have hit it, but she refrained. *Noblesse oblige.*

'*Julia!*' she said, with a rising inflection. 'There's only one Julia in our family.'

'Oh, you mean Julia?' said Lord Emsworth, enlightened. 'And what had Julia got to say for herself? She's at Biarritz, isn't she?' he said, making a great mental effort. 'Having a good time, I hope?'

'She's in London.'

'Oh, yes?'

'And she is coming here tomorrow by the two forty-five.'

Lord Emsworth's vague detachment vanished. His sister Julia was not a woman to whose visits he looked forward with joyous enthusiasm.

'Why?' he asked, with a strong note of complaint in his voice.

'It is the only good train in the afternoon, and gets her here in plenty of time for dinner.'

'I mean, why is she coming?'

It would be too much to say that Lady Constance snorted. Women of her upbringing do not snort. But she certainly sniffed.

'Well, really!' she said. 'Does it strike you as so odd that a mother whose only son has announced his intention of marrying a ballet-girl should wish to see her?'

Lord Emsworth considered this.

'Not ballet-girl. Chorus-girl, I understood.'

'It's the same thing.'

'I don't think so,' said Lord Emsworth doubtfully. 'I must ask Galahad.' A sudden idea struck him.

'Don't you like this Smith girl?'

'Brown.'

'Don't you like this Brown girl?'

'I do not.'

'Don't you want her to marry Ronald?'

'I should have thought I had made my views on that matter sufficiently clear. I think the whole thing deplorable. I am not a snob . . .'

'But you are,' said Lord Emsworth, cleverly putting his finger on the flaw in her reasoning.

Lady Constance bridled.

'Well, if it is snobbish to prefer your nephew to marry in his own class . . .'

'Galahad would have married her mother thirty years ago if he hadn't been shipped off to South Africa.'

'Galahad was—and is—capable of anything.'

'I can remember her mother,' said Lord Emsworth meditatively. 'Galahad took me to the Tivoli once, when she was singing there. Dolly Henderson. A little bit of a thing in pink tights, with the jolliest smile you ever saw. Made you think of spring mornings. The gallery joined in the chorus, I recollect. Bless my soul, how did it go? Tum tum tumpty tum . . . Or was it Umpty tiddly tiddly pum?'

'Never mind how it went,' said Lady Constance. One reminiscencer in the family, she considered, was quite enough. 'And we are not talking of the girl's mother. The only thing I have to say about Miss Brown's mother is that I wish she had never had a daughter.'

'Well, I like her,' said Lord Emsworth stoutly. 'A very sweet, pretty, nice-mannered little thing, and extremely sound on pigs. I was saying so to young Pilbeam only yesterday.'

'Pilbeam!' cried Lady Constance.

She spoke with feeling, for the name had reminded her of another grievance. She had been wanting to get to the bottom of this Pilbeam mystery for days. About that young man's presence at the Castle there seemed to her something almost uncanny. She had no recollection of his arrival. It was as if he had materialized out of thin air. And being a conventional hostess, with a conventional hostess's dislike of the irregular, she objected to finding that visitors with horrible moustaches, certainly not invited by herself, had suddenly begun to pervade the home like an escape of gas.

'Who is that nasty little man?' she demanded.

'He's an investigator.'

'A *what*?'

'A private investigator. He investigates privately.' There was a touch of quiet pride in Lord Emsworth's voice. He was sixty years old, and this was the first time he had ever found himself in the romantic role of an employer of private investigators. 'He runs the something detective agency. The Argus. That's it. The Argus Private Inquiry Agency.'

Lady Constance breathed emotionally.

'Ballet-girls . . . Detectives . . . I wonder you don't invite a few skittle-sharps here.'

Lord Emsworth said he did not know any skittle-sharps.

'And is one permitted to ask what a private detective is doing as a guest at Blandings Castle?'

'I got him down to investigate that mystery of the Empress's disappearance.'

'Well, that idiotic pig of yours has been back in her sty for days. What possible reason can there be for this man staying on?'

'Ah, that was Galahad's idea. It was Galahad's suggestion that he should stay on till after the Agricultural Show. He thought it would be a good thing to have somebody like that handy in case Parsloe tried any more of his tricks.'

'Clarence!'

'And I consider,' went on Lord Emsworth firmly, 'that he was quite right. I know it was Baxter who actually stole my pig, and you will no doubt say that Baxter is notoriously potty. But Galahad feels—and I feel—that it was not primarily his pottiness that led him to steal the Empress. We both think that Parsloe was behind the whole thing. And Galahad maintains—and I agree with him—that it is only a question of time before he makes another attempt. So the more watchers we have on the place the better. Especially if they have trained minds and are used to mixing with criminals, like Pilbeam.'

'Clarence, you're insane!'

'No, I am not insane,' retorted Lord Emsworth warmly. 'I know Parsloe. And Galahad knows Parsloe. You should read some of the stories about him in Galahad's book—thoroughly well-documented stories, he assures me, showing the sort of man he was when Galahad used to go about London with him in their young days. Are you aware that in the year 1894 Parsloe filled Galahad's dog Towser up with steak and onions just before the big Rat contest, so that his own terrier Banjo should win? A fellow who stuck at nothing to attain his ends. And he's just the same today. Hasn't changed a bit. Look at the way he stole that man Well-beloved away from me—the chap who used to be my pig-man before Pirbright. Fellow capable of that is capable of anything.'

Lady Constance spurned the grass with a frenzied foot. She would have preferred to kick her brother with it, but one has one's breeding.

'You are a perfect imbecile about Sir Gregory,' she cried. 'You ought to be ashamed of yourself. So ought Galahad, if it were possible for him to be ashamed of anything. You are behaving like a couple of half-witted children. I hate this idiotic quarrel. If there's one thing that's detestable in the country, it is being on bad terms with one's neighbours.'

'I don't care how bad terms I'm on with Parsloe.'

'Well, I do. And that is why I was so glad to oblige him when he rang up about his nephew.'

'Eh?'

'I was delighted to have the chance of proving to him that there was at least one sane person in Blandings Castle.'

'Nephew? What nephew?'

'Young Montague Bodkin. You ought to remember him. He was here often enough when he was a boy.'

'Bodkin? Bodkin? Bodkin?'

'Oh, for pity's sake, Clarence, don't keep saying "Bodkin" as if you were a parrot. If you have forgotten him, as you forget everything that happened more than ten minutes ago, it does not matter in the least. The point is that Sir Gregory asked me as a personal favour to engage him as your secretary . . .'

Lord Emsworth was a mild man, but he could be stirred.

'Well, I'm dashed! Well, I'm hanged! The man steals my pigman and engineers the theft of my pig, and he has the nerve . . .'

'. . . and I said I should be delighted.'

'What!'

'I said I should be delighted.'

'You don't mean you've done it?'

'Certainly. It's all arranged.'

'You mean you're letting a nephew of Parsloe's loose in Blandings Castle, with two weeks to go before the Agricultural Show?'

'He arrives tomorrow by the two forty-five,' said Lady Constance.

And as she had thrown her bomb and seen it explode and had now reached the front door and had no wish to waste her time listening to futile protests, she swept into the house and left Lord Emsworth standing.

He remained standing for perhaps a minute. Then the imperative necessity of sharing this awful news with a cooler, wiser mind than his own stirred him to life and activity. His face drawn, his long legs trembling beneath him, he hurried towards the lawn where his brother Galahad, whisky and soda in hand, reclined in his deck-chair.

4

C OOLED by the shade of the cedar, refreshed by the contents of the amber glass in which ice tinkled so musically when he lifted it to his lips, the Hon. Galahad, at the moment of Lord Emsworth's arrival, had achieved a Nirvana-like repose. Storms might be raging elsewhere in the grounds of Blandings Castle, but there on the lawn there was peace— the perfect unruffled peace which in this world seems to come only to those who have done nothing whatever to deserve it.

The Hon. Galahad Threepwood, in his fifty-seventh year, was a dapper little gentleman on whose grey but still thickly covered head the weight of a consistently misspent life rested lightly. His flannel suit sat jauntily upon his wiry frame, a black-rimmed monocle gleamed jauntily in his eye. Everything about this Musketeer of the nineties was jaunty. It was a standing mystery to all who knew him that one who had had such an extraordinarily good time all his life should, in the evening of that life, be so superbly robust. Wan contemporaries who had once painted a gas-lit London red in his company and were now doomed to an existence of dry toast, Vichy water, and German cure resorts felt very strongly on this point. A man of his antecedents, they considered, ought by rights to be rounding off his career in a bath-chair instead of flitting about the place, still chaffing head waiters as of old and calling for the wine list without a tremor.

A little cock-sparrow of a man. One of the Old Guard which dies but does not surrender. Sitting there under the cedar, he looked as if he were just making ready to go to some dance-hall of the days when dance-halls were dance-halls, from which in the quiet dawn it would take at least three waiters, two commissionaires and a policeman to eject him.

In a world so full of beautiful things, where he felt we should all be as happy as kings, the spectacle of his agitated brother shocked the Hon. Galahad.

'Good God, Clarence! You look like a bereaved tapeworm. What's the matter?'

Lord Emsworth fluttered for a moment, speechless. Then he found words.

'Galahad, the worst has happened!'

'Eh?'

'Parsloe has struck!'

'Struck? You mean he's been biffing you?'

'No, no, no. I mean it has happened just as you warned me. He has been too clever for us. He has got round Connie and persuaded her to engage his nephew as my new secretary.'

The Hon. Galahad removed his monocle, and began to polish it thoughtfully. He could understand his companion's concern now.

'She told me so only a moment ago. You see what this means? He is determined to work a mischief on the Empress, and now he has contrived to insinuate an accomplice into the very heart of the home. I see it all,' said Lord Emsworth, his voice soaring to the upper register. 'He failed with Baxter, and now he is trying again with this young Bodkin.'

'Bodkin? Young Monty Bodkin?'

'Yes. What are we to do, Galahad?' said Lord Emsworth.

He trembled. It would have pained the immaculate Monty, could he have known that his prospective employer was picturing him at this moment as a furtive, shifty-eyed, rat-like person of the gangster type, liable at the first opportunity to sneak into the sties of innocent pigs and plant pineapple bombs in their bran-mash.

The Hon. Galahad replaced his monocle.

'Monty Bodkin?' he said, refreshing himself with a sip from his glass. 'I remember him well. Nice boy. Not at all the sort of fellow who would nobble pigs. Wait a minute, Clarence. This wants thinking over.'

He mused awhile.

'No,' he said, 'you can dismiss young Bodkin as a hostile force altogether.'

'What!'

'Put him right out of your mind,' insisted the Hon. Galahad. 'Parsloe isn't planning to strike through him at all.'

'But Galahad . . .'

'No. Take it from me. Can't you see for yourself that the thing's much too obvious, much too straightforward, not young Parsloe's proper form at all? Reason it out. He must know that we would suspect a nephew of his. Then why is it worth his while to get him into the place? Shall I tell you, Clarence?'

'Do,' said Lord Emsworth feebly, gaping like a fish.

As the head of the family was standing up and he was sitting down, it was impossible for the Hon. Galahad to tap him meaningly on the shoulder. He prodded him meaningly in the leg.

'Because,' he said, 'he *wants* us to suspect him.'

'Wants us to suspect him?'

'Wants us to,' said the Hon. Galahad. 'He hopes by introducing Monty Bodkin into the place to get us watching him, following his every movement, keeping our eyes glued on to him, so that when the real accomplice acts we shall be looking in the wrong direction.'

'God bless my soul!' said Lord Emsworth, appalled.

'Oh, it's all right,' said the Hon. Galahad soothingly. 'A cunning scheme, but we're too smart to fall for it. We see through it and are prepared.' He gave Lord Emsworth's leg another significant prod. 'Shall I tell you what is going to happen, Clarence?'

'Do,' said Lord Emsworth.

'I can read Parsloe's mind like a book. A day or two after young Monty's arrival, there will be a mysterious stranger sneaking about the grounds in the vicinity of the Empress's sty. He will be there because Parsloe, taking it for granted that our attention will be riveted on young Monty, will imagine that the coast is clear.'

'God bless my soul!'

'And apparently the coast will be clear. We must arrange that. From now on, Clarence, you must not loaf about the Empress openly. You must conceal yourself in the background. And you must instruct Pirbright to conceal himself in the background. This fellow must be led to suppose that vigilance has been relaxed. By these means, we shall catch him red-handed.'

In Lord Emsworth's eye, as he gazed at his brother, there was the reverential look of a disciple at the feet of his master. He had always known, he told himself, that as a practical adviser in matters having to do with the seamier side of life the other was unsurpassed. It was the result, he supposed, of the environment in which he had spent his formative years. Membership of the old Pelican Club might not elevate a man socially, but there was no doubt about its educative properties. If it dulled the moral sense, it undoubtedly sharpened the intellect.

'You have taken a great weight off my mind, Galahad,' he said. 'I feel sure you are perfectly right. The only mistake I think you make is in supposing that this young Bodkin is harmless. I am convinced that he will require watching.'

'Well, watch him, then, if it will make you any happier.'

'It will,' said Lord Emsworth decidedly. 'And meanwhile I will be giving Pirbright his instructions.'

'Tell him to lurk.'

'Exactly.'

'Some rude disguise such as a tree or a pail of potato-peel would help.'

Lord Emsworth reflected.

'I don't think Pirbright could disguise himself as a tree.'

'Nonsense. What do you pay him for?'

Lord Emsworth continued dubious. Only God, he seemed to be feeling, can make a tree.

'Well, at any rate, tell him to lurk.'

'Oh, he shall certainly lurk.'

'From now on . . .' began the Hon. Galahad, and broke off to wave at some object in his companion's rear. The latter turned.

'Ah, that nice little Smith girl,' he said.

Sue had appeared on the edge of the lawn. Lord Emsworth beamed vaguely in her direction.

'By the way, Galahad,' he said, 'is a chorus-girl the same as a ballet-girl?'

'Certainly not. Different thing altogether.'

'I thought so,' said Lord Emsworth. 'Connie's an ass.'

He pottered away, and Sue crossed the turf to where the Hon. Galahad sat.

The author of the Reminiscences scanned her affectionately through his monocle. Amazing, he was thinking, how like her mother she was. He noticed it more every day. Dolly's walk, and just that way of tilting her chin and smiling at you that Dolly had had. For an instant the years fell away from the Hon. Galahad Threepwood, and something that was not of this world went whispering through the garden.

Sue stood looking down at him. She placed a maternal finger on top of his head, and began to twist the grey hair round it.

'Well, young Gally.'

'Well, young Sue.'

'You look very comfortable.'

'I am comfortable.'

'You won't be long. The luncheon gong will be going in a minute.'

The Hon. Galahad sighed. There was always something, he reflected.

'What a curse meals are! Don't let's go in.'

'I'm going in, all right. My good child, I'm starving.'

'Pure imagination.'

'Do you mean to say you're not hungry, Gally?'

'Of course I'm not. No healthy person really needs food. If people would only stick to drinking, doctors would go out of business. I can state you a case that proves it. Old Freddie Potts in the year '98.'

'Old Freddie Potts in the year '98, did you say, Mister Bones?'

'Old Freddie Potts in the year '98,' repeated the Hon. Galahad firmly. 'He lived almost entirely on Scotch whisky, and in the year '98 this prudent habit saved him from an exceedingly unpleasant attack of hedgehog poisoning.'

'What poisoning?'

'Hedgehog poisoning. It was down in the south of France that it happened. Freddie had gone to stay with his brother Eustace at his villa at Grasse. Practically a teetotaller, this brother, and in consequence passionately addicted to food.'

'Still, I can't see why he wanted to eat hedgehogs.'

'He did not want to eat hedgehogs. Nothing was farther from his intentions. But on the second day of old Freddie's visit he gave his chef twenty francs to go to market and buy a chicken for dinner, and the chef, wandering along, happened to see a dead hedgehog lying in the road. It had been there some days, as a matter of fact, but this was the first time he had noticed it. So, feeling that here was where he pouched twenty francs . . .'

'I wish you wouldn't tell me stories like this just before lunch.'

'If it puts you off your food, so much the better. Bring the roses to your cheeks. Well, as I was saying, the chef, who was a thrifty sort of chap and knew that he could make a dainty dinner dish out of his old grandmother, if allowed to mess about with a few sauces, added the twenty francs to his savings and gave Freddie and Eustace the hedgehog next day *en casserole*. Mark the sequel. At two-thirty prompt, Eustace, the teetotaller, turned nile-green, started groaning like a lost soul, and continued to do so for the remainder of the week, when he was pronounced out of danger. Freddie, on the other hand, his system having been healthfully pickled in alcohol, throve on the dish and finished it up cold next day.'

'I call that the most disgusting story I ever heard.'

'The most moral story you ever heard. If I had my way, it would be carved up in letters of gold over the door of every school and college in the kingdom, as a warning to the young. Well, what have you been doing with yourself all the morning, my dear? I expected you earlier.'

'I was talking to my precious Ronnie most of the time. He went off to catch his train about half an hour ago.'

'Ah, yes, he's going to young George Fish's wedding, isn't he? I could tell you a good story about George Fish's father, the Bishop.'

'If it's like the one about old Freddie Potts, I don't want to hear it. Well, after that I went to look for Lord Emsworth, because I had promised Ronnie to talk pig to him. But I saw Lady Constance with him, so I kept away. And then I came to see you, and found you talking together. You seemed to be having a very earnest conversation about something.'

The Hon. Galahad chuckled.

'Clarence has got the wind up, poor chap. About that pig of his. He thinks Parsloe is trying to put it on the spot or kidnap it.'

Sue looked round cautiously.

'You know who stole it that first time, don't you, Gally?'

'Baxter, wasn't it? The thing was found in his caravan.'

'It was Ronnie.'

'What!' This was news to the Hon. Galahad. 'That young Fish?'

She gave his hair a tug.

'You are not to call him "that young Fish".'

'I apologize. But what on earth did he do it for?'

'He was going to find it and bring it back. So as to make Lord Emsworth grateful, you see.'

'You don't mean that young cloth-head had the intelligence to think up a scheme like that?' said the Hon. Galahad, amazed.

'And I won't have you calling my darling Ronnie a cloth-head either. He's very clever. As a matter of fact, though, he says he got the idea from you.'

'From me?'

'He says you told him you once stole a pig.'

'That's right,' said the Hon. Galahad. 'Puffy Benger and I stole old Wivenhoe's pig the night of the Bachelors' Ball at Hammer's Easton in the year '95. We put it in Plug Basham's bedroom. I never heard what happened when Plug met it. No doubt they found some formula. Wivenhoe, I remember, was rather annoyed about the affair. He was a good deal like Clarence in that respect. Worshipped his pig.'

'What makes Lord Emsworth think that Sir Gregory is going to hurt the Empress?'

'Apparently Connie has gone and engaged his nephew as Clarence's secretary, and he thinks it's a plot. So do I. But personally, as I told Clarence, I feel that Parsloe is using young Monty Bodkin purely as a cat's paw.'

'Monty Bodkin!'

'The nephew. I'm convinced, from what I remember of him, that he isn't at all the sort of fellow . . .'

'Oh, Gally!' cried Sue.

'Eh?'

'Monty Bodkin coming here?' Sue stared in dismay. 'Oh, Gally, what a mess! Oh, I knew something was going to happen. I told Ronnie so, I've been feeling it for days.'

'My dear child, what's the matter with you? What's wrong with young Bodkin coming here?'

'I used to be engaged to him!' said Sue.

It seemed to the Hon. Galahad that advancing years and the comparative abstinence of his later life must have dulled his once keen quickness at the uptake. Sue's face had lost its colour, and anxiety and alarm were clouding her pretty eyes, and he could make nothing of it.

'Were you?' he said. 'When was that?'

'Two years ago . . . Two and a half . . . Three . . . I can't remember. Before I met Ronnie. But what does that matter? I tell you I used to be engaged to him.'

The Hon. Galahad was still fogged.

'But what's your trouble? What's all the agitation about? Why does it upset you so much, the idea of meeting him again? Painful associations, do you mean? Embarrassing? Don't want to awake agonizing memories in the fellow's bosom?'

'Of course not. It isn't that. It's Ronnie.'

'Why Ronnie?'

'He's so jealous. You know how jealous he is.'

The Hon. Galahad began to understand.

'He can't help it, poor darling. It's just the way he is. He makes himself miserable about nothing. So what *will* he do when Monty arrives? I know Monty so well. He won't mean any harm, but he'll come bounding in, all hearty and bubbling, and start talking of old times. "Do you remember—?" "I say, Sue, old girl, I wonder if you've forgotten—?" . . . Ugh! It will drive poor Ronnie crazy.'

The Hon. Galahad nodded.

'I see what you mean. That touch of Auld Lang Syne *is* disturbing.'

'Why, he tries to pretend he isn't, but Ronnie's jealous even of Pilbeam.'

Once more the Hon. Galahad nodded. A grave nod. He quite realized that a man who could be jealous of the proprietor of the Argus Inquiry Agency was not a man lightly to be introduced to former fiancés, especially of the type of Monty Bodkin.

'We must give this matter a little earnest consideration,' he said thoughtfully. 'You wouldn't consider taking a firm line and telling Ronnie to go and boil his head and not make a young fool of himself, if he starts kicking up a fuss?'

'But you don't understand,' wailed Sue. 'He won't kick up a fuss. Ronnie isn't like that. He'll just get very stiff and cold and polite and suffer in a sort of awful Eton and Cambridge silence. And nothing I do will make him any better.'

An idea struck the Hon. Galahad.

'You're sure you really are in love with this young Fish?'

'I wish you wouldn't . . .'

'I'm sorry. I forgot. But you are?'

'Of course I am. There's nobody in the world for me but Ronnie. I've told you that before. I suppose what you're wondering is how I came to be engaged to Monty? Looking back, I can't think myself. He's a dear, of course, and when you're about seventeen, you're so flattered at finding that anyone wants to marry you that it seems wrong to refuse him. But it never amounted to anything. It only lasted a couple of weeks, anyhow. But Ronnie will imagine it was one of the world's great romances. He'll brood on it, and worry himself ill, wondering whether I'm not still pining for Monty. He's just like a kid in that way. It'll spoil everything.'

'And we may take it as pretty certain that Monty will let it out?'

'Of course he will. He's a babbler.'

'Yes, that's how I remember him. One of those fellows you can count on to say the wrong thing. Reminds me rather of a man I used to know in the old days called Bagshott. Boko Bagshott, we called him. Took a girl to supper once at the Garden. Supper scarcely concluded when angry old gentleman plunges into the room and starts shaking his fist in Boko's face. Boko rises with chivalrous gesture. "Have no fear, sir. I am a man of honour. I will marry your daughter." "Daughter?" says old gentleman, foaming a little at the mouth. "Damn it, that's my wife." Took all Boko's tact to pass it off, I believe.'

He pondered, staring thoughtfully through his black-rimmed moncle at a spider which was doing its trapeze act from an overhanging bough.

'Well, it's quite simple, of course.'

'Simple!'

'Presents no difficulties of any sort, now that one gives it one's full attention. Ronnie won't be back from that wedding till late tomorrow evening. You must run up to London first thing in the morning and warn young Monty how the land lies. Tell him that when he arrives here he must meet you as a stranger. Pitch it strong. Explain about Ronnie's unfortunate failing. Drive it well into his head that your whole happiness depends on him pretending he's never met you before, and I should think you would have no trouble whatever. I wouldn't call Monty Bodkin particularly bright, but he ought to be able to handle a thing like that, if you make it perfectly clear to him what he's got to do.'

She drew a deep breath.

'You're wonderful, Gally darling.'

'Experienced,' corrected the Hon. Galahad modestly.

'But can I do it? I mean, the trains.'

'On your head. Eight-fifty from Market Blandings gets you to London about noon. Interview Monty between then and two-thirty. Catch the two forty-five back, and you get to Market Blandings somewhere around a quarter to seven. Take the station taxi, stop it half-way up the drive, get out and walk the rest, and you'll be in your room with an hour to dress for dinner, and not a soul knowing a thing about it. No, even better than that, because I remember Connie telling me there's a dinner-party on tomorrow night, so I suppose you won't have to show up till nearly nine.'

'But lunch? Won't they wonder where I am if I'm not at lunch.'

'Connie's lunching out. You don't suppose Clarence will notice whether you're there or not. No, the only point we haven't covered is, can you find Monty? Do you know his address?'

'He's sure to be at the Drones.'

'Then all is well. Why on earth you worry about these things, when you know you've got an expert like me behind you, I can't imagine. It's a pity about young Ronnie, though. That disposition of his to make heavy weather. Silly to be jealous. He ought to realize by this time that you love him—goodness knows why.'

'I know why.'

'I don't. Fellow's a perfect ass.'

'He's not!'

'My dear child,' said the Hon. Galahad firmly, 'if a man who doesn't know that he can trust you isn't a perfect ass, what sort of ass is he?'

5

IN supposing that she would be able to find her former fiancé at the Drones, Sue had not erred. Telephoning there from Paddington station shortly after twelve next morning, she was rewarded almost immediately by a series of sharp, hyena-like cries at the other end of the wire. To judge from his remarks, this voice from the past was music in Monty Bodkin's ears. Nothing, he gave her to understand, could have given him more pleasure than to get in touch after two years of separation with one whom he esteemed so highly. At his suggestion, Sue had got into a taxi, and now, across a table in the restaurant of the Berkeley Hotel, she was looking at him and congratulating herself on her wisdom in having arranged this meeting. A Monty unprepared for the part he had to play at Blandings Castle would, she felt, beyond a question have crashed into poor darling Ronnie's sensibilities like a high-powered shell. Over the preliminary cocktails and right through the smoked salmon he had been a sheer foaming torrent of 'Do you remembers' and 'That reminds mes'.

It seemed to Sue that she had a difficult task before her in trying to make clear to this exuberant old friend that on his arrival at the Castle he must regard the dear old days as a sealed book and herself as a complete stranger. Yet when a toothsome *truite bleue* had induced in him a sudden reverential silence and she was able at length to give a brief exposition of the state of affairs, she was surprised and pleased to gather from a series of understanding nods that he appeared to be following her remarks intelligently.

He finished the *truite bleue* and gave a final nod. It indicated a perfect grasp of the situation.

'My dear old soul,' he said reassuringly, 'say no more. I understand everything, understand it fully. As a matter of fact, Hugo Carmody had already tipped me off.'

'Oh have you seen Hugo?'

'I met him at the club, and he warned me about Ronnie. I had the situation well in hand. On arriving at Blandings I was planning to treat you with distant civility.'

'Then I needn't have come up at all!'

'I wouldn't say that. If Ronnie's so apt to go off the deep end at the slightest provocation, we can't be too much on the safe side. Even distant civility might have hotted him up.'

Sue considered this.

'That's true,' she agreed.

'Better to be perfect strangers.'

'Yes.' Sue gave a little frown. 'How beastly it's all going to be, though.'

'That's all right. I shan't mind.'

'I wasn't thinking about you. It seems so rotten, deceiving Ronnie.'

'You've got to get used to that. Secret of a happy and successful married life. I thought you meant that it would be rather agony you and me just giving each other a distant bow when they introduced us and then shunning one another coldly. And it does seem darned silly, what? I mean, we were very close to each other once. Can one altogether forget those happy days?'

'I can. And so must you. For goodness sake, Monty, don't let's have any of what Gally calls that touch of Auld Lang Syne.'

'No, no. Quite.'

'I don't want Ronnie driven off his head.'

'Far from it.'

'Well, do remember to be careful.'

'Oh, I will. Rely on me.'

'Thanks, Monty darling . . . What's the matter?' asked Sue, as her host gave a sudden start.

A waiter had brought up a silver dish and uncovered it with the air of one doing a conjuring trick. Monty inspected it with the proper seriousness.

'Oh, nothing,' he said as the waiter retired. 'Just that "Monty darling". It brought back the old days.'

'For goodness sake forget the old days!'

'Oh, quite. I will. Oh, rather. Most certainly. But it made me feel how rum life was. Life *is* rummy, you know. You can't get away from that.'

'I suppose it is.'

'Take a simple instance. Here are you and I, face to face across this table, lunching together like the dickens, precisely as in the dear old days, and all the time you are contemplating getting hitched up to R. Fish, while I am heart and soul in favour of an early union with Gertrude Butterwick.'

'What!'

'Butterwick. B for blister, U for ukulele . . .'

'Yes, I heard. But do you mean you're engaged, too, Monty?'

'Well, yes and no. Not absolutely. And yet not absolutely not. I am, as it were, on appro.'

'Can't she make up her mind?'

'Oh, her mind's made up all right. Oh, yes, yes, yes, indeed there's no doubt about good old Gertrude's mind, bless her. She loves me like billy-o. But there are wheels within wheels.'

'What do you mean?'

'It's an expression. It signifies . . . well, by Jove, now you bring up the point,' said Monty frankly, 'I'm dashed if I know just what it does signify. Wheels within wheels. Why wheels? What wheels? Still, there it is. I suppose the idea is to suggest that everything's pretty averagely complicated.'

'I understand what it means, of course. But why do you say it about yourself?'

'Because there's a snag sticking up in the course of true love. A very sizeable, jagged snag. Her blighted father, to wit, J. G. Butterwick, of Butterwick, Price, and Mandelbaum, export and import merchants.'

He swallowed a roast potato emotionally. Sue was touched. She had never ceased to congratulate herself on her sagacity in breaking off her engagement to this young man, but she was very fond of him.

'Oh, Monty, I'm so sorry. Poor darling. Doesn't he like you?'

Monty weighed this.

'Well, I wouldn't say that exactly. On two separate occasions he has said good morning to me, and once, round about Christmas time, I received a distinct impression that he was within an ace of offering me a cigar. But he's a queer bird. Years of exporting and importing have warped his mind a bit, with the result that for some reason I can't pretend to understand he appears to look on me as a sort of waster. The first thing he did when I ankled in and told him that subject to his approval I was about to marry his daughter was to ask me how I earned my living.'

'That must have been rather a shock.'

'It was. And a still worse one was when he went on to add that unless I got a job of some kind and held it down for a solid year, to show him that I wasn't a sort of waster, those wedding bells would never ring out.'

'You poor lamb. How perfectly awful!'

'Ghastly. I reeled. I stared. I couldn't believe the fellow was serious. When I found he was, I raced off to Gertrude and told her to jam her hat on and come round to the nearest registrar's. Only to discover, Sue, that she was one of those old-fashioned girls who won't dream of doing the dirty on Father. Solid middle-class stock, you understand. Backbone of England, and all that. So, elopements being off, I had no alternative but to fall in with the man's extraordinary scheme. I got my Uncle Gregory to place me with the Mammoth Publishing Company in the capacity of assistant editor of *Tiny Tots*. And if only I could have contrived to remain an assistant editor, I should be there now. But my boss went off on a holiday, silly ass, leaving me in charge of the sheet, and in a well-meant attempt to ginger the bally thing up a bit I made rather a bloomer in the Uncle Woggly department. The result being that a couple of days ago they formed a hollow square and drummed me out. And now I'm starting all over again at Blandings.'

'I see. I couldn't understand why you wanted to be Lord Emsworth's secretary. I was afraid you must have lost all your money.'

'Oh, no. I've got my money all right. And what,' demanded Monty, swinging an arm in a passionate gesture and hitting a waiter on the chest and saying 'Oh, sorry!' 'does money amount to? What *is* money? Fairy gold. That's what it is. Dead Sea fruit. Because it doesn't help me a damn towards scooping in Gertrude.'

'Is she an awfully nice girl?'

'An angel, Sue. No question about that. Quite the angel, absolutely.'

'Well, I do hope you will come out all right, Monty dear.'

'Thanks, old thing.'

'And I'm glad you didn't pine for me. I've felt guilty at times.'

'Oh, I pined. Oh, yes, certainly I *pined*. But you know how it is. One perks up and sees fresh faces. Tell me, Sue,' said Monty anxiously. 'I ought to be able to hold down that secretary job for a year, oughtn't I? I mean, people don't fire secretaries much, do they?'

'If Hugo could keep the place, I should think you ought to be able to. How are you on pigs?'

'Pigs?'

'Lord Emsworth . . .'

'Of course, yes, I remember now, Hugo told me. The old boy has gone porcine, has he not? You mean you would advise me to suck up to his pig, this what's-its-name of Blandings, to omit no word or act to conciliate it? Thanks for the tip. I'll bear it in mind.' He beamed affectionately at her across the table, and went so far as to take her hand in his. 'You've cheered me up, young Sue. You always did, I remember. You've got one of those sunny temperaments which look on the bright side and never fail to spot the blue bird. As you say, if a chap like Hugo could hold the job, it ought to be a snip for a man of my gifts, especially if I show myself pig-conscious. I anticipate a pleasant and successful year, with a wedding at the end of it. By which time, I take it, you will be an old married woman. When do you and Ronnie plan to leap off the dock?'

'As soon as ever Lord Emsworth lets him have his money. He wants to buy a partnership in a motor business.'

'Any opposish from the family?'

'Well, I don't think Lady Constance is frightfully pleased about it all.'

'Possibly it slipped out by some chance that you had been in the chorus?'

'It was mentioned.'

'Ah, that would account for it. But she's biting the bullet all right?'

'She seems resigned.'

'Then all is well.'

'I suppose so. And yet . . . Monty, do you ever get a feeling that something unpleasant is going to happen?'

'I got it two days ago, when my Lord Tilbury reached for the slack of my trousers and started to heave me out.'

'I've got it. I was saying so to Ronnie, and he told me not to be morbid.'

'Ronnie knows words like "morbid", does he? Two syllables and everything.'

'Monty, what is Ronnie's mother really like?'

Monty rubbed his chin.

'Haven't you met her yet?'

'No. She's been over in Biarritz.'

'But is returning?'

'I suppose so.'

' 'Myes. Post-haste, I should imagine. 'Myes!'

'For goodness sake, don't say "'Myes". You're making my flesh creep. Is she such a terror?'

Monty scratched his right cheekbone.

'Well, I'll tell you. Many people would say she was a genial soul.'

'That's what Ronnie said.'

'The jovial hunting type. Lady Di. Bluff goodwill, the jolly smile for everyone, and slabs of soup at Christmas time for the deserving villagers. But I don't know. I'm not so sure. I'll tell you this much. When I was a kid I was far more scared of her than I was of Lady Constance.'

'Why?'

'Ah, there you have me. But I was. Still, don't let me take the joy out of your life. For all we know, she may at this very moment be practising "O Perfect Love" on the harmonium. And now, I don't want to hurry you, but the sands are running out a bit. My train goes at two forty-five . . .'

'What?'

'Two-four-five, pip emma.'

'You aren't going to Blandings today . . . by the two forty-five?'

'That's right.'

'But I'm going back on the two forty-five.'

'Well, that's fine. We'll travel together.'

'But we mustn't travel together.'

'Why not? Nobody's going to see us, and we can be as distant as the dickens on arrival. Pleasant chit-chat as far as Market Blandings, and cold aloofness from there on, is the programme as I see it. It's silly to overdo this perfect stranger business.'

Sue, thinking it over, was inclined to agree with him. She had had one solitary railway journey that day, and was not indisposed for pleasant company on the way back.

'And if you think, young Susan,' said Monty, who, though chivalrous, could stand up for his rights, 'that I intend to wait on and travel by something that stops and shunts at every station, you err. It's a four hours' journey even by express. We'll just nip round to my flat and pick up my things . . .'

'And miss the train. No, thank you. I can't take any chances. I'll meet you at the station.'

'Just as you like,' said Monty agreeably. 'I was only thinking that if you came to my flat, I could show you sixteen photographs of Gertrude.'

'You can describe them to me on the journey.'

'I will,' said Monty. 'Waiter, laddishiong.'

It was as the hands of the big clock at Paddington station were pointing to two-forty that Lady Julia Fish made her way through the crowd on the platform, her progress rendered impressive by the fact that her maid, two porters, and a boy who mistakenly supposed that he had found a customer for his oranges and nut-chocolate revolved about her like satellites around a sun.

Towards the turmoil in her immediate neighbourhood she displayed her usual good-humoured disdain. Where others ran she sauntered.

Composedly she allowed one porter to open the door of an empty compartment, the other to place therein her bag, papers, novels, and magazines. She dismissed the maid, tipped the porters, and, settling herself in a corner seat, surveyed the bustle and stir without in an indulgent manner.

The ceremony of getting the two forty-five express off was now working up to a crescendo. Porters flitted to and fro. Guards shouted and poised green flags. The platform rang with the feet of belated travellers. And the train had just given a sort of shiver and began to move out of the station, when the door of the compartment was wrenched open and something that seemed to have six legs shot in, tripped over her, and collapsed into the seat opposite. It was a perspiring young man of the popinjay type, whose face, though twisted, was not so twisted that she was unable to recognize in him that Montague Bodkin who had once been so frequent a visitor at the home of her ancestors.

Monty had run it fine. What with hunting for a mislaid cigarette-case and getting held up in a traffic block in Praed Street, he had contrived this spectacular entry only by dint of sprinting the length of the platform at a rate of speed which he had not achieved since his university days.

But though warm and out of breath, he was still the *preux chevalier* who knew that when you have just barked the skin of a member of the other sex apologies must be made.

'It is quite all right, Mr Bodkin,' said Lady Julia as he made them. 'I am sorry I was in your way.'

Monty started violently.

'Gosh!' he exclaimed.

'I beg your pardon.'

'I mean—er—hullo, Lady Julia!'

'Hullo, Mr Bodkin.'

'Phew!' said Monty, dabbing agitatedly at his forehead with the handkerchief which so perfectly matched his tie and socks.

His distress was not caused entirely—or even to any great extent—by the reflection that he had just taken an inch of skin off the daughter of a hundred earls. That, no doubt, was regrettable, but what was really exercising his mind was the thought that Sue being presumably on the train and having presumably observed his rush down the platform would be coming along at any moment to see if he got aboard all right. It seemed to him that it was going to require all his address to handle the situation which her advent would create.

'Fancy running into you,' he said dismally.

'"Over me" would be a better way of putting it. I felt like some unfortunate Hindu beneath the wheels of Juggernaut. And where are you bound for, Mr Bodkin?'

'Eh? Oh, Market Blandings.'

'You are going to stay with your uncle at Matchingham?'

'Oh, no. I'm booked for the Castle. Lord Emsworth has taken me on as his secretary.'

'But how very odd. I thought you were working with the Mammoth Publishing Company.'

'I've resigned.'

'Resigned?'

'Resigned,' said Monty firmly. He was not going to reveal his Moscow to this woman.

'What made you resign?'

'Oh, various things. There are wheels within wheels.'

'How cosy!' said Lady Julia.

Monty decided to change the subject.

'I hear everything's much about the same at Blandings.'

'Who told you that?'

'Fellow named Carmody, who has been secretarying there. He said everything was much about the same.'

'What a very unobservant young man he must be! Didn't he mention that there had been an earthquake there, an upheaval, a social cataclysm?'

'I beg your . . . What was that?'

'Prepare yourself for a shock, Mr Bodkin. Ronnie is at Blandings, and with him a chorus-girl of the name of Brown, whom he proposes to marry.'

A little uncertain as to the judicious line to take, Monty decided to be astounded.

'No!'

'I assure you.'

'A chorus-girl?'

'Named Sue Brown. You don't know her, by any chance?'

'No. Oh, no. No.'

'I thought possibly you might.' Lady Julia looked out of the window at the flying countryside. 'Very trying for a parent. Don't you think so, Mr Bodkin?'

'Oh, most.'

'Still, I suppose it might have been worse. There is rather a consoling ring about that simple name. I mean, Sue Brown doesn't sound like a girl who will bring breach of promise actions when the thing is broken off.'

'Broken off!'

'It might so easily have been Suzanne de Brune.'

'But—er—are you thinking of breaking it off?'

'Why, of course. You seem very concerned. Or is this joy?'

'No—I—er—It just occurred to me that it might be a bit difficult. I mean, Ronnie's a pretty determined sort of chap.'

'He inherits it from his mother,' said Lady Julia.

It was during the silence which followed this remark that Sue entered the compartment.

At the moment of her arrival Monty was staring out of the window and Lady Julia had leaned back in her seat. There was nothing, accordingly, to indicate any connexion between the two, and Sue was just about to address to her old friend a cordial word of congratulation on his abilities as a sprinter, when the sound of the opening door caused him to turn. And so blank, so icy was the stare of non-recognition which she encountered that she sank bewildered on the cushions with all the sensations of one who, after being cut by the county, walks into a brick wall.

It was not long, however, before enlightenment came. Monty was a young man who believed in taking no chances.

'Nice and green the country's looking, Lady Julia,' he observed. 'Isn't it, Lady Julia?'

His companion gave it a glance.

'Very, considering there has been no rain for such a long time.'

'I should think Ronnie must be enjoying it at Blandings, Lady Julia.'

'I beg your pardon?'

'I say,' said Monty, spacing his words carefully, 'that your son Ronnie must be enjoying the green of the countryside at Blandings Castle. He likes it green,' explained Monty. And with another frigid stare at Sue he leaned back and puffed his cheeks out.

There was a pause. Monty had not wrought in vain. An electric thrill seemed to pass through Sue's small body. Her heart was thumping.

'I beg your pardon,' she said breathlessly. 'Are you Lady Julia Fish?'

'I am.'

'My name's Sue Brown,' said Sue, wishing that she could have achieved a vocal delivery a little more impressive than that of a very young, startled mouse.

'Well, well, well!' said Lady Julia. 'Fancy that. Quite a coincidence, Mr Bodkin.'

'Oh, quite. Most.'

'We were just talking about you, Miss Brown.'

Sue nodded speechlessly.

'I am losing a son and gaining a daughter, and you're the daughter, eh?'

Sue continued to nod. Monty, personally, considered that she was overdoing it. She ought, he felt, to be saying something. Something bright and snappy like . . . well, he couldn't on the spur of the moment think just what, but something bright and snappy.

'Yes,' said Lady Julia, 'I recognize you. Ronnie sent me a photograph of you, you know. I thought it charming. Well, you must come over here and tell me all about yourself. We will get rid of Mr Bodkin . . . By the way, you did tell me you had not met Miss Brown?'

'Definitely not. Certainly not. Far from it. Not at all.'

'Don't speak in that tone of horrified loathing, Mr Bodkin. I'm sure Miss Brown is a very nice girl, well worthy of your acquaintance. At any rate, you've met her now. Mr Bodkin, Miss Brown.'

'How do you do?' said Monty stiffly.

'How do you do?' said Sue with aloofness.

'Mr Bodkin is coming to Blandings as my brother's secretary.'

'Fancy!' said Sue.

'And now run along and look at the green countryside, Mr Bodkin. Miss Brown and I want to have a talk about all sorts of things.'

'I'll go and have a smoke,' said Monty, inspired.

'Do,' said Lady Julia.

Monty Bodkin sat in his smoking-compartment, well pleased with himself. It had been a near thing, and it had taken a man of affairs to avert disaster, but he had brought it off. Another half-second and young Sue would have spilled the beans. He was, as we say, pleased with himself, and he was also pleased with Sue. She had shown a swift grasp of the situation. There had been a moment when he had feared he was being too subtle, trying the female intelligence, notoriously so greatly inferior to the male, too high. But all had been well. Good old Sue had understood those guarded hints of his, and now everything looked pretty smooth.

He closed his eyes contentedly, and dropped off into a refreshing sleep.

From this he was aroused some half an hour later by the click of the door; and, opening his eyes and blinking once or twice, was enabled to perceive Sue standing before him.

'Ah! Interview over?'

Sue nodded and sat down. Her face was grave, like that of a puzzled child. Extraordinarily pretty it made her look, felt Monty, and for an instant there stole over him a faint regret for what might have been. Then he thought of Gertrude Butterwick and was strong again.

'I say, I did that distant aloofness stuff rather well, don't you think?'

'Oh, yes.'

'And pretty shrewd of me to grapple with a tricky situation so promptly and give you that instant pointer as to how matters stood?'

'Oh, yes.'

'What do you mean, Oh, yes? It was genius.' He looked at her with some intentness. 'You seem a shade below par. Didn't the interview go off well?'

'Oh, yes.'

'Don't keep saying "Oh, yes." What happened?'

'Oh, we talked.'

'Of course you talked, chump. What did you say?'

'I told her about myself, and—oh, you know, all that sort of thing.'

'And wasn't she chummy?'

She reflected, biting her lip.

'She was quite nice.'

'I know what that means—rotten.'

'No, she seemed perfectly friendly. Laughed a good deal and . . . well, just what you were saying. Lady Di. Bluff goodwill. But—'

'But you seemed to sense the velvet hand beneath the iron glove? No, dash it, that's not right,' said Monty, musing. 'The other way about it should be, shouldn't it? You got the impression that she was simply waiting till your back was turned to stick a knife in it?'

'A little. It's something about her eyes. She doesn't smile with them. Of course, I may be all wrong.'

Monty looked dubious. He lit a cigarette and puffed at it thoughtfully.

'No, I think you're right. I wish I didn't, but I do. I don't mind telling you that a second before you came in she was saying she was jolly well going to break the whole thing off.'

'Oh?'

'Of course,' Monty hastened to add consolingly, 'she hasn't got a dog's chance of doing it. There are few more resolute birds than Ronnie. But she'll try her damnedest. Tough eggs, that Blandings Castle female contingent. Odd that they should be so much deadlier than the male. Look at old Emsworth . . . old Gally . . . young Freddie . . . you've never met Freddie, have you? . . . All jolly good sorts. And against them you have this Julia, yonder Constance, and a whole lot more, all snakes of the first water. When you get to know that family better, you'll realize that there are dozens of aunts you've not heard of yet—far-flung aunts scattered all over England, and each the leading blister of her particular county. It's a sort of family taint. Still, as I say, old Ronnie is staunch. Nobody could talk him out of prancing up the aisle with the girl he loves.'

'No,' said Sue, her eyes dreamy.

'And now, pardon the suggestion, but wouldn't it be as well if you shoved off? Suppose she happened to come along and found us hobnobbing here like this?'

'I never thought of that.'

'Always think of everything,' said Monty paternally.

He closed his eyes again. The train rattled on towards Market Blandings.

6

IT was nearly an hour after the two forty-five had arrived at its destination that a slower and shabbier train crawled in and deposited Ronnie Fish on the platform of the little station of Market Blandings. The festivities connected with his cousin George's wedding and the intricacies of a railway journey across the breadth of England had combined to prevent an earlier return.

He was tired, but happy. The glow of sentiment which warms young men in love when they watch other people getting married still lingered. Mendelssohn's well-known march was on his lips as he gave up his ticket, and it was with a perceptible effort that he checked himself from saying to the driver of the station cab, 'Wilt thou, Robinson, take this Ronald to Blandings Castle?' Even when he reached his destination and found the hands of the grandfather clock in the hall pointing to ten to eight, his exuberance did not desert him. It was his pride that he could shave, bathe, and dress, always provided that nothing went wrong with the tie, in nine and a quarter minutes.

Tonight, all was well. The black strip of *crêpe-de-Chine* assumed the perfect butterfly shape of its own volition, and at eight precisely he was

standing in the combination drawing-room and picture-gallery in which
Blandings Castle was wont to assemble long before the evening meal.

He was surprised to find himself alone. And it was not long before
surprise gave way to a stronger emotion. For some minutes he wandered
to and fro, gazing at the portraits of his ancestors on the walls; but to a
man who has just come from a long and dusty train journey ancestral
portraits are a poor substitute for the old familiar juice. He pressed the
bell, and presently Beach the butler appeared.

'Oh, hullo, Beach. I say, Beach, what about the cocktails?'

The butler seemed surprised.

'I was planning to serve them when the guests arrived, Mr Ronald.'

'Guests? There aren't people coming to dinner, are there?'

'Yes, sir. We shall sit down twenty-four.'

'Good Lord! A binge?'

'Yes, sir.'

'I must go and put on a white tie.'

'There is plenty of time, Mr Ronald. Dinner will not be served till
nine o'clock. Perhaps you would prefer me to bring you an aperitif in
advance of the formal cocktails?'

'I certainly would. I'm dying by inches.'

'I will attend to the matter immediately.'

The butler of Blandings Castle was not a man who when he said
'immediately' meant 'somewhere in the distant future'. Like a heavy-
weight jinn, stirred to activity by the rubbing of a lamp, he vanished and
reappeared; and it was only a few minutes later that Ronnie was blos-
soming like a flower in the gentle rain of summer and finding himself
disposed for leisurely chat.

'Twenty-four?' he said. 'Golly, we're going gay. Who's coming?'

The butler's eyes took on a glaze similar to that seen in those of policemen giving evidence.

'His lordship the Bishop of Poole, Sir Herbert and Lady Musker, Sir
Gregory Parsloe-Parsloe . . .'

'What!'

'Yes, sir.'

'Who invited *him*?'

'Her ladyship, I should imagine, sir.'

'And he's coming? Well, I suppose he knows his own business,' said Ronnie dubiously. 'Better keep a close eye on Uncle Clarence, Beach. If you see him toying with a knife, remove it.'

'Very good, sir.'

'Who else?'

'Colonel and Mrs Mauleverer and daughter, the Honourable Major and Lady Augusta Lindsay-Todd and niece . . .'

'All right. You needn't go on. I get the general idea. Eighteen local nibs, plus the gang of six in residence.'

'Eight, Mr Ronald.'

'Eight?'

'His lordship, her ladyship, Mr Galahad, yourself, Miss Brown, Mr . . .' The butler's voice shook a little. '. . . Pilbeam . . .'

'Exactly. Six, you old ass.'

'There is also Mr Bodkin, sir.'

'Bodkin?'

'Sir Gregory Parsloe's nephew, Mr Ronald. Mr Montague Bodkin. You may recall him as a somewhat frequent visitor to the Castle during his school days.'

'Of course I remember old Monty. But you've got muddled. You've counted him in among the resident patients, when he's really one of the outside crowd.'

'No, sir. Mr Bodkin is assuming Mr Carmody's duties as his lordship's secretary.'

'Not really?'

'Yes, sir. I understand the appointment was ratified two days ago.'

'But that's odd. What does Monty want, sweating as a secretary? He's got about fifteen thousand a year of his own.'

'Indeed, sir?'

'Well, he had. Somehow or other we've not happened to run into each other much these last two years. Do you think he's lost it?'

'Very possibly, sir. A great many people have become fiscally crippled of late.'

'Rummy,' said Ronnie.

Then speculation on this mystery was borne away on a flood of sober pride. With a pardonable feeling of smugness, Ronnie Fish realized that his soul had achieved such heights of nobility that the prospect of a Monty Bodkin buzzing about the Castle premises in daily contact with Sue was causing him no pang of apprehension or jealousy.

Not so very long ago, such a thought would have been a dagger in his bosom. It was just the Monty type of chap—tall, lissom, good-looking, and not pink—that he had always feared. And now he could contemplate his coming without a tremor. Pretty good, felt Ronnie.

'Well, come along with your eight,' he said. 'That's only seven, so far.'

The butler coughed.

'I was assuming, Mr Ronald, that you were aware that her ladyship, your mother, arrived this evening on the two forty-five train.'

'What!'

'Yes, sir.'

'Good Lord!'

Beach regarded him solicitously, but did not develop the theme. He had a nice sense of the proprieties. Between himself and this young man there had existed for eighteen years a warm friendship. Ronnie as a child had played bears in his pantry. Ronnie as a boy had gone fishing with him on the lake. Ronnie as a freshman at Cambridge had borrowed five-pound notes from him to see him through to his next allowance. Ronnie, grown to man's estate, had given him many a sound tip on the races, from which his savings bank account had profited largely. He knew the last detail of Ronnie's romance, sympathized with his aims and objects, was aware that an interview of extreme delicacy faced him; and, had they been sitting in his pantry now, would not have hesitated to offer sympathy and advice.

But because this was the drawing-room, his lips were sealed. A mere professional gesture was all he could allow himself.

'Another cocktail, Mr Ronald?'

'Thanks.'

Ronnie, sipping thoughtfully, found his equanimity returning. For a moment, he could not deny it, there had been a slight sinking of the heart; but now he was telling himself that his mother had always been a cheery soul, one of the best, and that there was no earthly reason to suppose that she was likely to make any serious trouble now. True, there might be a little stiffness at first, but that would soon wear off.

'Where is she, Beach?'

'In the Garden Room, Mr Ronald.'

'I ought to go there, I suppose. And yet . . . No,' said Ronnie, on second thoughts. 'Might be a little rash, what? There she would be with her hair-brush handy, and the temptation to put me across her knee and . . . No. I think you'd better send a maid or someone to inform her that I await her here.'

'I will do so immediately, Mr Ronald.'

With a quiver of the left eyebrow intended to indicate that, had such a thing been possible to a man in his position, he would gladly have remained and lent moral support, the butler left the room. And presently the door reopened, and Lady Julia Fish came sailing in.

Ronnie straightened his tie, pulled down his waistcoat, and advanced to meet her.

The emotions of a young man on encountering his maternal parent, when in the interval since they last saw one another he has announced his betrothal to a member of the chorus, are necessarily mixed. Filial love cannot but be tempered with apprehension. On the whole, however, Ronnie was feeling reasonably debonair. He and his mother had laughed together at a good many things in their time, and he was optimistic enough to hope that with a little adroitness on his part the coming scene could be kept on the lighter plane. As he had said to Sue, Lady Julia Fish was not Lady Constance Keeble.

Nevertheless, as he kissed her, he was aware of something of the feeling which he had had in his boxing days when shaking hands with an unpleasant-looking opponent.

'Hullo, mother.'

'Well, Ronnie.'

'Here you are, what?'

'Yes.'

'Nice journey?'

'Quite.'

'Not rough, crossing over?'

'Not at all.'

'Good,' said Ronnie. 'Good.'

He began to feel easier.

'Well,' he proceeded chattily, 'we got old George off all right.'

'George?'

'Cousin George. I've just been best-manning at his wedding.'

'Ah, yes. I had forgotten. It was today, was it not?'

'That's right. I only got back half an hour ago.'

'Did everything go off well?'

'Splendidly. Not a hitch.'

'Family pleased, I suppose?'

'Oh, delighted.'

'They would be, wouldn't they? Seeing that George was marrying a girl of excellent position with ten thousand a year of her own.'

'H'r'rmph,' said Ronnie.

'Yes,' said Lady Julia, 'you'd better say "H'r'rmph!"'

There was a pause. Ronnie, who had just straightened his tie again, pulled it crooked and began straightening it once more. Lady Julia watched these manifestations of unrest with a grim blue stare. Ronnie, looking up and meeting it, diverted his gaze towards a portrait of the second Earl which hung on the wall beside him.

'Amazing beards those blokes used to wear,' he said nonchalantly.

'I wonder you can look your ancestors in the face.'

'I can't, as a matter of fact. They're an ugly crowd. The only decent one is Daredevil Dick Threepwood who married the actress.'

'You would bring up Daredevil Dick, wouldn't you?'

'That's right, mother. Let's see the old smile.'

'I'm not smiling. What you observed was a twitch of pain. Really, Ronnie, you ought to be certified.'

'Now, mother . . .'

'Ronnie,' said Lady Julia, 'if you dare to lift up your finger and say "Tweet-tweet, shush-shush, come-come," I'll hit you. It's no good grinning in that sickening way. It simply confirms my opinion that you are a raving lunatic, an utter imbecile, and that you ought to have been placed under restraint years ago.'

'Oh, dash it.'

'It's no good saying "Oh, dash it."'

'Well, I do say "Oh, dash it." Be reasonable. Naturally I don't expect you to start dancing round and strewing roses out of a hat, but you might preserve the decencies of debate. Highly offensive, that last crack.'

Lady Julia sighed.

'Why *do* all you young fools want to marry chorus-girls?'

'Read any good books lately, mother?' asked Ronnie, pacifically.

Lady Julia refused to be diverted.

'It's too amazing. It's a disease. It really is. Just like measles or whooping-cough. All young men apparently have to go through it. It seems only the other day that my poor father was shipping your Uncle Galahad off to Africa to ensure a cure.'

'I'll tell you something interesting about that, mother. The girl Uncle Gally was in love with . . .'

'I was a child at the time, but I can recall it so distinctly. Father thumping tables, mother weeping, and all that rather charming, old-world atmosphere of family curses. And now it's you! Well, well, one can only thank goodness that it never seems to last long. The fever takes its course, and the patient recovers. Ronnie, my poor half-wit, you can't really be serious about this?'

'Serious!'

'But, Ronnie, really! A chorus-girl.'

'There's a lot to be said for chorus-girls.'

'Not in my presence. I couldn't bear it. It's so *callow* of you, my dear boy. If this had happened when you were at Eton, I wouldn't have said a word. But when you're grown up and are supposed to have some sense. Look at the men who marry chorus-girls. A race apart. Young Datchet . . . That awful old Bellinger . . .'

'Ah, but you're overlooking something, my dear old parent. There are chorus-girls and chorus-girls.'

'This is your kind heart speaking.'

'And when you get one like Sue . . .'

'No, Ronnie. It's nice of you to try to cheer me up, but it can't be done. I regard the entire personnel of the ensembles of our musical comedy theatres as—if you will forgive me being Victorian for a moment—painted hussies.'

'They've got to paint.'

'Well, they needn't huss. And they needn't ensnare my son.'

'I'm not sure I like that word "ensnare" much.'

'You probably won't much like any of the words you're going to get from me tonight. Honestly, Ronnie. I know it hurts your head to think, but try to just for a moment. It isn't simply a question of class. It's the whole thing . . . the different view-point . . . the different standards . . . everything. I take it that your idea when you marry is to settle down and lead a normal sort of life, and how are you going to have that with a chorus-girl? How are you going to trust a woman of that sort of upbringing, who has lived on excitement ever since she was old enough to kick her beastly legs up in front of an audience and sees nothing wrong in going off and having affairs with everyman that takes her fancy? That sort of girl would be sneaking off round the corner the moment your back was turned.'

'Yes, Sue.'

Ronnie smiled indulgently.

'Wait till you meet her!'

'I have met her, thanks.'

'What?'

'She was in the train, and introduced herself.'

'But what was she doing in the train?'

'Returning here from London.'

'I didn't know she had gone up to London.'

'So I imagine,' said Lady Julia.

Not many minutes had passed since Ronnie Fish had been urging his mother to smile. With these words she had done so, but the fulfillment of his wish brought him no pleasure. The pink of his face deepened. There had come a tightness about his mouth. He had changed his mind about the desirability of keeping the scene light.

'Do you mind if I just get this straight?' he said coldly. 'A moment ago

you were talking about girls who ran off and had affairs . . . and now you
tell me you have met Sue.'

'Exactly.'

'Then you . . . had Sue in mind?'

'Exactly.'

Ronnie laughed, unpleasantly.

'On the strength, apparently, of her having gone up to London for the
day—to do some shopping or something, I suppose. I wouldn't call this
your ripest form, mother.'

'On the strength, if you really wish to know, of seeing her and young
Monty Bodkin lunching together at the Berkeley and finding them
together on the train . . .'

'Monty Bodkin!'

'. . . where they had the effrontery to pretend they had never met
before.'

'She was lunching with Monty?'

'Lunching with Monty and ogling Monty and holding hands with
Monty! Oh, for heaven's sake, Ronnie, do use a little intelligence. Can't
you see this girl is just like the rest of them? If you can't, you really must
be a borderline case. Young Bodkin came here today to be your uncle's
secretary. Two days ago he had some sort of employment with the Mammoth Publishing Company. He told me on the train that he had resigned.
Why did he resign? And why is he coming here? Obviously because this
girl wanted him here and put him up to it. And directly she hears it's settled, she takes advantage of your being away to sneak up to London and
talk things over with him. If there was nothing underhand going on, why
should they have pretended that they were perfect strangers? No, as you
said just now, I am *not* dancing round and strewing roses out of a hat!'

She broke off. The door had opened. Lady Constance Keeble came in.

In the doorway Lady Constance paused. She looked from one to the
other with speculation in her eyes. She was a veteran of too many fine
old crusted family rows not to be able to detect a strained atmosphere
when she saw one. Her sister Julia was clenching and unclenching her

hands. Her nephew Ronald was staring straight before him, red-eyed. A thrill ran through Lady Constance, such as causes the war-horse to start at the sound of the bugle. It was possible, of course, that this was a private fight, but her battling instinct urged her to get into it.

But there was in Lady Constance Keeble an instinct even stronger than that of battle, and that was the one which impelled her to act as critic of the sartorial deficiencies of her nearest and dearest. Years of association with her brother Clarence, who, if you took your eye off him for a second, was apt to come down to dinner in flannel trousers and an old shooting-jacket, had made this action almost automatic with the chatelaine of Blandings.

So now, eager for the fray, it was as the critic rather than as the warrior queen that she spoke.

'My dear Ronald! That tie!'

Ronnie Fish gazed at her lingeringly. It needed, he felt, but this. Poison was running through his veins, his world was rocking, green-eyed devils were shrieking mockery in his ears, and along came blasted aunts babbling of ties. It was as if somebody had touched Othello on the arm as he poised the pillow and criticized the cut of his doublet.

'Don't you know we have a dinner-party tonight? Go and put on a white tie at once.'

Even in his misery the injustice of the thing cut Ronnie to the quick. Did his aunt suppose him ignorant of the merest decencies of life? Naturally, if he had known before he started dressing that there was a big binge on, he would have assumed the correct costume of the English gentleman for formal occasions. But considering that he had been told only about two minutes ago . . .

'And a tail-coat.'

It was the end. If this woman's words had any meaning at all, it was that she considered him capable of wearing a white tie with a dinner-jacket. Until this moment he had been intending to speak. The thing had now passed beyond speech. Directing at Lady Constance a look which no young man ought to have directed at an aunt, he strode silently from the room.

Lady Constance stood listening to the echoes of a well-slammed door.

'Ronald seems upset,' she observed.

'It runs in the family,' said Lady Julia.

'What was the trouble?'

'I have just been telling him that he is off his head.'

'I quite agree with you.'

'And I should like now,' said Lady Julia, 'to apply the same remark to you.'

She was breathing quickly. The china-blue of her eyes had an enamelled look. It was thirty-five years since she had scratched Lady Constance's face, but she seemed so much in the vein for some such demonstration that the latter involuntarily drew back.

'Really, Julia!'

'What do you mean, Constance, by inviting that girl to Blandings?'

'I did nothing of the sort.'

'You didn't invite her?'

'Certainly not.'

'She popped up out of a trap, eh?'

Lady Constance emitted that sniff of hers which came so near to being a snort.

'She wormed her way into the place under false pretences, which amounts to the same thing. You remember that Miss Schoonmaker, the American girl you met at Biarritz and wrote to me about? You gave me the impression that you hoped there might eventually be something between her and Ronald.'

'I really can't understand what you are talking about. Why need we discuss Myra Schoonmaker?'

'I am trying to explain to you how this Brown girl comes to be at the Castle. About ten days ago I was in London, and I met Ronald in his car with a girl, and he introduced her to me as Miss Schoonmaker. I had no means of checking his statement. It never occurred to me to doubt it. I assumed that she really was Miss Schoonmaker, and naturally invited her to the Castle. She arrived, and she had not been here twenty-four hours when we discovered that she was not Miss Schoonmaker at all, but this chorus-girl of Ronald's. Presumably they had planned the thing between them in order to get her here.'

'And when you found out she was an impostor you asked her to stay on? I see.'

Lady Constance flushed brightly.

'I was compelled to allow her to stay on.'

'Why?'

'Because . . . Oh, Clarence!' said Lady Constance, with the exasperation which the sudden spectacle of the head of the family so often aroused in her. The ninth Earl had selected this tense moment to potter into the room.

'Eh?' he said.

'Go away!'

'Yes,' said Lord Emsworth, 'lovely.' As so frequently happened with him, he was in a gentle trance. He wandered to the piano, extended a long, lean finger, and stabbed absently at one of the treble notes.

The sharp, tinny sound seemed to affect his sister Constance like a pin in the leg.

'Clarence!'

'Eh?'

'Don't *do* that!'

'God bless my soul!' said Lord Emsworth querulously.

He turned from the piano, and Lady Constance was enabled to see him steadily and see him whole. The sight caused her to utter a stricken cry.

'Clarence!'

'Eh?'

'What—*what* is that thing in your shirt-front?'

The ninth Earl squinted down.

'It's a paper-fastener. One of those brass things you fasten papers with. I lost my stud.'

'You must have more than one stud.'

'Here's another, up here.'

'Have you only two studs?'

'Three,' said Lord Emsworth, a little proudly. 'For the front of the shirt, three. Dashed inconvenient things. The heads come off. You screw them off and then you put them in and then you screw them on.'

'Well, go straight up to your room and screw on the spare one.'

It was not often that Lord Emsworth found himself in the position of being able to score a debating point against his sister Constance. The fact that he was about to do so now filled him with justifiable complacency. It seemed to lend to his manner a strange, quiet dignity.

'I can't,' he said. 'I swallowed it.'

Lady Constance was not the woman to despair for long. A short, sharp spasm of agony and she had seen the way.

'Wait here,' she said. 'Mr Bodkin is sure to have dozens of spare studs. If you dare to move till I come back . . .'

She hurried from the room.

'Connie fusses so,' said Lord Emsworth equably.

He pottered back to the piano.

'Clarence,' said Lady Julia.

'Eh?'

'Leave that piano alone. Pull yourself together. Try to concentrate. And tell me about this Miss Brown.'

'Miss who?'

'Miss Brown.'

'Never heard of her,' said Lord Emsworth brightly, striking a D flat.

'Don't gibber, Clarence. Miss Brown.'

'Oh, Miss Brown? Yes. Yes, of course. Yes. Miss Brown, to be sure. Yes. Nice girl. She's going to marry Ronald.'

'Is she? That's a debatable point.'

'Oh, yes, it's all settled. I'm giving the boy his money and he's going into the motor business, and they're going to get married.'

'I want to know how all this has happened. How is it that this chorus-girl . . .'

'You're quite right,' said Lord Emsworth cordially. 'I told Connie she was wrong, but she wouldn't believe me. A chorus-girl is quite different from a ballet-girl. Galahad assures me of this.'

'If you will kindly let me finish . . .'

'By all means, by all means. You were saying—?'

'I was asking you how it has come about that everyone in this madhouse appears to have accepted it as quite natural and satisfactory that

Ronnie should be marrying a girl like that. She seems to be an honoured guest at the Castle, and yet, apart from anything else, she came here under a false name . . .'

'Odd, that,' said Lord Emsworth. 'She told us her name was School-bred, and it turned out she was quite wrong. It wasn't Schoolbred at all. Silly mistake to make.'

'And when that turned out, may I ask why you didn't turn *her* out?'

'Why, we couldn't, of course.'

'Why not?'

'Well, naturally we couldn't. Galahad wouldn't have liked it.'

'Galahad?'

'That's right. Galahad.'

Lady Julia threw up her arms in a passionate gesture.

'Is everybody crazy?' she cried.

Lady Constance came hurrying back into the room.

'Clarence!'

'You all keep saying "Clarence!"' said Lord Emsworth peevishly. '"Clarence . . . Clarence" . . . One would think I was a Pekingese or something. Well, what is it now?'

'Listen, Clarence,' said Lady Constance, speaking in a clear, even voice, 'and follow me carefully. Mr Bodkin is in the North Room. You know where the North Room is? On the first floor, down the passage to the right of the landing. You know which your right hand is? Very well. Then go immediately to the North Room, and there you will find Mr Bodkin. He has studs and will fit them into your shirt.'

'I'm dashed if I'm going to have my secretary dressing me like a nursemaid!'

'If you think that with sixteen people coming to dinner I am going to trust you to put in studs for yourself . . .'

'Oh, all right,' said Lord Emsworth. 'All right, all right, all right. Lots of fuss for nothing.'

The door closed. Lady Julia came out of the frozen coma into which her brother's words had thrown her.

'Constance!'

'Well?'

'Just before you came in, Clarence told me that the reason why this Brown girl was allowed to stay on at the Castle was that Galahad wished it.'

'Yes.'

'And we must all respect Galahad's wishes, must we not? I don't suppose,' said Lady Julia, mastering her complex emotions with a strong effort, 'that there are forty million people in England who think more highly of Galahad than I do. Tell me,' she went on with strained politeness, 'if it is not troubling you too much, how exactly does he come into the thing at all? Why Galahad? Why not Beach? Or Voules? Or the boy who cleans the knives and boots? What earthly business is it of Galahad's?'

Lady Constance was not by nature a patient woman, but she could make allowances for a mother's grief.

'I know how you must be feeling, Julia, and you can't be more upset about it than I am. Galahad, unfortunately, is in a position to dictate.'

'I cannot conceive of any possible position Galahad could be in which would permit him to dictate to me, but no doubt you will explain what you mean later. What I would like to know first is why he wants to dictate. What is this girl to him that he should apparently have constituted himself a sort of guardian angel to her?'

'To explain that, I must ask you to throw your mind back.'

'Better not start me throwing things.'

'Do you remember, years ago, Galahad getting entangled with a woman named Henderson, a music-hall singer?'

'Certainly. Well?'

'This girl is her daughter.'

Lady Julia was silent for a moment.

'I see. Galahad's daughter, too?'

'I believe not. But that explains his interest in her.'

'Possibly. Yes, no doubt it does. Sentiment is the last thing of which I would have suspected Galahad, but if the old love has lingered down the years I suppose we must accept it. All right. Very touching, no doubt. But it still leaves unexplained the mystery of why everybody here seems to be treating Galahad as if his word was law. You said he was in a position to dictate. Why?'

'I was coming to that. The whole thing, you see, turns on whether Clarence lets Ronald have his money or not. If he does, Ronald can defy us all. Without it he is helpless. And in ordinary circumstances you and I know that we could easily reason with Clarence and make him do the sensible thing and refuse to release the money . . .'

'Well?'

'Well, Galahad was clever enough to see that, too. So he made a bargain. You know those abominable Reminiscences he has been writing. He said that if Ronald was given his money he would suppress them.'

'What!'

'Suppress them. Not publish them.'

'Is *that* what you meant when you said that he was in a position to dictate?'

'Yes. It is sheer blackmail, of course, but there is nothing to be done.'

Lady Julia was staring, bewildered. She flung her hands up to her carefully coiffured head, seemed to realize at the last moment that a touch would ruin it, and lowered them again.

'Am I mad?' she cried. 'Or is everybody else? You seriously mean that I am supposed to acquiesce in my son ruining his life simply in order to keep Galahad from publishing his Reminiscences?'

'But, Julia, you don't know what they're like. Think of the life Galahad led as a young man. He seems to have known everybody in England who is looked up to and respected today and to have shared the most disgraceful escapades with them. One case alone, for example—Sir Gregory Parsloe. I have not read the thing, of course, but he tells me that there is a story in Galahad's book about himself when he was a young man in London . . . something about some prawns—I don't know what . . . which would make him the laughing-stock of the county. The book is full of that kind of story, and every story about somebody who is looked on today as a model of propriety. If it is published, it will ruin the reputations of half the best people in England.'

Lady Julia laughed shortly.

'I'm afraid I don't share your reverence for the feelings of the British aristocracy, Connie. I agree that Galahad probably knows the shady secrets of two-thirds of the peerage, but I don't feel your shrinking horror at the thought of the public reading them in print. I haven't the slightest objection in the world to Galahad throwing bombshells. At any rate, whatever the effect of his literary efforts on the peace of mind of the governing classes, I certainly do not intend to buy him off at the price of having Ronnie marrying any Miss Browns.'

'You don't mean that you are going to try to stop this marriage?'

'I most certainly am.'

'But, Julia! This book of Galahad's. It will alienate every friend we've got. They will say we ought to have stopped him. You don't know . . .'

'I know this, that Galahad can publish Reminiscences till he is blue in the face, but I am not going to have my son making a fool of himself and doing something he'll regret for the rest of his life. And now, if you will excuse me, Connie, I propose to take a short stroll on the terrace in the faint hope of cooling off. I feel so incandescent that I'm apt to burst into spontaneous flame at any moment, like dry tinder.'

With which words Lady Julia Fish took her departure through the french windows. And Lady Constance, having remained for some few moments in anguished thought, moved to the fireplace and rang the bell.

Beach appeared.

'Beach,' said Lady Constance, 'please telephone at once to Sir Gregory Parsloe at Matchingham. Tell him I must see him immediately. Say it is of the utmost importance. Ask him to hurry over so as to get here before people begin to arrive. And when he comes show him into the library.'

'Very good, m'lady.'

The butler spoke with his official calm, but inwardly he was profoundly stirred. He was not a nimble-minded man, but he could put two and two together, and it seemed to him that in some mysterious way, beyond the power of his intellect to grasp, all these alarms and excursions must be connected with the love-story of his old friend, Mr Ronald, and his new—but very highly esteemed—friend, Sue Brown.

He had left Mr Ronald with his mother. Then Lady Constance had gone in. A short while later, Mr Ronald had come out and gone rushing upstairs with all the appearance of an over-wrought soul. And now here was Lady Constance, after a conversation with Lady Julia, ringing bells and sending urgent telephone messages.

It must mean something. If Beach had been Monty Bodkin, he would have said that there were wheels within wheels. Heaving gently like a seaweed-covered sea, he withdrew to carry out his instructions.

The butler's telephone message found Sir Gregory Parsloe enjoying a restful cigarette in his bedroom. He had completed his toilet some little time before; but, being an experienced diner-out and knowing how sticky that anteprandial vigil in somebody else's drawing-room can be, he had not intended to set out for Blandings Castle for another twenty minutes or so. Like so many elderly, self-indulgent bachelors, he was inclined to shirk life's grimmer side.

But the information that Lady Constance Keeble wished to have urgent speech with him had him galloping down the stairs and lumbering into his car in what for a man of his build was practically tantamount to a trice. It must, he felt, be those infernal Reminiscences that she wanted to see him about: and, feeling nervous and apprehensive, he told the chauffeur to drive like the devil.

In the past two weeks, Sir Gregory Parsloe-Parsloe, of Matchingham Hall, seventh Baronet of his line, had run the gamut of the emotions. He had plumbed the depths of horror on learning that his old companion, the Hon. Galahad Threepwood, was planning to publish the story of his life. He had soared to dizzy heights of relief on learning that he had decided not to do so. But from that relief there had been a reaction. What, he had asked himself, was to prevent the old pest changing his mind again? And this telephone call seemed to suggest that he might have done so.

Of all the grey-haired pillars of Society who had winced and cried aloud at the news that the Hon. Galahad was about to unlock the doors of memory, it was probably Sir Gregory Parsloe who had winced most and cried loudest. His position was so particularly vulnerable. He had political ambitions, and was, indeed, on the eve of being accepted by the local Unionist committee as the party's candidate for the forthcoming by-election in the Bridgeford and Shifley Parliamentary Division of Shropshire. And no one knew better than himself that Unionist committees look askance at men with pasts.

Small wonder, then, that Sir Gregory Parsloe writhed in his car and, clumping up the stairs of Blandings Castle to the library in Beach's wake, sank into a chair and sat gazing at Lady Constance with apprehension on every feature of his massive face. Years of good living had given Sir Gregory something of the look of a buck of the Regency days. He resembled now a Regency buck about to embark on a difficult interview with the family lawyer.

Lady Constance made no humane attempt to break the bad news gently. She was far too agitated for that. Sir Gregory got it like a pail of water in the face, and sat spluttering as if it had actually been water she had poured over him.

'What shall we do?' lamented Lady Constance. 'I know Julia so well. She is entirely self-centred. So long as she can get what she wants, other people don't count. Julia is like that, and always has been. She will stop this marriage. I don't know how, but she will do it. And if the marriage is broken off, Galahad will have no reason for suppressing his abominable book. The manuscript will go to the publishers next day. What did you say?'

Sir Gregory had not spoken. He had merely uttered a wordless sound half-way between a grunt and a groan.

'Have you nothing to suggest?' said Lady Constance.

Before the Baronet could reply, if he would have replied, there was an interruption. The door of the library opened and a head inserted itself. It was a small, brilliantined head, the eyes beneath the narrow forehead furtive, the moustache below the perky nose a nasty little moustache. Having smiled weakly, it withdrew.

It was a desire for solitude that had brought P. Frobisher Pilbeam to the library. A few moments before, he had been in the drawing-room and had found its atmosphere oppressive. Solid county gentlemen and their wives had begun to arrive, and the sense of being an alien in a community where everybody seemed extraordinarily intimate with everybody else had weighed upon him, inducing red ears and a general sensation of elephantiasis about the hands and feet.

Taking advantage, therefore, of the fact that the lady with the weather-beaten face who had just asked him what pack he hunted with had had her attention diverted elsewhere, he had stolen down to the library to be alone. And the first thing he saw there was Lady Constance Keeble. So, as, we say, Percy Pilbeam smiled weakly and withdrew.

The actual time covered by his appearance and disappearance was not more than two or three seconds, but it had been enough for Lady Constance Keeble to give him one of the celebrated Keeble looks. Turning from this task and lowering the raised eyebrow and uncurling the curled lip, she was astonished to observe that Sir Gregory Parsloe was staring at the closed door with the aspect of one who had just seen a beautiful vision.

'What—what—what . . .'

'I beg your pardon?' said Lady Constance, perplexed.

'Good heavens! Was that *Pilbeam?*'

Lady Constance was shocked.

'Do you know Mr Pilbeam?' she asked in a tone which suggested that she would have expected something better than this from the seventh holder of a proud title.

Sir Gregory was not a man of the build that leaps from chairs, but he had levered himself out of the one he sat in with an animation that almost made the thing amount to a leap.

'Know him? Why, he's in the Castle because I know him! I engaged him to steal that infernal manuscript of your brother's.'

'What!'

'Certainly. A week or so ago. Emsworth called one morning with Threepwood to see me, and accused me of having stolen that dashed pig of his, and when I told him I knew nothing about it Threepwood got nasty and said he was going to make a special effort to remember all the discreditable things that had ever happened to me as a young man and put them in his book. So I ran up to London next day and went to see this fellow Pilbeam—he had acted for me before in a certain rather delicate matter—and found that Emsworth had asked him to come here to investigate the theft of his pig, and I offered him five hundred pounds if, when he was at the Castle, he would steal the manuscript.'

'Good gracious!'

'And then you told me the pig had been found and Threepwood was going to suppress the book, so I naturally assumed that the chap would have gone back to London. Why, if he's still here, the whole thing's simple. He must go ahead, as originally planned, and get hold of that manuscript and hand it over to us and we'll destroy it. Then it won't matter if this marriage you speak of takes place or not.' He paused. Animation gave place to concern. 'But suppose there are more copies than one?'

'There aren't.'

'You're sure? He may have had it typed.'

'No, I know he has not. He had never really finished the horrible thing. He keeps it in his desk and takes it out and adds bits to it.'

'Then we're all right.'

'If Mr Pilbeam can get possession of the manuscript.'

'Oh, he'll do that. You can rely on him. There isn't a smarter young fellow in London at that sort of thing. Why, he got hold of some letters of mine . . . but that is neither here nor there. I can assure you that if you engage Pilbeam to steal compromising papers, you will have them in the course of a day or two. It's what he's best at. You say Threepwood keeps the thing in a desk. Desks are nothing to Pilbeam. Those—er—those letters of mine . . . to which I alluded just now . . . those letters . . . perfectly innocent, you understand, but a wrong construction might have been placed upon one or two passages in them had they been published as the girl . . . as their recipient had threatened . . . Well, to cut a long story short, to secure them Pilbeam had to pretend to be the man come to inspect the gas meter and break into a safe. This will be child's play to him. If you will excuse me, I will go and find him at once. We must put the matter in hand without delay. What a pity he popped off like that. We could have had everything arranged by now.'

Sir Gregory hurried from the room, baying on the scent like one of his own hounds. And Lady Constance, drawing a deep breath, leaned back in her chair and closed her eyes. After all that had passed in the last twenty minutes, she felt the need to relax.

On her face, as she sat, there might have been observed not merely relief, but a sort of awed look, as of one who contemplates the inscrutable workings of Providence.

Providence, she now perceived, did not put even Pilbeams into the world without a purpose.

S UE stood leaning out over the battlements of Blandings Castle, her chin cupped in her hands. Her eyes were clouded, her mouth a thin red line of depression. A little furrow of unhappiness had carved itself in the smooth whiteness of her forehead.

It was an instinct for the high places, like that of a small, nervous cat which fears vague perils on the lower levels, that had sent her climbing to this eminence. Wandering past the great gatehouse where a channel of gravel divided the west wing of the castle from the centre block, she had espied an open door, giving on to mysterious stone steps; and mounting these, had found herself on the roof, with all Shropshire spread beneath her.

The change of elevation had done nothing to alter her mood. It was four o'clock of a sultry, overcast, oppressive afternoon, and sullen stillness had fallen on the world. The heatwave which for the past two weeks had been grilling England was in the uncomfortable process of working up to a thunderstorm. Shropshire, under a leaden sky, had taken on a sinister and a brooding air. The flowers in the gardens drooped forlornly. The lake was a grey smudge, and the river in the valley below a thread of sickly tarnished silver. Gone, too, was the friendly charm of the Scotch fir spinneys that dotted the park. They seemed now black and haunted and menacing, as if witches lived in crooked little cottages in the heart of them.

'Ugh!' said Sue, hating Shropshire.

Until this moment, except for a few cows with secret sorrows, there had been no living creature to mitigate the gloom of the grim prospect. It was as if life, discouraged by the weather conditions, had died out upon the earth. But as she spoke, shaking her head with the flicker of a grimace, she perceived on the path below a familiar form. It looked up, sighted her, waved, and disappeared in the direction of the gatehouse. And presently feet boomed hollowly on the stone stairs, and there came into view the slouch-hatted head of Monty Bodkin.

'Hullo, Sue. All alone?'

Monty, who seemed, like everything else, to be affected by the weather, puffed, removed his hat, fanned himself, and laid it down.

'Gosh, what a day!' he observed. 'You been up here long?'

'About an hour.'

'I've been closeted with that fellow Pilbeam in the smoking-room. Went in to fill my cigarette-case and got into conversation with him. He's been telling me all about himself. Interesting chap.'

'I think he's a worm.'

'He is a worm,' agreed Monty. 'But even worms, don't you think, are of more than passing interest when they run private inquiry agencies? Did you know he was a private detective?'

'Yes.'

'Now, there's a job I should like.'

'You would hate it, Monty. Sneaking about, spying on people.'

'But with a magnifying-glass, remember,' urged Monty. 'You don't feel that it makes a difference if you do it with a magnifying-glass? No? Well, perhaps you're right. In any case, I suppose it requires special gifts. I wouldn't know a clue if you brought me one on a skewer. I say, did you ever see such a day? I feel as if I were in a frying-pan. Still, I suppose one's as well off up here as anywhere.'

'I suppose so.'

Monty surveyed his surroundings with a sentimental eye.

'Must have been fifteen years since I was on this roof. As a kid you couldn't keep me off it. I smoked my first cigar behind that buttress. Slightly to the left is the spot where I was sick. You see that chimney-stack?'

Sue saw the chimney-stack.

'I once watched old Gally chase Ronnie twenty-seven times round that with a whangee. He had been putting tin-tacks on his chair. Ronnie had on Gally's chair, I mean, of course, not Gally on Ronnie's. Where is Ronnie, by the way?'

'Lady Julia asked him to take her to Shrewsbury in his two-seater, to do some shopping.'

Sue's voice was flat, and Monty looked at her inquiringly.

'Well, why not?'

'Oh, I don't know,' said Sue. 'Only, considering that she was at Biarritz for three months and then in Paris and after that in London, it seems odd that she should wait to do her shopping till she got to Shrewsbury.'

Monty nodded sagely.

'I see what you mean. A ruse, you think? A cunning stratagem to keep him out of the way? I shouldn't wonder if you weren't right.'

Sue looked out over the grey world.

'She needn't have bothered,' she said, in a small voice. 'Ronnie seems quite capable of keeping out of my way without assistance.'

'What do you mean by that?'

'Haven't you noticed?'

'Well, I'll tell you,' said Monty apologetically. 'What with being a good deal exercised about my lord Emsworth's questionable attitude and musing in my spare time on good old Gertrude, I haven't been much in the vein for noticing things. Has he been keeping out of your way?'

'Ever since we got back.'

'Oh, rot.'

'It isn't rot.'

'A girlish fancy, child.'

'It's nothing of the kind. He's been avoiding me all the time. He'll do anything to keep from being alone with me. And if ever we do happen to be alone together he's quite different.'

'How do you mean, different?'

'Polite. Horribly, disgustingly polite. All sort of stiff and formal, as if I were a stranger. You know that way he gets when he's with someone he doesn't like.'

Monty was concerned.

'I say, this wants thinking over. I confess that my primary scheme, on spotting you leaning over the ramparts, was to buzz up and pour out my troubles on your neck. But if this is really so, you had better do the pouring. As what's-his-name said to the stretcher-case, "Your need is greater than mine."'

'Are you in trouble, too?'

'Trouble?' Monty held up a warning hand. 'Listen. Don't tempt me. One more word of encouragement, and I'll be monopolizing the conversation.'

'Go on. I can wait.'

'You're sure?'

'Quite.'

Monty sighed gratefully.

'Well, it'll be a relief, I must own,' he admitted. 'Sue, old girl, I am becoming conscious of an impending doom. The future is looking black. For some reason which I am unable to fathom I don't seem to have made a hit with my employer.'

'What makes you think that?'

'Signs, Sue. Signs and portents. The old blighter bites at me. He clicks his tongue irritably. I look up and find his eyes fixed on me with an expression of loathing. You wouldn't think it possible that a man who could stick Hugo Carmody as a secretary for a matter of eleven weeks would be showing distress signs after a mere two days of me, but there it is. Why, I cannot say, but the ninth Earl obviously hates my insides.'

'Are you sure you aren't imagining all that?'

'Quite sure.'

'But it seems so unlike Lord Emsworth. I've always thought him such an old dear.'

'Precisely how I had remembered him from boyhood days. He used to tip me when I went back to school—tip me lavishly and with the kindest of smiles. But no longer. Not any more. He now views me with concern and dogs my footsteps.'

'Does *what*?'

'Dogs my footsteps. Tails me up, as they say at Scotland Yard. Do you recall that hymn about "See the hosts of Midian prowl and prowl around"? Well, that's what this extraordinary bloke does. For some strange reason of his own he has started watching me, as if he were suspecting me of nameless crimes. I'll give you an instance. Yesterday afternoon I had gone down to the ping-bin to chirrup to that pig of his in the hope of establishing cordial relations, as you advised, and as I approached the animal's lair I happened to glance round, and there he was peering out from behind a tree, his face alight with mistrust. Wouldn't you call that prowling?'

'It certainly seems like prowling.'

'It is prowling. Grade A prowling. And what, I am asking myself, will the harvest be? You may say, Oh, why worry? arguing that an Earl, on his own ground, has a perfect right to hide behind trees and glare at secretaries. But I go deeper than that. I look on the thing as a symptom, and a dangerous symptom. I contend that the Earl who hides behind trees today is an Earl who intends to apply the order of the boot tomorrow. And, my gosh, Sue, I can't afford to go getting the boot twice daily like this. If I don't stay put in some sort of job for a year, I fail to gather in Gertrude, and how am I to get another job if I lose this one? I'm not an easy man to place. I have my limitations, and I know it.'

'Poor old Monty!'

'"Poor old Monty" sums up the thing extraordinarily neatly,' agreed the haunted man. 'I'm sunk if this old bird fires me. And what makes it so particularly foul is that I haven't a notion what he's got against me. I've made a point of being so fearfully alert and obsequious and the perfect secretary generally. I've been simply fascinating. The whole thing's a mystery.'

Sue reflected.

'I'll tell you what to do. Why not get hold of Ronnie and ask him to ask Lord Emsworth tactfully . . .'

Monty shook his head.

'Not Ronnie. No. Not within the sphere of practical politics. Now, there's another mystery, Sue. Old Ronnie. Once one of my closest pals, and now frigid, aloof, distant. Says "Oh, yes?" and "Really?" when I speak to him, and turns away as if desirous of terminating the conversation.'

'Really?'

'And "Oh, yes?"'

'I mean, does he really seem not to like you?'

'He's as sniffy as dammit. And I can't . . . Great Scott, Sue,' cried Monty, struck with an idea, 'you don't suppose that by any chance he Knows All?'

'That you and I were once engaged? How could he?'

'No, that's right. He couldn't, could he?'

'Nobody here can have told him, because nobody knows. Except Gally, who wouldn't breathe a word.'

'True. It only occurred to me as a rather rummy coincidence that he's upstage like this with both of us. Why, if he does not Know All, should he be keeping out of your way, as you say he's doing?'

All Sue's pent-up misery found voice. She had not intended to confide in Monty, for she was a girl whom life had trained to keep her troubles to herself. But Ronnie had gone to Shrewsbury, and the heat was making her head ache, and the sky was looking like the under side of a dead fish, and she wished she were dead, so she poured out all the poison that was in her heart.

'I'll tell you why. Because his mother has been talking to him . . . never stopped since she got here . . . talking to him and nagging at him and telling him what a fool he is to think of marrying a girl like me, when there are dozens of girls in his own set . . . Oh, yes, she has. I know it just as if I had been there. I know exactly the sort of things she would say. And all quite true, too, I suppose. "My dear boy, a chorus-girl!" Well, so I am. You can't get away from that. Why should anyone want to marry me?'

Monty clicked his tongue. He could not subscribe to this.

'My dear old egg! Do it myself tomorrow, if not already earmarked elsewhere. I consider Ronnie dashed lucky.'

'That's sweet of you, Monty, but I'm afraid Ronnie doesn't agree with you.'

'Oh, rot!'

'I wish I could think so.'

'Absolute rot. Ronnie's not the sort of chap to back out of marrying a girl he's asked to marry him.'

'Oh, I know that. His word is his bond. We men of honour! My poor old Monty, you don't really think I would marry a man who has stopped being fond of me, simply because he's too decent to break the engagement? If there's one person I despise in the world, it's the girl who clings to a man when she knows it's only politeness that keeps him from telling her for goodness sake to go away and leave him in peace. If ever I really feel certain that Ronnie wants to be rid of me,' said Sue, staring dry-eyed at the menacing sky, 'I'll chuck it all up in a second, no matter how much it hurts.'

Monty shuffled uneasily.

'I think you're making too much of it all,' he said, but without conviction. 'If you boil it down, probably all that's happened is that the old chap's got a touch of liver. Enough to give anyone a touch of liver, weather like this.'

Sue did not reply. She had walked to the battlements and was looking down. Something in the aspect of her back seemed to tell Monty Bodkin that she was either crying or about to cry, and he did not know what to do for the best. The face of Gertrude Butterwick, floating between him and the sky, forbade the obvious move. A man with a Gertrude Butterwick on his books cannot lightly put his arms round other waists and murmur 'There, there!' into other ears.

He coughed and said, 'Er—well . . .'

Sue did not turn. He coughed again. Then, with a 'Well—I—er—ah . . .' he sidled to the stairs. The clang of the closing door came to Sue's ears as she dabbed at her eyes with the tiny fragment of lace which she called a handkerchief. She was relieved that he had gone. There are moments when a girl must be alone to wrestle single-handed with her own particular devils.

This she did, bravely and thoroughly. There was in her small body the spirit of an Amazon. She fought the devils and routed the devils, till presently a final sniff told that the battle had been won. Shropshire, which had been a thing of mist, became firmer in its outlines. She put away the handkerchief and stood blinking defiantly.

She was happier now. The determination to finish everything, if she saw Ronnie wanted it finished, had not weakened. It still lay rooted at the back of her mind. But hope had dawned again. She was telling herself that she understood Ronnie's odd behaviour. He was worried, poor darling, as who would not be with a woman of Lady Julia Fish's powerful personality going on at him all the time. And when a man is worried, he naturally becomes preoccupied.

The sound of a car drawing up on the other side of the house broke in upon her meditations. She hurried across the roof, her heart quickening.

She turned away, disappointed. It was not Ronnie, back from Shrewsbury. It was only a short, stout man who had driven up in the station taxi. A short, stout, stumpy man of no importance whatever.

So thought Sue in her ignorance. The stout man, had he known that he was being thus casually dismissed as negligible, would have been not only offended, but amazed.

For this visitor to Blandings Castle, for all that he arrived without pomp, driven to his destination by charioteer Robinson in that humble conveyance, the Market Blandings station taxi, was none other than George Alexander Pyke, first Viscount Tilbury, founder and proprietor of the Mammoth Publishing Company of Tilbury House, Tilbury Street, London.

There are men of the bulldog breed who do not readily admit defeat. Crushed to earth, they rise again. To this doughty band belonged George Alexander, Viscount Tilbury. He had built up a very large fortune chiefly by the simple method of never knowing when he was beaten, and the fact that he was now ringing the doorbell of Blandings Castle proved that the ancient spirit still lingered. He had come to tackle the Hon. Galahad Threepwood in person about those Reminiscences of his, and he meant to stand no nonsense.

Many men in his position, informed that the Hon. Galahad had decided to withhold his book from publication, would have felt that there was nothing to be done about it. They would have accepted the situation as one beyond their power to change, and would have contented themselves with grieving over their monetary loss and thinking hard thoughts of the man responsible. Lord Tilbury was made of sterner stuff. He grieved—we have seen him grieving—and he thought hard thoughts: but it never occurred to him for an instant not to do something about it.

A busy man, he could not get away from his office immediately. Pressure of work had delayed the starting of the expedition until today. But at eleven-fifteen that morning he had taken train for Market Blandings and, after establishing himself at the Emsworth Arms in that sleepy little town, had directed Robinson, of the station taxi, to take him on to the Castle.

His mood was one of stern self-confidence. The idea that he might fail in his mission did not strike him as even a remote possibility. He had only a dim recollection of the Hon. Galahad, for he had not met him for twenty-five years, and even in the old days had never been really an intimate of his, but he retained a sort of general impression of an amiable, easygoing man. Not at all the type of man to hold out against a forceful, straight from the shoulder talk such as he proposed to subject him to as soon as this door-bell was answered. Lord Tilbury had great faith in the magic of speech.

Beach answered the bell.

'Is Mr Threepwood in? Mr Galahad Threepwood?'

'Yes, sir. What name shall I say?'

'Lord Tilbury.'

'Very good, m'lord. If you will step this way. I fancy Mr Galahad is in the small library.'

The small library, however, proved empty. It contained evidence of the life literary in the shape of a paper-piled desk and a good deal of ink on the carpet and elsewhere, but it had no human occupant.

'Possibly Mr Galahad is on the lawn. He walks there sometimes,' said the butler indulgently, as one tolerant of the foibles of genius. 'If your lordship will take a seat . . .'

He withdrew, and began to descend the stairs with measured tread, but Lord Tilbury did not take a seat. He was staring, transfixed, at something that lay upon the desk. He drew closer—furtively, with a sidelong eye on the door.

Yes, his surmise had been correct. It was the manuscript of the Reminiscences that lay before him. Evidently its author had only just risen from the task of polishing it, for the ink was still wet on a paragraph where, searching like some Flaubert for the *mot juste*, he had run his pen through the word 'intoxicated' and substituted for it the more colourful 'pickled to the gills'.

Lord Tilbury's eyes, always prominent, bulged a trifle farther from their sockets. His breathing quickened.

Every man who by his own unaided efforts has succeeded in wresting a great fortune from a resistant world has something of the buccaneer in him, a touch of the practical, Do-It-Now pirate of the Spanish Main. In Lord Tilbury, as a younger man, there had been quite a good deal. And while prosperity and the diminishing necessity of giving trade rivals the elbow had tended to atrophy this quality, it had not died altogether. Standing there within arm's length of the manuscript, with the coast clear and a taxi waiting at the front door, he was seriously contemplating the quick snatch and the masterful dash for the open.

And it was perhaps fortunate, for sudden activity of the kind might have proved injurious to a man of his full habit, that before he could quite screw his courage to the sticking point his ear caught the sound of approaching footsteps. He drew back like a cat from a cream-jug, and when the Hon. Galahad arrived was looking out of the window, humming a careless barcarolle.

The Hon. Galahad paused in the doorway and stuck his black-rimmed monocle in his eye. Behind the glass the eye was bright and questioning. His forehead wrinkled with mental strain as he surveyed his visitor.

'Don't tell me,' he begged. 'Let me think. I pride myself on my memory. You're fatter and you've aged a lot, but you're someone I used to know quite well at one time. In some odd way I seem to associate you with a side of beef . . . Shorty Smith? . . . Stumpy Whiting? . . . No, I've got it, by gad! Stinker Pyke!' He beamed with honest satisfaction. 'Not bad, that, considering that it must be fully twenty-five years since I saw you last. Pyke. That's who you are. And we used to call you Stinker. Well, well, how are you, Stinker?'

Lord Tilbury's face had taken on an austere pinkness. He disliked the reference to his increased bulk and advancing years, and it is never pleasant for an elderly man of substance to be addressed by a name which even in his youth was offensive to him. He said as much.

'Well, all right. Pyke, then,' said the Hon. Galahad agreeably. 'How are you, Pyke? Good Lord, this certainly puts the clock back. The last time I saw you must have been that night at Romano's when Plug Basham started throwing bread and got a little over-excited, and one thing led to another and in about two minutes there you were on the floor, laid out cold by a dashed great side of beef and all the undertakers present making bids for the body. I can see your face now,' said the Hon. Galahad, chuckling. 'Most amusing.'

He grew more serious. His smile vanished. He shook his head sadly.

'Poor old Plug!' he sighed. 'A fellow who never knew where to stop. His only fault, poor chap.'

Lord Tilbury had not come a hundred and fourteen miles to talk about the late Major Wilfred Basham, a man who, even before the episode alluded to, had never been a favourite of his. He endeavoured to intimate this, but the Hon. Galahad when in reminiscent mood was not an easy man to divert.

'I took the whole thing up with him at the Pelican next day. I tried to reason with him. Throwing sides of beef about in restaurants wasn't done, I said. Not British. Bread, yes, I said. Sides of beef, no. I pointed out that all the trouble was caused by his fatal practice of always ordering a quart where other men began with pints. He saw it, too. "I know, I know," he said. "I'm a darned fool. In fact, between you and me, Gally, I suppose I'm one of those fellows my father always warned me against. But the Bashams have always ordered quarts. It's an old Basham family custom." Then the only way was, I said, to swear off altogether. He said he couldn't. A little something with his meals was an absolute necessity to him. So there I had to leave it. And then one day I met him again at a wedding reception at one of the hotels.'

'I . . .' said Lord Tilbury.

'A wedding reception,' proceeded the Hon. Galahad. 'And, by a curious coincidence, there was another wedding reception going on at the same hotel, and, oddly enough, their bride was some sort of connection of our bride. So pretty soon these two wedding parties began to mix and mingle, everybody happy and having a good time, and suddenly I felt something pluck at my elbow and there was old Plug, looking as white as a sheet. "Yes Plug?" I said, surprised. The poor, dear fellow uttered a hollow groan. "Gally, old man," he said, "lead me away, old chap. The end has come. The stuff has begun to get me. I have had only the merest sip of champagne, and yet I assure you I can distinctly see two brides.'"

'I . . .' said Lord Tilbury.

'A shock to the poor fellow, as you can readily imagine. I could have set his mind at rest, of course, but I saw that this was providential. Just the sort of jolt he had been needing. I drew him into a corner and talked to him like a Dutch uncle. And this time he gave me his solemn word that from that day onward he would never touch another drop. "Can you do it, Plug?" I said. "Have you the strength, the will-power?" "Yes, Gally," he replied bravely, "I can. Why, dash it," he said, "I've got to. I can't go through the rest of my life seeing two of everything. Imagine! Two book-ies you owe money to . . . Two process-servers . . . Two Stinker Pykes . . ." Yes, old man, in that grim moment he thought of you . . . And he went off with a set, resolute look about his jaw which it did me good to see.'

'I . . .' said Lord Tilbury.

'And about two weeks later I came on him in the Strand, and he was bubbling over with quiet happiness. "It's all right, Gally," he said, "it's all right, old lad. I've done it. I've won the battle." "Amazing, Plug," I said. "Brave chap! Splendid fellow! Was it a terrific strain?" His eyes lit up. "It was at first," he said. "In fact, it was so tough that I didn't think I should be able to stick it out. And then I discovered a teetotal drink that is not only palatable but positively appetising. Absinthe, they call it, and now I've got that I don't care if I never touch wine, spirits, or any other intoxicants again.'"

'I am not interested,' said Lord Tilbury, 'in your friend Basham.'

The Hon. Galahad was remorseful.

'I'm sorry,' he said. 'Shouldn't have rattled on. An old failing of mine, I'm afraid. Probably you've come on some most important errand, and here have I been yarning away, wasting your time. Quite right to pull me up. Take a seat, and tell me why you've suddenly bobbed up like this after all these years, Stinker.'

'Don't call me Stinker!'

'Of course. I'm sorry. Forgot. Well, carry on, Pyke.'

'And don't call me Pyke. My name is Tilbury.'

The Hon. Galahad started. His monocle fell from his eye, and he screwed it in again thoughtfully. There was a concerned and disapproving look on his face. He shook his head gravely.

'Going about under a false name? Bad. I don't like that.'

'Cor!'

'It never pays. Honestly, it doesn't. Sooner or later you're bound to be found out, and then you get it all the hotter from the judge. I remember saying that to Stiffy Vokes in the year ninety-nine, when he was sneaking about London calling himself Orlando Maltravers in the empty hope of baffling the bookies after a bad City and Suburban. And he, unlike you, had had the elementary sense to put on a false beard. Stinker, old chap,' said the Hon. Galahad kindly, 'is it worth while? Can this do anything but postpone the inevitable end? Why not go back and face the music like a man? Or, if the thing's too bad for that, at least look in at some good theatrical costumier's and buy some blond whiskers. What is it they are after you for?'

Lord Tilbury was beginning to wonder if even a volume of Reminiscences which would rock England was worth the price he was paying.

'I call myself Tilbury,' he said between set teeth, 'because in a recent Honours List I received a peerage, and Tilbury was the title I selected.'

Light flooded in upon the Hon. Galahad's darkness.

'Oh, you're *Lord* Tilbury?'

'I am.'

'What on earth did they make you a lord for, Stinker?' asked the Hon. Galahad in frank amazement.

Lord Tilbury was telling himself that he must be strong.

'I happen to occupy a position of some slight importance in the newspaper world. I am the proprietor of a concern whose name may be familiar to you—the Mammoth Publishing Company.'

'Mammoth?'

'Mammoth.'

'Don't tell me,' said the Hon. Galahad. 'Let me think. Why, aren't the Mammoth the people I sold that book of mine to?'

'They are.'

'Stinker—I mean Pyke—I mean Tilbury,' said the Hon. Galahad regretfully, 'I'm sorry about that. Yes, by Jove, I am. I've let you down, haven't I? I see now why you've come here. You want me to reconsider. Well, I'm afraid you've had your journey for nothing, Stinker, old man. I won't let that book be published.'

'But . . .'

'No. I can't argue. I won't do it.'

'But, good heavens! . . .'

'I know, I know. But I won't. I have reasons.'

'Reasons?'

'Private and sentimental reasons.'

'But it's outrageous. It's unheard of. You signed the contract. You were satisfied with the terms we proposed . . .'

'It's got nothing to do with the terms.'

'And you can't pretend that you are not in a position to deliver the book. There it is on your desk, finished.'

The Hon. Galahad took up the manuscript with something of the tenderness of a mother dandling her first-born. He stared at it, sighed, stared at it again, sighed once more. His heart was aching.

The more he reread it, the more of a tragedy did it seem to him that this lovely thing should not be given to the world. It was such dashed good stuff. Yes, if he did say it himself, such dashed good stuff. Faithfully and well he had toiled at his great task of erecting a lasting memorial to an epoch in London's history which, if ever an epoch did, deserved its Homer or its Gibbon, and he had done it, by George! Jolly good, ripping good stuff.

And no one would ever read the dashed thing.

'A book like this is never finished,' he said. 'I could go on adding to it for the rest of my life.'

He sighed again. Then he brightened. The suppression of his masterpiece was the price of Dolly's daughter's happiness. If it brought happiness to Dolly's daughter, there was nothing to regret, nothing to sigh about at all.

All the same, he did wish that his brother Clarence could have been of tougher fibre and better able, without assistance, to cope with the females of the family.

He put the manuscript away in a drawer.

'But it's finished,' he said, 'as far as any chance of its ever getting into print is concerned. It will never be published.'

'But . . .'

'No, Stinker, that's final. I'm sorry. Don't imagine I don't see your side of it. I know I've treated you badly, and I quite realize how justified you are in blinding and stiffing . . .'

'I am not blinding and stiffing. I flatter myself that I have under extreme provocation—succeeded in keeping this discussion on an amicable footing. I merely say . . .'

'It's no use your saying anything. Stinker.'

'Don't call me . . .'

'I can't possibly explain the situation to you. It would take too long. But you can rest assured that nothing you can say will make the slightest difference. I won't publish.'

There was a pregnant silence. Lord Tilbury's gaze, which had fastened itself, like that of a Pekingese on coffee-sugar, upon the drawer into which he had seen the manuscript disappear, shifted to the man who stood between him and it. He stared at the Hon. Galahad wistfully, as if yearning for that side of beef which had once proved so irresistible a weapon in the hand of Plug Basham.

The fever passed. The battle-light died out of his eyes. He rose stiffly.

'In that case I will bid you good afternoon.'

'You're not going?'

'I am going.'

The Hon. Galahad was distressed.

'I wish you wouldn't take it like this. Why get stuffy, Stinker? Sit down. Have a chat. Stay on and join us for a bite of dinner.'

Lord Tilbury gulped.

'Dinner!'

A harmless word, but on his lips it somehow managed to acquire the sound of a rich Elizabethan oath—the sort of thing Ben Jonson, in his cups, might have flung at Beaumont and Fletcher.

'Dinner!' said Tilbury. 'Cor!'

There are moments in life when only sharp physical action can heal the wounded spirit. Just as a native of India, stung by a scorpion, will seek to relieve his agony by running, so now did Lord Tilbury, fresh from this scene with one who seemed to him well fitted to be classified as a human scorpion, desire to calm himself with a brisk cross-country walk. Reaching the broad front steps and seeing before him the station taxi, he was conscious of a feeling amounting almost to nausea at the thought of climbing into its mildew-scented interior and riding back to the Emsworth Arms.

He produced money, thrust it upon the surprised Robinson, mumbled unintelligibly and, turning abruptly, began to stump off in a westerly direction. Robinson, having pursued him with a solid, silent, Shropshire stare till he had vanished behind a shrubbery, threw in his clutch and drove pensively homewards.

Lord Tilbury stumped on, busy with his thoughts.

At first chaotic, these began gradually to take shape. His mind returned to that project which he had conceived while standing alone in the small library. A single object seemed to be imprinted on his retina—that desk in which the Hon. Galahad had placed his manuscript.

He yearned for direct action against that desk.

Like all reformed buccaneers, he put up a good case for himself in extenuation of this resurgence of the Old Adam. To take that manuscript, he argued, would merely be to take that which was rightfully his. He had a legal claim to it. The contract had been signed and witnessed. Payment in advance had changed hands. Normally, no doubt, as between author and publisher, the author would have wrapped his work in brown paper, stuck stamps on it, and posted it. But if the eccentric fellow preferred to leave it in a desk for the publisher to come and fetch it, the thing still remained a legitimate business transaction.

And how simple the looting of that desk would be, he felt, if only he were staying in the house. From the careless, casual way in which the Hon. Galahad had put the manuscript in that drawer he had received a strong impression that he would not even bother to lock it. Anybody staying in the house . . .

Bitter remorse swept over Lord Tilbury as he strode broodingly through the heat-hushed grounds of Blandings Castle. He saw now what a mistake he had made in taking that proud, offended attitude with the Hon. Galahad. If only he had played his card properly, taken the thing with a smile, accepted that invitation to dinner and gone on playing his cards properly, he would almost certainly before nightfall have been asked to move his belongings from the Emsworth Arms and come and stay at the Castle. And then . . .

Of all sad words of tongue or pen, the saddest are these: It might have been. Groaning in spirit, Lord Tilbury walked on. And suddenly as he walked there came to his nostrils the only scent in the world which could have diverted his mind from that which weighed it.

He had smelt a pig.

To those superficially acquainted with them, it would have seemed incredible that George, Viscount Tilbury, and Clarence, Earl of Emsworth, could have possessed a single taste in common. The souls of the two men, one would have said, lay poles apart. And yet such was the remarkable fact. Widely though their temperaments differed in every other respect, they were both pig-minded. In his little country place in Buckinghamshire, whither he was wont to retire for recuperating over the week-ends, Lord Tilbury kept pigs. He not only kept pigs, but loved and was proud of them. And anything to do with pigs, such as a grunt, a gollop, or, as in this case, a smell, touched an immediate chord in him.

So now he came out of his reverie with a start, to find that his aimless wanderings had brought him to within potato-peel throw of a handsomely appointed sty.

And in this sty stood a pig of such quality as he had never seen before.

The afternoon, as has been said, was overcast. An unwholesome blight, like a premature twilight, had fallen upon the world. But it needed more than a little poorness of visibility to hide the Empress. Sunshine would have brought out her opulent curves more starkly, perhaps, but even seen through this grey murk she was quite impressive enough to draw Lord Tilbury to her as with a lasso. He hurried forward and stood gazing breathlessly.

His initial reaction to the spectacle was a feeling of sick envy, a horrible, aching covetousness. That was the effect the first view of Empress of Blandings always had on visiting fanciers. They came, saw, gasped, and went away unhappy, discontented men, ever after to move through life bemused and yearning for they knew not what, like men kissed by goddesses in dreams. Until this moment Lord Tilbury had looked on his own Buckingham Big Boy as a considerable pig. He felt now with a pang that it would be an insult to this supreme animal before him even to think of Buckingham Big Boy in her presence.

The Empress, after a single brief but courteous glance at this newcomer, had returned to the business which had been occupying her at the moment of Lord Tilbury's arrival. She pressed her nose against the lowest rail of the sty and snuffled moodily. And Lord Tilbury, looking down, saw that a portion of her afternoon meal, in the shape of an appetising potato, had been dislodged from the main *couvert* and had rolled out of bounds. It was this that was causing the silver medallist's distress and despondency. Like all prize pigs who take their career seriously, Empress of Blandings hated to miss anything that might be eaten and converted into firm flesh.

Lord Tilbury's pig-loving heart was touched. Envy left him, swept away on the tide of a nobler emotion. All that was best and humanest in him came to the surface. He clicked his tongue sympathetically. His build made it unpleasant for him to stoop, but he did not hesitate. At the cost of a momentary feeling of suffocation, he secured the potato. And he was on the point of dropping it into the Empress's upturned mouth, when there occurred a startling interruption.

Hot breath fanned his cheek. A hoarse voice in his ear said 'Ur!!' A sinewy hand closed vice-like about his wrist. Another attached itself to his collar. And, jerked violently away, he found himself looking into the accusing eyes of a tall, thin, scraggy man in overalls.

It was the time of day when most of Nature's children take the afternoon sleep. But Jas Pirbright had not slept. His employer had instructed him to lurk, and he had been lurking ever since lunch. Sooner or later, Lord Emsworth had told him, quoting that second-sighted man, the Hon. Galahad Threepwood, there would come sneaking to the Empress's sty a mysterious stranger. And here he was, complete with poison-potato, and Pirbright had got him. The Pirbrights, like the Canadian Mounted Police, always got their man.

'Gur!' said Jas Pirbright, which is Shropshire for 'You come along with me and I'll shut you up somewhere while I go and inform his lordship of what has occurred.'

Monty Bodkin, meanwhile, after parting from Sue on the roof, had been making his way slowly and pensively through the grounds in the direction of the Empress's headquarters. It was his intention to look in on the noble animal and try to do himself a bit of good by fraternizing with it.

He was not hurrying. The afternoon was too hot for that. Shropshire had become a Turkish bath. The sky seemed to press down like a poultice. Butterflies had ceased to flutter, and as he dragged himself along it was only the younger and more sprightly rabbits that had the energy to move out of his path.

Yet even had the air been nipping and eager, it is probable that he would still have loitered, for his mind was heavy with care. He didn't like the look of things.

No, mused Monty, he didn't like the look of things at all. Sheridan once wrote of 'a damned disinheriting countenance', and if Monty had ever read Sheridan he would have felt that he had found the perfect description for the face of the ninth Earl of Emsworth as seen across the table in the big library or peering out from behind trees. Not even in that interview with Lord Tilbury in his office at the Mammoth had he been surer that he was associating with a man who proposed very shortly to dispense with his services. The sack, it seemed to him, was hovering in the air. Almost he could hear the beating of its wings.

He came droopingly to the paddock where the Empress resided.

There was a sort of potting-shed place just inside the gate, and here he halted, using its surface to ignite the match which was to light the cigarette he so sorely needed.

Yes, he felt, as he stood smoking there, if he had any power of reading faces, any skill whatever in interpreting the language of the human eye, his latest employer was on the eve of administering the bum's rush. It seemed to him that even now he could hear his voice, crying 'Get out! Get out!'

And then, as the sound persisted, he became aware that it was no dream voice that spoke, but an actual living voice; that it proceeded from the shed against which he was leaning; and that what it was saying was not 'Get out!' but 'Let me out!'

He was both startled and intrigued. For a moment, his mind toyed with the thought of spectres. Then he reflected, and very reasonably, that a ghost that had only to walk a quarter of a mile to find one of the oldest castles in England at its disposal would scarcely waste its time haunting potting-sheds. There was a small window close to where he stood. Emboldened, he put his face to it.

'Are you there?' he asked.

It was a fair question, for the interior of the shed was of an Egyptian blackness. Nevertheless, it appeared to annoy the captive. An explosive 'Cor!' came hurtling through the air, and Monty leaped a full two inches. The thing seemed incredible, but if a fellow was to trust the evidence of his senses this unseen acquaintance was none other than—

'I say,' he gasped, 'that isn't Lord Tilbury, by any chance, is it?'

'Who are you?'

'Bodkin speaking. Bodkin, M. Monty Bodkin. You remember old Monty?'

It was plain that Lord Tilbury did, for he spoke with a familiar vigour.

'Then let me out, you miserable imbecile. What are you wasting time for?'

Monty was groping at the door.

'Right-ho,' he said. 'In one moment. There's a sort of wooden gadget that needs a bit of shifting. All right. Done it. Out you pop. Upsy-daisy!'

And with these words of encouragement he removed the staple, and Lord Tilbury emerged, snorting.

'Yes, but I say—!' pleaded Monty, after a few moments, anxious, like Goethe, for more light. This was one of the weirdest and most mysterious things that he had encountered in his puff, and it was apparently his companion's intention merely to stand and snort about it.

Lord Tilbury found speech.

'It's an outrage!'

'What is?'

'I shall have the fellow severely punished.'

'What fellow?'

'I shall see Lord Emsworth about it immediately.'

'About what?'

Briefly and with emotion Lord Tilbury told his tale.

'I kept explaining to the man that if he had any doubts as to my social standing your uncle, Sir Gregory Parsloe, who I believe lives in this neighbourhood, would vouch for me . . .'

Monty, who had been listening with a growing understanding, checking up each point in the narrative with a sagacious nod, felt compelled at this juncture to interrupt.

'My sainted aunt!' he cried. 'You say you offered the porker a spud? And then this chap grabbed you? And then you told him you were a friend of my Uncle Gregory? And now you're going to the Castle to lodge a complaint with Old Man River? Don't do it!' said Monty urgently, 'don't do it. Don't go anywhere near the Castle, or they'll have you in irons before you can say "Eh, what?" You aren't on to the secret history of this place. There are wheels within wheels. Old Emsworth thinks Uncle Gregory is trying to assassinate his pig. You are caught in the act of giving it potatoes and announce that you are a pal of his. Why, dash it, they'll ship you off to Devil's Island without a trial.'

Lord Tilbury stared, thinking once again how much he disliked this young man.

'What are you drivelling about?'

'Not drivelling. It's quite reasonable. Look at it from their point of view. If this pig drops out of the betting, my uncle's entry will win the silver medal at the show in a canter. Can you blame this fellow Pirbright for looking a bit cross-eyed at a chap who comes creeping in and administering surreptitious potatoes and then gives Uncle Gregory as a reference? He probably thought that potato contained some little-known Asiatic poison.'

'I never heard of anything so absurd.'

'Well, that's Life,' argued Monty. 'And, in any case, you can't get away from it that you're trespassing. Isn't there some law about being allowed to shoot trespassers on sight? Or is it burglars? No, I'm a liar. It's stray dogs when you catch them worrying sheep. Still, coming back to it, you *are* trespassing.'

'I am doing nothing of the kind. I have been paying a call at the Castle.'

The conversation had reached just the point towards which Monty had been hoping to direct it.

'Why? Now we're on to the thing that's been baffling me. What were you doing in these parts at all? Why have you come here? Always glad to see you, of course,' said Monty courteously.

Lord Tilbury appeared to resent this courtesy. And, indeed, it had smacked a little of the gracious seigneur making some uncouth intruder free of his estates.

'May I ask what you are doing here yourself?'

'Me?'

'If, as you say, Lord Emsworth is on such bad terms with Sir Gregory Parsloe, I should have thought that he would have objected to his nephew walking in his grounds.'

'Ah, but, you see, I'm his secretary.'

'Why should the fact you are your uncle's secretary—?'

'Not my uncle's. Old Emsworth's. Pronouns are the devil, aren't they? You start saying "he" and "his" and are breezing gaily along, and you suddenly find you've got everything all mixed up. That's Life, too, if you look at it in the right way. No, I'm not my uncle's secretary. He hasn't got a secretary. I'm old Emsworth's. I secured the post within twenty-four hours of your slinging me out of *Tiny Tots*. Oh, yes, indeed,' said Monty, with airy nonchalance, 'I very soon managed to get another job. Dear me, yes. A good man isn't long getting snapped up.'

'You are Lord Emsworth's secretary?' Lord Tilbury seemed to have difficulty in assimilating the information. 'You are living at the Castle? You mean that you are actually living—residing at Blandings Castle?'

Monty, thinking swiftly, decided that that airy nonchalance of his had been a mistake. Well meant, but a blunder. The sounder policy here would be manly frankness. He believed in taking at the flood that tide in the affairs of men which, when so taken, leads on to fortune. It was imperative that he secure another situation before Lord Emsworth should apply the boot; and he could scarcely hope to find a more propitious occasion for approaching this particular employer of labour than when he had just released him from a smelly potting-shed.

He replied, accordingly, that for the nonce such was indeed the case.

'But only,' he went on candidly, 'for the nonce. I don't mind telling you that I expect a shake-up shortly. I anticipate that before long I shall find myself once more at liberty. Nothing actually said, mind you, but all the signs pointing that way. So if by any chance you are feeling that we might make a fresh start together—if you are willing to let the dead past bury its dead—if, in a word, you would consider overlooking that little unpleasantness we had and taking me back into the fold, I, on my side, can guarantee quick delivery. I should be able to report for duty almost immediately, with a heart for any fate.'

Upon most men listening to this eloquent appeal there might have crept a certain impatience. Lord Tilbury, however, listened to it as though to some grand sweet song. Like Napoleon, he had had some lucky breaks in his time, but he could not recall one luckier than this—that he should have found in this young man before him a man who at one and the same time was living at Blandings Castle and wanted favours from him. There could have been no more ideal combination.

'So you wish to return to Tilbury House?'

'Definitely.'

'You shall.'

'Good egg!'

'Provided—'

'Oh, golly! Is there a catch?'

Lord Tilbury had fallen into a frowning silence. Now that the moment had arrived for putting into words the lawless scheme that was in his mind, he found a difficulty in selecting the words into which to put it.

'Provided what?' said Monty. 'If you mean provided I exert the most watchful vigilance to prevent any more dubious matter creeping into the columns of *Tiny Tots*, have no uneasiness. Since the recent painful episode, I have become a changed man and am now thoroughly attuned to the aims and ideals of *Tiny Tots*. You can restore my hand to the tiller without a qualm.'

'It has nothing to do with *Tiny Tots*.' Lord Tilbury paused again. 'There is something I wish you to do for me.'

'A pleasure. Give it a name. Even unto half of my kingdom, I mean to say.'

'I . . . That is . . . well, here is the position in a nutshell. Lord Emsworth's brother, Galahad Threepwood, has written his Reminiscences.'

'I know. I'll bet they're good, too. They would sell like hot cakes. Just the sort of book to fill a long-felt want. Grab it, is my advice.'

'That,' said Lord Tilbury, relieved at the swiftness with which the conversation had arrived at the vital issue, 'is precisely what I want to do.'

'Well, I'll tell you the procedure,' said Monty helpfully. 'You get a contract drawn up, and then you charge in on old Gally with your cheque-book . . .'

'The contract already exists. Mr Threepwood signed it some time ago, giving the Mammoth all rights to his book. He has now changed his mind and refuses to deliver the manuscript.'

'Good Lord! Why?'

'I do not know why.'

'But the silly ass will be losing a packet.'

'No doubt. His decision not to publish means also the loss of a considerable sum of money to myself. And so, as I consider that, the contract having been signed, I am legally entitled to the possession of the manuscript, I—er—I intend—well, in short, I intend to take possession of it.'

'You don't mean pinch it?'

'That, crudely, is what I mean.'

'I say, you do live, don't you? But how?'

'Ah, there I would have to have the assistance of somebody who was actually in the house.'

A bizarre idea occurred to Monty.

'You aren't suggesting that you want *me* to pinch it?'

'Precisely.'

'Well, lord-love-a-duck!' said Monty.

He stared in honest amazement.

'It would be the simplest of tasks,' went on Lord Tilbury insinuatingly. 'The manuscript is in the desk of a small room which I imagine is a sort of annexe to the library. The drawer in which it is placed is not, unless I am very much mistaken, locked—and even if locked it can readily be opened. You say you are anxious to return to my employment. So . . . well, think it over, my dear boy.'

Monty was plucking feebly at the lapel of his coat. This was new stuff to him. What with being invited to become a sort of Napoleon of Crime and hearing himself addressed as Lord Tilbury's dear boy, his head was swimming.

Lord Tilbury, a judge of men, was aware that there are minds which adjust themselves less readily than others to new ideas. He was well content to allow an interval of time for this to sink in.

'I can assure you that if you come to me with that manuscript, I shall only be too delighted to restore you to your old position at Tilbury House.'

Monty's aspect became a little less like that of a village idiot who has just been struck by a thunderbolt. A certain animation crept into his eye.

'You will?'

'I will.'

'For a year certain?'

'A year?'

'It must be for a year, positively guaranteed. You may remember me speaking about those wheels.'

In spite of his anxiety to enrol this young man as his accomplice and set him to work as soon as possible, Lord Tilbury was conscious of a certain hesitation. Most employers of labour would have felt the same in his position. A year is a long time to have a Monty Bodkin on one's hands, and Lord Tilbury had been consoling himself with the reflection that, once the manuscript was in his possession, he could get rid of him in about a week.

'A year?' he said dubiously.

'Or twelve months,' said Monty, making a concession.

Lord Tilbury sighed. Apparently the thing had to be done.

'Very well.'

'You will take me on for a solid year?'

'If you make that stipulation.'

'You will be prepared to sign a letter—an agreement—a document to that effect, if I draw it up?'

'Yes.'

'Then it's a deal. Shake hands on it.'

Lord Tilbury preferred to omit this symbolic gesture.

'Kindly put the thing through as soon as possible,' he said coldly. 'I have no wish to remain indefinitely at a rustic inn.'

'Oh, I'll snap into it. What rustic inn, by the way? I ought to have your address.'

'The Emsworth Arms.'

'I know it well. Try their beer with a spot of gin in it. Warms the cockles. All right, then. Expect me there very shortly, with manuscript under arm.'

'Good-bye, then, for the present.'

'Toodle-oo till we meet again,' said Monty cordially.

He watched Lord Tilbury disappear, then resumed his walk, immersed in roseate daydreams.

This, he reflected, was a bit of all right. There were no traces in his mind now of the scruples and timidity which had given him that slightly sandbagged feeling when this proposition had first been sprung upon him. He felt bold and resolute. He intended to secure that manuscript if he had to use a meat-axe.

In the shimmering heat-mist that lay along the grass it seemed to him that he could see the lovely face of Gertrude Butterwick gazing at him with gentle encouragement, as if she were endeavouring to suggest that he could count on her support and approval in this enterprise. Almost he could have fancied that the ripple of a lonely little breeze which had lost its way in the alder bushes was her silvery voice whispering 'Go to it!'

Writers are creatures of moods. Too often the merest twiddle of the tap is enough to stop the flow of inspiration. It was so with the Hon. Galahad Threepwood. His recent unpleasant scene with that acquaintance of his youth, the erstwhile Stinker Pyke, had been brief in actual count of time, but it had left him in a frame of mind uncongenial to the resumption of his literary work. He was a kindly man, and it irked him to be disobliging even to the Stinker Pykes of this world.

To send poor Stinker off with a flea in his ear was not, of course, the same as rebuffing, say, dear old Plug Basham or good old Freddie Potts, but it was quite enough to upset a man who always liked to do the decent thing by everyone and hated to say No to the meanest of God's creatures. After Lord Tilbury's departure the Hon. Galahad allowed the manuscript of his life-work to remain in its drawer. With no heart for further polishing and pruning, he heaved a rueful sigh, selected a detective novel from his shelf, and left the room.

Having paused in the hall to ring the bell and instruct Beach, who answered it, to bring him a whisky and soda out on to the lawn, he made his way to his favourite retreat beneath the big cedar.

'Oh, and Beach,' he said when the butler arrived with clinking tray, 'sorry to trouble you, but I wonder if you'd mind leaping up to the small library and fetching me my reading glasses. I forgot them. You'll find them on the desk.'

'No trouble at all, Mr Galahad,' said the butler affably. 'Is there anything else you require?'

'You haven't seen Miss Brown anywhere?'

'No, Mr Galahad. Miss Brown was taking the air on the terrace shortly after luncheon, but I have not seen her since.'

'All right, then. Just the reading glasses.'

Addressing himself to the task of restoring his ruffled nerves, the

Hon. Galahad had swallowed perhaps a third of the contents of the long tumbler when he observed the butler returning.

'What on earth have you got there, Beach?' he asked, for the other seemed heavily laden for a man who had been sent to fetch a pair of tortoiseshell-rimmed spectacles. 'That's not my manuscript?'

'Yes, Mr Galahad.'

'Take it back,' said the author, with pardonable peevishness. 'I don't want it. Good Lord, I came out here to forget it.'

He broke off, mystified. A strange, pop-eyed expression had manifested itself on the butler's face, and his swelling waistcoat was beginning to quiver faintly. The Hon. Galahad watched these phenomena with interest and curiosity.

'What are you waggling your tummy at me for, Beach?'

'I am uneasy, Mr Galahad.'

'You shouldn't wear flannel vests, then, in weather like this.'

'Mentally uneasy, sir.'

'What about?'

'The safety of this book of yours, Mr Galahad.' The butler lowered his voice. 'May I inform you, sir, of what occurred a few moments ago, when I proceeded to the small library to find your glasses?'

'What?'

'Just as I was about to enter I heard movements within.'

'You did?' The Hon. Galahad clicked his tongue. 'I wish to goodness people would keep out of that room. They know I use it as my private study.'

'Precisely, Mr Galahad. Nobody has any business there while you are in residence at the Castle. That is an understood thing. And it was for that reason that I immediately found myself entertaining suspicions.'

'Eh? Suspicions? How do you mean?'

'That some person was attempting to purloin the material which you have written, sir.'

'What!'

'Yes, Mr Galahad. And I was right. I paused for an instant,' said the butler impressively, 'and then flung the door open sharply and without warning. Sir, there was Mr Pilbeam standing with his hand in the open drawer.'

'Pilbeam?'

'Yes, Mr Galahad.'

'Good gad!'

'Yes, Mr Galahad.'

'What did you say?'

'Nothing, Mr Galahad. I looked.'

'What did *he* say?'

'Nothing, Mr Galahad. He smiled.'

'Smiled?'

'In a weak, guilty manner.'

'And then?'

'Still without speaking, I proceeded to the desk, secured the written material, and started to leave the room. At the door I paused and gave him a cold glance. I then withdrew.'

'Splendid, Beach!'

'Thank you, Mr Galahad.'

'You're sure he was trying to steal the thing?'

'The papers were actually in his grasp, sir.'

'He couldn't have been just looking for notepaper or something?'

A man of Beach's build could not look like Sherlock Holmes listening to fatuous theories from Doctor Watson, nor could a man of his position, conversing with a social superior, answer as Holmes would have done. The word 'Tush!' may have trembled on his lips, but it got no farther.

'No, sir,' he said briefly.

'But his motive? What possible motive could this extraordinary little perisher have for wanting to steal my book?'

A certain embarrassment seemed to grip Beach. He hesitated.

'Might I take the liberty, Mr Galahad?'

'Don't talk rot, Beach. Liberty? I never heard such nonsense. Why, we've known each other since we were kids of forty.'

'Thank you, Mr Galahad. Then, if I may speak freely, I should like to recapitulate briefly the peculiar circumstances connected with this book. In the first place, may I say that I am aware of its extreme importance as a factor in the affairs of Mr Ronald and Miss Brown?'

The Hon. Galahad gave a little jump. He had always known the butler as a man who kept his eyes open and his ears pricked up and informed himself sooner or later of most things that happened at the Castle, but he had not realized that his secret service system was quite so efficient as this.

'In order to overcome the opposition of her ladyship to the union of Mr Ronald and Miss Brown, you expressed your willingness to refrain from giving this volume of Reminiscences into the printer's hands—her ladyship being hostile to its publication owing to the fact that in her opinion its contents might give offence to many of her friends—notably Sir Gregory Parsloe. Am I not correct, Mr Galahad?'

'Quite right.'

'Your motive in making this concession being that you were apprehensive lest, without this check upon her actions, her ladyship might possibly persuade his lordship to refuse to countenance the match?'

'"Possibly" is good. You needn't be coy, Beach. This meeting is tiled. No reporters present. We can take our hair down and tell each other our right names. What you actually mean is that my brother Clarence is as weak as water, and that if it wasn't for this book of mine there would be nothing to stop my sister Constance nagging him into a state where he would agree to forbid a dozen weddings just for the sake of peace and quiet.'

'Exactly, Mr Galahad. I would not have ventured to put the matter into precisely those words myself, but since you have done so I feel free to point out that, the circumstances being as you have outlined, it would be very agreeable to her ladyship were this manuscript to be stolen and destroyed.'

The Hon. Galahad sat up, electrified.

'Beach, you've hit it! That fellow Pilbeam was working for Connie!'

'The evidence would certainly appear to point in that direction, Mr Galahad.'

'Probably Parsloe's sitting in with them.'

'I feel convinced of it, Mr Galahad. I may mention that on the night of our last dinner-party her ladyship instructed me with considerable agitation to summon Sir Gregory to the Castle by telephone for an urgent conference. Her ladyship and Sir Gregory were closeted in the library for some little time, and then Sir Gregory emerged, obviously labouring under considerable excitement, and a few moments later I observed him talking to Mr Pilbeam very earnestly in a secluded corner of the hall.'

'Giving him his riding orders!'

'Precisely, Mr Galahad. Plotting. The significance of the incident eluded me at the time, but I am now convinced that that was what was transpiring.'

The Hon. Galahad rose.

'Beach,' he observed with emotion, 'I've said it before, and I say it again—you're worth your weight in gold. You've saved the situation. You have preserved the happiness of two young lives, Beach.'

'It is very kind of you to say so, sir.'

'I do say so. It's no use our kidding ourselves. With that manuscript out of the way, those two wouldn't have a dog's chance of getting married. I know Clarence. Capital fellow—nobody I'm fonder of in the world— but constitutionally incapable of standing up against arguing women. We must take steps immediately to ensure the safety of this manuscript, Beach.'

'I was about to suggest, Mr Galahad, that it might be advisable if in future you were to lock the drawer in which you keep it.'

The Hon. Galahad shook his head.

'That's no good. You don't suppose a determined woman like my sister Constance, aided and abetted by this ghastly little weasel of a detective, is going to be stopped by a locked drawer? No, we must think of something better than that. I've got it. You must take the thing, Beach, and keep it in some safe place. In your pantry, for instance.'

'But, Mr Galahad!'

'Now what?'

'Suppose her ladyship were to learn that the papers were in my possession and were to request me to hand them to her? It would precipitate a situation of considerable delicacy were I to meet such a demand with a flat refusal.'

'How on earth is she to know you've got it? She doesn't ever drop into your pantry for a chat, does she?'

'Certainly not, Mr Galahad,' said the butler, shuddering at the horrid vision the words called up.

'And at night you could sleep with it under your pillow. No risk of Lady Constance coming to tuck you up in bed, what?'

This time Beach's emotion was such that he could merely shudder silently.

'It's the only plan,' said the Hon. Galahad with decision. 'I don't want any argument. You take this manuscript and you put it away somewhere where it'll be safe. Be a man, Beach.'

'Very good, Mr Galahad.'

'Do it now.'

'Very good, Mr Galahad.'

'And, naturally, not a word to a soul.'

'Very good, Mr Galahad.'

Beach walked slowly away across the lawn. His head was bowed, his heart heavy. It was a moment when a butler of spirit should have worn something of the gallant air of a soldier commissioned to carry dispatches through the enemy's lines. Beach did not look like that. He resembled far more nearly in his general demeanour one of those unfortunate gentlemen in railway station waiting-rooms who, having injudiciously consented at four-thirty to hold a baby for a strange woman, look at the clock and see that it is now six-fifteen and no relief in sight.

Dusk was closing down on the forbidding day. Sue, looking out over her battlements, became conscious of an added touch of the sinister in the view beneath her. It was the hour when ghouls are abroad, and there seemed no reason why such ghouls should not decide to pay a visit to this roof on which she stood. She came to the conclusion that she had been here long enough. Eerie little noises were chuckling through the world, and somewhere in the distance an owl had begun to utter its ominous cry. She yearned for her cosy bedroom, with the lights turned on and something to read till dressing for dinner time.

It was very dark on the stone stairs, and they rang unpleasantly under her feet. Nevertheless, though considering it probable that at any moment an icy hand would come out from nowhere and touch her face, she braved the descent.

Her relief as her groping fingers touched the comforting solidity of the door was short-lived. It gave way a moment later to the helpless panic of the human being trapped. The door was locked. She scurried back up the stairs on to the roof, where at least there was light to help her cope with this disaster.

She remembered now. Half an hour before, a footman had come up and hauled down the flag which during the day floated over Blandings Castle. He had not seen her, and it had not occurred to her to reveal her presence. But she wished now that she had done so, for, supposing the roof empty, he had evidently completed his evening ritual by locking up.

Something brushed against Sue's cheek. It was not actually a ghoul, but it was a bat, and bats are bad enough in the gloaming of a haunted day. She uttered a sharp scream—and, doing so, discovered that she had unwittingly hit upon the correct procedure for girls marooned on roofs.

She hurried to the battlements and began calling 'Hi!'—in a small, hushed voice at first, for nothing sounds sillier than the word 'Hi!' when thrown into the void with no definite objective; then more loudly. Presently, warming to her work, she was producing quite a respectable volume of sound. So respectable that Ronnie Fish, smoking moodily in the garden, became aware that there were voices in the night, and, after listening for a few moments, gathered that they proceeded from the castle roof.

He made his way to the path that skirted the walls.

'Who's that?'

'Oh, Ronnie!'

For two days and two nights grey doubts and black cares had been gnawing at the vitals of Ronald Fish. The poison had not ceased to work in his veins. For two days and two nights he had been thinking of Sue and of Monty Bodkin. Every time he thought of Sue it was agony. And every time his reluctant mind turned to the contemplation of Monty Bodkin it was anguish. But at the sound of that voice his heart gave

an involuntary leap. She might have transferred her affection to Monty
Bodkin, but her voice still remained the most musical sound on earth.

'Ronnie, I can't get down.'

'Are you on the roof?'

'Yes. And they've locked the door.'

'I'll get the key.'

And at long last she heard the clang of the lock, and he appeared at
the head of the stairs.

His manner, she noted with distress, was still Eton, still Cambridge.
Nobody could have been politer.

'Nuisance, getting locked in like that.'

'Yes.'

'Been up here long?'

'All the afternoon.'

'Nice place on a fine day.'

'I suppose so.'

'Though hot.'

'Yes.'

There was a pause. The heavy air pressed down upon them. In the
garden the owl was still hooting.

'When did you get back?' asked Sue.

'About an hour ago.'

'I didn't hear you.'

'I didn't come to the front. I went straight round to the stables.
Dropped mother at the Vicarage.'

'Yes?'

'She wanted to have a talk with the vicar.'

'I see.'

'You've not met the vicar, have you?'

'Not yet.'

'His name's Fosberry.'

'Oh?'

Silence fell again. Ronnie's eyes were roaming about the roof. He took
a step forward, stooped, and picked up something. It was a slouch hat.

He hummed a little under his breath.

'Monty been up here with you?'

'Yes.'

Ronnie hummed another bar or two.

'Nice chap,' he said. 'Let's go down, shall we?'

8

I F you turn to the right on leaving the main gates of Blandings Castle and follow the road for a matter of two miles, you will find yourself approaching the little town of Market Blandings. There it stands dreaming the centuries away, a jewel in the green heart of Shropshire. In all England there is no sweeter spot. Artists who come to paint its old grey houses and fishermen who angle for bream in its lazy river are united on this point. The idea that the place could possibly be rendered more pleasing to the eye is one at which they would scoff—and have scoffed many a night over the pipes and tankards at the Emsworth Arms.

And yet, on the afternoon following the events just recorded, this miracle occurred. The quiet charm of this ancient High Street was suddenly intensified by the appearance of a godlike man in a bowler hat, who came out of an old-world tobacco shop. It was Beach, the butler. With the object of disciplining his ample figure, he had walked down from the Castle to buy cigarettes. He now stood on the pavement, bracing himself to the task of walking back.

This athletic feat was not looking quite so good to him as it had done three-quarters of an hour ago in his pantry. That long two-mile hike had taxed his powers of endurance. Moreover, this was no weather for Marathons. If yesterday had been oppressive, today was a scorcher. Angry clouds were banking themselves in a copper-coloured sky. No breath of air stirred the trees. The pavement gave out almost visible waves of heat, and over everything there seemed to brood a sort of sulphurous gloom. If they were not in for a thunderstorm, and a snorter of a thunderstorm, before nightfall, Beach was very much mistaken. He removed his hat, produced a handkerchief, mopped his brow, replaced the hat, replaced the handkerchief, and said 'Woof!' Disciplining the figure is all very well, but there are limits. An urgent desire for beer swept over Beach.

He could scarcely have been more fortunately situated for the purpose of gratifying this wish. The ideal towards which the City Fathers of all English county towns strive is to provide a public-house for each individual inhabitant; and those of Market Blandings had not been supine in this matter. From where Beach stood, he could see no fewer than six such establishments. The fact that he chose the Emsworth Arms must not be taken to indicate that he had anything against the Wheatsheaf, the Waggoner's Rest, the Beetle and Wedge, the Stitch in Time, and the Jolly Cricketers. It was simply that it happened to be closest.

Nevertheless, it was a sound choice. The advice one would give to every young man starting life is, on arriving in Market Blandings on a warm afternoon, to go to the Emsworth Arms. Good stuff may be bought there, and of all the admirable hostelries in the town it possesses the largest and shadiest garden. Green and inviting, dotted about with rustic tables and snug summerhouses, it stretches all the way down to the banks of the river; so that the happy drinker, already pleasantly in need of beer, may acquire a new and deeper thirst from watching family parties toil past in row-boats. On a really sultry day a single father, labouring at the oars of a craft loaded down below the Plimsoll mark by a wife, a wife's sister, a cousin by marriage, four children, a dog, and a picnic basket, has sometimes led to such a rush of business at the Emsworth Arms that seasoned barmaids have staggered beneath the strain.

It was to one of these summerhouses that Beach now took his tankard. He generally went there when circumstances caused him to visit the Emsworth Arms, for as a man with a certain position to keep up he preferred privacy when refreshing himself. It was not as if he had been some irresponsible young second footman who could just go and squash in with the boys in the back room. This particular summerhouse was at the far end of the garden, hidden from the eye of the profane by a belt of bushes.

Thither, accordingly, Beach made his way. There was nobody in the summerhouse, but he did not enter it, having a horror of earwigs and suspecting their presence in the thatch of the roof. Instead, he dragged a wicker chair to the table which stood at the back of it, and, sinking into this, puffed and sipped and thought. And the more he thought, the less did he like what he thought about.

As a rule, when members of the Family showed their confidence in him by canvassing his assistance in any little matter, Beach was both proud and pleased. His motto was 'Service'. But he could not conceal it from himself that the Family had a tendency at times to go a little too far.

The historic case of this, of course, had been when Mr Ronald, having stolen the Empress and hidden her in a disused keeper's cottage in the west wood, had prevailed upon him to assist in feeding her. His present commission was not as fearsome an ordeal as that, but nevertheless he could not but feel that the Hon. Galahad, in appointing him the custodian of so vitally important an object as the manuscript of his book of Reminiscences, had exceeded the limits of what a man should ask a butler to do. The responsibility, he considered, was one which no butler, however desirous of giving satisfaction, should have been called upon to undertake.

The thought of all that hung upon his vigilance unnerved him. And he had been brooding on it with growing uneasiness for perhaps five minutes, when the sound of feet shuffling on wood told him that he had no longer got his favourite oasis to himself. An individual or individuals had come into the summerhouse.

'We can talk here,' said a voice, and a seat creaked as if a heavy body had lowered itself upon it.

And such was, indeed, the case. It was Lord Tilbury who had just sat down, and his was one of the heaviest bodies in Fleet Street.

When, a few minutes before, meditating in the lounge of the Emsworth Arms, he had beheld Monty Bodkin enter through the front door, Lord Tilbury's first thought had been for some quiet retreat where they could confer in solitude. He could see that the young man had much to say, and he had no desire to have him say it with half a dozen inquisitive Shropshire lads within easy earshot.

Great minds think alike. Beach, intent on an unobtrusive glass of beer, and Lord Tilbury, loath to have intimate private matters discussed in an hotel lounge, had both come to the conclusion that true solitude was best to be obtained at the bottom of the garden. Silencing his young friend, accordingly, with an imperious gesture his lordship had led the way to this remote summerhouse.

'Well,' he said, having seated himself. 'What is it?' It seemed to Beach, who had settled himself comfortably in his chair and was preparing to listen to the conversation with something of the air of a nonchalant dramatic critic watching the curtain go up, that that voice was vaguely familiar. He had a feeling that he had heard it before, but could not remember where or when. He had no difficulty, however, in recognizing the one which now spoke in answer. Monty Bodkin's vocal delivery, when his soul was at all deeply disturbed, was individual and peculiar, containing something of the tonal quality of a bleating sheep combined with a suggestion of a barking prairie wolf.

'What is it? I like that!'

Monty's soul at this moment was very deeply disturbed. Since breakfast-time that morning, this young man, like Sir Gregory Parsloe, had run what is known as the gamut of the emotions. A pictorial record of his hopes and despairs would have looked like a fever chart.

He had begun, over the coffee and kippers, by feeling gay and buoyant. It seemed to him that Fortune—good old Fortune—had amazingly decently put him on to a red-hot thing. All he had to do, in order to ensure the year's employment which would enable him to win Gertrude Butterwick, was to nip into the small library and lift the manuscript out of the desk in which, Lord Tilbury had assured him, it reposed.

Feeling absolutely in the pink, accordingly, and nipping as planned, he had fallen, like Lucifer, from heaven to hell. The bally thing was not there. Fortune, in a word, had been pulling his leg.

And here was this old ass before him saying 'What is it?'

'Yes, I like that!' he repeated. 'That's rich! Oh, very fruity, indeed.'

Lord Tilbury, as we have said, had never been very fond of Monty. In his present peculiar mood he found himself liking him less than ever.

'What is it you wish to see me about?' he asked, with testy curtness.

'What do you think I want to see you about?' replied Monty shrilly. 'About that dashed manuscript of Gally's that you told me to pinch, of course,' he said with a bitter laugh, and Beach, having given a single shuddering start like a harpooned whale, sat rigid in his chair; his gooseberry eyes bulging; the beer frozen, as one might say, on his lips.

Nor was Lord Tilbury unmoved. No plotter likes to have his accomplices bellowing important secrets as if they were calling coals.

'Sh!'

'Oh, nobody can hear us.'

'Nevertheless, kindly do not shout. Where is the manuscript? Have you got it?'

'Of course I've not got it.'

Lord Tilbury was feeling dismally that he might have expected this. He saw now how foolish he had been to place so delicate a commission in the hands of a popinjay. Of all classes of the community, popinjays, when it comes to carrying out delicate commissions, are the most inept. Search History's pages from end to end, reflected Lord Tilbury, and you will not find one instance of a popinjay doing anything successfully except eat, sleep, and master the new dance steps.

'It's a bit thick . . .' bellowed Monty.

'Sh!'

'It's a bit thick,' repeated Monty, sinking his voice to a conspiratorial growl. 'Raising hopes only to cast them to the ground is the way I look at it. What did you want to get me all worked up for by telling me the thing was in that desk?'

'It is not?' said Lord Tilbury, staggered.

'Not a trace of it.'

'You cannot have looked properly.'

'Looked properly!'

'Sh!'

'Of course I looked properly. I left no stone unturned. I explored every avenue.'

'But I saw Threepwood put it there.'

'Says you.'

'Don't say "says you". I tell you I saw him with my own eyes place the manuscript in the top right-hand drawer of the desk.'

'Well, he must have moved it. It's not there now.'

'Then it is somewhere else.'

'I shouldn't wonder. But where?'

'You could easily have found out.'

'Oh, yeah?'

'Don't say "Oh, yeah."'

'Well, what *can* I say, dash it? First you keep yowling "Shush" every time I open my mouth. Then you tell me not to say, "Says you". And now you beef at my remarking "Oh, yeah". I suppose what you'd really like,' said Monty, and it was plain to the listening ear that he was deeply moved, 'would be for me to buy a flannel dressing-gown and a spade and become a ruddy Trappist monk.'

This spirited outburst led to a certain amount of rather confused debate. Lord Tilbury said that he did not propose to have young popinjays taking that tone with him; while Monty, on his side, wished to be informed who Lord Tilbury was calling a popinjay. Lord Tilbury then said that Monty was a bungler, and Monty said, Well, dash it, Lord Tilbury had told him to be a burglar, and Lord Tilbury said he had not said 'burglar', he had said 'bungler', and Monty said, What did he mean, bungler, and Lord Tilbury explained that by the expression 'bungler', he had intended to signify a wretched, feckless, blundering, incompetent imbecile. He added that an infant of six could have found the manuscript, and Monty, in a striking passage, was making a firm offer to give any bloodhound in England a shilling if it could do better than he had done, when the argument stopped as abruptly as it had started. Childish voices had begun to prattle close at hand and it was evident that one of those picnic parties from the river was approaching.

'Cor!' said Lord Tilbury, rather in the manner of the moping owl in Gray's 'Elegy' under similar provocation.

One of the childish voices spoke.

'Pa, there's someone here.'

Another followed.

'Ma, there's someone here.'

The deeper note of a male adult made itself heard.

'Emily, there's someone here.'

And then the voice of a female adult.

'Oh dear. What a shame! There's someone here.'

The conspirators appeared to be men who could take a tactful hint when they heard one. There came to Beach's ears the sound of moving bodies. And presently, from the fact that the summerhouse seemed to have become occupied by a troupe of performing elephants, he gathered that the occupation had been carried through according to plan.

He sat on for some minutes; then, hurrying to the inn, asked leave of the landlord to use his telephone in order to summon Robinson and his station taxi. His mind was made up. He would not know an easy moment until he was back in his pantry, on guard. The station taxi would run into money, for Robinson, like all monopolists, drove a hard bargain; but if it would get him to the Castle before Monty it would be half a crown well spent.

'Robinson's taxi's outside now, Mr Beach,' said the landlord, tickled by the coincidence. 'A gentleman phoned for it only two minutes ago. Going up to the Castle himself he is. Maybe he'd give you a lift. You can catch him if you run.'

Beach did not run. Even if his figure had permitted such a feat, his sense of his position would have forbidden it. But he walked quite rapidly, and was enabled to leave the front door just as Monty was bidding farewell to a short, stout man in whom he recognized the Lord Tilbury who had called at the Castle on the previous day to see Mr Galahad. So it was he who had been egging young Mr Bodkin on to bungle!

For an instant, this discovery shocked the butler so much that he could hardly speak. That Baronets like Sir Gregory Parsloe should be employing minions to steal important papers had been a severe enough blow. That Peers should stoop to the same low conduct made the foundations of his world rock. Then came a restorative thought. This Lord Tilbury, he reminded himself, was no doubt a recent creation. One cannot expect too high a standard of ethics from the uncouth (*hoi polloi*) who crash into Birthday Honours lists.

He found speech.

'Oh, Mr Bodkin. Pardon me, sir.'

Monty turned.

'Why, hullo, Beach.'

'Would it be a liberty, sir, if I were to request permission to share this vehicle with you?'

'Rather not. Lots of room for all. What are you doing in these parts, Beach? Slaking the old thirst, eh? Drinking-bouts in the tap-room, yes?'

'I walked down from the Castle to purchase cigarettes at the tobacconist's, sir,' replied Beach with dignity. 'And as the afternoon heat proved somewhat trying . . .'

'I know, I know,' said Monty sympathetically. 'Well, leap in, my dear old stag at eve.'

At any other moment Beach would have been offended at such a mode of address and would have shown it in his manner. But just as he was about to draw himself up with a cold stare he chanced to catch sight of Lord Tilbury, who had retreated to the shadow of the inn wall.

On his marriage to the daughter of Donaldson's Dog-Biscuits, of Long Island City, N.Y., and his subsequent departure for America, the Hon. Freddie Threepwood, Lord Emsworth's younger son, who had assembled in the days of his bachelorhood what was pretty generally recognized as the finest collection of mystery thrillers in Shropshire, had bequeathed his library to Beach; and the latter in his hours of leisure had been making something of a study of the literature of Crime of late.

Lord Tilbury, brooding there with folded arms, reminded him of The Man With The Twisted Eyebrows in *The Caster-bridge Horror.*

Shuddering strongly, Beach climbed into the cab.

When two careworn men, one of whom has just discovered that the other has criminal tendencies, take a drive together on a baking afternoon, conversation does not run trippingly. Monty was thinking out plans and schemes; and Beach, in the intervals of recoiling with horror from this desperado, was wondering why the latter had called him a stag at eve. Silence, accordingly, soon fell upon the station taxi and lasted till it drew up at the front door of the castle. Here Monty alighted, and the taxi took Beach round to the back door. As he got down and handed Robinson his fare, the butler was conscious of an unwilling respect for the fiendish cunning of the criminal mind—which, having offered you a lift in a cab, gets out first and leaves you to pay for it.

He hastened to his pantry. Reason told him that the manuscript must still be in the drawer where he had placed it, but he did not breathe easily until he had seen it with his own eyes. He took it out and, having done so, paused irresolutely. It was stuffy in the pantry and he longed to be in the open air, in that favourite seat of his near the laurel bush outside the back door. And yet he could not relax with any satisfaction there, separated from his precious charge.

There is always a way. A few moments later he perceived that all anxiety might be obviated if he took the manuscript with him. He did so. Then, reclining in his deck-chair, he lit one of the cigarettes which it had cost him such labour to procure, and gave himself up to thought.

His moonlike face was drawn and grave. The situation, he realized, was becoming too complex for comfort.

The views of butlers who have been given important papers to guard and find that there are persons on the premises who wish to steal them are always clear-cut and definite. Broadly speaking, a butler in such a position can bear up with a reasonable amount of fortitude against the menace of one gang of would-be thieves. He may not like it, but he can set his teeth and endure. Add a second gang, however, and the thing seems to pass beyond his control.

Beach's researches in the library bequeathed to him by the Hon. Freddie Threepwood had left him extremely sensitive on the subject of Gangs. In most of the volumes in that library Gangs played an important part, and he had come to fear and dislike them. And here in Blandings Castle, groping about and liable at any moment to focus their malign attention on himself, were two Gangs—the Parsloe and the Tilbury. It made a butler think a bit.

To divert his mind, he began to read the manuscript. Being of an inquisitive nature, he had always wanted to do so, and this seemed an admirable opportunity. Opening the pages at random, therefore, and finding himself in the middle of Chapter Six ('Night-clubs of the Nineties'), he plunged into a droll anecdote about the Bishop of Bangor when an undergraduate at Oxford, and despite his cares was soon chuckling softly, like some vast kettle coming to the boil.

It was at this moment that Percy Pilbeam, who had been smoking cigarettes in the stable yard, came sauntering round the corner.

The stable yard had been a favourite haunt of Percy Pilbeam's ever since his arrival at the Castle. A keen motor-cyclist, he liked talking to Voules, the chauffeur, about valves and plugs and things. And, in addition to this, he found the place soothing because it was out of the orbit of the sisters and nephews of his host. You did not meet Lady Constance Keeble there, you did not meet Lady Julia Fish there, and you did not meet Lady Julia Fish's son Ronald there; and for Percy Pilbeam that was sufficient to make any spot Paradise enow.

He was also attracted to the stable yard because he found it a good place to think in.

He had been thinking a great deal these last two days. A self-respecting private investigator is always loath to admit that he is baffled, but baffled was just what Pilbeam had been ever since a second visit to the small library had informed him that the manuscript which he had been commissioned to remove was no longer in its desk. Like Monty, he felt at a loss.

It was all very well, he felt sourly, for that Keeble woman to say in her impatient, duchess-talking-to-a-worm way that it must be somewhere and that she was simply amazed that he had not found it. The point was that it might be anywhere. No doubt if he had a Scotland Yard search-warrant, a troupe of African witch-doctors and unlimited time at his disposal he could find it. But he hadn't.

A well-defined dislike of Lady Constance Keeble had been germinating in Percy Pilbeam since the first moment they had met. He was brooding upon that unpleasantly supercilious manner of hers as he turned the corner now. And he had just come to the conclusion, as he always came

on these occasions, that what she needed was a thoroughly good ticking
off, when he was suddenly jerked out of his daydreams by the sound of a
huge, reverberating, explosive laugh; and looking up with a start, espied
protruding over the top of a deck-chair a few feet before him an egg-
shaped head which he recognized as that of Beach, the butler.

We left Beach, it will be remembered, chuckling softly. And for a few
minutes soft chuckles had contented him. But in a book of the
nature of the Hon. Galahad Threepwood's Reminiscences the student is
sure sooner or later to come upon some high spot, some supreme expression of the writer's art which demands a more emphatic tribute. What
Beach was reading now was the story of Sir Gregory Parsloe-Parsloe and
the prawns.

'HA . . . HOR . . . HOO!' he roared.

Pilbeam stood spellbound. His had not been a wide experience of
butlers, and he could not recall ever before having heard a butler laugh—
let alone laugh in this extraordinary fashion, casting dignity to the winds
and apparently without a thought for his high blood-pressure and the
stability of his waistcoat buttons. As soon as the first numbing shock had
passed away, an intense curiosity seized him. He drew near, marvelling.
On tiptoe he stole behind the chair, agog to see what it could be that had
caused this unprecedented outburst.

The next moment he found himself gazing upon the manuscript of
the Hon. Galahad's Reminiscences.

He recognized it instantly. Ever since that attempt upon it which this
same butler had foiled, its shape and aspect had been graven upon his
memory. And even if that straggling handwriting had not been familiar
to him, the two lines which he read before uttering an involuntary cry
would have told him what it was that flickered before his eyes.

'Oof!' said Pilbeam, unable to check himself.

Beach gave a convulsive start, turned, and, looking up, beheld within
six inches of his eyes the face of the leading executive of the sinister
Parsloe Gang.

'Oof!' he exclaimed in his turn, and the deck-chair, as if in sympathy, also made an oof-like sound. Then, cracking under the strain, it spread itself out upon the ground.

Even under the most favourable conditions, the situation would have been one of embarrassment. The peculiar circumstances rendered it cataclysmic. Pilbeam, who had never seen a butler take a toss out of a deck-chair before, stood robbed of speech; while Beach, his heart palpitating dangerously, sat equally silent. He was frozen with horror. That the enemy should have succeeded in tracking him down already seemed to him to argue a cunning that transcended the human.

Rising with the manuscript clutched to the small of his back, if his back could be said to have a small, he began to retreat slowly towards the house. Continuing to recoil, he bumped into stone-work, and with an infinite relief found that he was within leaping distance of the back door. With a last, lingering look, of a nature which a sensitive snake would have resented, he shot in, leaving Pilbeam staring like one in a dream.

Almost exactly at the instant when he reached the haven of his pantry, Monty Bodkin, taking a thoughtful stroll on the terrace, suddenly remembered with a start of shame and remorse that he had left Beach to pay that cab fare.

One points at Monty Bodkin with a good deal of pride. Most young men in his position would either have dismissed the matter with a careless 'What of it?' or possibly even the still more ignoble reflection that a bit of luck had put them half a crown up; or else would have made a mental note to slip the fellow the money at some vague future date. For in the matter of Debts the young man of today wavers between straight repudiation and a moratorium.

But in a lax age Monty Bodkin had his code. To him this obligation was a blot on the Bodkin escutcheon which had to be wiped off immediately.

And so it came about that Beach, panting from his recent clash with the Parsloe Gang and in his dazed condition not having heard the door open, became suddenly aware of emotional breathing in the vicinity of his left ear and discovered that the right-hand man of the Tilbury Gang had now invaded his fastness.

It was a moment which would have tried the *morale* of the hero of a Secret Service novel. It made Beach feel like a rabbit with not one stoat but a whole platoon of stoats on its track. He had been sitting, relaxed. He now rose like a rocket and, snatching up the manuscript in the old familiar manner, stood holding it to his heaving chest.

Monty, who, like Pilbeam, had reacted strongly to the wholly unforeseen discovery of the precious object in the butler's possession, was the first to recover from the shock.

'What ho!' he said. 'Afraid I startled you, what?'

Beach continued to pant.

'I came to give you the money for that cab.'

Beach, though reluctant to take even one hand off the manuscript, was not proof against half-crowns. Cautiously extending a palm, he accepted the coin, thrust it into his pocket, and restored his grasp to the papers almost in a single movement.

'Must have given you a jump. Sorry. Ought to have blown my horn.'

There was a pause.

'I see you've got that book of Mr Galahad's there,' said Monty, with a rather overdone carelessness.

To Beach it seemed more than rather overdone. He had been manoeuvring with the open door as his objective, and he now took a shuffling step in that direction.

'Pretty good, I should imagine? Now, there's a thing,' said Monty, 'that I'd very much like to read.'

Beach had now reached the door, and the thought of having a clear way to safety behind him did something to restore his composure. That trapped feeling had left him, and in its stead had come a stern, righteous wrath. He stared at Monty, breathing heavily. A sort of glaze had come over his eyes, causing them to resemble two pools of cold gravy.

'You couldn't lend it to me, I suppose?'

'No, sir.'

'No?'

'No, sir.'

'You won't?'

'No, sir.'

There was a pause. Monty coughed. Beach, with an inward shudder, felt that he had never heard anything so roopy and so villainous. He was surprised at Monty. A nice, respectable young gentleman he had always considered him. He could only suppose that he had been getting into bad company since those early days when he had been a popular visitor at the Castle.

'I'd give a good deal to read that thing, Beach.'

'Indeed, sir?'

'Ten quid, in fact.'

'Indeed, sir?'

'Or, rather, twenty.'

'Indeed, sir?'

'And when I say twenty,' explained Monty, 'I mean, of course twenty-five.'

The sophisticated modern world has, one fears, a little lost its taste for the type of scene, so admired of an older generation, where Virtue, drawing itself up to its full height, scorns to be tempted by gold. Yet even the most hard-boiled and cynical could scarcely have failed to be thrilled had they beheld Beach now. He looked like something out of a symbolic group of statuary—Good Citizenship Refusing To Accept A Bribe From Big Business Interests In Connexion With The Contract For The New Inter-Urban Tramway System, or something of that kind. His eyes were hard, his waistcoat quivered, and when he spoke it was with a formal frigidity.

'I regret to say, sir, that I am not in a position to fall in with your wishes.'

And with a last stare, of about the same caliber as the last stare which he had directed at Percy Pilbeam, he moved in good order to the House-keeper's Room, leaving Monty plunged in thought.

Too often, when a man of Monty Bodkin's mental powers is plunged in thought, nothing happens at all. The machinery just whirs for a while, and that is the end of it. But on the present occasion this was not so. Love is the great driving force, and now it was as if Gertrude Butterwick had her dainty foot on the accelerator of his brain, whacking it up to unprecedented m.p.h. The result was that after about two minutes of intense concentration, during which he felt several times as if the top of his head were coming off, an idea suddenly shot out of the welter like a cork from the Old Faithful geyser.

It was obvious that, with Beach turning so unaccountably spiky as he had done, he could accomplish nothing further by his own efforts. He must put the matter into the hands of a competent agent. And the chap to apply to was beyond a question this bird Pilbeam.

Pilbeam, he reasoned, was a private detective. The job to be done, therefore, would be right up his street: for stealing things must surely be one of the commonplaces of a private detective's daily life. From what he could remember of his reading, they were always being called upon to steal things—compromising letters, Admiralty Plans, Maharajah's rubies, and what not. No doubt the fellow would be only too glad of the commission.

He went in search of him, and found him lying back in an armchair in the smoking-room. He had the tips of his fingers together, Monty noted approvingly. Always a good sign.

'I say, Pilbeam,' he said, 'are you in the market at the moment for a bit of stealthy stuff?'

'Pardon?'

'If so, I've got a job for you.'

'A job?'

Like Monty, Pilbeam had been thinking tensely, and, what with the strain on his brain and the warmth of the weather, was not feeling so bright as he usually did.

'You *are* a detective?' said Monty anxiously. 'You weren't just pulling my leg about that, were you?'

'Certainly I am a detective. I think I have one of my cards here.'

Monty inspected the grubby piece of pasteboard, and all anxiety left him. Argus Inquiry Agency. You couldn't get round that. Secrecy and Discretion Guaranteed. Better still. A telegraphic code address, too—Pilgus, Piccy, London. Most convincing.

'Topping,' he said. 'Well, then, coming back to it, I can put business in your way.'

'You wish to make use of my professional services?'

'If you're open for a spot of work at this juncture, I do. Of course, if you're simply down here taking a well-earned rest . . .'

'Not at all. I shall be glad to render you any assistance that is in my power. Perhaps you will tell me the facts.'

Monty was a little doubtful about the procedure. He had never engaged a private detective before.

'Do you want to know my name?'

'Isn't your name Bodkin?' said Pilbeam surprised.

'Oh, yes. Rather. Definitely. Only in all the stories I've read the chap who comes to the detective always starts off with a long yarn about what his name is and where he lives and who left him his money, and so forth. Save a lot of time if we can cut all that.'

'All I require are the facts.'

Monty hesitated again.

'It sounds so dashed silly,' he said coyly.

'I beg your pardon?'

'Well, bizarre, if you prefer the expression. Nobody could say it wasn't. Bizarre is the word that absolutely springs to the lips. It's about that book of Gally Threepwood's.'

Pilbeam gave a little jump.

'Oh?'

'Yes. You knew he had written a book?'

'Quite.'

'Well . . .' Monty giggled '. . . I suppose you'll think I'm a silly ass, but I want to get hold of it.'

Pilbeam was silent for a moment. He had not known that he had a rival in the field, and was none too pleased to hear it.

'You do think I'm a silly ass?'

'Not at all,' said Pilbeam, recovering himself. 'No doubt you have your reasons?'

It had just occurred to him that, so far from being a disconcerting piece of news, what he had heard was really tidings of great joy. He supposed, mistakenly, that Monty, who no doubt had many friends in high places, had been asked by one of them to take advantage of his being at the Castle to destroy the book. England, he knew, was full of men besides Sir Gregory Parsloe who wanted those Reminiscences destroyed.

The situation now began to look very good to Percy Pilbeam. He had only to secure that manuscript and he would be in the delightful position of having two markets in which to sell it. Competition is the soul of Trade. The one thing a man of affairs wants, when he has come into possession of something valuable, is to have people bidding against one another for it.

'Oh, I have my reasons all right,' said Monty. 'But it's a long story. Do you mind if we just leave it at this, that there are wheels within wheels?'

'Just as you please.'

'The thing is, a certain bloke—whom I will not specify—has asked me to get hold of this manuscript—for reasons into which I need not go—and . . . well, there you are.'

'Quite,' said Pilbeam, satisfied that the position was exactly as he had supposed.

Monty proceeded with more confidence.

'Well, that's that, then. Now we get down to it. I've just found out that the chap who's got the thing is—'

'Beach,' said Pilbeam.

Monty was astounded.

'You knew that?'

'Certainly.'

'But how on earth—?'

'Oh, well,' said Pilbeam carelessly, as one who has his methods.

Monty was now convinced that he had come to the right shop. This man was uncanny. 'Beach,' he had said. Just like that. Might have been a mind-reader.

'Yes, that's the strength of it,' he went on as soon as he had ceased marvelling. 'That's where the snag lies. Beach has got it and is hanging on to it like a limpet. He won't let me lay a finger on the thing. So the problem, as I see it . . . You don't mind me outlining the problem as I see it? . . .'

Pilbeam waved a courteous hand.

'Well, then, the problem, as I see it,' said Monty, 'is, how the hell is one to get it away from the blighter?'

'Quite.'

'That is, as you might say, the nub?'

'Quite.'

'Have you any ideas on the subject?'

'Oh, yes.'

'Such as—?'

'Ah, well,' said Pilbeam, a little stiffly.

Monty was all apologies.

'I see, I see,' he said. 'Naturally you don't want to blow the gaff prematurely. Shouldn't have asked. Sorry. But I can leave the matter in your hands with every confidence, as I believe the expression is?'

'Quite.'

'He might let you borrow the thing to read?'

'At any rate, I have no doubt that I shall find a way of getting it into my possession.'

Monty eyed him admiringly. Externally, Percy Pilbeam was not precisely his idea of a detective. Not quite enough of that cold, hawk-faced stuff, and a bit too much brilliantine on the hair. But as far as brain was concerned he was undoubtedly the goods.

'I bet you will,' he said. 'You can't run a business like yours without knowing a thing or two. I expect you've pinched things before.'

'I have occasionally been commissioned to recover papers, and so forth, of value,' said Pilbeam guardedly.

'Well, consider yourself jolly well commissioned now,' said Monty.

9

SAFE in the Housekeeper's Room, Beach sat gazing out of the window at the lowering sky. His chest was still rising and falling like a troubled ocean.

Too hot, felt Beach, too hot. Things were becoming too hot altogether.

His whole mind was obsessed by an insistent urge to get rid of these papers, the guardianship of which had become so hazardous a matter. The chase was growing too strenuous for a man of regular habits who liked a quiet life.

Nearly everything in this world cuts both ways. A fall from a deck-chair, for instance, is—physically—a painful experience. Against its obvious drawbacks, however, must be set the fact that it does render the subject nimbler mentally. It shakes up the brain. To the circumstance of his having so recently come down with a bump on his spacious trousers-seat must be attributed the swiftness with which Beach now got an idea that seemed to him to solve everything.

He saw the way out. He would hand this manuscript over to Mr Ronald. There was its logical custodian. Mr Ronald was the person most interested in its safety. He was, moreover, a young man. And the more he mused on the whole unpleasant affair, the more firmly did Beach come to the conclusion that the foiling of the Parsloe Gang and the Tilbury Gang was young man's work.

It would be necessary, of course, to apply to the Hon. Galahad for permission to take the step. If you went behind his back and acted on your own initiative after he had given you instructions, Mr Galahad could be quite as bad as any gang. Years of association with London's toughest citizens had given him a breadth of vocabulary which was not lightly to be faced. Beach had no intention of drawing upon himself the lightnings of that Pelican-Club-trained tongue. As soon as he felt sufficiently restored to move, he went in search of the Hon. Galahad and found him in the small library.

'Might I speak to you, Mr Galahad?'

'Say on, Beach.'

Clearly and well the butler told his tale. He recounted the scene at the Emsworth Arms, the subsequent invasion of his pantry by the man Bodkin, the proffered bribe. The Hon. Galahad listened with fire smouldering behind his monocle.

'The young toad!' he cried. 'Monty Bodkin. A fellow I've practically nursed in my bosom. Why, I can remember, when he was a boy at Eton, taking him aside as he was going back to school one time and urging him to put his shirt on Whistling Rufus for the Cesarewitch.'

'Indeed, sir?'

'And he notified me subsequently that, thanks to my kindly advice, he had cleaned up to the extent of eleven shillings—in addition to a bag of bananas, two strawberry ice-creams, and a three-cornered Cape of Good Hope stamp at a hundred to sixteen from a schoolmate who was making a book. And this is how he repays me!' said the Hon. Galahad, looking like King Lear. 'Isn't there such a thing as gratitude in the world?'

He expressed his disgust with a wide, passionate gesture. The butler, with his nice instinct for class distinctions, expressed his with one a little less wide and not quite so passionate. These callisthenics seemed to relieve them both, for when the conversation was resumed it was on a calmer note.

'I might have known,' said the Hon. Galahad, 'that a fellow like Stinker Pyke . . . what does he call himself now, Beach?'

'Lord Tilbury, Mr Galahad.'

'I might have known that a fellow like Lord Tilbury wouldn't give up the struggle after one rebuff. You don't make a large fortune by knuckling under to rebuffs, Beach.'

'Very true, Mr Galahad.'

'I suppose old Stinker has been up against this sort of thing before. He knows the procedure. The first thing he would do, after I had turned him down, would be to set spies and agents to work. Well, I don't see what there is to be done except employ renewed vigilance, like Clarence with his pig.'

Beach coughed.

'I was thinking, Mr Galahad, that if I were to hand the documents over to Mr Ronald . . .'

'You think that would be safer?'

'Considerably safer, sir. Now that Mr Pilbeam is aware that they are in my possession, I am momentarily apprehensive lest her ladyship approach me with a direct request that I deliver them into her hands.'

'Beach! Are you afraid of my sister Constance?'

'Yes, sir.'

The Hon. Galahad reflected.

'Well, I see what you mean. It would be difficult for you. You couldn't very well tell her to go and put her head in a bag.'

'No, sir.'

'All right, then. Give the thing to Mr Ronald.'

'Thank you very much, Mr Galahad.'

Infinitely relieved, Beach allowed his gaze, hitherto concentrated on his companion, to travel to the window.

'Storm looks like breaking at last, sir.'

'Yes.'

The Hon. Galahad also looked out of the window. It was plain that Nature in all her awful majesty was about to let herself go. On the opposite side of the valley there shot jaggedly across the sky a flash of lightning. Thunder growled, and raindrops began to splash against the pane.

'That fool's going to get wet,' he said.

Beach followed his pointing finger. Into the scene below a figure had come, walking rapidly. His interview with Percy Pilbeam had left Monty in that exhilarated frame of mind which demands strenuous exercise. Where Lord Tilbury, on a previous occasion, had walked because his heart was heavy, Monty walked because his heart was light. Pilbeam had filled him with the utmost confidence. He did not know how or when, but he felt that Pilbeam would find a way.

So now he strode briskly across the park, regardless of the fact that the weather was uncertain.

'Mr Bodkin, sir.'

'So it is, the young reptile. He'll get soaked.'

'Yes, sir.'

There was quiet satisfaction in the butler's voice. It was even possible, he was reflecting, that this young man might be struck by lightning. If so, it was all right with Beach. As far as he was concerned, Nature's awful majesty could go to the limit. He only wished that Pilbeam, too, were being exposed to the fury of the elements. He viewed members of gangs in rather an Old Testament spirit, and believed in their getting treated rough.

Ronnie was in his bedroom. When the heart is aching, there are few better refuges than a country-house bedroom. A man may smoke and think there, undisturbed.

Beach, tracking him down a few minutes later, found him well disposed to the arrangement he had come to suggest. He made no difficulties about accepting custody of the manuscript. Indeed, it seemed to Beach that he was scarcely interested. Listless was the word that occurred to the butler, and he put it down to the weather. He took his departure with feelings resembling those of the man who got rid of the Bottle Imp; and Ronnie, having thrown the manuscript into a drawer, resumed his seat and began thinking of Sue once more.

Sue! . . .

It wasn't that he blamed her. If she loved Monty Bodkin—well, that was that. You couldn't blame a girl for preferring one fellow to another.

All that stuff his mother had been saying about her being the typical chorus-girl fluttering from affair to affair was, of course, just a lot of pernicious bilge. Sue wasn't like that. She was as straight as they make 'em. It was simply that she had been dazzled by this blasted lissom Monty and couldn't help herself.

You were always reading about that sort of thing in novels. Girl gets engaged to bloke, thinking at the moment that he is what the doctor ordered. Then runs into second bloke and discovers in a sort of flash that she has picked the wrong one. No doubt, on that trip of hers to London she had happened to meet Monty accidentally in Piccadilly or somewhere and the thing had come on her like a thunderbolt.

It was what he had been expecting all along, of course. He had told her so himself. It stood to reason, he meant, that a terrific girl like her—a girl who practically stood alone, as you might say—was bound sooner or later to come across someone capable of cutting out a bally pink-faced midget who, except for getting a featherweight boxing Blue at Cambridge, had never done a thing to justify his existence.

Yes, that was about what it all boiled down to, felt Ronnie. He rose and went to the window. For some time now, in a subconscious sort of way, he had been dimly aware that there was something rummy going on outside.

He found himself looking out upon a changed world. The storm was now at its height. Torrents of rain were coursing down the glass. Thunder was booming, lightning flashing. A hissing, howling, roaring, devastated world. A world that seemed to fit in neatly with his stormy emotions.

Sue! . . .

Yesterday on the roof. Finding that hat and realizing that she and Monty had been up there together all the afternoon. He flattered himself that she couldn't possibly have detected anything from his manner—no, he had worn the good old mask all right—but there had been a moment, before he got hold of himself, when he had understood how those chaps you read about in the papers who run amok and slay two get that way.

Yes, reason might tell him that it was perfectly natural for Sue to be in love with Monty Bodkin, but nothing was going to make him like it.

The storm seemed to be conking out a bit. The thunder had rolled away into the distance. The lightning flashes had lost much of their zip.

Even the rain showed a disposition to cheese it. What had been a Niagara was now little more than a drizzle. And suddenly, watery and faint, there gleamed on the drenched stone of the terrace, a ray of sunshine.

It grew. Blue spread over the sky. Across the valley there was a rainbow. Ronnie opened the window and a wave of cool, sweet-smelling air poured into the room.

He leaned out, sniffing. And abruptly he became aware that the heavy depression of the last two days had left him. The thunderstorm had wrought its customary miracle. He felt like a man recovered from a fever. It was as if the whole world had suddenly been purged of gloom. A magic change had come over everything.

Birds were singing in the shrubberies below, and for two-pence Ronnie could have sung himself.

Why, dash it, he felt, he had been making a fat-headed fuss about absolutely nothing. He saw it all now. What had given him that extraordinary notion that Sue was in love with Monty was simply the foul weather. Of course there was nothing between them really. That lunch could easily be explained. So could that afternoon together on the roof. Everything could easily be explained in this best of all possible worlds.

And scarcely had he reached this conclusion when he perceived on the drive below him a draggled figure. It was Monty Bodkin, home from his ramble. He leaned farther out of the window, overflowing with the milk of human kindness.

'Hullo,' he said.

Monty looked up.

'Hullo.'

'You're wet.'

'Yes.'

'By Jove, you *are* wet!' said Ronnie. It hurt him to think that this brave new world could contain a fellow human being in such a soluble condition. 'You'd better go and change.'

'Yes.'

'Into something dry.'

Monty nodded, scattering water like a public fountain. He brushed the tangle of hair out of his eyes, and squelched on his way.

It was perhaps two minutes later that Ronnie, still aching with compassion, remembered that on the shelf above his wash-stand he had a bottle of excellent embrocation.

When once a man has reacted from a mood of abysmal depression, there is no knowing how far he will go in the opposite direction. In a normal frame of mind, Ronnie would probably have dismissed the moistness of Monty from his thoughts as soon as the other had left him. But now, in the grip of this strange feeling of universal benevolence, he felt that those few words of sympathy had not been enough. He wanted to do something practical, something constructive that would help to ward off the nasty cold in the head which this man might so easily catch as the result of his total immersion. And, as we say, he remembered that bottle of embrocation.

It was Rigg's Golden Balm, in the large (or seven-and-sixpenny) size, and he knew, not only from the advertisements, which were very frank about it, but also from personal trial, that it communicated an immediate warm glow to the entire system, averting catarrh, chills, rheumatism, sciatica, stiffness of the joints, and lumbago, and in addition imparted a delightful sensation of *bien-être*, toning up and renovating the muscular tissues. And if ever a fellow stood in need of warm glows and tonings up, it was Monty.

Seizing the bottle, he hurried off on his errand of mercy. He found Monty in his room, stripped to the waist, rubbing himself vigorously with a rough towel.

'I say,' he said, 'I don't know if you know this stuff! You might like to try it. It communicates a warm glow.'

Monty, the towel draped about him like a shawl, examined the bottle with interest. He sloshed it tentatively. This consideration touched him.

'Dashed good of you.'

'Not a bit.'

'You're sure it's not for horses?'

'Horses?'

'Some of these embrocations are. You rub them well in, and then you take another look at the directions and you see "For horses only," or words to that effect, and then you suffer the tortures of the damned for about half an hour, feeling as if you had been having a dip in vitriol.'

'Oh, no. This stuff's all right. I use it myself.'

'Then have at it!' said Monty, relieved.

He poured some of the fluid into the palm of his hand and expanded his torso. And, as he did so, Ronnie Fish uttered a quick, sharp exclamation.

Monty looked up, surprised. His benefactor had turned a vivid vermilion and was staring at him in a marked manner.

'Eh?' he said, puzzled.

Ronnie did not speak immediately. He appeared to be engaged in swallowing some hard, jagged substance.

'On your chest,' he said at length, in a strange, toneless voice.

'Eh?'

Eton and Cambridge came to Ronnie's aid. Outwardly calm, he swallowed again, picked a piece of fluff off his left sleeve, and cleared his throat.

'There's something on your chest.'

He paused.

'It looks like "Sue".'

He paused again.

'"Sue",' he said casually, 'with a heart round it.'

The hard jagged substance seemed to have transferred itself to Monty's throat. There was a brief silence while he disposed of it.

He was blaming himself. Rummy, he reflected ruefully, how when you saw a thing day after day for a couple of years or so it ceased to make any impression on what he rather fancied was called the retina. This heart-encircled 'Sue', this pink and ultramarine tribute to a long-vanished love, which in a gush of romantic fervour he had caused to be graven on his skin in the early days of their engagement, might during the last eighteen months just as well not have been there for all the notice he had taken of it. He had practically forgotten that it was still in existence.

It was a moment for quick thinking.

'Not "Sue",' he said. '"S.U.E."—Sarah Ursula Ebbsmith.'

'What!'

'Sarah Ursula Ebbsmith,' repeated Monty firmly. 'Girl I used to be engaged to. She died. Pneumonia. Very sad. Don't let's talk of it.'

There was a long pause. Ronnie moved to the door. His feelings were almost too deep for words, but he managed a couple.

'Well, bung-o!'

The door closed behind him.

S ue had watched the storm from the broad window-seat of the library. Her feelings were mixed. As a spectacle she enjoyed it, for she was fond of thunderstorms. The only thing that spoiled it for her was the knowledge that Monty was out in it. She had seen him cross the terrace in an outwardbound direction just as it began to break. The poor lamb, she felt, must be getting soaked.

Her first act, accordingly, when the rain stopped and that sea of blue began to spread itself over the sky, was to go out on to the balcony and scan the horizon, like Sister Ann, for signs of him. She was thus enabled to witness his return and to hear the brief exchange of remarks between him and Ronnie.

'Hullo.'

'Hullo.'

'You're wet.'

'Yes.'

'By Jove, you *are* wet. You'd better go and change.'

'Yes.'

'Into something dry.'

Considered as dialogue, not, perhaps, on the highest level. Reading it through, one sees that it lacks a certain something. But the noblest effort of a great dramatist could not have stirred Sue more. It seemed to her, as she listened, that a great weight had rolled off her heart.

It was the way Ronnie had spoken that impressed and thrilled. The kindly, considerate tone. The cheerful cordiality. For two days it had been as though some sullen changeling had taken his place; and now, if one could judge from the genial ring of his voice, the old Ronnie was back again.

She stood on the balcony, drinking in the fragrant air. It was astonishing what a change that healing storm had brought about. Shropshire, which yesterday had been so depressing a spectacle, was now an earthly Paradise. The lake glittered. The river shone. The spinneys were their friendly selves again. Rabbits were darting about in the park with all the old carefree abandon, and as far as the eye could reach there were contented cows.

She left the room, humming a little tune. Eventually, she would seek out Monty and make inquiries after his well-being, but her immediate desire was to find Ronnie.

The click of billiard-balls arrested her attention as she came to the foot of the stairs. Gally, probably, playing a solitary hundred up; but he might be able to tell her where Ronnie was. His voice during that conversation with Monty had seemed to come from one of the passage windows.

She opened the door, and Ronnie, sprawled over the table, looked up at her.

That tattoo-mark had settled things for Ronnie. It had swept away in an instant all the gay optimism brought by the passing of the storm. With a heart like lead, he had groped his way downstairs. The open door of the billiard-room had seemed to offer a means of diverting his thoughts temporarily, and he had gone in and begun to practise sombre cannons. For even if a man is leaden-hearted there is no harm in his brushing up his near-the-cushion game a bit. Indeed, it is an intelligent thing to do, for if the girl he loves loves another his life is obviously going to be pretty much of a blank for the next fifty years or so, and he will have to fall back for solace on his ambitions. One of Ronnie's ambitions was some day to make a flukeless break of thirty.

'Hullo,' he said politely, straightening himself and standing with cue at rest. Eton and Cambridge stood at his elbow, to help him through this ordeal.

No sense of impending disaster came to Sue. To her, this man was still the sort of modern Cheeryble Brother whom she had heard chatting so gaily out of the window.

'Oh, Ronnie,' she said, 'you can't stay indoors on an evening like this. It's simply lovely out.'

'Oh, yes?' said Eton.

'Perfectly wonderful.'

'Oh, yes?' said Cambridge.

Something seemed to stab at Sue's heart. Her eyes widened. A numbing thought had begun to frame itself. Could it be that that sunny geniality which she had so recently observed playing upon Monty Bodkin like a fountain was to be withheld from her?

But she persevered.

'Let's go for a drive in your car.'

'I don't think I will, thanks.'

'Then let's take a boat out on the lake.'

'Not for me, thanks.'

'Or the court might be dry enough for tennis by now.'

'I shouldn't think so.'

'Well, then, come for a walk.'

'Oh, for God's sake,' said Ronnie, 'let me alone!'

They stared at one another. Ronnie's eyes were hot and miserable. But they did not look hot and miserable to Sue. She read in them only the dislike, the sullen, trapped dislike of a man tied to a girl for whom he has ceased to feel any affection, so that merely to speak to her is an affliction to his nerves. She drew a deep breath, and walked to the window.

'Sorry,' said Ronnie gruffly. 'Shouldn't have said that.'

'I'm glad you did,' said Sue. 'It's better to come right out with these things.'

She traced little circles with her finger on the glass. A heavy silence filled the room.

'I think we might as well chuck it, don't you?' she said.

'Just as you say,' said Ronnie.

'All right,' said Sue.

She moved to the door. He hurried forward and opened it for her. Polite to the last.

Up in his bedroom, meanwhile, anointing his chest with Riggs's Golden Balm, Monty Bodkin had suddenly become amazingly cheerful.

'Tiddly-iddly-om, pom-POM,' he chanted, as blithely as any thrush in the shrubbery below.

A great idea had just come to him.

It was the embrocation that had done the trick. As he stood there enjoying the immediate warm glow and the delightful sensation of *bien-être*, it was as if his brain, as well as his muscular tissues, had been toned up and renovated. This bottle of embrocation, it suddenly occurred to him, was more than a mere three or four fluid ounces of stuff that smelled like a miasmic swamp—it was a symbol. If Ronnie was taking the trouble to bring him bottles of embrocation, it must mean that all was well between them; that that odd coldness had ceased to be; that his dear old pal, in a word, was once more a dear old pal. And if a man is a dear old pal, it stands to reason that he will be delighted to do a fellow a good turn.

The good turn Monty wanted Ronnie to do for him now was to go to Beach and use his influence with that obdurate butler to persuade him to cough up that manuscript.

It was not that Monty had lost faith in Pilbeam. No doubt, if given time, Pilbeam, exercising his subtle craft, would be able to secure the thing all right. But why go to all that trouble when you could take a short cut and work the wheeze quite simply without any fuss? Besides, there was the fellow's fee to be considered. These sleuths probably came pretty high, and a penny saved is a penny earned.

A room-to-room search brought him to where the Last of the Fishes was once more practising cannons. He approached him with all the happy confidence of a child entering the presence of a rich and indulgent uncle.

For Monty Bodkin was no mind-reader. He had detected no change in his friend's manner at the end of their recent interview. It had been awkward for a moment, no doubt, that business of the tattoo-mark, but he felt that his quick thinking had passed off a tricky situation pretty neatly, satisfactorily lulling all possible suspicions.

'I say, Ronnie, old lad,' he said, 'I wonder if you could spare me a moment of your valuable time?'

Ronnie laid the cue down carefully. For all that he had now resigned himself to the fact that Sue preferred this man to him, he was conscious of a well-defined desire to bat him over the head with the butt end.

White-hot knives were gashing Ronnie Fish's soul, and he could not but feel a very vivid distaste for the man responsible for his raw misery.

'Well?' he said.

It seemed to Monty that his friend was a bit on the chilly side, not quite the effervescing chum of the dear old embrocation days, but he carried on with only a momentary twinge of concern.

'Tell me, old man, how do you stand with Beach?'

'With Beach? How do you mean?'

'Well, does he feel pretty feudal where you're concerned? Would he, in fine, be inclined to stretch a point to oblige the young master?'

Ronnie stared bleakly. He had been prepared to be civil to this man who had wrecked his life, but he was dashed if he was going to spend the evening listening to him talking drip.

'What is all this bilge?' he demanded sourly. 'Come to the point.'

'Oh, I'm coming to the point.'

'Well, be quick.'

'I will, I will. Here, then, is the gist or nub. Beach has got something I badly want, and he refuses to disgorge. And I thought that perhaps if you went to him and did the Young Squire a bit—exerting your influence, I mean to say, and rather throwing your weight about generally—he might prove more . . . what's the word . . . begins with an A . . . amenable.'

Ronnie glowered wearily.

'I can't understand a damn thing you're talking about.'

'Well, in a nutshell, Beach has got that book of old Gally's and I can't get him to let me have it.'

'Why do you want it?'

Monty decided, as he had done when talking with Lord Tilbury by the potting-shed, that manly frankness was the only policy.

'You know all about that book?'

'Yes.'

'That Gally won't let it be published, I mean?'

'Yes.'

'And that he had signed a contract for it with the Mammoth Publishing Company?'

'No. I didn't know that.'

'Well, he did. And his backing out has rendered poor old Pop Tilbury, the boss of same, as sick as mud. Well, naturally, I mean to say, Old Tilbury had got serial rights and book rights and American rights and every other kind of rights including the Scandinavian, and you know what a packet there is in any literary effort that really dishes the dirt about the blue-gored. I should say, taking it one way and another, he stands to lose in the neighbourhood of twenty thousand quid if Gally sticks to his resolve not to publish. And so, to cut a long story s., old man, this Tilbury is so anxious to get hold of the manuscript that he states specifically that if I can snitch it from him he will take me back into his employment—from which, as I dare say you know, I was recently booted out.'

'I thought you resigned.'

Monty smiled sadly.

'That may be the story going the round of the clubs,' he said, 'but as a matter of actual fact I was booted out. There was a spot of technical trouble which wouldn't interest you and into which I will not go. Suffice it to say that we did not see eye to eye as regarded the conduct of the Uncle Woggly to his Chicks department, and my services were dispensed with. So now you get the run of the scenario. The thing is a straight issue. Let me grab this MS. and turn it in to the Big Chief, and I start working again at Tilbury House.'

'What do you want to do that for?'

'It's imperative. I must have a job.'

'I should have thought that you would have been happy enough here.'

'Ah, but I'm liable to get the sack here at any moment.'

'Too bad.'

'Quite bad enough,' agreed Monty. 'But it'll be all right if you can induce Beach to give up that manuscript. I shall then secure a long-term contract with old Tilbury and be in a posish to marry the girl I love.'

A strong convulsion shook Ronnie Fish. This, he considered, was pretty raw. A nice thing, taking a fellow's girl away from him and then coming to him to ask him to help him marry her. He had credited the other with more delicacy.

'You will, eh?' he said, after a pause to master his emotion.

'Positively. It's all fixed up.'

'Who is she?' asked Ronnie sardonically. 'Sarah Ursula Ebbsmith?'

'Eh? Oh, ah,' said Monty hastily. He had forgotten for the moment. 'No, not poor dear Sarah. Oh, no, no, no. She's dead. Tuberculosis. Very sad.'

'You told me it was pneumonia.'

'No, tuberculosis.'

'I see.'

'This is a new one. Girl named Gertrude Butterwick.'

Misunderstandings being always unfortunate, it was a pity, firstly, that Monty should have paused for a reverent second before uttering that sacred name and, secondly, that the girl of his dreams should have possessed a name which, one has to admit, sounded a little thin. In certain moods, a man whose mind is biased simply does not believe that there is such a name as Gertrude Butterwick. To Ronnie, noting that second's hesitation, it was just one this man had made up on the spur of the moment, even he not having the face to tell Sue's fiancé, as he supposed him still to be, that he wanted his assistance in taking Sue from him.

'Gertrude Butterwick, eh?'

'That's right.'

'Fond of her?'

'My dear chap!'

'And I suppose she's crazy about you?'

'Oh, deeply enamoured.'

Ronnie felt suddenly listless. What, he asked himself, did it matter, anyway? What did anything matter now?

Every man is tempted at times by the great gesture. This temptation had just come overwhelmingly upon Ronnie Fish. From the other's words he had become confirmed in his suspicion that somehow or other Monty since their last meeting must have lost all his money. Otherwise, why should jobs at Tilbury House be of such importance to him?

Unless he got that job at Tilbury House, he would not be able to marry Sue. And unless he, Ronnie Fish, helped him, he would not get it.

The Sidney Carton spirit descended upon Ronnie—with this difference, that where Sidney, if one remembers correctly, was rather pleased about the whole thing he himself felt bitter and defiant.

Monty had taken Sue from him. Sue had gone to Monty without a pang. All right, then. All jolly right. He would show them he didn't care. He would let them see the stuff Fishes were made of.

'Listen,' he said. 'There's no need to worry about Beach. He hasn't got that manuscript.'

'Oh, yes, he has. I saw him reading . . .'

'He gave it to me,' said Ronnie. He picked up his cue and shaped at the spot ball. 'You'll find it in the chest of drawers in my room. Take the damned thing if you want it.'

Monty gasped. No Israelite caught in a sudden manna-shower in mid-desert could have felt a greater mixture of surprise and gratification.

'My dear old man!' he began effusively.

Ronnie did not speak. He was practicing cannons.

THE passing of the storm had left the Hon. Galahad Threepwood at rather a loose end. He was not quite sure where he wanted to go or what he wanted to do. His favourite lawn, he knew, would be too wet to walk on, his favourite deck-chair too wet to sit in. The whole world out of doors, in fact, for all that the sun was shining so brightly, was much too moist and dripping to attract a man with his feline dislike of dampness.

After Beach had left him, he had remained for a while in the small library. Then, tiring of that, he had wandered aimlessly about the house, winding as many clocks as he could find. He was, and always had been, a great clock-winder. Eventually, he had drifted to the hall, and was now lounging on a settee there in the hope that, if he lounged long enough, somebody would come along with whom he might chat till it was time to dress for dinner. He always found this part of the evening a little depressing.

Up to the present, he had had no luck. Monty Bodkin had come downstairs, but after Beach's revelations he had no wish to do anything but glower sternly at Monty. Without attempting to draw him into conversation, though he had just remembered a thirty-year-old Limerick which he would have liked to recite to someone, he watched him go into the billiard-room, where the opening door showed a glimpse of Ronnie practising cannons. Presently, he had come out again and gone upstairs, followed as before by that stern eye.

'Young toad!' muttered the Hon. Galahad severely. He was shocked at Monty, and disappointed in him. He wished he had never given him that tip on the Cesarewitch.

Soon after this, Pilbeam had appeared, smiled weakly, and gone into the smoking-room. Here, again, there was nothing for the Hon. Galahad to work on. He had no desire to tell Limericks to Pilbeam. Apart from the fact that the fellow was conspiring with his sister Constance to steal his manuscript, he did not like the detective. Brought up in a sterner school of hairdressing, he disapproved of these modern young men who went about with their fungoid growth in sticky ridges.

It began to look to him as if in the matter of society he had but two choices open. Clarence, who would have appreciated that Limerick once he could have been induced to bring his mind to bear upon it, was presumably down at the sty making eyes at that pig of his; and Sue, the person he really wanted to talk to, seemed to have disappeared off the face of the earth. As far as he could see, he was reduced to the alternatives of going into the billiard-room and joining Ronnie, and of stepping up to the drawing-room and having a word with his sister Constance, who at this hour would no doubt be taking tea there. He was just about to adopt this second course, for he rather wanted a straight talk with Constance about that Pilbeam matter, when Sue came in from the garden.

Immediately, the idea of tackling Connie left him. He could do that at his leisure, and he was in the mood now for something pleasanter than a brother-and-sister dog-fight. Sue's bright personality was just the tonic he needed at this lowering point in the day's progress. He would be unable to tell her the Limerick, it not being that sort of Limerick, but at any rate they could talk of this and that.

He called to her, and she came over to where he sat. It was dim in the hall, but it struck him that she was not looking quite herself. The elasticity seemed to have gone out of her walk, that jaunty suppleness which he had always admired so in Dolly. But possibly this was merely his imagination. He was always inclined to read a fictitious sombreness into things when the shadows began to creep over the world and it was still too early for a cocktail.

'Well, young woman.'

'Hullo, Gally.'

'What have you been doing with yourself?'

'I was walking on the terrace.'

'Get your feet wet?'

'I don't think so. Perhaps I had better go up and change my shoes, though.'

The Hon. Galahad would have none of this. He pulled her down on to the settee beside him.

'Amuse me,' he said. 'I'm bored.'

'Poor Gally. I'm sorry.'

'This,' said the Hon. Galahad, 'is the hour of the day that searches a man out. It makes him examine his soul. And I don't want to examine my soul. I expect the thing looks like an old boot. So, as I say, amuse me, child. Sing to me. Dance before me. Ask me riddles.'

'I'm afraid . . .'

The Hon. Galahad gave her a sharp glance through his monocle. It was as he had suspected. This girl was not festive.

'Anything the matter?'

'Oh, no.'

'Sure?'

'Quite.'

'Cigarette?'

'No, thanks.'

'Shall I turn on the radio? There may be a lecture on Newts.'

'No, don't.'

'There *is* something the matter?'

'There isn't, really.'

The Hon. Galahad frowned. Then a possible solution occurred to him.

'I suppose it's the heat.'

'It was hot, wasn't it. It's better now.'

'You're under the weather.'

'I am a little.'

'Thunderstorms often upset people. Are you afraid of thunder?'

'Oh, no.'

'Lots of girls are. I knew one once who, whenever there was a thunderstorm, used to fling her arms round the neck of the nearest man, hugging and kissing him till it was all over. Purely nervous reaction, of course, but you should have seen the young fellows flocking round as soon as the sky began to get a little overcast. Gladys, her name was. Gladys Twistleton. Beautiful girl with large, melting eyes. Married a fellow in the Blues called Harringay. I'm told that the way he used to clear the drawing-room during the early years of their married life at the first suspicion of a rumble was a sight to be seen and remembered.'

The Hon. Galahad had brightened. Like all confirmed raconteurs, he took on new life when the anecdotes started to come briskly.

'Talking of thunder,' he said, 'did I ever tell you the story of Puffy Benger and the thunderstorm?'

'I don't think so.'

'It was one time when Plug Basham and I and a couple of other fellows had gone to stay with him in a cottage he had down in Somersetshire, for a bit of fishing. Puffy, I ought to tell you, was one of those chaps who are always drawing the long bow. Charming man, but a shocking liar. He had a niece he was always bragging about. His niece could do this, and his niece could do that. She was one of these business girls—must have been about the first of them—and he was very proud of her. And one day when we had been driven indoors by a thunderstorm and were sitting round yarning, he happened to mention that she was the quickest typist in England.'

Sue was leaning forward with her chin in her hands.

'Well, we said "Oh, yes!" and "Fancy!" and so on—the fellow was our host—and there the thing would have ended, no doubt, only Puffy, who could never let anything alone, went on to say that this girl's proficiency as a typist had had a most remarkable effect on her piano-playing. It wasn't that it had improved it—it had always been perfect—but it had speeded it up quite a good deal. "In fact," said Puffy, "you won't believe this, but it's true, she can now play Chopin's Funeral March in forty-eight seconds!"

'This was a bit too much for us, of course. "Not forty-eight seconds?" said somebody. "Forty-eight seconds," insisted Puffy firmly. He said he had frequently timed her on his stop-watch. And then Plug Basham, who was always an outspoken sort of chap, took the licence of an old friend to tell Puffy he was the biggest liar in the country, not even excluding Dogface Weeks, the then champion of the Pelican Club. "It isn't safe sitting in the same house with you during a thunderstorm," said Plug. "Why isn't it safe sitting in the same house with me during a thunderstorm?" said Puffy. "Because at any moment," said Plug, "the Almighty is liable to strike it with lightning. That's why it isn't safe." "Listen," said Puffy, a good deal worked up. "If my niece Myrtle can't play Chopin's Funeral March in forty-eight seconds, I hope this house *will* be struck by lightning this very minute." And by what I have always thought rather an odd coincidence, it was. There was a sort of sheet of fire and a fearful crash, and the next thing I saw was Puffy crawling out from under the table. He seemed more aggrieved than frightened, I remember. He gave one reproachful look up at the ceiling, and then he said in a peevish sort of voice, "You do take a chap so dashed literally!"'

He paused.

'Yes?' said Sue.

Most raconteurs would have found the observation a little dampening. The Hon. Galahad was no exception.

'How do you mean, yes?' he asked, with something of the querulousness exhibited on that other occasion by Puffy Benger.

'Oh, I'm sorry,' said Sue with a start. 'I'm afraid . . . What were you saying, Gally?'

The Hon. Galahad took her chin firmly and, tilting her face up, stared accusingly into her eyes.

'Now, then,' he said, 'no more of this nonsense about there being nothing the matter. What's the trouble?'

'Oh, Gally!' said Sue.

'Good God!' cried the Hon. Galahad, stricken with the cold horror that comes upon a man who finds he is holding the chin of a crying girl.

. . .

It was a stern, hard-faced Galahad Threepwood who entered the billiard-room some ten minutes later. His hair seemed to bristle, his
black-rimmed monocle to shoot forth flame.

'Ah, there you are!' he observed curtly, as he closed the door.

Ronnie looked up wanly. Since the departure of Monty Bodkin, he
had been sitting hunched up in a corner, staring at nothing.

'Hullo,' he said.

Despite the fact that his own company had been the reverse of enjoyable, he did not welcome his uncle's arrival. He was fond of the Hon.
Galahad, but at the moment had no wish for his society. What a man on
the rack wants is solitude. He supposed that the other had come to suggest a friendly game of snooker, and the mere thought of playing friendly
games of snooker with anyone made him feel sick.

'I was just off,' he said, to nip this project in the bud.

The Hon. Galahad swelled like a little turkey-cock. His monocle was
now a perfect searchlight.

'Just off be damned!' he snorted. 'You sit down and listen to me. Just
off, indeed! You can go off when I've finished talking to you, and not
before.'

Ronnie abandoned the snooker theory. Plainly it did not cover the
facts. His moroseness had become tinged with bewilderment. It was
many years since he had beheld his good-natured relative in a mood like
this. It seemed to bring back the tang of the brave old days of chimney-
stacks and whangees. He could think of nothing in his recent conduct
that could have caused so impressive an upheaval.

'Now, then,' said the Hon. Galahad, 'what's all this?'

'That's just what I was going to ask,' said Ronnie. 'What *is* all this?'

'Don't pretend you don't know.'

'But I don't know.'

'It's no good taking that attitude.' The Hon. Galahad jerked his thumb
at the door. 'I've just been talking to young Sue out there.'

A thin coating of ice seemed to creep over Ronald Fish.

'Oh, yes?' he said politely.

'She's crying.'

'Oh, yes?' said Ronnie, still politely, but with those white-hot knives at work on his soul again. His mind was divided against itself. Part of it was pointing out passionately that it was ghastly to think of Sue in tears. The other part was raising its eyebrows and shooting its cuffs and observing with a sneer that it was blowed if it could see what *she* had to cry about.

'Crying, I tell you! Crying her dashed eyes out!'

'Oh, yes?'

The Hon. Galahad Threepwood was himself an Old Etonian, and in his time had frequently had occasion to employ the Eton manner to the undoing of his fellow-men. There were grey-haired bookies and elderly card-sharps going about London to this day, who still felt an occasional twinge, as of an old wound, when they recalled the agony of seeing him stare at them as Ronnie was staring and of hearing him say 'Oh, yes?' as Ronnie was saying it now. But this did not make his nephew's attitude any the easier for him to endure. The whole point of the Eton manner, as of a shotgun, is that you have to be at the right end of it.

He brought his fist down on the billiard-table with a thump.

'So you're not interested, eh? You don't care? Well, let me tell you,' said the Hon. Galahad, once more maltreating the billiard-table, 'that I do care. That girl's mother was the only woman I ever loved, and I don't propose to have her daughter's happiness ruined by any sawn-off young half-portion with a face like a strawberry ice who takes the notion into his beastly turnip of a head to play fast and loose with her. Understand that!'

There were so many ramifications to this insult that Ronnie was compelled to take them in rotation.

'I can't help it if my face is like a strawberry ice,' he said, electing to begin with that one.

'It ought to be much more like a strawberry ice. You ought to be blushing yourself sick.'

'And when,' said Ronnie, feeling on safe ground here, 'you talk about sawn-off half-portions, may I point out that I'm about an inch taller than you are?'

'Rot!' said the Hon. Galahad, stung.

'I am.'

'You're certainly not.'

'Measure you against the wall,' insisted Ronnie.

'I'll do nothing of the sort. And what the devil,' demanded the Hon. Galahad, suddenly aware that the main issue of debate was becoming shelved, 'has that got to do with it? You may be a giraffe, for all I care. The point I am endeavouring to make is that you are breaking this girl's heart, and I'm not going to have it. She tells me your engagement is off.'

'Quite right.'

Once more the Hon. Galahad smote the green cloth.

'You'll smash that table,' said Ronnie.

There flashed into the Hon. Galahad's mind the story of how old Beefy Muspratt, with some assistance, actually had smashed a billiard-table in the year ninety-eight; and such is the urge to the raconteur's ruling passion that he almost stopped to tell it. Then he recovered himself.

'Curse the table!' he cried. 'I didn't come here to talk about tables. I came to tell you that, if you care to know what a calm, unprejudiced observer thinks of you, you're an infernal young snob . . . and a hound . . .'

'What!'

'. . . . and a worm,' went on the Hon. Galahad, as pink himself now as any pink-faced nephew. 'Do you think I can't see what's happened? If you want to know, Sue told me herself. Told me in so many words, out there in the hall just now. You're such a wambling, spineless, invertebrate jellyfish that you've let your mother talk you into breaking off this engagement. You've allowed her to persuade you that that poor child isn't good enough for you.'

'What!'

'As if Dolly Henderson's daughter wasn't good enough for the finest man in the kingdom—let alone a . . .'

On the brink of becoming a little personal again, the Hon. Galahad found himself interrupted. This time it was Ronnie who had thumped the table.

'Don't talk such absolute dashed nonsense!' thundered Ronnie. 'You don't suppose I broke off the engagement, do you? Sue broke it off herself.'

'Yes, because she could see that you wanted to get out of it and, being the splendid girl she is, wasn't going to cheapen herself by hanging on to a man who was obviously dying to be rid of her.'

'I like that! Dying to be rid of her! I . . . I . . . Why, damn it!'

'You aren't telling me you're still fond of her?'

'What do you mean, still? And what do you mean, fond of her? Fond of her! My God!'

The Hon. Galahad was astounded.

'Then what on earth have you been going about for these last few days like a spavined frog? Treating her as if . . .'

His manner softened. He began to see daylight. He could not lay his hand gently on his nephew's shoulder, for they were at opposite sides of a regulation-sized billiard-table. But he infused a gentle hand-laying into his voice.

'I see it all! You were worrying about something else; is that it? Or was it the heat? Anyhow, for some reason you allowed yourself to be odd in your manner. My dear boy, when you get to my age you'll know better than to take chances like that. Never be odd in your manner with a woman. Don't you realize that, even under the best of conditions, there's practically nothing that won't make a sensitive, highly strung girl break off her engagement? If she doesn't like her new hat . . . or if her stocking starts a ladder . . . or if she comes down late to breakfast and finds all the scrambled eggs are finished. It's like servants giving notice. I had a man back in the nineties—Spatchett, his name was—who used to give me notice every time he backed a horse that didn't finish in the first three. Why, he gave me notice once purely and simply because his wife's sister had had a baby. I never paid any attention to it. I knew it was just a form of emotional expression. Where you or I would have lit a cigarette, Spatchett gave notice. And it's the same with women. No doubt Sue saw you brooding and assumed that love was dead. Well, this has certainly eased my mind, Ronnie, my dear boy. I'll go and explain things to her at once.'

'Half a minute, Uncle Gally.'

'Eh?'

Pausing half-way to the door, the Hon. Galahad saw that a peculiar expression had come into his nephew's face. An expression a little like that of a young Hindu fakir who, having settled himself on his first bed of spikes, is beginning to wish that he had chosen one of the easier religions.

'I'm afraid it isn't quite so simple as that,' said Ronnie.

The Hon. Galahad drew in the slack of his monocle, which in the recent excitement had fallen from his eye. He screwed the thing into place, and surveyed his nephew inquiringly.

'What do you mean?'

'You've got it all wrong. Sue doesn't love me.'

'Nonsense!'

'It isn't nonsense. She's in love with Monty Bodkin.'

'What!'

'It's all settled between them that they're going to get married.'

'I never heard such . . .'

'Oh, it's perfectly true,' said Ronnie, his mouth twisting. 'I'm not blaming her. Nobody's fault. Just one of those things. Still, there it is. She's crazy about him. She went up to London to meet him the moment I was out of the place, just because she couldn't keep away from him. She got him to apply for Hugo's job as Uncle Clarence's secretary, just because she was so keen to have him here. She was up on the roof with him all yesterday afternoon. And . . .' Ronnie had to pause for a moment here to control his voice '. . . he's got her name tattooed on his chest, with a heart round it.'

'You don't mean that?'

'I saw it myself.'

'Well, I'm dashed! Hurts like sin, that sort of thing. I haven't heard of anybody having a girl's name tattooed on him since the year ninety-nine, when Jack Bellamy-Johnstone . . .'

Ronnie held up a restraining hand.

'Not now, uncle, if you don't mind.'

'Most amusing story,' said the Hon. Galahad, wistfully.

'Later on, what?'

'Well, yes, perhaps you're right,' admitted the Hon. Galahad. 'I suppose you're not in the mood for stories. It was simply that poor old Jack fell in love with a girl named Esmeralda Parkinson-Willoughby and had the whole thing tattooed on his wish-bone, and the wounds had scarcely healed when they quarrelled and he got engaged to another girl called May Todd. So if he had only waited . . . However, as you say, that is neither here nor there. Ronnie, my dear boy,' said the Hon. Galahad, 'this beats me. I had always looked on you as a pretty average sort of young poop, but never, never would I have imagined that you could have allowed yourself to believe all that drivel . . .'

'Drivel!'

'Perfect drivel. You've got hold of the wrong end of the stick entirely. Suppose Sue did go to London . . .'

'There's no supposition about it. My mother saw her and Monty lunching together at the Berkeley.'

'She would. Dashed Nosey Parker. Sorry, my boy. Forgot she was your mother. Still, she was my sister before you were ever born or thought of, and I hope a man can call his own sister a Nosey Parker. What did she tell you?'

'She said . . .'

'All right. Never mind. I can guess. No doubt she's been filling you up with all sorts of stories. Well, now you can hear the truth. Young Sue had nothing whatever to do with Monty Bodkin coming here. The first she heard of his having been taken on as Clarence's secretary was from me, and the news absolutely bowled her over. I can see her now, looking at me like a dying duck and saying here was a nice bit of box-fruit because she had once, when a mere child, been engaged to the fellow . . .'

'What!'

'Certainly. Years ago. Before she ever met you. Only lasted a week or two, as far as I can gather, and she was glad to get out of it. But there the fact was. She had been engaged to him, and he was coming here, and if he wasn't tipped off to keep the thing dark he would be sure to say something tactless about the old days, and that would upset you, because you were such a blasted jealous half-wit, always ready to make heavy weather about nothing. She asked me what she ought to do. I gave her the only possible advice. I told her to rush up to London before you got back, get hold of Monty, and tell him to keep his mouth shut. Which she did. That is how she came to be in London that day, and that is why she was lunching with him. So there you are. The whole thing, you observe, done from start to finish in the kindliest spirit of altruism, with no other motive than to preserve your peace of mind. Perhaps this will be a lesson to you in future not to give way to jealousy, which I have always said and always shall say is one of the dashed silliest . . .'

Ronnie was staring, perplexed in the extreme.

'Is this true?'

'Of course it's true. If you can't see by this time that Sue is a girl in a million—pure gold—and that you've been treating her abominably . . .'

'But she was up on the roof with him.'

The childishness of this seemed to nettle the Hon. Galahad. He uttered a sound which was rather like Lord Tilbury's 'Cor!'

'Why shouldn't she be up on the roof with him? Must people be in love with one another just because they are up on roofs together? I was up on that roof with you once, but if you thought I was in love with you you must have been singularly obtuse. It's been a grief to me for years that you were so nippy round that chimney-stack. Sue in love with young Bodkin, indeed! Why, Monty Bodkin is engaged himself. She told me so. To a girl named Gertrude Butterwick. Butterwick,' said the Hon. Galahad musingly. 'I used to know several Butterwicks. I wonder if she would be any relation to old Legs Butterwick, who used to paint his face with red spots to make duns who called at his rooms think he'd got smallpox.'

A shuddering groan burst from the lips of Ronnie Fish.

'Oh, gosh, what a fool I've made of myself!'

'You have.'

'I'm a hound and a cad.'

'You are.'

'I ought to be kicked.'

'You ought.'

'Of all the . . .'

'Hold it,' urged the Hon. Galahad. 'Don't waste all this on me. Tell it to Sue. I'll fetch her.'

He darted from the room, to return a moment later, dragging the girl behind him.

'Now!' he said authoritatively. 'Do your stuff. Tie yourself in knots at her feet, and ask her to kick you in the face. Grovel before her on your wretched stomach. Roll about the floor and bark. And while you're doing it I'll be stepping up to the drawing-room and having a word with your mother and my sister Constance.'

A stern, resolute look came into the Hon. Galahad's face.

'I'll spoil their tea and shrimps!' he said.

I n the drawing-room, however, when he arrived there after taking the stairs three at a time in that juvenile way of his which gout-crippled contemporaries so resented, he found only his sister Julia. She was seated in an armchair, smoking a cigarette and reading an illustrated weekly paper. The tea which he had hoped to spoil was in the process of being cleared away by Beach and a footman.

She looked contented, and she was feeling contented. Ronnie's growing gloom during the past two days had not escaped her. In a mood to be genial to everybody, even to one on whom she had always looked as the Family Blot, she welcomed the Hon. Galahad with a pleasant nod.

'You're late, if you've come for tea,' she said.

'Tea!' snorted the Hon. Galahad.

He stood fuming until the door closed.

'Now, then, Julia,' he said, 'I want a word with you.'

Lady Julia raised her shapely eyebrows.

'My dear Galahad! This is very menacing and ominous. Is something the matter?'

'You know what's the matter. Where's Connie?'

'Gone to answer the telephone, I believe.'

'Well, you'll do to start with.'

'Galahad, really!'

'Put down that paper.'

'Oh, very well.'

The Hon. Galahad strode to the hearthrug and stood with his back to the empty fireplace. Racial instinct made him feel more authoritative in that position. He frowned forbiddingly.

'Julia, you make me sick.'

'Indeed? Why is that?'

'What the devil do you mean by trying to poison young Ronnie's mind against Sue Brown?'

'Really, Galahad!'

'Do you deny that that is what you have been doing ever since you got here?'

'I may have pointed out to him once or twice the inadvisability of marrying a girl who appears to be in love with another man. If this be treason, make the most of it. Surely it's a tenable theory?'

'You think she's in love with young Bodkin?'

'Apparently.'

'If you will step down to the billiard-room,' said the Hon. Galahad, 'I think you may possibly alter your opinion.'

Something of Lady Julia's self-confidence left her.

'What do you mean?'

'Touching,' said the Hon. Galahad unctuously. 'That's what it was. Touching. It nearly made me cry. I never saw a more united couple. All their doubts and misunderstandings cleared away . . .'

'What!'

'Locked in each other's arms, weeping on each other's chests . . . you ought to go down and have a look, Julia. You'll be in plenty of time. It's evidently going to be one of those non-stop performances. Well, anyway, that's the first thing I came up here to tell you. You have been taking a lot of trouble to ruin this girl's happiness these last few days, and now you are getting official intimation that you haven't succeeded. They are all right, those two. Sweethearts still is the term.'

The Hon. Galahad spread his coat-tails to the invisible blaze and resumed.

'The other thing I came to say is that there must be no more of this nonsense. If you have objections to young Ronnie marrying Sue, don't mention them to him. It worries him and makes him moody, and that worries Sue and makes her unhappy, and that worries me and spoils my day. You understand?'

Lady Julia was shaken, but she had not lost her spirit.

'I'm afraid you must make up your mind to having your days spoiled, Galahad.'

'You don't mean that even after this you intend to keep making a pest of yourself?'

'You put these things so badly. What you are trying to say, I imagine, is do I still intend to give my child a mother's advice? Certainly I do. A boy's best friend is his mother, don't you sometimes think? Ronnie, handicapped by being virtually half-witted, may not have seen fit to take my advice as yet; but if in the old days you ever had a moment to spare from your life-work of being thrown out of shady night-clubs and were able to look in at the Adelphi Theatre, you may remember the expression "A time will come!"'

The Hon. Galahad stared at this indomitable woman with something that was almost admiration.

'Well, I'm dashed!'

'Are you?'

'You always were a tough nut, Julia.'

'Thank you.'

'Always. Even as a child. It used to interest me in those days to watch you gradually dawning on the latest governess. I could have read her thoughts in her face, poor devil. First, she would meet Connie and you could almost hear her saying to herself "Hullo! A vicious specimen this one." And then you would come along, all wide, innocent blue eyes and flaxen curls, and she would feel a great wave of relief and fling her arms round you; thinking "Well, here's one that's all right, thank God!" Little knowing that she had just come up against the stoniest-hearted, beastliest-natured, and generally most poisonous young human rattle-snake in all Shropshire.'

Lady Julia seemed genuinely pleased at this tribute. She laughed musically.

'You are silly, Galahad.'

The Hon. Galahad adjusted his monocle.

'So your hat is still in the ring, eh?'

'Still there, my dear.'

'But what have you got against young Sue?'

'I don't like chorus-girls as daughters-in-law.'

'But, great heavens above, Julia, surely you can see that Sue isn't the sort of girl you mean when you say "chorus-girls" in that beastly sniffy way?'

'You can't expect me to classify and tabulate chorus-girls. I haven't your experience. They're all chorus-girls to me.'

'There are moments, Julia,' said the Hon. Galahad meditatively, 'when I should like to drown you in a bucket.'

'A butt of malmsey would have been more in your line, I should have thought.'

'Your attitude about young Sue infuriates me. Can't you see the girl's a nice girl . . . a sweet girl . . . and a lady, if it comes to that.'

'Tell me, Gally,' said Lady Julia, 'just as a matter of interest, *is* she your daughter?'

The Hon. Galahad bristled.

'She is not. Her father was a man in the Irish Guards, named Cotterleigh. He and Dolly were married when I was in South Africa.'

He stood for a moment, his mind in the past.

'Fellow told me about it quite casually one day when I was having a drink in a Johannesburg bar,' he said with a far-off look in his eyes. '"I see that girl Dolly Henderson who used to be at the Tivoli has got married," he said. Out of a blue sky . . .'

Lady Julia took up her paper.

'Well, if you have no further observations of interest to make . . .'

The Hon. Galahad came back to the present.

'Oh, I have.'

'Please hurry, then.'

'I have something to say which I fancy will interest you very much.'

'That will make a nice change.'

The Hon. Galahad paused a moment. His sister took advantage of the fact to interject a question.

'It isn't by any chance that, if this marriage of Ronnie's is stopped, you will publish those Reminiscences of yours, is it?'

'It is.'

Lady Julia gave another of her jolly laughs.

'My dear man, I had all that days ago from Constance. And my flesh didn't even creep a bit. It seems to agitate Connie tremendously but speaking for myself I haven't the slightest objection to you publishing a dozen books of Reminiscences. It will be nice to think of you making some money at last, and as for the writhings of the nobility and gentry . . .'

'Julia,' said the Hon. Galahad, 'one moment.'

He eyed her intently. She returned his gaze with an air of faintly bored inquiry.

'Well?'

'You are the relict of the late Major-General Sir Miles Fish, C.B.E., late of the Brigade of Guards.'

'I have never denied it.'

'Let us speak for a while,' said the Hon. Galahad gently, 'of the late Major-General Sir Miles Fish.'

Slowly a look of horror crept into Lady Julia's blue eyes. Slowly she rose from the chair in which she had been reclining. A hideous suspicion had come into her mind.

'When Miles Fish married you,' said the Hon. Galahad, 'he was a respectable—even a stodgily respectable—Colonel. I remember your saying the first time you met him that you thought him slow. Believe me, Julia, when I knew dear old Fishy Fish as a young subaltern, while you were still poisoning governesses' lives at Blandings Castle, he was quite the reverse of slow. His jolly rapidity was the talk of London.'

She stared at him, aghast. Her whole outlook on life, as one might say, had been revolutionized. Hitherto, her attitude towards the famous Reminiscences had been, as it were, airy . . . detached . . . academic is perhaps the word one wants. The thought of the consternation which they would spread among her friends had amused her. But then she had naturally supposed that this man would have exercised a decent reticence about the pasts of his own flesh and blood.

'Galahad! You haven't . . .?'

The historian was pointing a finger at her, like some finger of doom.

'Who rode a bicycle down Piccadilly in sky-blue underclothing in the late summer of '97?'

'Galahad!'

'Who, returning to his rooms in the early morning of New Year's Day, 1902, mistook the coal-scuttle for a mad dog and tried to shoot it with the fire-tongs?'

'Galahad!'

'Who . . .'

He broke off. Lady Constance had come into the room.

'Ah, Connie,' he said genially. 'I've just been having a chat with Julia. Get her to tell you all about it. I must be going down and seeing how the young folks are getting on.'

He paused at the door.

'Supplementary material,' he said, focusing his monocle on Lady Julia, 'will be found in Chapters Three, Eleven, Sixteen, Seventeen, and Twenty-one, especially Chapter Twenty-one.'

With a final beam, he passed jauntily from the room and began to descend the stairs.

In the billiard-room, the scene which he had rightly described as touching was still in progress. He wished he could take a snapshot of it to show to his sister Julia.

'That's right, my boy,' he said cordially. 'Capital!'

Ronnie detached himself and began to straighten his tie. He had not heard the door open.

'Oh, hullo, Uncle Gally,' he said. 'You here?'

Sue ran to the Hon. Galahad and kissed him.

'I shouldn't,' said the gratified but cautious man. 'He'll be getting jealous of me next.'

'There is no need,' said Ronnie with dignity, 'to rub it in.'

'Well, I won't, then. Merely contenting myself with remarking that of all the young poops I ever met . . .'

'He is not a poop!' said Sue.

'My dear,' insisted the Hon. Galahad, 'I was brought up among poops. I spent my formative years among poops. I have been a member of clubs which consisted exclusively of poops. You will allow me to recognize a poop when I see one. Moreover, we won't argue the point. What I want to talk about now is that manuscript of mine.'

A wordless cry broke from Ronnie's lips.

'Poop or no poop,' proceeded the Hon. Galahad, 'he has got to guard that manuscript with his life. Because if ever there were two women who would descend to the level of the beasts of the field to lay their hooks on it . . .'

'Uncle Gally!'

'Ronnie, darling,' cried Sue, 'what is it?'

She might well have asked. The young man's eyes were fixed in a ghastly stare. His usually immaculate hair was disordered where he had thrust a fevered hand through it. Even his waistcoat seemed ruffled.

'. . . they are your mother and Lady Constance,' proceeded the Hon. Galahad, who was never an easy man to interrupt. 'And here's something that will surprise you. Young Monty Bodkin is after the thing, too. Young Bodkin has turned out to be an A1 snake in the grass, I'm sorry to say. He's under orders from the man who runs the firm that was going to publish my book to pinch it and take it to him—Lord Tilbury. I used to know him years ago as Stinker Pyke. Why they ever made young Stinker a peer . . .'

'Uncle Gally!'

A little testily the Hon. Galahad allowed the stream of his eloquence to be diverted at last.

'Well, what is it?'

A sort of frozen calm, the calm of utter despair, had come upon Ronnie Fish.

'Monty Bodkin was in here just now,' he said. 'He wanted that manuscript. I told him where it was. And he went off to get it.'

No joy in the world is ever quite perfect. *Surgit*, as the old Roman said, *aliquid amari*. Monty Bodkin, having removed the manuscript from Ronnie's chest of drawers and gloated over it and taken it to his room and, after gloating over it again, deposited it in a safe place there, found his ecstasy a little dimmed by the thought of the awkward interview with Percy Pilbeam which now faced him. He was a young man who shrank from embarrassing scenes, and it seemed to him that this one threatened to be extremely embarrassing. Pilbeam, he realized, would have every excuse for being as sore as a gumboil.

Look at the thing squarely, he meant to say. A private detective has his feelings. He resents being made a silly ass of. If you commission him to do something, and then buzz off and do it yourself, pique inevitably supervenes. Suppose Sherlock Holmes, for instance, had sweated himself to the bone to recover the Naval Plans or something, and then the Admiralty authorities had come along and observed casually, 'Oh, I say, you know those Naval Plans, old man? Well, don't bother about them. We've just gone and snitched them ourselves.' Pretty sick the poor old human bloodhound would have felt, no doubt. And pretty sick in similar circumstances Monty anticipated that Percy Pilbeam was going to feel. He did not like the job of breaking the news at all.

However, it had to be done. He found the proprietor of the Argus (Pilgus, Piccy, London) in the smoking-room, massaging his moustache, and with some trepidation proceeded to edge into the agenda.

'Oh, there you are, Pilbeam. I say . . .'

The investigator looked up. It increased Monty's feeling of guilt to note that he had evidently been thinking frightfully hard. He had a sort of boiled look.

'Ah, Bodkin, I was just coming to find you. I have been thinking . . .'

Monty's tender heart bled for the fellow, but he supposed it was kindest to let him have it on the chin without preamble.

'I know you have, my poor old sleuth,' he said. 'I can see it in your eye. Well, I've got a bit of bad news for you, I'm afraid. What I came to tell you was to switch off the brain-power. Stop scheming. Put the mind back into neutral. I'm taking you off the case.'

'Eh?'

'I'm sorry, but there it is. You see, what with one thing and another, I've been and got that manuscript myself.'

'What!'

'Yes.'

There was a long pause.

'Well, that's fine,' said Pilbeam. 'I hope you have hidden it carefully?'

'Oh, yes. It's shoved away under the bed in my room. Right up against the wall.'

'Well, that's fine,' said Pilbeam.

His attitude occasioned Monty much relief. He had braced himself up to endure reproaches, to wince beneath recriminations. It seemed to him extraordinarily decent of the man to take it like this. He was dashed, indeed, if he could remember ever having met anyone who, under such provocation, had been so extraordinarily decent.

'What are you going to do with it?' asked Pilbeam.

'I'm taking it down to the Emsworth Arms to a fellow of the name of Tilbury.'

'Not Lord Tilbury?'

'That's right,' said Monty, surprised. 'Do you know him?'

'Before I opened the Argus, I was editor of *Society Spice*.'

'No, really? Fancy that. Before he booted me out, I was assistant editor of *Tiny Tots*. It seems to bring us very close together, what?'

'But why does Lord Tilbury want it?'

'Well, you see, he has a contract with Gally for the book, and when Gally refused to publish he saw himself losing the dickens of a lot of money. Naturally he wants it.'

'I see. He ought to give you a pretty big reward.'

'Oh, I'm not asking him for money. I've got lots of money. What I want is a job. He promised to take me back on *Tiny Tots* if I would get the thing for him.'

'You are leaving here, then?'

Monty chuckled amusedly.

'You bet I'm leaving here. I expect the sack any moment. I'd have got it yesterday, all right,' said Monty, with another chuckle, 'if old Emsworth had happened to come along when I was working on the door of that potting-shed.'

'What was that?'

'Rather amusing. I found old Tilbury locked up in a species of shed yesterday afternoon. Apparently he had been caught in conversation with that pig of the old boy's, offering it potatoes and so forth, and was suspected of trying to poison the animal. So they shut him up in this shed, and I came along and let him out. Just imagine how quick I should be leaving if Emsworth knew that I was the chap who flung wide the gates.'

'My word, yes!' said Pilbeam, laughing genially.

'He'd throw me out in a second.'

'He certainly would.'

'Rummy, his attitude about that pig,' said Monty musingly. 'A few years ago, he used to be crazy about pumpkins. I suppose, if you really face the facts, he's the sort of chap who has to be practically off his rocker about something. Yesterday, pumpkins. Today, pigs. Tomorrow, rabbits. This time next year, roosters or rhododendrons.'

'I suppose so,' said Pilbeam. 'And when are you thinking of taking this manuscript to Lord Tilbury?'

'Right away.'

'I wouldn't do that,' said Pilbeam, shaking his head. 'No, I don't think I would advise you to do that. You want to wait till everybody's dressing for dinner. Suppose you were to run into Threepwood.'

'I never thought of that.'

'Or Lady Constance.'

'Lady Constance?'

'I happen to know that she is trying to get that manuscript. She wants to destroy it.'

'I say! You certainly find things out, don't you?'

'Oh, one keeps one's ears open.'

'I suppose you've got to, if you're a detective. Well, I do seem properly trapped in the den of the Secret Nine, what? I'd better not make a move till dressing for dinner time, as you say. I'm glad you gave me that tip. Thanks.'

'Don't mention it,' said Pilbeam.

He rose.

'You off?' said Monty.

'Yes, I've just remembered there is something I want to speak to Lord Emsworth about. You don't know where he is, do you?'

'Sorry, no. The ninth doesn't confide in me much.'

'I suppose he's in the pigsty.'

'You can tell him by his hat,' said Monty automatically. 'Yes, I imagine he would be. Anything special you wanted to see him about?'

'Just something he asked me to find out for him.'

'In your professional capacity, do you mean? Pilgus, Piccy, London?'

'Yes.'

'Is he employing your services, then?'

'Oh, yes. That's why I'm here.'

'I see,' said Monty.

This made him feel much easier in his mind. If Pilbeam was drawing a nice bit of cash from old Simon Legree, it put a different complexion on everything. Naturally, in that case, he wouldn't so much mind being done out of the Bodkin fee.

Still, he did feel that the fellow had behaved most extraordinarily decently.

Lord Emsworth was not actually in the pigsty, but he was quite near it. It took more than a thunderstorm to drive him from the Empress's side. A vague idea that he was getting a little wet had caused him to take shelter in the potting-shed during the worst of the downpour, but he was now out and about again. When Pilbeam arrived, he was standing by the rails in earnest conversation with Pirbright. He welcomed the detective warmly.

'You're just the man I was wanting to see, my dear Pilbeam,' he said. 'Pirbright and I have been discussing the question of moving the Empress to a new sty. I say Yes, Pirbright says No. One sees his point, of course. I quite see your point, my dear Pirbright. Pirbright's point,' explained Lord Emsworth, 'is that she is used to this sty and moving her to a strange one might upset her and put her off her feed.'

'Quite,' said Pilbeam, profoundly uninterested.

'On the other hand,' proceeded Lord Emsworth, 'we know that there is this sinister cabal against her well-being. Attempts have already been made to nobble her, as I believe the term is. They may be made again. And my view is that this sty here is in far too lonely and remote a spot for safety. God bless my soul,' said Lord Emsworth, deeply moved, 'in a place like this, a quarter of a mile away from anywhere, Parsloe could walk in during the night and do her a mischief without so much as taking the cigar out of his mouth. Where I was thinking of moving her, Pirbright would be within call at any moment. It's near his cottage. At the slightest sign of anything wrong, he could jump out of bed and hurry to the rescue.'

It was possibly this very thought that had induced the pig-man to say 'Nur' as earnestly as he had done. He was a man who liked to get his sleep. He shook his head now, and a rather bleak look came into his gnarled face.

'Well, there is the position, my dear Pilbeam. What do you advise?'

It seemed to the detective that the sooner he gave his decision the sooner the unprofitable discussion would be ended. He was completely indifferent about the whole thing. Officially at the Castle to help guard the Empress, his heart had never been in that noble task. Pigs bored him.

'I'd move her,' he said.

'You really feel that?'

'Quite.'

A mild triumph shone from Lord Emsworth's pince-nez.

'There you have an expert opinion, Pirbright,' he said. 'Mr Pilbeam knows. If Mr Pilbeam says Move her, she must certainly be moved. Do it as soon as possible.'

'Yur, m'lord,' said the pig-man despondently.

'And now, Lord Emsworth,' said Pilbeam, 'can I have a word with you?'

'Certainly, my dear fellow, certainly. But before you do so I have something very important to tell you. I want to hear what you make of it. Let me mention that first, and then you can tell me whatever it is that you have come to talk about. You won't forget whatever it is that you have come to talk about?'

'Oh, no.'

'I frequently do. I intend to tell somebody something, and something happens to prevent my doing so immediately, and when I am able to tell it to them I find I have forgotten it. My sister Constance has often been very vehement about it. I recollect her once comparing my mind to a sieve. I thought it rather clever. She meant that it was full of holes, you understand, as I believe sieves are. That was on the occasion when—'

Pilbeam had not had the pleasure of the ninth Earl's acquaintance long, but he had had it long enough to know that, unless firmly braked, he was capable of trickling on like this indefinitely.

'What was it you wished to tell me, Lord Emsworth?' he said.

'Eh? Ah, yes, quite so, my dear fellow. You want to hear that very important fact that I was going to put before you. Well, I would like you to throw your mind back, my dear Pilbeam, to yesterday. Yesterday evening. I wonder if you remember my mentioning to you the extraordinary mystery of that man getting out of the potting-shed?'

'Certainly.'

'The facts—'

'I know.'

'The facts—'

'I remember them.'

'The facts,' proceeded Lord Emsworth evenly, 'are as follows. In pursuance of my instructions, Pirbright was lurking near this sty yesterday afternoon, and what should he see but a ruffianly-looking fellow trying to poison my pig with a potato. He crept up and caught him in the act, and then shut him in that shed over there, intending to come back after he had informed me of the matter and hale him to justice. I should mention that, after placing the fellow in the shed, he carefully secured the door with a stout wooden staple.'

'Quite. I . . .'

'It seemed out of the question that he could effect an escape—I am speaking of the fellow, not of Pirbright—and you may imagine his astonishment, therefore—I am speaking of Pirbright, not of the fellow—when, on returning, he discovered that that is just what had occurred. The door of the shed was open, and he—I am once more speaking of the fellow— was gone. He had completely disappeared, my dear Pilbeam. And here is the very significant thing I wanted to tell you. Just before you came up I got Pirbright to shut me in the shed and secure the door with the staple, and I found it impossible—quite impossible, my dear fellow—to release myself from within. I tried and tried and tried, but no, I couldn't do it. Now, what does that suggest to you, Pilbeam?' asked Lord Emsworth, peering over his pince-nez.

'Somebody must have let him out.'

'Exactly. Undoubtedly. Beyond a question. Who it was of course, we shall never know.'

'I have found out who it was.'

Lord Emsworth was staggered. He had always known in a nebulous sort of way that detectives were gifted beyond the ordinary with the power to pierce the inscrutable, but this was the first time he had actually watched them at it.

'You have found out who it was?' he gasped.

'I have.'

'Pirbright, Mr Pilbeam has found out who it was.'

'Ur, m'lord.'

'Already! Isn't that amazing, Pirbright?'

'Yur, m'lord.'

'I wouldn't have thought it could have been done in the time. Would you, Pirbright?'

'Nur, m'lord.'

'Well, well, well!' said Lord Emsworth. 'That is the most extraordinary . . . Ah, I knew there was something I wanted to ask you . . . Who was it?'

'Bodkin.'

'Bodkin!'

'Your secretary, young Bodkin,' said Pilbeam.

'I knew it!' Lord Emsworth shook a fist skywards, and his voice, as always in moments of emotion, became high and reedy. 'I knew it! I suspected the fellow all along. I was convinced that he was an accomplice of Parsloe's. I'll dismiss him,' cried Lord Emsworth, almost achieving an A in alt. 'He shall go at the end of the month.'

'It would be safer to get him off the place at once.'

'Of course it would, my dear fellow. You are quite right. He shall be turned out immediately. Where is he? I must see him. I will go to him instantly.'

'Better let me send him to you out here. More dignified. Don't go to him. Let him come to you.'

'I see what you mean.'

'You wait here, and I'll go and tell him you wish to see him.'

'My dear fellow, I don't want to put you to all that trouble.'

'No trouble,' Pilbeam assured him. 'A pleasure.'

I t is one of the distinguishing characteristics of your man of the world that he can keep his poise even under the most trying of conditions. Beyond a sort of whistling gasp and a sharp 'God give me strength!' the Hon. Galahad Threepwood displayed no emotion at Ronnie's sensational announcement.

He did, however, gaze at his nephew as if the latter had been a defaulting bookmaker.

'Are you crazy?' he said.

It was a question which Ronnie found difficult to answer. Even to himself, as he now told it, the story of that great gesture of his sounded more than a little imbecile. The best, indeed, that you could really say of the great gesture, he could not help feeling, was that, like so many rash acts, it had seemed a good idea at the time. He was bright scarlet and had had occasion to straighten his tie not once but many times before he reached the end of the tale. And not even the fact that Sue, with womanly sympathy, put her arm through his and kissed him was able to bring real consolation. To his inflamed senses that kiss seemed so exactly the sort of kiss a mother might have given her idiot child.

'You see what I mean, I mean to say,' he concluded lamely. 'I thought Sue had finished with me, so there didn't seem any point in holding on to the thing any longer, and Monty said he wanted it, and so . . . well, there you are.'

'You can't blame the poor angel,' said Sue.

'I can,' said the Hon. Galahad. He moved to the fireplace and pressed the bell. 'It would surprise you how easily I could blame the poor angel. And if there was time I would. But we haven't a moment to waste. We must get hold of young Monty without a second's delay and choke the thing out of him. We'll have no nonsense. I am an elderly man, past my prime, but I am willing and ready to sit on his head while you, Ronnie, kick him in the ribs. We'll soon make him—Ah, Beach.'

The door had opened.

'You rang, Mr Galahad?'

'I want to see Mr Bodkin, Beach. At once.'

'Mr Bodkin has left, sir.'

'Left!' cried the Hon. Galahad.

'Left!' shouted Ronnie.

'Left!' squeaked Sue.

'It is possible that he may still be in his bedchamber, packing the last of his effects,' said the butler, 'but I was instructed some little while ago that he was leaving the Castle immediately. There has been trouble, sir, between Mr Bodkin and his lordship. I am unable to inform you as to what precisely eventuated, but . . .'

A cry like that of a tiger leaping on its prey interrupted him. Through the open door the Hon. Galahad had espied a lissom form crossing the hall. He was outside in a flash, confronting it.

'You, there! You bloodstained Bodkin!'

'Oh, hullo.'

The Hon. Galahad, as his opening words had perhaps sufficiently indicated, had not come for any mere exchange of courtesies.

'Never mind the "Oh, hullo." I want that manuscript of mine, young Bodkin, and I want it at once, so make it slippy, you sheep-faced young exile from Hell. If it's on your person, disgorge it. If it's in your suitcase, unpack it. And Ronnie here and I will be standing over you while you do it.'

There was an infinite sadness in Monty Bodkin's gaze. He looked like a male Mona Lisa.

'I haven't got your bally manuscript.'

'Don't lie to me, young Bodkin.'

'I'm not lying. Pilbeam's got it.'

'Pilbeam!'

Monty's voice trembled with intense feeling.

'I told the foul, double-crossing little blister where it was, like a silly chump, and he went off and squealed to Lord Emsworth about my letting old Tilbury out of the potting-shed, and Lord Emsworth sent for me and fired me, and while I was out of the way, being fired, he nipped up to my room and sneaked the thing.'

'Where is he? Where is this Pilbeam?'

'Ah,' said Monty, 'I'd like to know myself. Well, good-bye, all. I'm off to the Emsworth Arms.'

He strode sombrely out of the front door and down the steps. A cough sounded behind the Hon. Galahad.

'Would there be anything further, sir?'

The Hon. Galahad drew a deep breath.

'No thank you, Beach,' he said. 'I think that perhaps this will be enough to be getting on with.'

12

A T the moment when Monty Bodkin and the Hon. Galahad Threepwood, two minds with but a single thought, were wondering where
he was and wishing they could have a word with him, Percy Pilbeam,
the manuscript under his arm, had just emerged furtively from the
back of the Castle. He did not wish to have anything to do with front
doors. Directly he had crawled out from under Monty's bed, dragging
his treasure trove after him, he had dusted his fingers and made for the
servants' staircase. This had led him through twisting by-ways to a vast
echoing stone passage, and from that to the back door was but a step. He
had not encountered so much as a housemaid.

In his bearing, as he hurried along the path that skirted the kitchen
garden—in the oily smirk beneath his repellent moustache, in the
jaunty tilt of his snub nose, even in the terraced sweep of the brilliantine swamps of his corrugated hair—there was the look of a man who
is congratulating himself on a neat bit of work. Brains, reflected Percy
Pilbeam—that was what you needed in this life. Brains and the ability to
seize your opportunity when it was offered to you.

He had a long walk before him. It was his intention, in order to avoid
meeting any interested party, to make a wide circle round the outskirts

of Lord Emsworth's domain and strike the road to Market Blandings near Matchingham. There, no doubt, he would be able to get a lift to the Emsworth Arms. Then, having seen Lord Tilbury and arrived at some satisfactory financial arrangement with him, he proposed to take the next train to London. He had his whole plan of campaign neatly mapped out.

The one thing he had not allowed for was a sudden change in the weather. When he had left the Castle, the sun had been shining; but now it was blotted out by a dark rack of clouds. Apparently some minor storm, late for the big event, had come hurrying up and intended to hold a private demonstration of its own. There was a tentative rumble over the hills, and a raindrop splashed on his face. Before he had reached the end of the kitchen garden, quite a respectable deluge was falling.

Pilbeam, like the Hon. Galahad, hated getting wet. He looked about him for shelter, and perceived standing by itself in a small paddock not far away a squat building of red brick and timber. A man not used to country life, he had no idea what it was supposed to be, but it had a stout tiled roof beneath which he could keep dry, so he hastened thither, arriving just in time, for a moment later the world had become a shower-bath. He retreated farther into his nook and sat down on some straw.

In such a situation, the only method of passing the time is to think. Pilbeam thought. And as he did so he began to revise that scheme of his of taking the manuscript straight to Lord Tilbury.

It was a scheme which he had adopted as seeming to be the only one open to him. He would vastly have preferred his original idea of holding an auction sale, with Lord Tilbury and Lady Constance Keeble raising each other's bids; but until now the fatal objection to that course had seemed to him to be that there was no safe place where he could store the goods till the auction sale was over.

A visitor at a country house with something to hide is a good deal restricted in his choice of *caches*. He is, indeed, more or less driven back to his bedroom. And a bedroom, as had been proved in the case of Monty Bodkin, is very far from being a safe-deposit. From the inception of their acquaintance, Pilbeam had been greatly impressed by Lady Constance's strong personality. A woman of action, he considered, if ever there was one. If she knew that he had the manuscript and deduced that it was hidden in his bedroom, he could see her acting very swiftly. She would have the thing in her hands in half an hour.

But suppose he were to hide it in some such place as that in which he was now sitting. Things would be very different then.

He glanced round the dim interior, and felt that he was on the right track. This building was a deserted building. It did not appear to be used for anything. Presumably no one ever came here. And even if someone did happen to wander in, it would be a simple matter to hide the manuscript . . . under this straw, for instance.

He rose and thrust the papers under the straw. He eyed the straw appraisingly. It had as innocent a look as any straw he had ever seen.

A shaft of sunlight played in the doorway. The brief storm was over. Well content, Percy Pilbeam came out and started to walk back to the Castle.

Beach met him in the hall.

'Her ladyship is expressing a desire to see you, sir,' said Beach, regarding him with restrained horror and loathing. The recent exchange of remarks between Monty Bodkin and the Hon. Galahad in his presence had confirmed the butler in his view that of all the human serpents that ever wriggled their way into a respectable castle this private investigator was the worst. Knowing what the manuscript of the Reminiscences meant to Mr Ronald and his betrothed, Beach, had he been younger and slimmer and in better condition and not a butler, could—for two pins—have taken Percy Pilbeam's unpleasant neck in his hands and twisted it into a lover's knot.

His physique and his circumstances being as they were, he merely delivered the message he had been instructed to deliver. As far as any hostile demonstration was concerned, he had to be content with letting his lip curl.

Percy Pilbeam, however, was feeling far too pleased with himself to be daunted by butlers' curling lips. On the present occasion, moreover, he was not aware that the other's lip *was* curling. He had noted the facial spasm, but attributed it to a tickling nose.

'Lady Constance?'

'Yes, sir. Her ladyship is in the drawing-room, awaiting you.'

What the proprietor of Rigg's Golden Balm embrocation would have described as the delightful sensation of *bien-être* began to leave Pilbeam. He stood there looking thoughtful. He twisted his moustache uneasily.

Now that the moment had actually arrived for confronting Lady Constance Keeble and informing her that he was proposing to double-cross her and hold her up and extract large sums of money from her, he felt unpleasantly weak about the knees.

'H'm!' said Percy Pilbeam.

And then suddenly he remembered that nature in her infinite wisdom has provided a sovereign specific against these Lady Constance Keebles.

'Well, then, I'll tell you what,' he said, inspired. 'Bring me a large bottle of champagne, and I'll look into the matter.'

Beach withdrew to execute the commission. His demeanour, as he passed from the hall, was downcast. There in a nutshell, he was feeling, you had the tragedy of a butler's life. His not to reason why; his not to discriminate between the deserving and the undeserving; his but to go and bring bottles of champagne to marcelled-haired snakes to whom he would greatly have preferred to supply straight cyanide.

The eternal conflict between duty and personal inclination, with duty, because one was a conscientious worker and took one's profession reverently, winning hands down.

Her sister Julia's report of her conversation with the Hon. Galahad, retailed to her immediately, upon the latter's departure, had strengthened Lady Constance Keeble's already firm view that something had got to be done without any more of what she forcefully described as dilly-dallying.

The fact that it was now three days since the task of securing the manuscript had been placed in Percy Pilbeam's hands and that he had to all appearances accomplished absolutely nothing seemed to her to argue dilly-dallying of the worst kind, if not actual shilly-shallying. She could not understand why Sir Gregory Parsloe seemed to entertain so high an opinion of this young man's abilities. So far as she had been able to ascertain, they were non-existent, and she said as much to Lady Julia, who agreed with her.

It was, therefore, to no warm-hearted assembly of personal admirers that Pilbeam some quarter of an hour later proceeded to betake himself. If his specific had acted a little less rapidly, he might have been frozen to the bone by the cold wave of aristocratic disapproval which poured over him as he entered the drawing-room. As it was, the sight of Lady Constance, staring haughtily from a high-backed chair like Cleopatra about to get down to brass tacks with an Ethiopian slave, merely entertained him. He thought she looked quaint. He was feeling just the slightest bit dizzy, but extraordinarily debonair. If Lady Constance at that moment had proposed a little part-singing, he would have fallen in with the suggestion eagerly.

'You want to see me, Beach says,' he observed, slurring the honoured name a little.

'Sit down, Mr Pilbeam.'

The detective was glad to do so. Spiritually, he was at the peak of his form, but as regards his legs there appeared to be some slight engine trouble.

'Now then, Mr Pilbeam, about that book.'

'Quite,' said Pilbeam, smiling benignly. This, he was feeling, was just the sort of thing he enjoyed—a cosy chat on current literature with cultured women. He was about to say so, when his eye, wandering to the wall, caught that of the fourth Countess—Emilia Jane, 1747–1815—and so humorous did her aspect seem to him that he lay back in his chair, laughing immoderately.

'Mr Pilbeam!'

Before the detective had time to explain that his mirth had been caused by the fact that the fourth Countess looked exactly like Buster Keaton, Lady Constance had gone on speaking. She spoke well and vigorously.

'I cannot understand, Mr Pilbeam, what you have been doing all this time. You know perfectly well the vital importance of getting my brother's book into our hands. The whole thing has been clearly explained to you both by Sir Gregory Parsloe and myself. And yet you appear to have done nothing whatever about it. Sir Gregory told me you were enterprising. You seem to me to have about as much enterprise as a . . .'

She paused to search her mind for fauna of an admittedly unenterprising outlook on life, and Lady Julia, who had been listening with approval, supplied the word 'slug'. The agitation which Lady Julia Fish had betrayed in the presence of her brother Galahad had passed. She had become her cool, sardonic self again. She was watching Pilbeam with a brightly interested eye, trying to diagnose the strangeness which she sensed in his manner.

'Exactly,' said Lady Constance, welcoming the suggestion. 'As much enterprise as a slug.'

'Less,' said Lady Julia.

'Yes, less,' agreed Lady Constance.

'Much less,' said Lady Julia. 'I've seen some quite nippy slugs.'

Pilbeam's amiability waned a little. He frowned. His mind was not at its clearest, but it seemed to him that a derogatory remark had been passed.

The Pilbeams had always been a clan to stand up for themselves. Treat them right and, if it suited their convenience, they would treat you right. But try to come it over them, and they could be very terrible. It was a Pilbeam—Ernest William of Mon Abri, Kitchener Road, East Dulwich—who sued his next-door neighbour, George Dobson, of The Elms, for throwing snails over the fence into his back garden. Another Pilbeam—Claude—once refused to give up his hat and umbrella at the Hornibrook Natural History Museum, Sydenham Hill. P. Frobisher was no unworthy kin of these sturdy fighters.

'Did you call me a slug?' he asked sternly.

'In a purely Pickwickian sense,' said Lady Julia.

'Ah,' said Pilbeam, his affability returning. 'That's different.'

Lady Constance resumed the speech for the prosecution.

'You have had three whole days in which to do something, and you have not even found out where the manuscript is.'

Pilbeam smiled roguishly.

'Oh, haven't I?'

'Well, have you?'

'Yes, I have.'

'Then why in the name of goodness, Mr Pilbeam,' said Lady Constance, 'did you not tell us? And why don't you do something about it? Where is it, then? You said it was not in my brother's desk. Did he give it to somebody else?'

'He gave it to Beash.'

'Beash?' Lady Constance seemed at a loss. 'Beash?'

'Reading between the lines,' said Lady Julia, 'I think he means Beach.'

Lady Constance uttered an exclamation which was almost a battle cry. This was better than she had hoped. She felt a complete confidence in her ability to impose her will upon the domestic staff.

'Beach?' Her eyes lit up. 'I will see Beach at once.'

Pilbeam chuckled heartily.

'You may see him,' he said, 'but a fat lot of good that's going to do you. A fat, fat, fat lot of good.'

Lady Julia had completed her diagnosis.

'Forgive the personal question, Mr Pilbeam,' she said, 'but are you slightly intoxicated?'

'Yes,' said Pilbeam sunnily.

'I thought so.'

Lady Constance was less intrigued by the detective's physical condition than the mystical obscurity of his speech.

'What do you mean?'

'A little blotto,' explained Pilbeam. 'I've just had a bollerer champagne, and, what's more, I had it on an empty stomach.'

'Are you interested in Mr Pilbeam's stomach, Constance?'

'I am not.'

'Nor I,' said Lady Julia. 'Let us waive your stomach, Mr Pilbeam, and get back to the point. Why will it do us a fat lot of good seeing Beach?'

'Because he hasn't got it.'

'You seemed to suggest that he had.'

'So he had. But he hasn't. He gave it to Ronnie.'

'My son, do you mean?'

'That's right. I always think of him as Ronnie.'

'How sweet of you.'

'He tried to break my neck once,' said Pilbeam, throwing out the information for what it was worth.

'And of course that forms a bond, doesn't it?' said Lady Julia sympathetically. 'So now Ronnie has the manuscript?'

'No, he hasn't.'

'But you said he had.'

'I said he had, and he had, but he hasn't. He gave it to Bonty Modkin.'

'Oh, the man's impossible,' cried Lady Constance.

Pilbeam looked about him, but could see no man. Some mistake, probably.

'What is the good of wasting any more time on a person in his condition? Can't you see he's just maundering?'

'Wait a minute, Connie. I may be wrong, but I think something will soon emerge from the fumes. Everybody seems to have been handing Galahad's great work to somebody else. A little patient inquiry, and we may discover to whom Mr Bodkin handed it.'

Pilbeam laughed a ringing laugh.

'"Handed it" is good. Oh, very good, indeed. Considering that I had to crawl under his bed to get it.'

'What!'

'Gave my head a nasty bump, too, on the woodwork.'

'Do you mean to say, Mr Pilbeam, that all this time we've been talking *you* have got my brother's manuscript?'

'I told you something would emerge, Connie.'

'Yes, Connie,' said Pilbeam, 'I have.'

'Then why in the name of goodness could you not have said so from the first? Where is it?'

'Ah, that's telling,' said Pilbeam, wagging a playful finger.

'Mr Pilbeam,' said Lady Constance, with all the Cleopatrine haughtiness at her command, 'I insist on knowing what you have done with it. Kindly let us have no more of this nonsense.'

She could not have taken a more unfortunate attitude. The detective's resemblance to a roguish, if slightly inebriated, pixie vanished and in its place came pique, mortification, resentment, anger and defiance. His beady little eyes hardened, and from them there peeped out the fighting spirit of that Albert Edward Pilbeam who once refused to pay a fine and did seven days in Brixton jail for failing to abate a smoky chimney.

'Oh?' he said. 'Oh? It's like that, is it? Let me tell you, Connie, that I don't like your tone. Insist, indeed! A nice way to talk. I've got that manuscript hidden away somewhere where you won't find it, let me inform you. And it's going to stay there till I take it to Tilbury . . .'

'What *is* he talking about?' asked Lady Constance despairingly. Tilbury to her suggested merely a small town in Essex. She had a vague recollection that Queen Elizabeth had once held a review there or something.

But Lady Julia, with her special knowledge of Tilburies, had become suddenly grave.

'Wait,' she said. 'This is beginning to look a little sticky. I wouldn't take it to Lord Tilbury, Mr Pilbeam, really I wouldn't. I'm sure, if we only talk it over sensibly, we can come to some arrangement.'

Pilbeam, who had risen and was now tacking uncertainly towards the door waved a hand and clutched at a table to restore his balance.

'Too late,' he said. 'Too late for that. Been insulted. Don't like Connie's tone. I was going to sit and let you bid against each other, but too late, too late, too late, because I've been insulted. No further discussion. Tilbury gets it. He's waiting for it at the Emsworth Arms. Well, good-by-ee,' said Percy Pilbeam, and was gone.

Lady Constance turned to her sister for enlightenment.

'But I don't understand, Julia. What did he mean! Who is this Lord Tilbury?'

'Only the proprietor of the publishing concern with whom Gally signed his contract, my angel. Nothing more than that.'

'You mean,' cried Lady Constance, aghast, 'that if the manuscript gets into his hands, he will publish it?'

'That's it.'

'I won't allow him to. I'll get an injunction.'

'How can you? He'll stand on the contract.'

'Do you mean, then, that nothing can be done?'

'All I can suggest is that you telephone to Sir Gregory Parsloe and get him over. Tell him to come to dinner. He seems to have some influence with that little fiend. He may be able to talk him round. Though I doubt it. He's in a nasty mood. I rather wish sometimes, Connie,' said Lady Julia meditatively, 'that you were a little less of the *grande dame*. It's wonderful to watch you in action, I admit—one seems to hear the bugles blowing for the Crusades and the tramp of the mailed feet of a hundred steel-clad ancestors—but there's no getting away from it that you do put people's backs up a bit.'

Down at the Emsworth Arms, a servitor informed Lord Tilbury that he was wanted on the telephone. He walked to the instrument broodingly. The Bodkin popinjay, he presumed, that broken reed on which he had foolishly supposed that it would be possible to lean. He prepared to be a little terse with Monty.

Ever since his interview with Monty in the garden of the Emsworth Arms, Lord Tilbury had found his thoughts turning wistfully to the one man of his acquaintance who could have been relied upon to put through this commission of his. During the years when P. Frobisher Pilbeam had worked on his staff as editor of *Society Spice* Lord Tilbury had never actually asked him to steal anything, but he had no doubt at all that, if adequately paid, Percy would have sprung to the task. And now that he had blossomed out as a private investigator it was probable that he would spring to it with an even greater readiness. All that afternoon Lord Tilbury had been wondering whether the solution of the whole thing would not be to send Pilbeam a wire, telling him to come at once.

What deterred him was the reflection that it would be impossible to get him into the Castle. You cannot insert private inquiry agents in country houses as if you were slipping ferrets down a rabbit-hole. This it was that had made him abandon the roseate dream. And it was the fact that he had been compelled to abandon it that lent additional asperity to his manner as he now took up the receiver.

'Yes?' he said curtly. 'Well?'

A rollicking voice nearly cracked his ear-drum.

'Hullo, there, Tilbury! This is Pilbeam.'

Lord Tilbury's eyes seemed to shoot out suddenly, like a snail's. This was the most amazing coincidence he had ever experienced. More a miracle, he felt with some awe, than a mere coincidence.

'Speaking from Blandings Castle, Tilbury.'

'What!'

The receiver shook in Lord Tilbury's hands. Was this what was known as the direct answer to prayer? Or—taking the gloomier view—was he undergoing some aural hallucination?

'Speaking from Blandings Castle, Tilbury,' repeated the voice. 'You don't mind me calling you Tilbury, do you, Tilbury?' it added solicitously. 'I'm a bit tight.'

'Pilbeam!' Lord Tilbury's voice shook. 'Did I really understand you to say that you were speaking from Blandings Castle?'

'Quite.'

A man capable of building up the Mammoth Publishing Company is not a man who wastes time in unnecessary questions. Others might have asked Pilbeam how he had got there, but not Lord Tilbury. He could do all that later.

'Pilbeam,' he said, 'this is providential! Kindly come to me here as soon as possible. There is something I wish you to do for me. Most urgent.'

'A commission?'

'Yes, a commission.'

'And what,' inquired the voice, playfully, yet with a certain metallic note, 'is there in it for me?'

Lord Tilbury thought rapidly.

'A hundred pounds.'

A hideous noise sent his head jerking back. It was apparently a derisive laugh. When it was repeated more softly a moment later, he recognized it as such.

'Two hundred, Pilbeam.'

'Listen, Tilbury. I know what it is you want me to do. Oh, yes, I know. Something to do with a certain book . . .'

'Yes, yes.'

'Then let me tell you, Tilbury, that I've been offered five hundred in another quarter, and can easily work it up to the level thousand. But, seeing it's you, I won't sting you for more than that. Think on your feet, Tilbury. One thousand is the figure.'

Lord Tilbury thought on his feet. There were few men in England whom the prospect of parting with a thousand pounds afflicted with a greater sensation of nausea, but he could speculate in order to accumulate. And in the present case, what was a mere thousand? A sprat to catch a whale.

'Very well.'

'It's a deal?'

'Yes. I agree.'

'Right!' said the voice, with renewed cheeriness. 'Be in after dinner tonight. I'll bring the thing down with me.'

'What!'

'I say I'll bring the you-know-what to you after dinner tonight. And now *a river*-whatever-it-is, Tilbury, old cock. *Au revoir*, Tilbury. I'm feeling rather funny, and I think I'll get a bit of sleep. Ay tank I go home, Tilbury. Pip-pip!'

There was a click at the other end of the wire. Pilbeam had hung up.

Fingers tried the handle of Pilbeam's bedroom door. A fist banged on the panel. The detective looked up frowningly from the bed on which he lay. He had been on the point of sinking into a troubled doze.

'Who's that?'

'Open this door and I'll show you who it is.'

'Is that old Gally?'

'Damn your impudence!'

'What do you want?'

'A little talk with you, young man.'

'Go away, old Gally,' said Pilbeam. 'Don't want any little talks. Trying to get to sleep, old Gally. Tell 'em I shan't be down to dinner. Feeling funny.'

'You'll feel funnier if I can get in.'

'Ah, but you can't get in,' Pilbeam pointed out.

And, laughing softly to himself at the wit and cleverness of the retort, he sank back on the pillows and closed his eyes again. The handle rattled once more. The door creaked as a weight was pressed against it. Then there was silence, broken shortly by a rhythmic snoring.

Percy Pilbeam slept.

13

DARKNESS had fallen on Blandings Castle, the soft, caressing darkness that closes in like a velvet curtain at the end of a summer day. Now slept the crimson petal and the white. Owls hooted in the shadows. Bushes rustled as the small creatures of the night went about their mysterious business. The scent of the wet earth mingled with the fragrance of stock and of wallflower. Bats wheeled against the starlit sky, and moths blundered in and out of the shaft of golden light that shone from the window of the dining-room. It was the hour when men forget their troubles about the friendly board.

But troubles like those now weighing upon the inmates of Blandings Castle are not to be purged by meat and drink. The soup had come and gone. The fish had come and gone. The entrée had come and was going. But still there hung over the table a foglike pall of gloom. Of all those silent diners, not one but had his hidden care. Even Lord Emsworth, who was not easily depressed, found his meal entirely spoiled by the fact that it was being shared by Sir Gregory Parsloe-Parsloe.

As for Sir Gregory himself, the news communicated to him over the telephone by Lady Constance Keeble an hour before had been enough to ruin a dozen dinners. His might have been, as his whilom playmate, the Hon. Galahad Threepwood, had made so abundantly clear in Chapters Four, Seven, Eleven, Eighteen, and Twenty-four of his immortal work, a frivolous youth, but in his late fifties he was taking life extremely seriously. Very earnest was his wish to represent the Unionist party as their Member for the Bridgeford and Shifley Parliamentary Division of Shropshire: and if Pilbeam fulfilled his threat of taking that infernal manuscript to Lord Tilbury, his chances of doing so would be simply *nil*. He knew that local committee. Once let the story of the prawns appear in print, and they would drop him like a hot brick.

He had come tonight to reason with Pilbeam, to plead with Pilbeam, to appeal to Pilbeam's better feelings, if such existed. And, dash it, there was no Pilbeam to be reasoned with, to be pleaded with, or to be appealed to.

Where *was* the dam'feller?

The same question was torturing Lady Constance. Where was Pilbeam? Could he have gone straight to Lord Tilbury after taking his zigzag departure from the drawing-room.?

It was Lord Emsworth who put the question into words. For some moments he had been staring down the table over the top of his crooked pince-nez in a puzzled manner like that of a cat trying to run over the muster-roll of its kittens.

'Beach!'

'M'lord?' said that careworn man hollowly. Foxes were gnawing at Beach's vitals, too.

'Beach, I can't see Mr Pilbeam. Can you see Mr Pilbeam, Beach? He doesn't seem to be here.'

'Mr Pilbeam is in his bedchamber, m'lord. He informed the footman who knocked at the door with his hot water that he would not be among those present at dinner, m'lord, owing to a headache.'

The Hon. Galahad endorsed this.

'I knocked at his door just before the dressing gong went, and he said he wanted to go to sleep.'

'You didn't go in?'

'No.'

'You should have gone in, Galahad. The poor fellow may be feeling unwell.'

'Not so unwell as he would have felt if I could have got in.'

'You think you would have made his headache worse?'

'A good deal worse,' said the Hon. Galahad, taking a salted almond and giving it a hard look through his monocle.

The news that Pilbeam was on a bed of sickness acted on three members of the party rather as the recent rain had acted on the parched earth. Lady Constance seemed to expand like a refreshed flower. Lady Julia did the same. Sir Gregory Parsloe, in addition to expanding, gave such a sharp sigh of relief that he blew a candle out. Three pairs of eyes exchanged glances. There was the same message of cheer in each of them. If Pilbeam had not taken the irrevocable step, those eyes said, all might yet be well.

'God bless my soul,' said Lord Emsworth solicitously, 'I hope he isn't really bad. These infernal thunderstorms are enough to give anyone a headache. I had a slight headache myself before dinner. I'll run up and see the poor chap as soon as we've finished here. My goodness, I don't want Pilbeam on the sick list now, of all times,' said Lord Emsworth, with a glance at Sir Gregory so full of meaning that the latter, who was lifting his wine-glass to his lips, shied like a startled horse and spilled half its contents.

'Why now, particularly?' asked Lady Julia.

'Never mind,' said Lord Emsworth darkly.

'I only asked,' said Lady Julia, 'because I, personally, consider that all times are good times for Mr. Pilbeam to have headaches. Not to mention botts, glanders, quartan ague, frog in the throat and the Black Death.'

A soft, sibilant sound, like gas escaping from a pipe, came from the shadows by the sideboard. It was Beach expressing, as far as butlerine etiquette would permit him to express, his adhesion to this sentiment.

Lord Emsworth, on the other hand, showed annoyance.

'I wish you wouldn't say such things, Julia.'

'On the spur of the moment I couldn't think of anything worse.'

'Don't you like Pilbeam?'

'My dear Clarence, don't be fantastic. Nobody *likes* Mr Pilbeam. There are people who do not actually put poison in his soup, but that is as far as you can go.'

'I disagree with you,' said Lord Emsworth warmly. 'I regard him as a capital fellow, capital. And most useful, let me tell you. Attempts are being made,' said Lord Emsworth, once more sniping Sir Gregory with a penetrating eye, 'by certain parties whom I will not name, to injure my pig. Pilbeam is helping me thwart them. Thanks to his advice, I have now put my pig where the parties to whom I allude will not find it quite so easy to get at her. Let me tell you that I think very highly of Pilbeam. I've a good mind to send him up half a bottle of champagne.'

'Making the perfect example of carrying coals to Newcastle.'

'Eh?'

'Oh, nothing. 'Twas but a passing jest.'

'Champagne is good for headaches,' argued Lord Emsworth. 'It might make all the difference to Pilbeam.'

'Are we to spend the whole of dinner talking of Mr Pilbeam and his headache?' demanded Lady Constance imperiously. 'I am sick and tired of Mr Pilbeam. And I don't want to hear any more of that pig of yours, Clarence. For goodness sake let us discuss some reasonable topic.'

This bright invitation having had the not unnatural effect of killing the conversation completely, dinner proceeded in an unbroken silence. Only once did one of the revellers venture a remark. As Beach and his assistants removed the plates which had contained fruit salad and substituted others designed for dessert, Lady Julia raised her glass.

'To the body upstairs—I hope,' she said.

Percy Pilbeam, however, was not actually dead. At the precise moment of Lady Julia's toast, almost as if he were answering a cue, he sat up on his bed and stared muzzily about him. The fact that the room was now in darkness made it difficult for him to find his bearings immediately, and for perhaps half a minute he sat wondering where he was. Then memory returned, and with it an opening-and-shutting sensation in the region of the temples which made him regret that he had not gone on sleeping. Even if he had had the Black Death to which Lady Julia had so feelingly alluded, he could not have felt very much worse.

There are heads which are proof against over-indulgence in champagne. That of the Hon. Galahad Threepwood is one that springs to the mind. Pilbeam's, however, did not belong to this favoured class. For a while he sat there, wincing at each fresh wave of agony; then, levering himself up, he switched on the light and hobbled to the wash-stand, where he proceeded to drink deeply out of the water-jug. This done, he filled the basin and started to give himself first-aid treatment.

Presently, a little restored, he returned to the bed and sat down again. Endeavouring to recall the events which had led up to the tragedy, he found that he could do so only sketchily. One fact alone stood out clearly in his recollection—to wit, that in some way which he could not quite remember he had been insulted by Lady Constance Keeble. A great bitterness against Lady Constance began to burgeon within Percy Pilbeam, and it was not long before he reached the decision that, cost what it might, she must be scored off. There would be no auction sale. As soon as he felt physically capable of moving, he would take that manuscript to Lord Tilbury at the Emsworth Arms.

At this point in his meditations the house was blown up by a bomb. Or, what amounted to much the same thing as far as the effect on the nervous system was concerned, there was a knock at the door.

'May I come in, my dear fellow?'

Pilbeam recognized the voice. He could not be rude to his only friend at Blandings Castle. He swallowed his heart again, and unlocked the door.

'Ah! Sitting up, I see. Feeling a little better, eh? We all missed you at dinner,' said Lord Emsworth, beginning to potter about the room as he pottered about all rooms which he honoured with his presence. 'We wondered what had become of you. My sister Julia, if I remember rightly, speculated as to the possibility of your having got the Black Death. What put the idea into her head, I can't imagine. Absurd, of course. People don't get the Black Death nowadays. I've never heard of anyone getting the Black Death. In fact,' said Lord Emsworth, with a burst of confidence, dropping into the fireplace the hair-brush which he had been attempting to balance on the comb, 'I don't believe I know what the Black Death *is*.'

A sense of being in hell stole over Percy Pilbeam. What with the clatter of that brush, which had set his head aching again, and his host's conversation, which threatened to make it ache still more, he was sore beset.

'No doubt all that has happened,' proceeded Lord Emsworth, moving the soap-dish a little to the left, the water-bottle a little to the right, a chair a little nearer the door, and another chair a little nearer the window, 'is that that thunderstorm gave you a headache. And I was wondering, my dear fellow, if a breath of fresh air might not do you good. Fresh air is often good for headaches. I am on my way to have a look at the Empress, and it crossed my mind that you might care to come with me. It is a beautiful night. There is a lovely moon, and I have an electric torch.'

Here, Lord Emsworth, pausing from tapping the mirror with a buttonhook, produced from his pocket the torch in question and sent a dazzling ray shooting into his companion's inflamed eyes.

The action decided Pilbeam. To remain longer in the confined space of a bedroom with this man would be to subject his sanity to too severe a test. He said he would be delighted to come and take a look at the Empress.

Out on the gravel drive he began to feel a little better. As Lord Emsworth had said, it was a beautiful night. Pilbeam was essentially a creature of the city, with urban tastes, but even he could appreciate the sweet serenity of the grounds of Blandings Castle under that gracious moon. So restored did he feel by the time they had gone a hundred yards or so that he even ventured on a remark.

'Aren't we,' he asked, 'going the wrong way?'

'What's that, my dear fellow?' said Lord Emsworth, wrenching his mind from the torch, which he was flashing on and off like a child with a new toy. 'What did you say?'

'Don't you get to the sty by crossing the terrace?'

'Ah, but you've forgotten, my dear Pilbeam. Acting on your advice, we moved her to the new one just before dinner. You recollect advising us to move her from her old sty?'

'Of course. Quite. Yes, I remember.'

'Pirbright didn't like it. I could tell that by the strange noises he made at the back of his throat. He has some idea that she will feel restless and unhappy away from her old home. But I was particularly careful to wait and see that she was comfortably settled in, and I could detect no signs of restlessness whatever. She proceeded to eat her evening meal with every indication of enjoyment.'

'Good,' said Pilbeam, feeling distrait.

'Eh?'

'I said "good."'

'Oh, "good"? Yes, quite so. Yes, very good. I feel most pleased about it. As I pointed out to Pirbright, the risk of leaving her in her old quarters was far too great to be taken. Why, my dear Pilbeam, do you know that my sister Constance had actually invited that man Parsloe to dinner tonight? Oh, yes, there he was, at dinner with us. No doubt he had persuaded her to invite him, thinking that, having got into the place, he would be able to find an opportunity during the evening of slipping away and going down to the sty and doing the poor animal a mischief. A nice surprise he's going to get when he finds the sty empty. He won't know what to make of it. He'll be nonplussed.'

Here Lord Emsworth paused to chuckle. Pilbeam, though not amused, contrived to emit on his side something that might have passed as a mirthful echo.

'This new sty,' proceeded Lord Emsworth, having switched the torch on and off six times, 'is an altogether more suitable place. As a matter of fact, I had it built specially for the Empress in the spring, but owing to Pirbright's obstinacy I never moved her there. I don't know if you know these Shropshire fellows at all, Pilbeam, but they can be as obstinate as Scotsmen. I have a Scots head gardener, Angus McAllister, and he is intensely obstinate. Like a mule. I must tell you some time about the trouble I had with him regarding hollyhocks. But Pirbright can be fully as stubborn when he gets an idea into his head. I reasoned with him. I said, "Pirbright, this sty is a new sty, with all the latest improvements. It is up to date, in keeping with the trend of modern thought, and, what is more—and this I consider very important—it adjoins the kitchen garden . . ." '

He broke off. A sound beside him in the darkness had touched his kindly heart.

'Is your head hurting you again, my dear fellow?'

But the bubbling cry which had proceeded from Percy Pilbeam had not been caused by pain in the head.

'The kitchen garden?' he gasped.

'Yes. And that is most convenient, you see, because Pirbright's cottage is so close. No doubt you have seen the place if you have ever strolled round by the kitchen garden. It is made of stout red brick and timber, with a good tiled roof . . . In fact,' said Lord Emsworth, flashing his torch, 'here it is. And there,' he went on with satisfaction, 'is the Empress, still feeding away without a care in the world. I told Pirbright he was all wrong.'

The Empress might have been without a care in the world, but Percy Pilbeam was very far from sharing that ideal state. He leaned on the rail of the sty and groaned in spirit.

In the light of the electric torch, Empress of Blandings made a singularly attractive, even a fascinating, picture. She had her noble head well down and with a rending, golluping sound was tucking into a late supper. Her curly little tail wiggled incessantly, and ever and anon a sort of sensuous quiver would pass along her Zeppelin-like body. But Percy Pilbeam was in no frame of mind to admire the rare and the beautiful. He was trying to adjust himself to this utterly unforeseen disaster.

He had only himself to blame—that was what made it all the more bitter. If he had not so casually given his casting vote in favour of shifting this infernal pig to new quarters, he would not now have been faced by a problem which every moment seemed to become more difficult of solution.

For Pilbeam was afraid of pigs. He seemed to remember having read somewhere that if you go into a pig's sty and the pig doesn't know you it comes for you like a tiger and chews you to ribbons. Greedy though he was for Lord Tilbury's gold, something told him that never, no matter how glittering the reward, would he be able to bring himself to go into that sty in quest of the manuscript, guarded as it now was by this ravening beast. The Prodigal Son might have mixed with these animals on a clubby basis, but Percy Pilbeam knew himself to be incapable of imitating him.

How long he would have stood there, savouring the bitterness of defeat, one cannot say. Left to himself, probably quite a considerable time. But his reverie had scarcely begun when it was shattered by a cry at his elbow.

'God bless my soul!'

It seemed to Pilbeam for an instant that he had come unstuck. He clutched the rail, quivering in every limb.

'What on earth's the matter?' he demanded, far more brusquely than a guest should have done of his host.

An agitation almost equal to his own was causing the torch to wobble in Lord Emsworth's hands.

'God bless my soul, what's that she's eating? Pirbright! Pirbright! Can you see what she's eating, Pilbeam, my dear fellow? Pirbright! Pirbright! Can it be *paper*?'

With a febrile swoop Lord Emsworth bent through the rails. He came up again, breathing heavily. The light of the torch came and went like a heliograph upon something which he held in his hand.

Galloping feet sounded in the night.

'Pirbright!'

'Yur, m'lord?'

'Pirbright, have you been giving the Empress paper?'

'Nur, m'lord.'

'Well, that's what she's eating. Great chunks of it.'

'Ur, m'lord?' said the pig-man, marvelling.

'I assure you, yes. Paper. Look! Well, God bless my soul,' cried Lord Emsworth, at last steadying the torch, 'I'm dashed if it isn't that book of my brother Galahad's!'

14

AT about the moment when Lord Emsworth had knocked at Percy Pilbeam's door to inquire after his health and make his kindly suggestion of a breath of fresh air, his sister Lady Constance Keeble, his sister Lady Julia Fish, and his neighbour and guest Sir Gregory Parsloe-Parsloe were gathered together in the drawing-room, talking things over and endeavouring to come to some agreement as to the best method of handling the situation which had arisen.

The tone of the meeting had been a little stormy from the very outset. Owing to the suddenness of his summons to the Castle and the difficulty of explaining things over the telephone, all that Sir Gregory had known till now was the bare fact that Pilbeam had obtained possession of the manuscript and was proposing to deliver it to Lord Tilbury. Informed over the coffee cups by Lady Julia that the whole disaster was to be attributed to her sister Constance's tactless handling of the fellow, he had drawn his breath in sharply, gazed at Lady Constance in a reproachful manner, and started clicking his tongue.

Any knowledgeable person could have guessed what would happen after that. No woman of spirit can sit calmly and have a man click his tongue at her. No hostess, on the other hand, can be openly rude to a guest. Seeking an outlet for her emotions, Lady Constance had begun to quarrel with Lady Julia. And as Lady Julia, always fond of a family row, had borne her end of the encounter briskly, before he knew where he was Sir Gregory became aware that he had sown the wind and was reaping the whirlwind.

We mention these things to explain why it happened that there was a certain delay before G.H.Q. took the obvious step of trying to establish communication with Percy Pilbeam. More than a quarter of an hour had elapsed before Sir Gregory was able to still the tumult of battle with these arresting words:

'But, I say, dash it all, don't you think we ought to see the feller?'

They acted like magic. Angry passions were chained. Good things about to be said were corked up and stored away for use on some future occasion. The bell was rung for Beach. Beach was dispatched to Pilbeam's room with instructions to desire him to be so good as to step down to the drawing-room for a moment. And the end of it all was that Beach returned and announced that Mr Pilbeam was not there.

Consternation reigned.

'Not there?' cried Lady Constance.

'Not *there*?' cried Lady Julia.

'But he must be there,' protested Sir Gregory. 'Fellow goes to his room with a headache to lie down and have a sleep,' he proceeded, arguing closely. 'Stands to reason he must be there.'

'You can't have knocked loudly enough, Beach,' said Lady Constance.

'Go up and knock again,' said Lady Julia.

'Hit the dashed door a good hard bang,' said Sir Gregory.

Beach's demeanour was respectful but unsympathetic.

'Receiving no response to my knocking, m'lady, I took the liberty of entering the room. It was empty.'

'Empty?'

'Empty!'

'You mean,' said Sir Gregory, who liked to get these things straight, 'there wasn't anybody *in* the room?'

Beach inclined his head.

'The bedchamber was unoccupied,' he assented.

'He may be in the smoking-room,' suggested Lady Constance.

'Or the billiard-room,' said Lady Julia.

'Having a bath,' cried Sir Gregory, inspired. 'Fellow with a headache might quite easily go and have a bath. Do his headache good.'

'I visited the smoking-room and the billiard-room, m'lady. The door of the bathroom on Mr Pilbeam's floor was open, revealing emptiness within. I am inclined to think, m'lady,' said Beach 'that the gentleman has gone for a walk.'

The awful words produced a throbbing silence. Only too well could these three visualize the direction in which, if he had taken a walk, Percy Pilbeam would have taken it.

'Thank you, Beach,' said Lady Constance dully.

The butler bowed and withdrew. The silence continued unbroken. Sir Gregory walked heavily to the window and stood looking out into the night. It almost seemed to him that across that starry sky he could see written in letters of flame the story of the prawns.

Lady Constance gave a shuddering sigh.

'We shan't have a friend left!'

Lady Julia lit a cigarette.

'Poor old Miles! Bang goes *his* reputation!'

Sir Gregory turned from the window.

'Those Local Committee chaps will give the nomination to old Bill-ing now, I suppose.' His Regency-buck face twisted with injured wrath. 'Why the devil need the feller have been in such a hurry? Why couldn't he at least have let me *talk* to him? I brought my cheque-book with me specially. He knows I'd have given him five hundred pounds. I'll bet he won't get that from this Tilbury of his. I've met Tilbury. I've heard stories about him. Mean man. Tight with his money. Pilbeam'll be lucky if he gets a couple of hundred out of him.'

'A pity you put his back up like that, Connie,' said Lady Julia suavely. 'I don't suppose now he cares about the money so much. What he wants is to be nasty.'

'What I think a pity,' retorted Lady Constance, with the splendid Keeble spirit, 'is that Sir Gregory ever mentioned the matter to a man like this Pilbeam. He might have known that he was not to be trusted.'

'Exactly,' said Lady Julia. 'An insane thing to do.'

This unexpected alliance disconcerted Sir Gregory Parsloe. He spluttered.

'Well, I had had dealings with the fellow before on a . . . on a private matter, and had found him alert and enterprising. I just went and engaged him naturally, as you would engage anyone to do something. It never occurred to me that he wasn't to be trusted.'

'Not even after you saw that moustache?' said Lady Julia. 'Well, there's just one gleam of comfort in this business, Connie. We shall now be able to talk to Clarence and put a stop to any nonsense of his giving Ronnie his money.'

'That's true,' said Lady Constance, brightening a little.

As she spoke, the door opened and Percy Pilbeam came in.

Everybody, as the poet so well says, is loved by someone, and it is to be supposed, therefore, that somewhere in the world there were faces that lit up when even Percy Pilbeam entered the room. But never, not even by his mother, if he had a mother, nor by some warm-hearted aunt, if he had a warm-hearted aunt, could he have been more rapturously received than he was received now by Lady Constance Keeble, by Lady Julia Fish, and by Sir Gregory Parsloe-Parsloe, Bart, of Matchingham Hall, Salop. Santa Claus himself would have had a less enthusiastic welcome.

'Mr Pilbeam!'

'Mr *Pilbeam*!'

'Pilbeam, my *dear* chap!'

'Come in, Mr Pilbeam!'

'Sit down, Mr Pilbeam!'

'Pilbeam, my dear fellow, a chair.'

'How is your headache, Mr Pilbeam?'

'Are you feeling better, Mr Pilbeam?'

'Pilbeam, old man, I have a cigar here which I think you will appreciate.'

The investigator looked from one to the other with growing bewilderment. Though an investigator, he could not deduce what had caused this exuberance. He had come to the room expecting a sticky ten minutes, and had forced himself to face it because business was business and, now that that ghastly pig had transferred almost the entire manuscript of the Hon. Galahad's Reminiscences to its loathsome inside, it was from the group before him alone that he could anticipate anything in the nature of a cash settlement.

'Thanks,' he said, accepting the chair.

'Thanks,' he said, taking the cigar.

'Thanks,' he said, in response to the inquiries after his health. 'No, it isn't so bad now.'

'That's good,' said Sir Gregory heartily.

'Splendid,' said Lady Constance.

'Capital,' said Lady Julia.

These paeans of joy concluded, there occurred that momentary hush which always comes over any gathering or assembly when business is about to be discussed. Pilbeam's eyes were flickering warily from face to face. He had got to do some expert bluffing, and was bracing himself to the task.

'I came about—that thing,' he said, at length.

'Exactly, exactly, exactly,' cried Sir Gregory. 'You've been thinking it over and . . .'

'I'm afraid I was a little abrupt, Mr Pilbeam,' said Lady Constance winningly, 'when we had our last little talk. I was feeling rather upset. The weather, I suppose.'

'You did say you had your cheque-book with you, Sir Gregory?' said Lady Julia.

'Certainly, certainly. Here it is.'

There came into Pilbeam's eyes the gleam which always came into them when he saw cheque-books.

'Well, I've done it,' he said, in what he tried to make a cheery, big-hearted manner.

'Done it?' cried Lady Constance, appalled. The words conveyed to her a meaning different from that intended by their speaker. 'You don't mean you have taken . . .?'

'You wanted that manuscript destroyed, didn't you?' said Pilbeam. 'Well, I've done it.'

'What?'

'I've destroyed it. Torn it up. As a matter of fact, I've burned it. So . . .'

said Pilbeam, and cut his remarks off short on the word, filling out the hiatus with a meaning glance at the cheque-book. He licked his lips nervously as he did so. He was well aware that the conference had now arrived at what Monty Bodkin would have called the nub.

The committee of three evidently felt the same. There was another silence—an awkward silence this time, pulsing with embarrassment and doubt. It is always so embarrassing for well-bred people to tell a fellow human being that they do not believe him. Moreover, any intimation on the part of these particular well-bred people that they thought this man was lying to them would most certainly wound that sensitiveness of his which it was so dangerous to wound.

On the other hand, could they pay out large sums of money to a man with a moustache like that, purely on the off-chance that he might for once be telling the truth? The committee paused on the horns of a dilemma.

'Ha h'r'm'ph!' said Sir Gregory, rather neatly summing up the sentiment of the meeting.

Percy Pilbeam displayed an unforeseen amiability in this delicate situation.

'Of course, I don't expect you to take my word for it,' he said. 'Naturally you want some sort of proof. Well, here's a bit of the thing which I saved to show you. The rest is a pile of ashes.'

From his breast pocket he produced a tattered fragment of paper and handed it to Sir Gregory. Sir Gregory, after wincing with some violence, for by an odd chance the fragment happened to deal with the story of the prawns, passed it to Lady Constance. Lady Constance looked at it, and gave it to Lady Julia. The tension relaxed.

'It is not quite what we intended,' said Lady Constance. 'Naturally we expected you to bring the manuscript to us, so that we could destroy it with our own hands. Still . . .'

'Comes to the same thing,' argued Pilbeam.

'Yes, I suppose it does not really matter.'

Glances flitted to and fro like butterflies. Sir Gregory looked at Lady Constance, seeking guidance. Lady Constance silently consulted Lady Julia. Lady Julia gave a quick nod. Sir Gregory having noted it and looked at Lady Constance again and received a nod from her, went to the writing-table and became busy with pen and ink.

Chattiness ensued. Something of the atmosphere of a Board Room at the conclusion of an important meeting had crept into the air.

'I am sure we are all very much obliged to you,' said Lady Constance.

'But tell me, Mr Pilbeam,' said Lady Julia, 'what caused this sudden change of heart?'

'Pardon?'

'Well, when you left us before dinner, you seemed so determined to . . .'

'Oh, Clarence!' cried Lady Constance, with the exasperation which the head of the family's entry into a room so often caused her. He would, she felt, choose this moment to come in and potter.

But for once in his life Lord Emsworth was in no pottering mood. The tempestuous manner of his irruption should have told Lady Constance that. His demeanour and the tone of his remarks now enabled her to perceive it. Quite plainly, something had occurred to stir him out of his usual dreamy calm.

'Who moved my books?' he demanded fiercely.

'What books?'

'I keep a little book of telephone numbers on the table in the library, and it's gone. Ha,' said Lord Emsworth. 'Beach would know.'

He leaped to the fireplace and pressed the bell.

'You'll break your neck if you go springing about like that on this parquet floor,' observed Lady Julia languidly. 'Why skip ye so, ye high hills?'

Lord Emsworth returned to the centre of the room. He was glaring in what his sister Constance considered an extremely uppish manner. He seemed to her to have got quite above himself.

'Do go away, Clarence,' she said. 'We are talking about something important.'

'And so am I talking about something important. Once and for all, I insist on having my personal belongings respected. I will not have my things moved. My little book of telephone numbers has gone. I suppose you've got it, Connie. Took it to look up some number or other and couldn't be bothered to put it back. Tchah!' said Lord Emsworth.

'I have not got your wretched little book,' said Lady Constance wearily. 'What do you want it for?'

'I want to ring up that fellow.'

'What fellow?'

'That fellow what's-his-name. The vet. It's a matter of life and death. And I've forgotten his number.'

'What do you want the vet for?' asked Lady Julia. 'Are you ill?'

Lord Emsworth stared.

'What do I want the vet for? When the Empress has been eating that paper?'

'What paper does the Empress take in?' said Lady Julia. 'I've often wondered. Something sound and conservative, I suppose. Probably the *Morning Post*.'

'What *are* you talking about, Clarence?' said Lady Constance.

'Why, about the Empress eating that book of Galahad's, of course. Hasn't Pilbeam told you?'

'What!'

'Certainly. Went to her sty just now and found her finishing the last chapters. How the thing got there is more than I can tell you. Ink and paper! Probably poisonous. Ha, Beach!'

'M'lord?'

'Beach, what is that vet's telephone number? You know what I mean. The telephone number of what's-his-name, the vet.'

'Matchingham 2-2-1, m'lord.'

'Then get him quickly and put him through to the library. Tell him my pig has just eaten the complete manuscript of my brother Galahad's Reminiscences.'

And, so saying, Lord Emsworth made a dart for the door. Finding Beach in the way, he sprang nimbly to the right. The butler also moved to the right. Lord Emsworth dashed to the left. So did Beach. From above the mantelpiece the portrait of the sixth Earl looked down approvingly on these rhythmical manoeuvres. He, too, had been fond of the minuet in his day.

'Beach!' cried Lord Emsworth, passionate appeal in his voice.

'M'lord?'

'Stand still, man. You aren't a jumping bean.'

'I beg your lordship's pardon. I miscalculated the direction in which your lordship was intending to proceed.'

This delay at such a time had robbed Lord Emsworth of the last vestiges of prudence and self-control. On the polished floor of the drawing-room only a professional acrobat could have executed without disaster the bound which he now gave. There was a slithering crash, and he came to a halt against a china-cabinet, rubbing his left ankle.

'I told you you would come a purler,' said Lady Julia, with the satisfaction of a Cassandra, one of whose prophecies has at last been fulfilled. 'Hurt yourself?'

'I think I've twisted my ankle. Beach, help me to the library.'

'Very good, m'lord.'

'Ronnie has some embrocation, I believe,' said Lady Julia.

'I don't want embrocation,' snarled the wounded man, as he hopped from the room on the butler's supporting arm. 'I want a doctor. Beach, as soon as you've got the vet, get a doctor.'

'Very good, m'lord.'

The door closed. And, as it did so, Lady Constance, her lips set and her eyes gleaming with a fierce light, walked to where Sir Gregory stood gaping, took the cheque from his fingers, and tore it across.

A passionate cry rang through the room. It came from the lips of Percy Pilbeam.

'Hi!'

Lady Constance gave him one of the Keeble looks.

'Surely, Mr Pilbeam, you do not expect to be paid for having done nothing? Your instructions were to deliver the manuscript to myself or to Sir Gregory. You have not done so. The agreement is, therefore, null and void.'

'Spoken like a man, Connie,' said Lady Julia, with approval.

The investigator was staring helplessly.

'But the thing's destroyed.'

'Not by you.'

'Certainly not,' said Sir Gregory, with animation. He could follow an argument as well as the next man. 'Not by you at all. Eaten by that pig.'

'Just an Act of God,' put in Lady Julia.

'Exactly,' agreed Sir Gregory. 'A very good way of putting it. Act of God. No obligation on our part to pay you a penny.'

'But . . .'

'I am sorry, Mr Pilbeam,' said Lady Constance, becoming queenly. 'I see no reason to discuss the matter further.'

'Especially,' said Lady Julia, 'as we have a very urgent matter to discuss with Clarence, Connie.'

'Why, of course. I was forgetting that.'

'I wasn't,' said Lady Julia. 'You will forgive us for leaving you, Sir Gregory?'

Sir Gregory Parsloe was looking like a Regency buck who has just won a fortune on the turn of a card at Wattier's.

'By all means, Lady Julia. Certainly. As a matter of fact, I think I'll be getting along.'

'I'll order your car.'

'Don't bother,' said Sir Gregory. 'Don't need a car. Going to walk. The relief of knowing that that infernal book isn't hanging over my head any longer . . . phew! I think I'll walk ten miles.'

His eye fell on the tattered fragment of paper on the table. He gathered it up, tore it in half, and put the pieces in his pocket. Then, with the contented air of a man out of whose life stories of prawns have gone for ever, he strode briskly to the door.

Percy Pilbeam continued to sit where he was, looking like a devastated area.

15

WHILE these events were in progress at Blandings Castle, there sat in the coffee-room of the Emsworth Arms in Market Blandings a young man eating turbot. It was the second course of a belated dinner which he was making under the reproachful eye of a large, pale, spotted waiter who had hoped to be off duty half an hour ago.

The first thing anyone entering the coffee-room would have noticed, apart from the ozone-like smell of cold beef, beer, pickles, cabbage, gravy, soup, boiled potatoes and very old cheese which characterizes coffee-rooms all England over, would have been this young man's extraordinary gloom. He seemed to have looked on life and seen its hollowness. And so he had. Monty Bodkin—for this decayed wreck was he—was in the depths. It is fortunate that the quality of country hotel turbot is such that you do not notice much difference when it turns to ashes in your mouth, for this is what Monty's turbot was doing now.

He had never, he realized, been exactly what you might call sanguine when making his way to the Emsworth Arms to plead with Lord Tilbury to act like a sportsman and a gentleman. All the ruling of the form-book, he knew, was against him. And yet he had nursed, despite the whisperings of Reason, a sort of thin, sickly hope. This hope the proprietor of the Mammoth had slain dead within five minutes of his arrival.

When Monty had claimed consideration on the ground that it was through no fault of his own that he was not charging in, manuscript in hand, Lord Tilbury had remained mute and stony. When he had gone on to point out that Pilbeam could not have got the thing but for him, Lord Tilbury had uttered a sharp, sneering snort. And when, as happened a little farther on in the scene, Monty had called his former employer a fat, double-crossing wart-hog, the latter had terminated the interview by walking away with his hands under his coat-tails.

So Monty dined broodingly, his heart bowed down with weight of woe. Silence reigned in the coffee-room, broken only by the breathing of the waiter, a man who would have done well to put himself in the hands of some good tonsil specialist.

Optimist though he was by nature, Monty Bodkin could not conceal it from himself that the future looked black. Unless the senior partner of Butterwick, Mandelbaum and Price relented—a hundred to one shot— or Gertrude Butterwick jettisoned her sturdy middle-class prejudices and decided to defy her father's wishes—call this one eighty-eight to three— that wedded bliss of which he had dreamed could never be his. It was an unpleasant thought for a man to have to face, and one well calculated to turn to ashes the finest portion of turbot ever boiled, let alone the rather obscene-looking mixture of bones and eyeballs and black mackintosh which the chef of the Emsworth Arms had allotted to him.

Roast mutton succeeded the turbot and became ashes in its turn, as did the potatoes and brussels sprouts which accompanied it. The tapioca pudding, owing to an accident in the kitchen, was mostly ashes already. Monty gave it one look, then flung down his napkin with a Byronic gesture and, declining the waiter's half-hearted suggestion of a glass of port and a bit of Stilton, dragged himself downstairs and out into the garden.

Pacing the wet grass, he found his mind turning to thoughts of revenge. He was a kindly and good-tempered young man as a general rule, but conduct like that of Percy Pilbeam and Lord Tilbury seemed to him simply to clamour for reprisals. And it embittered him still further to discover at the end of ten minutes that he was totally without ideas on the subject. For all he could do about it, he was regretfully forced to conclude, these wicked men were apparently going to prosper like a couple of bay trees.

In these circumstances there was only one thing that could heal the spirit, viz. to go in and write a long, loving letter of appeal to Gertrude Butterwick, urging her to follow the dictates of her heart and come and spring round with him to the registrar's or Gretna Green or somewhere. With this end in view, he proceeded to the writing-room, where he hoped to be able to devote himself to the task in solitude.

The writing-room of the Emsworth Arms, as of most English rural hotels, was a small, stuffy, melancholy apartment, badly lit and very much in need of new wallpaper. But it was not its meagre dimensions nor its closeness nor its dimness nor the shabbiness of its walls that depressed Monty as he entered. What gave him that grey feeling was the sight of Lord Tilbury seated in one of the two rickety armchairs.

Lord Tilbury was smoking an excellent cigar, and until that moment had been feeling quietly happy. His interview with Bodkin M. before dinner had relieved his mind of a rather sinister doubt which had been weighing on it. Until Monty had informed him of what had occurred, he had been oppressed by a speculation as to whether the voice which had spoken to him on the telephone had been the voice of Pilbeam or merely that of the alcoholic refreshment of which Pilbeam was so admittedly full. Had he, in short, really got the manuscript? Or had his statement to that effect been the mere inebriated babbling of an investigator who had just been investigating Lord Emsworth's cellar? Monty had made it clear that the former and more agreeable theory was the correct one, and Lord Tilbury was now awaiting the detective's arrival in a frame of mind that blended well with an excellent cigar.

The intrusion of a young man of whom he hoped he had seen the last ruffled his placid mood.

'I have nothing more to say,' he observed irritably. 'I have told you my decision, and I see nothing to be gained by further discussion.'

Monty raised his eyebrows coldly.

'I have no desire to speak to you, my good man,' he said loftily. 'I came in here to write a letter.'

'Then go and write it somewhere else. I am expecting a visitor.'

It had been Monty's intention to ignore the fellow and carry on with the job in hand without deigning to bestow another look on him. But having gone to the desk and discovered that it contained no notepaper, no pen, not a single envelope, and in the inkpot only about a quarter of an inch of curious sediment that looked like black honey, he changed his mind.

He toyed for an instant with the idea of taking one of the magazines which lay on the table and sitting down in the other armchair and spoiling the old blighter's evening; but as those magazines were last-year copies of the *Hotel Keepers Register* and *Licensed Victuallers Gazette* he abandoned the project. With a quiet look of scorn and a meaning sniff he left the room and wandered out into the garden again.

And barely had he strolled down to the river and smoked two cigarettes and thrown a bit of stick at a water-rat and strolled back and thrown another bit of stick at a noise in the bushes, when the significance of Lord Tilbury's concluding remark suddenly flashed upon him.

If Lord Tilbury was expecting a visitor, that visitor obviously must be Pilbeam. And if Pilbeam was coming to the Emsworth Arms to see Lord Tilbury, equally obviously he must be bringing the manuscript with him.

Very well, then, where did one go from there? One went, he perceived, straight to this arresting conclusion—that there the two blisters would be in that writing-room with the manuscript between them, thus offering a perfect sitter of a chance to any man of enterprise who cared to dash in and be a little rough.

A bright confidence filled Monty Bodkin. He felt himself capable of taking on ten Tilburies and a dozen Pilbeams. All he had to do was bide his time and then rush in and snatch the thing. And when he had got it and was dangling it before his eyes, would Lord Tilbury take a slightly different attitude? Would he adopt a somewhat different tone? Would he be likely to reopen the whole matter, approaching it from another angle? The answer was definitely in the affirmative.

But first to spy out the land. He remembered that the window of the writing-room had been open a few inches at the bottom. He tiptoed across the grass with infinite caution. And just as he had reached his objective a voice spoke inside the room.

'You hid it? But are you sure it is safe?'

Monty leaned against the wall, holding his breath. He felt like the owner of a home-made radio who has accidentally got San Francisco.

The Pilbeam who had borrowed Voules's motor-bicycle and ridden down to the Emsworth Arms and now faced Lord Tilbury in the writing-room of that hostelry was a very different Pilbeam from the gay telephoner of before dinner. The telephoning Pilbeam had been a man who gave free rein to a jovial exuberance, knowing himself to be sitting on top of the world. The writing-room Pilbeam was a taut and anxious gambler, staking his all on one last throw.

After that painful scene in the drawing-room, it had taken the detective perhaps ten minutes to realize that, though all seemed lost, there did still remain just one chance of saving the day. If he were salesman enough to dispose of that manuscript to Lord Tilbury, sight unseen, without being compelled to mention that it was no longer—except in a greatly transmuted state inside Empress of Blandings—in existence, all would be well.

There might possibly be a little coldness on the other's side next time they met, for Lord Tilbury, he knew, was one of those men who rather readily take umbrage on discovering that they have paid a thousand pounds for nothing, but he was used to people being cold to him and could put up with that.

So here he was, making his last throw.

'You hid it?' said Lord Tilbury, after the detective in a brief opening speech had explained that he had not come to deliver the goods in person. 'But are you sure it is quite safe?'

'Oh, quite.'

'But why did you not bring it with you?'

'Too risky. You don't know what that house is like. There's Lady Constance after the thing and Gally Threepwood after the thing and Ronnie

Fish and . . . well, as I said to Monty Bodkin this afternoon, a fellow trying to smuggle that manuscript out of the place is rather like a chap in a
detective story trapped in the den of the Secret Nine.'

A little gasp of indignation forced itself from Monty's outraged lips.
This, he felt, was just that little bit that is too much. He had been modestly proud of that crack about the Secret Nine. Not content with pinching his manuscripts, this dastardly detective was pinching his nifties. It
was enough to make a fellow chafe and Monty chafed a good deal.

'I see,' said Lord Tilbury. 'Yes, I see what you mean. But if you hid it
in your bedroom . . .'

'I didn't.'

'Then where?'

The crucial moment had arrived, and Pilbeam braced himself to cope
with it.

'Ah!' he said. 'I think, perhaps, before I tell you that, we had better just get the business end of the thing settled, eh? If you have your
cheque-book handy . . .'

'But, my dear Pilbeam, surely you do not expect me to pay before . . .?'

'Quite,' said the detective, and held his breath. His stake was on the
board and the wheel had begun to spin.

It seemed to Monty that Lord Tilbury also must be holding his breath,
for there followed a long silence. When he did speak, his tone was that of
a man who has been wounded.

'Well, really, Pilbeam! I think you might trust me.'

'"Trust nobody" is the Pilbeam family motto,' replied the detective
with a return of what might be called his telephone manner.

'But how am I to know . . .?'

'You've got to trust me,' said Pilbeam brightly. 'Of course,' he went on,
'if you don't like that way of doing business, well, in that case, I suppose
the deal falls through. No hard feelings on either side. I simply go back
to the Castle and take the matter up with Sir Gregory Parsloe and Lady
Constance. They want that manuscript just as much as you do, though,
of course, their reasons aren't the same as yours. They want to destroy
it. Parsloe's original offer was five hundred pounds, but I shall have no
difficulty in making him improve on that . . .'

'Five hundred pounds is a great deal of money,' said Lord Tilbury, as if he were having a tooth out.

'It's not nearly as much as a thousand,' replied Pilbeam, as if he were a light-hearted dentist. 'And you agreed to that on the telephone.'

'Yes, but then I assumed that you would be bringing . . .'

'Well, take it or leave it, Tilbury, take it or leave it,' said the detective, and from the little crackling splutter which followed the words Monty deduced that he was doing what we are so strongly advised to do when we wish to appear nonchalant, lighting a cigarette. 'Good!' he said a moment later. 'I think you're wise. Make it open, if you don't mind.'

There was a pause. The heavy breathing that came through the window could only be that of a parsimonious man occupied in writing a cheque for a thousand pounds. It is a type of breathing which it is impossible to mistake, though in some respects it closely resembles the sound of a strong man's death agony.

'There!'

'Thanks.'

'And now—?'

'Well, I'll tell you,' said Pilbeam. 'It's like this. I didn't dare hide the thing in the house, so I put it carefully away in a disused pigsty near the kitchen garden. Wait. If you'll lend me your fountain pen, I'll draw you a map. See, here's the wall of the kitchen garden. You go along it, and on your left you will see this sty in a little paddock. You can't mistake it. It's the only building there. You go in and under the straw, where I'm putting this cross, is the manuscript. That's clear?'

'Quite clear.'

'You think you will be able to find it all right?'

'Perfectly easily.'

'Good. Well, now, there's just one other thing. The merest trifle, but you want to be prepared for it. I said this pigsty was disused, and when I put the manuscript in it so it was. But since then they've gone and shifted that pig of Lord Emsworth's there, the animal they call the Empress of Blandings.'

'What?'

'I thought I had better mention it, as otherwise it might have given you a surprise when you got there.'

The momentary spasm of justifiable indignation which had attacked Lord Tilbury on hearing this piece of information left him. In its place came, oddly enough, a distinct relief. In some curious way the statement had removed from his mind a doubt which had been lingering there. It made Pilbeam's story seem circumstantial.

'That is quite all right,' he said as cheerfully as could be expected of a man of his views on parting with money so soon after the writing of a thousand-pound cheque. 'That will cause no difficulty.'

'You think you can cope with this pig?'

'Certainly. I am not afraid of pigs. Pigs like me.'

At these words, Monty found his respect for a breed of animal which he had always rather admired waning a good deal. No animal of the right sort, he felt, could like Lord Tilbury.

'Then that's fine,' said Pilbeam. 'I'd start at once if I were you. Are you going to walk?'

'Yes.'

'You'll need a torch.'

'No doubt I can borrow one from the landlord of this inn.'

'Good. Then everything's all right.'

There came to Monty's ears the sound of the opening and closing of a door. Lord Tilbury had apparently left to begin the business of the night. For a moment Monty thought that Pilbeam must have left, too, but after a brief silence there came through the window a muttered oath, and, peeping in, he saw that the detective was leaning over the writing-desk. The ejaculation had presumably been occasioned by his discovery that there was no paper, no envelope, no pen, and only what a dreamer could have described as ink.

And such, indeed, was the case. Percy Pilbeam was a man who believed in prompt action. He intended to dispatch that cheque to his bank without delay.

He rang the bell.

'I want some ink,' Monty heard him say. 'And a pen and some paper and an envelope.'

He had placed the cheque on the desk before making the discovery of its lack of stationery. He now picked it up and stood looking at it lovingly.

He was well pleased with himself. It was a far, far better thing that he had done than he had ever done, felt Pilbeam. He wondered how many men there were who would have snatched victory out of defeat like that. He reached for his unpleasant moustache and gave it a complacent tug.

And, as he did so, over his shoulder there came groping a hand. The cheque was twitched from his grasp. And, turning, he perceived Monty Bodkin.

'Hell!' cried Pilbeam, aghast.

Monty did not reply. Actions speak louder than words. With a severe look, he tore the cheque in two pieces, then in four, then in eight, then in sixteen, then in thirty-two. Then, finding himself unable to bring the score up to sixty-four, he moved to the fireplace and, still with that austere expression on his face, dropped them in the grate like a shower of confetti.

After that first anguished cry Pilbeam had not spoken. He stood watching the tragedy with a frozen stare. It seemed to him that he had spent most of his later life looking at people tearing up cheques made out to himself. For one brief instant the battling spirit of the Pilbeams urged him to attack this man with tooth and claw, but the impulse faded. The Pilbeams might be brave, but they were not rash. Monty was some eight inches taller than himself, some twenty pounds heavier, and in addition to this had a nasty look in his eye.

He accepted the ruling of Destiny. In silence he watched Monty leave the room. The door closed. Percy Pilbeam was alone with his thoughts.

Monty strolled into the lounge of the Emsworth Arms. It was empty, but presently Lord Tilbury appeared, hatted, booted, and ready for the long trail. Monty eyed him sardonically. He proposed very shortly to put a stick of dynamite under this Lord Tilbury.

'Going out?' he said.

'I am taking a walk, yes.'

'God bless you!' said Monty.

He followed Lord Tilbury with his eye. Shortly he was going to follow him in actual fact. But that could wait. He knew that he could give that stout, stumpy man five minutes' start and still be at the tryst before him. And in the meantime there was grim work to be done.

He went to the telephone and rang up Blandings Castle.

'I want to speak to Lord Emsworth,' he said, in one of those gruff assumed voices that sound like a bull-frog with catarrh.

'I will put you through to his lordship,' replied the more melodious voice of Beach.

'Do so,' said Monty, sinking an octave. 'The matter is urgent.'

16

Lord Emsworth had taken his twisted ankle to the library and was lying with it on one of the leather-covered settees. The doctor had come and gone, leaving instructions for the application of hot fomentations and announcing that the patient was out of danger. And as the pain had now entirely disappeared it might have been supposed that the ninth Earl's mind would have been at rest.

This, however, was far from being the case. Not only was he anxiously awaiting the veterinary surgeon's report on the paper-filled Empress, which was enough to agitate any man ill accustomed to bear up calmly under suspense, but to add to his mental discomfort his two sisters, the Lady Constance Keeble and the Lady Julia Fish, had gathered about his sick-bed and were driving him half mad with some nonsense about his nephew Ronald's money.

However, for some time he had been adopting the statesman-like policy of saying 'Eh?' 'Yes?' 'Oh, ah?' and 'God bless my soul' at fairly regular intervals, and this had given him leisure to devote his mind to the things that really mattered.

Paper . . . Ink . . . wasn't ink a highly corrosive acid or something?

And could even the stoutest pig thrive on corrosive acids? Thus Lord Emsworth when his thoughts took a gloomy trend.

But there were optimistic gleams among the grey. He recalled the time when the Empress, mistaking his carelessly dropped cigar for something on the bill of fare, had swallowed it with every indication of enjoyment and had been none the worse next day. Also Pirbright's Sunday hat. There was another case that seemed to make for hopefulness. True, she had consumed only a mouthful or two of that, but to remain in excellent health and spirits after eating even a portion of the sort of hat that Pirbright wore on Sundays argued a constitution well above the average. Reviewing these alimentary feats of the past, Lord Emsworth was able to endure.

But he wished that Beach would return and put an end to this awful suspense. The butler had been dispatched with the vet to the sty to bring back his report, and should have been here long ago. Lord Emsworth found himself yearning for Beach's society as poets of a former age used to yearn for that of gazelles and Arab steeds.

It was at this tense moment in the affairs of the master of Blandings that Monty's telephone call came through.

'Lord Emsworth?' said a deep, odd voice.

'Lord Emsworth speaking.'

'I have reason to believe, Lord Emsworth . . .'

'Wait!' cried the ninth Earl. 'Wait a moment. Hold the line.' He turned. 'Well, Beach, well?'

'The veterinary surgeon reports, m'lord, that there is no occasion for alarm.'

'She's all right?'

'Quite, m'lord. No occasion for anxiety whatsoever.'

A deep sigh of relief shook Lord Emsworth.

'Eh?' said the voice at the other end of the wire, not knowing quite what to make of it.

'Oh, excuse me. I was just speaking to my butler about my pig. Extremely sorry to have kept you waiting, but it was most urgent. You were saying—?'

'I have reason to believe, Lord Emsworth, that an attack is to be made upon your pig tonight.'

Lord Emsworth uttered a sharp, gargling sound.

'What!'

'Yes.'

'You don't mean that?'

'Yes.'

'Oh, do hurry, Clarence,' said Lady Constance, who wished to get on with the business of the evening. 'Who is it? Tell him to ring up later.'

Lord Emsworth waved her down imperiously, and continued to bark into the telephone's mouthpiece like a sea-lion.

'Tonight?'

'Yes.'

'What time tonight?'

'Any time now.'

'What!'

('Oh, Clarence, do stop saying "What" and ring off.')

'Yes, almost immediately.'

'Are you sure?'

'Yes.'

'God bless my soul! What a ghastly thing! Well, I am infinitely obliged to you, my dear fellow . . . By the way, who are you?'

'A Well-wisher.'

'What?'

('Oh, Clar-*ence!*')

'A Well-wisher.'

'Fisher?'

'Wisher.'

'Disher? Beach,' cried Lord Emsworth, as a click from afar told him that the man of mystery had hung up, 'a Mr A. L. Fisher or Disher—I did not quite catch the name—says that an attack is to be made upon the Empress tonight.'

'Indeed m'lord?'

'Almost immediately.'

'Indeed, m'lord?'

'Don't keep saying "Indeed, m'lord", as if I were telling you it was a fine day! Can't you realize the frightful—? And you, Connie,' said Lord Emsworth, who was now in thoroughly berserk mood, turning on his sister like a stringy tiger, 'stop sniffing like that!'

'Really, Clarence!'

'Beach, go and bring Pirbright here.'

'He shall do nothing of the kind,' said Lady Constance sharply. 'The idea of bringing Pirbright into the library!'

It was not often that Beach found himself in agreement with the chatelaine of Blandings, but he could not but support her attitude now. Like all butlers, he held definite views on the sanctity of the home and frowned upon attempts on the part of the outside staff to enter it—especially when, like Pirbright, they smelt so very strongly of pigs. Five minutes of that richly scented man in the library, felt Beach, and you would have to send the place to the cleaner's.

'Perhaps if I were to convey a message to Pirbright from your lordship?' he suggested tactfully.

Lord Emsworth, though dangerously excited, could still listen to the voice of Reason. It was not the thought of the pig-man's aroma that made him change his mind—the library, in his opinion, would have been improved by a whiff of bouquet de Pirbright—but that deep, grave voice had said that the attack was to take place almost immediately, and in that case it would be madness to remove the garrison from its post even for an instant.

'Yes,' he said. 'A very good idea. Much better. Yes, capital. Excellent. Thank you, Beach.'

'Not at all, m'lord.'

'Go at once to Pirbright and tell him what I have told you, and say that he is to remain in hiding near the sty and spring out at the right moment and catch this fellow.'

'Very good, m'lord.'

'He had better strike him over the head with a stout stick.'

'Very good, m'lord.'

'So we shall wind up the evening with a nice murder,' said Lady Julia. 'Eh?'

'Don't pay any attention to me, of course. If you like to incite pig-men to brain people with sticks, it's none of my affair. But I should have thought you were taking a chance.'

Lord Emsworth seemed impressed.

'You think he might injure Parsloe fatally?'

'Parsloe!' Lady Constance's voice caused a statuette of the young David prophesying before Saul to quiver on its base. 'Are you off your head, Clarence?'

'No, I'm not,' replied Lord Emsworth manfully. 'What's the use of pre-tending that you don't know as well as I do that it's Parsloe who is making this attempt tonight? The way you let that fellow pull the wool over your eyes, Constance, amazes me. What do you think he wheedled you into inviting him to dinner for? So that he could be on the premises and have easy access to the Empress, of course. I'll bet you find he has sneaked off while you were not looking.'

'Clarence!'

'Well, where is he? Produce Parsloe! Show me Parsloe!'

'Sir Gregory left the house a few minutes ago. He wished to take a walk.'

'Take a walk!' This time it was Lord Emsworth's voice that rocked the young David. 'Beach, there isn't a moment to lose! Hurry, man, hurry! Run to Pirbright and say that the blow may fall at any moment.'

'Very good, m'lord. And in the matter of the stick—?'

'Tell him to use his own judgement.'

Lord Emsworth sank back on his settee. His mental condition resem-bled that of a warrior who, crippled by wounds, must stay in his tent while the battle is joined without. He snorted restlessly. His place was by Pirbright's side, and he could not get there. He put his foot to the floor and tentatively leaned his weight upon it but a facial contortion and a sharp 'Ouch!' showed that there was no hope. Pirbright, that strong shield of defence, must be left to deal with this matter alone.

'I'm sure everything will be quite all right, Clarence,' said Lady Julia, who believed in the methods of diplomacy, silencing with a little gesture her sister Constance, who did not.

'You really feel that?' said Lord Emsworth eagerly.

'Of course. You can trust Pirbright to see that nothing happens.'

'Yes. A good fellow, Pirbright.'

'I expect that when Sir Gregory sees him,' said Lady Julia, with a steady, quelling glance at her sister, who was once more sniffing in rather a marked manner, 'he will run away.'

'Pirbright will?' said Lord Emsworth, starting.

'No, Sir Gregory will. There is nothing for you to worry about at all. Just lie back and relax.'

'Bless my soul, you're a great comfort, Julia.'

'I try to be,' said Lady Julia virtuously.

'You've made me feel easier in my mind.'

'Splendid,' said Lady Julia, and with another little gesture she indicated to Lady Constance that the subject was now calmed and that she could proceed.

Lady Constance gave her a masonic glance of understanding.

'Julia is quite right,' she said. 'There is no need for you to worry.'

'Well, if you think that, too . . .' said Lord Emsworth, beginning to achieve something like that delightful feeling of *bien-être*.

'I do, decidedly. You can dismiss the whole thing from your mind and give me your attention again.'

'My attention? What do you want my attention for?'

'We were speaking,' said Lady Constance, 'of this money of Ronald's and the criminal folly of allowing him to have it in order that he may make a marriage of which Julia and I both disapprove so very strongly.'

'Oh, that?' said Lord Emsworth, the glow beginning to fade.

He looked at the door wistfully, feeling how easy a task it would have been, but for this ankle of his, to disappear through it like an eel and not let himself be cornered again before bedtime.

Cornered, however, he was. He leaned back against the cushions and women's voices began to beat upon him like rain upon a roof.

. . .

D own at the Emsworth Arms, Monty Bodkin had just decided to make a small alteration in the plan of action which he had outlined for himself. It had been his original intention, it may be recalled, to follow Lord Tilbury to the trap which he had prepared for him, so that, lurking in the background—probably with folded arms, certainly with a bitter sneer of triumph on his lips—he might have the gratification of witnessing his downfall. But when, wearying of the Wisher-Fisher-Disher controversy, he hung up the receiver and left the telephone booth, he found this project looking less attractive to him.

A man who is by nature a light baritone cannot conduct a conversation for any length of time in a deep bass without acquiring a parched and burning throat. Monty came out of the booth feeling as if his had been roughly sandpapered, and the thought of that two and a half mile walk to the Castle and its little brother, the two and a half mile walk back, intimidated him. The more he thought of it, the less worth while did it seem to him to go to all that fearful sweat simply in order to see the scruff of Lord Tilbury's neck grasped by a pig-man. Far better, he felt, to toddle along to the bar-parlour and there, over a soothing tankard, follow the scene with the eye of imagination.

Thither, accordingly, he made his way, and presently, seated in a corner with a stoup of the right stuff before him, was lubricating his tortured vocal chords and exchanging desultory chit-chat with the barmaid.

For himself, gripped as he still was by that melancholy which torments those who have loved and lost, Monty would have preferred to be allowed to meditate in silence. But as he happened to be the only customer in the place at the moment, the barmaid, a matronly lady in black satin with a bird's nest of gold hair on her head, was able to give him her full attention, and her social sense urged her to converse. On such occasions she very rightly regarded herself as a hostess.

They spoke, accordingly, of the weather, touching on such aspects of it as the heat before the storm, the coolness after the storm, the violence of the storm, its possible effect on the crops and what always happened to the barmaid's digestive organs when there was thunder. It was after she had finished a rather lengthy description (one which would, perhaps, have interested a physician more than a layman) of what she had suffered earlier in the summer through rashly eating cucumber during a storm that Monty happened to mention that he had been caught in the downpour.

'Not reely?' said the barmaid. 'What, were you out in it?'

'Absolutely,' said Monty. 'I got properly soaked.'

'But what a silly you must be, if you'll excuse me saying so,' observed the barmaid, 'not to have took shelter in a shop or somewhere. Or were you taking one of those country hikes?'

'I was in the park. Up at Blandings.'

'Oh, are you up at the Castle?' said the barmaid, interested.

'I was then,' said Monty, with reserve.

The barmaid polished a glass.

'There's a great to-do up there,' she said. 'I expect you've heard?'

'A to-do?'

'About his lordship's pig. Eating all that paper.'

'Eh?'

'Oh, you haven't heard?' said the barmaid, gratified. 'Oh, yes, his lordship is terribly upset. I had it from Mr Webber, the vet, who stepped in for a quick one on his way up there. He'd just been phoned for, extremely urgent. About half an hour ago, it was.'

'Paper?'

'That's what Mr Webber said. Some book his lordship's brother had been writing, he said, and somehow, he said, it had got into this pig's sty, and the pig had eaten it. That's what he said. Though how a book could have got into a pigsty, is more than I can tell you.'

The barmaid broke off to attend to a customer who came in for a stout-and-mild, and Monty was able to wrestle in silence with this extraordinary piece of news.

So that was why Pilbeam had been so urgent in demanding cash in advance! From the confused welter of Monty's thoughts there emerged a clear realization that there must be a lot of hidden good in Percy Pilbeam that he had overlooked. A man with the resource and initiative to extract a thousand pounds from Lord Tilbury for a piece of property which he knew to be in the process of being digested by a pig was surely a man of whom one wished to see more, a fellow one would like to know better. As he reviewed that scene in the writing-room and remembered the confidence with which the detective had stated his terms, the gallant nonchalance of that take-it-or-leave-it of his which had sent Lord Tilbury scrambling for his cheque-book, something very like a warm affection for Percy Pilbeam began to burgeon in Monty. He did his hair in a pretty gruesome way, and there was no question but that that moustache of his was a bit above the odds—nevertheless, he definitely felt that he would like to fraternize with the man.

He saw now—what had puzzled him before—why that cheque-tearing stuff had gone so big. At the moment of the cheque's destruction, Monty, like Ronnie Fish on another occasion, had intended merely the great gesture. Even while his fingers were busy, he was feeling that he was accomplishing little of practical value, because all the fellow had to do was to go and get another cheque from Lord Tilbury. But this news put an entirely different aspect on the matter. Obviously, Lord Tilbury would not do any more cheque-writing now. The great gesture had landed Pilbeam squarely in the soup, he realized, and, oddly enough, he felt remorseful.

He could now see the thing from Pilbeam's point of view. With a sum like a thousand pounds at stake, could the fellow be blamed for stooping to some fairly raw work? Was he not almost justified in going a bit near the knuckle in his methods? Absolutely, felt Monty as he sipped his tankard.

What with this dawning of the big, broad outlook and the excellence of the Emsworth Arms draught ale, he began to be conscious of an almost maudlin change in his attitude towards the investigator. Anyone who could send Lord Tilbury two and a half miles on a fool's errand was Monty's friend. More like a brother the detective now seemed than the tripe-hound he had once supposed him.

At this moment, just as he was at his mellowest, the man in person came into the bar-parlour.

'Good evening, sir,' said the barmaid in her spacious way. As with so many barmaids, there was always a suggestion in her manner of being somebody who was bestowing the Freedom of the City on someone.

'Evening,' said Pilbeam.

He caught sight of Monty in his corner, and frowned. If Monty had begun to warm to him, it was plain that he was nowhere near warming to Monty. He eyed him sourly. His intention had apparently been to consume liquid refreshment in the bar-parlour, but the sight of the person who had so recently impaired his finances made him change his mind. One does not drink in an atmosphere poisoned by a man who has just robbed one of a thousand pounds.

'I want a double whisky,' said Pilbeam. 'Send it into the writing-room, will you?'

He stalked out. The barmaid, whose manner during their brief conversation had shown impressments, jerked a rather awed thumb at the door.

'See that feller?' she said. 'Know who he is? Mr Voules, the chauffeur up at the Castle, was telling me. He runs a big detective agency in London. Employs hundreds and hundreds of skilled assistants, Mr Voules says. Sort of spider, if you get my meaning, sitting in his web and directing the movements of his skilled assistants.'

'Good gosh!' cried Monty.

'Yes,' said the barmaid, pleased at his emotion. She polished a glass with something of an air.

But Monty's emotion had been caused by something of which she was not aware. Where she beheld a good-gosher who good-goshed from sheer astonishment at her sensational information, this young man's good-goshing had not been due to surprise. It was that bit about the skilled assistants that had wrenched the ejaculation from Monty's lips. Those two words had given him the idea of a lifetime.

Thirty seconds later he was in the writing-room, the detective looking up at him like a startled basilisk.

'I know, I know,' said Monty, rightly interpreting the message in his eye. 'But I've got a bit of business to talk over. I can do you a spot of good, Pilbeam.'

It would be too much to say that the investigator's eye melted. It still looked like that of a basilisk. But at these words it became that of a basilisk which reserves its judgement.

'Well?' he said.

Monty perpended.

'It's a little difficult to know where to begin.'

'As far as I'm concerned,' said Pilbeam, his feelings momentarily overcoming his business instinct, 'you can begin by getting out of here and breaking your ruddy neck.'

Monty waved a pacific hand.

'No, no,' he urged. 'Don't talk like that. The wrong attitude, old soul. Not the right tone at all.'

At this moment there entered a lad in shirt-sleeves bearing the investigator's double whisky. The interruption served to enable Monty to marshal his thoughts. When the lad had withdrawn, he began to speak fluently and with ease.

'It's like this, my dear old chap,' he said, paying no heed to an odd noise which proceeded from his companion, who appeared not to like being called his dear old chap. 'I seem to recollect mentioning to you this afternoon that as far as my affairs were concerned there were wheels within wheels. Well, there are. Not long ago I became betrothed to a girl, and her ass of a father won't let me marry her unless I get a job and hold it down for a year. And, dash it, my every effort to do so seems to prove null and void, if null and void is the expression I want. No,' said Monty, gently corrective, 'it isn't a bit of luck for the girl. It's very tough on the girl. She loves me madly. On the other hand, being a sort of throwback to the Victorian age, she won't go against her old dad's wishes. So I've got to have that job. I tried being assistant editor of *Tiny Tots*. No good. The boot. I became secretary to old Emsworth. Again no good. Once more the boot. And this is the idea that struck me just now, listening to the conversation of that female who works the beer-engine out there. You run a detective agency. You employ hundreds of skilled assistants. Well, come on now, be a sport. Employ me!'

The only reason why Percy Pilbeam did not at this point interject a blistering comment on the proposal thus put before him was that three such comments entered his mind simultaneously, and in the effort to decide which was the most blistering he drank some whisky the wrong way. Before he had finished choking, Monty had gone on to speak further. And what he went on to say was so amazing, so arresting, that the investigator found himself choking again.

'There's a thousand quid in it for you.'

Percy Pilbeam at last contrived to clear his vocal chords.

'A thousand quid?'

'Oh, I've got packets of money,' said Monty, misreading the look in those watering eyes and taking it for incredulity. 'I'm simply ill with the stuff. If money had been the trouble, there never would have been any trouble, if you follow what I mean. That hasn't been the difficulty. What's been the difficulty has been the extraordinary mental attitude of J. G. Butterwick. He insists . . .'

An astonishing change had come over the demeanour of P. Frobisher Pilbeam. One has seen much the same thing, of course, in the film of Jekyll and Hyde, but on a much less impressive scale. His scowling face had melted into a face that glowed as if lit by some inner lantern. Aesthetically, he looked equally unpleasant whether scowling or smiling, but Monty was far from being in the frame of mind to regard him from the austere standpoint of a judge in a Beauty Competition. He saw the smile, and his heart leaped within him.

Pilbeam had still to wrestle with his emotions for a moment before he could speak.

'You'll pay a thousand pounds to come into my Agency?'

'That exact figure.'

'For a thousand pounds,' said Pilbeam simply, 'you can be a partner, if you like.'

'But I don't like,' said Monty urgently. 'You're missing the idea. This has got to be a job. I want to be a skilled assistant.'

'You shall be.'

'For a year?'

'For ten years, if you want to.'

Monty sat down. There was in the simple action something of the triumph and exhaustion of the winner of a Marathon race. He stared in silence for a moment at a framed advertisement of Sigbee's Soda ('It Sizzles') which was assisting the wallpaper to impart to the room that note of hideousness at which hotel-keepers strive.

'Butterwick's her name,' he said at length. 'Gertrude Butterwick.'

'Yes?' said Pilbeam. 'Where's your cheque-book?'

'Her eyes,' said Monty, 'are grayish. And yet, at the same time blue-ish.'

'I bet they are,' said Pilbeam. 'In one of your pockets, perhaps?'

'About her hair,' said Monty. 'Some people might call it brown. Chest-nut has always seemed to me a closer description. She's tallish, but not too tall. Her mouth . . .'

'I'll tell you,' said Pilbeam. 'Let me get a sheet of paper.'

'You want me to draw you a picture of her?' said Monty, a little doubtfully.

'I want you to write a cheque for me.'

'Oh, ah, yes, I see what you mean. My cheque-book's upstairs in my suitcase.'

'Then come along,' said Pilbeam buoyantly, 'and I'll help you unpack.'

B each sat in his pantry, sipping brandy. And if ever a butler was entitled to a glass of brandy, that butler, he felt, was himself. He rolled the stuff round his tongue, finding a certain comfort in the fiery sting of it.

His heart was heavy. It was a kindly heart, and from the very first it had been deeply stirred by the stormy romance of Mr Ronald and his young lady. He wished that life were as the writers of the detective sto-ries, to which he had become so addicted, portrayed it. In those, no mat-ter what obstacles Fate might interpose in the shape of gangs, shots in the night, underground cellars, sinister Chinamen, poisoned asparagus and cobras down the chimney, the hero always got his girl. In the pres-ent case Beach could see no such happy ending. The significance of the presence in the library of Lady Constance Keeble and Lady Julia Fish had not escaped him. He feared that it meant the worst.

Eighteen years of close association with Clarence, Earl of Emsworth, had left the butler with a very fair estimate of his overlord's character. He wished well to everyone—Beach knew that. But where viewpoints clashed and arguments began, a passionate desire for peace at any price would undoubtedly lead him to decide in favour of whoever argued loudest. And eighteen years of close association with Lady Constance Keeble told Beach who, on the present occasion, that would be.

He saw no hope. Sighing despondently, he helped himself to another glass of brandy. Usually at this hour he drank port. But port to him was a symbol. He never touched it till dinner was over and the coffee served, and it signified that the responsibilities of his office were at an end and that until the morrow should bring its new cares and duties his soul was at rest. Port tonight would have been quite unsuitable.

Sighing again and about to start sipping once more, he became aware that he was no longer alone. Mr Ronald had entered the room.

'Don't get up, Beach,' said Ronnie.

He sat down on the table. His face had a pinkness deeper than its wont. There was a repressed excitement in his manner. The butler was reminded of that other occasion, ten days ago, when this young man had come into his pantry looking much the same as he was looking now and, having announced that he intended to steal his lordship's pig, had proceeded to cajole him into becoming his accomplice and helping him to feed the animal. The weighing machine in the servants' bathroom had informed Beach that he had lost three pounds in two days over that little affair.

'Bad show, this, Beach.'

Beach stirred mountainously. Solicitude shone from his prominent eyes. It has already been mentioned that Beach in the drawing-room and Beach in his pantry were different entities. He was now in his pantry, where he could cast off the official mask and be the man with whom a younger Ronnie had once played bears on this very floor.

'Extremely, Mr Ronald. Then you have heard?'

'Heard?'

'The unfortunate news.'

'You were there when I heard it. In the hall.'

The butler rolled his eyes, to indicate that there was something much more Stop Press than that.

'The Empress has eaten Mr Galahad's book, Mr Ronald.'

'What!'

'Yes, sir. Somebody apparently left it in her sty, and she was devouring the last of it when his lordship found her.'

'Pilbeam!'

'So one would be disposed to imagine, Mr Ronald. No doubt he had employed the sty as a hiding-place.'

'And it's gone?'

'Quite gone, Mr Ronald.'

'And Aunt Constance knows about it?'

'I fear so, Mr Ronald.'

Ronnie's face became a little pinker.

'Well, it doesn't make much odds. There was never any chance of recovering it from Pilbeam. That's why I . . . I think I could do with a spot of that brandy, Beach.'

'Certainly, sir. I will get you a glass. Why you . . . you were saying, Mr Ronald?'

'Oh, just a sort of decision I came to. This is good stuff, Beach.'

'Yes, sir.'

'A sort of decision,' said Ronnie, sipping pensively. 'I don't know if you noticed that I was a bit quiet at dinner?'

'You did strike me as somewhat silent, Mr Ronald.'

'I was thinking.'

'I see, sir.'

'Thinking,' repeated Ronnie. 'Doing a bit of avenue-exploring. I came to this decision with the fish.'

'Indeed, sir?'

'Yes. And I think it will work, too.'

Ronnie swung his legs for a while without speaking.

'Have you ever been in love, Beach?'

'In my younger days, Mr Ronald. It never came to anything.'

'Love's a rummy thing, Beach.'

'Very true, sir.'

'Sort of keys you up, if you understand me. Makes you feel you'd stick at nothing. Take any chance. To win the girl you love, I mean.'

'Quite so, sir.'

'Go through fire and water, as you might say. Brave every peril.'

'No doubt, sir.'

'Got another dollop of that brandy, Beach?'

'Yes, sir.'

'Well, there it is,' said Ronnie, emptying his glass and holding it out for fresh supplies. 'Half-way through the fish course I made up my mind. Now that that manuscript has gone, I'm up against it. At any moment Aunt Constance will be at Uncle Clarence, telling him not to give me my money.'

The butler coughed commiseratingly.

'I rather fancy, Mr Ronald, that her ladyship was in the act of doing so when I entered the library not long ago.'

'Then by this time she has probably clicked?'

'I very much fear so, Mr Ronald.'

'Right!' said Ronnie briskly. 'Then there's nothing left but strong measures. The time has come to act, Beach.'

'Sir?'

'I'm going to steal that pig.'

'What, *again*, Mr Ronald?'

Ronnie eyed him affectionately.

'Ah, you remember that other time, then?'

'Remember it, Mr Ronald? Why, it was only ten days ago.'

'So it was. It seems years. Not that I can't recall every detail of it. I haven't forgotten how staunchly you stood by me then, Beach. You were splendid.'

'Thank you, sir.'

'Wonderful! Marvellous!' continued Ronnie in an exalted voice. 'I doubt if there has ever been anybody who came out of an affair better than you did out of that one. A sportsman to the finger-tips, that's what you showed yourself. And don't,' said Ronnie earnestly, 'think that I didn't notice it, either. I appreciated it very much, Beach.'

'It is very kind of you to say so, sir,' said the butler, his head swimming a little.

'You're a fellow a fellow can rely on.'

'Thank you, sir.'

'Through thick and thin.'

'Thank you, sir.'

'When I got this idea of stealing the Empress this second time, Miss Brown said to me, "Oh, but you can't ask Beach to help you again." And I said, "Of course I can. Apart from the fact that Beach and I have been pals for eighteen years, he's devoted to you." And she said, "Is he?" and I said, "You bet he is. There's nothing in the world Beach wouldn't do for you." And she said, "The darling!" Just like that. And you should have seen the look in her eyes as she said it, Beach. They went all soft and dreamy. I believe if you had been there at the moment she would have kissed you. And I shall be greatly surprised,' said Ronnie, with the air of one offering a treat to a deserving child, 'if, when everything is over and you've been as staunch as you were before and chipped in and done your bit again, as you did then, she doesn't do it.'

All through this moving address the butler had been shaking and rumbling in a manner which would have reminded an eyewitness irresistibly of a volcano on the point of finding self-expression. His eyes had bulged, and his breathing was coming in little puffs.

'But, Mr Ronald!'

'I knew you would be pleased, Beach.'

'But, Mr Ronald!'

Ronnie eyed him sharply.

'Don't tell me you're thinking of backing out?'

'But, sir!'

'You can't at the last moment like this, after all our plans have been made. It would upset everything. I can't act without you. You wouldn't let me down, Beach?'

'But, sir, the risk!'

'Risk? Nonsense.'

'But, Mr Ronald, his lordship was notified on the telephone in my presence not half an hour ago that an attempt was to be made upon the Empress tonight. I have only just returned from seeing Pirbright and conveying his lordship's instructions to him to be on his guard.'

'Well, that's fine. Don't you see how this fits in with our plans? Pirbright will be waiting for this chap. He will catch him. And then what will he do, Beach? He will march him off to Uncle Clarence, leaving the coast absolutely clear. While he's gone we nip in and collar the animal without the slightest danger of inconvenience.'

The butler puffed silently.

'Think what it means, Beach! My happiness! Miss Brown's happiness! You aren't going to go through the rest of your life kicking yourself at the thought that a little zeal, a little of the pull-together spirit on your part would have meant happiness for Miss Brown?'

'But if I were detected, sir, my position would be so extremely equivocal.'

'How can you be detected? Pirbright won't be there. Nobody will be there. I only need your help for about five minutes. This isn't like the last time. I'm not planning to hide the Empress somewhere and feed her. This is the real, straight kidnapping stuff. Just five minutes of your time, Beach, just five little minutes and you can come back here and forget all about it.'

Strong tremors continued to shake the butler's massive frame.

'Really only five minutes, Mr Ronald?' he said pleadingly.

'Ten at the outside. I forgot to tell you, Beach, that one of the things Miss Brown said about you was that you reminded her of her father. Oh, yes, and that you had such kind eyes.'

The butler's mouth opened. Lava might have been expected to flow from it, for his resemblance to a volcano had now become exceptionally close. But it was not lava that emerged. What did so was a strangled croak. This was followed by a remark which Ronnie did not catch.

'Eh?'

'I said "Very good," Mr Ronald,' said Beach, looking as if he were facing a firing squad.

'You'll do it?'

'Yes, Mr Ronald.'

'Beach,' said Ronnie with emotion, 'when I'm a millionaire, as I expect to be a few years after I've put my money in that motor business, the first thing I shall do is to come to this pantry with a purse of gold. Two purses of gold. Dash it, a keg of gold. I'll roll it in and knock off the lid and tell you to wade in and help yourself.'

'Thank you, Mr Ronald.'

'Don't thank *me*, Beach. You're the fellow who's entitled to all the gratitude that's going. And, talking of going, shall we be? There isn't a moment to lose. Shift ho, yes?'

'Very good, Mr Ronald,' said the butler in a strange, deep, rumbling voice, not unlike that of Mr A. L. Disher on the telephone.

17

LADY Julia Fish gave a little yawn and moved towards the door. For ten minutes she had been listening to her sister Constance express her views on the subject under discussion, and she was not a woman who accepted contentedly a thinking rôle in any scene in which she took part. If Connie had a fault—and offhand she could name a dozen—it was that she tended to elbow her associates out of the picture at times like this. Standing by and acting as a silent audience bored Lady Julia.

'Well, if anybody wants me,' she said, 'they'll find me in the drawing-room.'

'Are you going, Julia?'

'There doesn't seem much for me to do round here. I feel that I am leaving the thing in competent hands. You speak for me. The voice is the voice of Constance, but you can take the sentiments, Clarence, as representing the views of a syndicate.'

Lord Emsworth watched her go without much sense of consolation. It is better, perhaps, to have one woman rather than two women making your life an inferno, but not so much better as to cause an elderly gentleman of quiet tastes to rejoice to any very marked extent.

'Now, listen, Clarence . . .'

Lord Emsworth stifled a moan, and tried—a task which the deaf adder of Scripture apparently found so easy—to hear nothing and give his mind to the things that really mattered.

He shifted restlessly on his settee. Surely soon there ought to be news from the Front. By this time, if Mr Disher was to be believed, the assault should have been made and, one hoped, rolled back by the devoted Pirbright.

Musing on Pirbright, Lord Emsworth became a little calmer. A capital fellow, he told himself, just the chap to handle the emergency which had arisen. Not much of a conversationalist, perhaps; scarcely the companion one would choose for a long railway journey; a little on the 'Ur' and 'Yur' side; but then who wanted a lively and epigrammatic pig-man? The point about Pirbright was that, if silent, he had that quality which so proverbially goes with silence—strength.

The door opened.

'Well, Beach?' said Lady Constance with queenly displeasure, for nobody likes to be interrupted in moments of oratory. 'What is it?'

Lord Emsworth sat up expectantly.

'Well, Beach, well?'

A close observer, which his lordship was not, would have seen that the butler had recently passed through some soul-searing experience. His was never a rosy face, but now it wore a pallor beyond the normal. His eyes were round and glassy, his breathing laboured. He looked like a butler who has just been brought into sharp contact with the facts of life.

'Everything is quite satisfactory, m'lord.'

'Pirbright caught the fellow?'

'Yes, m'lord.'

'Did he tell you what happened?'

'I was an eye-witness of the proceedings, m'lord.'

'Well? Well?'

'Oh, Clarence, must we really have all this now?'

'What? What? What? Of course we must have it now. God bless my soul! Yes, Beach?'

'The facts, m'lord, are as follows. In pursuance of your lordship's instructions, Pirbright had placed himself in concealment in the vicinity of the animal's sty, and from this post of vantage proceeded to keep a keen watch.'

'What were you doing there?'

The butler hesitated.

'I had come to lend assistance, m'lord, should it be required.'

'Splendid, Beach. Well?'

'My cooperation, however, was not found to be necessary. The man arrived . . .'

'Parsloe?'

('Clarence!')

'No, m'lord. Not Sir Gregory.'

'Ah, an accomplice.'

('Oh, Clarence!')

'No doubt, m'lord. The man arrived and came to the rails of the sty, where he remained for a moment . . .'

'Nerving himself! Nerving himself to his frightful task.'

'He seemed to be manipulating an electric torch, m'lord.'

'And then—?'

'Pirbright sprang out and overpowered him.'

'Excellent! And where is the fellow now?'

'Temporarily incarcerated in the coal-cellar, m'lord.'

'Bring him to me at once.'

'Clarence, do we want this man, whoever he is, in here?'

'Yes, we do want him in here.'

Beach coughed.

'I should mention, m'lord, that he is considerably soiled. In order to overpower him, Pirbright was compelled to throw him face downwards and rest his weight upon him, and the ground in the neighbourhood of the sty had been somewhat softened by the heavy rain.'

'Never mind. I want to see him.'

'Very good, m'lord.'

The interval between the butler's retirement and reappearance was spent by Lady Constance in sniffing indignantly and by Lord Emsworth in congratulating himself that a sense of civic duty and a lively apprehension of what his sister would say if he resigned that office had kept him a Justice of the Peace. Representing, as he did, the majesty of the Law, he was in a position to deal summarily with this criminal. He would have to look it up in the book of instructions, of course, but he rather fancied he could give the chap fourteen days without moving from this settee.

The door had opened again.

'The miscreant, m'lord,' announced Beach.

With a final sniff, Lady Constance dissociated herself from the affair by withdrawing into a corner and opening a photograph album. There was a scuffling of feet, and the prisoner at the bar entered, trailing like clouds of glory Stokes, first footman, attached to his right arm, and Thomas, second footman, clinging like a limpet to his left.

'Good God!' cried Lord Emsworth, startled out of his judicial calm. 'What a horrible-looking brute!'

Lord Tilbury, though resenting the description keenly, would have been compelled, had he been able at the moment to look in a mirror, to recognize its essential justice. Beau Brummell himself could not have remained spruce after lying in four inches of mud with a six-foot pig-man on top of him. Pirbright was a man who believed that a thing well begun is half done, and his first act had been to thrust Lord Tilbury's face firmly below the surface and keep it there.

A sudden idea struck Lord Emsworth.

'Beach!'

'Did Pirbright say if this was the same fellow he shut up in the shed yesterday?'

'Yes, m'lord.'

'It is?'

'Yes, m'lord.'

'God bless my soul!' cried Lord Emsworth.

This pertinacity appalled him. It showed how dangerous the chap was. None of that business here of the burned child dreading the potting-shed. No sooner was this fellow out of that mess than back he came for a second pop, as malignant as ever. The quicker he was put safely way behind the bars of Market Blandings' picturesque little prison, the better, felt Lord Emsworth.

He was interrupted in this meditation by a voice proceeding from behind the mud.

'Lord Emsworth, I wish to speak to you alone.'

'Well, you dashed well can't speak to me alone,' replied his lordship with decision. 'Think I'm going to allow myself to be left alone with a fellow like you? Beach!'

'M'lord?'

'Take that thingummajig,' said Lord Emsworth, indicating the young David prophesying before Saul, 'and if he so much as stirs hit him a good hard bang with it.'

'Very good, m'lord.'

'Now, then, what's your name?'

'I refuse to tell you my name unless you will let me speak to you alone.'

Lord Emsworth's gaze hardened.

'You notice how he keeps wanting to get me alone, Beach.'

'Yes, m'lord.'

'Suspicious.'

'Yes, m'lord.'

'Stand by with that thing.'

'Very good, m'lord,' said the butler, taking a firmer grip on David's left leg.

'Hallo,' said a voice. 'What's all this? Ah, Connie, I thought I should find you here.'

Lord Emsworth, peering through his pince-nez, perceived that his brother Galahad had entered the room. With him was that little girl of Ronald's. At the sight of her Lord Emsworth found his righteous wrath tinged with a certain embarrassment.

'Don't come in here now, Galahad, there's a good fellow,' he begged. 'I'm busy.'

'Good God! What on earth's that?' cried the Hon. Galahad, his monocle leaping from his eye as he suddenly caught sight of the mass of alluvial deposits which was Lord Tilbury.

'It's a horrible chap Pirbright found sneaking into the Empress's sty,' explained Lord Emsworth. 'Parsloe's accomplice, whom you warned me about. I'm just going to give him fourteen days.'

This frank statement of policy decided Lord Tilbury. For the second time that day he thought on his feet. Passionately though he desired to preserve his incognito, he did not wish to do so at the expense of two weeks in jail.

'Threepwood,' he cried, 'tell this old fool who I am.'

The Hon. Galahad had recovered his monocle.

'But, my dear chap,' he protested, staring through it, 'I don't know who you are. You look like one of those Sons of Toil Buried by Tons of Soil I once saw in a headline. Are you somebody I've met?' He peered more closely and uttered an astonished cry. 'Stinker! Is it really you, my poor old Stinker, hidden away under all that real estate? I can explain all this, Clarence. I think first, perhaps, though, it would be as well to clear the court. Pop off, Beach, for a moment, if you don't mind.'

'Very good, Mr Galahad,' said Beach, with the disappointed air of a man who is being thrown out of a theatre just as the curtain is going up. He put down the young David and, collecting eyes like a hostess at a dinner-party, led Thomas and Stokes from the room.

'Is it safe, Galahad?' said Lord Emsworth dubiously.

'Oh, Stinker—Pyke, I mean—Tilbury, that is to say, is quite harmless.'

'What did you say his name was?'

'Tilbury. Lord Tilbury.'

'*Lord* Tilbury?' said Lord Emsworth, gaping.

'Yes. Apparently they've made old Stinker a peer.'

'Then what was he doing trying to kill my pig?' asked Lord Emsworth, perplexed, for he had a high opinion of the moral purity of the House of Lords.

'He wasn't trying to kill your blasted pig. You came after that manuscript of mine, eh, Stinker?'

'I did,' said Lord Tilbury stiffly. 'I consider that I have a legal right to it.'

'Yes, we went into all that before, I remember. But abandon all hope, Stinker. There isn't any manuscript. The pig's eaten it.'

'What!'

'Yes. So unless you care to publish the pig . . . .'

There was too much mud on Lord Tilbury's face to admit of any play of expression, but the sudden rigidity of his body told how shrewdly the blow had gone home.

'Oh!' he said at length.

'I'm afraid so,' said the Hon. Galahad sympathetically.

'If you will excuse me,' said Lord Tilbury, 'I will return to the Emsworth Arms.'

The Hon. Galahad took his soiled arm.

'My dear old chap! You can't possibly go to any pub looking like that. Beach will show you to the bathroom. Beach!'

'Sir?' said the butler, manifesting himself with the celerity of one who has never been far from the keyhole.

'Take Lord Tilbury to the bathroom, and then telephone to the Emsworth Arms to send up his things. He will be staying the night. Several nights. In fact, indefinitely. Yes, yes, Stinker, I insist. Dash it, man, we haven't seen one another for twenty-five years. I want a long yarn with you about the old days.'

For an instant it seemed as if the proud spirit of the Pykes was to flame in revolt. Lord Tilbury definitely drew himself up. But he was not the man he had been. Every man, moreover, has his price. That of the proprietor of the Mammoth Publishing Company at this moment was a hot bath with plenty of soap, a sprinkling of bath-salts, and well-warmed towels.

'Kind of you,' he said gruffly.

Like the mountain reluctantly deciding to come to Mahomet, he followed Beach from the room.

'And now, Connie,' said the Hon. Galahad, 'you can put that book down and come and join the party.'

Lady Constance moved with dignified step from her corner.

'I suppose,' said the Hon. Galahad, eyeing her unfraternally, 'you've been nagging and bullying poor old Clarence till he doesn't know where he is?'

'I have been giving Clarence my views.'

'You would. I suppose the poor devil's half off his head.'

'Clarence has been listening very patiently and attentively,' said Lady Constance. 'I think he understands what is the right thing for him to do in this matter—a matter which I must say I would prefer to discuss, if we are going to discuss it, in private.'

'You mean you don't want Sue here?'

'I should imagine that Miss Brown would find it less embarrassing not to be present.'

'Well, I do want her here,' said the Hon. Galahad. 'I brought her specially. To show her to you, Clarence.'

'Eh?' said Lord Emsworth, jumping. He had been dreaming of pigs.

'To show her to you, I said. I want you to take a look at this little girl, Clarence. Get those dashed pince-nez of yours straight and examine her steadily and carefully. What do you think of her?'

'Charming, charming,' said Lord Emsworth courteously.

'Isn't she just the very girl any sensible man would choose for his nephew's wife?'

'My dear Galahad!' said Lady Constance.

'Well?'

'I cannot see what all this is leading to. I imagine that nobody is disputing the fact that Miss Brown is a pretty girl.'

'Pretty girl be dashed! I'm not talking about her being a pretty girl. I'm talking of what anybody with half an eye ought to be able to see when he takes one look at her—that she's all right. Just as her mother was all right. Her mother was the sweetest, straightest, squarest, honestest, jolliest thing that ever lived. And Sue's the same. Any man who marries Sue is in luck. Damn it all, the way you women have been going on about him, one would think young Ronnie was the Prince of Wales or something. Who *is* Ronnie, dash it? My nephew. Well, look at me. Do you mean to assert that a fellow handicapped by an uncle like me isn't jolly lucky to get *any* girl to marry him?'

This sentiment so exactly chimed in with her own views that for once in her masterful life Lady Constance had nothing to say. She seemed vaguely to suspect a fallacy somewhere, but before she could investigate it her brother had gone on speaking.

'Clarence,' he said, 'take that infernal glassy look out of your eyes and listen to me. I realize that you hold the situation in your hands. You can't have been hearing Connie talk for any length of time without knowing that. This little girl's happiness depends entirely on what you make up your woolly, wobbly mind to do. Nobody is more alive than myself to the fact that young Ronnie, like all members of this family, is worth about twopence a week in the open market. He's got to have capital behind him.'

'Which he won't have.'

'Which he will have, if Clarence is the man I take him for. Clarence, wake up!'

'I'm awake, my dear fellow, I'm awake,' said Lord Emsworth.

'Well, then, does Ronnie get his money or doesn't he?'

Lord Emsworth looked like a hunted stag. He fiddled nervously with his pince-nez.

'Connie seems to think. . .'

'I know what Connie thinks, and when we're alone I'll tell you what I think of Connie.'

'If you are simply going to be abusive, Galahad . . .'

'Nothing of the kind. Abusive be dashed! I am taking great pains to avoid anything in the remotest degree personal or offensive. I consider you a snob and a mischief-maker, but you may be quite sure I shall not dream of saying so . . .'

'How very kind of you.'

'. . . until I am at liberty to confide it to Clarence in private. Well, Clarence?'

'Eh? What? Yes, my dear fellow?'

'It's a simple issue. Are you going to do the square thing or are you not?'

'Well, I'll tell you, Galahad. The view Connie takes . . .'

'Oh, damn Connie!'

'Galahad!'

'Yes, I repeat it. Damn Connie! Forget Connie. Drive it into your head that the view Connie takes doesn't amount to a row of beans.'

'Indeed! Really! Well, allow me to tell *you* Galahad . . .'

'I won't allow you to tell me a thing.'

'I insist on speaking.'

'I won't listen.'

'Galahad!'

'May I say something?' said Sue.

She spoke in a small, deprecating voice, but if it had been a bellow it could scarcely have produced a greater effect. Lord Emsworth, in particular, who had forgotten that she was there, leaped on his settee like a gaffed trout.

'It's only this,' said Sue, in the silence. 'I'm awfully sorry to upset everybody, but Ronnie and I are motoring to London tonight, and we're going to get married tomorrow.'

'What!'

'Yes,' said Sue. 'You see, there's been so much trouble and misunderstanding and everything's so difficult as it is at present that we talked it over and came to the conclusion that the only safe thing is to be married. Then we feel that everything will be all right.'

Lady Constance turned majestically to the head of the family.

'Do you hear this, Clarence?'

'What do you mean, do I hear it?' said Lord Emsworth with that weak testiness which always came upon him when family warfare centred about his person. 'Of course I hear it. Do you think I'm deaf?'

'Well, I hope you will show a little firmness for once in your life.'

'Firmness?'

'Exert your authority. Forbid this.'

'How the devil can I forbid it? This is a free country, isn't it? People have a perfect right to motor to London if they want to, haven't they?'

'You know quite well what I mean. If you are firm about not letting Ronald have his money, he can do nothing.'

The Hon. Galahad seemed regretfully to be of this opinion, too.

'My dear child,' he said, 'I don't want to damp you, but what on earth are you going to live on?'

'I think that when he hears everything, Lord Emsworth will give Ronnie his money.'

'Eh?'

'That's what Ronnie thinks. He thinks that when Lord Emsworth knows that he has got the Empress . . .'

Lord Emsworth rose up like a rising pheasant.

'What! What? What's that? Got her? How do you mean, got her?'

'He took her out of her sty just now,' explained Sue, 'and put her in the dicky of his car.'

Even in his anguish Lord Emsworth had to stop to inquire into this seemingly superhuman feat.

'What! How on earth could anyone put the Empress in the dicky of a car?'

'Exactly,' said Lady Constance. 'Surely even you, Clarence, can see that this is simply ridiculous . . .'

'Oh, no,' said Sue. 'It was quite easy, really. Ronnie pulled—and a friend of his pushed.'

'Of course,' said the Hon. Galahad, the expert. 'What you're forgetting, Clarence, what you've overlooked is the fact that the Empress has a ring through her nose, which facilitates moving her from spot to spot. When Puffy Benger and I stole old Wivenhoe's pig the night of the Bachelor's Ball at Hammer's Easton in ninety-five, we had to get her up three flights of stairs before we could put her in Plug Basham's bedroom . . .'

'What Ronnie says he thinks he'll do,' proceeded Sue, 'is to take the Empress joy-riding . . .'

'Joy-riding!' cried Lord Emsworth, appalled.

'Only if you won't give him his money, of course. If you really don't feel you can, he says he's going to drive her all over England . . .?'

'What an admirable idea!' said the Hon. Galahad with approval. 'I see what you mean. Birmingham today, Edinburgh tomorrow, Brighton the day after. Sort of circular tour. See the country a bit, what?'

'Yes.'

'He ought to take in Skegness. Skegness is so bracing.'

'I must tell him.'

Lord Emsworth was fighting to preserve what little sanity he had.

'I don't believe it,' he cried.

'Ronnie thought you might not. He felt that you would probably want to see for yourself. So he's waiting down there on the drive, just outside the window.'

It was not at a time like this that Lord Emsworth would allow a trifle like an injured ankle to impede him. He sprang acrobatically from the settee and hopped to the window.

From the dicky of the car immediately below it the mild face of the Empress peered up at him, silvered by the moonlight. He uttered a fearful cry.

'Ronald!'

His nephew, seated at the wheel, glanced up, tooted the horn with a sort of respectful regret, threw in his clutch, and passed on into the shadows. The tail-light of the car shone redly as it halted some fifty yards down the drive.

'I'm afraid it's no good shouting at him,' said Sue.

'Of course it isn't,' agreed the Hon. Galahad heartily. 'What you want to do, Clarence, is to stop all this nonsense and give a formal promise before witnesses to cough up that money, and then write a cheque for a thousand or two for honeymoon expenses.'

'That was what Ronnie suggested,' said Sue. 'And then Pirbright could go and take the Empress back to bed.'

'Clarence!' began Lady Constance.

But Lord Emsworth in his travail was proof against any number of 'Clarence's!' He had hopped to the desk and with feverish fingers was fumbling in the top drawer.

'Clarence, you are not to do this!'

'I certainly am going to do it,' said Lord Emsworth, testing a pen with his thumb.

'Does this miserable pig mean more to you than your nephew's whole future?'

'Of course it does,' said Lord Emsworth, surprised at the foolish question. 'Besides, what's wrong with his future? His future's all right. He's going to marry this nice little girl here; I've forgotten her name. She'll look after him.'

'Bravely spoken, Clarence,' said the Hon. Galahad approvingly. 'The right spirit.'

'Well, in that case . . .'

'Don't go, Connie,' urged the Hon. Galahad. 'We may need you as a witness or something. In any case, surely you can't tear yourself away from a happy scene like this? Why, dash it, it's like that thing of Kipling's . . . how does it go . . .?

> '"We left them all in couples a-dancing on the decks,
> We left the lovers loving and the parents signing cheques,
> In endless English comfort, by County folk caressed,
> We steered the old three-decker . . ."'

The door slammed.

'" . . . to the Islands of the Blest,"' concluded the Hon. Galahad. 'Write clearly, Clarence, on one side of the paper, and don't forget to sign your name, as you usually do. The date is August the fourteenth.'

18

THE red tail-light of the two-seater turned the corner of the drive and vanished in the night. The Hon. Galahad polished his monocle thoughtfully, replaced it in his eye, and stood for some moments gazing at the spot where it had disappeared. The storm had left the air sweet and fresh. The moon rode gallantly in a cloudless sky. The night was very still, so still that even the lightest footstep on the gravel would have made itself heard. The one which now attracted the Hon. Galahad's attention was not light. It was the emphatic, crunching thump of a man of substance.

He turned.

'Beach?'

'Yes, Mr Galahad.'

'What are you doing out at this time of night?'

'I thought that I would pay a visit to the sty, sir, and ascertain that the Empress had taken no harm from her disturbed evening.'

'Remorse, eh?'

'Sir?'

'Guilty conscience. It was you who did the pushing, wasn't it, Beach?'

'Yes, sir. We discussed the matter, and Mr Ronald was of the opinion that on account of my superior weight I would be more effective than himself in that capacity.' A note of anxiety crept into the butler's voice. 'You will treat this, Mr Galahad, as purely confidential, I trust?'

'Of course.'

'Thank you, sir. It would jeopardize my position, I fear, were his lordship to learn of what I had done. I saw Mr Ronald and the young lady go off, Mr Galahad.'

'You did? I didn't see you.'

'I had taken up a position some little distance away, sir.'

'You ought to have come and said good-bye.'

'I had already taken leave of the young couple, sir. They visited me in my pantry.'

'So they ought. You have fought the good fight, Beach. I hope they kissed you.'

'The young lady did, sir.'

There was a soft note in the butler's fruity voice. He drew up the toe of his left shoe and rather coyly scratched his right calf with it.

'She did, eh? "Jenny kissed me when we met, jumping from the chair she sat in." I'm full of poetry tonight, Beach. The moon, I suppose.'

'Very possibly, sir. I fear Mr Ronald and the young lady will have a long and tedious journey.'

'Long. Not tedious.'

'It is a great distance to drive, sir.'

'Not when you're young.'

'No, sir. Would it be taking a liberty, Mr Galahad, if I were to inquire if Mr Ronald's financial position has been satisfactorily stabilized? When I saw him, the matter was still in the balance.'

'Oh, quite. And did you find the Empress pretty fit?'

'Quite, Mr Galahad.'

'Then everything's all right. These things generally work themselves out fairly well, Beach.'

'Very true, sir.'

There was a pause. The butler lowered his voice confidentially.

'Did her ladyship express any comment on the affair, Mr Galahad?'

'Which ladyship?'

'I was alluding to Lady Julia, sir.'

'Oh, Julia? Beach,' said the Hon. Galahad, 'there are the seeds of greatness in that woman. I'll give you three guesses what she said and did.'

'I could not hazard a conjecture, sir.'

'She said "Well, well!" and lit a cigarette.'

'Indeed, sir?'

'You never knew her as a child, did you, Beach?'

'No, sir. Her ladyship must have been in the late twenties when I entered his lordship's employment.'

'I saw her bite a governess once.'

'Indeed, sir?'

'In two places. And with just that serene, angelic look on her face which she wore just now. A great woman, Beach.'

'I have always had the greatest respect for her ladyship, Mr Galahad.'

'And I'm inclined to think that young Ronnie, in spite of looking like a minor jockey with scarlatina, must have inherited some of her greatness. Tonight has opened my eyes, Beach. I begin to understand what Sue sees in him. Stealing that pig, Beach. Shows character. And snatching her up like this and whisking her off to London. There's more in young Ronnie than I suspected. I think he'll make the girl happy.'

'I am convinced of it, sir.'

'Well, he'd better, or I'll skin him. Did you ever see Dolly Henderson, Beach?'

'On several occasions, sir, when I was in service in London. I frequently went to the Tivoli and the Oxford in those days.'

'This girl's very like her, don't you think?'

'Extremely, Mr Galahad.'

The Hon. Galahad looked out over the moon-flooded garden. In the distance there sounded faintly the plashing of the little waterfall that dropped over fern-crusted rocks into the lake.

'Well, good night, Beach.'

'Good night, Mr Galahad.'

• • •

Empress of Blandings stirred in her sleep and opened an eye. She thought she had heard the rustle of a cabbage-leaf, and she was always ready for cabbage-leaves, no matter how advanced the hour. Something came bowling across the straw, driven by the night breeze.

It was not a cabbage-leaf, only a sheet of paper with writing on it, but she ate it with no sense of disappointment. She was a philosopher and could take things as they came. Tomorrow was another day, and there would be cabbage-leaves in the morning.

The Empress turned on her side and closed her eyes with a contented little sigh. The moon beamed down upon her noble form. It looked like a silver medal.